HEART OF FLAMES

ALSO BY NICKI PAU PRETO

Crown of Feathers

A CROWN OF FEATHERS NOVEL

HEART OF FLAMES

NICKI PAU PRETO

SIMON PULSE

NEW YORK   LONDON   TORONTO   SYDNEY   NEW DELHI

SIMON PULSE

An imprint of Simon & Schuster Children's Publishing Division

1230 Avenue of the Americas, New York, New York 10020

First Simon Pulse hardcover edition February 2020

Text copyright © 2020 by Nicki Pau Preto

Jacket illustration copyright © 2020 by Kekai Kotaki

All rights reserved, including the right of reproduction in whole or in part in any form.

SIMON PULSE and colophon are registered trademarks of Simon & Schuster, Inc.

For information about special discounts for bulk purchases, please contact

Simon & Schuster Special Sales at 1-866-506-1949 or business@simonandschuster.com.

The Simon & Schuster Speakers Bureau can bring authors to your live event.

For more information or to book an event contact the Simon & Schuster Speakers Bureau

at 1-866-248-3049 or visit our website at www.simonspeakers.com.

Jacket designed by Tiara Iandiorio

Interior designed by Mike Rosamilia

The text of this book was set in Adobe Garamond Pro.

Manufactured in the United States of America

2 4 6 8 10 9 7 5 3 1

Library of Congress Cataloging-in-Publication Data

Names: Pau Preto, Nicki, author.

Title: Heart of flames / by Nicki Pau Preto.

Description: First Simon Pulse hardcover edition. | New York : Simon Pulse, 2020. |

Series: Crown of feathers | Summary: "Veronyka, Tristan, and Sev must stop the advancing

empire from destroying the Phoenix Riders"—Provided by publisher.

Identifiers: LCCN 2019023375 | ISBN 9781534424654 (hardcover) | ISBN 9781534424678 (eBook)

Subjects: CYAC: Magic—Fiction. | Sex role—Fiction. | Secret societies—Fiction. | Human-animal relationships—

Fiction. | Phoenix (Mythical bird)—Fiction. | Sisters—Fiction. | Fantasy.

Classification: LCC PZ7.1.P384 He 2020 | DDC [Fic]—dc23

LC record available at https://lccn.loc.gov/2019023375

TO DEREK,

❧

who truly is my ride-or-die,
and who would gladly follow me
into the flames

A phoenix is safe inside its shell,
resting in a bed of flame and ash.
But that is not what firebirds are for.
Rise, child of Axura, and spread
your wings.

—*"Wings," from* A Book of Songs and Poems
*by Hector, famed poet and playwright,
published 119 AE*

- CHAPTER I -
VERONYKA

VERONYKA KICKED AS HARD as she could at Tristan's face.

They were in the training yard, and the evening sun was casting purple shadows across the stronghold walls, setting the golden phoenix statue atop the temple ablaze with light.

The dinner bell had rung, and the rest of the apprentices and masters had finished their training for the day. Those who remained were packing up and putting away practice weapons or watching idly as Veronyka and Tristan circled each other.

They were sparring, and though Veronyka hated the attention, she'd told Tristan she wouldn't quit for the day until she'd beaten him *once*. So far, she was zero for five, and she was getting tired.

Tristan dodged her kick as easily as he'd dodged the others, stepping out of range while Veronyka stalked after him.

"Why don't we pick this up tomorrow?" he asked, panting slightly. Only *just* slightly. Meanwhile, Veronyka was a sweating, gasping mess.

She wanted to answer him—*no*, they couldn't wait until tomorrow. The final details from the attack on the Eyrie had trickled in over the past few weeks, putting numbers and names to the deaths, damages . . . and the missing.

And this was just the start.

Things were going to get worse before they got better; the empire wouldn't forget them after such a narrow defeat . . . and Veronyka had to be ready. She'd been practicing as hard as she could, pushing herself in flying and weapons and yes, combat. It was her weakest skill and therefore required the most effort and attention.

Veronyka had to make sure that when the empire returned—when the next battle was fought—she wouldn't be sidelined. And the only way to guarantee that didn't happen was to become a Master Rider. To pass the very tests Tristan had struggled with weeks before—and had trained months to conquer.

Despite her skill in flying and her powerful animal magic, Veronyka was so far behind in combat, so utterly out of her element, that it was all she could do to remain on her feet.

But she wouldn't give up. Couldn't.

In response to Tristan's offer to quit for the day, Veronyka tightened her mental walls and kicked again.

Because it wasn't *just* the combat that had Veronyka struggling. She couldn't fight Tristan like she could the others, because while her shadow magic was always reaching for minds and hearts, when it came to Tristan, it was like water being sucked down a whirlpool. She had to actively fight it, aware that every touch, every moment of eye contact, might be the thing that broke them both wide open. It was like fighting two opponents at once.

Tristan shook his head with a slight smirk, leaping effortlessly out of reach.

Veronyka swallowed, her throat dry as the sand under her feet, and tried to focus.

For weeks now, the combat lessons had been her worst, the things she dreaded most of all. There was no one for her to match up with, no one the same size and skill level. So she took a constant beating. Her only advantages were her speed and the fact that she was a small target.

She was also unpredictable. Not on purpose, but from lack of expertise.

Occasionally, it worked in her favor, catching her opponents off guard.

Everyone except for Tristan. When they sparred, sometimes it felt like *he* was the one with shadow magic. He anticipated her moves so easily, was able to counterstrike flawlessly, and adapted almost instantly to everything she threw at him.

Of course, if she *really* wanted to win, she could open her mind to him and anticipate *his* every thought and movement. Like she had during the attack on the Eyrie. Their connection had been heady and powerful, but then they'd been working *together* to achieve a goal. She'd also lost consciousness when she'd let their bond get away from her outside the breeding enclosure the day before that. It was too dangerous, and it was also exactly the kind of thing her sister, Val, would do.

Veronyka shook her head. The more she opened herself to him, the more she opened herself to Val—and that was the last thing she needed right now.

Veronyka just had to get *one* win under her belt for the day, one win so she could go to dinner with her head held high.

Most fights ended by a person getting hit with a pin or hold, taking too much damage to continue, or being shoved from the ring. So far, Tristan had managed to pin her three times and knock her out of the chalk the other two.

As he regained his balance across the ring, Veronyka studied him.

Underneath the padding he wore his usual training gear, the fitted tunic and worn leather as much a part of him as his curling brown hair and dimpled smile. There was a difference in him, though, a sense of surety that wasn't there before. The battle for the Eyrie had changed him—it had changed them all—and he seemed more confident in himself now, though the only difference in his outward appearance was a strip of red-dyed leather that wrapped around his biceps, indicating his position as a patrol leader, and a fine white scar that split his bottom lip—a souvenir from the attack.

"Come on, Tristan," called Anders from the sidelines, grinning widely. "Put this apprentice in her place."

The others laughed and jeered, and Tristan's jaw clenched. He'd never been great at handling teasing, and since Anders's taunt was technically directed at *her*, Tristan was taking it even worse than usual.

Veronyka knew the words were meant in fun. Anders and Tristan had only recently been elevated from apprentices, after all, but there were others who she suspected enjoyed the heckling with more malice. Latham, another apprentice turned Master Rider, smirked from just behind Anders, a coldly amused glint in his eye, and Fallon's second-in-command, Darius, whispered behind his hand into his patrol leader's ear. Many of them had been distant toward her ever since she'd revealed the fact that she was Veronyka, not Nyk, and she could tell they were suspicious of her closeness with Tristan. Even now . . . the masters rarely trained with the apprentices—at least not like this, one-on-one—but Tristan was helping Veronyka because she'd asked him when her lessons were done. The others saw it as favoritism, as special treatment. Maybe even something more.

"Shut it, Anders," Tristan practically growled, tossing his sweat-soaked hair off his forehead in agitation.

"Or stuff it at dinner," Veronyka piped up, trying to defuse the situation. Anders guffawed, but he didn't leave. Nobody did.

Veronyka and Tristan had sparred together often and knew each other's habits and tendencies probably better than they knew their own. Tristan was a careful fighter, observant and thoughtful about his attacks, learning his opponent before he made a move. But he could be baited. Anders had just proven that.

If Tristan could be lured into making a mistake, Veronyka might be able to squeak out of this with a win.

Still, she hesitated. While Tristan was calm and disciplined, Veronyka was wild and impatient—and he knew it. It was usually *her* fault she lost; Tristan just watched and waited for her to mess up, then capitalized on whatever opening or vulnerability she presented. But in order to bait him, she had to make a move.

Because of her short height, Veronyka favored kicks over punches, her legs having a farther reach than her arms. Skirting around him and angling her body, Veronyka prepared for a left kick to Tristan's ribs. She avoided his eyes—it was the surest way to open a shadow magic connection—and kept her gaze on Tristan's upper body, the angle of his shoulders and the position of his hands, held loosely at his sides.

As soon as her knees bent and her foot left the ground, Tristan's muscles tensed—his right arm tightening, preparing to block the blow, while his shoulders turned, angling his body away from her.

But Veronyka *didn't* kick. At least, not from her feet. She dropped into a crouch at the last second and swung out her foot with a kick aimed at Tristan's legs, not his torso.

She glanced up in time to see his eyes bug out and his body twist as he tried to adapt.

Veronyka's foot struck Tristan's calf, and the crowd that surrounded them oohed as his leg was taken out from underneath him.

But rather than falling backward out of the circle—her true goal—or collapsing onto his side, Tristan fell *forward*.

Onto her.

She'd only managed to clip one of his legs as he'd tried to leap over her kick, and now Tristan was stumbling toward her, and her only choice was to roll to the side.

She missed his impact with the ground by inches, but was defenseless as she tried to get away.

He leapt onto Veronyka's exposed back, slipping his arms around her middle and across her chest. Hands locked together, he gave a hard pull, drawing them both backward into the sand. In the blink of an eye he had turned *her* attack into *his* dominant position. As he lay on his back with Veronyka pinned against his chest, Tristan was a heartbeat away from pressing his forearm against her windpipe in a choke hold. She scrambled to the side, making the angle more difficult, but Tristan took the new opportunity she presented by throwing his leg over her body and climbing on top of her.

Veronyka squirmed, kicking and taking wild swings at his head, forcing him to duck and cover, but he still managed to get into position, his thighs on either side of her hips as he straddled her.

Being close like this caused Veronyka's mental barriers against him to shake and tremble. Her magic wanted him, reached for him often, seeking any excuse to strengthen their link. There were certain triggers—eye contact, touch, and sensory details like smell and sound—that weakened her walls one stone at a time. Add them all together, and it was an assault her mind couldn't withstand.

He lowered his head toward her chest, making it impossible for her to strike him as he got inside her guard. He was adjusting his position, regaining his balance, her wildly flailing legs no longer unseating him.

His heavy breath rang in her ears, his chest rising and falling and pressing against her own. His damp tunic and sweat-curled hair smelled of soap and salt and sunshine—smelled of Tristan—and Veronyka tried her best to jerk away. But he was holding her fast, and when she lifted her face and their eyes met, the stones of her mental walls came crumbling down.

The link between them burst open, as swift and certain as river water cascading through a dam. Her magic surged, and her mind filled with his thoughts, so loud and clear that they drowned her own.

He was aware of her in the same way she was aware of him. Her smell, her feel—all of it put Tristan on high alert, but not for the same reasons his presence rattled her. Well, not entirely. It wasn't just shadow magic she protected against, wasn't just a mental connection she feared.

Heedless of the consequences, Veronyka shoved at Tristan's chest, twisting and squirming—panicked and desperate for escape.

But her recklessness made her vulnerable, as she'd known it would. She realized with frustration that she'd exposed herself to an arm lock, and her breath hitched as she waited for Tristan to seize the chance. All he had to do was shift his weight, reposition himself so they were perpendicular to each other, then grab her wrist and pull against his chest, hyperextending the elbow. A simple move; a second's work.

Only, he didn't.

Tristan was frozen, and Veronyka frowned at him a moment before bucking her hips, sending him off-balance and slipping to the side. She squirmed out from underneath him and turned around, watching as he got slowly to his feet.

Silence had descended over the training yard, heavy with confusion. Tristan had *let* her go, had let the chance to pin her pass him by. He'd even let her get back to her feet.

He was panting now, sand stuck to the sweat coating his forearms and legs.

Their eyes met again, but she didn't need their mental connection to confirm her suspicions.

He'd wanted to shelter her from the pain and humiliation of losing in front of all the others.

He'd wanted to protect her.

It reminded her of when he'd tried to keep her out of the fighting during the attack on the Eyrie; it reminded her of Commander Cassian keeping the Riders locked up safe while the world around them fell apart. Worst of all, it made her think of Val, always supposedly "protecting" her, so thoroughly and so fiercely that Val wound up hurting Veronyka far worse than if she'd just let Veronyka know the truth, if she'd just treated her as an equal.

Anders and the others were watching, and there was no way they'd missed his hesitation. Tristan had gone easy on her, and they all knew it.

With something like a snarl, Veronyka lunged for Tristan. He had no choice not to fight her now, no opportunity to waver.

He absorbed her attack, using her momentum against her. Twisting his upper body—and hers along with it—he threw her over his hip, sending her flat to her back on the sand.

The wind was knocked from her lungs, and as she struggled to her feet, she saw the chalk line underneath her.

She'd been tossed from the ring. Veronyka let her head fall back to the ground, her eyes squeezed shut.

Zero for six.

ⱳ   ⱳ   ⱳ

Later, Veronyka took out her frustration in the saddle. It was what she did most nights when she couldn't sleep.

As an apprentice, she was supposed to sleep in the barracks inside the stronghold, and Xephyra inside the Eyrie. That separation was a part of Rider training, meant to strengthen the bond over distance, but Veronyka hated it. She always slept better next to Xephyra and had tried to sleep inside the Eyrie more than once, but was usually shooed off by Ersken, who did late-evening and early-morning rounds. Veronyka and Tristan often spent time at night on the ledge outside his rooms, cleaning armor or just hanging out with their bondmates. One time Veronyka accidentally fell asleep there after Tristan had gone in to bed, and it hadn't been Ersken who'd discovered her, but the commander himself. His suspicious look—and curious glance at his son's closed door—told her she'd better get out of there quick and avoid such a run-in in the future. People already gave them strange looks for their close friendship, which had begun when she was a stable *boy* and now culminated with her being a girl, an apprentice with a full-grown mount, *and* his underwing. She didn't need the rumor that she slept outside his door like a lovesick puppy dog added to the mix.

Veronyka had slept in the barracks ever since, and instead focused on strengthening her bond to Xephyra, particularly pushing their ability to communicate. Not only did they constantly test their range, but Veronyka also pushed her phoenix to use words when communicating rather than just thought and feeling. It was partly to keep their link strong and secure while they were separated, but also because of what had happened with Val after Xephyra's death. It sickened Veronyka to know that not only had Val manipulated Veronyka's connection to her bondmate to control Xephyra, but that Veronyka herself hadn't felt Xephyra's return because she'd blocked all thoughts of her phoenix to ease her own pain. If she'd been open, if their bond had been stronger and their ability to communicate more honed . . . maybe Veronyka would have known about Xephyra's resurrection sooner.

They practiced all day, sending words to each other whenever they were apart—eating or sleeping or distracted by other things—but the best test of their bond always came when they practiced *together.* Exercises like the obstacle course Tristan had done to finish out his apprenticeship were such an example, but Veronyka wasn't there yet in her training. Besides, she and Xephyra both preferred *flying.*

Veronyka waved to the perimeter guards and the Rider on patrol—currently Beryk—but everyone was well used to her late-night flights by now. She and Xephyra soon arrived at their destination, a practice course called Soth's Fury. The series of caves were filled with tight, narrow spaces that tested a Rider's ability to maneuver at high speeds, and they'd installed targets throughout to make a challenging run for any would-be warrior to hit them with arrow or spear.

Veronyka loved Soth's Fury, and she and Xephyra were getting better and better at navigating its darkest depths.

Ready? Veronyka asked as they approached the mouth of the caves.

Xephyra didn't reply so much as give a surge of excitement and adrenaline. An obvious *yes,* but Veronyka pushed her to communicate more clearly.

Words, Xephyra, Veronyka pressed.

Xephyra huffed beneath her. *Aeti,* she said at last.

Veronyka rolled her eyes, fighting back a grin. Whenever Xephyra grew tired of Veronyka's constant pushing, she rebelled. In this instance, choosing to reply in ancient Pyraean rather than common Trader's Tongue.

You think this is funny? Veronyka asked, going for stern but not quite managing it. There was no hiding your emotions from your own bondmate, after all.

Sia, Xephyra replied smugly. That was a northern Arborian dialect that she'd picked up from Anders, who sang old Arborian songs to the other Riders and translated them for anyone who'd listen. Most people didn't, but apparently Xephyra did.

Are you finished? Veronyka asked, the gaping mouth of the entrance drawing steadily nearer.

Verro. That was . . . Ferronese, maybe? How Xephyra had picked *that* up, Veronyka had no idea. She couldn't help it; she laughed as they dove down into the dark.

Veronyka had flown through the caverns many times and felt comfortable there, despite the dank echoes and shifting shadows that made it a somewhat spooky place. There were targets positioned at intervals within the caves, providing a variety of different shots for a mounted archer to hit. They were metallic, so they reflected sunlight—or phoenix fire—but were still difficult to spot, not to mention the fact that some were better suited to a spear throw or even a short sword or dagger, if the Rider was daring enough to fly so close.

And Veronyka was.

Her favorite part of the course was a stretch of targets that alternated between those she could hit on phoenix-back and those she could only hit on foot—partially obscured by rocky outcrops or tilted at an impossible angle. To get them all, the Rider must leap from their phoenix's back, run across uneven rocky ground to strike the target, then leap back onto their bondmate to grab their bow and continue on to the next target. It was nearly impossible, and required pinpoint precision and top-notch communication.

Veronyka gripped her reins as they barreled through the narrow opening. They weren't true reins—they didn't lead to a bridle and bit in Xephyra's mouth like a horse's reins did—but were meant to act as handholds and restraints, allowing inexperienced Riders to remain safely attached to their mounts during flight, and for more advanced flyers, they allowed a Rider to stand or reposition themselves. Veronyka had seen Fallon, the second patrol leader, fly *upside down*, using his reins to hold his body tight to his phoenix, defying gravity.

Veronyka was usually a no-nonsense flyer during lessons and drills, but after her failure in the ring today, she was determined to push herself and try her hand at some theatrical acrobatics of her own.

They moved swiftly into the labyrinthine caves, the stony walls closing in on them. They were smooth and high, like columns of dripping wax, while spiky stalagmites rose from the ground, some so large they had to be dodged as they whipped past. The shadows grew thick and cool around them, while trickles of water could be heard in the distance, remnants of some long-ago river rush.

Veronyka withdrew her bow, and through the bond she told Xephyra which targets she wanted and in what order, loosing arrow after arrow into the metallic bull's-eyes. Since it was pitch-black in the caverns, Xephyra emitted a faint glow to light the way.

Soth's Fury was divided into three courses in varying levels of difficulty, and though she knew it was foolish, Veronyka followed the most challenging route, each target marked by a circle of vivid purple paint around its edge like the tips of Xephyra's plumage.

While the start was easy enough, the course became more difficult with every target they passed. Up ahead, the stretch of concealed targets loomed, and Veronyka braced herself.

Telling Xephyra to slow her pace ever so slightly, Veronyka tightened her handhold and carefully pulled her feet from the stirrups until she was squatting on Xephyra's back. Her phoenix flapped her wings as little as possible, keeping her flight steady, but still Veronyka wobbled and struggled for balance.

The first concealed target appeared, tucked into a crevice above a narrow ledge and hidden behind a stalagmite that jutted from the ground. Veronyka braced herself, waiting.

Now, she said to Xephyra, leaping to the right as her phoenix flew left, just missing the stalagmite by inches. Veronyka slipped and stumbled as she tried to regain her footing, but she couldn't slow down—momentum was all that was keeping her on such a scant foothold. She careened forward, whipping out a dagger and hitting the target with a resounding thud, before hurtling past it and leaping out into the empty air of the cavern.

But then Xephyra was there, as Veronyka had known she would be. She slammed hard into the saddle, but even the pain couldn't dim the feeling of triumph coursing through her veins.

Xephyra swung her neck around to look at Veronyka, and her dark eyes danced with fiery pleasure.

Good? she asked, turning back around and soaring gracefully between rocky spires.

Aeti, Veronyka replied, and Xephyra crooned.

Afterward, they sat on their favorite slab of stone and watched as the sun began to rise in the distance.

Veronyka leaned against Xephyra, her body exhausted and her thoughts still, finally finding the peace she failed to get alone at night. After a while something stirred in the back of her mind, and Veronyka knew that Tristan was awake.

Just like that, her peace was shattered.

Everything about her bond to Xephyra made Veronyka feel better, stronger, and more alive. Her bond to Tristan did too. But she couldn't let it. Being bonded to another human was dangerous. . . . Veronyka had learned that lesson the hard way. She kept trying to forget about it, kept hoping that it would resolve itself or fade into the background. Tristan deserved to know that a magical link existed between them that gave her insight into his thoughts and feelings, but it was hard to face telling him that *without* any words of comfort or reassurance.

Why, yes, Tristan, I can hear your thoughts and sense your feelings—and no, I have no idea how to stop it. You're scared? Me too.

Veronyka knew nothing of shadow magic and only the barest fragments of how to strengthen or weaken its power. The only person who had the answers she sought was Val, and reaching out to her was a risk Veronyka couldn't take.

She glanced down at her wrist, where a braided bracelet sat. It was her own hair she'd cut off weeks ago, black and shining with a heavy coat of *pyraflora* resin, along with a single braid of Val's vibrant red. There among the strands were beads and trinkets Veronyka had collected throughout her childhood, as well as a single, heavy golden ring.

It belonged to Val—or rather, Avalkyra Ashfire, the fierce warrior queen who had died almost two decades before and had been resurrected into the girl Veronyka had until recently thought was her sister.

The ring was tied into the braids so that only the simple golden band was visible, while the front, with Avalkyra Ashfire's seal, was hidden from view.

The revelation that her sister, Val, wasn't her sister at all had left Veronyka feeling utterly lost and adrift. Family had always been a fraught concept for her—how could it not be, with someone like Val as a sibling?—but at least she'd known where she belonged and who she was, however unimportant. Now that she'd discovered her *maiora* who'd raised her was actually Ilithya Shadowheart, Avalkyra Ashfire's spymaster, and that Val was actually the Feather-Crowned Queen herself, Veronyka had to question everything she'd ever been told about her life. And the most pressing question of all? If Val was Avalkyra Ashfire, then who was Veronyka?

Only Val knew for sure, and she was not only elusive and self-serving—she was dangerous. Veronyka had seen firsthand what Val could do with shadow magic, and she feared opening herself up to her once-sister. What if Val just fed her more lies? What if Val sent more jarring dreams and memories? What if she *didn't*, and Veronyka never, ever learned the whole truth?

And what if Val tried to take hold of Xephyra again? Veronyka knew it was possible, and she was more aware than ever of the complicated web that shadow and bond magic wove between her and the ones she cared about.

Like Xephyra. And Tristan.

Veronyka knew she had to protect herself, but she had to protect *them* most of all.

And the best way to do that—the only way she knew how to do that—was to block Val out completely. To block shadow magic completely.

To pretend neither existed.

But as Veronyka mounted up and headed back to the Eyrie—Tristan's presence a warm glow in her mind and heart and Val's a cold shadow that followed her everywhere she went—she knew that to block shadow magic was to block animal magic, to block Xephyra, and that was something Veronyka simply couldn't do.

Soth's Fury is a series of caverns named by the ancient Pyraean people who that believed the south wind—called Soth—was wicked and vengeful, blowing storms and chaos up into the mountains from the valley below. Only Soth could carve such deep, destructive paths through the mountain, creating shadowy places in the world where Axura's light could not touch.

Soth was more superstition than true god, at least to the people of Pyra, and a product of lower rim communities who mingled more with the valley civilizations and their diverse, wide-reaching pantheon.

The word itself has similarly unknown origins, and most historians believe that the god may have been adopted from the mysterious Lowland civilization that was later wiped out by Lyra the Defender and her Red Horde after the Lowlanders tried to invade Pyra.

The tradition of naming nature gods is a popular custom of the Arborian people, possibly suggesting a unified ancestry with the Lowland civilization. For example, the people of Arboria pray to Nors, the fair north wind, for good weather and safe travel to this day.

—"Weather and Nature Deities," from *Obscure Gods and Goddesses of the Golden Empire*, by Nala, Priestess of Mori, published 84 AE

There once was a girl born from a legacy of ash and fire.
Except she had none of it. How cruel to have such ancestors,
to have such a name, and yet possess no claim to any of it.

- CHAPTER 2 -
AVALKYRA

AVALKYRA STARED AT THE remains of her fire.

She should have used it to cook her dinner or warm her hands. Something useful. Instead she'd used it to incubate *another* phoenix egg . . . and that phoenix egg had failed to hatch. Yet again. Now it was nothing but a cold, dead stone amid the ashes, like so many others before it.

It was the same egg she'd taken from the Eyrie, right out of that soldier's satchel. Avalkyra had saved it for this place, for the ruins of Aura. Hoping, maybe, that it would make a difference. That something, or maybe even someone, would help her. But no. Avalkyra had to do everything herself. It had always been this way.

Avalkyra stood inside a vast, echoing chamber of some crumbling temple. There were pillars of carved marble standing like trees in an Arborian forest, their tall, wide trunks disappearing high above her, the ceiling canopy untouched by the light of her small fire. It might have been a holy place once, but now, like everything in Aura, it felt more like a tomb. There was no escaping that feeling, no matter if she stood in a bakery or a bathhouse—every building held that haunted, hollowed-out feeling.

If possible, outside was worse.

Though Avalkyra didn't hold with superstition, the wind *did* howl through the buildings, lifting the hair on the back of her neck and causing strange echoes and moans. Dried leaves scattered, whispering across the ground, while the air still held the scent of ash and smoke and ruin.

Avalkyra took a deep, lung-filling breath. Then she kicked out, connecting with the egg and sending it flying into the shadows, where it ricocheted off the nearest pillar before tumbling down a short flight of stairs.

It sent up a delicious racket, piercing the endless, eerie silence, but Avalkyra didn't feel satisfied. All she felt was the ache in her foot.

She pursed her lips, staring down at the remains of the fire again. Then she kicked the ashes and bones and smoking embers, too, covering herself in soot and fully dispersing the last evidence of her hours of hard work—and her failure.

Avalkyra straightened. *Now* she felt better.

Leaving that hallowed place, Avalkyra stepped out into the dark, ghostly ruins. An archway rose above her, one of hundreds sparkling with veins of silver and gold and standing at least twice her height and ten times as wide. They marked the footpaths in and out of the city's main square, which featured columned entryways and ornately carved facades excavated from the rock of the mountain, appearing like gemstones from the raw, jagged surroundings.

Contrary to popular belief, Aura *could* be reached on foot. Not everyone in ancient Pyra had a phoenix, and the early settlers had lived here long before they had flaming firebirds. The landscape was steep and dangerous, and that was why the ancient Pyraeans had built roads *inside* the mountain. There were endless tunnels all over Pyrmont, from the highest peaks down to the Foothills. They didn't all connect—at least not anymore, after centuries of neglect and cave-ins—but Avalkyra had found them during the Blood War. Some could be accessed by caves or mines, others through fallen arches and crumbling doors like those that dotted the *Sekveia*. The empire had searched for her secret lairs for years, necks craned to the sky, and never thought to look below their feet. Her bases were never found; her defenses never breached.

Well, not by *soldiers*. There was *one* person who had managed to find her there . . . but she was no warrior.

The paths inside the mountain had been dark and treacherous, but Avalkyra had had old maps to guide her and rope to climb with. It had taken weeks, but then she was here, standing among these fabled ruins.

Everywhere she looked there were monuments to phoenixes and feathers and fire, and everything was shot through with gold. The grandeur put even Marble Row and the gods' plaza in Aura Nova to shame, and yet . . . there was sadness among the grandeur. Despair.

Everything was still, and empty, and quiet. Nothing soft and permeable remained. No rippling banners with the Ashfire sigil or tallow candles burning low in open windows. There were no shouts or laughter, no crackle of a cook fire. Even the scent of life was missing—baking bread or fresh Fire Blossoms. Nothing grew in this rocky landscape, and all the window boxes and public gardens were barren.

It was an empty city, a mausoleum.

It was a graveyard.

Avalkyra had searched everywhere for the storied Ashfire crowns—said to grace the dead queens' memorial stones—but they refused to reveal themselves to her. Somehow, it felt personal, as if her ancestors were hiding not only their earthly relics but their secrets as well. Surely in a *millennium*, one of them had struggled with her animal magic and her place in the world?

At the center of the ruins was the Everlasting Flame—or rather, the cold, empty pit that was all that remained of it—the truest monument to death Avalkyra had ever seen. She walked there now, drawn to it in a way she could not explain. Perhaps it was the devastation of it, the sense of something dead and destroyed but still there, despite everything. Something that refused to fade away completely.

It, too, was surrounded by archways, larger and grander than the others.

At first she'd thought they were all the same, replicated over and over again from some ancient mold. But now that she'd walked the ruins for several weeks, she was beginning to note distinct, deliberate differences. The phoenix above her now had a vast wingspan, while she'd seen others that were smaller in size. The height of the crests, the length of their feathers . . . insignificant details, maybe, but Avalkyra began to suspect these archways were dedicated to specific phoenixes who had come and gone. Her theory was proven correct when she found an archway outside the temple with its inscription intact:

Here flew Xauriel, bondmate of Friya. May her eternal flame burn bright.

There were thirteen archways that surrounded the Everlasting Flame, and Avalkyra was certain they were meant to commemorate the First Riders and their mounts. Ignix. Cirix. Roxana. There should have been fourteen, but there was an open space that told her one had likely collapsed. Their inscriptions were gone, smoothed away from years of wind and sun and rain. It even snowed sometimes, up here at Pyrmont's summit. And these pillars were a thousand years old.

Avalkyra hated them. She hated the ancient Riders and their loyal mounts, hated the phoenixes carved on every available surface. Aura was a wasteland of crumbling temples, towering sculptures, and wide, soaring walkways—and all of it was marred with a constant reminder of what she did not have. What she could never have *again*, it seemed.

She'd had a phoenix, once: Nyx. Fierce and reliable. Avalkyra didn't romanticize the bond like Veronyka did—Nyx had been a useful ally. A means to an end. But she'd been strong and steadfast. And yes, loyal. Until the end.

But the end hadn't *been* the end, had it? And while Avalkyra had clung desperately to life, Nyx had left her all alone.

At times like these, Avalkyra missed Veronyka and her endless hope. Or was it Pheronia's company she craved? Sometimes it was hard to tell. The two were so similar.

And yet . . . she had lost Pheronia, even before she'd died. Avalkyra had pushed her sister too far when she murdered Pheronia's scheming mother, and Pheronia had finally severed contact. Letters unanswered. Treaties unsigned. She'd tried to backtrack, to mend their fractured relationship—because of

Veronyka, Avalkyra now knew, though she hadn't at the time—but it had been too late. In some ways, Veronyka was the peacemaker. The thread that bound Pheronia and Avalkyra together even still. If Pheronia hadn't been pregnant . . . if there hadn't been a baby . . . they both would have died in that war, and there would be no Ashfires left in the world.

Veronyka the Peacemaker, like Queen Elysia herself.

Avalkyra snorted.

She hadn't lost Veronyka yet. Avalkyra had given the girl her space, but with shadow magic between them, separation was an illusion. No distance was too great. Avalkyra would make Veronyka *hers* again.

Avalkyra had had time to think about it—too much time—and decided that she'd finally figured out the mistake she'd made. She had always assumed Pheronia understood what needed to be done, that she was a vital part of the future Avalkyra saw for herself—for them both. Yet Avalkyra had never come out and asked her sister. She'd never said the words, assuming the words didn't *need* to be said. But maybe they did.

You and I are meant to rule together. Join me, sister. The world is ours.

After years of strife and separation, when they'd come face-to-face again, it had been too late. Those dreams had been dashed.

But this time . . . Veronyka was different. Things were different.

She was a shadowmage, after all, and a Phoenix Rider. She was more than Pheronia could have ever been, and together they would be truly unstoppable.

But that same magic that made Veronyka strong had also convinced Avalkyra that the words didn't need to be spoken—that they understood each other because of their bond. And so she'd made the same mistake she'd made with Pheronia. Despite all the ways Veronyka was superior to Pheronia, she hadn't been raised with the knowledge of who and what she was. She didn't understand that they were chosen, destined to rule.

She still didn't know.

It had been too dangerous to risk when she was young, her shadow magic wild and unpredictable. And now? Avalkyra had given Veronyka pieces of what she needed, but not the whole picture. Until she had a plan of her own, revealing to Veronyka her true heritage would only complicate matters.

Avalkyra thought she'd had a plan—hatch a phoenix, raise it until it was big enough to fly, then start gathering her allies and make her move on the capital. This had been her plan for years. For a lifetime. And it had failed repeatedly, spectacularly, over and over again.

Avalkyra needed a new plan, but no matter how she looked at it, she needed a phoenix. What kind of Ashfire queen would she be without one? She'd be like poor, powerless Pheronia.

No, Avalkyra needed a phoenix to ride into battle, a fiery beacon to light the night and warn the empire of her second coming. Without that, she'd be a shadow of her former self. A pale comparison.

Maybe she already was.

While her shadow magic was as strong as ever, honed over two lifetimes, her animal magic felt weakened. Whisper thin. Whatever she'd gained in shadows, she'd lost in her desperate bid for new life. She could not give these phoenixes what they sought. No matter how much life she gave them, no matter the heaps of bones and white-hot pyres, they refused to come forward.

Then, as if summoned there by thought alone, the endless, haunted silence was punctuated by a distant, steady pump.

Wingbeats.

For a wild moment Avalkyra thought it was Nyx—a stupid, foolish thought. Nyx had not come back. The bond endured—Veronyka and her phoenix had proven that. If Nyx were alive, Avalkyra would feel it.

No, this phoenix was larger than Nyx. Older. A female, her long purplish feathers marked her as a centennial—possibly many times over, so dark was her plumage—and her beak was narrower, her neck longer. As for the crown atop her head . . . well, it put Avalkyra's crown of feathers to shame.

A surge of anger blossomed in her stomach. She would fashion a new crown and take the feathers from this phoenix's corpse if she wanted. She was Avalkyra Ashfire. She was a *queen*. None would shine brighter or burn hotter than her.

Avalkyra glowered at the creature as it landed before her, anger still bubbling in her stomach and clawing its way up her throat.

Though the phoenix was impressive in both size and age, she did not seem . . . stable. There was something broken and fractured in her eyes, in her twitching, erratic movements. She kept tilting her head or darting her gaze this way or that . . . as if looking for something, and Avalkyra was not it.

Unlike most phoenixes, who emanated light and warmth and sparking energy, this creature felt dark and cold and wary.

"Who are you?" Avalkyra asked. Minutes passed, and when the silence continued to stretch on, Avalkyra pushed out with her magic. *Tell me who you are!* she demanded, but the phoenix's mind rebelled against her touch. She had impressive strength, and yet there were also gaps along the barriers of her mind . . . cracks and fissures. These weren't born from ineptitude or inexperience. No, the weakness in this phoenix's defenses came from trauma.

Centuries of trauma.

And deep within Avalkyra came the knowledge that while the body might endure or be resurrected anew, the mind did not survive so many lives unscathed.

"What do you want?" she asked instead, though she wasn't sure why. Why should she care what this old bag of bones wanted? "I am your queen, phoenix, and here in my domain you will answer me."

Those words got the firebird's attention. Her gaze, which had been wandering off to the side, snapped back onto Avalkyra with sharpened focus.

Ashfire, she said. Not a question.

"Yes," Avalkyra said faintly. The word had boomed inside her mind, loud, clear, and echoing, like a massive bronze bell.

More ash than fire, the phoenix said, fixing her with a single, unblinking stare, before shifting her wings and looking around once more.

Avalkyra stared. She'd never heard a phoenix speak like that, playing with words and meanings like a human would. And yet there was something otherworldly about this creature's voice too. It was cold—detached in a way that felt like hatred, and Avalkyra *knew* hatred.

Then the phoenix added, almost as an afterthought, *It is no wonder that you fail.*

Was she . . . ? Had the phoenix seen Avalkyra's attempt at hatching an egg? Fury pulsed through her veins. She lashed out, a searing pulse of shadow magic that met against the phoenix's fractured walls and broke through.

The phoenix reared back, shaking her head and screeching loudly.

Avalkyra reveled in the sound.

"I am ash *and* fire, and Nefyra's blood runs in my veins, phoenix. Remember to whom you speak."

There was silence for a time, and the phoenix seemed almost . . . stunned.

Nefyra, she said carefully, as if relearning the word. She shook her head again slowly, then more violently, before taking to the sky with a sudden screech and the flap of angry wings.

Avalkyra watched her go, wondering how many more broken things she'd find in Aura and sickened to realize that she was one of them.

A part of her had expected to find dozens of phoenixes in the ruins, living here in retreat from the world. But if there were others, they remained hidden.

Like cowards.

Like *her.*

What was she doing up here anyway? There was no luck to be found, no magical cure to her inability to hatch an egg and claim a bondmate. Instead there was this decrepit old phoenix here to taunt her. To show Avalkyra what she could never have again.

She thought back to the cold ashes of Xephyra's resurrection pyre, when Avalkyra had managed to use her connection to Veronyka to exploit the bond between the girl and her phoenix.

Avalkyra had found a way to control Xephyra without a bond of her own; even with her animal magic failing, she had done it.

Why not again?

Of course, that had been different. She'd utilized Veronyka's bond to Xephyra and her own bond to Veronyka, which connected them all in unexpected ways. As far as Avalkyra could tell, the creature she'd just met had no Rider, and even if she did, Avalkyra would not be bonded to them.

But there were other ways to control . . . ways that involved shadow magic. Shadow magic was typically the realm of human minds, but she'd broken through the phoenix's mental barrier just now, hadn't she? And she'd done that not with animal magic, but with shadow.

While the magic of the living was the realm of light and life and *bonds*, the magic of the shadows created a different kind of link. A bind. It was one way, a claiming rather than a union. And while it cost the binder less than a bond—they didn't have to give access to their own mind in return—the results were similar enough for Avalkyra's purposes.

She stared after the phoenix, still visible in the distance. A wavering speck, the creature silhouetted against the stars—a flicker of potential and possibility.

"Come back," Avalkyra said. The words were quiet, and though there was no immediate response—and the phoenix surely could not hear her at this distance—Avalkyra was certain that she would return. Their paths would cross again, and Avalkyra would make it count.

Calm certainty settled over her.

What had she done all her life when the world refused to give her what she needed? What she *deserved*?

She had taken it.

Maybe her plans weren't so unattainable after all: first a phoenix, then Veronyka . . . then, the empire.

Perhaps it was time for Veronyka to know the truth after all.

Maybe with the knowledge of who she was, Veronyka would finally accept her place at Avalkyra's side. Then she'd leave those so-called Phoenix

Riders—leave the Eyrie and her protections—and together they'd finish what Avalkyra and Pheronia had started a lifetime ago.

She would need proof, though. . . . It had taken her signet ring and a carefully chosen memory to validate her own truth to Veronyka, and so Avalkyra would need more than just words. There had been too many years and too many lies between them for Veronyka to trust anything she said.

Yes, Avalkyra would need proof.

And she knew exactly where to get it.

Unwanted, they called her. Ordinary.
Powerless. And she believed them, believed
the lies they told her about herself.

- CHAPTER 3 -
SEV

SEV SAT ALONE IN the small chamber. In truth, it wasn't small at all—it was actually a series of rooms with a bedchamber, a sitting room, and a private washroom—but everyone called it the small chamber, since it was the smallest of half a dozen long-term-care rooms in the infirmary wing of the palatial estate of Lord Rolan, governor of Ferro.

Sev shook his head, trying to understand how he'd gotten here.

When he'd left the Phoenix Riders, his confidence that he could do what he'd promised faltered with every step. He was *willingly* returning to the empire, to his position as a soldier, when he'd only just gotten free of them. It was hard to believe he'd volunteered for this.

As hard as it was to believe he'd gotten involved with Trix, the Feather-Crowned Queen's spymaster, and her ridiculous rebellion. The thought brought a rueful smile to Sev's face. It had been the best decision of his life, and his footsteps had lightened somewhat after that.

Before he'd left the Eyrie, Commander Cassian had helped him form a plan, including a travel route that would avoid the Phoenix Rider sweeps. They'd decided together that Sev should return to the Vesperaean Caves— the place where his regiment had congregated before the attack—in order to scrounge for supplies and see if there were any survivors.

"We can't give you anything," the commander had warned, "or have you looking too well cared for upon your return. We've salvaged what we could of your original clothing, but the tunic was too far gone. You'll have to claim you pilfered one from a corpse—or stole one from a traveler."

Sev had sighed then, beginning to realize what exactly it was that he'd signed up for.

"And your shoulder wound will rouse suspicion," the commander had continued, unaware of—or maybe uninterested in—Sev's distaste for what lay ahead.

"It couldn't be any more authentic," Sev argued, looking down at his bandaged shoulder, which was stiff and aching, though the bone-deep heat that radiated from it was lessening somewhat. "It proves I was a part of the attack and not some turncoat or deserter." Or spy.

"Yes, and it was expertly tended by Greta, a priestess of Hael, a healer you couldn't hope to find anywhere in Pyra—nor could you afford her even if you did."

A sense of foreboding had uncoiled in Sev's belly. "I could say I found a village healer, or went to a temple near the border—"

"And if you find one of your fellow soldiers at the caves and don't get the chance?" the commander said, shaking his head. "I've spoken with Greta. Your wound has done well, and she thinks it's healed sufficiently enough that you likely won't risk true infection if you remove the bandages and replace them with dirty scraps of linen. You will also apply this salve periodically," he said, unscrewing the lid of a small ceramic jar. The scent was quite nice, floral and sweet. "It is made from ivy and bleeding heart. Apply it to the surface of the wound only. It will cause the skin to redden and swell and prevent it from knitting together for the duration of the jour-ney. Ensure you lose it before you enter the empire's border. This will set you back several weeks, but it is our best option to avoid suspicion."

Sev took the salve, already dreading the increased pain that was sure to come.

"You will tell them the arrow shaft was removed by one of the empire's healers during the battle, before he was killed. There were a handful positioned within each regiment—we found several bodies near the switchback stair and down by the bluffs. We've retrieved one of their bags, though they were woefully undersupplied. Bandages, thread and needle for stitching, and a poppy tincture to numb pain. You will carry one of their bags with you as evidence."

After that Sev had donned his dirty, bloodstained clothes and rubbed his skin with dirt. Before he knew it, he was making his way back down the mountain.

Now he was tucked into a four-poster bed, a plush down-filled mattress beneath him and soft wool covers piled three high overtop. These rooms were meant for use by the estate's residents, with all the comforts a governor's family would expect in case they were forced to spend weeks under care by a healer.

A pitcher of mint-and-lemon-flavored water sat on his bedside table, and Sev was scrubbed and fed and wrapped in fresh bandages. Ever since his arrival he'd been treated kindly, graciously—like a valiant hero come home from war. Because of the nature of his recovery, Sev had been assigned this private chamber, had a healer checking in on him twice daily, plus servants he could summon with the shake of a bell.

Sev knew he was being treated better than most soldiers who returned from battle, no matter their wounds, and it made him extremely uneasy— like a beast fattened up before being sent to the slaughter.

But today, at long last, he was to meet directly with Lord Rolan. He had been in the capital when Sev first arrived but had apparently left word that any returning soldiers from Pyra be given the best possible treatment. Sev had gleaned since that there had been quite a few survivors before him who had already been questioned and sent to their new posts, not to mention the one *he'd* arrived with.

When Sev had first returned to the Vesperaean Caves, they had been deserted. Or so he'd thought. The Riders had already been through to burn the corpses and dispose of the spoiled food, and the llamas had gone as well—though Sev wasn't sure if they'd broken free to roam Pyrmont or if they had been snatched up by surviving soldiers or the Riders. A part of him had been hoping to see some evidence of Kade, to find some hint or hope that he might have gotten away, but there was nothing. He'd even searched for Kade's tags among the ashes in the funeral pyre, dread heavy inside his chest, terrified of what he might find. When his search turned up empty, he'd released a shaky sigh of relief.

He'd just been considering camping in the caves for the night when a voice had rung out in the growing twilight.

Sev had whirled around, pain lancing through his reaggravated wound, to find himself face-to-face with an unfamiliar man covered in angry red burns and with a short sword in hand. Sev scrabbled for his own weapon, but he needn't have bothered. He was a soldier, the same as Sev, and had been a part of the supplementary forces that had arrived the night of the botched poisoning. He'd taken one look at Sev's wound, said, "Better cold steel than hot fire" with a wolfish grin, and the two had traveled together for the rest of the trip back to the empire.

Over the following days Sev had thought often of Trix and Kade. It made him feel worse sometimes, but once he moved past the darker memories that would cause his breath to hitch and his throat to ache, he'd remember something that made him smile or laugh. Trix's sharp tongue and Kade's quiet humor. He'd remember the *point* of all this, and sleep would come a bit easier.

After years of fear and complacency, hiding among those who should have been his enemies, Sev's life now had purpose and direction. He was hiding again, but this time it was for the greater good. It had been devastating to lose Trix and Kade, and the only thing Sev could do to make it hurt less was to finish what they had started: protect the last remnants of the Phoenix Riders—the order his own parents had died fighting for—and bring down men like Lord Rolan.

He'd been the one to send secret forces into Pyra with the express purpose of slaughtering the Phoenix Riders, and it was generals like him who had sent swarms of soldiers to kill his parents.

If Sev was going to be the one to survive, his life had to mean something. It had to. How did he deserve life when people like his parents, like Kade and Trix, did not?

Despite their wounds and their meager supplies, Sev and the soldier made good time, walking through the gates to Lord Rolan's estate in the center of Orro a mere three weeks after the fighting had finished. The other man had been in much better shape than Sev, and after a quick perusal by Hestia, the healer, was smeared with ointment and sent back out again. Sev's wound required more thorough treatment. Even after Hestia had done what she could to bring the severe redness and swelling down on the injury, Sev had very limited movement in the shoulder, as well as a constant, radiating ache that caused the surrounding muscle to tighten with tension along his neck and back. She'd given him the kind of look that told Sev he'd never be fully healed again, but she still visited daily to apply poultices and salves and help Sev stretch the stiff joint.

After one extremely painful session that left Sev sweating and dizzy, Hestia gave him a heavy dose of sedative and left him to his spiraling fears that he'd be no good to Rolan without his arm, and that he'd be discharged or locked in jail to serve out his remaining years owed to the empire.

Sev couldn't let that happen. He needed to be here, where he could be useful for the Phoenix Riders. Commander Cassian had asked for evidence, proof that Lord Rolan had planned the attack on the Riders and employed a spy of his own—an apprentice named Elliot—after kidnapping the boy's sister to blackmail him for information. If Sev wasn't *near* Rolan, he would be utterly useless, and he would have handed himself back to the empire's military for nothing.

As the medicine had dragged him toward sleep, Sev closed his eyes and thought of Trix and Kade until the darkness closed in.

That had been several days ago, and now Sev waited inside his rooms for the governor himself to arrive. For his fate to be decided.

A servant knocked before opening the door and announcing Lord Rolan, governor of Ferro.

Sev pushed a slow breath out through his lips. No matter the role he played or the things he might be forced to do, he would remember who he truly was and what he was fighting for.

After another painful treatment session that afternoon, Sev had been ordered by Hestia to remain in bed. He felt foolish and uncomfortable as Lord Rolan strode in, wondering if the man would think him lazy if he didn't get up and salute. But as Sev moved to stand, Rolan quickly waved him off.

"The healer has informed me of your condition," he said, pausing at the foot of Sev's bed. The servant who'd announced him rushed forward to draw a chair from the adjoining sitting room and place it next to Sev's bedside. "Some wine, Bertram," Rolan added, taking a seat. The servant bowed and backed out of the room.

Lord Rolan was probably in his forties, fair haired and light skinned, though his cheeks and forearms were a ruddy golden color, which told Sev this councilman spent a lot of time in the sun. He had crow's-feet around his green eyes, and despite the fact that he smiled, his gaze was hard and cold as he settled into the chair next to Sev.

His clothes were dusty and travel worn, but clearly expensive, and Sev got the impression he'd leapt from his horse and come directly to this room. That was a shocking amount of courtesy from a governor of the empire to a lowly foot soldier.

Before Rolan could speak, the servant, Bertram, returned with a decanter of wine and two cups, leaving them on the side table before bowing out again. Rolan poured two cups, then handed one to Sev.

"Nothing like a long day's ride to drum up a thirst," Rolan said, downing several gulps. Before Sev could take more than a sip—it was the best wine he'd ever tasted—Rolan had finished his cup and put it back onto the tray. "It's Sevro, isn't it?" he asked, his tone businesslike.

"Yes, Lord Rolan, sir."

"I want to thank you, Sevro, for your service and for sustaining such a wound while in my employ. The province of Ferro—and the entire Golden Empire—is in your debt."

"Oh, you're welcome, my lord. I was only doing my duty."

Rolan nodded, but he looked pensive. "I'm afraid that duty is not yet done. We did not accomplish what we set out to do in Pyra, and now we must consider our next move. I have called a Grand Council meeting to address the Phoenix Rider threat, and in the meantime I will shore up our defenses along the border and prepare for a counterstrike."

Sev blinked. *Were* the Riders planning a counterstrike? He felt suddenly, laughably underinformed. He knew that was the point—he was a spy, after all, and if he were found out and questioned, the less he knew, the less he could give away. But if the Riders were planning on attacking anyway . . . Sev had to wonder if his goal here—finding proof of Rolan's attack—was still relevant.

"A Grand Council meeting, sir?" Sev asked, adopting his slow, simpleton voice.

"Oh, it's just a meeting of the entire council—some fifty members, when last I checked—in which a member may present an issue to be discussed so that a course of action might be determined."

Sev's mind raced. If Commander Cassian was hoping to bring proof of Rolan's attack to the council as a means of undermining the governor, it seemed Lord Rolan was one step ahead. Surely Rolan wouldn't willingly face the council if he knew he was subject to punishment for attacking Pyra without their consent? Something was off here.

"And *you* called it?" Sev pressed, brow scrunched up, as if trying to understand an extremely complex concept. "To ask for help, sir? For your next move?"

Sev knew he was being too curious, speaking out of turn and asking for information that he, as a lowly foot soldier, had absolutely no right to. But Lord Rolan was refilling his cup and seemed distracted enough that he answered without much thought.

"I'll need their help if I'm to wage war. If I cannot eliminate the Phoenix Rider threat on my own, I will entreat my fellow governors to put soldiers and resources toward the cause. Of course, I must convince them there is, in fact, a threat—but that is another matter entirely."

How could Lord Rolan convince the council that the Phoenix Riders were a threat if they weren't?

Sev's heart sped up to match the pace of his thoughts. He was missing something, some important piece of Rolan's plans. But knowing about the Grand Council was at least something he could report back to Commander Cassian.

"Now, for the issue at hand," Rolan said, snapping Sev out of his thoughts. Something in the man's tone made a trickle of foreboding slip down Sev's spine.

"Of the surviving soldiers, you are only the second from Captain Belden's regiment."

The second . . . Only *two* soldiers had survived from more than two hundred who'd first set out? The shock of it made the blood drain from Sev's face. It shouldn't have surprised him—Trix had intended to poison them all—but it was strange to speak of it here, in this cozy room, miles away from the blood and carnage.

"Who else?" Sev asked, his voice hoarse.

"Officer Yara," Rolan said, head tilted as he studied Sev. "She was unharmed, and I have taken her statement. While the majority of my soldiers died in the fighting, many were sickened—and some killed—by the antics beforehand." The botched poisoning. "But as she was attending Captain Belden for much of the night in question, her information is limited. And I need to pass down judgment."

"Judgment, sir?" Sev asked faintly.

"Only two soldiers lived, but there were some bondservant survivors as well. Officer Yara escorted them back to the province with the help of soldiers from the other regiments as they fled after the fighting."

Sev's stomach clenched so painfully he lurched forward. Bondservant survivors?

"And so I will need your help identifying them—separating the loyal servants from the traitors. I'm afraid my store of animages has been drastically depleted. I'd hate to waste good help."

Waste. That meant death. Sev's blood turned to ice in his veins as he realized what Rolan was asking. He might have to point the finger at his fellow conspirators or lie and risk his own position in Rolan's good graces.

"Can I count on you, Sevro?" Rolan asked softly.

"Yes, my lord."

What if he recognized some of them? What if they recognized *him* and knew of his role in the poisoning? Would they point the finger at Sev to save themselves?

And, most pressing of all—what if Kade was among them?

As soon as Rolan left, Sev climbed from his bed and opened the window in his sitting area. The sky was purple outside, still clinging to the last vestiges of the day's saturated sunlight, though most of the view was obscured by a large, leafy tree.

Sev paced for several minutes, until a gray pigeon fluttered onto the ledge. She was plain and unremarkable-looking—and that was the point. With a smile, Sev used a bit of magic to greet her and unearthed a piece of bread he'd hidden from his dinner. He broke it into pieces and set them on the windowsill. As the bird pecked and cooed, Sev flipped up the edge of the plush green-and-gold rug in the center of the room. It was beautiful and expensive, stitched with the horse-and-scythe pattern that was popular among the Stellan-made textiles.

There, hidden under the carpet, was a loose tile. Sev pried it up, revealing a leather-wrapped parcel. Inside there was paper and ink. As the wind rustled the leaves outside his window, filling his room with warm summer air and the bright citrus tang of Rolan's lemon trees, he began his letter to Commander Cassian.

The foundation of the Phoenix Rider order is the First Riders, legendary figures who fought alongside Nefyra Ashfire, the First Rider Queen, against Nox's army of strixes. Until this day, Phoenix Riders claim descent from those mighty warriors, though proof of such a bloodline would be nearly impossible to verify, as the First Riders existed a thousand years ago.

What do survive are the myths and legends of their heroic deeds, as well as their personal emblems or sigils. They were often painted onto flags or stamped into leather, passed down on rare artifacts generation after generation.

Despite their noble history, the ancient Rider lines slowly died out. By the time of the Blood War, the only remaining descendants of the First Riders included members of the Ashfire, Flamesong, and Strongwing families. After the Blood War, which saw the death of both Pheronia and Avalkyra Ashfire—as well as the death of the Pyraean governor Adara Strongwing—only the Flamesongs remain.

THE FIRST RIDERS
and THEIR MOUNTS

ASHFIRE

Nefyra
Rider of Ignix

LIGHTBRINGER

Callysta
Rider of Cirix

STRONGWING

Siytara
Rider of Ajax

BRIGHTBLAZE

Adalyn
Rider of Axalea

SMOKEWIND

Halyn
Rider of Meraxis

DAWNSTAR

Talliya
Rider of Ximena

HEARTLIGHT

Roza
Rider of Roxana

COLDFLAME

Myra
Rider of Lexara

FLAMESONG

Oriyana
Rider of Xhea

NIGHTSTAR

Kiyana
Rider of Xelda

FLEETFEATHER

Devyn
Rider of Xariah

STARFALL

Natalya
Rider of Elexa

SUNFLARE

Inara
Rider of Ixiya

SKYFIRE

Eelya
Rider of Niaxi

—*A History of the First Riders*, the Morian Archives, **147** AE, updated **171** AE

She was not measured on her own merit or skills.
She was forever standing behind her sister, and
the brightest lights turn all else to darkness.

- CHAPTER 4 -

VERONYKA

AFTER YET ANOTHER SLEEPLESS night, Veronyka made her exhausted way to her Pyraean language lessons held in the commander's study and meeting room.

Though Veronyka generally loved learning, she was growing more and more impatient in her classes, grouped together as she was with the youngsters while the other Riders were out flying patrols. They no longer had to hide their existence. . . . All of Pyra, and certainly many beyond, knew of their presence here thanks to the battle at the Eyrie. The very battle she'd fought in, the same as Tristan and the others, and yet she was forced to remain behind with apprentices who couldn't even ride. She itched to be out there with Xephyra, but how could she hope to be elevated to Master Rider when Tristan kept embarrassing her inside the ring?

If she had to remain out of the field, she should at least be spending her time honing her combat skills rather than spending her days going over things she already knew.

Veronyka was the oldest of the new recruits, and she already had a firm grasp on ancient Pyraean. The result was that she often found herself as an assistant to their instructor—a retired tutor from Arboria and a non-Rider. While Petyr—who had disliked Veronyka since she was Nyk and they'd worked together in the stables—would rather eat soaptree leaves than ask for her help, the others, particularly the girls, were eager to have her input.

They were the one bright spot in her schedule. Of the ten new recruits, three were girls, and Veronyka did what she could to support them. She made sure the girls knew they could come to her about anything, and Xephyra was extra gentle with them whenever they approached her with awe, thrilled at the idea that their own phoenixes would grow so big.

When Veronyka wasn't helping out, their tutor let her spend their lessons reading by herself in the library, a separate room where the commander kept the majority of his books, scrolls, and other valuable items from his time as the governor of Ferro.

Veronyka loved the library: the silence, the solitude, and the precious volumes of Phoenix Rider lore that she'd never encountered before. Poems and biographies, atlases and art history books—all of it was there, and she delved hungrily into the dusty pages. It was strange to realize that this was likely a fraction of the books the commander and Tristan had had in their home library in Ferro, but it was a wealth of knowledge for Veronyka.

If she had loved Phoenix Rider history before, it was nothing like the fervor she felt now. Rather than reading aimlessly, chasing tales of thrilling battles or scandalous romance, Veronyka looked for anything and everything she could find about Avalkyra Ashfire.

Admittedly, there wasn't much. The commander had been exiled soon after the end of the Blood War, and all mention of Phoenix Riders was forbidden in the aftermath of Avalkyra's rebellion. No doubt the Morian Archives had made record of the events of the war, but that information wasn't allowed to be shared or made public. Besides a few propaganda pamphlets distributed by both sides, the commander had little about the Blood War. What he *did* have were books about Avalkyra's childhood, particularly tomes dealing with the question of succession between Avalkyra and Pheronia, as well as several volumes dedicated to the Ashfire line, including histories, genealogies, and even books of myths and legends.

Veronyka tore through them hungrily, the name "Avalkyra" jumping out at her every time she found it on a page. Unfortunately, the books didn't tell her much she didn't already know—the sisters were close until the death of Pheronia's mother, the Queen Regent Lania of Stel. Her death was an unsolved mystery, but most people, Pheronia included, believed Avalkyra was to blame. Avalkyra fled justice and set up in Pyra, and that was the beginning of the end for her and her Phoenix Riders.

Veronyka was particularly interested in the genealogy books with their complicated family trees and descriptions of the First Riders and their descendants. Though she'd already been through most of these volumes, Veronyka found herself absently seeking *her* name instead of Avalkyra's, as if she might find some ancient ancestor or family to which she belonged. She studied the Ashfire line most closely of all. Could she be a relative? A distant cousin? It would explain why Val had bothered to raise her, even if it wouldn't explain much else. She didn't allow herself to hope but rather studied the pages with a detached, almost clinical interest. And of course she found nothing, tracing from Nefyra Ashfire all the way down to Avalkyra and Pheronia, the last members of the royal line.

Most all of the Ashfires had been Phoenix Riders, and Xephyra stirred with interest in the back of Veronyka's mind as she pored over lists of bonded pairs or famous phoenixes.

Xephyra, her phoenix said through the bond, a question or a promise, maybe, that her name would one day be among these legends.

Xephyra, bondmate of Veronyka, Veronyka replied. After Xephyra's surge of satisfaction, the link between them quieted again.

While most Riders outshone their mounts in terms of fame and notoriety, there were some phoenixes that stood out and gained reputations of their own, or pairs that were always listed together. Cirix, the first male phoenix, was particularly well known because he'd been resurrected no less than five times, bonding with various descendants of his first bondmate, Callysta, over a period of two hundred years. Nefyra and Ignix were the first-ever Phoenix Riders and so were often named together, and Ignix had been a mated pair with Cirix throughout his many lives. Queen Genya's mount, Exiline, was famously large, her wingspan measuring nearly eight meters wide. It earned her the nickname General's Shadow, for the wide swath of darkness that slid over the ground, marking her passing in the sky.

Though these tales were her favorites, Veronyka put the familiar volume aside. For the first time since she'd begun lessons, she sought books and scrolls on a different subject matter: shadow magic. She knew it wasn't a recognized magical discipline, and the odds of finding anything on it in Cassian's library were extremely low, but she had to try. After the events of the previous day's combat lessons, Veronyka was more determined than ever to get it under control.

In truth, she wanted nothing more than to tell Tristan about it—to spew all her fears and worries and bring down the last of the barriers between them. But those barriers . . . they were her last scraps of self-preservation. She didn't know how to explain the way the magic scared her, the way Val wielded it with such precision . . . the way it made her feel vulnerable and unsafe in her own mind. And then there was Val, too—her true identity something else she hadn't yet told him. But wouldn't opening up to him make the bond between them stronger? Or would telling him *help* Veronyka get their link under control?

Veronyka spent the entire lesson and half of her lunch break shifting through all the books she could find on magic, to no avail. She had better luck with the volumes of myths and legends, reading between the lines about witches using mysterious spells or ancient queens who controlled their subjects with unknown magical powers. Still, none of it helped Veronyka. There were no "how to" chapters, no practical information or advice.

But as she hastily reshelved the books before afternoon lessons, hoping to sneak into the dining hall for a quick lunch, Veronyka realized that there *was* someone besides Val she could ask about shadow magic: Morra, the stronghold's cook, who was a veteran Phoenix Rider from the Blood War—and a shadowmage herself.

Veronyka would have to reveal her own shadow magic in the process, but she knew in her heart that Morra wouldn't shun or shame her. Maybe she could give Veronyka some basic information and guidance.

Maybe she could teach her to stop being scared of her own magic.

Veronyka didn't get a chance to speak to Morra in private until after dinner.

She walked through the empty dining hall, the benches placed atop the long wooden tables so that the floor could be swept, while the fireplaces that ran along the far wall burned low.

On the other side, Morra was alone in the kitchens, hunched over the counter as she finished whatever prep needed doing before the morning. The fireplaces separated the cooking area from the dining hall, casting her work space into flickering orange and yellow light.

Hearing Veronyka's hesitant footsteps, she turned.

Veronyka didn't say anything, just sank onto a stool, trying to figure out how to broach the topic. Morra set aside the bowls of dough she was preparing for the morning baking and surveyed Veronyka, who was twisting her hands together nervously.

"I think I could use something to warm me up. What about you?" Morra asked, glancing over her shoulder as she opened a container and dropped leaves into a teapot. She didn't wait for Veronyka to answer, instead filling the pot from the still-hot kettle over the hearth and placing the steaming, fragrant pot before them. Thankfully it wasn't Morra's infamous pungent healing tea, but instead something that smelled sweet and floral. Morra filled their cups and leaned her crutch against the wall before easing into a seat beside Veronyka. They drank in silence for several moments.

"Morra . . . you're a shadowmage, aren't you?" Veronyka asked, abandoning pretense.

Morra glanced over her shoulder, but the place was deserted. Obviously people knew Morra was Commander Cassian's top choice for interrogations, but Veronyka doubted many of them understood her gift or what it was called. As Veronyka's recent research attested, it had historically been treated with a lot of fear and superstition, or ignored altogether, no matter that Nefyra herself had supposedly been a shadowmage.

"And if I am?" Morra asked carefully.

"The thing is . . . I am too."

Veronyka braced herself for anger, but Morra wore a grim, resigned expression. There was a whisper of magic against Veronyka's mental barriers, but no push or intrusion. It was more questing, confirming . . . like an acknowledgment rather than an invasion. "I thought you might be. I wasn't sure if you knew you were, though. There's many that don't. I sure didn't, when I first started hearing other people's minds as a child. Thought I was losing my mind instead." She smiled cajolingly, and Veronyka nodded, surprised by the tears filling her eyes. Veronyka had known, thanks to Val, but the magic had never brought her anything but trouble.

Well, that wasn't true. Though it was fraught and dangerous, her link to Tristan had brought her a connection to another person more powerful than anything she'd experienced before. And now that she had no sister or grandmother . . . that bond was more than just a complication. It was like what she had with Xephyra.

It was like family.

"Hey, now, it's all right, young one. It's all right," Morra murmured, pulling Veronyka into a hug. She smelled of cinnamon and fresh-baked dough, and Veronyka wanted to sink into her and disappear. "It's a hard gift, there's no mistaking it. And people often don't understand. You were wise to keep it to yourself."

Veronyka pulled away, wiping at her eyes. "What do you mean?"

Morra paused. "Well . . . besides the fact that many are suspicious of it," she began thoughtfully, "it's made more powerful by familiarity." Icy dread slipped down Veronyka's spine. She knew this, but hearing it confirmed was worse somehow. "It's harder to control with the people you're closest to," Morra conceded, speaking slowly, as if carefully choosing each word. "It's the same as animal magic in that regard. But if the people around you *know* you have it—it will be worse still."

"What? How?" Veronyka asked desperately.

Morra sighed heavily, fiddling idly with her teacup on the table before her. "Do you remember when you first discovered you were an animage? Not when you were little, using your magic unconsciously. I mean when you *knew* you had magic and how it worked."

Veronyka paused, thinking of her first animal magic memory—in which Val set a snake on her to test her magic—but quickly banished the thought. Even then she hadn't known what she was doing; she'd reached out and calmed the snake on instinct. "Okay, yes. I was probably around seven years old. I didn't understand why this stray dog followed me everywhere, and my grandmother told me it was because of my magic."

"And did it solve the problem? Stop the stray from following you?" Morra pressed, and Veronyka began to see her meaning.

"No . . . There were five strays following me the next day."

Morra nodded gravely. "That is often how it goes for young magelings. Animal magic is a *social* magic. It's always reaching, seeking . . . and shadow magic is no different. Once we are aware of it, our mind can't help but push out curiously, trying to test its limits. Did you experience something similar when you learned of your shadow magic?"

Veronyka thought hard on that . . . and realized the first shadow magic dream she ever had was on the heels of Val telling her about her second, darker magical gift. The girls had been waiting outside a market stall while their *maiora* haggled, when Veronyka had overheard the vendor say that the fish was days old and about to turn. Or at least, she'd *thought* she overheard it. When she tugged her grandmother's sleeve and told her the fish was bad, Val and her *maiora* had shared a knowing look. Apparently the vendor hadn't said those words at all, but *thought* them. Later, Val told Veronyka the truth of what she was, and that night Veronyka had dreamed she was flying in a sky set on fire.

"Yes," Veronyka admitted. "So you're saying that if I tell anyone . . ."

"They'll be more susceptible—especially if they are a mage themselves. Their senses will seek you out, will search for you even within the confines of their own minds. And if you both are reaching, the connection will be that much stronger."

Panic fluttered against Veronyka's chest at Morra's words. Her connection to Tristan was already too strong—it was a bond.

"But knowing has to be better than not knowing in the end, right?" she pressed, trying to put words to what she was thinking. "Even though my magic was more out of control when I first realized I had it, it eventually got stronger *because* I knew about it. Surely a trained animage—or shadowmage—is more capable than an untrained one, and you can't be trained without knowing about your gift. Wouldn't telling someone be the primary step in making them more resistant?"

Morra tapped her fingers against her lips thoughtfully. "Not sure anyone's ever tried to teach a person without shadow magic how to defend against it. You'd have to be a shadowmage to do that, and what shadowmage wants to weaken themselves in such a way?"

"This one," Veronyka muttered. "I hate shadow magic."

Morra dropped her hand. "I understand, but I'm afraid it's up to you, Veronyka. To hone your gift. Sharpen it. Then you need not worry about using it by accident against someone you care about."

"Could you teach me? How long would it take?" Veronyka said eagerly, but Morra gave her a sad, pitying look.

"It took me twenty years to get to a place where I didn't fear my magic getting away from me, and I'm still learning. I also happen to think your magic is stronger than mine, given the way you've tricked me in the past, young and untrained as you are."

Veronyka lowered her gaze, disappointed but also slightly guilty. She wasn't entirely untrained, though most of what Val had taught her was piecemeal and meant only to hold her back. Veronyka had learned some things through observance and others in self-defense, but it still wasn't enough. And she didn't have twenty years, not with Val on the prowl and her bond to Tristan getting stronger every day.

"Chin up," said Morra, laughter in her voice. "There's no shame in outwitting me—and you wouldn't be the first. Avalkyra Ashfire was a shadowmage. I'm sure of it. The way her patrol obeyed her, the way they flew in battle . . . There was more to it than mere chemistry. I wouldn't be surprised if they knew the truth of her ability—it would have made her control over them nearly complete."

Unease boiled in Veronyka's stomach. She'd wavered so long in telling Tristan about her magic, and now that she was trying to muster the courage to do it, she was realizing that she couldn't. The thought of making their bond stronger when her control was so erratic? She couldn't do that to him. She had to lie if only to protect him.

It occurred to Veronyka that Val had probably told her about her shadow magic for the very same reason Veronyka *wasn't* telling Tristan: She'd wanted to make Veronyka more completely under her control. She'd hounded Veronyka to guard her mind and not project her thoughts, but she'd done nothing to help Veronyka protect herself from Val's influence. Her dark mood plummeted even further at the thought.

"What if I didn't use it at all?" Veronyka asked, a flicker of hope kindling in her chest. She'd already suspected that the best way to protect herself and those she was bonded to was to pretend she didn't have this kind of magic at all—and Morra had basically just confirmed it. The problem was, she didn't know *how*. "What if I blocked it completely? There must be a way to do that without blocking my animal magic. And the less I use shadow magic, the weaker it will get, right?"

"Pretending something doesn't exist doesn't make it go away," Morra said warningly, but she saw the shining desperation in Veronyka's eyes. "The thing is, there are side effects to blocking out magic, Veronyka. It can come out when you least expect it, no matter how well you close it off, and you weaken your ability to detect and deal with it properly when you do. It's a muscle. If you ignore it, you weaken it. If you do not use your legs, eventually they will atrophy, and there may come a time when you need to run for your life—and you will not be able to."

"But shadow magic isn't life and death," Veronyka said, but Morra did not seem to agree. She frowned, pouring herself another cup of tea. "Please, Morra?" Veronyka begged.

Morra sighed. "How do you imagine your magic?" she asked, leaning back and wrapping her hands around the warm mug. "How do you see it in your mind?"

Veronyka was surprised by the question, but eager at the prospect that Morra might be willing to teach her after all. She thought for a moment. "I see it like a river, and my mind is a stone tower in the center of the rush. If I want to protect myself, or block out the chatter of people and animals, I shore up the stones, reinforcing the walls so no water—or magic, I guess— gets through. It used to work for me, but . . ." She shrugged, avoiding Morra's eye. She didn't want to explain what was happening between her and Tristan—that there were *doors* in her stone tower—if she could help it.

"One river, for both animal and shadow magic?" Morra asked, and Veronyka nodded. "Well, that's part of the problem right there. It's two rivers."

"Two rivers . . . ," Veronyka repeated, rocking back slightly in her chair. "But whenever I open myself up to animals, humans get in too."

"That's because of the way you've trained yourself to understand it. Your mind shapes the magic, not the other way around. It's no wonder you're having such trouble. Up here," she said, tapping her own temple, "I've got a fine Pyraean house with red shutters and a domed roof, and two dusty roads on either side: one for animals, one for humans. You need to separate the two in your mind, learn to tell the difference between them. Do that, and blocking out one and not the other should be rela- tively easy—not that I'd recommend it," she added sternly. "You will have to face it eventually, Veronyka, and I fear you will not be well equipped when you do."

But Morra didn't understand. Veronyka wasn't dealing with the usual kind of magical influence—loud rooms and crowds of strangers. She had *two* human bonds, and the web that was tangling between them was too dangerous to let remain. If she could block out Val and Tristan, she'd never have to worry about Val intruding upon her mind or her own mind accidentally intruding upon Tristan's. It was worth any sacrifice, worth any struggle she might one day face, to have safety and security now.

Veronyka considered the possibilities as she toyed idly with her bracelet.

It was more than just the bond, though. Val's presence in her mind was more than just magic. Val was constantly in her thoughts, even when she wasn't magically in her mind. Veronyka understood suddenly that she couldn't block one without blocking the other. Val and shadow magic were intertwined in Veronyka's mind, just like the rivers of her magic. She couldn't block shadow magic but continue to think of Val, and vice versa; thinking of Val meant thinking about shadow magic—their link and their shared past.

To let go of her magic, Veronyka would have to let go of Val, of the possibility of getting any answers about her past and her identity. It was a tough thing to swallow, but she would have to live with it. She hardly knew anything about the dead Phoenix Rider parents Val had invented for her all those years ago, so what was the difference?

As for Val—or rather, Avalkyra—Veronyka didn't know what to do with that information anyway. The Ashfires had *lost* the throne, after all, and the empire had changed. The Phoenix Riders were rebuilding, but was there room for a queen among them when they had suffered as much as anyone at the hands of the Ashfires?

Until Val came forward and tried to stake her claim—which she no doubt had delusions of doing—Veronyka saw no reason to concern herself with it. Val had been Avalkyra Ashfire for sixteen years already, even if in secret, and all she'd tried to do was get a phoenix—and she had failed. As far as Veronyka knew, Avalkyra Ashfire was a ghost, just like the Feather-Crowned Queen. A shadow, a legacy . . . nothing that mattered *now*. The empire—the world—had moved on without her, and maybe Veronyka needed to as well.

The Ashfires were a part of the past—and so was Val. Maybe Veronyka needed to leave her there. What good was it to dwell on a past she couldn't change, on an identity she couldn't know? She would block her shadow magic, bury it down deep, and do the same with Val, too. With all of it.

Distantly, a bell chimed the watch change, and Veronyka got to her feet. "Thanks, Morra. For helping—and for not yelling at me."

Morra chuckled, but her amusement faded as she considered Veronyka. In a gesture Veronyka could only describe as motherly, the woman reached out and tucked a strand of Veronyka's now chin-length hair behind her ear. "It's difficult being special—" she began, but Veronyka immediately cut her off.

"I'm not special."

Morra dropped her hand and rolled her eyes, all motherly tenderness gone. "*Different*, then. But you are, Veronyka. And when you finally figure it all out, well . . . you'll be something fierce."

Despite the stress and the worry and fear, Veronyka couldn't help it— she grinned.

*But it was in that darkness that the girl learned to find
her own way in the world. To find her own strength.
That girl, daughter, was me.*

- CHAPTER 5 -

ELLIOT

ELLIOT WALKED THE STRONGHOLD alone.

He was used to being alone these days, so utterly at ease with closing himself off from everything and everyone that the thought of actually being a Rider again—of laughing and training and sleeping next to his fellow apprentices—filled him with something close to dread.

Of course, Elliot had been alone long before he'd been exposed for spying on the Riders. He'd been alone since the day that man, Captain Belden, showed up at his front door and made plain the conditions upon which Elliot would be allowed to become a Rider in the first place—and all it would cost him and his family if he failed.

And he *had* failed. His father was under constant watch from whoever had been pulling Belden's strings, and his sister . . .

Elliot squeezed his eyes shut.

A low croon reverberated in the back of his mind, thrumming through the bond, just as a similar throaty sound emanated from the beak of the creature flying above him.

Jaxon. Elliot sighed, glancing up at his phoenix. Sometimes he forgot that he was never *truly* alone, despite how it felt. He did have a bondmate, for better or—as he'd come to think of it lately—worse. Jax deserved more than a bondmate who was filled with self-loathing and constantly moping about. He deserved better than a Rider who was never allowed to actually ride.

Jax continued to try to bolster Elliot through their connection, though his positive mood flickered and faltered, reminding Elliot that every bleak, sour thought that crossed his own mind took up residence in his bond-mate's head as well.

Elliot clenched his fists, guilt twisting his stomach. Everything—he made *everything* worse. For his family. For the Riders. For his own damned bondmate.

Walking with his shoulders hunched, Elliot passed beneath the strong-hold gate under the watchful eye of the guards stationed above, then through the dark village, pools of golden light emanating from the windows of the modest houses, where the families that grew the crops and worked as guards and servants enjoyed the quiet evening hours together.

Elliot felt their hatred, their wariness of him, even as he knew he moved as a shadow, barely seen or noticed. He'd been forgotten. Written off. A traitor, a betrayer, but a scorpion without its sting. Belden, the man he'd reported to, was dead, and Elliot's duplicitous ways had been exposed. Those first few weeks, Beryk had watched Elliot's every move, but it soon became clear Elliot had no intentions of resuming his role as a spy, plus no ability to do so besides—his access to important information was nonexistent, and his contact with the messenger pigeons completely cut off.

After some time had passed, Elliot had mustered the courage to plead on Jaxon's behalf and had earned this small freedom: He was allowed to escort his bondmate outside the village each night, where Jaxon could fly in peaceful solitude over the rolling plains of tall summer grass while Elliot watched him from the ground.

It wasn't like flying *together*. It was nothing of that same exhilaration and unity, that blissful emptiness that took over Elliot's mind and made it all about the here and now, the movement, the flight. But it was something.

As soon as Elliot cleared the village walls—still smelling of fresh lumber and paint, even weeks after the attack—the tightness in his shoulders eased slightly. Jax soared higher, up into the stars, and Elliot stood alone, hands in his pockets.

Out here, he was alone in the good way—away from suspicious eyes and judgmental scowls. The grass had grown over the scorched and churned-up earth, so he could almost forget that when the soldiers had come to kill them all, he'd been on the wrong side. He'd given the soldiers the information they needed to plan their attack, to avoid the patrols, and to all but seal their victory over the Phoenix Riders, over everyone Elliot had come to know and respect.

He hated the decisions he'd made, but what else could he have done? He railed at it, the injustice of what had happened to him. He'd been forced to choose, to pick between his family—his baby sister—and his new friends. But it hadn't really been a choice at all. He'd tried to keep his distance from the people he was meant to betray to make the pain of what he was doing easier, but it hadn't worked.

Elliot didn't just hate his decisions. . . . He hated himself. Hated that Jaxon was bound to him. His bondmate should leave, fly away and be free.

His vision glistened and sparkled with unshed tears, and he stared up at the stars.

"Do you hear me?" he shouted at his bondmate, who sensed his obvious distress and redirected midflight to land in front of Elliot. Elliot released a shuddering breath and lowered his voice. When Jax leaned forward, nudging at Elliot's chest, Elliot shoved his bondmate roughly away. "You should leave."

"Are you talking to me?" came a voice from directly behind Elliot, so close at hand that he literally jumped. He whipped around, stepping subconsciously in front of Jax as if to protect him, when his mind had already pieced together what his sight confirmed: The speaker was a young girl. Pale, freckled skin. Tangled blond hair. Surrounded by a veritable menagerie and holding what was clearly a homemade spear.

"I—what? No, no I'm not," Elliot said, still collecting himself after she'd so badly startled him. He cleared his throat and swiped hastily at his eyes, when he realized that this was the girl who assisted Ersken with the phoenixes—the girl who was blind. He puffed out his cheeks with a breath of relief. She hadn't caught him crying—she hadn't seen his tears at all. "I didn't see you there. I was just taking Jax out for some exercise."

She frowned at him—or at least, in his general direction. Her head was tilted slightly, as if she were listening to or sensing her surroundings rather than really seeing them. There was a bird perched atop her head, a pair of dogs trailing after her, and as she brushed absently at her shoulder, Elliot realized there was a mangy ginger cat hiding underneath her hair, scrawny and feral-looking, with a missing ear and tail.

Her hand stilled, as if she'd realized something. "Jax. You're Elliot, then?" she asked, and Elliot's stomach plummeted. "The one . . . ," she continued, face scrunched up, and Elliot stared at his feet, waiting for her to finish.

The one who spied. The one who betrayed us. The one who's grounded indefinitely and will probably never be allowed to fly with the others again.

". . . whose sister is missing."

Elliot looked up. Every time Riella was mentioned—usually brusquely by the commander, one of a dozen loose ends for him to tie up, and no more—it felt like getting punched in the stomach. But for some reason, when this girl said "sister," Elliot didn't feel the word like a blow. Maybe it was her tone—deliberate and without pretense—or maybe it was the fact that she had remembered him not as the person who had done bad things, but instead, as the person who'd had bad things done to him. The person who was *missing* something.

The person who was missing *someone.*

Elliot nodding, then, remembering himself, added, "Yes."

"Riella," the girl said brightly, as if pleased with herself for remembering the name. One of the dogs started gnawing on the bottom of her spear, which she seemed to use as a walking stick. Rather than shoo the dog away, she lobbed the stick across the field, and both dogs barked and chased after it.

"That's right," Elliot said as he watched the dogs fighting over the narrow piece of wood.

"My name's Sparrow," she said, then frowned. "It's not so pretty as Riella . . . ," she mused. "But it's mine." Again, her simple words about Elliot's sister went straight to his chest, but not in a bad way.

Sparrow bent to put the cat onto the ground, causing the bird that perched on her head to shift and ruffle its feathers. A lightning bolt of realization zipped through him. He'd seen this girl before—not just in the stronghold, but in Vayle, with Veronyka. She'd been trying to steal from the bloody wagon, or at least he'd thought she was. He was probably just paranoid. When you were constantly plotting deception and hiding your intentions, you tended to think others were as well. She had probably just been trying to get herself in with the Riders like Veronyka, who'd soon taken on the disguise of Nyk.

Nyk. Veronyka had lied to everyone and concealed the fact that she'd already had a bondmate. She'd deceived the Riders, the same as Elliot, but no one hated her. At least, not the way they hated him. They were wary of her, maybe. But she wasn't grounded. She wasn't punished.

But she *didn't lead the empire to their doorstep;* she *didn't put everyone's lives in danger.*

The day he'd first met Veronyka and Sparrow in Vayle had also been the night that Elliot had slipped off to meet with Captain Belden, refusing to give any more information until he had assurances that Riella was okay. The snake of a man had given Elliot some scrap of a letter with no trace of his sister in the words or the penmanship.

The knowledge that it might have all been for nothing was like broken glass prickling over Elliot's skin. Had his dreams of saving his sister been lost even then? Had they ever been possible, or had Riella been dead as soon as those soldiers marched her out their front door, Elliot's father holding him back as he kicked and yelled and fought?

Elliot glared at the girl before him, in no mood to talk—or think—about Riella.

"It's late. You . . ." He paused, not sure what to say but determined to end the conversation. "You should go back inside."

Sparrow stilled before him, as if she weren't unused to being spoken to rudely but was still taken aback by it. "Too quiet inside," she said. "And *he* wants me to stay."

She was nodding her chin over Elliot's shoulder, where Jaxon stood. Elliot stared at his bondmate, who was blinking bright, curious eyes at Sparrow and inching closer to her.

A stab of something like annoyance throbbed in Elliot's stomach. He reached out and placed a hand on his phoenix's warm neck, meaning to stop his movement. It ached to touch Jax this way, to be this close and yet unable to mount up and ride. But Jax needed his exercise, not to stand around and play with some half-wild animage. And the last thing Elliot needed—or wanted—was this girl hanging around. This girl, who was probably the same age as Riella and even reminded Elliot of her a bit—the dirty knees and scraggly hair and constant parade of animals.

"What he *wants*," Elliot said, his voice hard, "is to fly while he has the chance."

"Maybe," Sparrow said, her tone light and conversational, as if she didn't notice—or didn't care—how rude Elliot was being. "Maybe he wants to be friends."

Elliot snorted. "There are no friends for us here."

"You could *make* friends," Sparrow pointed out, her calm voice becoming more and more maddening to Elliot with every word she spoke.

"In case you didn't hear, I betrayed all my friends, Sparrow. So now we have no one," he said, fighting for composure, all while Sparrow's eyes were wide and unseeing and filled with understanding well beyond her years. He turned away, continuing to pet Jax, but it was an automatic gesture, something to do with his hands to stop them from shaking. "I ruined everything—I hurt everyone, and Riella's . . ." He trailed off, unable to finish.

When Elliot turned back around, Sparrow was standing close behind him. Her brow was furrowed, but after a moment's consideration, she scooped up the cat from the ground—where it was twisting between her legs—and shoved it none too gently into Elliot's chest.

Elliot scrambled to catch the creature as it mewled reproachfully and scrabbled with sharp claws against his tunic. He realized upon closer inspection that it was barely more than a kitten, and it was missing one of its legs as well as its ear and tail. His magic went out to the animal, calming it, and Jax released a slow, steady pulse of soothing heat.

"That's Carrot," Sparrow said, nodding at the cat. "She fought in the attack on the stronghold, brave as a mountain lion, and she lost her ear, her tail, and her leg—but she's still here. I lost . . ." Sparrow swallowed, and for the first time that night, she looked uncertain. Vulnerable. "I lost Chirp, my best friend. But I'm still here. I can't bring Chirp back, and I can't change that he fought to protect me and died. But I can take care of Carrot. And Ash," she added, gesturing to the pigeon that had been riding on her head, one of its wings gone, "and Lucky and Larry." Behind her, the two dogs, similarly scarred and wounded as Carrot, ambled around as best they could.

"I can still do good things," Sparrow continued. "No matter how much I miss Chirp. No matter how much I blame myself for what happened to him. Maybe, one day, the good things will make up for the bad things. If not out here," she said, gesturing around them, "then maybe in here," she finished, pointing to her chest.

Elliot bit his tongue. He wanted to rage at her that he hadn't lost some *bird*, he'd lost his sister, but then he shot an apologetic look at Jax, whose expression was baleful. He sighed, staring down at the cat. There was something about this girl that had gotten under his skin . . . something about her words that made him second-guess himself.

"It's not the same thing. Your friend, your Chip—"

"*Chirp,*" she corrected, her lips pursed. "What kinda name is Chip for a bird?"

What kinda name is Carrot for a cat? he wanted to say but didn't. "Right—well, Chirp, he chose to fight for you, didn't he? But Riella didn't *choose* to be taken as a hostage. The Riders didn't *choose* to give up information in the hopes of securing her release. I did all that. I've done so much damage, and there's no fixing it. There's no undoing it or making up for it."

Sparrow considered this as Elliot bent to put Carrot into the tall grass. The dogs bounced over, biting and snapping and hoping for another playmate—but Carrot turned up her nose and batted the nearest pup away. Elliot watched, a smile tugging at the corner of his mouth. He had to admit that the animals lightened his dark mood. He'd almost forgotten what they were talking about when Sparrow finally spoke.

"Maybe you can't undo it or fix it. But you hurt people," she said, and Elliot's chest tightened. Yes, he'd hurt people. He'd led soldiers to their doorstep. "You let your commander down. You made your friends sad."

Elliot wasn't sure he'd use the word "sad," but then again, he did sense that the others didn't hate him as much as they were disappointed in him. He'd betrayed their *trust* more than anything else. And he supposed that had made them sad.

"If you want to oversimplify it for the sake of your argument, sure," he said with a sigh.

Sparrow ignored the sarcastic comment. "Then what you have to do is easy."

"What?" Elliot asked with a laugh. The sound was rusty, as if he hadn't done it in so long, his throat had forgotten how. "Make them happy?" It was ridiculous. Juvenile. The words of a child.

As if he could really make them all forget—and forgive—what he'd done, simply by trying to make them happy. How could that ever be enough?

Sparrow nodded gravely. "You don't just make them happy. You show them you still care."

*When I was young, my sky had three suns: my mother, my father,
and my sister. I thought I would bask forever in their warm glow,
our lives together like fixed points in a never-changing universe.
But it was not meant to be.*

- CHAPTER 6 -

TRISTAN

IT WAS SEVERAL DAYS before Tristan had a chance to be alone with
Veronyka. Not that he would've known what to say even if he *had* been
alone with her. Guilt gnawed at him—both for holding back during their
sparring match and for finally defeating her. In front of everyone. But Veronyka was far too hard on herself. She expected to be at Tristan's level after
only a few short weeks of training, when he'd had *years* of practice. No one
else asked it or expected it of her; rather, she asked it of herself.

And yet Tristan understood her drive. They were all feeling a bit restless, a bit antsy in the wake of the empire's attack. Somehow, they had made
it through—thanks in no small part to Veronyka's bravery and quick thinking. Everyone in the stronghold and village had come together to defend
this place, and while new camaraderie blossomed, fear and anxiety weren't
far behind.

Like Veronyka, Tristan was desperate to get out there and actually *do*
something after the attack. So far, the Master Riders were only doing patrols
and sporadic safety checks at local villages. They weren't exacting revenge on
the empire or planning some grand retaliation.

They were doing almost nothing at all. He hated it, and he knew
Veronyka did too. How much worse would her helplessness be when she

couldn't even leave the Eyrie on more than practice runs or training missions? No wonder she was on edge.

While Tristan had gotten his promotion and his own patrol, Veronyka's position was more difficult to define. She was technically a new recruit, but Xephyra was over three months old, and they had been riding even before she was officially taken on. Veronyka had well-honed bond magic and a strong connection with her phoenix, but she was behind in things like combat and weapons training. She was also Nyk the stable boy turned Veronyka, the new Rider apprentice. She was the same person, yet somehow different, and it seemed that people didn't know exactly how to treat her, Tristan among them. Even helping her seemed to make things worse—his hesitation during the fight was a prime example.

It was late evening when Tristan found Veronyka sitting on the walkway outside his new Master Rider quarters, the sky a dusky purple as it hung over the expanse of the Eyrie. The rest of the walkways, stacked in tiers like the seating of an amphitheater, were dark and quiet, save for the shuffling of feathers as a phoenix settled in to sleep for the night.

She was hunched over his armor, treating the leather with *pyraflora* resin anywhere it had thinned or worn off—part of her underwing duties. The smell was pungent, and despite the growing twilight, she worked by the glow of two phoenixes: Xephyra and Rex, nestled on either side of her.

Rex was the first to note Tristan's approach, shaking out his wings and tilting his head in Tristan's direction.

Absorbed in her work, Veronyka didn't look up or notice his presence. "Steady, Rex. You're making the light dance. . . ."

Something about the way she addressed Tristan's bondmate, with affection and familiarity, made Tristan's chest swell.

"Maybe you shouldn't be working until it's dark," Tristan offered after watching her for several silent moments. Veronyka twisted to look up at him.

Her face fell, and she immediately looked away, avoiding his gaze—as she had every day since their last match in the ring. Tristan couldn't figure out if it was anger or embarrassment or something else entirely, but he was tired of guessing. With a pat on Rex's rump and a jerk of his chin, Tristan dismissed his bondmate, who ruffled his feathers in haughty indignation, taking to the air only to flutter around Veronyka's other side and settle next to Xephyra instead. Tristan smiled, knowing Rex's reaction was mostly a performance, thanks to their bond. He promised candied ginger—Rex's favorite—tomorrow, and his bondmate perked up considerably.

"So," Tristan said, easing down onto the ground next to Veronyka. He glanced at her, features cast into profile thanks to Xephyra's glow. Her hair had grown a bit since she'd first arrived here—well, since Tristan first took her as a captive. The memory made him smile now. He thought of the way she'd constantly challenged him and made him better. She'd been Nyk then, and when he'd discovered that she'd been lying about who she was, he'd feared he'd lost the person he knew. The person he was rapidly growing more-than-friendship feelings for. But Veronyka *was* Nyk, and Nyk was Veronyka. His feelings hadn't changed. They continued to grow with each passing day.

Her shoulders shifted slightly—she was aware of his presence but unwilling to face him. "So," she said in response, head still bowed over her work.

Veronyka's hair was blacker than night, silken and shiny, often falling into her eyes or whipping in the wind. Tristan loved the wildness of it, and he could picture her in a few years, head heavy with beads and braids commemorating all her achievements. He never doubted that she would get there, *knew* that it would happen . . . but maybe *she* didn't. Maybe that was why her perceived failure cut so deep. She had been through more to become a Rider than anyone he knew: years of constant fear and poverty, the death of her bondmate—by her sister's own hand, which Veronyka had only recently revealed to him. He'd disliked Val before, but now just the thought of her was enough to make Tristan's blood boil. He could only imagine how Veronyka felt about her, having to flee their home and pretend to be a boy, not to mention the reappearance of her phoenix and the battle for the Eyrie. She had come so far, but she still wasn't there. Tristan understood the feeling, if only marginally, and had wanted to make things easier for her, but since when had Veronyka ever wanted anything easy?

She continued to ignore him, so Tristan reached across her and snatched the leather armor, flinging it unceremoniously to his other side. Her mouth opened, scandalized—she was far more careful and meticulous with his gear than he was—and he grinned. She smiled too, but reluctantly.

Tristan's face fell, and he sighed. "You're mad at me," he said.

"No, I'm not," she said at once.

He stared expectantly at her, brows raised. She didn't look at him, but made a sudden lunge for the armor, diving across his lap. He caught her, a laugh rumbling in his chest at her determination, and reached back to knock the leather off the walkway and down into the echoing caverns of the Eyrie a hundred feet below.

"*Tristan,*" Veronyka scolded, but she was smiling. No damage would come to it, and Tristan could get it tomorrow.

They were still pressed together, Veronyka leaning across his body, Tristan with one arm wrapped around her—at first to pull her back, but now that arm held her close. Her body coiled with tension, as if always ready for action . . . or prepared for attack. Tristan knew it was Val who had made her this way, and his anger toward the girl flared again, hot and fierce.

Veronyka finally looked up at him, their eyes catching and holding. He felt something, a pull or tug that seemed to reach deep down into the pit of his stomach. Next to them, Xephyra crooned softly, and Veronyka pulled away.

"I'm not mad," she said, putting the lid back onto the jar of resin and wiping her hands on a rag. "Not at you."

"At who?" Tristan asked, sitting up and fixing his tunic, which had been pulled askew. He wanted to touch her again, but her demeanor was still distant. She was talking to him, at least. "Not yourself."

"No. Yes. I . . ." She blew a puff of air out through her lips, causing pieces of her hair to flutter. "I'm mad at everyone and everything. Aren't you?"

Tristan was taken back by the question, but before he could answer, Veronyka continued.

"I just want to be able to contribute."

"But you will—you already do," Tristan protested.

She lifted an eyebrow at him. "Tristan . . . nothing's happening. People are missing, the villages are crumbling . . . and I'm just sitting here. *We're* just sitting here. And when something finally *does* happen, if I'm not a Master Rider . . . if I can't even *compete* with the Master Riders"—she darted a glance at him before continuing—"then what? I don't want to be left behind."

Tristan sighed and leaned back, his head resting against the stone wall and his legs stretched out before him. Her concerns were valid. His father was cautious almost to the point of inaction, though Tristan knew in his heart that Commander Cassian was no coward. He did things for a reason, but he rarely let people in on those calculations. They were too limited in number to strike back at the empire—at least in the military sense—but surely there were other things to be done. They could recruit foot soldiers or hire mercenaries, set up a border defense or take residence in one of the remaining outposts from before the war. Their existence now felt like the taut string on a drawn bow, and Tristan wanted to be ready when the arrow was loosed.

But of course, Tristan also knew that when the time came, the commander would be unlikely to allow new recruits to join in the fighting. Unless the circumstances were dire, like the surprise attack on the Eyrie. Ten fully trained Riders were more potent than fifteen untrained, and the more practice and experience the apprentices got before their next battle, the more likely that they would survive beyond it.

"Well, like you said, nothing's happening, which means there's still time."

This didn't seem to please her. He supposed it was small consolation, the kind of assurance his father had given him over and over again as he strove to rise in the Rider ranks.

The kind of reassurance Tristan had hated too.

"It's not just that," Veronyka said, staring down at her hands where they sat in her lap. "Why did you hold back during the last match?"

"So you *are* mad at me," Tristan said, and she didn't contradict him. "I . . . ," he began, searching for words. He'd expected this from her, but he still didn't know what to say. "I'm not exactly sure."

She cast him a pointed look, crossing her arms, and he knew he'd have to do better than that.

He cleared his throat. "I was tired, and everyone was watching, and . . ."

"Were you trying to make it easier for me?" she asked, agitation coloring her voice. "Were you trying to let me win?"

"No, I never intended—I wasn't thinking. I just hesitated for a sec—"

"You didn't think I *could* win, did you?" she demanded angrily. "You thought I was destined to lose, and you didn't want to embarrass me in front of everyone, so you went easy on the poor, incompetent *girl*."

"No! I didn't go easy on you," Tristan said at once. "I know that I hesitated," he added quickly, "but I fought hard before that. And I didn't hold back because you're a girl," he said, hurt that she'd think so little of him. "It was because you're you."

Her rage faltered. "What do you mean? I don't want special treatment."

Tristan looked away from her, heat crawling up his cheeks. He was glad it was dark. "I knew how much you wanted to win—how hard you've been working. And I guess that compromised me." She continued to stare at him, uncomprehending, so he plowed on. "I know you don't want special treatment, but you are special—to me."

Her lips parted, but no words came out. She turned away, looking toward Xephyra and Rex, who were huddled together several feel away. Both their glows had dimmed; the only light came from the lanterns hung on regular intervals along the walkway, and the distant, icy stars.

When she finally did speak, her voice was soft, a whisper across his skin. "The thing is . . . you've always hated the way your father treated you differently. Good or bad . . . it feels like you're protecting me. But that's not—that's not why I'm here. That's not what I want from you."

What do you want? Tristan was desperate to ask, but he was afraid of the answer. They'd spent hours alone together since the battle for the Eyrie, when her secrets were laid bare and they had grown closer to each other. But once the dust settled, nothing more had happened between them. And he wanted it to. He hated when they were apart and couldn't wait until she graduated and joined his patrol. They were short one Rider, and Tristan had yet to name a second-in-command. That position was Veronyka's, and it would be waiting for her whenever she was ready.

Tristan wanted her by his side always. Did she not want the same?

"I'm sorry," he whispered, avoiding her gaze.

She nodded, though it seemed more in resignation than anything else. "Latham's always saying how you favor me, and I overheard him whispering to Petyr after the match that you were afraid to hit me."

"I hit you all the time!" Tristan said, outraged, and her lips twitched in a smile. "In training, obviously," he muttered, realizing the way his words sounded. He'd accidentally given her a black eye two weeks ago, and the barest hints of green still colored her golden-brown skin. He'd been horrified at first, but Veronyka had only touched the swelling gently before smiling, wearing the purple bruises like a badge of honor. "And Petyr's just jealous."

"It doesn't matter," Veronyka said. "This place is too small, and everyone loves gossip. One day I'm the stable boy Nyk, the next I'm a girl, a brand-new apprentice—and the commander's son's favorite. You know what they'll say, how they'll spin it. They'll say that we're—that you and I . . ."

She trailed off, and silence fell between them.

"So what if we were?" Tristan asked, and when her eyes widened, he hastily continued. "I mean, it used to happen all the time, didn't it? Mated pairs, or whatever." Her eyes were round as plates now, and Tristan's cheeks were hotter than Rex in a fire dive. He rubbed a hand against the back of his neck, glancing away from her and forcing a determinedly nonchalant shrug. "Let them talk."

The truth was, the other apprentices had been gossiping about Veronyka and Tristan since she'd first arrived. While Latham would occasionally moon about girls and Anders would laugh and tease and try to push everyone's buttons, Tristan had always been more reserved. He'd never shown much interest in the others—for friendship or romance—but then Nyk the new stable boy turned up and the two became inseparable. It didn't matter that it was his father's order that started it; they'd seen the way Tristan looked at Nyk, noticed the change that Veronyka never could because she hadn't known him before. No matter how innocent their relationship—even though Tristan had long wished it were otherwise—something about being the commander's solitary, standoffish son made him an entertaining target, and they loved to try to get a rise out of him.

"It's different for you," Veronyka said. "You're the one in power. I'm the one who looks like I'm clinging to your phoenix tail."

Rex let out a reproachful croak and shuffled forward; Veronyka smiled at him, patting his outstretched beak.

Tristan watched them, thinking over her words. He realized it was exactly how he'd felt being the commander's son, as if no matter how hard he worked or how well he performed, everyone would assume he'd been given an easy path.

"Anyone who sees you fly will know that you've earned every single thing you have—and you'll earn much more, before all this is done," he said, hoping to reassure her, but there was a heaviness settling into his stomach. If just being *friends* compromised Veronyka's integrity and her hopes for the future, how could Tristan ever hope for anything more?

"All my life," she began, "my s-sister"—she stuttered slightly on the word—"treated me like I was made of glass. Not precious, but fragile. Useless."

"I do *not* think you're useless," Tristan interrupted, and she smiled widely. His stomach leapt at the sight.

"I know," she said, before the grin slipped off her face. "I just . . . I hate this, Tristan. I hate sitting here . . . I *feel* useless."

Her voice was tired now as she leaned back against the wall, staring off into the distance. Heart fluttering, Tristan reached for her, his fingers crawling across the cool stone to find hers in the dark. She stiffened at first, only to grip his hand hard.

"Yeah," Tristan said, sliding closer to her and gently tracing his thumb across her knuckles. "Me too."

After walking Veronyka back to the apprentice barracks, Tristan roamed the stronghold. It was well after dinner, and the place was deserted.

He was considering walking the ramparts or visiting Wind in the stables when he spotted his father cutting across the cobblestones toward the dining hall. Tristan hastened his footsteps to catch up to him, surprised to see him out so late. His father usually retired early to work, the lantern glow from his chambers spilling out the windows and into the courtyard well into the night.

His father turned at the sound of Tristan's footsteps. "Tristan," he said in surprise, his brows furrowing. "What are you doing out here at this late hour? Did Beryk send you?"

"No one sent me," Tristan assured him. "I was just . . ." He trailed off. He wasn't really doing anything.

The commander's gaze roved his face, and in a surprising act of perceptiveness, he nodded toward the dining hall. "Care to join me for a nightcap?"

"Sure," Tristan said, slightly dumbfounded as he followed his father through the doors and toward the high table. Late-night drinks were for the commander and his second, or maybe Fallon, the other patrol leader. With a jolt, Tristan realized that *he* was a patrol leader now, on the same level as these other Master Riders.

A servant was wiping down the long tables that filled the hall, but otherwise, the place was deserted.

"Some rockwine, if you please," the commander asked when the servant wandered over, "and whatever is left from dinner—there's no need to reheat."

While his father took a seat at the head of the high table, Tristan sat next to him, the long planked surface stretching out before them. The servant returned quickly, carrying a tray of assorted cakes and meat pastries, along with two ceramic cups and a chilled decanter dotted with beads of condensation from the warm summer air.

His father took the liberty of pouring—a healthy measure for himself and a lesser amount for his son. Tristan smirked, but he took the cup gratefully. They'd never shared a drink like this before, as if they were old friends. As if they were equals. It made him think of Veronyka.

"How did you manage being my father *and* my commander these past years? How did you remain neutral?"

His father wore a somewhat dubious expression, popping a bite of a pastry into his mouth and dusting his hands. "I'm not sure I did," he said, casting his son an appraising look. "I've *tried* to be fair, and when I knew I couldn't be, well . . . I didn't go easier on you, did I? I went harder. I asked more of you than of anyone else, so there could be no question. An imperfect solution, but I knew you were up to the challenge, no matter how much you resented me for it."

The corners of his father's mouth quirked, and Tristan copied him. It did seem funny, now that he was on the other side of it. But this was where he'd gone wrong with Veronyka, inadvertently or not. He'd tried to make things easier for her, and that had made everything worse.

"What about you and my mother? You were the governor, plus her patrol leader. Didn't people whisper and gossip? And what about other mated pairs? Did the First Riders resent Queen Nefyra for having Callysta as her lover and her second?"

The commander considered Tristan over the edge of his cup. "Your interest in this subject matter . . . it has to do with our stable-boy-turned-apprentice, Veronyka?"

Tristan nodded stiffly, embarrassment tingling up and down his neck. He'd never in his life talked to his father about anything so personal, but the fact that his father guessed so easily meant that it wasn't just the new masters and young apprentices who'd noted his and Veronyka's behavior.

His father took a drink, studiously avoiding Tristan's eyes as he asked, "*Are* you a mated pair?"

"No!" Tristan blurted, wanting to melt away into the floorboards. "No, I mean . . . not yet. Maybe never. I just . . ." Axura above, he was talking to his *father* about mating with Veronyka. *Mating*, like animals. The prickling sensation crawling up his back was almost painfully hot. "We have a relationship outside of our roles as Riders, and I'm in a position of authority over her. I need to find a way to make it work so that people don't think I'm favoring her in some way. I don't want them to grow to resent her—especially after the whole 'Nyk' thing."

Tristan knew that Riders had romances with one another all the time. *That* wasn't the issue. If he were an apprentice, there would be no issue at all. Or maybe he was kidding himself. He was still the commander's son, wasn't he? Maybe there was no way for Tristan to become entangled with another Rider without causing some kind of scandal.

"You know your mother and I fought alongside each other for years before it became something more. In truth, I was meant to marry a Stellan girl—some councilman's daughter. My father had set it up for me, but then I met your mother. Well, I'm sure you remember that Olanna was not a woman to be ignored."

His father smiled wistfully, and an ache radiated from Tristan's chest. Sometimes he thought he could remember his mother, but other times he was certain he'd invented an image of her, pieced together from stories told by his nursemaid and his father, or people like Morra. He supposed that it might even be better than the real thing, because their words were colored with love, but he couldn't help but feel grief for the lack of his own memories.

His father pushed aside the plate of pastries and refilled his cup. When Tristan slid his forward, Cassian hesitated before smiling slightly and topping him off as well—a larger pour than before. "We were never a mated pair—our bondmates were not suited to each other—but our romance was well known. I won't say that it was easy. In fact, it was exceedingly difficult trying to stay away from your mother—if only for a time. Not that she would have me, at first. She was beloved among her fellow Riders, talented and bright and beautiful. Well born too, with ancestors all the way back to Oriyana Flamesong. I was one in a long line of hopeful suitors. So rather than press her, I made my case over time. Looking back, I think this is why we made such a strong match. We developed a friendship, a foundation, and didn't allow our feelings to distract us from our duty. There was no resentment or regret. Just as Callysta earned her reputation as a dazzling flyer and devastating warrior before she devoted herself to Nefyra, your mother was Olanna Flamesong long before she was my wife."

Tristan drank from his cup. He'd never heard his father say so much about his mother, about the time before the war. Maybe it was the wine, or maybe it was a newfound closeness he was feeling, but the blazing embarrassment that had burned his flesh moments before now felt as warm and comfortable as a hearth fire.

His father spoke easily, but now his tone turned hesitant. "If it is real, Tristan, and not a passing fancy," he began, and waved off Tristan's open-mouthed attempts to deny anything so frivolous. "I said *if*. If it is real, it will be all the sweeter for the waiting."

Waiting. The thought was not an encouraging one. Weren't they doing enough of that already?

"Has there been any news from the empire?" he asked, changing the subject.

His father cast a wary gaze around the dining hall, but the servant who had brought their meal was gone, and they were alone. Commander Cassian knew that when Tristan asked for news, he meant news from the spy, Sev. It had taken a while to get the information out of his father once Tristan realized the soldier was gone and had left no word of his plans or whereabouts. It had actually been Fallon who'd let it slip during a Riders Council meeting, and Tristan had the sinking feeling that if Fallon hadn't brought it up, he still wouldn't know what had become of the animage soldier.

But after their conversation tonight, Tristan felt like he and his father had crossed some invisible barrier—that the commander was finally starting to see Tristan as a man and not a boy.

"Nothing of note," his father said dismissively, but seeing the look on his son's face, he sighed good-naturedly. "These things take time, Tristan, and often the information we glean takes even longer to piece together into something usable."

They left the dining hall soon after, his father to his rooms inside the administrative building that had become his home, and Tristan to the Eyrie.

The rockwine sang in his veins as he approached the archway, and he veered right, toward the apprentice barracks. He lingered outside the building, staring at the window where he knew Veronyka's hammock hung. He stood there for a long time, imagining tapping on the windowpane or crawling in through the open shutter. What would happen then? His heart raced at the thought, but then he remembered his father's words.

We developed a friendship, a foundation, and didn't allow our feelings to distract us from our duty. There was no resentment or regret.

The last thing Tristan wanted was for Veronyka to resent him. He'd almost crossed that line during their most recent match, when his feelings for her had become a problem, a barrier to her success. He couldn't risk it. Maybe his father was right and waiting would make it sweeter.

Tristan walked away, past the scorched walls and still-charred remnants of what had once been a storage shed. Maybe his father was wrong and waiting was going to get them all killed.

Later, I realized my parents were more like falling stars,
destined to light my world for only the briefest of moments.
There and then gone again, my life colder after their passing.
Except, of course, for my sister.

- CHAPTER 7 -
SEV

FOUR DAYS LATER, SEV was set to meet with Lord Rolan in the governor's rooms instead of his own. If Sev thought the small chamber he was sleeping in was grander and more finely appointed than anywhere he'd had the privilege of entering before, Rolan's personal suite of rooms was a palace in and of itself.

There was marble everywhere, from the shining white floors to the fountain in the center of courtyard gardens, visible out the open double doors, to the massive fluted columns with their gilded capitals carved in flowers and twisting vines. Golden sculptures were perched on pedestals and in carved niches, while the fabrics ranged from the thick velvet hangings on Rolan's bed, embroidered with silver thread, to the whisper-thin silk tulle curtains stirring in the evening breeze.

Sev had seen grandeur in the rest of the compound—even the plates and cups were beautiful pieces of art that he was terrified to drop—but the corridors where soldiers and servants prowled were different from those Lord Rolan used, the walls punctuated with paintings and niches of statuary and the floor plush with rugs.

Rolan's personal attendant, Bertram, met Sev at the door and quickly guided him into a side chamber. It was a bare-bones room—probably once used for storage—and featured a simple wooden desk and three chairs, as well as a second door in the opposite wall, which undoubtedly led into the servant corridors.

The walls were pristine, as if they had been newly painted, and the lingering scent of lemon and pine oil told Sev that the room had recently been scrubbed down. Something about the stark plaster and the windowless walls caused apprehension to tighten his gut. This was no longer a simple storage space . . . it was an interrogation chamber.

Rolan was already seated. He waved Sev toward the chair next to him, and Sev sat gingerly, unease prickling his skin and making his shoulder, wrapped in a sling, ache.

He had been thinking about this moment every day since their first meeting, running through the possibility of who he might be faced with and how he would respond. He didn't want to condemn anyone, and his instincts told him to fall back on his old trick—playing dumb—but if he declared them all innocent, or said he didn't know anything, wouldn't Rolan become suspicious? What if Rolan started to question *Sev's* loyalty? Not only would his life be in danger, but his mission here as a spy would be over before it had even begun.

Sev didn't want to lie and claim someone was guilty when they weren't. . . . But what if they *were*? What if he came face-to-face with some of his fellow conspirators?

His instincts warred with one another, old and new.

The *old* Sev would have looked out for himself no matter what, but he didn't want to be that way anymore. But if Sev's *new* self served a greater purpose—protecting the Phoenix Riders and opposing the empire—then it was his duty to do whatever he could to help, which in this case meant remaining in place as a spy. Which circled back around to self-preservation.

Sev's head spun. In order to be better, he had to do his worst.

Bertram had barely shut the door behind Sev when a firm knock came from the other.

"Enter," Rolan called, and one of the estate's guards opened the door wide, ushering in an old, bent-backed and gray-headed bondservant. He had leathery brown skin and short bristly hair, and even when he straightened, he barely reached the guard's shoulder. He took the chair opposite them at the guard's command, placing his bound wrists on the table before them. The knuckles were knobby, and his fingers twitched and trembled.

Sev remembered him at once, though they'd never spoken a word to each other. The tightness in his stomach eased. This man was innocent, and whatever Sev might be willing to do to protect himself, condemning an innocent man wasn't it.

Rolan looked at Sev expectantly, while the man stared at the table, refusing to meet Sev's gaze. Luckily, Sev's *other* instincts kicked in—the ones that had him noticing every detail and memorizing every face. He knew this bondservant was innocent, and he could prove it.

"Well, Sevro?" Rolan prodded. "Do you remember this man?"

"Yes," Sev said, and Rolan straightened beside him. "He was part of the hunting party. A fisherman." It was a rare ability among animages, communicating with fish, but this man could get fish to swim directly into whatever nets or baskets he had set up. He spoke little and kept mostly to himself. "And the night of the attack, he was finishing the salt-trout rations for the return journey. No fish was served that night."

The bondservant seemed surprised by Sev's words, and the tremor in his hands lessened. Maybe he expected nothing good from a soldier. Sev remembered thinking the same thing, once.

Rolan's face was inscrutable. He glanced down at a sheaf of papers he'd brought in with him, as if confirming Sev's story against the details written there.

"Did you happen to catch his name, Sevro?"

"Alastor," Sev said, and Rolan nodded. He gestured to the guard standing by the door, who helped the bondservant to his feet and led him back out the door they'd come through.

Before Sev could guess what would happen to Alastor, another knock sounded on the door, and the guard returned with a young woman. She was probably only a few years older than Sev's eighteen, and despite having her hands bound like the old man before her, she held her chin high.

Sev studied her face, but he didn't recognize her. Her expression was defiant, if a bit cowed by Rolan's cool, indifferent stare.

"I've never seen her before, my lord."

"She was stationed with the secondary forces and would have arrived around the time the poisoning took place," Rolan said, glancing down at his papers once again. "We are assuming the poisoning was at the hands of Captain Belden's bondservants, but I wish to be thorough. You never saw her near the cook fires or food stores?"

Sev shook his head. "No, sir."

"Very well," Rolan said, though his voice sounded more tired than relieved as he bent over his papers and waved the girl and the guard away. Sev tried to read over Rolan's shoulder and thought he caught the words "return to" before the governor leaned back and Sev hastily withdrew his gaze.

The third bondservant was a plump woman who wept throughout the meeting, and the fourth was a burly man with an unkempt beard and forearms as thick as tree trunks. Neither had been involved, as far as Sev knew, and he did his best to recount where he last remembered seeing them or their assignments on the day's duty rosters. It was a delicate balance—Sev knew more than the average soldier would, so he had to be vague in some instances and more specific in others.

He measured each word he spoke, hoping every time the door closed that it would be the last time—while secretly, desperately hoping that it wouldn't be, that there would be just one more survivor. . . .

Even that was selfish, though. In a perfect world, Kade wouldn't be caught—he'd have run as far from the war and the empire as possible. In some ways that was easier. . . . Sev could imagine him living somewhere safe in Pyra, free from bondage, but the hard part was that he'd never know for sure. The hard part was imagining the *other* possibility if Kade didn't turn up today, the far more likely possibility that Kade had died like so many others that night. That Sev would never see him again.

Rolan took notes, asking questions here and there, but it seemed that their full stories had already been recounted and recorded—likely by Officer Yara—and Sev was acting as confirmation for the details.

He wasn't sure if he should be relieved that none of Trix's true conspirators had been caught, or if this meant that they'd all likely been executed atop Pyrmont.

When the door opened for the fifth time, Sev's heart plummeted.

This was someone he knew—and not the person he'd secretly been hoping for.

The man who shuffled into the room had steely gray hair and eyes to match. His skin was a deep, ruddy shade that came from a lifetime in the sun, and his thin body was wiry with age and decades of hard work. Sev recalled that he'd been a breeder of Stellan horses in the south but hadn't been a registered animage and so owed fifteen years of back taxes. He'd probably be a bondservant until he died.

Sev remembered him; he'd been part of the hunting party—the worst duty for an animage, being forced to lure animals to the slaughter over and over again.

He'd also been a supporter of Trix. He'd helped to harvest the *pyraflora*— Trix's poison of choice—while out on hunting trips, and Sev had seen him whispering with Trix many times throughout their long journey up Pyrmont.

As soon as the man's eyes fell on Sev, he stiffened in recognition, causing the soldier who held his arms to shove him more aggressively toward his seat, as if the man had been resisting his grip rather than reacting to the sight of Sev sitting there on the opposite side of the table.

Just as Sev had seen him with Trix, so too had he seen Sev.

His name was Ulric. They had never spoken, but Sev saw a familiar hatred in his eyes—the hatred he himself had carried toward soldiers, toward the empire, for most of his life—and knew that this was not going to go like the rest. For him to see Sev alive and well while he was imprisoned—and the majority of his co-conspirators dead—was obviously too much for Ulric to bear. His eyes glinted dangerously, near the point of looking deranged, and Sev understood in that instant that this man wanted to bring Sev down, his own life be damned.

"All right, Sevro, let's——"

"That man is a traitor!" Ulric said, voice tight with suppressed rage as he cut Lord Rolan off. The room went silent. The soldier who'd deposited Ulric into his chair stepped forward, as if ready to apprehend the bondservant, though he glanced to Rolan for instruction.

Rolan held up a hand to the soldier, halting his movement, before turning his attention to Ulric. "I do not recall asking you to speak."

Ulric laughed, a rasping bark that echoed in the cramped space. "No, but I will," he said, the laughter dying as abruptly as it had begun. He leaned forward in his chair. "He's one of us. He's a traitor, and here he sits next to his lord, a war hero, while the rest of us bow and bend and scrape."

Out of nowhere, he lunged for Sev, but his hands came up short, missing their target—Sev's throat—by inches, thanks to the soldier, who leapt forward and took hold of the back of Ulric's tunic.

Sev reared back anyway, almost toppling over in his chair, but Rolan gripped his good shoulder to steady him.

When it was clear he'd not be able to move again, Ulric spat instead. It landed on Sev's chest, and he clenched his jaw to stop from reacting. He was breathing heavily, the accusations stinging, despite the fact that he understood them. This man thought Sev had gotten away with it—which he had—but that he'd decided to return to his masters in the empire without a backward glance. Maybe he expected Sev to turn him in—Sev would have too, if faced with an empire soldier in his position—but what made Sev's stomach twist painfully was the realization that now he *had* to do exactly what the man expected him to. He had to discredit Ulric's claims.

"He was one of hers!" Ulric shouted, struggling against the soldier's hold, though he was weak and easily restrained. "That old woman needed a soldier. She needed one of them near the animals. She——"

Sev lurched to his feet, turning his fear and panic into outward anger.

"Shut your mouth, beast-talker," he snapped, having heard the slur count-less times and never once expecting to say it himself, and with such vitriol. With such hate. But he had to stop Ulric from speaking, stop him from saying something that Sev couldn't explain away.

He turned to Lord Rolan. "This man was a member of the hunting party—and he resented it. He—" Sev hesitated, his stomach clenched like a fist. "He wanted to work with the pack animals instead. Asked me to put in a good word, as if I'd put my neck out for a *mageslave*. I thought he just hated the hunt, but he must've wanted to be near the food supplies."

Ulric bared his teeth in a snarl. "She didn't need me there when she already had—"

Rolan said, in a bored voice, "Subdue him."

There was a loud thump—a fist to the jaw—and Ulric sagged dazedly in his seat, his lip bloody.

Rolan turned an expressionless face to Sev. "And the night of the poi-soning?"

Sev felt as if he stood on a precipice, overlooking an expanse of dark, endless emptiness below. Could he do it? Could he cross that line and make that leap?

Did he have a choice? This was spying, wasn't it? Ruthlessness. Fear-lessness. Trix had said she was ready every day for her own death—but she didn't talk about how many times she'd defeated death. How many others she had condemned to die in her stead.

Trix never talked about how hard it was to be good at surviving when it seemed so many others were good at dying.

Sev swallowed thickly and stepped over the edge.

"He was lurking near the cook fires," he said, acid roiling in his belly, "and now I think on it, they decided to serve stew last minute—and *he* butchered the venison they used. He must have convinced the servants to change the menu and poisoned the meat when he couldn't get at the other food stores."

It was true that they had been serving venison stew that night, among other things. And it was true that the stewpots were poisoned. Sev didn't know if Ulric had helped with the actual poisoning, but he had been involved in making the poison itself. He *was* guilty.

But so was Sev, and never had his position in this world—both as a soldier and as an animage—been clearer than when Rolan took his account without question, turned a look of disgust toward Ulric, and sent him and his soldier guard away. Where was Ulric going? To be locked up? To be killed? Sev would probably never know.

Chest heaving, he fought to get his breath under control.

With his eyes on his papers, Rolan handed Sev a handkerchief—meant for the spit that had spattered across his tunic. Sev accepted numbly, wiping all evidence of what had just happened away.

"Thank you, my lord," he said as soon as his voice was under control. He lowered himself back into his chair. It creaked.

Rolan nodded, shuffling his papers.

Sev was suddenly exhausted. His shoulder ached—whatever medicine Hestia had given him was wearing off—and he longed for solitude. Deep down, the ghostly wisp of hope he'd been clinging to that maybe, maybe he'd get to see someone else today was slowly dissipating like smoke in the wind.

"Well, Sevro, that's—oh, no," Rolan said, coming to a final page and squinting down at it. "It seems we've got one more. . . ."

Sev stopped listening. Anticipation flared to life inside him, and some-how he *knew*, even before the knock sounded and the tall, broad-shouldered bondservant was shoved into the chair opposite them.

Sev stared, just barely managing to tamp down on his wild, swirling emotions, eyes boring into the top of the bondservant's head. Slowly, as if it weighed a hundred pounds, the bondservant lifted his chin. Molten amber eyes, sharply carved jawline, and the unmistakable scowl of Kade.

The breath whooshed from Sev's lungs. Badly healing scabs and faded bruising marred the skin of Kade's face and knuckles—he had clearly been fighting—and his eyes were cold and distant . . . until they landed on

Sev. Something warm flickered inside. Something as bright and sudden as lightning.

Sev wanted to cry. He wanted to laugh. He wanted to say a prayer to Teyke or Anyanke or whoever had pulled this off.

But then he realized the terrible danger Kade was in. What had just happened to Ulric would be nothing if Sev couldn't get Kade out of this unharmed. If the gods had brought them together only to rip them apart again, Sev didn't think he could bear it.

Kade was guilty, just as Ulric had been. But he wasn't fool enough to shout accusations and goad Sev into revealing the truth. He would know that Sev was trying to save him.

Wouldn't he?

There was something questioning in Kade's eye . . . something uncertain. He had doubted Sev all along, hadn't he? Was it so surprising that he'd doubt Sev now, safe and cared for by their enemies?

"Yes," Sev found himself saying, even before Rolan prompted him. "I know him."

Rolan waited expectantly, while Kade had gone still as a statue. "We were positioned together with the pack animals."

"The pack animals that carried the food stores?" Rolan asked, moving to make a note on his papers.

Sev nodded. "Yes, sir. But," he continued, "the bondservant was reassigned halfway through our journey." No need to mention *why* he was moved—or where—unless Rolan asked. "He was nowhere near the food or the preparations. What's more," Sev added, when Rolan continued to frown, "he saved my life."

"He did?" Rolan repeated, glancing at Kade. "How?"

Sev couldn't tell him the truth—but as any good liar will tell you, it's best to stick as close to the truth as possible.

"One of the bondservants was trying to escape and came up behind me with a knife drawn. This one hit the attacker over the head with a piece of wood."

"He attacked one of his own?" Rolan asked, sounding almost impressed.

Kade's expression turned dark—or rather, dark*er.* Sev doubted anyone but him would notice the subtle shift at the suggestion that he would turn against his fellows.

"He did," Sev said, trying to shoot Kade an apologetic look while Rolan's attention was on his papers. "But then we got separated in the chaos, and I didn't know what had become of him."

"How do you know he didn't kill that bondservant to cover his own actions?"

Sev considered his words. "I don't," he said at last, shrugging. He had to be careful how he played this, else Rolan would know that there was more between them than Sev was letting on. That Sev was keenly invested in the outcome of this particular interrogation. "I just know he was nowhere near the food that night."

"Indeed," said Rolan, leaning back in his chair to consider Kade. He nodded, and the guard moved to escort Kade from the room.

Sev stared at the man. Was that it—was Kade off the hook?

As Kade was pulled to his feet, they shared a look—a bare instant in which so much needed to be said but couldn't be—and then he was gone again, the heavy door swinging shut behind him.

*We were not meant to orbit one another, or to pass in and
out of each other's skies. We were always destined to collide,
leaving heartbreak and desolation in our wake.*

- CHAPTER 8 -
VERONYKA

SOMEHOW—POSSIBLY THANKS TO HIS new position as patrol
leader, but more probably because of his guilt over their last combat
match—Tristan managed to get Veronyka on his patrol for a visit to Vayle.

It was a temporary assignment. She wasn't actually a part of their patrol
or a Master Rider. She wasn't approved for active duty, but she was apparently more than welcome to help with menial labor.

They were being sent to check in with the Vayle villagers and to survey
damages. While Rushlea and Petratec had been the main targets during
the empire's diversionary attacks, when the soldiers had fled, they'd burned
and pillaged on their way back down the mountain. A patrol of Riders
had returned the next day to chase them off and force their retreat, but by
that time most of the damage was done—not to mention the new damages
inflicted by their pursuit.

Fallon's patrol had been stationed in Rushlea for two weeks to oversee
repairs, and even the commander's patrol had spent several days in Petratec.
Because Vayle was farthest—and had suffered the least damage—they'd
been put last on the list.

"I know why he's sending me," Tristan said, smiling and shaking his
head as he stuffed a few extra tunics inside his travel bag. They were in

his Master Rider chambers, early-morning sunlight spilling in from the open door. The rest of his patrol would be meeting them atop the phoenix plinth in several moments, and Veronyka was already packed. "The people of Vayle aren't happy. They've sent two messengers plus I don't know how many pigeons requesting some face time. He doesn't want to deal with it."

He was obviously talking about his father, the commander. But while such a situation would have made Tristan angry just a few short weeks ago, now he seemed more . . . amused. He and his father were definitely on better terms than they had been when Veronyka arrived at the Eyrie, and she was glad for him. He had proved something to his father and to himself, and he deserved this newfound confidence. Now he could laugh at being made to do grunt work and not feel insulted or belittled by it.

"We'll be there for two days tops, helping with cleanup and meeting with their leaders." He closed his satchel and swung it over his shoulder, peering down at her. He looked a bit uneasy. "I know it's not a real patrol," he said, "but it's something."

"And I'm grateful," Veronyka said. She was still disappointed in her current situation, but Tristan was right—this was real work out there in the real world. Maybe she'd be able to prove her worth outside the combat ring.

Veronyka had been working hard on what Morra had told her about shadow and animal magic, separating the two "rivers" in her mind and tightening the stones on the shadow magic side of her mental tower. It was difficult without actually using shadow magic to sense vulnerabilities, but Veronyka did the best she could. She hadn't slipped into Tristan's mind or sensed Val since she'd started doing it, but she knew her mind was far from airtight. Guarding herself constantly was exhausting, but she thought—or maybe hoped—that she was beginning to get the hang of it.

As they made their way to the phoenix plinth to saddle their bondmates and head out, Veronyka remembered how close Vayle was to the cabin she'd shared with Val. Was there any chance Val was still living there . . . ? She wrenched her mind away from thoughts of her once-sister. The temptation to think about Val was like the flickering, dancing allure of an open flame: enticing, mesmerizing—and likely to leave her burned.

Maybe Veronyka needed a concrete way of releasing Val. . . . She glanced down at her braided bracelet, thinking. How was she supposed to forget Val entirely when she wore a reminder—the red lock of hair and golden signet ring—on her wrist every single day? A visit to the cabin might be the perfect way to say goodbye. To leave Val and the objects that represented her behind. Maybe then she'd be able to let go of thoughts of her own mysterious identity and the sister who wasn't a sister at all. She'd get some closure, and then she'd be able to move forward.

As Veronyka and Tristan saddled their mounts, the other Riders in Tristan's patrol slowly turned up, greeting them with exhausted stretches and wide yawns.

Besides Tristan there was Ronyn, a no-nonsense local with a heavy brow and thick, muscled arms; Anders, a joker from Arboria with curling brown hair and large ears; Latham, the gossip who was often by Anders's side, his pale golden hair shining in the morning sun; and finally Lysandro, who was Ferronese and a distant cousin of Tristan's. Apparently Tristan and his father had been living with Lysandro's family in the Foothills for years before making the Eyrie their home and base of operations. While Anders beamed and Ronyn nodded politely at her, the others seemed surprised by her presence. Latham scowled.

"Since we are a Rider short of a full patrol, Commander Cassian allowed me to bring along an apprentice, so I chose my underwing, Veronyka," Tristan said, speaking in his authoritative voice. No one made any comment or objection, so he continued. "We're going to fly a southeastern route, staying clear of the river and the road, and land in the tree cover just north of Malka's ruined outpost. We'll make camp there and come at Vayle on foot. They're expecting us, but we don't want to announce our presence armed and on phoenix-back. We might be their allies, but I doubt we'll receive the warmest welcome."

"It's gotta be better than at Petratec," Anders muttered, shaking his head. "I flew extra supplies out, and I thought they were gonna shoot me down from the sky."

"They're trying to protect themselves," said Ronyn, whose family was from Petratec. "I cannot blame them."

"I can," Anders said indignantly, adjusting a wrist guard. "Or I *would have*, if they'd filled me full of holes."

Ronyn rolled his eyes and cuffed Anders across the back of his head. Anders grinned.

"Harder next time," Latham said through a yawn, and Anders shoved him.

Tristan let them get their jokes in before bringing the conversation back to the issue at hand. "We'll fly in a standard *trivol*—a three-Rider arrowhead pattern," he added to Veronyka, who hadn't yet learned all the flight combinations. "I'll take first lead with Veronyka and Lysandro."

Veronyka was pleased to be flying with Tristan, and Lysandro too seemed excited to fly next to the patrol leader. Lysandro was a year younger than Veronyka, and though Tristan didn't seem to notice, it was clear he idolized his older cousin. He constantly looked to Tristan for cues on how to act or behave, and he took heart from Tristan's smallest gestures of approval and affection. Flying next to Tristan in a *trivol* meant he was flying in a position usually held by a second-in-command.

It meant Veronyka was as well.

"Ronyn," Tristan continued, "you'll run point with Anders and Latham."

Everyone nodded, returning to their phoenixes for a last check of fastenings and straps. The sky was a pearly shade of pink toward the east, the stars and shadows chased away by Axura's coming dawn. There was a feeling in the air, a crackle of energy and anticipation.

Veronyka hopped into the saddle, Tristan on Rex in front of her and Lysandro just beside.

Once everyone was mounted up, Tristan leapt, disappearing over the edge of the plinth before soaring back up into the sky. Lysandro followed, and then Veronyka. Her stomach swooped with the drop, only to tingle with adrenaline as they shot back up into the sky. She took a deep, chest-filling breath, the misty morning air cool and refreshing against her skin. The sky was wide and welcoming, the view endless and unobstructed all around.

Inside her mind, Xephyra's sleepy thoughts filtered through the bond. *More lessons?* she asked, getting better and better with her vocabulary and communication skills.

No, Veronyka said, grinning. *This is the real thing.*

It was the longest journey Veronyka had taken on phoenix-back.

Xephyra seemed to enjoy the extended flight—they'd flown long hours before, but usually in circuits while training in the gullies and peaks around the Eyrie. Here, the landscape changed beneath them, the entirety of Pyra unfolding far below. Rock and river and tree, all of it familiar and yet different observed from above. Everything seemed minuscule, almost like toys dotting the ground below, and yet the sky . . . the sky seemed to grow and expand, endless blue in all directions.

Veronyka marveled that she had done the same journey on foot. It seemed so painfully slow, plodding on step after step, when, with one powerful pump of her wings, Xephyra could traverse hours' worth of foot travel.

Of course, the wind currents often set them slightly off course—they didn't fly straight and true like an arrow—and they couldn't pump their wings and fight against the updrafts the entire time or they'd quickly grow exhausted. Still, a journey that had taken Veronyka almost a full week took Xephyra and the rest of the phoenixes about seven hours, not including their midday stop for food and rest.

By the time they reached Malka's ruined outpost outside Vayle, the afternoon sun was turning the landscape into a haze of citrus hues—warm orange and golden lemon. Even the trees and grass were rich in the summer sunlight, as green as a fresh-sliced lime.

As the Riders dismounted and began to make camp, a strange, uneasy feeling settled over Veronyka. It seemed it had been a lifetime since she'd stood in this spot, thinking her dreams dashed for good. Then Sparrow had found her, and when Beryk turned up, a new path presented itself. She was closer to the cabin, to her old life with Val, than she had been in months. Yet it seemed longer given all the ways things had changed, not only in her life, but in her heart and mind as well.

But there was so much that remained unanswered, so much that only Val could tell her. A familiar stirring tickled the edges of her awareness, like a brush of wingbeats. Val's doorway. A part of her was always there in Veronyka's mind; Veronyka simply had to reach for it.

She clenched her jaw and forced thoughts of Val from her mind before shoring up the stones inside her mental walls. But no matter how sturdy she made them, she didn't know how to board up a doorway. She'd tried stacking stones around it. She'd tried imagining mud and planks of sturdy wood. . . . But whatever she did, Veronyka knew the door was there, that there was no way of erasing it entirely. This was doubly hard when trying to block someone who had the gift themselves, someone who was always seeking any crack or sliver of vulnerability. Someone who had a door in her walls made just for them.

"Veronyka?" Tristan said, cutting into her thoughts. He put a hand on her shoulder, and she jumped.

"Oh—hi," she said, so focused on closing off her magic that she hadn't heard his approach. But just like with Val, Tristan's door was always there. When she gave him her full attention, uncertainty radiated out from him, an anxious humming through their bond—no matter how hard Veronyka tried to block it. He rubbed a hand along the back of his neck, ruffling his soft brown curls. Behind him the others had begun to make camp within the ruins of the outpost.

"We usually sleep together, two per tent," he began, and Veronyka nodded, having seen the camping supplies before. "Since we're only five, I usually take the last tent by myself. . . ." He faltered, and Veronyka understood at once. She was now their sixth member, and there was only one available tent to sleep in—his.

Tristan leaned in slightly, lowering his voice. "I brought an extra tent," he said, his brow furrowed, "but I know that looks like I'm giving you special treatment. But if we sleep in the tent *together*"—he cleared his throat— "that looks like special treatment too. I . . ." He trailed off, looking totally at a loss. It was almost funny—or it would have been, if they hadn't so recently been discussing this very issue. She was their first female trainee, and she hated how it made her stand out. Even here, on a simple overnight mission, there were issues. Complications. *Problems.*

Sometimes Veronyka wished she'd just kept up the Nyk facade. At least then she could have fit in with the others in some way, even if it was a lie. Now she was new, a girl, *and* she was Tristan's favorite. The idea would have thrilled her endlessly once—and it still did, down deep in her stomach— but it also made her feel isolated.

And the worst part was, proper or not, part of her wanted to sleep in Tristan's tent. He was her best friend, the person she felt closest to. The idea of sleeping side by side . . .

Veronyka shook her head. "Thanks, Tristan, but I'll sleep outside with Xephyra," she said, nodding at her bondmate, who was currently snuffling her beak along the ground at the edges of the clearing, Rex close by.

"No—I'll do that," Tristan said hastily, guilt flickering across his face and through their connection, as if he regretted that he hadn't thought of it first. Veronyka closed her eyes and pressed her fingers to her temples, pushing his feelings from her mind. She didn't know if Morra's advice was truly helping her, but she had to trust it, and to be content with the fact that even if her control over their connection wasn't getting better, it wasn't getting worse, either.

She looked up to find Tristan frowning at her, as if confused by her gestures.

Veronyka forced a smile, her chest tight. "Just a bit of a headache," she murmured, glancing away. "You can't sleep outside and give me the tent— that's special treatment, remember? If you usually sleep in a tent, then that's what you'll do. Honestly, I don't mind. It's summer, and if it gets a bit cold, Xephyra will keep me warm."

His jaw worked at that comment, and her stomach clenched at the thought that maybe he'd liked the idea of sleeping side by side too—that he wanted to be the one to keep her warm.

"Come on," she said, avoiding his gaze. "Let's help set up."

They walked into the village first thing the following morning, taking in the empire's destruction for the first time. Their feet scraped against the gravel as they traversed the quiet streets, so different from the bustling village Veronyka remembered. Villagers huddled in corners or watched them from inside darkened windows, the entire place strangely cold and lifeless.

Veronyka's insides felt hollow. There were scorch marks everywhere—on the finely painted shutters and the smooth stone walls, on the surrounding trees, and even on the fishing boats moored near the bridge.

And the bridge. It was gone.

It had been a massive wooden archway, stretching across the wide bend of the Aurys, its planks worn smooth after decades of feet and wagon wheels.

Now it was a blackened skeleton, the barest framework remaining on both sides, like hunched old folks reaching in vain across the river's dark depths.

There was more. All along the riverbank and in seemingly random places across the village were bunches of flowers.

Veronyka understood the meaning at once.

The delicate, pale-white Star Flowers, or *stellaflora*, were here to commemorate the dead, whose souls would rise into the sky to live among the stars.

Then there were the spiky black Shadow Blooms, more commonly called deathmaidens after the servants of the goddess Nox, who took lost souls to the dark realms. These flowers were meant to protect, to lure the deathmaidens and distract them, allowing the missing loved ones a chance to make it home.

Veronyka swallowed. So many flowers . . . so many dead and lost.

Next to her, Tristan had gone ashen, the warm olive of his skin almost gray in the early-morning light. All of them wore similar expressions of shock and grief. They hadn't known it was this bad. . . . And how could they? Commander Cassian hadn't sent anyone. Even the numbers that had been reported didn't match—or maybe they just didn't convey—what they saw here.

A spark of anger blistered Veronyka's chest, even as she tried to reason with herself. Rushlea and Petratec had suffered *worse* damage. They couldn't be everywhere at once. But they could be more places if they had more Riders. Veronyka might not be perfect, but she was capable, and she shouldn't be held back just to pass some arbitrary tests. If she'd known it was this bad, she would have asked to fly back and help out herself.

Still, the frustration was there, along with the guilt, a fiery cocktail licking up her throat. Low croons echoed down from the outpost clearing, where the phoenixes remained out of sight but always connected to their bondmates' emotions.

Heat brushed Veronyka's skin—Tristan, his hands balled into fists by his sides. Compassion overwhelmed her anger when she realized that no matter whose fault this was, no matter that it was his father's decision to delay their arrival here, Tristan was the one who would answer for it.

Though she knew it was dangerous, Veronyka reached out and put a hand on his shoulder. She meant only to steady him—she didn't open herself or reach with her magic, but as she took slow, deep breaths, Tristan's own heaving chest hitched, then slowed, mirroring hers. Was that shadow magic, or just the comfort of a friend?

Veronyka dropped her hand, and Tristan turned to the others. "There will be a town meeting in the cookhouse this morning. All are invited. I'll need someone to take notes—Lysandro?" he asked, looking to his cousin, who nodded at once, a satchel with ink and paper already in hand.

"What about the rest of us?" asked Ronyn, glancing uneasily around at the villagers who were now drifting out of their homes, whispering and pointing at the newcomers or walking purposefully toward the cookhouse. There was an air of hostility—or at least wariness—in the way they regarded the Phoenix Riders, as if wondering what new harm they might bring down on the village.

"We'll get started," Veronyka said, looking between them. She didn't know about the others, but she had lived through tenement fires, burglars, raids, and riots before. She'd lost count of how many times she'd scavenged wood from junk heaps to repair broken window shutters or helped her *maiora* scrub ash and charcoal from their walls. They were so used to the possibility that everything could go to pieces overnight that they buried their valuables—such as they were—into the dirt floor, ensuring no harm from fire or thieves could come to them.

When they all turned to her with blank stares, she continued. "We'll need to clear out the damaged wood, figure out what can be salvaged or repurposed and what can be burned. If we can get our hands on some distilled vinegar—the cookhouse or anyone who's willing to donate from their reserves—we can make a solution with water and lemon and get scrubbing some of these stone exteriors. . . ."

Tristan looked like he could kiss her. His face softened, his eyes bright with suppressed emotion—half gratitude, half relief. She knew that if the Riders were out here working—no matter how seemingly menial the task—everything would go easier for him inside.

Her cheeks heated at the intensity of his emotion and the way it begged to push through the barriers of her mind, but in truth, she wasn't doing this for him.

She was doing it for the people of Vayle.

No matter how bleak things had felt whenever a wave of fires decimated an entire sector of the Narrows, it was in the moments after, when neighbors joined together to clean and build and salvage what they could, that Veronyka had felt truly connected to the world around her. When she felt she belonged somewhere. It was fleeting, perhaps, but it had taught her the power of togetherness.

The villagers had made a start—patches of buildings showed evidence of scrubbing, and most of the burned wood and debris had been cleared away—but it was easy to see how they'd been derailed. With no bridge, Vayle's trade and commerce with the other villages must have screeched to a halt. That wasn't to mention the way most of Pyra would have suffered when news of the empire soldiers spread through the countryside. Travel was practically nonexistent with or without a functional bridge, and many had been wounded—or worse—during the attacks. Villages like Vayle were trying to get back to business as usual, which for some meant rebuilding livelihoods from the ground up. It was still summer, but no doubt their winter stores were taking a hit as the people tried to piece their lives back together.

"Yes." Tristan nodded vigorously at Veronyka before turning to the others. "Let's get it done," he said, before straightening his shoulders and striding toward the cookhouse with Lysandro.

To her intense surprise, Ronyn, Anders, and Latham turned to her, as if awaiting orders. "Any of you cleaned anything before?" she asked.

Anders and Latham glanced uneasily at each other, and Ronyn rolled his eyes. "My *maiora* had me scrubbing floors before I could walk," he said, and Veronyka grinned.

"Okay. Anders and Latham, go get your axes and gloves from camp and start taking down what's left of this bridge. Separate the wood into three piles: good, salvageable, and scrap. Make sure to save any metal nails or hinges. Once that's done, see if the villagers will let you take down their damaged doors and shutters. Ronyn, you'll come with me. Time to see if those muscles are good for more than just fighting."

Ronyn gave a wolfish grin. "There won't be a spot of soot when I'm through."

"Good," Veronyka said, smiling widely. "We'll make your *maiora* proud."

They worked well into the evening, until darkness prevented them from continuing. While the day had begun as a solitary effort by the Riders, by afternoon, children were gathering nails and refilling water buckets, while strong young adults helped carry planks of wood and scrubbed buildings and old folks were forcing cups of water and fresh crusts of bread into their hands. The atmosphere in the village had shifted from one of tension and mistrust to the satisfied companionship of a team effort.

Tristan and Lysandro were still locked away inside the cookhouse; Tristan had left the building once at midday, ensuring that the Riders were fed and that there were no squabbles and concerns in the village before returning, tired-eyed but determined, to his meeting with their leaders.

Back at camp they'd built a fire in the ring of ruins. The tents were pitched around it, their canvas walls rippling in the evening breeze.

Veronyka had been nervous to be alone with Tristan's patrol now that the work was done, worried that her presence as an outsider would make things a bit awkward or tense. But the long day—and the fact that Veronyka had been an integral part of their effort—had forged a sense of camaraderie between them. The others seemed less wary of her presence, and they shared food and drink as if it were natural for her to be among them. As if she were accepted.

Later, while the others were settled inside their tents or slouched just outside, staring drowsily into the flames, Veronyka sat near the mouth of their camp so she could see down the slope toward Vayle, where golden lantern lights twinkled in the darkness. Rex and Xephyra were nearby, gnawing quietly on fallen branches from nearby walnut trees, keeping their beaks sharp as they tried to get to the sweet sapwood underneath.

Rex stopped abruptly, dropping his branch onto the earth with a thud as he raised his head, staring in the direction of the road. Footsteps and low whispers could be heard as Tristan and Lysandro finally made their return.

Rex leapt forward to greet his bondmate, while Lysandro's mount, a more hesitant creature, fluttered excitedly just behind. Tristan clapped Lysandro on his back when they parted ways just outside the light of the campfire, murmuring words of thanks, and Lysandro's face lit with pride as he joined the others.

"Hey, Rex," Tristan said, patting his phoenix gently along his neck and receiving an affectionate nuzzle in return. After a quick survey of his bondmate, Rex ruffled his feathers in satisfaction and tried to return to his branch—but Xephyra had taken it up in his place and was now trying to keep both branches to herself. The two scuffled and squawked—Xephyra standing guard while Rex tried to bait and draw her out—until eventually Rex managed to steal Xephyra's original branch, and she kept his—leaving them right back where they'd started, with a branch apiece.

"How did it go?" Veronyka asked, starting to get to her feet, but Tristan was slumped down on the ground next to her before she could stand, leaning against the heap of packs and supplies that Veronyka had been using as a seat. Their backs were to the fire, where Lysandro could be heard recounting the day's events to Ronyn and Latham, who poked their heads out from their tents, trying to listen over the sound of Anders's snores.

"It was . . . well—they were angry, at first. And I can't blame them. Most of that damage wasn't from soldiers. It was from us."

Veronyka nodded as Tristan shrugged out of his formal Rider uniform—a leather vest stamped with spread wings that tied down the middle with red-dyed laces. It was a remnant of before the war, a formal, decorative bit of armor that identified a soldier as a Rider and indicated their rank and position. It deliberately resembled the Ashfire sigil and was almost as old. The Riders hadn't worn them under Cassian's new regime until recently, when he'd wanted to present a united—and slightly more impressive—front to the locals in the wake of the empire's attack. Even Veronyka had one, simpler and less finely made than Tristan's and stamped with a single wing to indicate she was still an apprentice.

Tossing the leather aside, Tristan stretched and settled back more comfortably in the soft brown tunic he'd been wearing underneath.

"I mostly just listened to their stories. They want to be heard, to feel like we care. They're scared, I think—scared there'll be more attacks, that Pyra will become a battleground again like it was during the war." He sighed heavily, ruffling his hair as he sank lower into the packs. "I have to thank you, Nyk," he muttered, voice drifting off. *"Veronyka,"* he corrected, straightening slightly and darting a glance in her direction. She could just make out the edge of his face in the darkness, brows arched apologetically, but she only smiled. She'd told him he could call her whatever he wanted, and she meant it. She even missed the moniker from time to time. Seeing that she wasn't upset, he continued. "They warmed considerably to me when they heard what you guys were doing . . . with all the cleanup." He yawned widely. "They have plans for a new bridge already drawn up, plus an estimate of the supplies they think they need." He paused. "I don't know what help the commander will give them."

Veronyka leaned next to him, their shoulders just barely brushing together. Her body was heavy with fatigue, but there was a peacefulness that came with it. She'd done something of value today—they all had—and it eased some of the restlessness that had been gnawing at her for weeks.

"Even if he refuses to send more aid, we're not expected back for another day at least, right?"

"Right," Tristan said through another yawn. "I didn't expect to finish our meetings in a single day."

"So we'll stay tomorrow, finish whatever we can?"

His head bobbed up and down. "Yeah . . . I think they'd appreciate that. It's the least we can do, after everything. Plus, they want to meet you."

"Me?" Veronyka asked in surprise.

He smiled, a flash of teeth in the darkness. "The local girl who became a Phoenix Rider."

Tristan went quiet after that, and Veronyka settled down deeper onto her pack. She supposed she *was* a local, in a way, though she wasn't from Vayle originally.

Or am I?

Veronyka had no idea. Still, she felt strong ties to this place—to the cabin she and Val had shared. It would be good to see it again, even if it brought up painful memories. Veronyka needed to see it. She needed to say goodbye.

Tristan's slow, steady breathing filled the silence as the campfire burned low. Before long Rex shuffled over, huddling down next to him and burying his face under his wing. Warmth enveloped Veronyka as Xephyra settled into a similar position on her other side.

They slept there, under the stars, while the tent beside them stayed empty.

Pyraean folktales claim that during the Dark Days, every time a strix fell from the sky, a deathmaiden was born. They were shadows made solid, darkness personified, who took on the form of the dead and haunted battlefields. Instead of letting the dead find their place among the stars, the death-maidens tried to ensnare the lost souls and lead them into the endless black abyss of the dark realms.

This concept likely originated from the clusters of black flowers that cover the upper reaches of Pyrmont, shifting and whispering in the breeze, their color so deep and dark that they seem to absorb light. Superstitious locals likely saw these Shadow Blooms as deathmaidens themselves, and believed their presence was meant to mark some ancient battle fought long ago where a strix had fallen from the sky.

Others maintained that the death of a strix merely lured the deathmaidens, and from this belief arose the custom of using Shadow Blooms as a means to draw and distract the deathmaidens, helping lost souls avoid their clutches and find peace in the heavens.

—*Myths and Legends of the Golden Empire and Beyond*, a compilation of stories and accounts, the Morian Archives, 101 AE

*Sometimes I think we were nothing more than two
lost girls with the weight of an empire on our narrow
shoulders. What might we have been if we'd been born
in a different time . . . under different stars?*

- CHAPTER 9 -

VERONYKA

THE NEXT DAY WENT by in a blur. Veronyka and Ronyn continued their cleaning efforts, while Tristan scouted local forests for ideal trees to supply wood for the bridge, and Anders, Latham, and Lysandro helped build a small shed to store their burgeoning supplies and tallied materials.

Before Veronyka knew it, the sun was dipping low in the sky, and Tristan's patrol was walking back to the campsite.

Veronyka's muscles ached, and the others complained of splinters and sore backs—but it was in a familiar, companionable way. Their group was in high spirits, and they had the night to themselves before they left the following morning.

She had hoped to find an opportunity that day to hop on Xephyra and sneak down to the cabin, but time had gotten away from her, and she was too tired to fly tonight.

Veronyka was walking next to Tristan at the back of the group as they made their way to camp. "Are we leaving first thing tomorrow?" she asked.

"Probably. We've done all we can for now, and I want to get my report to the commander as soon as possible. Why?"

Veronyka wavered. She'd told Tristan a bit about her upbringing, but he didn't know everything she had discovered relating to Val after the battle at the Eyrie. It was hard to explain what she intended to do—to bury her past and her connection to Val, literally and figuratively—but she knew he'd support her regardless.

"I thought I might go to my old house. Just for a visit. I don't think my sister lives there anymore, but . . ."

The last time she'd been in that cabin, she'd left Val—and Xephyra's cold ashes—inside. And though Tristan didn't know everything about Veronyka and Val, he knew that Val had poisoned Xephyra, and he'd seen her cruel, calculating ways firsthand in their short acquaintance at the Eyrie. He understood their relationship was fraught and that Veronyka might find solace—or closure—in seeing the home they'd once shared.

Tristan straightened. "There should be time for that. How far is it?"

"Probably an hour both ways on phoenix-back."

Tristan nodded as he considered. "If we fly before sunrise, we could make it back before the others are up and moving," he said, indicating the rest of his patrol.

"We?" Veronyka asked, hope mingling with reluctance inside her chest. She relished the idea of not having to step over that threshold alone, but at the same time, she wasn't sure she wanted Tristan to see the squalor she'd been living in.

"Of course—I mean, if you'll let me," he said, slowing his pace as he read the hesitance on her face. "If you'd rather go alone—"

"No," Veronyka said, deciding on the spot. "No, I wouldn't."

"Good." He smiled in relief. "Then we better get some shut-eye. We'll leave in a few hours."

Ronyn was on watch as they quietly saddled and mounted their phoenixes, the sky dark and still as a held breath as it waited for the coming dawn. Tristan explained that they were visiting Veronyka's house—the whole patrol knew she was from the area—and Ronyn nodded, seated on a fragment of the crumbling stone wall, his phoenix perched beside him.

Like the journey from the Eyrie to Vayle, Veronyka marveled at how, in what seemed a few short wingbeats, they had traveled a distance that she had slogged for hours on foot.

With every pump of Xephyra's wings, a lead weight settled heavier and heavier in Veronyka's stomach. Any moment now that domed roof would become visible between the trees. Now that she was nearly there, Veronyka didn't know if she had the strength to face it all again.

A low croon reverberated through Xephyra's chest when she spotted the cabin in the distance, and flashes of confusion and painful memories rippled through the bond.

"It's okay," Veronyka mumbled, closing her eyes as nausea overtook her.

It's okay, Xephyra repeated back to her.

Veronyka didn't know if they were comforting each other or themselves, but the link between them settled somewhat, and she opened her eyes again in time to see them slow their pace and circle around the cabin, descending until both phoenixes came in to land on the soft grass that filled the clearing.

Veronyka forced slow breaths through her lips, her insides quivering uncomfortably. She didn't know how long she sat there, steeling herself, but it was Tristan's voice that drew her back from the brink.

"Veronyka?" he said softly. He was standing next to Xephyra, a hand outstretched. Veronyka knew he wasn't aware of their link, but she suspected some sense of her feelings reached him, even if he thought he was only guessing at her emotions.

She pushed out one last huff of breath, then clenched her fists. It was just a building—dark, quiet, and deserted. She could do this. She needed to do this.

Veronyka reached down and took Tristan's hand; his expression cleared as he helped her from the saddle before giving Xephyra an affectionate pat along her neck. She still seemed agitated to Veronyka—though she leaned into Tristan's touch—and even Rex was restless, jostling his wings and craning his neck to dart glances into every part of the clearing.

Veronyka swallowed—was this more of their tangled shadow magic web? Her emotions bleeding into Tristan and then into Rex? Or could Rex sense Xephyra's disquiet in some sort of phoenix instinct?

"Stay out of trouble, you two," Tristan said to them both, and they began picking their way through the tall grasses, ferreting for acorns or fruit that had fallen from the nearby trees.

Tristan stood next to Veronyka, who hadn't moved from where she'd dismounted, several yards away from the side of the house. It looked the same—utterly unchanged—yet she knew in her heart that it was abandoned. The stack of firewood that leaned against the back wall was depleted, the plants that grew in front of the door were tall and untrampled, and no smoke or hint of ash touched the air around them.

She tugged at her bracelet, running her fingers over familiar beads and the cool, smooth weight of the ring.

"Are you ready?" Tristan whispered, hand dropping to the knife at his belt as he headed toward the door.

"Wait," Veronyka said, gripping his arm and holding him back. She unhooked her own dagger—Sev's, stolen by Val in this very clearing—and gripped it tightly, stepping around Tristan to open the door herself. "Let me."

Tristan nodded and looked to her, waiting.

Veronyka straightened her spine and turned the handle.

The door creaked on its hinges, retreating into the darkness and leaving a slice of moonlight in its wake. Veronyka held her breath as she crossed over the threshold, and she felt Xephyra with her, tense and uncertain. The house was surprisingly cold, as if the empty, ashen hearth in the center of the room sucked heat away instead of emanating it, as most fireplaces should. It was like a gaping void of nothing and everything. This was where Veronyka's life had changed forever.

The cabin looked smaller now than it had before, as if the lives that filled it had expanded the very architecture, their hearts becoming *its* heart, their bodies creating space rather than using it up.

Veronyka wandered in, trailing a finger along the wall as she took in every detail: their broken cooking pot was still here, along with some moldering food supplies. Bits of rice were scattered under the window where, without the wooden shutters, forest creatures had wandered in to scavenge what little they could. Old footsteps—human and animal— dotted the dirt floor, and the walls were caked with soot and grime, the scent bitter on the air.

A snap and hiss drew her attention to the doorway, where Tristan held a lit lantern aloft. She didn't know when he'd retrieved it, but he strode into the room—his broad shoulders making the place look, if possible, even tinier—and brought clear, golden light with him. Their shadows danced and flickered across the walls.

"It's even worse than I remember," Veronyka said, her voice hoarse. "Though I guess some of that is my fault. I burned the shutters myself, though they were broken to begin with. It was a pretty lousy home."

Tristan put the lantern onto the edge of the hearthstones, then came to stand in front of her. He put his large hands on her shoulders, turning her slightly to face him. "Home isn't a building," he said as soon as their eyes met. "Home is . . ." He cast about as if searching for words. "It's like a bond. It's a place you feel safe; it's the people who make it that way."

Veronyka nodded, unwelcome tears pricking the back of her eyes. She'd had the same sort of thoughts about bonds, about how they gave her something like family. The places had changed, but Veronyka had felt at home in her life when she was with her family, which had included her *maiora*; her bondmate, Xephyra—and even her once-sister, Val.

And she felt at home with Tristan, too.

None of them were truly related to her, but they were all still family.

She sniffed and swiped at her eyes. Tristan watched her do it, his gaze catching and snagging on her every movement. He hesitated, his hands shifting slightly on her shoulders, and Veronyka didn't know if he intended to drop them or raise them up to her face.

Before he could do either, distant voices cut through the silence. They both flinched, pulling away from each other.

Tristan tilted his head toward the open door, while Veronyka reached with her magic for the phoenixes in the clearing outside. The voices were too far to be easily distinguished, but they seemed to be getting louder, which meant they were getting closer. It wasn't dawn yet, but the darkness around them was growing lighter, hazier, as if the sun weren't too far off.

Hide, Veronyka said to Xephyra and Rex, as Tristan took another step toward the open door.

"I'll head them off," Tristan whispered. *Stay here,* he mouthed, before slipping out the door and closing it behind him.

Veronyka listened carefully as Tristan's footsteps receded. She wasn't worried about her and Tristan—she was worried about their phoenixes. If those were empire soldiers strolling through the wilds, she doubted they'd be talking loudly and giving away their position. Then again, the men who'd tried to rob this very cabin several months back hadn't been discreet either. A flutter of anxiety pressed against her breast. What if they *were* soldiers and Tristan was about to face them on his own?

His voice pierced through their low, rumbling chatter, and Veronyka heard a mix of people, old, young—even children—in reply. She relaxed. Just travelers, then, not soldiers. Tristan laughed and joked with the group, and Veronyka thought she heard him say something about coming from Vayle. She blew a slow breath out through her lips, reminded Xephyra and Rex to stay hidden, and peered back around the cabin.

Veronyka stared dejectedly at the cramped, empty space, then looked down at the braided bracelet with its gleaming golden ring on her wrist. It was time. She would leave it here, bury it along with her thoughts of Val, of her past, and her lost identity. Veronyka would leave it all behind.

As she searched for a likely place, her attention lit on the hearthstones, the usual place they would bury their belongings back in Aura Nova. If she could slide one of those up, it would be a ready-made hole, deep and easily reburied.

But as Veronyka moved closer, she could see that the stones were slightly uneven and awkwardly placed—as if they'd already been removed and then returned without much care.

Veronyka shoved the cold bricks and heaps of ash aside, revealing a second layer of stones beneath. She dug her fingernails in between them, finally prying up one of the blocks to reveal a deep earthen hole. Inside was the edge of a lacquered wooden box.

Her heart skipped a beat. Veronyka *knew* that box. . . . It was the very same one their grandmother used when they lived in Aura Nova. But they'd fled that home with nothing but the clothes on their backs. Hadn't they?

"Diyu ma, xe Nyka."

Veronyka whipped around in alarm. Val stood just inside the window, half her face in shadow, thanks to the lantern's stark light. It was as if she'd materialized out of thin air, yet despite her relaxed posture and easy words, her eyes flashed with something like surprise as they bored into Veronyka.

"Val," Veronyka said, standing, her heart clenched—not in surprise, but something closer to dread. It felt as though, deep down, she had known this would happen. Had she wanted it to? Seeing Val went against everything Veronyka was trying to achieve, and yet . . . there was something right about seeing her again, *here.* For a strange moment, the cabin felt like home again. "Or I guess I should say Avalkyra," she said, keeping her voice steady, no matter how emphatically her heart pounded. "Yes, it has been a long time."

"I'm glad you're keeping up on your Pyraean," Val said, unhitching herself from the wall. "And you may call me Val, if you wish. For now."

"For now?" Veronyka asked, wary of Val's every movement, all her senses on high alert. Xephyra was inching closer to the cabin outside, even as Veronyka told her to stay back.

"Someday soon you'll call me queen."

Veronyka wasn't shocked by Val's words. She'd known somewhere deep inside that if Val was indeed Avalkyra, then she'd have one goal in mind above all others—and that goal would involve a crown.

"And what will you call me?" Veronyka asked, unable to help herself. "Who am I to you? Not your sister."

"Not my sister," Val conceded slowly, as if weighing her words very carefully. "You'll have to come with me if you want to know more."

Veronyka gritted her teeth. It was so unfair that Val should hold such information as if it were *hers*, as if Veronyka's identity didn't belong to Veronyka herself. As if she didn't have a right to it.

"Then," Val said, taking a tentative step forward, "once we're together, we can—"

"We can *what*?" Veronyka demanded. "*You* can become queen while I watch from the sidelines? Is that what you wanted all this time? An audience? Someone smaller and weaker to make you feel superior?"

A spasm of frustration crossed Val's face as she looked away. "No," she said, her gaze roving the gloomy hovel. When she turned her eyes back to Veronyka, they were wide. Almost pleading. "Come with me, and I'll tell you everything. I promise."

Promise. Veronyka shrank back from the word. What did promises mean to Val anyway? Before Veronyka could reply, Val's gaze darted downward. It was the barest flicker of her eyes, but Veronyka knew somehow that Val was staring at the hole in the hearth—and the box Veronyka had unearthed there.

Maybe there *was* another way to know more.

Veronyka lunged toward the box just as Val did the same.

They collided in the dirt, and Veronyka was reminded of the last time they were here—when Veronyka struggled against Val to try to save Xephyra as she choked and spluttered on a poisoned date.

She sensed Xephyra now, fluttering outside the cabin, frantic and confused and fighting against Veronyka's request to stay hidden and safe.

The last time they'd clashed, Veronyka had been easily overpowered—young and afraid and inexperienced.

She might still be some of those things—especially when she considered that Val was no regular sixteen-year-old—but she'd been sparring with Tristan for weeks now.

And she wasn't going down without a fight.

Veronyka's hands were on the box in the hearth, and Val was clawing at her wrists. Rather than leaning away from her, Veronyka angled her body toward Val and shoved her shoulder into Val's chest, breaking Val's hold and sending her stumbling.

Veronyka wrenched the box up from the dirt, but already Val was reaching for her with renewed ferocity. Veronyka tried to run, but Val grabbed her by the throat, dragging her backward.

The harder Val fought, the more certain Veronyka became that there were answers inside this box. That there was something vitally important within her grasp. She could not let it go.

Veronyka swung wildly, her elbow connecting with Val's jaw—though she'd had to relinquish her two-handed grasp on the box to do it. Val took hold of Veronyka's hair next, jerking hard, but Veronyka's palms were slippery with dirt, and at the sudden jolt, the box flew out of her hand . . .

. . . and landed in the open doorway, where Tristan now stood.

Val let out a snarl of frustration, releasing Veronyka's hair and backing to the far side of the cabin.

"You don't understand," Val said, panting from exertion. "We need to speak alone. There's so much I have to say . . . so much to explain. You need me."

The words were ones Val had spoken often in Veronyka's life, and one of those times had been right here, in this room, after Xephyra was dead and Veronyka was preparing to run away.

"No, I don't," Veronyka said, her voice cold and sharp as shards of ice.

Val hesitated, glancing at Tristan, who scowled as he loomed in the doorway, then back at Veronyka. If she wanted another fight, this was one she wouldn't win. "You know where to find me," she said, tapping her temple once, softly, before slipping out the window and disappearing into the darkness.

But I am glad we had each other, my sister
and me. Even at the very end, I was glad.

- CHAPTER 10 -
TRISTAN

"WAS . . . WAS THAT YOUR SISTER?" Tristan asked, still shocked by the scene he'd inadvertently stepped into. He knew it was Val—Tristan didn't think he'd ever be able to forget her—but his mind had gone blank, and he didn't know what else to say.

Veronyka was dirty and disheveled, her hair wild, and bloody tracks like fingernail gouges trailed along her arms and hands.

She didn't answer. Instead she walked over and picked up a box from where it had landed mere feet in front of him. It looked to be made from wood and coated in some kind of shining lacquer, the surface plain and unmarked. She clutched it to her chest, and the contents rattled and shifted inside. Her face was oddly expressionless, her eyes wide and dark but distant.

"Are you okay?" Tristan pressed, seeing more scratches and scrapes and the torn edge of her tunic. They'd been fighting when he'd arrived, though he only saw Val releasing her grip on Veronyka's hair.

"I'm—yes," she said, her voice shaky.

"What—" Tristan began, but he was cut off when something barreled into his back, causing him to stumble forward.

Xephyra was behind him in the doorway, too large to fit through the narrow frame but frantic to get to her bondmate.

Tristan moved out of the way, giving room for Veronyka to step outside.

Xephyra backed up, but only enough to allow Veronyka through. She crooned low in her throat, and Veronyka buried her face into her bondmate's neck. That told Tristan more than anything else how rattled Veronyka was, despite her lack of tears or outward fear.

He suffered a strange pang of jealousy as he watched them. He couldn't begrudge Veronyka the comfort of her bondmate, but he longed to be the one she turned to—the one who made things all right for her.

Rex was visible just behind Veronyka and Xephyra, a spectator to this quiet moment, the same as Tristan. Rex nudged his mind, making sure Tristan was okay, and he nodded, coming outside to join them.

At last Veronyka and Xephyra separated, though Veronyka kept a hand on her phoenix's neck.

Xephyra straightened, swiveling her head from side to side—as if seeking something—before shaking out her feathers with a squawk.

"I know," Veronyka said apologetically, smiling up at her bondmate. "But it's not like you could fit through the door."

Tristan frowned, knowing Veronyka was speaking aloud to include him—to make it okay for him to speak too.

"Are you sure you're all right?" he asked, coming to stand before her. Rex sidled up to him, his presence a wordless comfort. "Both of you?" he pressed, looking up at Xephyra. She cocked her head.

"Yes," Veronyka said, more firmly this time. "It's just that . . . this is where it happened. Where Val . . ." She trailed off, and both Veronyka and Xephyra seemed to lean into each other unconsciously.

Tristan looked back in through the open door of the cabin, though he wasn't really seeing it. All he could see was red. Of course this was where it had happened. This was where they'd been living before Veronyka ran away. She had told him how Val poisoned her bondmate, determined that they should raise their phoenixes together—or not at all. The story haunted him, so much so that he was ashamed to admit he'd tried to *forget* it. But

Veronyka couldn't. And she'd come here anyway, willing to face it with a strength and fearlessness Tristan could only dream of.

An ache in his palms told Tristan he was clenching his hands into fists so tightly he was in danger of drawing blood. He released his grip with difficulty and swallowed back a number of angry, useless comments. *I hate your sister. I hate that she did that to you.*

"It's okay," Veronyka said softly, and Tristan refocused his attention on her. She was looking at him with empathy, *consoling* him, and it occurred to him to wonder what other awful things Veronyka had had to endure in her life at Val's hands—and how she could have come out the way she had: kind, compassionate, and full of brilliant light.

"It's not okay," Tristan said, his throat tight.

"No," Veronyka agreed with a sigh, casting a sidelong glance up at Xephyra, whose head had dipped slightly. "But we're stronger now—stronger because of her."

Tristan couldn't argue with that. He reached out to put a hand on Veronyka's shoulder, and to his surprise, Rex extended his neck to nudge his head against Xephyra at the exact same time. It was a comforting gesture, one he'd seen the phoenixes give each other occasionally, but it still surprised him the way their actions mirrored one another.

He thought suddenly of mated pairs, and heat swept his face, but luckily Veronyka wasn't looking at him. Rex was butting Xephyra so hard that she bumped into Veronyka, and when Xephyra squawked and snapped playfully at Rex, Veronyka laughed.

The tension lightened somewhat, Veronyka glanced down at the box in her hand, as if only just remembering she had it.

"Is that why you wanted to come back? For that?"

Veronyka shook her head. "I didn't even know it was here."

"What's in it?" Tristan asked, though he got the impression it was a loaded question.

"I don't know," Veronyka said thoughtfully. Then her face hardened. "But if Val wanted it, there must be something important."

Tristan didn't know what to say to that. There was so much between Veronyka and Val that he didn't understand, and he knew, somehow, that he shouldn't ask about. It was clear that Veronyka was still sorting out her own feelings on the matter, even though Val had killed Xephyra here, in this very building. The fact of the matter was, Veronyka loved Val, and there was something wonderful about the fierceness of it—that she *could* love Val, even after everything she'd done.

"So what news from the travelers?" Veronyka asked, putting the box into Xephyra's saddlebag—or trying to, as Rex and Xephyra were nipping and jostling and making it difficult for her. Tristan leaned over to help, holding the bag steady so Veronyka could rearrange a few items to fit the box inside.

Tristan's hand dropped. He'd forgotten. "We need to get back to the Eyrie immediately."

"What, why? What happened?" she asked, turning around and leaving the box hanging halfway out of the bag.

"Empire soldiers have been spotted along the border."

As they prepared to fly back to camp, Tristan filled Veronyka in on all he'd heard from the travelers. It had been a family of Pyraean tinkers who had a connection to the Office for Border Control that allowed them to travel in and out of the empire, visiting Runnet and Vayle along with some of the smaller communities scattered between them—before returning again. This time while passing through Runnet they'd heard some rumors of groups of soldiers collecting along the border in the west, near Ferro.

"How many?" Veronyka asked.

"Hundreds, apparently," Tristan said grimly, Veronyka's dire face mirroring his own initial reaction.

"Do we know what direction they were going?" Veronyka asked as she climbed into her saddle. "What their target is?"

Tristan settled into his own saddle. "Wherever they go—whatever damage they do—I think it's safe to say their target is us."

They returned to camp and packed up quickly, making their return to the Eyrie only a bit later than Tristan had originally intended. He decided not to share the news of the soldiers with the rest of his patrol. They would find out eventually, and he didn't want them to suggest doing the thing he very much wanted to do himself—which was to head south toward the border and find out more. Tristan's orders had been to fly straight to Vayle and then to fly right back. Even visiting Veronyka's cabin was technically forbidden, and he knew the commander would be furious if they tried to scout empire soldier movements without first reporting to him. Tristan's position as patrol leader was still very much new—and his father wouldn't hesitate to strip the honor if Tristan failed to perform his duties correctly.

He also didn't want to cause a panic among the local villagers. No doubt they'd hear the news from the traveling tinkers when they arrived later that day, but Tristan didn't want to be there when they did. He knew they'd demand answers that he couldn't give.

Not yet, he told himself firmly. His father couldn't ignore this. He'd been resisting action for weeks, but he could do so no longer.

By late afternoon, they were flying past the perimeter patrol and signaling their approach. The sun was hot and low in the sky, and a steady trail of perspiration trickled down Tristan's back despite the brisk winds from Rex's speedy flight. Of course, it wasn't just the weather that was making Tristan sweat. He was about to face his first real challenge as a patrol leader, his first chance to speak up and—hopefully—have his opinions heard. So far he'd been quiet in their Rider Council meetings, trying to listen and learn and prove to his father that promoting him wasn't a mistake.

Now he had vital information to share, and it was exhilarating to finally be a part of the decision making.

When they touched down inside the Eyrie, Veronyka moved to unsaddle Rex—a general part of her duties as underwing was to help with tasks such as this—but Tristan grabbed her outstretched hand.

"Lys, do you mind?" he asked, calling out to his cousin and gesturing to Rex *and* Xephyra.

"You got it," Lysandro replied with a nod, dropping his saddle to the ground and reaching for Rex. Veronyka hesitated. Lysandro was a master, after all, and she was an apprentice—and Latham stood nearby, eyebrows raised in silent reproach. But Tristan ignored them.

"Come on," Tristan said to Veronyka, tugging her arm. "We've got news to report."

Eventually she nodded and wiped her hands down her front, as if nervous, but Tristan didn't know why. They'd learned about the soldiers together, so it seemed only natural to bring her. Besides, Tristan always felt bolstered when she was around, more certain in his convictions than he was when he was by himself with his father.

He actually smirked a bit as he led the way inside the stronghold. If Tristan didn't have the nerve to stand up for what was right, he knew Veronyka would. They had a Rider Council meeting scheduled upon his patrol's return, and Tristan was eager to disclose what he'd learned.

When they arrived in his father's meeting room, Beryk was already there, head bowed over some documents his father had splayed on the table.

"Ah, Tristan, come in," his father said, spotting him in the doorway. "We'll have to finish reviewing the budget later," he said to Beryk before gathering the papers and putting them on the sideboard. "How was—" He paused, noting for the first time that Veronyka had entered the room behind Tristan.

Before he could say more, Fallon and Darius arrived, glancing around at the somewhat awkward silence.

"This is a Rider Council meeting," the commander said at last. "Veronyka, will you please excuse us?"

Tristan gripped Veronyka's arm. "We have important news to share with the council."

His father frowned. "Surely you can relay the details on your own, Tristan. We have other matters to disc—"

"Empire soldiers have been spotted on the Pyraean border," Tristan blurted. "Near Ferro. We got word from a family of travelers." The room stilled, tension filling the empty silent spaces. Tristan glanced at Veronyka, then plowed on. There were details he hadn't told her yet either. "There haven't been any attacks yet, but groups of soldiers have been seen as far east as Runnet, and some animages have been reported missing." It was a common tactic of the empire—the kidnappings done by soldiers and raiders alike. Animages were worth money on the black market, and they were easy targets in a place like Pyra. "Obviously, the attack at the Eyrie was only the beginning."

Tristan expected uproar. He expected shock and rage and dozens of questions.

Instead, every head in the room swiveled to his father. Tristan's insides felt hollow.

"You knew?" Tristan asked, his mouth dry.

"I . . . suspected," the commander clarified. "Sit, Tristan, and we'll talk. Veronyka, if you don't mind—"

"*No,*" Tristan snapped, jerking out not one chair but two. "She stays."

Veronyka's eyes were wide, looking between father and son, uncertain. Tristan felt a stab of guilt for putting her in such a position, but he'd be damned if he bowed to his father's wishes—no matter how seemingly trivial. He'd die of thirst before he took a cup of water right now, if his father suggested it.

"Why exactly?"

"She's my second," Tristan said, before he realized what he was saying. Heat crept over the back of his neck and along his ears, but he refused to back down. His father knew what was between them—knew that there was more to their relationship than that.

"She cannot be your second—she's not even a Master Rider yet," his father said, voice flat with suppressed impatience.

Tristan didn't dare look at Veronyka when he spoke. "I don't care. She'll be a Master Rider eventually. And when she is, the position will be waiting for her." Finally he looked at Veronyka, whose face was frozen in shock. "If she wants it," he added, though Veronyka didn't respond.

Tristan shifted his focus to his father, whose nostrils were flared as he fought for composure. Next to him, Beryk looked somewhat exasperated. He was used to the way the commander and his son conflicted with each other, no matter the issue. Darius smirked, arms crossed as he took in the scene with mild amusement, but Fallon had a measuring look on his face. Tristan couldn't be certain, but Fallon seemed almost impressed that he was standing his ground.

The commander sighed heavily, and Tristan knew the fight was won— at least for now. Still, Veronyka didn't move a muscle until the commander gestured for her to take a seat. She did, followed by Fallon and Darius.

"So," Tristan continued, "why do I get the feeling you already knew about the soldiers?" He was trying to give his father a chance to explain, but his anger was simmering in his chest, ready to ignite.

"I didn't know," the commander insisted, "but I guessed."

"Based on what? We're not flying patrols any farther south than Vayle."

"You know I have sources of information beyond my Riders," his father said calmly.

"You said there hadn't been any news from Sev." There, a flicker in the commander's eyes, and Tristan knew that his father had lied to him in the dining hall. Lied directly to his face. After everything they'd been through . . . Tristan couldn't believe he was back here again.

Calm as the mountain, he said inside his head. He was beginning to think the words were better suited to his father than to him. Calm as the mountain. Stoic as the mountain. Cold and hard and unfeeling as this gods-forsaken mountain.

"No," the commander corrected. "I said there had been nothing of note."

"You didn't think that empire soldiers on our borders was *noteworthy*?"

"I told you I didn't know about the soldiers, Tristan."

"No, but you assumed. Why?"

Tristan looked around. He wasn't just angry. He was embarrassed, because he could tell by the look on Beryk's, Fallon's, and Darius's faces that they knew whatever it was his father was keeping from him. It hurt that his new position as a patrol leader was being taken as some kind of joke—that even Beryk and Darius, who ranked lower than Tristan, were kept in the commander's confidences when he was not.

But more than that, it hurt because Tristan had been feeling closer to his father lately. After he'd put Tristan in charge during the attack, after he'd promoted him and given him a patrol, Tristan had thought they were moving out of the rigid boxes his father had forced them into. Then they'd talked in the dining hall, speaking about things that the two had never shared with each other before. He'd thought that they were finally relating man to man, not just father to son, but now he felt like a child again. Had that all been a cover, a way to distract Tristan or make him think he was in his father's confidences, only so he could conceal whatever he wanted from his naive, trusting son?

"We have received news from the empire, but it's nothing we can yet act upon."

"*What* news?" Tristan gritted out.

"There will be a Grand Council meeting," Beryk said, cutting into the conversation at last.

"A Grand Council?" Tristan repeated, looking between them. He'd heard the term before. . . . If he wasn't mistaken, his mother had been condemned to death by the Grand Council.

The commander nodded. "Lord Rolan—the man responsible for the assault on the Eyrie—called it himself," his father said, voice tight. "Instead of waiting for the news of his unsanctioned attack on Pyra to reach the council and sway them against him, Rolan has decided to double down."

"What does that mean?" Tristan asked blankly.

"It means that when the Grand Council meets in several weeks' time, Rolan will present Pyra as a lawless place. He will say the Freelands are dangerous and that the Phoenix Riders in particular are a threat to the border lords, the northern provinces, and the empire in general."

Tristan glanced around. "How will he do that?"

"By proving it. This is mostly speculation, but I think that until the

Grand Council meets, Rolan will do everything in his power to cause strife, bloodshed, and general terror along the border. He will use every resource he possesses, including sizable coffers, influence over important officials, and of course, his soldiers. By the time the governors and council members meet, it won't matter who started it—they will finish it."

"So he means to provoke us?" Tristan tried to wrap his head around the backward strategy. "He plans to attack us, to bring the violence and destruction into our lands until we have no choice but to defend ourselves? Then he would paint *us* as the villains?" he asked incredulously.

"You have to understand . . . by the time they meet, the council will have heard rumors, smelled the smoke and seen the fires—even if they are not our own. They will be afraid, and won't care about right and wrong. They'll care about damaged lands and lost incomes. About their own safety." The commander's voice was bitter, and this show of emotion helped calm Tristan's own frustration. At least his father was admitting to something—revealing something. "Most of them, anyway," he added with a sigh. "Certainly a majority vote, which is all Rolan needs."

"Isn't the border under surveillance?" Tristan asked. "How are hundreds of soldiers crossing without anyone inside the empire raising the alarm? They can't all be in on his plans. . . ."

"If you'll recall," the commander said gravely, "Elliot's father works for the Office for Border Control."

"And Rolan has his daughter—Elliot's sister," Tristan said, stunned.

"I fear it goes beyond letting a few hundred soldiers pass undocumented," Beryk added. "The office also has several seats on the Grand Council; Rolan will try to guarantee at least one vote in his favor."

"Elliot's father doesn't currently have a seat," the commander corrected, "but no doubt Rolan hopes to make use of his connections there all the same."

"So what can we do?" Tristan asked the room at large.

His father got to his feet, rubbing his chin thoughtfully as he paced the room. "We cannot properly defend the border," he said, and Tristan immediately opened his mouth to object. The commander silenced him with a hand. "But we can establish a perimeter deeper into Pyra. If we can hold that position, we should be able to keep the majority of the people in Pyra safe—"

"But not all of them," Tristan interjected. His father spoke over him.

"—while ensuring we don't play directly into Rolan's hands. He wants Phoenix Riders seen 'terrorizing' the border. We will not give him that."

"So we let them do what they want? Run unchecked while we watch from a safe distance?"

"What would you have me do, Tristan? Line up our *seventeen* Master Riders opposite the empire's hundreds? Or would you have me send the hatchlings as well? Shall we fight battles on multiple fronts, leaving the rest of the province unprotected? We'll be slaughtered."

"Better us than the civilians caught in between. Have you seen what happened in Rushlea and Petratec?" Tristan demanded. "Here," he said, grabbing his report from where he'd left it on the table and flinging it across the surface, where accounts of the damages and the missing or dead were listed plain for all to see. "Look at what happened to Vayle. We can't leave these people to fend for themselves when it's because of *us* that they're in danger in the first place. We should position Riders in each of the villages at the very least, and some of the stronghold guards too, if we can spare them."

The commander studied Tristan. "We cannot position Riders in every village—*but*," he added, before Tristan could object, "we'll position some in Vayle. And we'll garrison Prosperity."

Prosperity was an ancient outpost updated and heavily expanded by Queen Ellody during her Reign of Prosperity. It actually wasn't far from Veronyka's cabin or from Vayle. Tristan could already see the rough line his father was drawing across Pyra and expected they'd also send patrols along the *Sekveia*, giving them a foothold centrally as well as west and east.

"And what about the Grand Council?" Tristan asked.

"If Rolan intends to argue his case at the Grand Council, then I will argue ours."

Tristan glanced around at the others. While they still did not appear surprised by the news, they definitely seemed uneasy about it.

"You mean to go into the empire to represent us? But . . . they'll kill you on sight!" This time, when Tristan looked at the others, they avoided his gaze entirely. "You were banished, weren't you? Never allowed to return. You can't just fly down there. You'd be playing right into their hands."

"You forget I was once one of these politicians. I know how they think, and I'm certain I can sway enough votes to give us a chance."

Tristan clenched his hands into fists. His father's arrogance was so absolute it was impossible to penetrate—like trying to see through a brick wall.

"They do not want a war, despite appearances," the commander continued. "If there's one thing the council hates to lose—besides a battle—it's gold, and there is nothing more costly than war."

"You trusted these people before!" Tristan shouted, lurching to his feet and causing his chair to scrape loudly against the floor. "You turned yourself in after the Blood War, and look what happened! You lost your position and your wife."

Tense silence descended over the room, thick and stifling.

His father's jaw worked. "Your mother made her own choices, Tristan. I would not presume to take credit for them."

Or blame, Tristan thought darkly. "Who's going to be stationed at Prosperity?" he asked. "I'd like to volunteer my patrol."

"Absolutely not," the commander said. "Prosperity will be the main hub of our defense. I cannot put our greenest patrol on the front lines. And besides," he continued, his tone one of grim victory, "you've forgotten a crucial detail. Your patrol is a Master Rider short. It would be irresponsible of me to send you out undermanned and underprepared."

"We could audition a new master," Tristan said, scrambling for ideas. "It's not unheard of during wartime. Avalkyra Ashfire was elevated to Master Rider—and commander—during the Stellan Uprising."

"A formality," the commander said with a dismissive wave of his hand.

"She'd already been leading her own patrol for four years. It is hardly the same—"

"I could audition."

Tristan turned to see Veronyka on her feet beside him. She swallowed thickly, her eyes round as coins, but her mouth was set in a determined line.

"Perfect," Tristan said, a challenge on his face, daring his father to pull out some other excuse. Before the war, Riders studied for nearly a decade, beginning as a child right through to the end of their adolescence. But now they had to accelerate the entire process, and with the empire already moving on them? They would have to adapt. Even though soldiers trained for years, in the face of war and invasion, every farmer and peasant who could hold a weapon was a soldier too. Was this any different? Veronyka was a capable flyer and good with a bow. She could keep up in the air and wouldn't slow the others down. And when *not* matched with Tristan, she was pretty good in a fight.

And beyond all that, she was Tristan's best friend and most trusted Rider. There was no better choice.

The commander scrubbed a hand across his face. "She's had barely two months of training. You can't possibly—"

"Who better? All the others are too young or less skilled than she is. Her phoenix is strong and flies well with the flock. And most of all, she's willing."

"Please," Veronyka said, her voice quiet but strong. "I can do this."

The commander fixed them both with a cold, inscrutable stare. He glanced at Beryk, who was frowning, and then to Fallon, whose brows were lifted as if he thought it was a decent idea. Darius looked skeptical.

"Fine," the commander said, his expression hard. "Your entire patrol will participate, as is the custom when an apprentice is auditioned before properly completing their training. If you can perform as a team and complete the assigned trials, Veronyka will be elevated to Master Rider. Then we can discuss Prosperity. The tests will be first thing tomorrow."

Ears ringing, Tristan strode for the door. After a nod of thanks to the commander, Veronyka followed.

ↄ   ↄ   ↄ

Tristan paused in the shadowy hallway. Things were finally happening—maybe not exactly as he wanted, but thanks to Veronyka, they still had a shot at being a real part of the defense effort.

He turned to her. Their eyes met, and a sparkling, kinetic energy crackled between them. She was staring at him with an intense look on her face. "I—you were amazing in there," she said, lips lifting at the corners with a secret smile. Tristan had the sudden, dizzying urge to lean forward and taste it. "Thank you for supporting me."

Tristan lifted his gaze from her mouth. "Always," he said, and she smiled more widely.

"I won't let you down," she promised, her expression turning serious.

"I know you won't," he said. "You never do."

They continued to stare at each other, and Tristan felt oddly pulled toward her, as if the world were tilting beneath his feet and gravity was dragging him inexorably forward. Could he kiss her, here—now?

"I've—I'm gonna go for a walk, I think," she said abruptly, and the pull ceased.

Tristan shook his head slowly, trying to banish the memory of that strange feeling, and nodded.

Veronyka turned to go, then stopped, facing him again. "And thanks for the other thing." Tristan frowned, unsure what she meant. She bowed her head, smiling shyly again. "When you said that I was your second."

"Right," he said, forgetting that bit of boldness. His cheeks grew hot, and he was grateful for the shadows.

"I do, by the way. Want it, I mean. More than anything."

Tristan beamed.

Prosperity was the common name for Queen Ellody's outpost. The original structure dates back to Queen Lyra the Defender and was used most notably during the Lowland Invasion. It was later restored by Queen Ellody and named for her Reign of Prosperity.

Though the Pilgrimage Road wouldn't be built for another ten years by Ellody's pious son, King Justyn, the roots of the tradition of traveling to important religious and historical sites in Pyra began during Ellody's reign. Some say it was the restoration of Queen Lyra's outpost that launched the tourist industry in Pyra and thus led to the building of the Pilgrimage Road. Looking for a way to give back to her mother's homeland, Queen Ellody took the opportunity to enhance the out-of-use outpost's beauty and celebrate the grandeur of the Ashfire queens and their glorious reign.

The main tower is covered in relief sculptures that rise from the ground all the way to the pinnacle in a continuous spiral frieze, depicting important events throughout history, starting at the bottom with the battle between Axura's phoenixes and Nox's strixes and culminating in Queen Elysia's crowning in Aura Nova. The outpost also features a small temple to Axura, plus a second, shorter tower that is all that remains of the original structure.

With Pyra's separation from the empire at the start of the Blood War, Prosperity has been lost to the pilgrims and travelers who had been visiting it for decades. Rumor has it that the outpost did come into use again during Avalkyra Ashfire's rebellion—not by Riders, but by smugglers instead.

—"Pyraean Art and Architecture," from *Sights Along the Pilgrimage Road* by the Ministry of Tourism in Pyra, published 56 AE, updated 172 AE

My sister taught me there is more than one
kind of fire. There is the fire that consumes,
and there is the fire that illuminates.

- CHAPTER II -

ELLIOT

TO ELLIOT'S ANNOYANCE, SPARROW returned every evening after their first meeting, as if it were the most normal thing in the world for a young girl to walk around an empty field alone at night.

Well, not *alone*. Elliot was there, though he did his best to ignore her. And of course she always had about a dozen animals with her too.

Most of the time she'd wander the grassy plain aimlessly, throwing sticks for dogs to chase or laying out handfuls of seed for flocks of birds to peck at. She even brought treats for Jax sometimes, though she made no direct mention of it. Instead Jax would pause abruptly in his exercise to fly over to her, ferreting his beak around in the grass or poking it into her palms, Sparrow giggling in delight.

Elliot hated the sound, the way she snorted and squealed like a pig, but he couldn't deny the way Jaxon's pleasure lightened his own heavy heart. Really, Elliot suspected Sparrow knew exactly what she was doing, getting to him through his bondmate.

It was a low, dirty trick.

Or maybe it was just kindness. Elliot had trouble telling the difference sometimes. The day Beryk turned up at his father's house, Elliot had thought all his wildest dreams were coming true. He'd even convinced

Riella, who loved animals but hated fighting, how much fun it would be to go together. Little did he know he was playing right into the empire's hands. Little did he know how that kindness would turn to ashes in his mouth.

The strange thing was that no matter how late Elliot stayed with Jax, Sparrow stayed later. He had a sneaking suspicion she was sleeping out there, lying flat on the grass, hemmed in on all sides by whatever animals she'd brought with her—and some, Elliot was certain, who had wandered to her out of the wilds, drawn like a moth to a flame. Literally—he'd seen moths circling her head, avoiding hungry beaks but never veering far.

Despite his best efforts, Elliot had been thinking a lot about what Sparrow had said to him that first night. *Show them you still care.*

Elliot knew much of what Sparrow had said was born from naive innocence, but her last few words had really struck home. Ever since his lies had been revealed, Elliot had withdrawn from the others. He answered questions, spoke when spoken to, but otherwise kept to himself. He'd thought he was doing them all a favor—they hated him, but he was a bonded Rider. They needed him but couldn't really *use* him. Elliot knew that they had no idea what to do with him, so he'd stayed out of their way. But what if his detached, automatic obedience was actually working against him? Was there a chance they all looked at him, with his emotionless expression and bowed head, and saw not a person cowed and paying for his crimes, but someone who had given up?

The idea troubled him to no end. If it were up to Elliot, he'd be in on every Rider Council meeting. He'd be helping them find Riella, devising plans and strategies and working double—triple—patrol shifts. He knew he couldn't, but were there other ways? Could he somehow show them all that he was not just sorry, but that he had so much more to give?

Beryk had convinced the commander that Elliot could be of use as his assistant, though he helped with only the most basic of tasks, not trusted with anything to do with money or sending letters or even the schedules of the other Riders. Elliot had been doing his duties exactly how Beryk told him to do them—no more, no less. He was afraid that if he stepped a toe out of line, if he did *anything* he wasn't specifically instructed to do, he'd be punished.

Elliot tried to imagine an assistant like that—one that had to be told how and when to do everything. Someone who could, but *wouldn't*, anticipate tasks, get ahead of schedule, or add helpful input or suggestions. His heart sank. He suspected he was more hindrance than help to Beryk, who had been so good to him even *after* the truth of his betrayal was revealed. Elliot realized with painful certainty that Beryk had the impression that he no longer cared.

Elliot had to change that.

It was a week after he'd first spoken to Sparrow that Elliot saw his chance.

They were still two days away from his monthly meeting with Beryk, in which they tallied supplies and checked them against the previous year's numbers, adjusting their amounts as necessary before reordering.

It was something Elliot used to do alone but had now become one of a dozen other things Beryk was forced to take on in the face of Elliot's betrayal. Elliot hated that Beryk, the person who'd fought for his right to stay here, was the one being punished most of all. They'd never become *close*, not when Elliot was keeping his guard up and so much about himself a secret, but Beryk was a good, honest man, and he deserved better.

While Elliot was no longer allowed to see the books—they held much of the Eyrie's financial accounts—he could easily tally their existing supplies on his own. It was the most time-consuming of their tasks, and something he was quite certain they wouldn't mind him doing. The only danger with Elliot being alone in the cellar was that he might slip out the underground tunnels and escape, but ever since the attack from the empire, the exterior gate had been locked, and only Commander Cassian had the key. And it wasn't as if he were counting coins or jewels. Elliot would be counting sacks of grain, jars of preserves, and barrels of wine. He certainly couldn't steal them—how on earth would he sneak around with a fifty-pound sack of grain?—and though the temptation to drink himself into oblivion alone in the cellars wasn't nonexistent, he'd wake up to far more trouble than it was worth.

And so after his other duties were done the day before his official count with Beryk, Elliot crept down into the storage room and counted through the night.

The next morning he handed a harassed and exhausted-looking Beryk the list of sums, and the man frowned at it for several long, bewildered seconds. Then, for first time in weeks, he smiled—a grateful, slightly baffled smile, one that told Elliot that he'd made things easier for Beryk. That he'd made a difference.

It was then that Elliot realized what he had to do. He couldn't undo what he'd done or fix much of what he'd broken, but he could be useful. He could *try*.

He could show them he still cared.

Thanks to Elliot's eagerness to help Beryk, they finished the reorders with time to spare, and Elliot's high spirits made him less inclined to wait for the cover of darkness. He felt he'd earned the time with his bondmate, and Jax deserved to fly again in the sun.

Elliot was elated, as light as a phoenix feather as he strolled the village streets and left through the gate, running his hands through the lush, waist-high grasses. He was startled, but not altogether surprised, to see Sparrow leave the village not long after him.

His usual annoyance at her arrival was gone; if anything, Elliot was feeling a bit smug at his accomplishments that day. As she approached, however, his mood faltered slightly. Sparrow looked, if possible, even smugger than him.

"What?" he demanded as soon as she was in earshot.

"*What* what?" she repeated, a toothy grin on her face.

Elliot crossed his arms. "What are you smiling about? And what are you doing out here so early? Did you . . . follow me?"

"How would I do that?" she asked sweetly. "Can't see nothing, can I?"

Elliot scowled, shifting his gaze to the animals that accompanied her:

Carrot again, prowling a bit awkwardly alongside her, a glossy-winged raven with a nasty scar on his face tangled in Sparrow's hair, and one of the baby goats, bleating and leaping around, causing Carrot's fur to stand on end in fear or annoyance. Elliot considered each of them, then decided the raven was the culprit—the one who'd obviously seen Elliot pass and led Sparrow here. They were extremely intelligent, sneaky, and when he reached out with his magic, the creature rebuffed his questions with a haughty squawk.

Guilty as charged, Elliot thought darkly. "Why are you smiling, then?" he persisted.

She shrugged. "Heard you helped Beryk today. Saved him loads of time. He was right pleased."

"How . . . how could you have heard that?"

Sparrow shrugged again. "I hear everything."

Elliot considered her. The words should have been funny, coming from this half-wild girl with messy hair and bare feet, but they weren't. Maybe she *did* hear everything. Maybe *she* should have been the spy.

He sighed. There was no point in denying it. "I thought about what you said . . . about showing them I still care."

Sparrow's face lit with pleasure as he spoke. Elliot found his own lips quirking up in the corners, despite himself.

His good humor soon faded as he considered what lay before him.

"Beryk was easy, though. I know how to help him—I trained to do his job for a year. But the others . . . the commander . . . he won't be so simple."

Sparrow tilted her head as if mulling over his words, then turned abruptly away. The raven, who had been combing his beak idly through her hair, leapt down into her hands.

He croaked, snapping his beak several times.

"I know," Sparrow muttered to the bird, lifting it higher so their faces were on a level. "But he won't want to . . ."

Elliot stared.

Was . . . was she talking to the bird? About him? And was he talking *back*? While Jaxon might be able to communicate in something close to human-style speech through their bond, Elliot had never had another creature convey meaning anywhere close to a way that could be considered conversational. Maybe it was just Sparrow, choosing to respond as if the creature were human.

After several more whispered words and a definitive squawk, Sparrow turned away from the raven, raising her face toward Elliot.

"Oh, good," Elliot said. "Your private meeting is over."

"It is," Sparrow said gravely, missing his sarcasm.

"And what did your raven familiar advise?" Elliot asked solemnly. It seemed nothing—not even Sparrow's constant intrusion—could put a damper on his good mood.

"It's almost dark, isn't it?" she asked, ignoring his question.

Elliot looked around. The sun had disappeared over the distant peaks of Pyrmont, and twilight was fast descending. "Almost, yeah." He cast a sidelong glance at Sparrow. "Why?"

"The commander's in a Rider Council meeting," she said, and Elliot just shook his head. How she knew that, he had no idea, but he believed her.

"And you think I should bring them snacks and cold beverages?" he asked.

She definitely caught his tone that time and crossed her arms over her chest. "Not unless you wanna be a serving wench," she said flatly, and Elliot grinned. "I think you should climb the roof and listen at the window."

The smile slipped from Elliot's face.

"You *do* realize this is why I'm grounded, don't you?" Elliot said ten minutes later, scrambling after Sparrow across the roof of the administrative building. She'd left her spear behind on the ground, the shaft bitten and dented after the dogs used it as a chew toy the other night but still intact.

He didn't mean to follow her—not even back into the village, never mind onto the roof of the stables, across the storage sheds, and onto the sun-warmed tiles of the commander's private residence. But here he was, trying to stop *her* from doing the very thing that he was now doing. "I was a spy," he huffed out, panting slightly from the exertion of the climb.

"We're not spying," Sparrow said with an airy wave of the hand, surprisingly nimble for a person who couldn't see, making quick work of the climb and scampering across the tiles on featherlight feet. While she'd left Carrot and the goat behind, the raven was still with her—and Elliot suspected he was the one helping her navigate the treacherous surroundings. With night rapidly falling around them, Elliot couldn't see much either, and he was stumbling and staggering far worse than her.

They had waited outside the stables, Elliot arguing vehemently against her mad plans, until the roof of the Rider Council meeting room was dark enough to hide their prowling shadows. It was full night now, the only light the lanterns that hung along the walls below.

"We're not?" Elliot asked dubiously.

"Nope. Just listening," she said, reaching the apex of the roof. There she stopped, seeming to get her bearings.

"To stuff we're not supposed to," he pressed, catching his breath as he joined her.

Sparrow turned to face him. "Exactly," she said, smiling brightly before turning and making slower progress down the other side of the sloping roof.

"So, spying," Elliot muttered.

They'd already had several variations of this argument, but no matter what he said, Sparrow refused to budge, insisting she was going to make the climb anyway. Elliot didn't know how to just let her go while she did something so dangerous—she was blind, after all—so he followed her, though now that he'd done the thing, he was quite certain she hadn't needed his help in the slightest. Except for the spying, of course. She'd said he "might" make a useful assistant since he had "working peepers," and that had made Elliot smirk just long enough to realize he was in it, whatever the outcome.

As they neared the edge of the roof, Elliot reached out instinctively, gripping Sparrow's arm as they crept toward the drop. Voices rose from somewhere below, and he guessed they were perched directly above the commander's window.

Fear, sudden and fierce, rooted him to the spot. The air froze in his lungs. What was he *doing*? If he was seen, if somebody caught him . . . Elliot didn't care about himself, about destroying his chances of ever being a Rider again—though the thought of what that would mean for Jax made his heart lurch painfully. The only thing that mattered to him was his sister. And if Elliot angered the commander . . . maybe he'd decide her rescue wasn't worth the effort. Or worse, maybe he'd think Elliot deserved it for defying him once again.

"Sparrow," he whispered faintly, his lungs still arrested in his chest. "I can't be here. I can't—" He clamped his mouth shut as a single voice separated from the general murmur.

". . . looks like we'll need to adjust morning patrol?" That was Fallon, the second patrol leader.

"Indeed," said another voice—the commander's familiar, steady intonation. "All three of us will need to attend the audition."

Audition? Elliot frowned, leaning closer, despite his recent apprehension. Next to him Sparrow was motionless, but he knew she listened as closely as he did.

"Right—Darius can take point," Fallon answered, and there was a soft scrape of chair legs, as if he were pushing back from the table and getting to his feet. "I'll make the arrangements now, if we're all finished here?"

"We are," said the commander. There were murmured goodbyes, along with scuffing boots, clinking glasses, and the whisper of loose papers.

Elliot was secretly relieved. The meeting was over; it was time to get out of there. He crouched, preparing to stalk away, when Sparrow found the edge of his tunic and tugged him back down.

"Not done," she whispered, so softly he had to squint at her mouth in the darkness to catch her words. Not done?

A door shut in the room below. There were several moments of silence in which Elliot was certain they'd all left, but then Beryk's measured voice floated out into the night.

"I think you should reconsider, Cassian."

"What—telling Tristan? You know he can't be involved in this." Elliot leaned forward. The commander was keeping things from Tristan? Not only was he Tristan's father, but Tristan was a patrol leader.

"Not just Tristan. All of it. The risks—"

"—will be well worth it, Beryk, if my plan succeeds."

"That is a large *if*, Cassian," Beryk said, his tone steady. "It is just as likely to fail."

"It won't."

Elliot had never heard such steel in the commander's voice. He was always a strong-minded, self-assured man. Poised, powerful, and in control. But this . . . There was a dangerous edge to his voice, a coldness, that brought to mind the blade of a knife. And when you walked that line . . . one slip was all it took.

"What next, then, Commander?" Beryk asked briskly, all his dire warnings forgotten.

There was a soft squeaking sound like a drawer being opened and shut again, then more shuffling papers.

"There are nearly fifty members of the Grand Council, and it's safe to say these"—a stack of papers thwapped onto the table—"are sympathetic to Lord Rolan, while *these*"—another rustle of pages—"are supportive of animages, Pyra, and the Phoenix Rider cause."

The Grand Council? Elliot had heard about the ruling body in the empire and knew they met very sparingly—and only to vote on matters of utmost importance. Clearly there was a meeting coming, and something to do with Pyra and the Phoenix Riders was at stake.

"Some of these allies, however," the commander continued, "are border lords, and they may change their minds if Rolan's antics result in too much damage to property or income. And there are these, who I know virtually nothing about and cannot predict their allegiances."

"Mostly Stellan delegates . . . ," came Beryk's thoughtful voice. "But Rolan isn't very popular in his own province."

"No," the commander conceded, "but he still has some influence there. War in the northern provinces will matter little to Stel and will allow them to charge twice as much for their exports as agriculture in Ferro and Arboria North takes a hit. By my estimation, Lord Rolan stands to win the vote by a margin of ten. If we eliminate these five, plus—"

There was a sharp intake of breath. "That's too many, Cassian. There has to be a way to sway some of these others. . . ."

"We can try, Beryk, but unless we know how some of these Stellan representatives and border lords intend to vote, we can't risk it."

Silence descended.

The commander was obviously trying to get a handle on voting numbers to swing the results in his favor. Results that had to do with *war*? And then his use of the word "eliminate" made Elliot's heartbeat speed up, but there was something else that had caught his attention—this time in a good way.

Elliot had lived in Aura Nova for most of his life; his father worked in the Office for Border Control and split his time between their home in the city and his offices along the northern border. But originally they were from the south. Elliot's family hailed from Stel, and his great-aunt on his mother's side was an important political figure in the province.

Important enough to vote on the Grand Council.

Elliot had only met his great-aunt twice, but she was a staunch supporter of animages and had represented a dissenting faction in Stel during the Blood War—she had refused to send soldiers or supplies to aid in the war against Avalkyra Ashfire. She still moved in those circles, which meant the commander had more allies on the Grand Council than he realized.

Elliot could *help* him, give him information he most certainly needed. But how to do so without revealing that he'd been eavesdropping?

"We'll have to put that aside for now. There's still the matter of contacting the members of the council who we know will vote in our favor and ensuring they are apprised of the situation and willing to intercede, should we need them to."

The conversation died down after that. For a while there was only the sound of papers and the scratch of a writing implement, followed by low murmurs that were impossible to overhear. Then Beryk excused himself, though the lantern remained lit, its steady glow visible even after Elliot and Sparrow climbed back down and waited in the shadows behind the building until the dinner bell rang.

As they merged with the crowd, Elliot was lost in thought.

Whatever the commander was doing, it had something to do with Lord Rolan, a war, and a Grand Council vote.

It made very little sense to Elliot—but it didn't need to. He had information the commander could use, and now he just had to find a way to give it to him.

My sister also taught me that there is more than one kind of ash.
There are the ashes of destruction—all that is left after a blaze—
and there are the ashes of rebirth. The ashes of a remade
world . . . the fertile ground upon which new life grows.

- CHAPTER 12 -
SEV

IT HAD BEEN DAYS since Sev was forced to face Kade and the rest of the surviving bondservants, and his heart was still racing. He knew that the bondservants who had been deemed innocent had been released, thanks to the early-morning gossip exchange that happened in the soldiers' mess hall during breakfast, but he didn't know where Kade had been assigned. He could have been sent to a number of other places in Ferro—or to other places in the empire besides—but Sev was desperate to talk to him again. About the plan, of course, but there was much more he had to say.

As for Ulric . . . Sev didn't hear any news of him and was ashamed to admit he was afraid to ask.

After Kade had left the interrogation room, Rolan told Sev he'd receive his new assignment within the week. Because of his injury, Sev had feared he'd be sent away—that he'd be deemed unfit for service—but instead he was stationed at the estate as a general guard under the healer's care until he recovered.

It was an easy, comfortable posting inside a walled, heavily defended property. His job would be standing in doorways or walking down halls. A perfect position for someone who needed to gather information.

That, at least, Sev knew how to do. What came after was harder. He needed to find evidence of Rolan's attack on Pyra—he'd have to find letters, documents . . . anything that proved that Rolan had acted without the council's permission. How Sev would manage that, he wasn't sure, but he'd have to try.

A soft knocking reverberated through his room, and Sev sat bolt upright from where he'd been lying on his bed, staring at the lantern light as it danced across his ceiling. He was still living in the small chamber in the medical wing, despite the fact that Hestia had told him he could remove the sling for his first shift on duty.

Sev tilted his head—listening hard. It was too late for a visitor, and the knock hadn't come from the doorway or even the windowsill. It had come from the wall in his sitting room.

Sliding off his bed, he tiptoed into the adjoining chamber. There was a tapestry hanging on the wall opposite the window, and Sev brushed it aside, running his fingertips along the wood paneling. He had checked every inch of this room as soon as he was back on his feet—it was how he'd found the loose tile under the rug—and had already been over this wall. He'd knocked on it himself, sensing that it was thinner than the rest—that there might be a hallway or a room beyond. He suspected it was for the servants to access the rooms for cleaning, or for the healer to use while attending a long-term patient, though whenever he was visited by Hestia, she used the front door.

So while Sev knew a passage was there, he'd been unable to find the latch or lock to open it.

Apparently, it was on the other side.

He had only just pressed his ear to its surface when something inside clicked, and the panel slid open. Sev leapt back, scrambling at his hip for a knife, but he'd already removed his padded vest and weapons belt.

Not that he needed them.

Kade materialized before him, stepping out of the darkness of the passage and into the glow of the lantern light.

Sev gaped at him, standing mere feet away. He had cleaned up since their last meeting: new tunic, shaved jaw, and the bruises on his face had turned from dark purple to faint green.

He still looked a little worse for wear, but he also looked like himself, like Kade. He looked . . . perfect.

Sev's breath hitched, and he lurched forward, throwing his arms around him. *Gods*, he was alive, alive and unhurt—for the most part. He smelled of soap and freshly laundered clothes, and underneath that, the familiar scent of Kade—dark and rich, like honey fresh from the comb.

After a moment of apparent surprise, the tension left Kade's body and he hugged back, the force of it squeezing the air from Sev's lungs and jostling his stiff shoulder. Sev grimaced and flinched, and Kade stepped away at once, face apologetic.

"Right, your shoulder," he said, obviously remembering their last meeting, when Sev's arm had been bound in a sling. "What happened?" he demanded.

"Arrow," Sev forced out through clenched teeth. While he was getting used to the constant, dull throb, when he moved his shoulder the wrong way, a stab of sharp pain lanced through all the way down to the joint. Certain movements were impossible altogether.

With a hesitant glance, Kade pulled aside the loose tunic Sev wore to reveal the bandaging on his shoulder. The wound itself was closed up, but Hestia liked to put a poultice on at night to help with inflammation. Sev was getting used to the scent of the crushed seed and poppy-flower paste, though he was self-conscious of the smell now that Kade was here.

Kade's amber gaze was fixed on his shoulder, and Sev felt suddenly vulnerable, his tunic tugged low, revealing a large swath of his chest.

Heat swept Sev's body, and he shifted the collar back into place. "I can't believe you're here," he said at last, filling the silence between them.

"Thanks to you," Kade said, smiling slightly as he turned to close the hidden door. It slid quietly back into place, and Sev realized that the panel didn't need to be opened or unlocked, it just needed to be pulled inward and to the side on its tracks—or pushed, when coming from his side of the passage.

Kade walked farther into the room, looking around. "They've got you well appointed, haven't they?"

Sev gestured dejectedly at his shoulder. "I'm still being treated. Apparently I'm lucky to be alive."

Kade gave him a funny look. "We all are." His gaze raked Sev's body before he added, "I'm glad they're taking good care of you."

The words sounded almost protective, and something warm blossomed inside Sev's chest.

"I just don't understand," Kade said, his features twisted in confusion. "How did you come to be here? What happened that night?"

Sev realized there was a lot they needed to catch up on. As far as Kade knew, Sev was just here again by accident, stumbling and bumbling and surviving as he'd always done. Sev was eager to prove him wrong, to show that he'd changed.

He gestured to the couch, and Kade lowered himself into a seat, waiting for Sev to take the chair opposite.

The wood creaked as Sev leaned forward, scrubbing a hand across his face. "I don't even know where to begin."

"Begin with Ilithya," Kade said, and so Sev did. He recounted everything that happened the night of Ilithya's failed revolt. How, after Kade had disappeared into the forest, drawing off the soldiers, Sev took the phoenix eggs to her, hoping she could help him. Only Captain Belden had gotten to her first. Her poison had killed him, in the end—the news brought a dark smile to Kade's lips—and she'd told Sev to flee before she was executed.

"I took the arrow as I ran from the campsite. It was like fire in my back, my lungs . . . but I just kept going, all night in the dark. I climbed higher and higher until I ran into their perimeter guard. They took me to the Riders' hideout—Azurec's Eyrie. I warned them of the attack and delivered the eggs."

"You did it," Kade said, his expression one of somewhat unflattering disbelief. "You really did it."

"We did it," Sev corrected. "I was just the messenger boy."

The corner of Kade's mouth lifted before his brows lowered in confusion. "I still don't know how you wound up back here. Did they turn you in?"

Sev shook his head. "I offered myself up to their leader." He looked around the room, listening for any sounds in the outside halls or nearby rooms, but all was silent. He lowered his voice all the same. "I told them I'd be their spy."

This time, Kade's brows shot up to the ceiling. "That was very brave, Sev."

Sev snorted. "More like stupid, you mean. What was it Trix said to me?" He squinted as he tried to remember the correct phrasing. "'War has a way of making regular people into heroes.'"

Kade nodded. "Ilithya was very wise."

"I disagreed," Sev said, smiling slightly. "I said it made us into fools."

Kade chuckled, a warm sound that filled the space between them. "You aren't wrong."

Sev's smile slipped. "We need her. I'm no Trix. I'm no Shadowheart."

"That's okay," Kade said kindly, and Sev shook his head.

"No, it's not. We lost a spymaster and got stuck with me instead. I have to be better—I have to do what she would have done. Otherwise . . ."

"Otherwise what? You don't deserve to be here—to be alive? You don't mean that."

Sev shrugged, avoiding Kade's eye. "What happened to you?" he asked, wanting to change the subject and curious to know how Kade had survived this mess as well.

Kade's eyes narrowed, and Sev suspected he noticed the deflection but allowed it. "I lost those two soldiers that chased me," Kade began. "I got as much of a head start as I could, then climbed one of the trees and hid." Sev thought about the time Trix had convinced him to climb a tree, and his lips twitched into a sad smile. "But when the sun rose, the soldiers started sweeping the forest—I could hear them—and I knew I had to make a run for it. They caught me near the river and rounded me up with the others. They chained us together—I didn't know any of them, though. The others must have escaped or . . ." He trailed off. Escaped or been killed. "Then they left us there, in the caves. I thought . . ." Kade swallowed, his eyes dark. "I thought that we might die there, chained together. Then, when I heard sounds the next day, I hoped the Riders might find us." He laughed bitterly. "But it was a group of soldiers who'd fled the battle when it was clear they would lose. They fetched us and whatever supplies they could carry and headed back down the mountain."

Sev had since learned that while there had been only a few dozen survivors combined from the main attacking force, there had been a third regiment made up of bandits and mercenaries that had been charged with the diversionary tactics at the Pyraean villages. From what Sev had heard, they had fled into the wilds of Pyra or through the Foothills into Arboria North and had yet to return.

"I can't believe Ilithya's gone," Kade said sadly, staring unseeing at the low table between them.

Sev hesitated. "There was something she said, right—right before," he said, struggling to find the words. "She said that Avalkyra Ashfire lived."

Kade didn't seem shocked or surprised. He just sighed heavily, expelling a breath through his nostrils. "There was a time when I believed her—when her promises of the dead queen's resurgence gave me hope. But now? If she truly does live and she's left us all to this fate . . . then I'm not sure she's a queen I'd want to bow to."

Sev hadn't thought about it like that. If she was indeed alive, where was she now? Unless the Riders were hiding her? But Sev had told the commander Ilithya's words. . . . He had seemed genuinely startled, and even a little bit disturbed. Sev doubted she was with them. If Avalkyra Ashfire was alive, she must be somewhere else. Meanwhile, the last breath of the Phoenix Riders continued to fight her war. Kade was right. . . . That wasn't a leader worth following.

"So, Rolan has you assigned to the estate?" Sev asked, unable to keep the hopeful note from his voice.

"In my old post," he said, a soft smile lighting his face. "His dogs love me."

"Of course they do," Sev said with a smirk. The weight that had been pressing on him since his arrival eased somewhat. He wasn't alone in this; he had Kade.

And this time they were on the same side from the beginning.

"What're you—" Kade began, then froze, tilting his head slightly to listen. He stared at the window, where a second later, a pigeon landed on the ledge, a scroll tied to its foot.

"It must be from the commander," Sev said, getting to his feet. He took the scroll from the bird's leg, and it began to stroll along the sill, pecking hungrily. "Sorry, little one. I haven't—"

But then Kade was there, drawing a biscuit from his pocket. He cracked off a corner and left the pieces for the pigeon, who cooed happily.

"What's it say, then?" he prodded.

"Oh, right," Sev muttered, withdrawing his attention from Kade and returning to the sitting room, where the lantern light was brightest. Reclaiming his seat, he unfurled the letter onto the short wooden table at its center, while Kade stood above him. "It's written in code. One of Trix's old ciphers."

Kade's eyes roved the page. "So you need . . ."

"The key," Sev said, getting onto his knees and lifting the corner of the rug to reveal his hidden compartment. Kade looked impressed, watching with interest as Sev opened the lockbox and revealed the supplies within, including a copy of an ancient Pyraean Epic poem. The commander said it was in use during Avalkyra Ashfire's rebellion, and it was a code Ilithya would have been familiar with. Though utilizing an existing cipher was somewhat of a risk in case others in the empire had already cracked it, he thought it would be valuable to Sev in case he found any of her old contacts or materials. Besides, copies of *The Pyraean Epics* were extremely rare ever since the council's purge of phoenix-related art and artifacts.

Together they bent over the letter, transcribing it onto a fresh sheet of paper. Kade helped, pointing to words when Sev had trouble finding them. Finally they leaned back, the translated message sitting on the table next to the coded original.

Sev frowned. "He's sent me new orders," he said, before clearing his throat and reading aloud. He wasn't the best reader, though his mother had taught him when he was young. He hadn't had much use for reading on the streets of Aura Nova, and it wasn't until he became a soldier that his ability to read had become an asset again. Many soldiers couldn't, and merely learned how to recognize their names on duty rosters or to sign out weapons and supplies. Sev's ability to read had afforded him some measure of control—and his ability to gather information had been the thing that drew Trix's notice in the first place.

"'In light of the Grand Council meeting,'" he began self-consciously, aware of Kade watching him, "'forget your original mission and focus instead on learning more about the governor's next moves.'"

"The Grand Council . . . ?" Kade asked. "What's that?"

"It's a meeting of the full Council of Governors—all fifty members," Sev answered. "The commander sent me here to find evidence against Rolan; his attack on the Phoenix Riders wasn't sanctioned by the council. But now that Rolan's called the Grand Council, he's obviously not intending to hide the fact that he attacked, but instead convince them all that the attack was necessary—that the Phoenix Riders are a danger to the empire. That they must be destroyed. Only, he wants the council to help him do it."

"He wants war," Kade said, voice hushed.

Sev nodded distractedly. He'd thought it was going to be hard enough finding evidence for what Rolan had already done, but learning what he had *yet* to do . . . How would Sev manage that?

Something Rolan had said during their first meeting weighed on Sev.

I must convince them there is, in fact, a threat.

Lord Rolan wanted a war, and in order to get it, he had to convince the council that the Phoenix Riders were a threat. But how?

"He doesn't say anything about the hostage," Sev said, glancing down at the original coded letter in case he'd missed something. He hadn't.

"Hostage?" Kade asked.

Sev frowned. "There's a girl," he said. "Her brother was one of the Riders, and Captain Belden took her hostage to force him to spy."

Kade's eyebrows rose. "And this Rider spy told the commander and the others?"

Sev nodded.

"Do you think she still lives?"

The question sent an icy spear into Sev's heart. He hadn't considered that. "He didn't come forward until right before the battle," Sev said, convincing himself as much as Kade. "I don't think anyone here would know he'd defected. . . ." He sighed. "I guess we need to focus on Lord Rolan for now."

Kade tilted his head at Sev. "We?" he asked, though his tone was light.

"If you want," Sev said hurriedly.

Kade surveyed Sev as he had done countless times before, his gemstone eyes glimmering in the lamplight.

"So, what do you say?" Sev prodded, trying to keep the hope from his voice. "Are you in?"

Kade grinned. "I'm in," he said, and Sev smiled so hard his face hurt.

They sat in a comfortable silence, with nothing but the sound of the wind in the trees outside Sev's window and the clucking of the messenger pigeon picking its way across the sill.

"I should go," Kade said eventually, getting to his feet. "I've an early start tomorrow."

Sev stood as well. "How will we . . . ," he began, but Kade nodded at the concealed door.

"I'll come as often as I'm able. Every night, if I can. Leave a lantern lit in your sitting room if you are in and alone—I can see it through the doorframe. If you don't, I'll assume you're with someone and will return later."

They looked at each other, and there was still so much unsaid between them that Sev didn't know where to begin. "I'm so glad you're here" was all he managed, his throat constricting slightly on the words. He didn't *just* mean here in this room—or here in Rolan's estate. He meant *here, alive*, when Sev had already said his goodbyes.

"Me too," Kade whispered, rare softness in his face again. He gripped Sev's good shoulder, the warm press of his hand lingering before he stepped around Sev, crossing the room to pull aside the tapestry. With a last glance over his shoulder, he stepped into the shadowy corridor and slid the panel back into place.

Sev burned the letter and its translation before packing away his supplies and putting out the lantern. He fell back onto his bed, staring at the ceiling once more, wishing he'd had the courage to ask Kade to stay.

After the defeat of Nox and her children, the fearsome strixes, the people of the world rejoiced. They believed their war against the darkness was over, which was true.

But there were battles yet to be fought.

Famine came after the Dark Days, and it was in this time that sister phoenixes Xatara and Xolanthe were hatched, born from a First Rider bloodline.

Despite their strength and vigor, Xatara and Xolanthe found themselves Rider-less in the first year of their lives, having both lost their bondmates to hunger.

They did not despair, though, because in the death of their Riders, they found purpose.

No sooner had the ashes of their bondmates cooled than Xatara and Xolanthe took to the sky in search of food. They traveled far and wide, down deep into the valley where all was wild and dangerous. They fought great hairy beasts with curling horns and giant, scaly creatures that breathed fire. They even fought men who lived among those fantastic creatures, waiting with traps and snares and poison-tipped darts.

At last they found what they were looking for: a tree growing from a thrust of stone in the middle of the valley, with two fat, bright-red fruits dangling from its boughs. They each took one in their beak and flew home, where the villagers rejoiced to see them return, for phoenixes didn't often remain after their bondmates had died.

The humans sliced open the fruits and found golden seeds inside. Though the highest reaches of Pyrmont were barren and little grew there, when the villagers planted the golden seeds in the rocky ground, they took root immediately: one grew into the first Fire Blossom tree and the other into the first phoenix fruit tree.

Xatara and Xolanthe were celebrated as heroes and remained among their people and their phoenixes. Some say they bonded again, years later, while others insist they remained as guardians over the two trees, ever watchful.

Whatever their fates, the Pyraean villagers never went hungry again.

—"Xatara and Xolanthe," from *The Pyraean Epics*, Volume 2, circa 460 BE

*My sister taught me many things. Would for you,
my daughter, to have a sister such as her. She would
teach you life's hard lessons. Some on purpose. Some by
accident. And some simply by virtue of who she is.*

- CHAPTER 13 -
VERONYKA

IT WAS LATE BY the time Veronyka stepped out into the stronghold, alone for the first time all day. She cast a glance over her shoulder toward the commander's administrative building, but Tristan was nowhere in sight.

She sighed and rubbed her forehead, rebuilding her mental barriers.

It had been a close call.

Despite how hard she'd been working on blocking her shadow magic lately, her emotions were suddenly raw—Val, the lockbox, the soldiers, and now a chance to become a Master Rider. Tristan had supported her, stood by her, and then they'd been alone in that dark hallway. . . .

He'd wanted to kiss her—she'd heard him think it. She hadn't realized how much she'd opened herself to him until that moment, and she'd been forced to get away from him. Immediately.

Because Veronyka wanted to kiss him, too, and it seemed that even the thought of it was enough to rattle the connection between them. To make it tremble and shake. Would she *ever* be able to have that kind of closeness with Tristan? Or was their romantic relationship doomed before it had even begun?

No. Veronyka refused to believe that. She'd get it under control. She had to.

Their bond was difficult for her to wrap her brain around. It wasn't like her bond with Xephyra, because that went both ways. Even her bond with Val was something they were both aware of. But Tristan didn't see what was happening between them, had no control over his own mind and thoughts, and that felt like a horrible betrayal of trust.

But she couldn't tell him. Not if she didn't want to make things worse than they already were.

Not if she wanted to pass the trials the next day and achieve her goals.

If she'd been eager to become a Master Rider before, she was downright frantic now. Not only would she have the chance to join Tristan's patrol, but she'd do so as his *second*. It was everything she wanted. The empire was mobilizing, soldiers had been sighted, and the Phoenix Riders were finally, *finally* going to leave the Eyrie and prepare to defend the people of Pyra.

And Veronyka needed to be a part of it.

But then there was the lockbox. Veronyka had gone to the cabin to bury her past, not unearth it. She'd been ready to turn her back on the questions that plagued her, to do what needed to be done to strengthen herself and block her shadow magic, and now?

Without deciding to do it, Veronyka's walked into the Eyrie. She found her saddlebags, stored with the others, and carefully withdrew the box.

It had no keyhole or visible opening mechanism. She had memories of seeing this box in her *maiora's* hands, remembered the contrast of her pale, wrinkled fingers against its smooth dark surface. After the mob took Ilithya and they'd run for their lives, Val must have returned to their ransacked home in the Narrows for it.

And then she'd returned again to their cabin in the woods. Whatever this lockbox contained, it was obviously important.

Veronyka needed sleep. The next day's tests would be difficult, and her entire future hung in the balance. But the past was here, literally in her grasp. She didn't know what she expected to find, but she knew she couldn't wait to check. If she found some answers to the questions that had been plaguing her—or at the very least, learned something of what Val was planning to do—it would give Veronyka some semblance of control. It would make her feel less powerless.

Then she could let go of some of the weight that was holding her down. She could let go of Val, too. Maybe having some answers would make blocking her shadow magic easier. Maybe it would quiet her mind and put her at ease.

And if it was nothing? She could shelve her disappointment and focus on the tests tomorrow.

Veronyka wended her way through the village streets. The metalworker's forge was still and quiet, the scent of quenched flames and cooling iron lingering on the evening breeze. Heat emanated from the stall as Lars cleaned his tools and prepared to shut down for the day. Veronyka's heart leapt to see that he hadn't yet abandoned his shop, and she hurried forward.

When he spotted Veronyka, he paused in untying his apron. "Did I miss an order today?" he asked, assuming she was there on behalf of the Riders. "I thought those harness repairs weren't needed until the end of the week."

"No, you didn't miss anything," she said, smiling and putting her box onto his long wooden counter. "I was hoping you might have a tool for opening a lockbox?"

His gaze lit on it, and a frown creased his brow. He approached, tossing his apron onto the counter and leaning down for a closer look. Lars was both tall and wide, his hands as big as Veronyka's head, and the box looked like some child's trinket as he lifted it for further examination. "Y'know, *traditionally*, it's a key that opens a lockbox," he said, a twinkle in his eye, though his expression turned quizzical as he rotated the box and found no lock. "Who'd you steal this from, then?" he asked.

"It's not stolen," she said quickly, though she realized that technically wasn't true.

"There's no opening mechanism that I can see, but there are the hinges," he said, running a thick finger along the metal hardware. "I could pry it open along the seams, but that might damage whatever's inside."

Without thinking, Veronyka snatched it back from him, and Lars raised his hands as if to show he hadn't done any damage—yet. Veronyka was desperate to get inside the box, but damaging the contents would completely defeat the purpose. There had to be another way.

Before she could say anything, Old Ana sidled up to Lars's stall. She was a plump, kind-looking woman, her graying black hair pinned atop her round face and her brown skin smudged with earth. She smiled warmly at them both before she slammed a pair of gardening shears onto the counter. "It's happened again, you great brute. I thought I told you I needed my clippers to *cut*, not to lock up every time I try to use them."

Lars turned a baleful look at Veronyka as he took the shears, sighing heavily. Veronyka smirked. Ana reminded her of her *maiora*, brusque and with a sharp tongue, and it always amused her to see the woman barking at a man nearly three times her size.

"And I told *you*, Sweet Ana, that these shears are no good for thinning out your stubborn rosebushes. You'll need a handsaw for that."

"Don't try to butter me up, Lars. It's *Old* Ana to you and everyone else. Either make me a handsaw that fits in my apron or unstick those shears."

Lars shook his head and smiled, disappearing into the back of his stall for some of his tools.

Old Ana watched him, a wistful smile on her face. "I tell you, Nyka, if I were thirty years younger, that man would be tending more than my shears, if you know what I mean."

Veronyka pulled a face, and Ana cackled. She was the only person to use the Pyraean diminutive of her name, just as Val had done, but Veronyka didn't mind. Maybe it was because she associated Ana with her grandmother, or maybe it was because some part of her missed the familiarity of it.

"What's that you've got there? A Pyraean puzzle box?"

Veronyka looked down at the lockbox in her hand. "Puzzle box?" she asked, having never heard the term before.

Ana reached for it, and Veronyka reluctantly handed it over. With surprising deftness, Ana squinted and prodded, her hands—stained with decades of dirt across knuckles and under fingernails—sliding expertly over its dark, shiny surface.

"Aha," she said, turning it so the front faced Veronyka, with the hinge on the other side. Rather than pulling up at the seam, Ana slid the front panel *sideways*, and something clicked. Then she opened the lid as easily as one would open a chest.

Veronyka's eyes bulged, landing on the piles of papers inside. She reached for it, but Ana was already closing and relocking it. She guided Veronyka's hand along the panel, showing her how she'd done it, and Veronyka nodded her thanks, her heart racing.

"Something valuable in there, I take it?" Ana said, noting Veronyka's breathless excitement.

"I hope so," Veronyka answered, clutching the box to her chest before hurrying away.

With the other apprentices already inside the barracks, Veronyka wandered the stronghold, uncertain, before deciding on the stables as the best place to be alone. Well, to be away from *people*, at any rate.

Xephyra nudged at her mind, telling her to come to the Eyrie, but even at night there were too many people about. That was where the Master Riders slept, after all, and she didn't want to chance a run-in with Tristan.

Veronyka's second favorite animal at the Eyrie, Tristan's horse, Wind, welcomed her warmly—eventually. At first he was his usual prickly self, having taken her almost three-day absence rather personally. He kept turning away from her, bending his long neck so far he was practically looking behind himself—until she promised him apples for the next three days to make up for it. With a huff and a snort, he suffered her pats and affection, before slipping back into a doze.

Veronyka sank down onto the straw-strewn ground, placing a freshly lit lantern next to her.

This was the very stall Veronyka had hidden in weeks before, only to be found by Tristan—and soon after, the commander. She hoped neither would disturb her now.

With a shaky breath, she slid back the panel the way Ana had shown her and lifted the lid.

The golden light revealed a stack of papers—some thick and professionally inscribed, others covered in smudged charcoal or bleeding ink. While most were written in the Trader's Tongue, some were in ancient Pyraean.

Veronyka frowned, lifting the papers to find some heavy with wax seals or tied together with string, while smaller scraps slipped out from between the pages. Surely some had been torn from books or collections, while others looked like personal letters or notes. Her mind spun as she took it all in, unsure where to begin or what to make of it. She glanced at the topmost page, which was an excerpt from *The Pyraean Epics* documenting the history of Nefyra and the First Riders. Underneath that was a square of paper so thin it was translucent, its messily scrawled words—part of a song or poem?—faded and difficult to decipher.

It seemed a strange assortment of papers, and Veronyka wondered what Val could want with them, especially when, upon further inspection, it was clear that her *maiora* had gathered them. Her grandmother had some training as a healer, so people were often coming and going from the back door of their Narrows apartment. That wasn't the only reason people came to see her, though. She was a collector—a spy, Veronyka now knew—asking after people and places, hoarding bits of news and snippets of gossip. It had always seemed so arbitrary to Veronyka, because she couldn't see past the surface details. Why should they care if the butcher's son had gambling debts? But her *maiora* saw more, and like a seamstress with scraps of fabric, she would line up the edges and sew together their tangled threads into something new and whole.

The butcher's son was eventually charged with murder, but most people—her grandmother among them—knew he'd been so desperate for money he'd agreed to dispose of a body for one of the most powerful gang leaders in the Narrows, then been caught and blamed for the crime.

"Guard your secrets like you guard your flesh and blood, Veronyka," her grandmother had said after accosting the messenger boy who'd been shouting the news along the tightly packed streets. "A secret in the wrong hands is as good as a blade in the back."

Veronyka was certain that her grandmother wouldn't have left these documents in such a state. Val must have rummaged through the box's contents, taking what she wanted without a care in the world for their grandmother's efforts. And yet . . . she'd obviously left something behind, or else why would she have come back for it? Val was not the sentimental sort.

Just as when she was a child, Veronyka had trouble seeing the whole picture. There must be some purpose to all this . . . some reason for the collection.

She leaned back and started dividing the documents into piles based on content and form—scraps from history books in one pile, handwritten notes in another. There were stacks of letters wrapped in twine and some official-looking documents with crumbling bits of wax on them.

The act of sorting the items was soothing, and Veronyka didn't read in too much detail, finding the endless pages overwhelming. Her thumping heart began to ease, and it was nice to feel like she was back in the apartment with her grandmother, helping sort her papers in the warm lantern light. Her chest ached with the loneliness of it, the yearning that could never be fulfilled.

She was halfway through the stack when a piece of paper with a long list of names—written in her grandmother's hand—caught her eye.

There were nearly a dozen names in total, some underlined while others were circled or crossed out, and underneath each were scribbled notes indicating last-known whereabouts, political affiliations, former associates, and living family.

Beside each person on the list was a secondary name. A phoenix name.

Veronyka's hands shook. This was a list of Phoenix Riders. And judging by the notes beneath, they were Riders who had survived the Blood War.

Aidan and Alaxor.

Alexiya and Himn.

Cillian and Voxol.

Doriyan and Daxos.

Sidra and Oxana.

Or at least, they were *thought* to have survived the war. Veronyka's soaring heart plummeted as she saw, written next to some of the names in bold, black ink: *Deceased. Missing. Deceased.*

These people must have been unaccounted for after the fighting, when this list was made. Then their status was updated one by one.

All those who had been deemed dead or missing had an *X* beside their information. It was, sadly, most of the list.

Veronyka scanned the names more closely, but they were unfamiliar. Most of the names she knew from recent history belonged to those who had died fiery, explosive deaths.

Like Avalkyra Ashfire.

Reading the details below the names, she saw that things had been added over time by different hands in different inks—presumed locations changed, or family and affiliations.

Had Ilithya been looking for these Riders on Val's behalf, hoping for friends and allies to rebuild her army? Veronyka had a hard time imagining Val appealing directly for help, especially when she was phoenix-less and living in poverty. Still, Val had disappeared from time to time, and so had her *maiora.* Val, of course, gave no excuse or reason, but Veronyka had always assumed it had been about phoenix eggs. Her grandmother, on the other hand, would leave to "deliver a baby" or gather herbs and supplies for her medicines, giving her days to do what she needed for her queen.

Veronyka had often wondered why they'd stayed in Aura Nova all those years, and she thought she finally had her answer. Travel was banned, and they didn't have the proper paperwork to leave, but Veronyka and Val had bribed their way out of the empire eventually. Surely, someone as intelligent and resourceful as her *maiora* could have done the same in a fraction of the time. But looking at this list, the majority of the people who were crossed out had been living in the capital city or elsewhere in the empire—unable, Veronyka could only assume, to leave thanks to their status as Phoenix Riders. Aura Nova was centrally located, so it made sense strategically for them to stay.

Veronyka closed her eyes, trying to imagine the roller coaster of emotions Val must have gone through each time Ilithya left only to return with a frown or a shake of the head. Those who had been assumed alive were then labeled dead, usually along with their phoenixes, while others' locations changed over and over again.

Then there were those who had been deemed loyal, only to have that word viciously scratched out. How many had refused to join or listen to Ilithya? How many hated Avalkyra Ashfire for what she had done?

A few were *not* crossed out, though—three total—and Veronyka didn't know if that was because Val hadn't approached them yet or if their allegiances were still uncertain.

Why had Val always insisted that all the Phoenix Riders were dead when she clearly knew otherwise? Maybe she suspected Veronyka would badger her to seek them out. Maybe Val didn't want to acknowledge their existence when they refused to support her.

Veronyka read the list again. Though they were different ages and with varying levels of skill and experience, all three of the Riders who weren't crossed out had one thing in common: their last-known whereabouts were in Pyra. Though the empire had marched into the province after the Blood

War and turned every village and settlement inside out looking for surviving Riders, most animages in hiding today found being outside the empire safer than being within it. Commander Cassian certainly agreed, as did these exiled Riders.

Did they know about the commander and his burgeoning Rider army? Did they care? And if confronted with the choice between him and a resurrected queen, who might they choose?

With a yawn, Veronyka put the list aside, shuffling absently through the remaining documents and letters until she reached the last page.

Her heart leapt into her throat. Her name was on it—she recognized it immediately, even though the paper was upside down. Fully awake again, she rotated the official-looking document, signed and stamped with a wax seal, to see that it was a birth certificate.

Veronyka's brain stuttered, her vision blurring as she stared and stared but couldn't seem to *see*.

Regular people didn't get birth certificates. They were reserved for those with wealth or position, those who had to worry about lands and rights and inheritance. Those with titles.

And then . . . just below her name was another name. A surname. These, too, were given only to the empire elite—and only where custom dictated.

Veronyka Ashfire.

Her heart was spasming now, thumping so painfully that Veronyka struggled to swallow. It constricted her airways. It made her head swim.

Underneath her name—was it *her* name?—was another. A familiar one.

Of course it was that name. The only name in the world that could inspire love, loyalty, and most of all, hatred, from the Feather-Crowned Queen herself.

Pheronia Ashfire.

And next to it was the word "mother."

Veronyka's thoughts whirled, running through dates and timelines while her chest heaved, her heart convulsing against her lungs, suffocating her. There was no father listed, no explanation. This wasn't a story or a letter, meant to charm and inspire. This was a legal document. Cold. Indifferent. It didn't care that it held the weight of the world in its ink-and-wax edict. It didn't care that it proved Veronyka's whole life was a lie.

Below the names was a birth date—not the birth date Veronyka had celebrated her whole life. Yet this date was well known to her, as it was to everyone.

It was the day of the Last Battle in Aura Nova. The end of the Blood War. The end of everything.

And the beginning. *Her* beginning.

CERTIFICATE OF BIRTH

THIS DOCUMENT CERTIFIES
THAT
VERONYKA ASHFIRE
WAS BORN ON
THE TWENTY-FIRST DAY OF
THE NINTH MOON,
170 AE, IN AURA NOVA,
THE GOLDEN EMPIRE

TO

MOTHER: PHERONIA ASHFIRE

FATHER: _____

NOTARIZED BY: *Cedric, Grand Council Lawmaker*

WITNESSED BY: *Ilithya, Acolyte of Hael*

And make no mistake—in my life with Avalkyra Ashfire,
I learned a great deal. If only some of those hard lessons
could be unlearned. If only they were not necessary.

- CHAPTER 14 -
VERONYKA

VERONYKA LURCHED TO HER feet, the sudden movement making her head spin . . . or maybe it was something else.

Frantic wingbeats brushed against her mind—Xephyra, trying to break through—but Veronyka blocked her out. She tried to calm herself, to *breathe*, but all she managed were short, shallow inhalations. Her feelings were a tangled mess, as if there was a disconnect between her brain and her body.

The words swam before her vision. Veronyka Ashfire. Veronyka Ashfire.

Val, she said in her mind, seeking out that locked, barred door between them. Suddenly nothing else mattered. Not the dangers of shadow magic, not the work she'd been putting in day after day to keep herself and the people around her safe. Her desperation was a clawed beast inside her.

The word echoed in the emptiness of her mind. The silence was worse somehow. She'd never felt more alone.

Avalkyra Ashfire! she screamed, her heart pumping harder, faster, ratcheting up her bloodstream.

Yes, xe Nyka? came the cool, calm reply. Veronyka had forgotten the way it felt to have another inside her mind. She did not like it.

It was startling to have Val's voice so near while her body was somewhere else entirely. Distantly, Veronyka understood that this shouldn't be possible, that shadow magic was limited by things like proximity, the same way animal magic was.

This, what was happening now, was the *bond* at work.

Is it true? Veronyka demanded, the memory of the birth certificate filling her mind's eye.

She sensed Val's slightly bored, slightly angry reaction. Though she'd known Veronyka would find the certificate, she hadn't wanted her to.

You know it is, she answered.

Is that all you have to say, Aunt? Veronyka growled, heat rising inside her. *Is that all you have to say to me?*

What would you like me to say, Veronyka? she answered, and for once, her tone lacked sarcasm or disdain. *Would you like me to tell you that I'm sorry? That I never meant to hurt you? I want no more empty words between us.*

Of course Val saw apologies and remorse as empty words. *I want you to tell me why.*

Val shrugged, the picture of her becoming clearer in Veronyka's head the longer they spoke. She wasn't actually seeing Val, she didn't think, but rather, seeing a mental projection of her memory of Val—the way Veronyka always imagined her. Red hair and braids. Black eyes as cold and dark as the River Aurys at night.

I did not think you were ready, Val answered.

Liar, Veronyka said.

Fine, Val said, voice flat. *I didn't tell you because I think you are weak and emotional and I did not want to break you.*

Veronyka's lips pulled back from her teeth in a snarl, but before she could reply, there was a sudden rush of color and sound. The stables drifted away as visions from a battlefield descended around Veronyka like a curtain of heavy rainfall.

Clashing metal and screams—human and phoenix—pierced the night, while fire slashed through the darkness of the

world, rippling and cracking like flags in the wind. High
above, burning phoenixes crisscrossed the sky, swirling and
diving and falling to their deaths. Veronyka could smell the
smoke, could feel the heat of flames on her skin.

There was pain, too—in Veronyka's bones and in her
heart. Pain that did not belong to her.

This was another of Val's memories.

Veronyka withdrew her focus from the battle, looking down to see
her—or rather, Val's—blood-soaked hands. And beneath her lay a body.

A girl, almost the same age Veronyka was now—her
black hair sticking to her forehead with sweat, while a
phoenix-feather-fletched arrow protruded from her chest.
Blood stained the fabric of her fine shirt, and there was a
swell beneath it—her belly round with child.

Mother, *Veronyka thought, just as Val's lips whispered,*
"Sister."

Pheronia reached for Val, dragged her down, and
pressed Val's hands to her stomach. Veronyka felt it, felt
herself inside, struggling to live as the light of her mother's
life flickered out.

Veronyka reared back from the vision, slamming into the wall behind
her, blinking as the stables came back into view. She wiped her hands over
her legs, the sticky heat of her mother's blood still warm on her skin.

See? Val said idly, her voice slowly fading away. *The truth is not for the*
faint of heart.

There's nothing faint about my heart, Avalkyra Ashfire! Veronyka shouted.
Do you hear me? But there was no reply, nothing but silence in the darkened
corners of her haunted mind.

Tell me why you wanted it! Veronyka asked, frantic now. There was so much she needed to know, and their conversation had been cut far too short. *Tell me why—*

"Avalkyra Ashfire?" came a voice, surprisingly near at hand. Veronyka spun around to find Sparrow standing at the open door to Wind's stall. Her hair was mussed as usual, thanks in part to the raven perched atop her head. She stared just to the left of Veronyka, at the stable wall, unable to actually see her, but instead sensing her location by sound—or by the raven's helpful instructions.

Veronyka's heart was hammering—she hadn't realized she'd spoken aloud. "What are you doing here?" she asked, though the stables weren't exactly private. Sparrow had just as much a right as Veronyka to be here at all hours of the night.

"Just been listenin' around," Sparrow answered with a shrug.

Listenin' around? Veronyka thought, perplexed, but shook away her confusion. "I—I must have nodded off," she said, hastily crouching down to gather her papers and stuff them back into the box. "It was a bad dream."

Sparrow nodded, as if she knew all too well the plague of nightmares. It made Veronyka feel guilty for lying to her when she'd been very much awake during the exchange she'd just had with Val. With Avalkyra Ashfire . . . her *aunt*.

"I better get to the barracks," Veronyka said, standing with the lockbox. How she intended to sleep after what she'd just learned . . . She squeezed the thoughts from her mind. She couldn't afford to go to pieces now, with her audition for Master Rider the next day.

You wouldn't need to audition if you told them the truth, came a voice from the back of Veronyka's mind. It sounded like Val's—cold and imperious—but Veronyka knew it was her own voice, her own thought. *You are an Ashfire. You are a queen.*

"A-are you coming too?" she asked Sparrow, trying to pick up the fraying threads of their conversation while swallowing down the panic that was rising like a tide in her chest. She glanced out the nearest window, at the inky, star-spattered sky. How long had she been here?

"Nah. Don't like the barracks. Might go for another walk with this fine fellow," she said, stroking the raven's shining black feathers. Upon closer inspection, Veronyka saw that the bird's face was slashed by a long scar, blinding one eye and leaving a pale, jagged line down to his chest.

"What's his name?" Veronyka asked, unable to help herself. Maybe Sparrow had found a new companion to take the place of Chirp. She seemed happier than Veronyka had seen her since the attack. She actually looked taller, too, and even her clothes—though dirty and torn in several places—seemed to fit her better, the short, scrawny, half-wild girl Veronyka first met several months ago slowly fading away. Well, partially, anyway. She still had a bird tangled in her hair, after all.

Sparrow snorted. "Won't tell me. I think he likes it best when I call him 'fine fellow,'" she said.

Despite her distraction, Veronyka laughed. "Nice to meet you, Fine Fellow," she said, and Sparrow grinned. "I've gotta go," Veronyka said, scanning the ground to make sure she'd gotten all her papers before they exited Wind's stall together.

Got to, came Val's imagined reproach inside Veronyka's mind. Val. Avalkyra. Sister. Queen. *Aunt.*

Sparrow strolled in the direction of the village gate, and Veronyka wondered idly if she sometimes slept outside or in the stables rather than in the servant barracks. Veronyka didn't know for certain, but she suspected that Sparrow had been homeless before she'd come here. She'd likely slept in far worse places than Veronyka and Val ever had, and she did so with a smile.

Veronyka clutched the lockbox to her chest. She wished, for the first time in her life, that she was the same nobody she'd always thought she'd been.

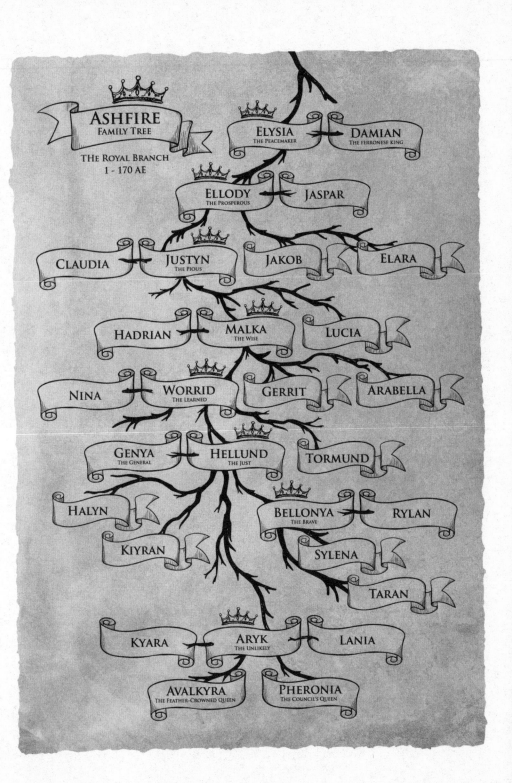

When our father died, I learned
what it was to stand together.

- CHAPTER 15 -
AVALKYRA

THERE'S NOTHING FAINT ABOUT my heart, Avalkyra Ashfire!

Veronyka's words rang in Avalkyra's ears long after she'd broken off their contact.

With a frustrated curse, Avalkyra forced the phoenix she'd been riding to land. It was dark and she couldn't see, but she trusted the creature enough to make sure they didn't die on the way down.

They landed—roughly—and the instant she stumbled from the phoenix's back, Avalkyra fell to her knees and retched.

The phoenix squawked and skittered several feet away, shaking out her wings and tossing her head.

"Be silent," Avalkyra said, voice ragged. She was too spent to use what little energy she had left on more shadow magic commands. It had taken everything she had to speak to Veronyka through their bond just now, and even then, she'd feared she might lose control over the creature beneath her and fall from the sky to her death.

She sighed. Veronyka had discovered the truth. Avalkyra had known it was coming. . . . As soon as Veronyka had taken the lockbox, she'd known it was only a matter of time.

Now Veronyka knew who she was, and still she remained tucked away safe inside the Eyrie, out of Avalkyra's reach. If the realization of her true identity wasn't enough to draw Veronyka out, Avalkyra feared nothing would be.

With a shaky breath, Avalkyra took in her surroundings. A quiet copse of trees with moonlight streaming through the leaves, and no sign of human habitation. She let her head droop. They should be safe here, for now.

It had taken Avalkyra several days to figure it out, and even now that she thought she had a handle on it, it didn't make what she was doing easy. Putting a shadow magic bind on a phoenix was no small thing. Phoenixes and humans communicated through *animal* magic, not shadow magic—except that was exactly what Avalkyra was doing.

It didn't make sense and it shouldn't have worked, and yet it did. This was no ordinary phoenix, old as she was, and Avalkyra was no ordinary shadowmage. They said shadow magic was born of death; her mother's death gave her shadow magic in her first life, and her own death gave her shadow magic in her second. Two deaths. Did that make her magic twice as strong? She wasn't sure, but she'd had decades to hone and master her dark gift. She might as well make use of it.

Avalkyra thought back to the first time she'd seen the phoenix, standing there among the ruins. Something about her behavior—her speech and mannerisms—had seemed strange to Avalkyra. Strange, and oddly *human*.

The phoenix had lived for centuries, Avalkyra guessed, her tail feathers longer than Avalkyra was tall. The creature had lived, and lost, and seen much. Too much, perhaps. Avalkyra thought about it often, about how much a single soul could endure. How much *she* could endure.

That was when she realized why she thought the creature seemed human.

It was her sadness.

A Morian priestess had explained to her once that shadow magic was a communion between minds of equal intelligence. That was why it worked only on humans and not animals, who were less intelligent.

Avalkyra had known there and then that while the priestess might *study* shadow magic, she certainly didn't have it. Forgetting the fact that phoenixes were highly intelligent, her statement had still rung false. First of all, Avalkyra could use her shadow magic on any fool without the natural mental instincts—or instruction—to defend against it. And second, she'd come to understand the connection not as a meeting of like minds but as a meeting of shared experiences. Not necessarily in a literal sense, but all humans shared a certain understanding about life and death that most animals never could. That was, after all, the primary distinction between human and animal: awareness of mortality.

And that sadness, that *darkness* that came with death, was an integral part of humankind.

Shadow magic was darkness that sought other darkness. Avalkyra and Veronyka connected so easily because they were both human, but also because they shared so many memories—many of them dark and difficult—and surviving those trials had bound them together permanently.

Animal magic, on the other hand, was life seeking life, always searching for a flicker or a spark.

While humans and animals shared that spark of life, what they did not always share was the darkness.

Even phoenixes, intelligent and magical as they were, did not view death the way humans did. How could they? They were capable of resurrection, of living for hundreds of years without ever having to face the idea of dying. How could they possibly relate to the brief flicker of life that was humanity?

The most obvious way was through a magical bond. Sure, phoenixes *could* die in battle, but it had been a millennium since they'd fought in wars of their own against the strixes. Now if they fought, it was alongside their humans and for human matters. Through their bondmates, phoenixes began to understand concepts like language, strategy, and social custom. They also became aware of death—of the eventuality of their bondmate's and the possibility of their own, both constant worries in the back of their human's mind.

The phoenix before Avalkyra, however old she was, had clearly lived long among humans. Her internal speech was highly developed, if a bit scattered, and she understood words and their context beyond mere conversation, possessing a self-awareness Nyx had never come close to in all her years at Avalkyra's side.

This phoenix had also surely been bonded, because it was that loss, that sorrow, that permeated her mind and her presence. Perhaps she had bonded more than once or had lived through many wars and battles. Whatever it was, this creature *knew* death, grasping its cold finality. And as a result, her mind was *dark*, darker than most phoenixes.

That was the thing Avalkyra had clung to when she'd punched her way into the phoenix's mind. That was the bridge that spanned the distance between them. It had taken several attempts, but Avalkyra had done it; she'd broken down the phoenix's mental barriers and put the bind in place. It wasn't the same as a bond, where the link provided insight into thoughts and feelings and identity like an open door into the mind. It was more like a *hole*, a puncture wound in the walls of the creature's defenses. If the phoenix's mind was a stronghold, Avalkyra's shadow magic was a battering ram.

But it was tiring. A phoenix's will wasn't easily bent and broken, and Avalkyra was in a state of near-constant exhaustion.

She still felt faint and shaky—nausea was a rare symptom of magic overuse—but the night air cooled her brow and after several moments gathering herself, she got to her feet. No matter the cost, she couldn't give up now, not when the possibilities unfurled before her. If she could make this work, she'd be the first Phoenix Rider in history without a bond.

If anyone could do it, Avalkyra Ashfire could.

Her plans were starting to come together at long last—or at least, they had been. She'd finally gotten her phoenix—untempered, unbound, and practically uncontrollable, but hers nonetheless—and she'd been on the way to get what she needed to lure Veronyka to her side once more. But by luck or ill fate, Veronyka had gotten there first.

For almost seventeen years Avalkyra had guarded her secrets, hoarding them like precious treasure. First, she hadn't understood who or what she was, some not-quite-child confused by a past life that haunted her day and night. So she'd developed a habit of gathering useless trinkets—bits of rocks shaped like arrowheads and dirty brown feathers from the doves that clustered outside the orphanage window—trying to put her life together like a puzzle without all the pieces. As she grew older, Avalkyra learned to call down messenger pigeons to steal letters and to pick pockets along the busy Narrows streets or the docks along the Fingers. At that point she'd had a better idea of what she was looking for, and by the time she'd found Ilithya's hovel with Veronyka inside, Avalkyra had a pouch filled with coins, a piece of true Pyraean obsidian, a rusted Ferronese steel knife, and an old leaflet distributed by the Council of Governors announcing her death at the end of the war.

Ilithya already had a cache of her own, and together they had swelled its contents, building a story of the past and looking for a way to rewrite the future. Ilithya was the one who had found the letters between Pheronia and Avalkyra, stolen from the locked drawers of private collectors, and she had also ensured that Veronyka's birth certificate was authenticated before she absconded with both the child and the official documentation. She'd made a bloody mess to retrieve Avalkyra's signet ring, leaving bodies and burning buildings in her wake.

But as Avalkyra's memories grew stronger, the box had become something she dreaded to look at or think about . . . a weak, washed-out version of what had once been. A reminder when she didn't want to be reminded, and evidence of the things she couldn't forget no matter how hard she tried.

Still, Avalkyra had protected it, clutching that box from one run-down apartment to the next, just as she'd clutched Veronyka's hand, and when Ilithya was swallowed by that mob, Avalkyra had returned to the scene of the crime and dug those buried treasures up from the dirt.

But sometimes the lockbox was safer when it *wasn't* with her—like when she'd set out after Veronyka at the Eyrie—so she'd left it buried inside their cabin. Veronyka didn't know the man who owned it would never return, thanks to a quiet knife in the dark delivered by Avalkyra's steady hand, and besides, she hadn't thought Veronyka would have the guts to return to that cursed cabin, the place where her bondmate had died.

Except that she had.

Avalkyra had gone back to unearth the past as she'd done countless times before, only to find Veronyka was there. It was almost a boon—and despite her frustration with the girl, Avalkyra's heart had leapt at the sight of her. If she'd been alone, Avalkyra *knew* she could have talked her around, convinced Veronyka to stay while she explained the truth of who they were and what they were meant to do.

Of course, old habits were like phoenixes—rising again and again—and the next thing she knew, they were locked together like snarling beasts. Avalkyra was fighting for something valuable beyond measure—their future—and Veronyka was fighting because she was angry and afraid and knew that if Avalkyra wanted the box, it was worth fighting for.

Despite Veronyka's ferocity, Avalkyra would have won that fight and won Veronyka to her side if the commander's son hadn't turned up and shifted the confrontation in Veronyka's favor. Avalkyra'd had no choice then but to flee and hope they didn't give chase. Avalkyra Ashfire might have once been the greatest flyer of her generation, but with a bucking phoenix controlled by a bind and not a bond, she was lucky not to plummet from the sky every time they leapt into the air, never mind fly in evasive maneuvers with two mounted Riders in pursuit.

What would Veronyka do with the information? What *could* she do? She was a part of Commander Cassian's flock, sworn to follow his orders like some soldier lackey and *not* the Ashfire princess that she was, to whom all of them should bend a knee and bow in supplication.

Despite this fact, instinct told Avalkyra that Veronyka wouldn't share her discovery with the commander. She didn't want to be different, to be above those she thought of as friends, and she had long since learned not to trust Avalkyra. She might even convince herself the information was false, anything to deny the terrible truth. Avalkyra had felt it when they'd connected, Veronyka's horror and reluctance to have her entire life ripped out from underneath her, what little autonomy she'd managed to glean for herself torn away and put in the hands of a politician like the commander.

She would probably tell his son, though.

Foolish, sentimental girl. How was Avalkyra to get her out of the Eyrie now?

Then again, Veronyka's discovery *did* provide opportunity. By allowing Avalkyra into her mind just now, Veronyka had left herself exposed. She'd been guarding herself relentlessly since their parting outside the Eyrie—even their encounter at the cabin had not shaken her resolve—but with this one moment of openness, Veronyka had shown Avalkyra that she was scared, confused, and most of all, *compromised*. Even now, with her own shadow magic weakened, Avalkyra could sense Veronyka in a way she hadn't since they'd lived together. This tendril of connection wouldn't last long, but Avalkyra might just be able to exploit it. To plant seeds and sow doubt.

But even if Avalkyra utilized this link while they still had it, there was nothing she could reveal that was any more valuable than what Veronyka already knew. She could lie, but even if that succeeded in luring Veronyka out, it would not *keep* her, and Avalkyra had learned her lesson in that regard.

Veronyka was a Phoenix Rider now. She would not be so easy to control as she'd once been, and everything hinged on them being together—permanently. This time when Veronyka joined her, it would be for good.

She had to give Veronyka something worth fighting for.

The problem was, Veronyka didn't see herself as an Ashfire yet. She didn't covet the throne, didn't feel the legacy in her blood or the weight of the crown atop her head.

She would, Avalkyra knew, but she didn't yet. So what did she feel?

Suddenly Avalkyra understood. Veronyka was the same girl she'd always been deep down. And that girl was an orphaned animage living in squalor. Veronyka still remembered—was barely removed from—a life when she was barefoot and hungry, longing for the power to rescue not only herself, but others as well. She'd never seen her circumstances as temporary, as something to be suffered until the inevitable payoff, as Avalkyra had.

This was why Veronyka had wanted to be a Phoenix Rider in the first place: to protect, to save, to champion the weak and powerless.

To offer Veronyka a throne now would be pointless—she did not want it. She did not understand the big picture. No, Avalkyra had to offer her something tangible and closer to home . . . and that home and heart was Pyra, the land where she'd found friends and acceptance and purpose.

It was the place Avalkyra must strike, the place that Veronyka was most vulnerable.

Already it was happening—the attack at the Eyrie was proof of that. War was coming, and Avalkyra would simply nudge it along.

If Pyra had to burn for Veronyka to be by Avalkyra's side, so be it.

Loath as she was to admit it, Avalkyra needed help. She needed to contact whoever had orchestrated the attack on the Eyrie in the first place, and provide what assistance she could to move the war along. To do that she needed information, but unfortunately, her spymaster was dead.

Still . . . there were others who yet lived. Those Avalkyra hadn't been able to face without a phoenix at her command.

People she could trust. Friends.

No, not friends. Allies.

And Avalkyra knew just where to find one.

She took to the sky once more and it was nearing dawn by the time she steered her mount down for the second landing of the night, this time more carefully. She proceeded on foot, leaving the phoenix behind as she picked a path through the trees.

She was west of the River Aurys, deep in the uninhabited parts of Pyrmont. While most of the mountain was hard and untamed, covered in gnarled trees and jagged, rocky slopes, there was the occasional stretch of rolling hills that the locals farmed expertly, carving out stepped fields or terraces and making the most of the limited land. As Avalkyra walked out from the tree cover, it was clear the expanse of wide, gently climbing steps had once been such a farm, though the earth had shifted and softened over time, the local flora overtaking whatever cultivated crops had once grown here. The result was a staggered, swishing plain of tall grass and wildflowers, shimmering silver in the moonlight.

Avalkyra snorted. Trust a Stellan to find the flattest, grassiest part of the mountain as her hiding place.

At the far edge of the clearing there was a partially collapsed structure—once a small farmhouse, maybe—and though it was utterly dark and quiet, Avalkyra made her way toward it. The night was warm, but she wore a cloak, the hood pulled up to conceal her face.

They weren't far from a small trading post that some said was as old as the *Sekveia* and served as a rest stop for the kinds of travelers who avoided the road—generally poachers, bandits, and hermits hiding away from the rest of civilization. There were some farmers still living off the land in these parts, existing in near-total isolation save for when they marched to the trading post to sell their produce and share news.

One such farmer was peddling runner beans to an informant of Ilithya Shadowheart's, and brought word of a fierce warrior woman with a strange Stellan haircut and surprising green eyes living out in the wilds. She also happened to have a rather distinct scar that bisected her left eyebrow and carved deeply into her cheek below.

Rumor had it she was an outlaw, a brigand or raider.

But Avalkyra and Ilithya knew the truth: She was a Phoenix Rider.

Avalkyra had given her that scar during a sparring session when they were children. Sidra had been a lost puppy when she arrived at Phoenix Rider training, rejected by her family for being an animage and desperate to prove herself. She'd gotten into fights, argued with the instructors, and barely a week after her arrival, challenged Princess Avalkyra to a duel during their lessons. She'd lost the fight *and* earned an ugly scar, but Avalkyra had been impressed by her boldness and determination. And like any stray, when Avalkyra showed a kind hand and eventually invited Sidra to join her patrol, Sidra had returned that gesture with fierce loyalty. She wasn't the most talented or the most intelligent, but her hunger to serve and remain by Avalkyra's side couldn't be replaced.

As Avalkyra drew near the building, there was a soft rustling in the copse of trees behind the dilapidated farmhouse. She lifted her head and cast wide with her exhausted shadow magic . . . but she sensed nothing. She tried again, this time with animal magic, and thought she felt a whisper of familiarity.

Before she could do more, her shadow magic leapt forth of its own accord, warning her of a presence not in front of her, but behind. She stepped left as an object whistled through the air, turning just in time to see a heavy staff slice mere inches past her head.

Though it was dark, she knew her attacker was a woman. Not only was it evident in her shape and stature, but her movements were familiar too.

Avalkyra had her hood up, and her attacker didn't pause to demand she state her business. She swung again, this time in a low sweep meant to take out Avalkyra's legs.

Without even thinking, Avalkyra leapt, and it was like they were back at Rider training, sparring again. The staff whipped beneath her feet, and as the momentum carried it wide, her opponent left her body exposed. Avalkyra kicked out hard, landing a blow across the woman's middle and delighting in the sound of impact and the way the breath whooshed from her lungs. The woman didn't stagger or slow, but drew the staff forward again, this time relying on brute strength over surprises or tricks. She took the butt of the wooden stick and lunged forward, aiming a blow that, if it landed, would likely crack Avalkyra's ribs.

But it did not land.

Avalkyra knew this move—she'd dodged it countless times before—and so she didn't step backward, which would have only delayed the inevitable, or try to duck or block it. She merely turned her body, shrinking the target and allowing the staff to slip by her, harmless as a summer breeze.

The woman hesitated then—just for a fraction of a second—and let out a growl of frustration as she jerked the staff sideways. The impact was more of a shove than a blow, and Avalkyra absorbed it against her stomach before putting both hands onto the smooth wood and wrenching it from her attacker's grasp.

Startled as she was by actually landing a hit, the staff slipped easily from her fingers, and Avalkyra smiled in triumph as she swung the weapon—plain, but well crafted—around her head in a lazy spin before swiping downward in a diagonal slash and hitting the woman's shoulder with an echoing crack. As she staggered, Avalkyra swiped her feet out from under her—using the same sequence of moves the woman had tried and failed to execute—before leveling the butt of the weapon at her face and looming over her.

She waited, the woman panting and clutching at her shoulder, though Avalkyra hadn't dealt a severe injury.

When it was clear Avalkyra had the upper hand and the woman wasn't going to try anything drastic, Avalkyra lowered the weapon to the ground, holding it like a walking stick, and drew back her hood.

The sun was cresting the distant peaks of Pyrmont, casting hazy pearlescent light across the grassy clearing, sparkling on specks of dew like a field of earthbound stars and causing Avalkyra's hair to glow red as the dawn.

"Sidra of Stel," Avalkyra said at last. "You've aged terribly."

Sidra stared up at her, heavy brow furrowed with incomprehension. She ignored the jibe, her eyes roving Avalkyra's face, trying to understand how her dead queen could be standing before her, even younger than she'd been when she died. Her gaze latched onto Avalkyra's red hair, darting between it and Avalkyra's eyes and back again. Something flickered in Sidra's expression.

"Impossible . . . ," she murmured.

No, Avalkyra said, using what little magical energy she had left. The adrenaline that had spiked during their fight was ebbing away, leaving her weary and depleted. *Not impossible.*

"My queen," Sidra whispered, as though barely daring to believe it.

She scrabbled onto one knee and lowered her head in a bow.

A sense of rightness, of long-awaited justice, expanded in Avalkyra's chest. This was how it was meant to be: Avalkyra standing proud, a queen once more, and her loyal subjects bowing before her.

It soon became clear that Sidra's homage was more than just subservience—more than fealty. As Sidra offered her body to Avalkyra's service, she also offered her mind.

It was a promise Avalkyra had demanded of her entire patrol. Shadow magic could be forced on almost anyone—though magical minds were often easier, open and searching as they were—but that took effort and skill and time.

Something powerful happened, however, when a shadowmage was invited in. Knowledge of shadow magic made a mind more susceptible to its influence, and if that person chose to *welcome* that magic inside . . . well, it made putting a bind in place much easier. Avalkyra had put binds on her entire patrol, and she would do it again, one by one.

Avalkyra let her magic flow into Sidra. Then she drew it back out again, leaving the bind in her wake. She was surprised at how easy it was. Tiring, yes. Draining—definitely. But not hard. Sidra's mind was willing, and though Avalkyra's original bind had disappeared upon her death, Sidra's mind recognized the sensation and absorbed her magic quickly.

Avalkyra knew it was a risk—she could barely hold her bind on the phoenix, never mind create a new one—and she had other, more pressing needs for her shadow magic. But this was important. Avalkyra couldn't afford to trust anyone, even the warriors who had been in her inner circle, and with Sidra's bind in place, she could turn her focus to other matters. To Veronyka.

"What news?" she asked, striding into the farmhouse and helping herself to the food and water she found in a cold box under the window. She took a seat on Sidra's bed and waited.

It was an old routine between them, a request for an informal report. Sidra might not have been a true spy, but Avalkyra had often handed her thya to use as she saw fit. The woman was observant, had a good memory, and was utterly devoid of her own ambitions. As reliable a servant as Avalkyra could hope for even without the bind—and with it, she was virtually infallible.

Sidra joined her inside, though she remained standing at attention.

"War is brewing," Sidra said, and Avalkyra waved her on.

"Tell me."

When we faced our first battle during the Stellan Uprising,
I learned that even when we were on the same side, we stood for
opposing ideals. While Avalkyra was skilled at ripping bodies
apart, I was skilled at putting them back together.

- CHAPTER 16 -
TRISTAN

THE DAY WAS NOTHING but clear blue skies, warm golden sun, and the crisp, scented breeze swishing through the tall grasses that lined the field outside the village. Tristan couldn't have asked for better conditions for Veronyka to gain her Master Rider status and for the rest of his patrol to prove they were ready to do something real at last.

When Tristan told his patrol about the soldiers near the border and the commander's plans to garrison the Prosperity outpost, they'd all jumped at the chance. When he'd explained that they had to audition a sixth member the following morning in order to do it, they were *less* enthusiastic. He knew they were tired from travel and a bit uncertain that Veronyka could be the sixth member they needed. She was fairly new, after all. But the fact of the matter was, even without Tristan's belief in her and his desire to have her as part of his patrol, she was their best shot.

He'd been up most of the night, alternating between worrying about the trials and fuming about the argument with his father. He knew Cassian wasn't telling him the full truth. It was infuriating. And his plans for the Grand Council were downright foolish. How could he think the council would let him *fly* into the empire, into the capital city, and argue his case? It was surely a trap. Worst of all, Tristan couldn't shake the feeling that even if they *did* pass the tests today and become a full patrol, his father would still try to keep them as far away from the action as possible. The commander spoke constantly of Tristan's patrol's lack of experience and yet balked at the idea of giving them a chance to *gain* any. They'd held Azurec's Eyrie against a surprise attack of hundreds of empire soldiers—surely that counted for something?

Veronyka stood next to Tristan as they waited for the last few stragglers to turn up. He tried to catch her eye, to gauge how she was feeling, but she only gave him a vague nod and looked away. Was she regretting this audition? The pressure was extreme, but he had never known her to back down from a challenge.

Maybe she was just nervous. This meant more to her than it did to any of them; it was a fast track to becoming a Master Rider, and Tristan knew how badly she wanted that. There was external pressure too. Veronyka's success would allow Tristan's entire patrol to be more involved, and surely she felt that added weight.

Tristan tried to give her space, turning his attention to the rest of the group. Beryk stood at the front with Elliot beside him. They were short-handed enough after the attack, so despite Elliot's betrayal, Beryk used him as an assistant to aid with his steward duties, as well as other odd jobs around the Eyrie and stronghold.

Tristan had no idea how Elliot felt about it all. He usually walked around with his head down and his shoulders slumped, avoiding eye contact and rarely speaking. The other apprentices gave Elliot a wide berth, and Tristan himself had trouble truly forgiving him.

When the commander had first recruited Elliot, he'd intended for him to round out the newest patrol when the time came. Obviously, that plan had not come to fruition. If it had, they wouldn't be having these trials to begin with.

As they waited for everyone to turn up, some of the other Riders spoke in low whispers about the soldiers and the empire's next move, their expressions a mix of frowning concern and stiff-jawed focus. Tristan even caught the words "Grand Council," and while the information about the soldiers was common knowledge—it wasn't as if they could hide the fact when local travelers were spreading the news and Prosperity was about to be garrisoned—discussion of the Grand Council meeting was more limited. As far as Tristan knew, his father didn't want it widely known. . . . But then again, gossip traveled quickly in an isolated place like Azurec's Eyrie.

Tristan was about to call for a halt to the whispering when Beryk cast a stern gaze over the group. The mutterings fell silent, but not before everyone in the vicinity had caught the words—including Elliot and several guards who had helped set up.

The commander and Fallon were last to arrive, and would act as judges for the trials that were to come. Fallon's phoenix was saddled and perched nearby; Tristan suspected he'd be watching whatever flying they did from the air.

"We'll be doing three separate tests today," Beryk announced, hooking his thumbs in his belt. "Flying, archery, and hand-to-hand combat. These are the basics for any Phoenix Rider and essential skills for warriors facing active duty. Flight is, of course, our greatest advantage, and so we'll begin there with a relay race."

A ripple of excitement swept their group, and Tristan cast a glance at Veronyka. Flight was definitely her strongest skill apart from her command of animal magic, though the two were related. With a good start, her confidence would be high for the remainder of the trials. It was the best he could have hoped for.

"You'll perform a circuit of the Eyrie, following the flags into the tunnels of Soth's Fury, before looping back around to make the handoff here, at the finish line," Beryk continued, indicating a series of green flags that rippled in the breeze. "If the baton hits the ground or you fail to complete the run in the allotted time, you will fail. Also, you'll all be blindfolded, which means you'll be required to use your bond if you want to make it through. Patrol leader," he said, nodding to Tristan, "strategize with your team and determine the order. We'll begin in ten minutes."

Elliot handed out blindfolds while Tristan assigned positions. Anders was the fastest of their group, followed closely by Veronyka. Ronyn was the slowest but sure with his handoffs, and Lysandro's mount had good speed but tired easily. Tristan and Latham fit somewhere in the middle.

"Anders, how do you feel about starting?" Tristan asked, "with Latham right behind you?" Anders perked up, tossing a smug smile at Latham.

"How does it feel to always be second best?" Anders asked. "I hope you enjoy the view of my backside."

"It's better than your front," Latham said with a smile. Anders's mouth dropped open in mock outrage, and Lysandro snorted.

"Lys, you go after Latham, and you'll hand off to Ronyn. Then it's me, with Veronyka bringing us home." Going last was a high-pressure position, but Veronyka thrived in such situations. Besides, they needed to finish strong.

Veronyka nodded, knotting her blindfold and sliding it up onto her forehead, but she didn't look at him—there was no smile or light in her eyes.

"Are you okay?" Tristan asked in a low voice, as the others went about checking their mounts and adjusting their saddles. "Is something wrong?"

"Everything's . . ." She closed her eyes for a breath, then opened them again. Her voice was stronger this time when she spoke. "Everything's fine."

But everything *wasn't* fine—Tristan could feel it.

Anders mounted his phoenix and waited near the edge of the field while the rest of them milled around to watch. There was a green flag attached to a thrust of the stone, indicating the start and finish line as well as where the handoffs would occur. Anders twirled the smooth metal rod in his hands as he sat in the saddle, completely at his ease. Latham stood nearby, hissing playful taunts and jeers at the back of Anders's head while Anders grinned widely, apparently enjoying every minute of it.

"Ready?" Beryk called, looking first to Anders, who raised a hand before tugging down his blindfold, then over to the commander and Fallon, who nodded. Fallon climbed into his saddle and took to the air, flying toward the caverns. "Three—two—one," he said, before putting his thumb and forefinger to his lips and letting out a short, sharp whistle.

Anders was off in a gust of wind and flapping wings. While Tristan and the others watched him zip across the rocky landscape before disappearing from view, Latham took up Anders's vacated place near the starting line. When Anders made his return, Latham would take to the sky and prepare for the handoff.

While flying was similar with or without the blindfolds—they just had to mirror with their mounts and hang on tight—it was the handoff that became challenging. Not only did they have to trust their phoenix's vision, as well as sync their pace and timing perfectly, but they had to reach dangerously forward or backward on their saddles without actually being able to see. There were varying strategies: Some Riders chose to fly above or below during the handoff, with the lower Riders standing in their stirrups while the upper Rider had to dangle from the side of their saddle. Sometimes a side-by-side handoff could be achieved if both phoenixes carefully stilled their wings and rode the wind during the seconds it took for their Riders to make contact.

This was another reason why a close bond was so important. If a baton was fumbled or one of the strategies failed to work, a close pair could adjust and alter their approach while a lesser pair would fail. This was also why they did their handoffs so high in the air . . . it gave them time to recover if a baton was dropped.

No matter how much they bickered and teased, when Anders rounded the far end of the Eyrie and approached the starting line, Latham pulled down his blindfold and took to the air, a look of serious concentration on his face. Tristan knew he was the least supportive of Veronyka, and it was a relief to see him taking the trials seriously. As soon as Anders slapped the baton into his hand, he tore off, a red streak in the blue sky.

Anders swooped around and landed with a flourish, smiling and tearing off his blindfold while the others clapped him on the back. His phoenix stood just behind him, shaking out his wings and setting off waves of heat after the short but intense flight.

Lysandro lined up next, with Ronyn on deck. All the while, Tristan was aware of Veronyka at the edges of the field behind him, like a storm cloud he could sense on the horizon even before it was visible.

Every time he looked back at her, she was scowling, her face screwed up and her lips moving, as if she were muttering to herself or talking to Xephyra, who remained close to her side. In fact, he'd distinctly seen her say the words "leave me alone." It was an odd thing to do—talking aloud when you had a bond—but Tristan himself had done it before, and he'd seen Veronyka do it too, though he doubted very highly she'd ever say such words to Xephyra.

The weirdest thing about it all was the way he thought he could *hear* her, even across the field. He could definitely hear something, but with the others cheering and shouting loudly, he couldn't figure out *how*.

Tristan sidled over to her. "Can you . . . ? Will you tell me what's bothering you?"

She shook her head slightly, as if bothered by a pesky fly. "It's nothing, Tristan."

Tristan frowned and tried to think what it could be, his mind combing over everything that had happened the previous day—Val and soldiers and Master Rider auditions—but he felt like he was forgetting something important. "Wait," he said suddenly, realizing with a jolt exactly what it must be. "The lockbox—did you . . . ?"

As soon as he said the word "lockbox," Veronyka flinched and darted a glance in his direction. It was the first time she'd looked at him properly all day, and to his surprise, the moment was followed by a strange, weightless sensation. A wave of dizziness reared up, accompanied by dark splotches speckling his vision.

"You're up," she said, breaking their eye contact and nodding toward the others. Lysandro had returned and Ronyn was in the air, so Tristan walked over to the starting line. His light-headedness had passed, and though Veronyka was clearly dealing with something, Tristan did his best to shake it off. Whatever she needed, even if it was space *away* from him, he would give it. The audition was what mattered now.

They were making good time, and barring any screwups, they would pass this first trial. Maybe then Veronyka would loosen up and forget whatever was troubling her.

Rex had difficulty standing still as they awaited Ronyn, and Tristan knew it was his own feelings filtering through the bond. Tristan had been restless since yesterday, and a night of tossing and turning hadn't changed that. They were both eager to get into the air and leave their stress and worry behind.

Ronyn rounded the corner, approaching at a steady pace. Tristan and Rex took to the air, and already Tristan felt lighter and more at ease. He tugged the blindfold over his eyes, and the world around him grew dark as he reached with his magic for Rex. There was a shimmer, like looking through a darkened veil as shafts of light and color filtered through. Then a blink, and they were mirrored, the world around him vibrant and strange with his phoenix's superior, but still different, sight.

They flew up and down in place high above the crowd as Tristan acclimated to seeing the world through his phoenix's eyes. The shouts below grew louder, and he nudged his bondmate, who turned to watch Ronyn's approach. Rex pumped his wings hard, propelling them forward. They had to match Ronyn's speed to make for an easier handoff, plus keep their spacing tight for the simple front to back hand off—made possible by their combined heights. This was the hardest part. Rex couldn't fly forward *and* look back at the same time, so Tristan had to extend his arm and trust that Ronyn and his phoenix would do the rest.

Luckily, Ronyn's height made the exchange quick and painless, and when the baton slipped into the center of Tristan's palm, Rex flapped his wings with a shriek of excitement, taking off after the flag-marked route.

The wind whipped through Tristan's hair, and his muscles tensed and bunched, adjusting and reacting to Rex's bursts of movement. He relied on feel as much as sight, because Rex wasn't seeing the saddle or stirrups. When his bondmate banked hard, Tristan leaned opposite, distributing his weight while keeping a careful hold on the baton.

They entered the cool darkness of Soth's Fury, the exhaustion Tristan had been keeping at bay growing palpable as their flight wore on. Another wave of dizziness gripped him, and there was a kind of humming in his ears that he figured was just the strange echoes of the narrow stone passages playing tricks on him. Still, relief swept through him when the heat of the sun slid over his skin as they emerged from the cavern, rounding the Eyrie before making their way back toward the field outside the village. He heard yelling and cheering from below, the others watching the race more intently now as the final lap approached.

Ahead, Veronyka was already in the air, Xephyra pumping her wings in a lazy bob. Xephyra was large for her age, but it was her combination of size and agility that made her so fast. Her Rider was light, as well, which helped even more.

As they drew near and Xephyra began her forward motion, Tristan stared at Veronyka, her hand stretched backward. He frowned. There was a darkness to her shape, a shadowy aura that pulsed from the inside out, like a reverse lantern. He'd never seen such a thing through Rex's eyes before, and they mirrored all the time.

It was jarring and strange, but Tristan shook the vision aside and focused. While Ronyn's height and reach had given them an advantage, Veronyka was the opposite, and so Tristan had to cover more ground than usual. He leaned forward in his saddle, while Rex flattened and steadied his flight, allowing Tristan to extend himself over his bondmate's head. It was difficult to maintain balance without sight and with one hand clenching the metal baton, but slowly Tristan steadied himself and reached.

The instant he felt the warm brush of Veronyka's fingers, the knot of fear in his chest loosened—only to twist again more tightly and painfully than before. Veronyka fumbled the baton, as if she'd felt something too, and Rex saw her stagger in her saddle. As soon as their skin had touched, the shadows that surrounded Veronyka expanded like greedy, clawing hands— reaching for him. He didn't know if he was seeing it with Rex's eyes or with his magic, but everything about it felt wrong.

"Tristan?" Veronyka said sharply, but her voice sounded very far away. He thought he heard another voice, an unwanted one, though he had no idea whose it was. He reared back from it, forgetting the baton, forgetting the race and the fact that he was hundreds of feet in the air.

He forgot everything he'd ever known as the darkness closed in, swallowing him whole.

"Tristan!" someone shouted, desperate fear in their voice, while a guttural shriek rumbled from underneath him as he fell, weightless, into shadows.

And when my mother was murdered
and my sister was guilty, I learned
what it was to stand alone.

CHAPTER 17

VERONYKA

VERONYKA TORE OFF HER blindfold just in time to see Tristan fall limply from Rex's back. The phoenix screeched and turned in midair, but his momentum was carrying him one way, while the wind carried Tristan the other.

Tristan was unconscious and falling helplessly through the air, and it was all her fault.

Ever since Veronyka discovered her birth certificate, ever since her world blew up around her and she reached for her once-sister without a second thought—without an ounce of hesitation—Val had been inside her head.

A whisper here, a comment there. Just enough to taunt Veronyka but not enough to give her anything she actually wanted or needed. What she *needed* was to focus on her audition and be made a Master Rider. What she wanted . . . that was harder.

Yes, she wanted answers, and Val promised them—at a price, of course. With Val there was always a price.

I'll tell you everything, Veronyka, if you join me. I'm the only one who can help you.

I'm the only one who knows. Who understands.

Leave the Eyrie and join me.

Veronyka had tried to rebuild her walls, tried to keep Val out—but she had invited Val into her mind, and that had weakened her defenses. Then there was the part of her that wanted what Val was offering—the truth about her past—so desperately she thought she'd choke on the words when she refused.

You know I won't abandon my place here. Leave me alone.

Your place? Veronyka, you are an Ashfire. . . . Your place is where you will it. It is your birthright.

As the day wore on, it was clear their connection was flickering and fading away—partially from Veronyka's efforts and partially from the natural deterioration of the previous day's link—and Veronyka suspected Val was doing whatever she could to maintain the contact. Her intrusions became more insistent, more pressing, trying to widen and restabilize the channel.

Your place is with me.

Leave me alone, Veronyka said, over and over again. And so Val tried a different tack.

I guess with soldiers on the move, she began idly, *you'll be flying out soon anyway.*

Veronyka hadn't responded to that. Val was baiting her, trying to pull her attention—trying to offer information Veronyka didn't have. Information Veronyka would give up everything for.

Oh dear. I do hope they don't plan to leave you behind. . . .

How did Val know? How did she always know the way to Veronyka's heart—and why did she always do *damage* when she got there?

And then, just as she and Tristan were about to complete their handoff . . .

We could do it together, you know. . . . We could save lives, save the world. You and I together could change everything. . . .

There was power in Val's words—they'd pulled and dragged at Veronyka. It was almost enough to rob her of her consciousness, but she'd been so preoccupied with keeping Val out of her mind and herself in the saddle that she hadn't thought about Tristan, who shared her mind and was just as vulnerable as her but had no idea about it or how to protect himself.

Their hands had touched, the skin-on-skin contact blasting their connection wide open, and now he was plummeting from his phoenix's back.

Veronyka didn't think; she acted. Tristan had barely left his saddle before she turned in her seat and leapt after him.

She fell, the wind tearing at her hair and clothes and roaring in her ears. Fear gripped her stomach as the ground rushed toward her, but she kept her gaze focused on Tristan.

He was still unconscious, his limp body twisting and flailing in the air, catching the wind and slowing his fall. Arms pinned to her sides and head dipped toward the ground, Veronyka pelted after him like an arrow, catching up easily. When she was near enough, she extended an arm and reached, gripping his tunic and releasing a half gasp, half sob. Just as she wrapped her arms around his chest and her legs around his waist, Xephyra became visible in her peripheral vision, diving right after Veronyka had. Thanks to the bond, she'd understood at once what Veronyka intended to do and had hastened to play her part.

Xephyra caught up to them, then blurred past, slipping underneath in one fluid motion.

Their speed matched, Veronyka gripped the saddle and pressed herself and Tristan against it, eyes closed and heart hammering. Xephyra spread her wings, catching the wind and slowing their descent.

Only, they weren't slowing fast enough.

The crowd below gasped, and Veronyka opened her eyes to see Xephyra trying desperately to pull back up again, but the ground was rushing toward them, and impact was seconds away.

We're not going to make it, Veronyka thought desperately. The sounds from the crowd below changed, shifting from shock and confusion to shouts of alarm. Veronyka clung to the saddle, bracing them both for impact.

But the panic Xephyra had been projecting ceased, and she spoke to Veronyka in a calm, self-assured tone. *We will.*

Before Veronyka could say anything else, an earsplitting shriek sounded from above. She craned her neck to see Rex swooping down, his shadow falling over them and his clawed feet descending.

His claws sank into the saddle on either side of Tristan and Veronyka, and once he had them in his grip, he threw his wings wide, just as Xephyra had done.

Wind buffeted them as they slowed, the combined efforts of both phoenixes' wingspans doing what one alone could not. Xephyra and Rex pulled up mere inches from the ground, sweeping back around to slow their speed and control their flight. Rex released his grip on the saddle, and Xephyra turned in a wobbly arc before coming to a landing.

Veronyka drew herself up so she could get a better look at Tristan, but he remained unconscious. The other Riders crowded around as Veronyka slid from the saddle—or tried to. Rex had taken up a defensive position, screeching at anyone who got too near his bondmate.

Veronyka opened her mouth to speak, but it was Xephyra who intervened, screeching loudly to draw Rex's attention, Tristan still lying across her back. Rex stared at his bondmate, then tossed his head angrily before stepping aside. Veronyka gaped at the pair of them, at their easy shorthand and the stunning rescue they'd managed together. It occurred to her that as she and Tristan grew closer, their bond strengthening, the same thing was happening between Xephyra and Rex. The thought was a melancholy one, considering she'd been doing her best to deny them that same closeness.

Elliot had already run for the healer, while everyone whispered and muttered and called Tristan's name. The commander pushed to the front, pulling Tristan down from Xephyra's back and carrying him, like a child, into the village.

Veronyka hung back, her heart clenched painfully and her hands trembling. Xephyra nudged her and crooned low in her throat, but it was no good.

When Tristan woke up, she'd have some explaining to do.

Veronyka remained by Tristan's bedside in the Eyrie for the rest of the day, Rex and Xephyra hovering just outside the door. The healer had decided, after checking his vitals, that Tristan was simply exhausted. Their journey to Vayle—along with the days of work and fielding villager complaints—had clearly left him overtaxed. Beryk and the commander, who had both remained nearby as she assessed him, nodded their agreement, happy with this most simple of excuses.

Veronyka, however, knew the truth. *She* had done this. Well, she and Val.

The healer had ordered rest—as well as a pot of Morra's pungent herbal tea—for him, and been on her way.

The commander had turned to Veronyka, who lingered nearby. "Thank you," he said, somewhat hoarsely, his face pale.

Heat rose in Veronyka's cheeks, but he didn't need to thank her. She'd do anything for Tristan. "Of course, sir," she said, unable to meet his eye and uncomfortable with his gratitude. It was her fault; fixing her mess was the *least* she could do.

He cast a look over his shoulder at his son, then sighed. "Despite your impressive individual performance, however, I'm afraid this counts as a failure," he said regretfully. When Veronyka continued to stare at him, confused, he added, "For the trials."

Oh. *Right.* Her hopes and dreams. Her chance at becoming a Master Rider and joining Tristan's patrol so they could garrison Prosperity outpost. After everything she'd discovered the night before, Veronyka's life as a Rider felt extremely far away. This news should sting, but right now she couldn't seem to muster the feeling. She'd almost *killed* Tristan. Nothing else really mattered.

She bowed her head, at a loss for what to say, but that act of resignation seemed to be enough.

"The rules are very clear on the matter," he continued. "A Master Rider can only be tested early as a part of a full patrol, and a failure in any one of the trials results in a team failure. You may audition again in six weeks or continue on with your regular lessons and be elevated to master when you are deemed ready by your instructors."

Veronyka nodded, and the commander turned to go, Beryk waiting for him by the door. He hesitated, putting a hand on her shoulder. "You'll stay with him?" he asked softly, and she looked up into his familiar light brown eyes. *Tristan's* eyes.

"Yes, sir," she said, and he squeezed her shoulder appreciatively before departing.

The other Riders checked in throughout the day, even Elliot, and Morra brought Tristan's tea herself.

Xephyra kept prodding at Veronyka through the bond—*Okay? Okay? Okay?*—and Veronyka wasn't sure if she was asking about Veronyka herself or asking about Tristan on Rex's behalf. The growing closeness between the two phoenixes was one more thing Veronyka couldn't think about right now. The last few hours had been a startling whirlwind, and the only way she knew how to keep going was to stay busy and stop herself from dwelling.

That didn't make it easy. Veronyka had decided that who Val was didn't matter anymore. She'd been determined not to let the past, the mystery of her own identity, weigh her down as she moved into her future. She knew that in order to block her shadow magic, she had to block it all.

But now? How could she? Val was still her family—and would have been regardless of what that birth certificate said—but now Veronyka was an Ashfire. The royal line. Descended from queens.

The line was broken. That was what everyone thought.

The queens had failed; the empire belonged to the Ashfires no longer.

Veronyka thought of the Ashfire family tree. . . . She thought of the two branches splitting: Pheronia on one side, Avalkyra on the other. And now Veronyka on one side, Avalkyra on the other.

Why did it feel like her identity was just another way for her to be controlled by Val? Another reason for Val to lay claim to her and her life? Veronyka didn't want that legacy. . . . She didn't want to be a queen. She didn't want a war. She wanted peace. She wanted to protect others like her, to make the world safe for animages again. Veronyka wanted to fly in a flock, to be a part of the Phoenix Rider resurgence, to stand *among* her fellows with pride and confidence, not *above* them.

She never wanted to be isolated again. And to be Val's sister . . . to be Avalkyra's sister . . . was to be alone. To stand apart. It was everything Val needed and nothing Veronyka wanted.

To pass the time, Veronyka had helped remove Tristan's armor and cleaned the leather, she'd gotten fresh hot water for Morra's tea when the first pot got cold and rinsed the cool cloth on Tristan's forehead every time it went dry. She'd made sure Rex and Xephyra were fed and trusted in her bondmate to comfort Rex just as she was comforting Tristan.

She'd also tended her mental walls brick by agonizing brick, focusing on the minute details of the task and not on how easily Val had breached her walls or when she might choose to do it again. Veronyka had opened herself to Val, and she feared there was no turning back. She had been thoughtless, reaching out to Val the way she had, and ultimately selfish, too.

She was not alone in her mind—she had to remember that. Veronyka didn't exist in a vacuum; she was inextricably linked to those around her, and she'd endangered them. Things could have been much worse, too. What if Xephyra had been the one to lose consciousness? What if all three of them—Veronyka, Xephyra, *and* Tristan—had gone under?

The thought made a shudder rack her body. Veronyka needed to stop listening to other people and start listening to herself. Morra counseled caution and seclusion, while Val had taught lies and defenses and impenetrable walls—even as she used her magic to manipulate and control. One felt like cowardice and the other felt like giving in to the darkest part of herself. Neither would work for her.

Veronyka would do the only thing that made sense—the right thing, no matter the cost to herself. She'd be open and honest and give Tristan what he deserved: the truth. They'd figure this out. They *had* to. They were in this together, and it was too late to pretend otherwise. Awareness might make him vulnerable, but it was also the key to self-defense.

Next to her, Tristan stirred. He looked younger in sleep, despite the ghost of stubble that shadowed his jawline. His hair was plastered to his forehead and temples, sweat combined with the damp cloth the healer had ordered placed there. Seizing upon the distraction, she reached across him to remove it, intending to rinse it with fresh water and reapply, when his hand reached up to grab her wrist. Her pulse jumped in her throat—both with relief and wild fear. He was awake. He was okay.

It was time to talk.

His eyes opened, hooded and drowsy, though they fixed on her. He held her hand pinned to his forehead, before his arm slackened slightly, drawing her palm down the side of his face to rest against his cheek.

"Strange dreams . . . ," he murmured, voice hoarse.

"Here," Veronyka said, tugging her arm free to grab hold of the tea. She'd had the presence of mind to have them send a warmer along with the most recent pot. Morra had also sent food—Veronyka had been there all day—but she'd had no appetite.

She held a cup of tea under his nose, and he drew back as soon as the tendrils of steam reached him, causing the towel on his forehead to slip off his face. He jerked his head side to side.

"Not that again," he said, more alert now, and Veronyka held back a smile. Anyone who'd been the slightest bit ill or tired in the stronghold had been subjected to Morra's pungent tea. "Water?" he asked hopefully, and Veronyka obliged.

Tristan emptied his cup before handing it back to her and scrubbing a hand across his face. He glanced past her, taking in his darkened room.

"What time is it?"

"After dinner," Veronyka said, staring at the cup in her hands. Dread was a living thing inside her chest. *Tell him tell him tell him.*

"What happened?" he muttered, sinking back against his pillows.

Veronyka swallowed. "I . . . There's something I need to tell you."

The tone of her voice made him pause. He tried to sit up straighter, but his body was still boneless with exhaustion.

Veronyka blew out her cheeks, putting the cup on the side table and rubbing her suddenly clammy hands against her thighs. "Have you ever heard of shadow magic?"

His eyes flickered, and he nodded. "Morra has it, I think."

A small wave of relief swept through Veronyka. This wasn't going to be easy, but at least he wasn't among the people who thought it some mythical ability, or worse, a superstitious curse. She didn't have to convince him it existed, at least.

She only had to convince him to forgive her for lying about it—lying to him. Again.

"Yes, she does," Veronyka said, sitting forward on her chair. She swallowed thickly. "And so do I."

He continued to stare at her, his face surprisingly opaque. But just as Morra had promised, his mind reached out of its own accord, seeking her—seeking a foreign presence within its borders. She clenched her jaw and blocked him, but the surge of connection had been bright and powerful as a spark from a flint stone.

She could sense his wariness, his desire to draw himself in, even as his mind did the exact opposite.

"That's how I was able to trick Morra when I first arrived. How I convinced her I was Nyk, not Veronyka. Nobody knows I have it except for her," she continued, trying to read his expression again and failing. "And now you. And Val. She has it as well."

He reacted to that news, a jump of his brows before they furrowed and his attention turned inward.

"That's why you always felt strange around her," Veronyka continued. "She was meddling in your mind."

"She was?" he asked, voice flat. "How do you know that? Were you in there as well?"

"No, of course not! I mean, not on purpose . . ."

A spasm of anger or hurt flickered across his features, there and then gone, but she had seen it. She had *felt* it. And there was still more she had to own up to.

"I know she was in there because she was always in my mind too. She and I . . . we have a connection. A permanent one. It's sort of like a bond,

I think, but without all the good stuff like openness and trust. I never purposely went into your mind—I swear. It just started happening sometimes. The thing is, I have to guard against it *constantly*, and even then, sometimes it's not enough."

Emotion was rising in Veronyka's throat, constricting her airways. He was pulling away from her. She could feel it through their connection. But she had to plow on, had to tell him everything if she ever had any hope of him trusting her again. She spoke faster, determined to get it all out, no matter how much it hurt to have him look at her the way he was right now . . . like he was looking at a stranger.

"It's just like with animal magic. It can get away from you sometimes. And Val, she never taught me anything—she never wanted me to be able to wield it against her."

"Against her?" he repeated.

"She's . . . she's not what she seems."

"And neither are you."

Veronyka looked down. The words stung, causing tears to prick at the back of her eyes.

"Why are you telling me now?" he asked, arms crossing over his chest. "Is that why I blacked out today? Were you using it against me, trying to . . . I don't know, control me somehow?"

"No, Tristan!" she said, gaping at him, her heart breaking at the idea that he could think so little of her. Didn't he know who she was at all? Hadn't *she* been the one to convince *him* that using magic to command was wrong and ineffectual? "I would never, ever use it that way. Not on you, not on anyone."

He seemed to realize that he'd hurt her, opening his mouth, only to clamp it shut and stare around the room, as if searching for words.

"All that's ever happened between us is accidental slipups. Like that night before the attack on the Eyrie when I passed out in front of the breeding enclosure. When one of us is running high emotionally, it sort of sucks me in—makes the magic harder to control. There's also the fact that we're so . . . familiar with each other. It creates a link, like the one I have with Val."

"You and I are linked?" he asked faintly. "What does that mean? Is that permanent? Is it—"

He sounded horrified to be tied to her in such a way, making her fracturing heart sink into her stomach.

"I don't know, Tristan. All I know is that I have a link to you and a link to Val. I've been blocking her out for weeks, blocking my shadow magic entirely. . . ." She stopped. "I was trying to, anyway. But I screwed up and let her in, and I couldn't get her out again," Veronyka said, panic rising inside her. "Then suddenly you and I touched—that strengthens a connection—and the next thing I knew . . . I almost fainted too. I managed to put up walls and protect myself, but I forgot mine wasn't the only mind in danger—that Val has access to you *through* me. I forgot to protect us both. I'm sorry."

Tristan stared at the floor. "First my father, now you. Why doesn't anybody tell me the truth?" he said, lurching to his feet. He was a bit unsteady, but he was able to use the wall for support.

Veronyka's insides turned to ice at his words. He thought she was the same as his father? Nothing he'd said or done had ever made her feel so cold.

"I didn't tell you," she began, after several weighted moments. Her voice quivered slightly, so she cleared it before continuing. "I didn't tell you because Morra warned me against it."

He turned to look at her then, as if surprised, though he made no comment.

"I was struggling—trying to block it, but it wasn't working. I asked her for advice, and she told me that it was too dangerous to tell you."

"And when was this?"

Veronyka looked down. "A little over a week ago, I guess. The day after our last time sparring."

"Veronyka, I've known you for *months*. You had all that time before you talked to Morra to tell me. How could you keep this from me for so long? After everything we've been through . . ."

"It's *because* of everything that happened, everything with my sister. . . . I was afraid to lose you. I couldn't stand to lose anyone else."

Tristan was shaking his head, though Veronyka didn't know if he was denying her words or trying to cast the memory of them aside. "I don't know how I'm supposed to trust you. Every few weeks, some new secret comes out. I feel like I don't even know you."

Veronyka let out a snort of mirthless laughter as she got to her feet. "You know what, Tristan? You're not the only one."

He frowned, taking a slight step back, startled by her bright, angry tone. "What are you talking about?"

"What am I talking about? Well, let me see." She dug into her trouser pocket, where she'd stuffed the birth certificate. *Her* birth certificate. "You wanted to know what was in the lockbox? Well, here it is," she said, throwing it at him.

Tristan crouched down to pick it up, eyes on her as he carefully unfolded the paper. He finally looked down to read it, and only when his gaze dropped did she find the courage to speak again. "Looks like I'm not who *I* thought I was either. And you know what else? My *sister*, Val? She's not my sister at all. She's my aunt."

He looked up at her, his face leached of color. He blinked, as if trying to understand her words. The birth certificate named Pheronia Ashfire as her mother, and Veronyka watched as Tristan slowly made the connection. "Your aunt . . ."

"Yes, my aunt. Avalkyra Ashfire."

"But—Val, she's way too young. . . ."

"She was resurrected after the Last Battle. I know it—I've *seen* it," she hissed, pointing at her temple. "At least shadow magic is good for something."

"Veronyka," Tristan said, regret in his tone.

But Veronyka didn't want to hear it. She didn't want kind words or a hundred questions. "So don't talk to me about secrets," she choked out, her throat so tight it hurt.

She turned away from him, stifling a sob as she wrenched open the door.

Xephyra, Veronyka said through the bond, but her phoenix was already waiting outside the door, Rex beside her.

Without another word or backward glance, Veronyka leapt onto Xephyra's back and they soared into the sky.

Day 9, Sixth Moon, 168 AE

Dear Lexi,

I was happy to receive your last letter. . . . I know you are eager to prove yourself, but there is little glory to be found in war. If you'd ever actually fought in one, you'd understand. Maybe someday, impyr.

I've been lucky; I'm not on the front lines of the uprising. Instead I'm in service to Princess Pheronia as her personal bodyguard. She is fiercer than I expected, though I shouldn't be surprised, her being an Ashfire and all. She's not like the others—not like her sister. They say Ashfires are like phoenixes: Get too close, and you're likely to be burned.

But Pheronia's fire is warm and her heart is good. You'd like her.

Practice hard, Lex—especially with your spear, which needs work. You never know when you might have to do the real thing.

-Theryn

*Always I had been in her shadow, until the day
she left for good and took the light with her.
There were no suns left in my sky.*

- CHAPTER 18 -
VERONYKA

XEPHYRA WASN'T SADDLED, SO Veronyka clung to her feathers and buried her face into the warmth of her phoenix's neck. Xephyra nudged her mind just in time for Veronyka to wave to the perimeter guard. Then they were beyond sight of the Eyrie, flying through the endless starry sky.

Before Veronyka realized it, Xephyra landed at their favorite spot, a narrow slab of stone just outside the entrance to Soth's Fury. It offered a wide vista of the mountainside, with soaring peaks and cascading valleys all around them. They weren't far from the Eyrie, but being here gave the illusion of solitude.

Even though they'd landed, Veronyka couldn't seem to make herself dismount. She just lay there, gripping Xephyra's feathers in a way that was probably uncomfortable for her bondmate, but she made no complaint.

Okay? Xephyra asked again, and though the word was simple, Veronyka felt the complex emotions attached to it. Xephyra knew that Veronyka hadn't been okay all day—or the previous night. Xephyra didn't fully understand what the birth certificate meant because Veronyka hadn't explained it to her, but she could tell something was very wrong.

"M'okay," Veronyka murmured into her feathers, but they both knew it was a lie. Still, Xephyra's desperate concern for her was enough to make

Veronyka slide from her back onto the cold stone ground. There she sat, knees pressed to her chest, while Xephyra tucked in behind her, a warm wall with a beating heart that Veronyka could lean against no matter what.

No matter what, Xephyra parroted, but Veronyka knew she meant it.

And suddenly, sitting there under the endless expanse of velvet night and jeweled stars, Xephyra at her back, Veronyka's heart felt a little bit lighter. The loneliness that had engulfed her at Tristan's reaction eased somewhat. She was never alone, thanks to Xephyra.

Her bondmate practically purred with pride, and Veronyka laughed—until distant wingbeats drew her attention.

Veronyka squinted, quickly mirroring to borrow Xephyra's superior vision, and straightened at the sight of Rex approaching with a figure on his back.

Xephyra didn't seem surprised at all, and when Veronyka blinked away their connection and stared up at her, she sensed a distinctly guilty conscience.

"You told him?" Veronyka demanded, meaning Rex. How else could they have found her and Xephyra so easily?

Xephyra tossed a wing in an attempt at innocence, but the human gesture didn't quite work on her, and she wound up looking twitchy.

"Traitor," Veronyka muttered, and Xephyra nudged her in a cajoling sort of way.

I know, Veronyka said, nudging back. She needed to face him sooner or later.

Tristan dismounted several feet away. He looked a bit stiff from his day in bed, but he'd at least had the forethought to saddle his mount.

"You shouldn't be flying," Veronyka said as soon as he approached. "If the commander knew—"

"What the commander doesn't know won't kill him," he said shortly, putting aside his reins.

"Still," she pressed stubbornly. "You could have fallen."

Rex snorted indignantly, as if offended that Veronyka would suggest he'd drop his bondmate twice in the same day.

Sorry, Rex, she said with animal magic. Though phoenix minds were generally closed and well guarded, Rex had opened himself to her many times before—not to mention whatever closeness now bound them thanks to her link to Tristan—and he heard her words. He huffed and relaxed his stance, and when Xephyra fluttered over to him, Tristan edged toward Veronyka.

He was smiling as he glanced back at his bondmate, but when he turned to Veronyka, his expression faltered.

He settled warily onto the ground next to her.

Veronyka held her breath. She wanted to run, to hide, to pretend the last few hours had never happened.

"I . . . ," Tristan began. "I don't know what to say."

"Then why are you here?" she said, surprised at the hardness in her words. She leapt to her feet, not wanting him to see the pain in her face. He scrambled after her, and a hand shot out, grabbing her wrist. She prepared to wrench herself free, reminded for a terrible moment of Val, of the way she'd pinch and squeeze and grip Veronyka until she bent to Val's will, like hot metal under a metalsmith's hammer.

Instead she shoved him, and he released her.

"Veronyka, please," he said. He didn't move to block or touch her again. He just waited, hand still outstretched.

Veronyka expelled a breath through her nostrils and looked at him. There were tears sparkling in his eyes, his expression anguished. His fingers twitched and trembled, as if he wanted to touch her again. Instead he stepped toward her, asking, hopeful, but fearful of rebuke.

Veronyka's own vision swam. She squeezed her eyes shut and stopped resisting. She fell into his arms, where he held her gently for a heartbeat before sighing and squeezing her tight. She thought of Val again. For all her dragging and pulling and demanding, all the ways their bodies had come into contact—and conflict—with each other over the years, Val had never given herself to Veronyka like this. Never offered herself at all. With Val, everything was take, take, take.

"I'm so sorry," Tristan whispered, his voice thin. His head dipped when he spoke, his chin pressed into the crook of her neck.

"I'm sorry too," Veronyka choked out.

"Please, *don't*," Tristan said, somewhat harshly. He drew back slightly and shook his head. "I'm the one who should be sorry. I can't believe how selfish I am."

"You're not," Veronyka began, but stopped when Tristan released his grip on her arms. He lowered himself onto his left knee, his right hand pressed against his heart.

"What are you doing?" she demanded, looking wildly around, but except for their bondmates, they were very much alone. "Tristan, stop," she ordered, tugging his arm, trying to pull him to his feet. Was this what he thought she wanted, for him to bow before her?

He resisted, his features grave. "This isn't because you're heir to the throne and far, far outrank me," he said, a hint of a smile playing on his lips before he grew serious once more. "It's because this is what you deserve—what you've always deserved."

"I don't want someone *beneath* me," Veronyka snapped.

"It's not about being beneath you," he said calmly. "It's about loyalty."

"Loyalty? What are you—" Veronyka froze, her eyes rounding as realization dawned. She stared at him again, at the left knee and right hand against his chest. He wasn't just kneeling. . . . He was swearing an oath. It was a gesture from ancient Pyra, a ceremony of fealty between Riders. Those who were on a patrol together would kneel before one another—no matter their rank or status. Queens knelt to their subjects, and patrol leaders to their second-in-commands. Val had described the custom to Veronyka in exquisite detail. Not because she loved or admired it, but because she loathed it.

Of course, Val had never known what it was to trust another person. It required a leap of faith, a risk.

It meant admitting that you were not superior.

And Veronyka was not Val.

Her chest swelling with some unnamed emotion, Veronyka copied him, lowering herself onto her knee and pressing her hand to her heart. It was a position of vulnerability, meant to show complete trust.

It was a statement, a symbol—a promise.

Tristan's eyes were warm as he watched her kneel opposite him. He heaved a great breath, his tone still heavy with regret. "Of all the stuff I said . . . comparing you to my father, asking if you'd used it against me or if you'd tried to control me, saying that you weren't who I thought you were . . ." It was clear that it pained him to recount his words, but he did so anyway, determined to finish. "I think the worst thing I did was make you think I didn't trust you. So that's why I'm doing this. I trust you," he said. "Completely."

Veronyka's throat constricted. She nodded, unable to speak around the lump in her throat.

He reached out for her—she took his hand, and they helped each other to their feet. Veronyka looked at him properly for the first time. His hair was sticking up at odd angles and he was dressed in the same wrinkled tunic and trousers he'd been sleeping in. He was usually perfectly pressed and groomed, and her heart warmed at the sight of him this way.

He gave her a rueful look. "I'm sorry I made everything about me. Only child," he said, pointing to his chest with a smirk.

Me too, Veronyka realized. Then again, she and Val had grown up together *as* sisters, no matter their true parentage, and who knew what other relatives of hers might be hiding out there. It was enough to make her head spin.

He reached into his pants pocket. "Here," he said, handing over a piece of folded paper—her birth certificate. Veronyka's stomach hardened with embarrassment at the childish way she'd thrown it at him.

"Thanks," she muttered, stowing it away without looking at it.

"About my reaction?" Tristan said abruptly, filling the silence. "I was— well . . . I don't mean to make excuses, but the idea that *you* can see into my mind and know every embarrassing, highly personal detail about my thoughts and feelings, especially as they relate to you, is, well, frankly . . . terrifying."

Oh. Veronyka hadn't really thought about it that way. She imagined how she'd feel if Tristan were able to see the way she looked at—and thought about—*him*, and burning heat rose in her face so fast she felt like a kettle boiling over.

"I didn't—I don't know anything about that. I mean, not really . . . That's not how it works. It's the same as animal magic. When you connect with an animal, you don't know everything about them, right?"

"No," Tristan conceded. "But I usually know how they feel about me."

Veronyka opened her mouth—but what could she say? Yes, she'd sensed something of his feelings before, but she was always fighting against their connection. The last time they'd been linked for longer than a brief flash was during the attack on the Eyrie. Needless to say, Tristan had had other things on his mind.

"It doesn't matter," Veronyka said. "I made a mistake, letting Val in—it won't happen again. I've been learning to block it."

"Does that work?" Tristan asked delicately, brow furrowed. "Blocking it?"

Veronyka snorted, overcome suddenly with a fit of laughter. Of course it wasn't working—he'd almost died today because of how spectacularly it *wasn't* working—but it was sweet of him to ask, to pretend that she wasn't as big a mess as she was.

He frowned more deeply at her, obviously unnerved by her bizarre behavior. He smiled eventually, but it was a crooked, quizzical thing.

She sighed, letting the laughter go. "No, not really."

Tristan straightened. "That's because you've been doing it all alone."

"What do you mean?"

"Well, you said we're, uh, bonded?" he asked, struggling to find the words. Veronyka nodded uneasily, and Tristan swallowed, fighting to keep a reaction from his features. "Then it's up to both of us to figure this out. It's like our bond with our phoenixes," he said, gesturing over his shoulder at Rex and Xephyra, whose heads popped up at them in unison. "We didn't figure those bonds out on our own, did we?"

Nope, said Xephyra smugly, and Veronyka gave her a wry grin before refocusing on Tristan. His tone, his expression . . . Tristan was giving her everything she needed right now: positivity, hope, and the prospect that she wasn't alone in this.

"But you don't have shadow magic," she said. "I don't know if you really can."

"I can try. And now that I know . . ." He wavered, glancing at her from beneath his lashes before looking away. "I can do my part. Avoid eye contact, touching you . . ." He cleared his throat. "Whatever you need."

Veronyka's stomach turned sour. He was right. Even if he couldn't help with the shadow magic portion, now that they both knew the risks, they could each do their best to avoid triggering her magic. It wasn't perfect, but it was better than nothing—better than what she'd been doing before.

She had to embrace what she'd always known: that they were stronger together.

"You told me you don't like being protected," Tristan said, recalling their conversation inside the Eyrie after their last sparring match, "but you've taken it upon yourself to protect me. That's not fair." He raised his brows in mock rebuke.

Veronyka twisted her mouth and nodded. "You're right. Thank you, Tristan. I . . . It won't be forever. I'll find a way, so we can . . ." She trailed off, a tingle of embarrassment climbing up her neck, and let him fill in the words: *I'll find a way so we can touch again.*

Tristan frowned as he sorted through her words. Then a slow smile crawled across his face, flashing his dimples. Veronyka's stomach swooped in response.

They stood in comfortable silence for a few moments before Tristan spoke. "So," he said, casting her a scrutinizing look, "are you okay?"

"Am *I* okay?" she repeated with a laugh. "You're the one who almost fell to his death today."

He didn't smile. "And you're the one whose entire life just got blown apart. I'd say we're even."

"I guess you have a point," she said in resignation, staring across the rocky landscape.

"Will you tell me?" he asked. "All of it? Or is that, I don't know . . . dangerous? With the bond and all?"

"I don't care," Veronyka replied with a shake of her head. "I don't want any more secrets between us. I'll tell you everything."

"I won't tell anyone," he said solemnly. "I promise."

Veronyka smiled. "I know."

The tradition of kneeling to swear fealty to fellow Phoenix Riders dates all the way back to Queen Nefyra. She knelt before her chosen Riders one by one, just as she'd knelt before Axura herself. It eventually became a part of several important Pyraean ceremonies, including the assignment of patrol positions and marriage rites.

When disputes arose between neighboring communities, it was common for the arguments to be settled and peace treaties sealed by their leaders kneeling opposite each other.

Queen Elysia brought the tradition with her to the valley, and the act was immortalized in a famous tapestry called *The Queen Who Knelt*, which once hung in the throne room of the Nest and has since been moved to the Morian Archives.

It featured Queen Elysia kneeling before her King Consort, Damian. He knelt as well, the two promising an alliance that would unite their people and serve as the foundation for the empire. For every king Elysia conquered or allied with, she would kneel, offering her loyalty, and if they wanted to keep their positions—and their heads—they would do the same.

—*Social and Political Customs of the Pyraean Queens*, the Morian Archives, 111 AE

But alone I finally understood what it was to be
an Ashfire. I did not want to rule, but we do
not always choose our destinies. Being an Ashfire
was not a choice, but a responsibility.

- CHAPTER 19 -

ELLIOT

AFTER EAVESDROPPING WITH SPARROW and overhearing some of the commander's plans, Elliot expected it to take several days to devise a way to relay the information about his great-aunt and the Grand Council. He had to make it seem natural—like something that he'd decided to tell the commander all on his own. He couldn't just stride up to the man the very next day and blurt out his family tree.

Or at least, that was what he'd thought.

It turned out that Elliot *could* in fact approach the commander the next day, and it was thanks to the gossip he overheard from his fellow Riders during the morning's Master Rider audition.

Beryk had enlisted Elliot's help with the proceedings, and it wasn't long before he heard why they were suddenly auditioning a new master: Empire soldiers had been sighted along the border. Tristan's patrol was a Rider short—a spot that had surely been meant for Elliot, and something he tried not to be resentful about—and they discussed both the soldiers and the Grand Council meeting within earshot that very morning. Beryk had quickly silenced the talk, but it was enough for Elliot to broach the topic with the commander without raising suspicion. While deliberately eavesdropping was one thing, accidentally overhearing gossip was something else.

His plans were derailed slightly after the events of the day, however, which included not only a failed trial, but a near-death fall by the commander's own son. After the commotion and Veronyka's brilliant diving rescue, Tristan had been carted off to his rooms by the healer, followed closely behind by Veronyka, the commander, Beryk, Fallon, and the members of Tristan's patrol. Elliot had never felt the divide between himself and those who had been his fellow apprentices as he had then, as they rushed off together and he was left behind. So he'd stood rooted to the spot, fists clenched and emotions held in check, until everyone else was gone. Then he'd cleaned up after them, doing what they needed him to, and when word had reached him that Tristan would make a full recovery, Elliot enjoyed his relief alone.

It was late by the time he worked up his courage to see the commander. The corridors and grounds were quiet, but Elliot knew the commander would be working inside his office well into the night. He paused outside the door, golden lantern light spilling around the gaps, before knocking softly.

He regretted his decision at once and was just turning away when the handle jiggled and the door swung wide.

"Elliot," the commander said in surprise as Elliot jerked back around and straightened.

"Sir."

They stood in awkward silence.

"Is there something you need?" the commander asked, looking a bit uncomfortable. He glanced down the hall. "Has Beryk sent you?"

Elliot shook his head. "I . . . overheard some rumors, and it made me think of something. Something I thought might be of help to you."

The commander's expression shifted with every word—dubious, then a flash of resignation at the spread of gossip inside the Eyrie, and then, finally, a spark of interest. "Come in."

Rather than settling in at the opposite side of the table, the commander took the chair nearest to the door and gestured for Elliot to do the same. He didn't want to sit—his anxiety and adrenaline made him want to run laps or loose arrows, anything to release the pent-up energy funneling through his limbs—but he did, perching uneasily on the edge.

It was the first time he'd been alone with the commander since his lies had been revealed, and Elliot was having a hard time looking the man in the face. It was also difficult being in this room again, where he had been subjected to hours upon hours of questioning. At least Beryk and Morra had been there, and though their presence wasn't meant to be a comfort to him, it had been. Even Beryk's disappointed face and Morra's intense, unnerving interrogation were better than being alone with cold, hard, intimidating Commander Cassian.

Those had been hard days, reliving every excruciating detail of his betrayal. Because of his fear of being caught by the Riders, Elliot had foolishly burned all his early letters. Later, when he'd begun to question the veracity of Captain Belden's claims and his sister's whereabouts, he'd decided to keep some of the missives, but they weren't of much use. Without all the letters to paint a complete picture, the scraps of requests and information proved only that *someone* wanted information about the Riders. They weren't signed, weren't sealed or authenticated, and they didn't explain the terms of their deal. Still, Elliot had turned over what he had—including the false letter from his sister that Elliot assumed was written by Belden himself—and relayed everything he could remember of the rest.

Elliot thought he had given all he could—but maybe he had a bit more to offer.

"What were these rumors you heard, Elliot?" the commander asked.

"About the Grand Council, sir. I heard the other—the Riders talking about it," he said. It felt wrong to insinuate that he was a Rider when he hadn't ridden in weeks. "They said there would be a meeting."

The commander pursed his lips. "There will be—though I do wish my Riders would be more discreet."

Elliot didn't want to get the Riders into trouble, so he hastened to continue. "Well, sir, it got me thinking about my aunt."

"Your aunt?"

"My great-aunt, actually. Emilia of Stel. She's the Minister of Trade in Stel and so has a seat on the Grand Council." The commander perked up considerably at that, confirming that it was a fact he didn't know. "As a minister, she actually controls—"

"*Three* seats," the commander said, gaze sliding out of focus as he considered these ramifications.

"Yes, sir. One for herself and two others that she can appoint at will. I'm not sure if you recall, but during the war, Emilia allied with Stelarbor."

Elliot paused to let that information sink in.

Stelarbor was the southernmost city in the empire, on the border of Arboria South and Stel, and well known for their disinterest in war. Though technically in the province of Stel, they rarely sided with them politically. They hadn't supported the Stellan Uprising or the Stellan involvement in the Blood War, and were actually known to work against the Stellan agenda from time to time.

"That's right. . . . ," the commander said, looking at Elliot with new eyes. "I'd forgotten that a portion of Stel resisted the council and their push for a Stellan-blooded queen."

Elliot nodded eagerly. "They refused to send soldiers, weapons, or gold that might be used against the Phoenix Riders. Like Stelarbor, my great-aunt has always supported the animage cause. I thought it might be good to know that you had an ally where you might not have counted one before."

The commander leaned back. "Thank you, Elliot. I, well . . . I know this ordeal has been trying for you. It's good to know you're still with us, despite everything. That you still want to help where you can."

Elliot's chest swelled. "Of course, sir."

That night, when Sparrow arrived outside the village, Elliot was waiting for her. He marched toward her across the grass, and she stiffened as he reached her—either hearing his footsteps or perhaps warned by one of her animal friends, which tonight included a one-legged bluebird, a fluffy dog that helped the villagers herd their small of sheep, and what Elliot was pretty sure was a chameleon, its scaly head with its wide, swiveling eyes poking out from her tunic's front pocket.

"Elliot?" she said, not so much warily as in surprise—he never greeted or approached her at all.

"Yes," Elliot said. "It's me."

Then, without explanation or preamble, he took her by the waist—careful not to crush the lizard—and twirled her around. He'd done this with Riella countless times, and though it seemed to startle Sparrow at first—as well as the bluebird perched on her head, which took off with an indignant trill—a bubble of laughter burst from her mouth as she clung tighter, giggling maniacally.

"Thank you, thank you, a thousand times thank you!" Elliot sang to her, his voice sounding more like a triumphant yell than anything else. "Sparrow, you are a genius!" he shouted to the night sky before carefully slowing his pace and releasing her.

"I am?" she asked somewhat breathlessly, stumbling a bit as she regained her footing. Her spear lay on the grass behind her; she must have dropped it when he scooped her up. A good thing, too, or Elliot might have accidentally wound up stuck like a pig.

"You are," Elliot replied. "I—" Before he could say more, however, something large and furry slammed into his chest, bowling him over.

The wind was knocked from Elliot's lungs—from the initial shock of the impact, plus the fact that the fur ball was still standing on his rib cage. He struggled to draw air, while a growling muzzle was inches from his face.

"Ruff, no!" came Sparrow's voice, but it was Jax's interference that moved the sheepdog from Elliot's chest. With a sharp butt of his head, the animal was gone, and Elliot drew in a gasping breath.

Jax remained looming over Elliot in a protective stance. The phoenix didn't seem angry—there wasn't any heat or sparks—but he was certainly annoyed. He croaked low in his throat and puffed up his feathers until the dog, who'd still been circling nearby, tucked his tail between his legs and scampered off.

Once the dog was gone, Jax looked downward until his head filled Elliot's field of vision—that was until Sparrow's head bent over him, even nearer at hand.

"Is he dead?" she asked aloud—and Elliot wondered who she was talking to until Jax released a sound that could only be described as a laugh-snort.

"I'm fine," Elliot wheezed, raising himself up on his elbows. "What happened?" he asked, still feeling a bit dazed.

"Oh, well—you startled me," Sparrow explained, sounding chagrined. "It's not good to touch someone who can't see. Not without asking," she clarified. "Ruff was just tryin' to teach you some manners is all."

Elliot grimaced. "I'm an idiot," he said, his cheeks heating in embarrassment. Of course she'd be surprised when he started spinning her around out of nowhere. "I wasn't thinking. I'm sorry, Sparrow. I was just grateful, I guess, and—"

"It's okay," Sparrow interrupted, fidgeting with the hem of her tunic. The bluebird returned, fluttering onto the girl's shoulder, and that seemed to settle her a bit. "Is that why you spun me, then?" she asked, brow furrowed. "To say thank you?"

Elliot got to his feet and dusted off the dirt and grass from his clothes. "I—well, no. I mean yes? I spun you because I was happy. You were right about showing them I still care. I spoke to the commander just now, and I think I really helped him."

"Did you spin him, too?"

"Gods, no," Elliot said, aghast. Then he burst out laughing. She seemed genuinely puzzled, but her expression lightened at the sound. He eventually sighed. "Sorry, Sparrow, I . . . I used to spin my sister like that."

"Riella?" Sparrow prompted.

"Yeah. I haven't felt like doing that in a long time. Since they told me I would be a Rider."

Sparrow seemed to consider his words for a long time. "Did Riella like it?"

"She loved it," Elliot said, his mood turning a bit melancholy again. "I guess . . . ," he began, suddenly self-conscious. "I guess you probably hated it."

"No," Sparrow said, shaking her head firmly. Then she smiled at him. "I loved it too."

Though Elliot felt lighter than he had in months after helping Beryk and giving important information to Commander Cassian, he knew he had a long way to go to make up for his past.

And so he chipped away at it, one day at a time.

When Anders broke a string on his lyre at dinner, lamenting that he'd have to order replacements from Arboria because the instrument wasn't commonly used in Pyra, Elliot spoke to one of the locals from Petratec. They had a popular troupe that often visited the Eyrie on festival days, including a band of minstrels, and with some digging Elliot was able to discover a harpist who could sell him extra strings. With Beryk's approval, Elliot ordered the replacements Anders needed, and they arrived the next day.

Anders was so surprised by the gesture that he'd laughed and gripped Elliot by both shoulders, planting a kiss on each cheek—a popular greeting in Arboria, or so Elliot had been told. He suspected Anders was just affectionate, but Elliot was pleased all the same. Anders played twice as long and sang twice as loud that night . . . and Elliot worried he'd maybe gone backward in earning his fellow Riders' affection. Luckily, no one seemed to blame him.

Elliot had managed to use the prospect of Petratec visitors to spread more goodwill—Ronyn's older sister was one of the singers, and she accompanied the harpist to deliver the strings. Though Ronyn was technically on duty, when Elliot told him his sister would be visiting, he was able to get his patrol shift covered and eat lunch with her. Ronyn wasn't as easily won over as Anders, but he'd offered Elliot an appraising sort of look when he'd told Ronyn the news, and after he said goodbye to his sister at the village gates, he'd given Elliot an appreciative slap on the back. A small thing, maybe, but Ronyn had reacted as badly as any of them at the news of Elliot's betrayal, and Elliot knew it would take more than one simple gesture to earn his trust and affection. Still, it was like Sparrow had said: He couldn't undo his mistakes or fix all the wrongs he'd done, but he *could* show them he was trying.

After that it was staying late to help Lysandro clean up the training yard and offering to unsaddle Fallon's and Darius's mounts when they returned late from a patrol and had to rush to a meeting.

Elliot even helped out the youngsters when he could, watching their lessons in bow or spear and offering an extra hand when needed. No task was beneath him, no job too petty or too insignificant. Before long he found joy not just in repaying his fellow Riders, but in being involved in everything again. He was an outsider, yes, but he wasn't banished entirely. He was still a part of this world.

While finding ways to help most of his fellow Riders had been fairly easy, Elliot struggled with Latham. They had never been close, never joked and laughed or even sat in easy silence together. Latham had a brash and prickly nature, and when they had talked as apprentices, they'd often bickered. And things had only gotten worse between them since the attack.

Latham had been more distant and irritable than usual, and at first Elliot had thought it was just toward him. And why shouldn't it be? The attack was Elliot's fault, and it seemed obvious that they should all blame him. Latham and his phoenix, Xane, hadn't been harmed during the fighting, but that didn't mean Elliot didn't deserve the cold shoulder.

When Elliot noticed Latham's contemptuous treatment of Veronyka—whose true identity had been revealed soon after the battle—Elliot had assumed Latham's disdain wasn't so much for the battle as it was for a pair of liars in their midst.

Elliot had believed this theory true until he'd taken a good look at Xane.

The phoenix reminded him very much of Jaxon in those first few weeks after Elliot's betrayal was made known. Xane was drooping and listless, his fire not as hot and his feathers not as bright. There was something wilting about him, like a flower dying on its stem.

Elliot didn't have the right words for it, didn't know the complex psyche of a creature like a phoenix, even though he was bonded to one. But what he did know was that sadness hit them particularly hard, especially sadness as it related to death. It made sense; phoenixes were immortal if not slain and could resurrect if they chose. For them, death was a distant, unknowable thing, and when they did encounter it . . . they did not bounce back easily.

Clarity shot through Elliot. There had been so much death and destruction during the attack, and while none of the bonded Riders had died, one of the *phoenixes* had. Xolanthe—sometimes called Xoe for short.

And unless Elliot was mistaken, Xane was Xolanthe's son.

It was hard to tell of it was Latham's bad mood infecting Xane, as it had been for Jax and Elliot, or if it was Xane's sadness leaking into Latham.

It troubled Elliot. For while he had gotten out of his own spiraling depression—he had Sparrow to thank for that—he didn't know how to help Latham and Xane. Their problem wasn't as simple as temporary illness or even as uncertain as Elliot's punishment and his sister's whereabouts; their problem was death. Irrevocable, since Xolanthe had burned in the pyre and not come back. Final.

He'd seen the others try to cheer Latham; Anders's lyre songs had been loud and lewd—usually Latham's favorites—but nothing seemed to get through to him. Elliot decided to focus his efforts on Xane instead. What could a phoenix want—or need—to move on from the death of another phoenix? Xolanthe might have been Xane's mother, but Latham had hatched her egg, and mother and son had been separated for all of Xane's life. Was it possible he mourned Xoe because he never knew her?

It was a long shot, but it was something.

After his duties with Beryk were complete, Elliot journeyed down into the bottom of the Eyrie, where the hatchlings slept. While most of the new phoenixes were old enough to fly, they were still young and vulnerable to things like predators or getting lost out in the wilderness, and so Ersken monitored their flight and kept them inside the Eyrie after dark. They spent their days with their soon-to-be Riders, strengthening their bonds and learning to work and communicate together, and they spent their nights sleeping and eating in a group, much as the adult phoenixes did.

They huddled in little clusters, ten hatchlings in total, varying in age from nearly two months to just over two weeks. Most of them couldn't yet make their own flames, so Ersken kept braziers burning through the night despite the warm summer weather. There was nothing a phoenix loved so much as heat.

Elliot walked among the fiery pools of light, the rustle of feathers and low, throaty chirps cutting through his echoing footsteps.

He hadn't seen Sparrow upstairs, either out on the field while Jax flew, or inside the dining hall. He suspected she was down here somewhere, but it was Ersken he sought.

Sparrow, however, found him first.

"What did I tell you?" she whispered vehemently, her spear whipping out of nowhere to stop Elliot in his tracks. Sparrow stepped into the glow of the nearest brazier, which lit the gnarled strands of her hair in shades of red and orange, making her head look like it was on fire.

"I . . . ," Elliot croaked, oddly chastened by the fierceness of her face and the gleaming point of her spear.

"Told you to let them be when they're sleeping! Told you they need rest, not—" She faltered suddenly and tilted her head to the side. The one-legged bluebird was with her again, perched on her shoulder and chirruping softly into her ear. Sparrow straightened. "Oh," she said, lowering her spear and allowing it to hit the ground with a thunk.

Elliot realized she didn't know it was him. "Expecting someone else?" he asked in amusement, and her puzzled expression cleared.

"Elliot!" she said, and he didn't miss the delight on her face. It made his stomach twist with a strange mix of emotion, both happiness and loss. It must be something to do with Riella again—no one except her ever lit up when they saw him. "I thought it was Petyr," she muttered. "Can't tell talons from tails."

Elliot chuckled, scrubbing a hand along the back of his neck. "I was hoping to catch Ersken—is he still awake?"

Sparrow snorted. "Old man never sleeps, no matter how much I tell him he needs his rest."

Elliot grinned—he couldn't help it. "Do you call him 'old man' when you do it?" he asked.

Sparrow shrugged. "What else am I gonna call him? He's no fresh hatchling."

"That *might* have something to do with it," he said dryly, but Sparrow was already moving. As she stepped through the pools of brazier light, he caught the darting tail of a cat winding its way through the phoenixes and leading the way to Ersken's workroom.

Inside, while Sparrow fed the cat from a bowl on Ersken's table, Elliot asked about phoenix mental health.

"'Scuse me?" Ersken said, raising his bushy eyebrows.

"Ever since the attack on the Eyrie, I've noticed that Xane . . . he hasn't been the same. And I thought it might be because of his mother. Did you . . . ? Do you know much about Xolanthe?"

Ersken cocked his head, squinting slightly. "What do you mean?"

Elliot shrugged, watching as Sparrow went about her business—though he knew she was listening. "I thought . . . maybe you could tell Xane about his mother—about Xoe. What she was like." He paused, searching for the right words. "I'm not sure he knows how to grieve for her when he hardly knew her. Maybe if he knows what she was like, if she was happy . . ."

Ersken's curious expression turned wary. "I won't lie to him. His mother was in a cage, and she died in a battle."

"I know," Elliot hastened to say. "But, well . . . I know you were fond of her. There has to be a reason for that. And even though she died fighting . . . she chose that, at least. And from what I hear, if it weren't for her . . ."

"I doubt you and I'd be here talkin' about her." He huffed a breath, and his gaze flicked to the table where Sparrow stood. It was covered with an assortment of knickknacks, including a handful of vivid red phoenix feathers. One of them was tipped in brilliant, iridescent purple. Could it be Xoe's?

Ersken's attention shifted back to Elliot. "I'll try."

Together, Ersken, Elliot, and Sparrow made their way to the top of the Eyrie, where the adult phoenixes roosted.

It wasn't hard to find Xane, alone on a ledge outside Latham's door. Jax was nearby, sensing Elliot's approach, but he too was alone. The other phoenixes avoided Jax just as their bondmates avoided Elliot, and that isolation was on display now as the rest of the phoenixes bunched together the same way the hatchlings did.

As they neared Xane, Ersken stuck out a hand, telling Elliot and Sparrow to hang back—though of course Sparrow didn't see it. Elliot tugged her tunic, pulling her aside as Ersken edged warily forward.

Xane straightened, shaking out his wings, but the challenging squawk died in his throat as his eyes landed on the feather in Ersken's outstretched hand.

Footsteps sounded, and Latham's door was wrenched open—no doubt he could sense his bondmate's curiosity or distress. Latham was half-dressed, tugging on his tunic as he stepped onto the walkway.

"What do you think—" he started. He too stopped when his eyes fell on the phoenix feather. Latham's scowling expression shifted, landing on Ersken. Then he turned and spotted Elliot and Sparrow standing on the other side of the doorway.

Ersken indicated that Elliot should deal with Latham, then turned his attention back to Xane, taking a seat next to the phoenix and laying the feather between them.

"What is he . . . ?" Latham began, and Elliot drew his attention.

"That was Xoe's," Elliot said softly, so as not to disturb Ersken and Xane. As it was, all he could hear was the low rumble of Ersken's voice, while Xane blinked at him, bright and curious.

Latham turned on him, his expression accusatory.

"I thought . . . I asked Ersken if he'd bring it to Xane," Elliot continued. It felt a bit self-serving to claim credit for the work Ersken was doing, but if it backfired—and there was still a chance it would—Elliot wanted the blame to land squarely on him. "And if he'd talk about her."

"Talk about her?" Latham repeated flatly. His eyes were dark shadows, the moon above providing only the barest illumination.

"About Xoe. Ersken knew her best . . . knew her better than Xane, and I thought . . ." Elliot paused, looking around Latham to where Ersken sat. Xane had settled down again, listening avidly to what Ersken said, gaze fixed on the feather. "I thought Xane should know what she was like. I thought it might make it easier to . . . let go."

Latham took an angry step toward Elliot, who reached back for Sparrow, pressing her protectively behind him. But before Latham could do more than grip the front of Elliot's tunic, a low croon sounded from Xane. Latham whirled around, staring at his phoenix. Then he glanced back at Elliot, releasing his grip. They were close enough now that Elliot could see the haunted, slightly desperate look in Latham's eyes. . . . It was something close to hope.

"I think he wants you to hear this too," Ersken called out. Latham started nodding, then turned away from Elliot and came to sit next to his phoenix. They leaned together, both staring at that single shining feather, and the gentle murmur of Ersken's voice filled the silence once more.

Remembering his lesson from earlier, Elliot withdrew his arm from where it was still pressed against Sparrow. "Sorry," he whispered. Luckily her cat friend hadn't joined them, else they might have gotten tripped up in the scuffle with Latham. As it was, only the bluebird remained, perched atop her head. "We should go."

Elliot turned and walked along the dark ledge toward the archway that led out into the stronghold, Sparrow behind him. There he paused, looking back at the small group.

"I hope . . . ," he began, then hesitated. What *did* he hope? That he'd done the right thing? That he'd made things better and not worse? He glanced down at Sparrow, who was stroking the bluebird's feathers and waiting patiently for him to continue. "I thought it would be better than not knowing," Elliot said at last. "This way they can grieve properly."

"Grieve properly," Sparrow repeated thoughtfully. "I had a family, you know," she said matter-of-factly. "Two brothers and two sisters. I was the oldest, but I couldn't work in the shop"—she pointed at her eyes—"so they couldn't keep me. Gave me to Miseriya to be an acolyte, but I hated being inside all the time," she said with a shudder. "I ran away. Didn't know where I was . . . didn't know how to get back home. If . . ." She hesitated, picking at a knot in the wood of her spear. "If I could know more, if I could remember, I would. Even if it hurt—I would want to know. I think what you did . . . I think it was very kind."

Elliot walked back to his room, wondering who he was really doing it all for and deciding he didn't care either way. Whatever it took to keep the warm glow inside his chest, he'd do it.

Avalkyra Ashfire wanted to rip more than bodies apart. . . .
She wanted to tear the whole world asunder. And so it
was up to me to piece it back together.

- CHAPTER 20 -
SEV

LORD ROLAN'S ESTATE WAS huge, spanning multiple wings and floors. Sev and Kade decided that their best course of action for the time being was to get familiar with it and the people inside. And though finding the hostage Riella was no longer his mission, Sev kept an eye out for her just the same.

While Kade explored the servant passages, Sev wandered the main halls and soldiers' haunts. He walked every corridor and stairwell, peered into every room and closet and cupboard, learning not just the layout, but the very heartbeat of the house—memorizing the schedules, habits, and hangouts of the occupants from the guards to the governor himself—but found nothing useful for spying on Lord Rolan or uncovering his war plans.

Kade filled in the gaps in Sev's knowledge, doing his best to settle back into his old role among the estate's bondservants, many of whom were likely acquainted with Ilithya one way or another. The problem was, Trix's allies—especially those who had been on the Pyra mission—didn't have a high survival rate. If any of her surviving associates knew anything of value, they weren't talking. Kade also reported that the servant passages that led directly into the governor's suite of rooms were cut off from the rest—likely to avoid potential assassination or, even worse, *common* servants coming and going—and Bertram, Lord Rolan's personal attendant, was the only member on the staff who had access to them. He slept in an adjoining chamber, took his meals alone, and never left the estate for personal matters.

"He's actually a bondservant," Kade had said, when they met on the third night since their reunion. "A *freed* one. Rolan forgave all his transgressions and offered him a paid position."

Sev's brows rose, impressed, but Kade shook his head.

"Don't get too excited. He didn't do it out of the goodness of his heart. Bertram is apparently a cousin. From what I've overheard, Rolan only freed him to remove the stain from their family, and he offered the job as attendant so he could guarantee Bertram's loyalty. One false move and he'll be back in bondage again. He also personally manages Rolan's messenger birds, so there's no chance of intercepting any, like we'd hoped."

Sev cursed. He'd thought they could tap one of Ilithya's best sources of information, the mail, by bribing or making friends with whatever bondservant currently managed the messenger birds. But if they were handled entirely by Bertram, Rolan's loyal attendant and cousin, they'd have very little chance of plumbing that resource. Or of gaining access to Rolan's chambers through the servant passages.

Despite the fact that Rolan had put his stamp on things, the house seemed haunted by the ghost of the exiled governor and his family, no matter how many Stellan rugs and family trees Rolan hung up. The gardens were the legacy of Cassian's Pyraean—and fellow Phoenix Rider—wife, Olanna, planted with orange and lemon trees and clusters of bright Fire Blossoms. The ironwork benches were wrought with phoenix motifs, and the stonework paths swirled and coiled like plumes of fire. There was a fresco in the west hall that featured King Damian, an ancestor of Cassian and consort to Queen Elysia, which had been concealed behind a heavy tapestry depicting Lord Rolan's ancestor King Rol, and a wooden doorframe outside the private dining room was notched halfway up, marking the increasing age and height of Cassian and Olanna's son, Tristan. Though Sev hadn't yet seen it firsthand, there was apparently a phoenix roost atop the highest tower of the gleaming plaster-and-white-marble estate, enclosed with ornately carved columns and attached to an upper-story balcony, where phoenixes could perch and Riders could easily mount up.

Sev couldn't help but notice the fact that Lord Rolan and Commander Cassian were the descendants of King Rol and King Damian respectively, and that just as their ancestors had fought over lands and titles before the empire, so too did Rolan and Cassian clash. First, in a smaller way over this estate and its legacy, but also in a larger way over the lands they occupied and the borders that divided them. It seemed that all wars, no matter how ancient, never really ended.

While the building itself clung to the past, Sev wondered if its inhabitants *besides* Lord Rolan did too. Surely some of the servants had been here since Cassian was governor? And what of the soldiers? Could any of them be bought or convinced to divulge important information?

Sev had plenty of questions but no answers, and his frustration grew with every unoccupied room he found and every shift he spent watching Rolan attend to the dull affairs of state expected of any governor—paying wages, approving supply orders, ensuring they stored enough grain for the winter—and not defense strategy and warcraft. The most exciting thing Sev overheard was that there would be an order of Ferronese steel shipping in a few days. But those weapons were going *away* from Lord Rolan, not toward him. Another dead end.

The Grand Council was looming, and every day that slipped by without discoveries or breakthroughs felt like a failure. Sev needed time not only to get the information, but to send it to Cassian and for Cassian to act on it.

Sev needed to be more proactive. The question was, *how?*

Early one evening, he was waiting dutifully in his rooms after dinner for Hestia to come apply her nightly poultice. She'd told him he was doing well, and they would likely switch to a once-weekly application soon.

Sev had learned over the course of his treatment why Hestia was taking such "good care of him," as Kade had said. Sev had seen more seasoned and valuable soldiers receive much less, and he thought he'd finally begun to understand why.

Not only was Hestia a Ferronese local, but she'd lost her two sons during the Blood War. Every time she looked at Sev, something in her brusque face softened, and he was glad for his father's light eyes and his Ferronese name. She'd taken a liking to him at once and diligently cared for his wound, her affection gruff and no-nonsense, but also unwavering, as if he were as important to her as her own children. Sev wondered how they had died . . . if she'd treated them and failed, or if they'd never returned home from some faraway battlefield.

It was clear that she held sway within Lord Rolan's household. Not only did she give Sev top-notch medical treatment, but she showed her preference for him in ways that might go unnoticed if Sev weren't the sort of person who paid attention to details. The medicine she gave him was expensive, the bandages softest linen, his bed made with plump down-filled pillows and finely embroidered sheets. His rooms were cleaned every single day, and his laundry washed and pressed.

As a soldier, those last responsibilities should have been his own, but Sev suspected Hestia was getting him the kind of perks a sick or wounded member of the household would receive—not a lowly foot soldier. Lord Rolan's estate had an infirmary, but it was meant for wartime, when dozens of beds would be filled. It didn't make sense to put Sev there, alone, when treating him in a room like this was likely easier for Hestia and her assistants. Even still, she could have treated him in the soldier barracks at this point—but for some reason she kept him here, in comfort.

When Hestia found out Sev didn't have a "sweetheart," she took it upon herself to send very pretty serving girls instead of assistants to his rooms— always locals from Ferro—delivering teas or tinctures with a deep bow and a sweet smile. Hestia hadn't known Sev had no interest in blushing maidens, but she was no fool—before long she was sending handsome serving *boys* instead.

Sev would turn them away, red-faced and stammering, relieved when he was alone again and he could light his lantern and wait for Kade.

That night, Hestia arrived a bit later than usual, knocking on the door before letting herself in. One of her assistants accompanied her, delivering a tray of materials Hestia would need and then departing.

"I was wondering if you'd forgotten me," Sev teased after the door closed behind her assistant.

Hestia rolled her eyes. "So needy," she lamented, though her lips twisted in a smirk. "I'll have you know, I had a last-minute request from the governor himself. Mosquito bite ointment, so he can entertain on his terrace tonight," she added with a long-suffering sigh. "The man looks like he has a pox, but he refuses to dine indoors. He'd never admit it, being from Stel, but Ferro has the most beautiful summers in all the empire."

Sev had been around long enough to know that Lord Rolan took almost all his meals outside on his terrace. Sev assumed he did it for privacy—he closed the doors to the courtyard whenever he entertained, at any rate, leaving his guards to protect him from inside—but maybe Hestia was right and Rolan had a soft spot for the temperate weather.

What Sev wouldn't do to overhear some of those meetings—like the one that was probably happening tonight. No doubt that was where much of his scheming and plotting took place.

"So, how is the swelling tonight, Sevro?" Hestia asked, dusting off her hands—she'd been separating poppies from their stems and placing the flowers into a pestle and mortar for grinding—before peering down her nose sternly at Sev.

Sev was seated on his bed, legs over the side, and tried not to squirm under her watchful gaze. "It's not as bad as yesterday," he hedged. He was quite certain it was exactly the same as the day before and that Hestia would call him out on it at once.

"Hmph—a likely story," she said, sliding a pair of spectacles onto her nose and leaving her tray to come have a closer look. Sev was already shirtless, and it didn't take her long to spot the flushed redness of the skin—particularly around the scar tissue—and the limited movement of the joint as she lifted Sev's arm forward and to the side, one hand holding his wrist, the other gently supporting his elbow. "Were you straining yourself again?"

"Wouldn't dream of it," Sev said, shaking his head earnestly. Really, with the state his arm was in, putting on his tunic in the morning pushed his limits. He was fortunate to be posted to the estate, but even still, there were weapons to wield, doors to open, and duties like cleaning armor and sharpening blades to attend to. He was a soldier, after all.

After poking and prodding at his swollen joint, Hestia shook her head with obvious affection and returned to her tray. She added seeds to the heavy stone bowl, grinding them into powder along with the flowers, then poured in water from a jug. "You men are all the same—refuse to heed the healer's advice, no matter how practical."

Sev bowed his head, behaving appropriately chagrined.

"I remember—oh, nearly thirty years ago now—when young lord Cassian was bedridden with phoenix fever, he stayed in this very room," she began, and Sev listened intently. He didn't know that Hestia had served the previous governor as well. "Didn't matter that he was burning up, covered in sweat and not keeping food or fluids down; he still snuck out that window"— she jerked a thumb over her shoulder to indicate the window Sev used to send his letters to Cassian in the present—"every gods-cursed night, shimmying up a drainpipe and onto the roof. He'd climb halfway across the estate on those tiles just so he could spend a bit more time with his phoenix."

Sev's pulse jumped at her words, but she spoke them at the exact moment she'd taken a washcloth to his shoulder and clearly assumed his reaction was due to the cool water against his hot skin. Her brisk touch grew gentler, but Sev's thoughts were elsewhere—on the window and the drain- pipe and the roof. He tried to picture it, the rough layout of the estate and how every wing and courtyard—like the one Rolan had private meetings in—were connected by those bright terra-cotta tiles.

"The creature was just a hatchling then," Hestia continued, oblivious to Sev's revelation. "Barely able to fly—and it's a good thing, too. If he'd have been older, no doubt Cassian would've flown him and fallen to his death.

On my watch, no less. Governor Lucian would've had my hide. I told him to put locks on the outside, but he had a soft spot for his only child. Luckily, Cassian survived the fever unscathed."

Sev wrenched his mind back to the present and scrabbled for a response. "Luckily, or because of your expert care?" he asked, smiling sweetly.

She snorted. "Take that charm and flattery elsewhere, Sevro," she said. "It is wasted on me."

But Sev didn't think it was. Her treatment was careful and thorough—no cutting corners or rushing through—and she seemed happy and content as she chattered on about Cassian and his son, Tristan, and how all young Ferronese boys loved to run around wild and barefoot, no matter their birth. As she spooned the poultice paste onto a square of bandage and applied it to his shoulder, Sev listened, understanding that Hestia was really talking about her own sons, and doing it this way allowed her to remember them with less grief.

Finally his poultice was in place, and Sev allowed himself a small stab of guilt at all the hard work Hestia had put into it and his plans to rip it off almost as soon as she left the room. He'd hear it from her tomorrow when the swelling was worse than ever.

She apparently sensed something in Sev's edgy, slightly agitated mood, and favored him with a long look as she prepared to leave. "Another night alone in your rooms, Sevro?" she asked. "No plans to take a stroll into the city, or spend time in the soldiers' mess?"

Sev shook his head—he never truly spent his nights alone, but he obviously couldn't tell Hestia who visited him through the secret passage.

She frowned, then nodded, as if coming to a decision. "I'll send something for the pain so you can sleep," she said, standing in the open doorway, tray in hand. "Have a good night—but no . . . *overexertion*, okay, Sevro?"

She left, and something in her expression made Sev think she knew exactly what he planned to do—but how could she? A few minutes later he realized his mistake.

Another knock sounded—Hestia's promised sleep aid—and Sev shrugged into his unlaced tunic to answer it, glancing over his shoulder to make sure Kade wasn't emerging from behind the tapestry before opening the door.

It wasn't an assistant, however, but another of Hestia's handsome serving boys. Suddenly her questions about spending the night alone—and her warning not to overexert himself—held new, mortifying meaning. Had she gone straight to the servants' hall and sent him here?

He was familiar—having already been to Sev's rooms before—and the embarrassment Sev felt at the sight of him was enough to drive every other thought from his mind.

"Y-yes?" he asked.

The boy bowed slightly, his lithe frame elegant and sure—like an acrobat or a dancer. He raised a silver tray bearing not a medicinal tea or potion, but a bottle of orange-flavored liqueur. It was a popular drink in Ferro; Sev had never tasted it, but he could remember the smell of it on his father's breath when he'd uncorked their small, far less fine bottle the day Sev's grandfather died.

"Hestia advised that this would help with the pain—so you can sleep," the servant said, straightening and offering a knowing smile. That was when Sev realized there were *two* glasses on the tray. The boy moved to step into the room, but Sev panicked and cut him off, seizing the tray from his hands. The entire contents rattled dangerously, the boy's graceful movements making it all look far easier than it was.

"I—thank you very much," Sev said, struggling to keep the bottle steady. "I'll take it from here."

"Please, sir, it's my job to serve you."

Sev's eyes practically bugged out of his head at the double meaning in the boy's words.

"At least let me carry . . . ," the boy continued with a smile, but Sev hastily drew the tray out of his reach.

"No," Sev practically shouted. He swallowed. "I prefer to be alone tonight. Antony, was it?" he asked, trying to remember their introduction from earlier in the week.

The servant dropped his outstretched arms and nodded. "Yes, sir. Antony."

"Thank you for delivering this, Antony, and please send my . . . appreciation to Hestia. If you'll excuse me," he said, clumsily shifting the tray to one hand while closing the door with his other. Antony's smile was gone, replaced with a puzzled frown as the door swung shut. A boy who looked like that probably wasn't used to being turned down by anyone—never mind someone as bumbling and awkward as Sev.

He'd barely set the tray on the low table in the sitting room when Kade's voice spoke from behind him.

"Entertaining someone?" he asked, slipping silently into the room, the tapestry swishing inaudibly behind him. He glanced toward the door. "Did I interrupt?"

"Of course not—it was one of the servants."

"Antony?" he asked, and Sev was surprised at how well he could hear behind that wooden panel.

"Yes," Sev said, frowning slightly. Kade seemed . . . not angry, exactly, but agitated? And his amber eyes roved Sev's face before lowering to see the laces of his shirt hanging open and his chest exposed.

Sev cleared his throat, resisting the urge to tug his tunic closed. "Would you like some?" he asked, gesturing to the bottle—then grimaced. Sev had forgotten about the two glasses on the tray, and how that would look considering they'd been delivered by a handsome serving boy.

Kade's lip curled. "I don't think that was meant for me."

Was Sev imagining it, or was there *jealousy* in Kade's tone? He fought to keep a stupid grin from splitting across his face. "What does it matter?" he asked, his voice light. "I'm offering it to you."

"I'd rather not meet with you at night if that's when you prefer to have . . . *guests*," he said, as if the word were distasteful to him.

His tone was accusatory, but also questing, asking Sev to confirm or deny something.

"What's it to you if I have guests or not?" Sev countered.

Kade reared back slightly. "I don't—I'm not—" He was clearly flustered.

He pointed to the table. "The lantern was lit! I could have walked in on you."

"Walked in on me doing what, exactly?" Sev asked. He wanted Kade to say it, to say what he suspected and admit that it made him jealous.

Kade looked down, straightening his shoulders and expelling a breath in a huff. "What you do in your rooms is none of my business," he began, and disappointment settled in Sev's bones, making him feel heavy and tired. His shoulder throbbed. "But if I had been seen coming out of that passage . . ."

"The only thing I do in these rooms is sleep and wait for you," Sev said honestly. "And have my shoulder treated. Antony wasn't here as a guest, or at my request. Hestia sent him with the alcohol to help me sleep. And in case you hadn't noticed, I turned him away."

Sev took a step closer to Kade. How could he not see that Sev wanted nothing to do with the servant and everything to do with him?

"Only because you knew I was coming. If I wasn't . . ."

"Then I'd be drinking that bottle by myself and cursing you for my hangover come morning."

Kade smiled a bit at that, the tension loosening in his shoulders. He scrubbed at the back of his neck. "I think I'll take that drink now."

Sev grinned and reached for the bottle and glasses. "Better make it a quick one," he said, filling the cups and handing one to Kade. He took his with him as he walked over to the window and leaned out, seeking the drainpipe. "If we're going to get back before dawn."

"Before dawn . . . What're you talking about—and *what* are you doing?" Kade said, alarmed by the way Sev was leaning out of the frame.

He didn't answer, only leaned back inside the room, grinning. "Plotting our escape route."

After Sev explained what he intended them to do—namely, climb onto the roof, crawl across the sloping tiles, and locate Rolan's garden courtyard—Kade objected at once.

"You can barely lift your arm."

Sev ignored him. "How are you at climbing?" he asked, and Kade laughed, shaking his head.

"Better than you."

Now it was Sev's turn to laugh. "You're probably right," he said, unable to help the way his eyes fell to Kade's muscled arms and broad shoulders. Of the two of them, Kade had a true fighter's build, while Sev was thin and wiry. "But I'll do better once I get this off," he said, walking over to the bed. He settled down on it and began tugging off his tunic.

Kade looked away at once. "What are you doing?" he demanded for the second time that night.

"I'm taking off the poultice," Sev said, secretly pleased by the way Kade's jaw muscles twitched, revealing taut lines of tension along his neck. "It would go faster if you helped me."

Finally Kade lifted his gaze, and seeing that Sev had only gotten his tunic off partway—it always snagged on the bandages, and it was difficult to move his arm enough to slide it off—he stalked over.

Jaw still set, Kade tugged at the laces until they were completely free, before sliding his hand underneath the worn cotton and slipping it from Sev's shoulder. He was obviously being gentle because of the wound, but Kade's touch was warm—and his body so near—that Sev lost himself in the feeling of being undressed by him. Alone in this dark, quiet room.

Sev's pulse hammered in his throat, and he stared fixedly at the glowing lantern across the chamber. With his eyes out of the equation, the rest of Sev's senses seemed to rise in response, so every scratch of fabric, touch of skin, and trace of Kade's scent was all the more potent, like some heady cocktail ten times stronger than the alcohol on the tray.

Sev had already gotten his good arm out of the shirt, and now Kade finished tugging it off his bad arm and laid it carefully aside. He too was avoiding looking at Sev, keeping his eyes on the thick bandages that wrapped his shoulder.

He cleared his throat. "Now what?"

"There's a pin . . . ," Sev said, reaching up with his good hand and trying to locate it near the back of his shoulder. Kade had to step closer to see, his legs now pressed against the bed and bracketing Sev's leg on either side. He leaned forward, bare inches away, until his hand pressed over Sev's, halting it in its search.

"I see it," he murmured, his mouth so close to Sev's ear that Sev's entire body erupted in goose bumps. Could Kade see that? He didn't have time to worry, because then Kade's deft fingers were undoing the pin, and the compress began to unravel.

Kade put the pin aside and began unwrapping the length of bandage, under Sev's arm, then across his chest, again and again, passing it from one hand to the other, and leaning in close every time he had to tug it around Sev's back.

Sev swallowed, wondering if he'd bitten off more than he could chew with this arrangement. He wanted to stand up and get some space. . . . He wanted to pull Kade closer.

When cool air began to reach his skin through the thin layers of bandage, Sev figured he'd let this go on long enough. "I can, uh . . . ," he said, stopping Kade's hands as they passed in front of him and taking hold of the bandage. "I can finish."

Kade hesitated before nodding and relinquishing the linen. Sev pulled the rest of it off, giving an extra tug as the fabric stuck to his damp skin and the dark smear of the poultice residue. Sev bunched the bandages up in his hands, thinking about using them to wipe his skin, when Kade stepped back into his field of vision. Before Sev realized what was happening, Kade put a damp cloth against his bare shoulder and wiped the skin clean.

He was surprisingly tender, and Sev could do nothing but stare at him until the task was done.

"Thank you," he whispered. They looked at each other . . . and then Sev remembered he was shirtless and hastened to shrug back into his tunic. The poultice had already eased some of the ache in his joint, but he'd be putting it through the ringer before this night was through.

The climb was more challenging than Sev had anticipated. In order to get onto the roof, they had to actually stand on Sev's extremely narrow window ledge, then reach across the open air to the drainpipe that ran from the gutters above to the ground below. It was a good arm span away. Sev had new appreciation for the young Commander Cassian, whose youth—and delirious fever—must have made him fearless.

Kade went first, balancing effortlessly on the small ledge, his long arm easily reaching the pipe. He swung himself across, then shimmied up to the roof in under a minute. Sev was on the second floor, and luckily there wasn't a third in this wing of the estate. Kade hoisted himself silently over the edge and called for Sev to follow.

He had to reach with his bad arm for the pipe, which meant it was more of a controlled fall than an elegant jump. Pain lanced through him at the jarring movement, and the pipe rattled underneath his grip. When he had both hands and feet wrapped around the metal, he looked up to see Kade watching him anxiously.

Sev knew he didn't have time to waste and started moving as quickly and quietly as he could. Despite the fact that only his shoulder was wounded, Sev's entire arm felt weak, and his palm slipped as he tried to gain purchase. He was barely halfway up when he felt Kade's hand over his own.

"I have you," Kade said, tugging until Sev loosened his hold on the pipe and gripped Kade's hand instead.

With a shocking surge of strength, Kade lifted him bodily, and Sev almost cried out in surprise. He had a terrifying moment of dangling, his feet and hands connected to nothing, before Kade heaved him the rest of the way and Sev could take hold of the edge of the roof.

His bad arm trembled as he hoisted himself up, but Kade never released his grip—reaching for hand, arm, and tunic—until Sev was sprawled on the tiles next to him.

"You were right," Sev said, panting. He turned his head to the side to see Kade sitting next to him, his own chest rising and falling rapidly, arms resting on knees. Kade shot him a quizzical look. "You were better than me," Sev added, and a slow smile spread across Kade's face.

"Let's go," Sev said once he'd caught his breath, sitting up and looking behind him to get his bearings.

"What is it you're expecting to overhear?" Kade whispered, as they crouched low and cut across the sloping tiles. It was full dark, and most of the light from the compound glowed beneath them, not above. All that lit their path was moonlight. "You think Rolan shouts his war plans to the rooftops?"

"No," Sev said, casting a somewhat exasperated look over his shoulder. "But he *does* hold private meetings on his terrace, and apparently he's entertaining tonight. It's my best chance to hear something important."

Lord Rolan's rooms were a good distance from Sev's—no wealthy lord wants to sleep next to the medical wing—and they had to climb up to the third floor, then back down again to make it to the right part of the building.

At last they spotted the correct courtyard and climbed their way toward it. The space below was filled with greenery sliced through with stonework paths and metal benches, all connecting to a terrace that led directly into Rolan's rooms. The scent of lemon trees was heavy on the air, tainted with the tang of a charcoal brazier. Rolan often had at least one brazier lit, even in high summer, to keep some of the insects away. . . .

Which meant Rolan was in the courtyard, just as Hestia had said.

Before Sev could relay this information to Kade, voices reached them on the evening breeze, and Kade yanked him down flat across the tiles.

Sev grimaced as his shoulder collided with the sun-warmed tiles, but that didn't stop him from shooting a triumphant—and yes, smug—look at Kade before turning his attention to the conversation below. Kade rolled his eyes but followed suit.

They were directly above Rolan's marble dining table; there was a low murmur of voices, along with the clink and swirl of a glass being refilled from a decanter and the gentle scrape of metal cutlery on ceramic plates.

". . . the shipment is set to depart in two days," came a man's voice— Lord Rolan's. He spoke with energy, as if their conversation sparked excitement. "It will take another two days to reach the capital. Ideally, you will meet it halfway—well out of sight of local traffic. That should provide a nice counterbalance to our offensive across the border."

"Survivors?" The word was clipped, cool . . . and spoken by a woman. Sev didn't understand the question. What did survivors have to do with a shipment? But an offensive across the border . . . Sev thought he knew what *that* meant, at any rate.

Rolan's soldiers were about to mobilize.

"At least a few," Rolan replied easily. "Not too many, mind—we'll need them spreading fear and panic, not tales of their heroic escape."

"There will be nothing heroic in their tales, I assure you," the woman said, and a chill ran down Sev's spine.

"If you do as you say you will and deliver what you promise, I will handle the rest. Do we have an accord?" Rolan said, and Sev murmured a low curse. The words had a tone of finality about them; Sev and Kade had missed the majority of the conversation.

There was a scrape of chair across stone—Rolan was standing. Sev inched forward on the roof, craning his neck. He caught a glimpse of Rolan with his hand outstretched, while the woman, her head cloaked, remained in her chair. Someone else stood just behind her, positioned more like a guard or attendant than a dinner guest.

Next to him, Kade's attention was on the wider courtyard—as if he were looking for something in the bushes.

The woman finally stood—but made no move to reach for Rolan's hand.

"I always deliver what I promise," she said. Something in her cold, detached voice seemed oddly familiar to Sev, though he couldn't place it. It was hard to imagine how any woman he knew would be dining with the governor of Ferro.

Footsteps echoed up to them, followed by a creak of leather and jingle of something metallic. There was a rustle—the sound of dry leaves skittering across the ground—followed by a gust of warm wind.

Then two massive, winged creatures exploded into the sky.

Sev gaped, hardly daring to believe his eyes. *Phoenixes*. The cloaked woman sat astride one of their vast backs while her attendant or guard rode the other. They flew in the opposite direction, away from Sev and Kade, who watched, mouths hanging open, as the Riders disappeared into the night.

Numb with shock, they waited until Lord Rolan opened his balcony doors and returned to his chambers before crawling back to Sev's rooms.

They shimmied down the drainpipe at the same time, Kade first, then Sev directly after—so Kade could catch Sev if need be, and Sev couldn't find it in him to resent the coddling. His shoulder throbbed relentlessly, and he was already wondering if he could salvage the scraps of Hestia's poultice when he got back inside.

By the time they climbed through his window, they were both exhausted, and Kade had to get back to the bondservant quarters before his absence was noted. There wasn't time to discuss what they had seen and heard—not that Sev could make sense of it even if he had.

Had Commander Cassian sent a Phoenix Rider to treat with Lord Rolan? And if he had . . . why hadn't he warned Sev? And if he *hadn't* . . .

Sev scribbled down everything he could remember, then hastily converted the letter into code. Dawn light was filtering into his room by the time he finished the note and attached it to the messenger pigeon. He watched the bird disappear into the sunrise, then prepared for the day.

Either the commander was keeping Sev in the dark, or there was more than one band of Phoenix Riders in existence, and those Riders might just be fighting for the wrong side.

There is a Stellan saying that states "The dryer the earth, the deeper the roots," which suggests that the poorer the conditions, the harder one must fight for survival—and the stronger one becomes because of it. It is an interesting metaphor for the Stellans, who had to fight hard, constantly, for what little resources there were to be had. As a result, they are a hardy—and often misunderstood—people.

Of the so-called lesser kingdoms that existed in the era before the Golden Empire, one of the more famous is that of Rolland. It was led by Rol the Unruly—who would later earn the rather biased nickname Rol the Betrayer—whose kingdom was in the northwest of modern Stel, along the border with Ferro. Most of Rol's lands were in the arid desert and rocky land now called the Shadow Plains, stationed directly next to the Spine.

Unable to feed his people, King Rol sought to expand but had nowhere to go. To the south was the powerful kingdom of Qorlland, and to the east was the smaller, less powerful kingdom of Lunland. Rather than waste resources trying to overtake King Lun, King Rol forged an alliance with him and set his sights on Ferro, which was rich in land, minerals, and other much-needed resources. King Rol's efforts to peacefully take lands from the Ferronese king Damian were brutally rebuffed, and so open war soon broke out between them.

In the deciding battle, King Rol fought bravely and was on the cusp of victory when the tide was turned in favor of King Damian. King Rol had defeated him fairly, but before he could claim the Ferronese king's life—as was his right—the Pyraean queen, Elysia, and her sisters unjustly intervened, murdering Rol in cold blood and forever marring the great king's legacy.

—"Stellan Kings: A Noble History," by the Stellan Historical Preservation Alliance, published 58 AE

*While Avalkyra collapsed the economy and toppled the foundations
of the empire, I worked tirelessly to correct its course. When Avalkyra burned
fields of crops or poisoned granaries, I emptied my coffers to replenish
our stores and resow every field, but still it was not enough.*

- CHAPTER 21 -
VERONYKA

NEARLY A WEEK AFTER the failed trials, the commander summoned Tristan's patrol into his meeting room—Veronyka included. He gave the official word that Veronyka had not passed and would therefore not be elevated to Master Rider.

This surprised no one, but the news he delivered afterward did.

"We have received intelligence from an agent in place in the empire," he began, and Veronyka knew he was referring to Sev, their soldier-spy. "And it appears that Lord Rolan's soldiers will soon march. Since they are stationed along the border with Ferro, Fallon will run point from Prosperity. From there he and his patrol can watch the western front and keep an eye on the soldiers' movements. If there is an attack, we should be able to see it coming and engage in counter-maneuvers."

Counter-maneuvers? That seemed like a strange way to say "fighting back." Then again, maybe he had different strategies in mind . . . sabotage, ambushes, and other forms of guerrilla warfare.

The commander's gaze flicked around the room, settling on each of them in turn before lingering on Tristan. "Your patrol, on the other hand, will return to Vayle. I have reviewed your report, and I am approving the requested repairs to the bridge. You will supervise and aid in the rebuild, as well as patrol the region as our eastern front."

Veronyka watched Tristan for his reaction. He tilted his head, considering. With the soldiers massing in the west, they'd be tucked out of sight, away from the action. Still, it was better than remaining at the Eyrie, even farther away.

"I know it is not the mission you were hoping for," the commander continued, "but it is an important one. You'll be the face of our operation in the east to reassure the locals that we have everything in hand."

Tristan's patrol murmured and nodded their heads, but the commander wasn't done.

"There's something else as well."

His tone made Veronyka pause. He'd delivered their orders with his usual calm, efficient demeanor, but now he seemed almost . . . hesitant.

"Phoenix Riders have been spotted in the south. . . . Riders who are not a part of our flock."

Veronyka's heart lurched inside her chest—first with excitement, but then with something like dread. The commander's expression wasn't one of interest or cautious hope. While the group looked at one another, eyes wide and mouths open, Tristan fixed his father with a perceptive look.

"Who are they?" Tristan asked. He darted an uneasy look at Veronyka, and she wondered if he was thinking what she'd been thinking. . . . Could it be Val?

If not her, it could easily be one of the Riders from Ilithya's list, though Tristan didn't know about them yet. Veronyka had told him the lockbox was filled with documents and letters, but she hadn't gotten into specifics.

"I don't know anything about their identities; all I know is that there are two, and I have reason to believe that they have allied with the empire."

Silence.

"But . . . why?" asked Anders incredulously. Next to him, Ronyn's brow was low, and the looks of interest and excitement that had been on Latham's and Lysandro's faces dimmed.

"The information I have is scant and circumstantial," the commander said, shifting back into his authoritative tone. "But they were seen in Ferro, at the governor's estate, and I suspect we will be seeing them again before all this is over."

Veronyka swallowed, her mind racing. Surely it couldn't be Val. . . . She hated the empire and everyone in it.

"And what do we plan to do about it?" Tristan asked, arms crossed. "We should try to make contact with them, see if they're actually on his side, and if not—maybe they could be persuaded to join ours instead."

Hope ignited inside Veronyka. She could show the commander her list of surviving Riders—maybe he'd even let her help seek them out? Wishful thinking, but Veronyka couldn't help it.

The commander shook his head. "Whatever's happening with these other Phoenix Riders is happening *inside* the empire. Pyra is our domain, and it's where we must draw the line. Our forces are already severely outnumbered. We can't be lured into some wild-goose chase or into splintering our factions any more than they already need to be."

"But Commander—" Tristan interjected, but his father cut him off.

"We can't afford to fight two battles at once; we don't have enough warriors to watch the border, never mind what's happening beyond it. End of discussion."

Tristan's arms dropped to his sides, hands clenched into fists. Veronyka knew he wanted to disagree—she wanted to argue herself—but the commander wasn't *wrong*. Their resources were already spread so thin. Whatever those Phoenix Riders were doing, until it involved Pyra and the war . . . they just didn't have the time to deal with it. Unless . . . could *she* find the time?

In the quiet that followed Tristan and the commander's exchange, Latham raised his hand. "So . . . about Vayle," he said. "Is it all six of us? Even without passing the trials?"

Veronyka's face heated as everyone turned to look in her direction. She'd been wondering the same thing, though Latham's obvious distaste for the idea stung.

"My patrol is still a member short," Tristan pointed out, "and she came with us last time. She was a big part of why the villagers welcomed our presence."

Veronyka's chest tingled at the praise, though she wasn't sure Tristan's words were entirely true. She turned a wary look at the commander, who wore a mask of thinly veiled frustration. Veronyka suspected he was weighing whether the denial would be worth the fight that followed.

He bowed his head in acquiescence.

Veronyka's heart soared, and Tristan beamed at her as they rushed from the room. Maybe the commander didn't have the time and resources to investigate the Phoenix Rider sightings, but Veronyka did.

They flew to Vayle the very next day.

Part of the reason the villagers so eagerly wanted their help in construction was for the collection of wood. Most of the trees in Pyra were of the shorter, twisted variety, their crooked branches and knotted boughs poor material for building projects. There were some pockets of taller, straighter trees—likely brought to the region by settlers from Arboria North—including the nearby Silverwood to the south. With phoenixes, they could harvest trees from hours away, carrying the massive logs faster and more easily than they could hope to do by hand and horse-pulled cart. It would save days of time and effort, not to mention allow them to venture to copses of trees they wouldn't normally be able to reach.

Besides aiding in the rebuilding, Tristan's Riders were there to patrol. The first day was mostly setup and organization, but by the second they had begun to settle into a new routine, while Veronyka and Tristan began a routine of their own.

At night, after all their other chores and obligations were finished, they met at the edges of their camp to work on blocking shadow magic.

Spending so much time in each other's company was in some ways counterintuitive—every moment spent together was a moment bonding, literally and magically—but Veronyka needed to tell him what she knew about shadow magic so he could attempt to muster some kind of defense.

Admittedly, her own understanding of the subject was minimal, and even Morra had had nothing to offer on the prospect of teaching a non-shadowmage how to protect themselves, but Veronyka had to try. What she had with Tristan felt strangely territorial, as if she'd marked him as her own and he had no say in the matter. At least the bond between Veronyka and Val was something they both had power over, even if Val had cultivated and manipulated it without Veronyka's knowledge.

Veronyka wondered if bonds often formed between close-knit Riders and mated pairs, but unless one of them was a shadowmage, neither ever became aware of it. To them their link would be an instinct, a feeling . . . a gut reaction, nothing more.

Determined that Tristan should have *some* control of their connection, Veronyka used the concept of the mental safe house—storing unwanted memories or feelings inside an imaginary box at the back of one's mind—which she'd taught Tristan to use to keep his fear of fire in check, and built upon that idea.

But no matter how much Tristan practiced strengthening his mental barriers and blocking his mind, as soon as she touched him or looked into his eyes, the bond between them opened instantly.

Veronyka wondered if she was asking the impossible, if this was as hopeless and unnatural as a Rider attempting to block their bond with their phoenix.

But even if Veronyka couldn't find a way to block their bond, she had to at least find a way to control it. And for the time being, the only way she knew how to do that was to control her relationship with Tristan. They had to avoid the things that triggered their link, from extended time alone together to eye contact and touch. *All* kinds of touch.

She could see—even without their bond—that the prospect of these rigid rules and physical barriers was not something Tristan relished either. In fact, the entire thing would have been devastating, if not for Tristan's very real—and very recent—near-death experience. They *had* to take these precautions seriously, and their best comfort was to remind each other over and over again that these were temporary measures.

Just until the danger with Val passed and Veronyka's mind became a safe space again.

Just until Veronyka got a hold on her magic. Then they'd be able to be themselves again.

Neither of them said the obvious thing, that they had no idea how to make those eventualities happen. Veronyka didn't know if she'd ever be able to control her magic, and she couldn't imagine a world in which she was safe from Val unless Val was no longer in that world at all. She might have deluded herself before, but now, knowing the truth? Val would never let someone as valuable as Veronyka go.

We could save lives, save the world. You and I together could change everything. . . .

Did Val truly mean that? Did she still want them to be together, as she'd always claimed, even after everything that had passed between them? Or did she want to *use* Veronyka for some other purpose? Regardless, Val's sudden silence in Veronyka's mind—she hadn't sensed even a whisper of Val's presence since the relay race—felt like the calm before the storm, and she feared Val would turn up again at the worst possible time. Veronyka had to prepare herself.

The problem was, even without Val inside her head, Veronyka's mind was a confusing, muddled place of late.

Veronyka Ashfire.

Every time her thoughts wandered in the direction of that birth certificate and what it meant, she redirected them with a savage jerk. Even if Veronyka wanted to reveal herself and embrace her bloodline, it wasn't just about her. If she announced that she was an Ashfire, that act alone would push Val to do the same. They were bound by cause and effect, and the last thing Veronyka wanted was to add fuel to the fire of this impending war.

And if she did come forward . . . would anyone believe her? She had proof, but couldn't such things be forged? Even if people did believe her . . . what would happen next? Was she supposed to stroll into Aura Nova and take a seat on the vacant throne? Or worse, would she be expected to fight her way to that position? There was no way the council would want some orphan girl, raised as a peasant in the Narrows, to rule over them, royal bloodline or no. Then again, many of those same council members who would deem Veronyka unfit to rule might just change their tune if the choice was between her and the Feather-Crowned Queen, who'd wreaked years of havoc and had been *reborn* in order to seek her final, bloody vengeance.

In order to bring them all to their knees.

Was Val trying to rope Veronyka into helping her achieve this goal, or was Veronyka just another person to be defeated in the long line to the throne? Was that what Val had meant before the attack on the Eyrie, when she'd told Veronyka she hoped she'd "chosen the right side"? Were they on opposite sides by virtue of the same reason Avalkyra and Pheronia had been on opposite sides . . . because there could only be one? Or had Veronyka's mother been just as hungry to rule as Avalkyra was? Everything Val had ever told Veronyka about Pheronia painted her as someone spineless and weak. . . . But Veronyka had good cause to question that, now that she knew the truth about her sister.

Regardless of what had happened before, Veronyka knew that if she made *any* kind of bid for the throne, there would be blood. There would be war—the Blood War—all over again. So what were her choices? To take the secret to her grave? To stand aside and let Val claim what she'd come back for? Would that act of deference result in *less* death and destruction, or was Veronyka the only thing standing between Val and infinite, reckless power?

And what if Veronyka refused it—refused the identity she didn't want and the role Val forced her to play? That in itself felt more like a real choice than any of the others. Was living her life and refusing to fall into the place Val expected her to its own form of rebellion?

The thoughts were too much for her to wrap her brain around, and she couldn't talk to Tristan about it either. Not only would it counteract their attempts to block their bond, but she was afraid of what he might tell her to do . . . what he might expect of her. She could barely hold her own life together. . . . The idea that she might be expected to lead, to give orders and make decisions, was more than she could currently handle.

But there were other things she could focus on.

The lockbox held more than just her birth certificate, after all. The list of Phoenix Riders in hiding might be just the thing to help them investigate the sightings south of the border. Veronyka didn't know how old the list was, or how recently it had been updated, but it seemed like a good place to start.

If there were unknown, unchecked Phoenix Riders existing in the empire and beyond, the Riders on this list were obvious suspects. And if it wasn't any of them, they still might have information the commander's flock sorely needed.

Besides, the last-known whereabouts of one of the names on the list—Alexiya, Rider of Ximn—was listed as somewhere in the Silverwood. It seemed like a lost opportunity not to at least *try* to seek her out.

It was a risk, but one worth taking. Veronyka couldn't stand being shunted aside and left out of the war. Yes, they were helping the local villagers—and that mattered too—but if she could do more, she would.

The worst that could happen was a fight or a skirmish, but the best? Another ally for their fledgling flock? It was too good a chance to pass up, especially when it might mean taking allies away from the empire. Veronyka relished the idea of recruiting more Riders to their cause, swelling their ranks not just with apprentices and new hatchlings but with fully fledged Riders who had fought in and survived a war.

They'd made camp in the ruins of Malka's outpost again, and Veronyka waited until after dinner before she broached the topic with Tristan. The others—save for Ronyn, who was on patrol—were relaxing around the fire, the early-evening sun sinking below the tree line and casting dappled golden light over the clearing. Tristan was sitting with Lysandro, going over some lists of supplies.

"Tristan? Can I talk to you for a second?" Veronyka asked.

He glanced over his shoulder, squinting slightly into the sun. He opened his mouth, as if to ask for a minute, until he got a proper look at her face. His eyes latched onto hers before he remembered himself and they darted away. He seemed to see or sense that this was about something important, though, and turned back to his cousin. "You can finish this, Lys?" he asked, and Lysandro nodded. He looked quite happy to be deputized and took the sheaf of papers while Tristan stood.

"What's up?" he asked, falling into step beside Veronyka as she walked to the edge of the clearing, past the phoenixes, who were clustered together around fresh fruit the Riders had scattered for their evening meal.

Like usual lately, Veronyka was anxious being alone with Tristan, as if every second together was illicit—never mind that what she was about to propose meant spending even more time in each other's company.

Veronyka waited until they reached a thick, gnarled tree, pausing in its shadow. "I've been thinking . . . about those Phoenix Riders."

"The ones spotted in the south?"

"Yes . . . You remember how I found that birth certificate in the lockbox?"

"Vaguely," Tristan said dryly, leaning against the rough bark and crossing his arms over his chest.

Veronyka smirked before continuing. "And how I found other stuff too?"

Tristan stilled, his relaxed posture turning rigid. "Yes . . ."

Veronyka reached into her pocket. "One of the things I found was a list of Phoenix Riders that survived the war."

She passed it to him, her hands trembling slightly. Fear, excitement, she didn't know which, had sent her nerves to jangling, but whatever it was, she knew she had to act on it. Their skin touched, and she flashed back to the moment Tristan had fallen, limp, from his saddle. A wave of dizzying fear washed over her, and she snatched her hand back. Tristan remained still—perfectly, unnaturally still, and kept his focus on the paper.

"Veronyka," he said on a breath, unfolding the page, his eyes bugging. "This is . . ." He trailed off, and Veronyka understood. They'd thought they were alone in Pyra—in the empire—but apparently they were wrong.

"That hand," Veronyka said, pointing to the smaller, simpler script, "is Ilithya Shadowheart's. That," she said, pointing to the swooping, elegant—yet somehow wilder, less controlled—handwriting, "belongs to Val. *Avalkyra*."

Tristan frowned at the page, and Veronyka studied him. She was surprised at how easy it had been to convince Tristan that Val was indeed Avalkyra. After she'd told him everything she knew about herself and her sister—the memories and the dream visions included—in addition to what Morra had said about resurrections, Tristan had just nodded, slightly stunned. Apparently his Pyraean nursemaid had told him plenty of folktales and local superstitions.

"She and Ilithya must have made this list hoping to find allies," Veronyka continued. "I don't know how many Val went to herself. I think . . ." She trailed off, staring unseeing into the distance. "I think she was ashamed to show herself as she was—young, poor, and without a phoenix. So my *maiora*—Ilithya," she clarified, though she'd already told him about the spy's role in her upbringing, "did it instead. Obviously it didn't work, or Val would have an army of her own by now."

"We should send this to my father," Tristan said, somewhat reluctantly. They weren't on the greatest of terms after Cassian's most recent attempts to keep Tristan out of the loop.

"You heard him," Veronyka said reasonably. "He didn't want to discuss it. And I understand—he's got too much to manage and can't send people flying all over the empire looking for them. But maybe there's another way—a way we could help. Maybe we could do it for him."

"It would be dangerous, Veronyka. They could be the Riders that were spotted in the south. They could be working with the empire."

Veronyka tipped her head in acknowledgment. She knew there was a chance they weren't friendly, but there was also a chance they *were*.

"They *could* be," she conceded. "Or, if we play this right . . . they could be working with us instead."

Do you see the error of my ways yet, my daughter?
You cannot douse a fire by throwing water
at its flames. You have to go to the embers,
the kindling—the beating heart.

- CHAPTER 22 -

AVALKYRA

AVALKYRA SAT ASTRIDE HER phoenix, perched on a rolling hilltop and surveying the distant, winding strip of the Iron Road. It branched west off the Pilgrimage Road, which twisted south toward Aura Nova and north toward Pyra. The Iron Road was named after the ore that gained Ferro its fame and fortune and for the route that had been traveled for centuries, sending Ferronese steel weapons from the forges of Ferro into Aura Nova, then onto riverboats setting out for the rest of the empire.

A merchant caravan bearing just such a shipment currently made its slow progress along that same route, heading east on the Iron Road toward the capital. There were three wagons brimming with short swords, spear tips, and arrowheads, all made of the finest Ferronese steel and coming from Lord Rolan's own personal refineries. As governor of the province, he oversaw all production and approved all shipments, but he also had a personal stake in several mines and their corresponding forges. These weapons belonged to him.

And Avalkyra was about to steal them.

With a soft gust of wind, Sidra landed by her side. "No other travelers on the road, and only ten guards per wagon."

"Only ten?" Avalkyra repeated with a smirk. "Two against thirty is poor odds."

"For them, you mean."

"Yes," Avalkyra said, the blood rising inside her as the lust for battle pulsed through her veins. "For them."

After a few days of much-needed rest and a trip to Ferro, Avalkyra was feeling like herself again. Well, not exactly like herself. Things weren't quite what they had been—her loyal bondmate and full imperial flock of Phoenix Riders had been replaced with a temperamental *bind*mate and a single Phoenix Rider ally, but just a few weeks ago she'd had neither.

She needed to draw Veronyka and the rest of the Phoenix Riders into a war, and doing so with an army of one would have been relatively impossible. So she'd sought alliances. First a servant whose subservience could not be questioned. Then someone with soldiers and wealth and a position of power . . . someone who already had it out for Pyra and the Phoenix Riders.

After Avalkyra found Sidra and put her bind in place, the woman told Avalkyra all she knew about the politics of the day, about the recent attack in Pyra—and even better, the attacks that were allegedly to come. Soldiers had been spotted along the border, soldiers that belonged to none other than Lord Rolan of Stel, governor of Ferro and the man responsible for the first attack on Pyra. Then it was simply a short flight to Ferro, an anonymous bargain, and the pieces of her plan slowly moved into place.

And this was only the beginning. Soon she'd have Veronyka by her side and a crown atop her head.

But first there were things that needed doing.

"Tell me, why are we bothering with this again?" Sidra asked, her voice bored. Avalkyra was reminded of the old days, when they were young and impetuous and would make trouble just for fun, striking fear and intimidation into the hearts of any who would dare challenge Avalkyra and her mighty patrol. "These hapless merchants won't put up much of a fight."

"That's the point."

"An empire city would be far better sport."

"I won't risk injury or capture for *better sport*," Avalkyra said, still amused. "There are only two of us—we couldn't take a city and live to tell not died and come back only to rot away in some empire

 ression flickered, only just concealing a flash of fear. Avalkyra had explained to her—succinctly and with little embellishment—how she had come to be here, nearly seventeen years after her death at the end of the Blood War. Sidra accepted her story, but it was clear the notion unsettled her.

"There could be more," she said after she collected herself. "There are others who might join us, if we asked them. Doriyan fled the capital as well, and I'm quite sure Alexiya, that young Rider who—"

"That's enough," Avalkyra snapped, her good mood evaporating. She told herself her hackles were up because of Sidra's casual insubordination, but she knew it was that cursed name that had her on edge. She clenched her fists, gripping the reins of the spare phoenix saddle Sidra had given her. "You are too free with your opinions, Sidra of Stel."

"Forgive me, my queen."

Sidra bowed her head, chastised, and Avalkyra surveyed her before tightening her hold on the woman's mind, reminding her that she was a servant, a vassal, an agent of Avalkyra's will. Whatever errant thoughts Sidra might have had disappeared like smoke on the wind.

Avalkyra turned her attention back to the convoy, releasing her hold and appearing to forget the confrontation, but her mind continued to mull it over.

Though Sidra had knelt again before her queen and offered herself for the bind, Avalkyra had struggled to put the magical link in place. The original bind she'd put in decades ago had disappeared upon her death, leaving no trace behind, and despite the fact that Sidra's mind was open and unguarded, Avalkyra's magic was weakened with the constant effort it took to keep the ancient firebird beneath her under control.

There was also the link between herself and Veronyka, the connection Avalkyra had fought to keep open in the aftermath of the birth certificate discovery. Veronyka had rebelled against it, but Avalkyra had managed to keep the channel strong all through the night and into the following day.

She knew it would be hard to convince Veronyka to come see her—especially after the shock and betrayal that she was feeling in the face of the startling revelation of who she was. But it was worth trying, worth reminding Veronyka that she was there—always with her, always a bond away.

And when the attacks started to happen in earnest and her precious Commander Cassian *didn't* act or retaliate, she might remember that Avalkyra would. That *they* could. That the rules did not apply to them.

Their bond was stronger than anything Avalkyra had ever had with Nyx, even though Veronyka had spent most her life afraid of her power and unsure how to use it. Imagine if she were bold and fearless with her gift? They'd be inseparable, able to anticipate each other's every thought and feeling. They'd be bound to each other—forget the phoenixes.

They'd be unstoppable.

Avalkyra took a steadying breath. She had to be careful. It was her tenderness to Pheronia, her unwillingness to do what needed to be done, that had been her undoing in her first life.

She couldn't let things with Veronyka get as far as they had with Pheronia. She had to convince Veronyka that they belonged together; if Avalkyra was to remake the past, they must *both* be a part of it.

Avalkyra had to convince Veronyka that if she followed Avalkyra one last time, they could remake not just the past, but the whole world. They could be sister queens. Avalkyra could teach her so much, could walk the halls of the Nest and tell a thousand stories about Pheronia and Avalkyra and about Ashfires long gone.

For now Veronyka's mind was locked tight again, and so Avalkyra had to trust in the other plans she'd made. She would hit Veronyka and the Riders where it hurt, and she would draw them out, one way or another.

Whatever it took, she would have Veronyka by her side again. For the alliance and for the future they'd build together.

Whatever it took.

It was late evening by now, and she and Sidra waited in silence, watching the merchant wagons until they had full cover of darkness. Not for stealth, but rather for showmanship. There was nothing quite so spectacular—or so terrifying—as a fiery phoenix battle at night, and this little attack wasn't a military move or a show of strength. It was a performance, an act, a proclamation to all that the Phoenix Riders were indeed back . . . and they had it out for the empire.

That should have been the truth—the Phoenix Riders *should* have had it out for the empire—but the commander was a pacifist. He'd do whatever he could to avoid open war, which meant Avalkyra and her new allies would have to help the war along. They'd poke and prod, attack and harry at the border—never in open daylight, but at night, so their numbers could be skewed, their existence speculated at. Had it been two or twenty Riders who'd attacked an arms shipment and stolen its wares to fund their own military campaign? No one would know, and it was that uncertainty that would push these coddled empire lords into action.

"This should be quick," Avalkyra said into the darkness. Night had fallen at last. "But not too quick. We need them to spread tales of us."

"Blood and fire?" Sidra asked. It was their old battle cry—a mantra and a promise, repeated before every battle. There was only ever one reply.

"Ashes and ruin," Avalkyra said, and with a flap of wings and a crackle of flame, she made it so.

Day 19, Seventh Moon, 168 AE

Dear Theryn,

If you think there's little glory to be found in war, you're not doing it right. I know you're a soldier, but open a book sometime and tell me how else the heroes of old earned their legacies.

I can't believe you've been sent to fight in the Stellan Uprising but you're stuck babysitting a princess. "Pheronia's fire is warm and her heart is good"? Is this love poetry? If so, it is pitiful. I hope you do not share it with her. Even a spoiled princess shouldn't have to suffer such a verse.

Practice your poetry, Theryn, and leave the spear to me.

Lex

Crops and coffers
weren't my true problem.
Avalkyra Ashfire was.

- CHAPTER 23 -
VERONYKA

VERONYKA AND TRISTAN TOOK to the sky the following evening, before the cover of dark. They reasoned that an exiled Rider in recluse might not welcome visitors in the dead of night. This way they weren't sneaking up on their target but instead announcing themselves as would-be visitors.

Before they left, Tristan explained their errand to his patrol.

As it was, they had one Rider flying the perimeter of the village at all times, and they sent a *trivol* patrol at regular intervals to do a wider sweep of the area. When it was time for the next three-Rider group to leave, Tristan told Anders that he could sit this one out and that Tristan and Veronyka would handle it. He explained that Veronyka knew the area—having lived nearby—and that they intended to scout additional locations for logging.

Anders shrugged and settled back down on the grass next to the fire, while Latham shook his head. Veronyka knew that even though Anders was the one benefiting from the arrangement, Latham didn't miss the way Tristan always seemed to break the rules when it came to her. Veronyka sighed. It didn't matter that she had always tried to be friendly to Latham during their time at the Eyrie or whenever she went out with their patrol; he was plainly uninterested, and probably disliked her for the same reason some of the others did—because she had lied and for her closeness with

Tristan. So she brushed it off as best she could, reminding herself that what they were doing was more important than whatever resentment Latham held toward her.

Despite their excuse, Veronyka didn't know much about the Silverwood and had never actually been there. Luckily, Tristan had a variety of maps of the region, and they were able to quickly chart a course to the southeast.

Veronyka's hands shook for the entire flight. Her adrenaline was shooting through her veins like lightning. Of all the things that excited her about meeting an exiled Rider, she had to admit that very near the top of the list was the fact that the Rider they sought was a woman. Yes, there were female apprentices among their ranks at the Eyrie now, but Veronyka had never seen a female Master Rider before. Something in her heart caught fire at the idea of meeting someone who truly looked like the ancient queens of old.

Someone who looked like her.

Once they arrived at the edge of the Silverwood, they flew in sweeps, seeking cabins, caves, or any sign of habitation.

Veronyka felt the pressure to hurry; the sun was sinking below the hills in the distance, and soon they'd be unable to discern much in the shadows of the forest.

Out of nowhere, an arrow shaft whizzed past her and Xephyra as they swept low through a clearing. Her heart leapt into her throat as she followed its progress, her neck jerking to the side as it embedded itself into a tree with an echoing thud. Xephyra let out a burst of heat and sparks in response, and as Veronyka twisted in her saddle, looking back, a pair of eyes reflected her phoenix's light from the darkness of the tree canopy.

Veronyka's ears were ringing, but she told Xephyra to circle back around. That arrow had been fletched with red and purple feathers. Phoenix feathers. *This is who we're looking for.*

Though Veronyka had known this Rider might be an enemy, if she'd truly meant Veronyka harm, that arrow would be embedded in her chest, not a tree. This arrow had been a warning shot meant to draw their attention— not to actually hit them.

Still, her breath was shallow and uneven as she realized how differently things might have turned out, but Tristan was approaching fast—he must have heard the sound of the arrowhead striking the tree—and Veronyka hastened to wave him off, signaling for him to stop his pursuit and slow his pace. She was in no danger. At least, she didn't think so.

Xephyra landed in the clearing below and Veronyka dismounted, neck craned up at the trees. Tristan landed soon after, mouth set in a tight line, and reached for his bow. Veronyka gripped his arm—then released it at once. Why was it so hard to remember not to touch him? When he looked at her, she shook her head in warning instead. They were the trespassers here, and if they arrived bearing weapons, Veronyka feared their visit would end before it even began.

"Smart move," came a deep, silken voice from somewhere above.

They both froze and looked skyward, where the branches were so thick and dense that they could hardly see the sky. There was the barest sound, the scrape of boots on bark, but Veronyka couldn't actually see the woman.

"You draw that bow, *phoenixaemi*, and it'll be the last thing you do," she said, the words as slow and smooth as a caress. While *phoenixaeris* was the term for a "phoenix master," *phoenixaemi* translated roughly to "phoenix friend." It was usually meant to indicate apprentices or young, untested Riders, and carried with it the hint of derision or condescension—especially since Tristan was already a Master Rider.

"We mean you no harm," Veronyka said, stepping out of reach of the weapons strapped to Xephyra's saddle and indicating with a nod that Tristan should do the same. She raised her hands, showing she was unarmed.

There was a rustle, nearer at hand, and the woman appeared, crouched on a thick branch. She looked completely at ease, as comfortable in the soaring treetops as a wildcat.

"Baby Riders, here all alone," she crooned. "What makes you think I don't mean harm to you?" she asked, tilting her head to study them.

Veronyka licked her lips. She pointed in the direction of the tree where the woman had embedded her warning arrow mere moments before. "You already had a chance—you didn't take it. We just want to talk."

"Maybe I don't want to talk," she said, before swinging her weight down from the branch, hanging from her hands before dropping lightly to her feet. She approached them slowly, appraisingly, circling the pair of them like a hunter stalking its prey. She was startlingly beautiful, her long inky hair filled with braids and feathers and chunks of shining obsidian, the dozens of plaits threaded into a single, thicker braid that ran down her back. Her skin was brown like Veronyka's, but with cool, almost metallic undertones, making her look at home among the icy leaves of the Silverwood.

"We're older than you were when you flew your first mission," Veronyka said, her heart thumping wildly. "You are Alexiya, aren't you? My name is Veronyka, and this is Tristan."

The woman finished her circuit, coming to a stop directly in front of Veronyka, though her eyes lingered on Tristan. There was something curious and intent in her gaze that made Veronyka's stomach clench.

Ignoring the attempt at instructions, the woman fixed her glittering dark eyes on Veronyka. "Who sent you?"

"No one—we sent ourselves."

"How did you find me?"

Veronyka figured honesty was the best option—at least for now. "Ilithya Shadowheart."

Her entire body stilled at the name. "Is she coming as well?" she asked.

Veronyka shook her head, unable to mask the sadness on her face. "I— she's gone. Ilithya is gone."

"Then why do you do a dead woman's work?" she asked, and Veronyka suspected she was doing fishing of her own. "Surely you have better things to do—other battles to fight?"

"What do you know about our battles?" Veronyka asked, studying the woman's face for her reaction.

Her voice was unapologetic when she said, "I know you're fighting one you cannot win."

Veronyka bristled. "Is that why you're in hiding? Unwilling to fight if you know you might lose? Or have you thrown your lot in elsewhere?"

Veronyka's accusation of cowardice elicited little more than a clenched jaw and narrowed eyes, but the last words Veronyka spoke caused a chink in her impassive demeanor.

"Elsewhere?" she asked, frowning. She seemed genuinely puzzled, which went a long way to calming Veronyka's anger—and her anxiety. Whatever this woman was, Veronyka doubted she was allied with Lord Rolan or the empire.

The woman stared at them both, and when they didn't elaborate, she sighed.

"Very well then," she said, looking up at the patches of visible sky, gone purple and turquoise in the twilight. "It is getting dark. Your bondmates may follow through the air, but you will come with me."

"I don't make a habit of following nameless people to unknown locations," Veronyka said, arms crossed.

The woman smiled at her stubborn stance and shook her head, yielding at last. "You win, *impyr*. My name is Alexiya—as you well know. Now come." Then she disappeared into the shadow of the trees.

Veronyka hesitated, her victory marred with confusion. She frowned at Tristan. *Impyr* . . . she'd never heard that word before.

"It means 'little fire,'" he explained, properly reading her expression. "It was part of a song my nursemaid used to sing."

"Oh," Veronyka muttered as they sent their phoenixes to the sky and prepared to follow on foot.

She couldn't decide if it was meant as a compliment or an insult.

Alexiya melted into the forest, soundless, invisible as she darted between the thick, towering trunks. Veronyka and Tristan struggled to keep up, tripping over undergrowth and tangled, gnarled roots.

It was intensely silent among the ranks of the Silverwood, as if even the animals didn't dare to dwell here anymore. It had once been home to several smaller villages, but they had been abandoned. Just as the tall, dark trees concealed their own careful treads, so too did they conceal the footsteps of empire soldiers. The Silverwood became an alternate route into Pyra during the Blood War. It was traversed by countless regiments of empire soldiers in search of Avalkyra Ashfire's base, and any locals who didn't want to be caught in the crossfire were forced to flee.

Veronyka could feel the emptiness of this place—haunted by war—and it made a shiver slip down her spine. Above, Xephyra and Rex flew close to the canopy, though the gathering dark of night likely concealed their flight regardless.

Ahead, Alexiya stopped in front of a massive, towering trunk. She was nothing more than a shifting shadow in the dense darkness of the forest, but the barest light sparked and glimmered off the obsidian in her hair. To Veronyka's confusion, she began to climb. As Veronyka stepped up behind her, a ladder materialized out of the shadows, carved into the living wood. Craning her neck, Veronyka looked up, but she couldn't discern anything in the gloom.

She began to climb, Tristan behind her, and the higher they went, the more of the twilight crept in—or perhaps Veronyka's eyes were finally adjusting—slowly revealing planks of smooth, planed wood overhead. Veronyka climbed through a square opening in the boards, up into a world of frosted moonlight. They were near the tops of the trees, still protected by their thick foliage but able to see wide vistas on either side. To the west, the sky bled from magenta to violet, while to the east, inky darkness spread like a stain, obliterating all but the stars.

When Veronyka drew her gaze lower, a gasp escaped her lips. Despite the coming night, the last breath of the sun revealed a series of rope bridges extending from where they stood, like the Fingers from the Godshand in the valley. She was standing on a platform, closed in on all sides by a wooden railing, while the swaying footpaths connected five, six—ten wooden houses, built into the trees.

Veronyka had heard tell of such places in Arboria North, where the trees were twice the size of those that surrounded them, but she'd had no idea they'd made it into Pyra.

tood next to her, his face lit with the same wonder.

he houses appearing intact, not a single lantern flicker or titter .. ouund reached them. It appeared that, just as Veronyka had heard, these villages were abandoned.

"This way," said Alexiya, standing near the corner of the railing and making them jump. The platform was like the central hub for the rest of the paths, wrapping around the tree they'd climbed. Alexiya led them across one of the narrower bridges, and Veronyka traversed the swinging, swaying ropes with mild trepidation. There were waist-high handrails—which Alexiya completely ignored—while underfoot, short wooden planks were tied tightly together. Many were missing, and the failing light meant that Veronyka felt her way more than saw it.

By the time they reached the other end, Veronyka sensed, then saw, Xephyra and Rex circling in the wide-open space above. Alexiya, meanwhile, was standing within the doorway of a small house, so overgrown with leaves and vines that it was nearly invisible.

Before Tristan and Veronyka could step from the shaking bridge, however, a squawking, flapping shadow separated itself from the darkness above Alexiya's house.

The phoenix landed on the bridge directly before Veronyka, wings wide, causing her to stagger back into Tristan. Sparks puffed into the air, while the bird flapped frantically, as if seeking purchase on the rippling, wobbling bridge.

Above, Xephyra sensed Veronyka's alarm and screeched, preparing to dive, while Alexiya stepped forward and shoved exasperatedly at the phoenix's neck.

"Down, you ridiculous creature," she said, and the phoenix—a female called Ximn, Veronyka recalled from the exiled Rider list—allowed herself to be pushed from the bridge, falling for a moment only to extend her wings and loop back around in dizzying, erratic spirals. She bobbed up over the bridge again, chirruping at Veronyka and Tristan before darting out of Alexiya's grasp, only to zoom underneath and pop up on the other side.

Veronyka laughed, her initial fear gone. The phoenix was like a puppy deprived of company for too long and eagerly greeting her master—and her new friends—at the door.

Xephyra landed on the roof of the house, cocking her head curiously at Ximn, who landed next to her. Xephyra was wearing her haughtiest expression, neck tall and chest feathers puffed out, though the effect was somewhat marred by the way the other phoenix edged closer and closer before nipping playfully at Xephyra's feet. It didn't take long before the phoenixes were chasing and snapping at each other in the open space below the bridge, while Rex busied himself crunching on whatever food Alexiya had put atop the roof of the house for her bondmate.

"Shall we?" Alexiya said, laughter lightening her features. She pulled aside a curtain, and Tristan and Veronyka stepped inside the house. There was a snap and a hiss as Alexiya lit a series of lanterns, and Veronyka took in their surroundings as they slowly appeared in the lamplight.

The wood was definitely treated with some kind of stain or lacquer—maybe even the fire-resistant *pyraflora* resin the Riders favored—making the walls gleam molten in the flickering orange light. Despite the silver-gray exterior, the interior of the house was rich with color and texture, with soft layered rugs underfoot, shelves of shining pottery and assorted tools, and an impressive stash of weapons mounted on the far wall, including an obsidian-tipped spear, a twin-bladed battle-ax with leather grip and matching hatchet, and a sheathed short sword of the sort preferred by the foot soldiers of the empire.

The place was cozy and inviting, and beyond the main chamber was a connected set of rooms that appeared to be for sleeping. Cooking in villages like this could be tricky, and Veronyka suspected they had a single communal cookhouse, carefully guarded and protected against fire.

A squawk echoed from outside, and Alexiya shook her head. "Ximn," she said ruefully, gesturing that they should sit on the pile of plush cushions that were stacked in the opposite corner. She busied herself removing her bow and quiver of arrows and hanging them on the wall with the other weapons before gathering a set of three mismatched ceramic cups and a pitcher. "I'd like to say it's the seclusion that's made her so rambunctious, but she was always that way, even from an egg."

Veronyka considered the words, adding further evidence to the probability that Alexiya wasn't one of the Riders colluding with the empire. If she'd been flying in and around Ferro, she wouldn't be suffering from "seclusion," would she? And Sev had seen two Phoenix Riders, according to the commander.

Something about the phoenix's arrival had broken the tension between them, and Veronyka took the cup Alexiya offered as she settled opposite them on a short stool, resting her feet on an overturned bucket.

"And here I thought Xephyra was precocious," Veronyka said, taking a cautious sip—it was watered wine, sweetened with honey. "She never listened to a word I said in the beginning."

"That's the way it ought to be," Alexiya said. "A docile phoenix is a phoenix with a broken spirit. They're not like horses to be bent to our will."

Veronyka's impression of the woman soared, and she straightened slightly in her seat. Next to her, Tristan was eyeing Alexiya's weapons; meanwhile, Alexiya eyed *him*. Veronyka's good feelings dissipated.

"How did you find this place?" Tristan asked, unaware of Alexiya's intense interest. "I'd heard of the villages in the Silverwood but wouldn't have thought to look up."

"Well, that's the Arboria in me," she said, leaning back against the wall and staring up at the ceiling. "Stargazers, every one. At least, that's what Dad always said. We left Arboria when I was recruited."

"You left?" Veronyka asked, momentarily distracted. "Why?"

Alexiya shot her a lazy smile, though there was real hurt in her eyes. "Arborians like animages just fine—but *Phoenix Riders*, not so much." Veronyka frowned at that, and Alexiya explained. "Firebirds aren't a welcome sight in Arboria, the Land of Wood."

The literal translation of Arboria was the Land of *Trees*, but Alexiya had a valid point. Great swaths of forest covered almost the entirety of

Arboria North and quite a large amount of Arboria South. That, coupled with their use of treetop homes built entirely of wood, and Veronyka could understand how a bird made of fire might cause something of a panic. One phoenix in full flame could devastate the province. "Mom preferred her home and her son over her daughter and her husband, so Dad and I came to his homeland, Pyra. Still, I always missed my treetop bedroom, and sleeping so close to the stars."

Silence followed, and Alexiya continued to study Tristan over the rim of her cup.

Something about the way she stared at him made Veronyka uneasy. *Not because she's wildly beautiful,* she reassured herself. And definitely not because Veronyka was jealous. It was protectiveness, she was sure.

Mostly sure.

"I'm sorry we turned up like this," Veronyka said. "But, well—we *are* fighting battles, on multiple fronts. Unless you're living in complete isolation, I'm sure you've heard what happened by now. Empire soldiers, posing as raiders, slipped into Pyra and attacked Azurec's Eyrie, as well as some of the other villages, including Vayle."

"I heard." She paused, knuckles tightening on the handle of the pitcher before she put it aside. "We were on a hunting trip when it happened." Her expression went unfocused, and then she gazed down, as if through the floor. "They'd have slipped through the trees on their way back to the empire. They'd have passed right underneath me, if I were here. . . ." She lifted her face and stared at the wall of weapons.

Was that fear in her voice, for how close she'd come to being surrounded by soldiers—or regret that she'd missed the chance to fight them?

"I can't get into the details," Veronyka continued, "but we have reason to believe that those attacks were only the beginning."

Alexiya didn't react, just took up the pitcher and refilled her cup before settling back into her seat. "Does that *reason* have anything to do with the ranks of soldiers lining up along the border to Ferro?"

Tristan stiffened beside her, as if Alexiya's brusque tone were a matter of concern—but not to Veronyka. To her, this was a good sign. It meant Alexiya wasn't completely closed off and disinterested. It meant she still cared. But where she'd gotten that information felt equally important.

"How do you know about that? Do you often travel south?" she asked idly, though Alexiya's eyes narrowed—she could sense there was more to the question. Even if Alexiya wasn't one of the Riders that had been spotted in the empire, if she was in contact with those who had, she could still be dangerous.

"Travelers. Traders. I visit Runnet from time to time. I'd have to be a fool to fly farther south than that. Or have a death wish. Why?"

Veronyka glanced at Tristan but saw no reason to lie at this point. She didn't believe Alexiya was on Lord Rolan's side, and that meant they needed her to be on theirs. "Phoenix Riders have been sighted in the empire again . . . in Ferro. They were meeting with the governor, who happens to be the man responsible for the attacks on Pyra."

"Phoenix *Riders*, plural?" she asked.

Veronyka nodded. "Any guesses who they might be?"

Alexiya's lips twisted into a tight smile. "I have a couple."

"I know there are others in hiding," Veronyka continued. "Other survivors. I understand if you want to protect their privacy. . . ."

Alexiya snorted. "I know of only two other Riders who are in hiding, and I'd sooner see them dead than *protected*."

"Who?" Veronyka asked softly.

"Two of the *wilder* members of Avalkyra's patrol," Alexiya said with an airy hand. "Sidra of Stel and Doriyan—born in Rushlea. They had a bit of a reputation."

"For what?" Veronyka pressed, hands clenched. Sidra and Doriyan . . . they were two of the other Riders on Ilithya's list. If Alexiya wasn't one of the Phoenix Riders spotted in Ferro, it *might* have been them.

Alexiya shrugged, though for the first time she looked a bit uncomfortable. She shook her head. "Dark stuff. Whatever it was, they always did it together."

"A mated pair?" Tristan asked, but Alexiya shook her head.

"They liked each other well enough but were devoted entirely to Avalkyra Ashfire. It's what she demanded of her patrol."

Veronyka was reminded of what Morra had said, that Avalkyra might have used shadow magic on them.

"Was one of them Avalkyra's second?" Veronyka asked, struck suddenly by the question. It was hard to imagine her with a trusted companion—with anyone at all.

"She flew solo, *always*," Alexiya scoffed. "Maybe if her sister had had a phoenix, they'd have flown together, and Pheronia could have been her second-in-command. But of course, she did not. I wonder how much bloodshed might have been prevented if that girl had been an animage. . . . Then again, maybe there'd have been twice as much."

The thoughts echoed those that Veronyka had had about herself and Val, and she couldn't help the way her heart raced at the sudden mention of Pheronia. Her mother.

"I suppose she managed well enough even without the magic."

"What do you mean?" Veronyka asked somewhat breathlessly. She sensed Tristan staring at her face, but she ignored him.

"Pheronia wasn't the good little princess the council made her out to be, and she caused plenty of trouble on her own. She had a streak of defiance in her—she was an Ashfire, after all, and did what she wanted," Alexiya said, shaking her head. "Avalkyra tried to shut her away safely during the Stellan Uprising, and what did she do? Snuck out every night and worked in the medical tent. Avalkyra was all obstinance and blunt force, but Pheronia . . . she was charming and charismatic. She didn't have to force people to follow her. . . . They just did."

Veronyka drank in every drop of what Alexiya said. "You knew them?" she asked softly, afraid to bring Alexiya back to the present.

"Not really. I was too young to serve in the Stellan Uprising, but I heard rumors from the soldiers stationed there. I knew one of Pheronia's personal guards . . . ," she said, then cleared her throat, draining her cup.

"I fought for Avalkyra in the Blood War, like all the rest of us."

Us. Phoenix Riders. Alexiya's expression was bleak.

Veronyka had read the notes next to Alexiya's name on the exiled Rider list, including the details of her service to the empire and to Avalkyra Ashfire. Alexiya had been barely more than a child herself when the war began and had fled the empire before she was officially named a Master Rider. She'd participated in over a dozen skirmishes and battles, earning her place among their elite fighters, and had been the sole survivor of an empire raid on Runnet.

"This is why we're here—we want to protect Pyra and to protect the innocent people caught in the crossfire. To make sure what happened in Runnet never happens again."

Alexiya's dark eyes slid out of focus, hovering on a place in the middle distance—on nothing and everything. On past and present.

Runnet had once been the capital of Pyra. When the province separated, the town was too near the border to properly defend, though Avalkyra Ashfire did try, for a time.

When the empire sent a thousand soldiers marching down the Pilgrimage Road into Pyra, they easily overwhelmed the border town's defenses and slaughtered every last Phoenix Rider they could find, dragging them from the sky with nets and spearing them to the ground. Buildings were ransacked, crops and livestock burned.

Alexiya, fifteen at the time, was the only Rider to survive.

"We lost more than a *town* that day, baby Riders. *I* lost more. Their names are burned into my memory forever, and their faces . . . ," she said, then stopped, swallowing thickly. "I saw them all die."

Veronyka thought back to the battle at the Eyrie. So much death, so much blood and horror. And they had been *lucky*—they had survived, and ultimately, they had won the battle. But the memory of it was something she tried to keep at bay. It had, she realized, inadvertently made its way into her mental safe house, along with what Val had done to Xephyra. Some things were easier to forget than they were to remember.

"I'm sorry," Veronyka said, and she truly meant it. "I understand that when Ilithya came, you weren't interested in—"

"Weren't interested in what?" Alexiya demanded, removing her feet from the bucket and leaning forward. "In restarting the war that destroyed the Phoenix Riders and all but condemned animages across the empire to bondage? Do you think I'm proud of the devastation we wrought? That I want to take up Avalkyra Ashfire's flag and finish the job? Ilithya was talking madness when she came here, as bad as any half-copper gossip on an Aura Nova street corner. 'Avalkyra Ashfire lives; the bloodline isn't broken.'" Alexiya shook her head in disgust. "Everyone in the empire was absolutely certain they'd found some long-lost Ashfire, seeking for any advantage, any excuse to take the throne in some child's name."

Tristan's tension was a palpable force, pushing on the barriers of Veronyka's mind, but Alexiya didn't notice.

"We all know the Ashfire dynasty was barely clinging on *before* the war," Alexiya said. "King Aryk was called 'the Unlikely' for a reason; he was never meant to rule, and the line was almost wiped out entirely thanks to phoenix fever."

Veronyka had already noted this in her study of Commander Cassian's books—how the Ashfire line had slowly thinned over time. King Aryk, Avalkyra's father—Veronyka's grandfather—had inherited the throne from his sister, Queen Bellonya, when she and his two older siblings died. She'd had two daughters, but they'd died in infancy, and so the line had diverted. There were surely distant Ashfire cousins spread throughout the empire, descended from one of the other Five Brides, yet Elysia's line was all but gone. Besides, whatever others with Ashfire blood who still existed would have been raised so far from the throne that they'd have trouble gaining support. Just like Veronyka.

"We're not here for any of that—we're here for the people of Pyra."

"Who's this 'we' you keep speaking of? What about his father?" she asked, nodding her chin at Tristan.

He stared at her, a bit too slow in wiping the look of surprise from his face.

"What do you know about his father?" Veronyka demanded.

Alexiya snorted. "*Lord* Cassian, exiled governor of Ferro and current commander of the Phoenix Riders of Azurec's Eyrie?"

Veronyka swallowed. Apparently quite a bit.

"I could see it on you the moment you arrived," she said to Tristan, straightening her legs and leaning back against the wall. "Though I must say, I prefer the look of the son over the father. There's a splash of Pyra in him, and he's got some of Olanna's wild beauty."

Though she spoke about Tristan, her eyes were on Veronyka, a subtle smile playing on her lips. Veronyka suspected Alexiya saw a hint of what was between them and was enjoying needling them both. But then her expression turned thoughtful, her gaze searching.

"You, on the other hand . . . ," she murmured, eyes narrowing as they roved Veronyka's face, "I cannot place."

Terror flared up inside Veronyka. Alexiya had said she didn't know Pheronia or Avalkyra, but that didn't mean she hadn't seen their faces. And that their faces didn't look even a tiny bit like Veronyka's face.

"So, will you help us?" Veronyka blurted before Alexiya could spot another family connection.

"How?" Alexiya said, forgetting her intense scrutiny and dismissing Veronyka's words with a shrug. "The three of us are no army. Even your 'army' up at the Eyrie is no army. So what can we possibly do?"

"Protect the people," Veronyka said simply. "There's . . ."

She trailed off. A waft of smoke had reached her nostrils, and it wasn't the smell of burning wick and oil coming from Alexiya's lanterns.

It was the smell of wood. Green, living wood—the kind that gave off dense, choking smoke.

"What—" Tristan began, but then Alexiya was on her feet. She marched into one of the back rooms, which had a hatch that opened onto the roof. She was outside before Veronyka even fully entered the room, leaving moonlight spilling in from the opening and illuminating a short ladder. She and Tristan hastened to follow.

The roof above was conical, and Alexiya climbed to the summit before turning her gaze south. Veronyka followed her, and on the far side of the roof, Xephyra and the other phoenixes lifted their heads.

The landscape was dotted with distant, flickering pulses of light—fires, burning in the Silverwood. Veronyka thought of their earlier discussion about firebirds in the Land of Trees, and her heart clenched.

"What is it?" she found herself asking, though she already knew. One fire might be an accident—a lantern knocked over or a cook fire gotten out of control—but five, six . . . seven of them?

"It's an attack," Tristan said, stunned. "But *who* are they attacking? I thought no one lived here anymore."

"There are some small communities living at the edge of the Foothills," Alexiya said, her voice strange and distant. "They trade north and south of the border, mostly to places that don't see a lot of travelers."

"But why the fires? Do they mean to set the entire Silverwood ablaze?" Tristan demanded. "What's the point?"

"To make it look like Phoenix Riders did it," Veronyka said, casting a look at Alexiya to see her response.

She didn't argue.

"We need to get there," Veronyka said, tugging Tristan's arm. "Now."

She thought of the rest of Tristan's patrol—close, but not close enough to get there in time. Only minutes had passed, and already the fires were brighter, the scent of smoke almost stifling, even in the open air.

"Will you help us?" Veronyka asked Alexiya, as Tristan shuffled down the other side of the roof to mount Rex. He lifted the horn strapped to his saddle and blew—but they both knew his patrol was out of range. They were on their own.

Alexiya was rigid at the roof's apex. She looked down when Veronyka spoke but made no answer.

"They used to say one Phoenix Rider was worth fifty soldiers," Veronyka said as Tristan called her name and Xephyra shook out her wings, ready for a fight. "Let's prove it."

Shine now, little fire, the day is cold.
Shine now, little fire, the night is dark.
Shine now, little fire, in time you'll grow.
Shine now, little fire, and before long,
you'll be a little fire no more.

—Pyraean nursery rhyme

If I'd had the strength to confront Avalkyra,
I could have stopped a war. But instead I shielded my eyes,
unable to face my sister, my rival—my brightest sun—
until it was too late.

- CHAPTER 24 -
TRISTAN

DESPITE A FLICKER OF something in her eye, Alexiya didn't move at Veronyka's words. Didn't speak or react.

"Come on," Tristan called to Veronyka, fighting his own sinking disappointment. His mind was going a mile a minute—were these Rolan's soldiers too, or did he have other allies supporting his warmongering?—but he pushed his worries aside and focused. Flying was difficult for phoenixes in such tight quarters, with dense foliage and crisscrossing branches obscuring their wingbeats and their sight lines. Not to mention that phoenixes *ignited* during battle, and to do so here could have devastating consequences.

Of course, the fires already burned. That old fear reared up inside, rising in his chest and pressing onto his lungs.

"We need to get eyes on what's happening down there," Tristan said as Veronyka left Alexiya and climbed into Xephyra's saddle.

"We'll have to stay above the trees for now," Veronyka said, "and mirror for best visibility."

They flew toward the cluster of fires in the distance, Veronyka veering slightly west and Tristan east, hopefully giving them a full picture of what was happening below.

It wasn't good. Once Tristan mirrored with Rex, his vision grew better in the darkness. There were houses built among the roots of the towering trees at the edge of a clearing. Already some of the homes were burning, the inhabitants dark shadows running this way and that, screaming in fear and crying out for loved ones. The soldiers were easier to follow, most of them carrying torches and burning as they went.

Tristan swooped back around and sought Veronyka across the dark expanse of the sky. Her expression was bleak but determined as they brought their phoenixes together above the fray.

"Most of the villagers are running west," Veronyka said, pointing back the way she'd come. "I'll do what I can to steer them north. If we can get them to Alexiya's village . . ."

"They can take refuge in the tree houses," Tristan said. "We'll have a far easier time protecting them up there. And trunks that thick won't burn down easily."

Veronyka nodded. "Once they're out of reach of the soldiers, we can send for help."

"I'll try to cut off pursuit," Tristan said, wheeling Rex back around. He frowned. It would be ideal if they were a patrol of three—as they *should* have been if he hadn't left Anders behind and as they *could* have been if Alexiya had joined them. Tristan shook the thoughts aside—that didn't matter now. He and Veronyka would do what they could.

With one final look at each other—a lingering look that they shouldn't have shared if they were going to break this bond between them—they separated. Even as he dove among the trees, drawing his bow and nocking an arrow, a part of Tristan stayed with Veronyka. It had been this way since the attack on the Eyrie. Tristan always felt her presence, some awareness of her when she walked into a room or stepped up behind him, and he was coming to realize that it might have been the bond between them all this time. That even though he had no shadow magic, some part of him sensed its presence.

And that same part of him hated the idea of letting it go.

Tristan sighted several soldiers and loosed his arrows without lighting them. Rex was growing hot beneath him but was doing his best to keep his flames in check. Tristan felt his fear stirring, the part of him that hated fire—even the potential of it, the scent of it on his bondmate's feathers. But he fought the feeling back as he had learned to do before, focusing his mind on the mental safe house that Veronyka had help him build. The tremor in his hand ceased, and he drew another arrow.

Now that he'd hit a few soldiers, the others had noticed him—and those who hadn't, Rex alerted with a fierce, echoing shriek. Tristan wanted to draw as much attention as he could from the fleeing villagers and Veronyka, whom he could still see in the distance, flying low among the trees. Xephyra was emitting a soft glow, meant to act as a beacon for those who tripped and stumbled and struggled to find their way. Once she got the villagers to Alexiya's village and climbing the ladders, Tristan would join her, and together they could properly defend the entire group. The high ground was always ideal in a fight—especially a Phoenix Rider fight—and the soldiers would have difficulty reaching their targets, even with crossbows, if they were fifty feet above and protected by wooden platforms and thick walls.

While Tristan continued to loose arrows, he had to be cautious. Villagers were mixed in among the soldiers, and he had to hold his shot more than once because there were civilians in the way. Instead he nudged Rex to try diving directly at the soldiers, causing some to scatter and release their grip on the people they'd been terrorizing or dragging along in their wake.

He was just swooping around for another dive when a scream drew his attention to Veronyka and the escaping villagers.

Some soldiers had gotten behind him and were trying to drag the stragglers back, causing one of them to cry out in fear. He flew hard, Rex weaving between the low-hanging branches, and rather than Tristan firing arrows, Rex extended his claws and pulled up two soldiers by his talons before tossing them roughly aside. But even as the attackers at the end of the line scattered, a dozen more appeared out of the darkness, descending on the front of the line and blocking their escape.

They were surrounded.

The fires that were burning nearby were growing and spreading too, licking across the dry underbrush and climbing up the trees, the heat a palpable weight at Tristan's back. The smoke was becoming thick, clawing at his throat and making his eyes water as he tried to think.

He either had to abandon the back of the line and join Veronyka to fight their way forward, or he and Rex had to stay as they were, defending their position but unlikely to get a better one. Tristan did a hasty count—they'd run out of arrows before they killed all these soldiers, and then what? Their phoenixes would have to ignite and make more fire—fire they couldn't control or hope to rein in once it was let loose inside the dense forest. All would be ash and smoke, and the soldiers wouldn't be the only casualties.

Tristan nocked another arrow, but when he didn't release it, the soldiers grew bolder. Two separated from the pack, crossbows raised—and dropped before Tristan could aim his bow.

A battle cry rent the night, and Tristan looked up in surprise.

Alexiya descended from the darkness above, mounted on Ximn. She fired arrows with such rapid-fire precision that Tristan was struck momentarily frozen, watching as she took down half a dozen soldiers before he'd even realized what was happening.

Ximn landed, and Alexiya leapt from her saddle, firing two more arrows before swinging her bow around to knock one soldier to the ground, then pulling a dagger out of her belt to dispatch another.

The rest of the soldiers drew back as Ximn took flight again, swooping and diving around the cluster of villagers, creating a temporary barrier and snapping or clawing at any who drew too close. It was clear she, unlike Rex and Xephyra, was familiar with flying in the tight quarters of the Silverwood.

Alexiya nodded at Tristan, then gave a longer look to Veronyka—an acknowledgment of her alliance, of her choice to fight with them.

"This way," Alexiya shouted, pitching her voice for the villagers to hear and pointing just beyond the nearest trees. "There's a bunker in that low hill. Get your people inside and barricade the door." She turned to Veronyka and Tristan, who had flown over to meet her. "Come, together we'll—"

"We're not leaving them alone," Veronyka said, cutting her off. She glanced around at the villagers, who were coughing and holding one another, clearly frightened and confused and wary of the fires that pressed in on all sides.

Alexiya's face hardened. "The soldiers—the fires," she countered, but Veronyka shook her head.

"The people first. You know where the bunker is—you lead them."

Tristan stared, surprised—and impressed—that Veronyka had the confidence to order around a seasoned war vet like Alexiya. The two stared at each other, and Tristan was struck by the thought of Veronyka in the future, as beautiful as Alexiya, with braided hair trailing down her back, shimmering with twice as many trophies and symbols of excellence as Alexiya had.

And in that vision, she wore a crown.

Alexiya tilted her head a fraction of an inch, and then, to Tristan's surprise, she smiled.

"I will lead the villagers to safety. Give pursuit, if you can," Alexiya said, as Ximn came to land next to her. The soldiers had mostly scattered at this point, apparently unwilling to face off against the three Phoenix Riders, not to mention the growing flames. "But focus your attention on the fires. We need to smother the flames."

She leapt into the saddle, and Ximn took to the sky to hover in front of them.

Smother the flames? Tristan frowned and cast a curious look at Veronyka, who looked equally puzzled.

Alexiya's lips twisted into a sardonic smile. "Baby Riders," she muttered, somewhat indulgently. "Trust your bondmates—they'll know what to do."

Then she was off, calling out for the villagers to follow her, Ximn glowing faintly to light the way.

Veronyka and Tristan directed their phoenixes away from the villagers, keeping a wary eye out for soldiers who might have tried to circle around, but there were none. The fires burned so bright now that there were few places to hide, and the heat was sweltering.

It took all the strength Tristan possessed to fly *into* the flames instead of away from them, but he trusted his mental safe house and he trusted Veronyka, flying a few paces in front. It occurred to him that as patrol leader, he should be the one leading the charge. Maybe Veronyka recognized that facing fire like this would be hard for Tristan. Or maybe leadership was her natural state. It was in her blood, after all.

When they drew close to the heart of the nearest fires—the burning houses—Rex slowed down, copying Xephyra, and told Tristan to dismount through the bond.

Rex—what do you mean? Tristan asked, remaining in the saddle just long enough for Rex to try to buck him off impatiently. "Okay, okay," Tristan muttered, sliding off his phoenix's back and stumbling to the ground.

Saddle, Rex pressed, and Tristan hurried forward to fumble with the straps, just as Veronyka did beside him. As soon as the leather seat was off his back, Rex took to the air once more.

Tristan and Veronyka stood and watched, dumbfounded, as Rex and Xephyra flew into the burning, blistering flames. Yes, they were phoenixes—they could make fire hotter than this—but that came from their own bodies. This was harder to watch—harder to understand.

When Rex disappeared into the molten blue center of a nearby fire, Tristan took an unconscious step forward—something he never thought he'd be able to do. But to see Rex vanish like that . . . Tristan's heart thudded and his breath grew thin.

But as he watched, the fire diminished, its licking flames shrinking, drawing in on themselves, until Tristan could see Rex again. He was in the center of it all, but rather than seeing the fire explode outward from his feathers—as Tristan had seen time and time again—Rex was drawing the fire inward. He was absorbing it, making it a part of himself, and then stifling its power.

Xephyra was doing the same to another smoldering fire, and Tristan and Veronyka shared a look of complete and utter wonder.

"I didn't know a phoenix could do that," Veronyka said, her voice oddly hushed—as if they were in the presence of something divine and miraculous.

Maybe they were.

"Neither did I."

By the time they'd put out the fires, the sky was lightening to the east. Alexiya stood watch outside the bunker, which apparently was a common element in Arborian tree villages.

"In case of fire," Alexiya had explained, showing the large, underground cavern built into a hillock, rather spacious and filled with chairs, blankets, and old supplies.

They led the villagers north, through the trees and toward Vayle. Many of them wanted to return to their homes to scavenge for belongings, and some cried about missing pets or even family members. Veronyka's eyes were wide and pleading, but it was too dangerous to go back. They didn't know if the soldiers in the trees were alone, or possibly just the vanguard or forward scouts of a larger force. There were too many unknowns.

Still, when they reached the edge of the Silverwood and Latham—currently patrolling the village perimeter—descended, Tristan glanced back over his shoulder. It was light enough now that they could fly safely above the trees and see where the soldiers—and the missing people—had gone.

"I'll go," Veronyka said at once, but Alexiya pushed to the front.

"Let me," she said quietly—but firmly. "I know these parts. Go with your patrol. I will come back as quickly as I can."

Veronyka wavered, then nodded. Alexiya turned to Tristan next, and all he said was, "Be careful."

Then she was off.

Tristan faced Latham, who looked pale and furious as he took in Tristan's smoke-and-ash-covered appearance, but also relieved. Apparently

Tristan's patrol had been minutes from sending out a search for him and Veronyka. They had spotted the distant smoke and suspected that was what was delaying the pair of them on their return.

Latham led the way to the village, darting a curious look at Alexiya, who was flying back south, while Veronyka and Tristan took up the rear.

Despite everything—despite the anger and exhaustion pulling at his muscles—Tristan directed a tired smile at Veronyka. She cocked him a questioning eyebrow, and he nodded at Alexiya's retreating figure.

"Look who you've won to our side," he said.

Veronyka twisted in her saddle to stare after Alexiya, brow furrowed. "I think she'd have come anyway. She'd have followed the flames."

"She wasn't following the flames," Tristan said. "She was following you."

He'd done his best to forget everything Veronyka had told him about who she really was. In fact, he was trying not to think about a lot of things lately: that his father was lying to him again or how it had felt to black out and have no memory of falling helpless from his saddle. That wasn't to mention waking up to learn that he was bonded to Veronyka—oh, and that her full name was Veronyka Ashfire and she was heir to the empire.

But every now and then, the truth of who she was hit him so undeniably that he felt it was a wonder he hadn't spotted it before. The fact of the matter was, there *was* something queenly about Veronyka—something that set her apart from everyone else. Not arrogance or self-importance or entitlement. She was the kind of person who led by example, and like a lantern in the darkness, she made you want to follow.

It was strange; he usually read adoring histories and flowery epic poems with a cynical eye—surely kings and queens weren't always strong and beautiful and awe-inspiring. Maybe it was because he himself was descended from kings and his own father had been both a Phoenix Rider and a governor. Yes, he'd always looked up to and idolized the impressive commander, but he was also just a man, no more special or gods-chosen than Morra the cook or Lars the metalsmith.

But looking at Veronyka, suddenly he *believed* it . . . that some people were destined for greatness. That they were meant to rule and to lead.

Of course, he hadn't told *her* that. After she'd spilled everything to him, he'd followed her example in not mentioning anything about it. She wanted it kept secret, for starters, and he knew her entire sense of self was on fragile ground. That wasn't to mention the issue with the shadow magic.

Tristan knew it was wrong, but ever since he'd learned about it, he'd found himself wishing the link went two ways—that he could see into her heart and mind and understand *her* better. It was still a thrilling thing to fantasize about, even as he realized with chagrin that he would be a poor shadowmage, selfish and lacking in control.

In blazing flash of clarity, Tristan understood how that magic had shaped who Veronyka was—her emotional control, her compassion, and her relationship with her sister. Shadow magic had touched every part of her life, teaching her to guard herself and others. To be a protector. It had also taught her to fear the person she'd loved most—Val. Tristan hated the hard lessons she'd had to learn and hated himself for the way he'd reacted when she'd told him of her magic. As if the burden were *his* instead of what it truly was: a constant weight and responsibility pressing down on Veronyka every minute of every single day.

Maybe that was why it was supposedly the gift of queens, popular in the royal Ashfire line. They were built of stuff that was better than him.

When they arrived in the main square where the rest of his patrol— along with a cluster of villagers—waited, Tristan began issuing orders. The villagers rushed to get food and water and blankets, while Ronyn and Anders took to the sky to fly a circuit of the village and surrounding area to ensure they hadn't been followed.

Once the Silverwood survivors were divided up among the local cookhouse and inn, the remaining members of Tristan's patrol returned to camp.

He was preparing to debrief his Riders and figure out next steps— they'd need to send out a wider patrol as soon as Alexiya returned, find more permanent housing for the Silverwood refugees, and get word to both the commander at the Eyrie and to Fallon at Prosperity.

But Tristan had barely dismounted before Ronyn and Anders landed behind him—back from their quick flight around the village.

"What is it—did you find something?" Tristan asked, heart kicking against his ribs. Were there more soldiers descending upon them at this very moment?

"The surrounding area is secure. I was just making my return flight when a letter arrived," Ronyn said, handing over a sealed scroll. Tristan unwrapped it at once—it was from Fallon, who was already in place at Prosperity outpost.

"There's been an attack along the Iron Road," Tristan said, voice flat with shock.

Veronyka stepped forward. "Why would soldiers attack the Iron Road? That's in the empire."

Tristan lowered the letter, staring around at them all. "It wasn't soldiers. It was Phoenix Riders."

I thought I had failed,
and I was ready to give up hope.
But then there was you.

- CHAPTER 25 -
SEV

THE COMMANDER'S REPLY CAME just over a week later and carried disturbing news.

There had been another attack in Pyra—to the east, in the Silverwood along the border near Arboria North. A group of Phoenix Riders had managed to beat the soldiers back, but the damage was still substantial. And though he had no proof, the commander was certain that Lord Rolan was behind it.

Again, the governor's words from their first meeting rang in Sev's head: *I must convince them there is, in fact, a threat.* If Rolan wanted to convince the empire's other governors that the Phoenix Riders—and Pyra as a whole— were a threat, what better way than to stage fights up and down the border, drawing them out? Rolan had said he expected a Phoenix Rider counter-attack, but Commander Cassian was too smart a man to strike at the empire when their numbers were so few. Surely Rolan knew this and had decided to force the commander's hand.

When the empire's lords heard tell of phoenixes and fire so near their lands, it wouldn't matter who had started it—the empire would be sure to finish it.

Besides news of the attack in Pyra, the commander said that the Phoenix

Riders Sev had spotted were not his own—and furthermore, that another band of Phoenix Riders had allegedly attacked a merchant caravan traveling along the Iron Road and hauling valuable Ferronese steel weapons. This was surely the shipment Lord Rolan had been referring to in his meeting, and these were surely those same Phoenix Riders.

It felt like Commander Cassian was the informant, not the other way around, and Sev tried his best to make sense of the news. A stolen shipment of steel weapons going from Ferro into the capital meant lost income for the governor, who collected taxes on all items coming and going from the province. But when Sev considered all Rolan had said in the meeting, talking about survivors who could spread the tale, he realized that this too might be a means of waging war against Pyra by turning the Phoenix Riders into criminals—and diverting suspicion away from Rolan himself.

Sev wanted to know more, but as the attack along the Iron Road had happened within the empire, Commander Cassian made it clear that it was a matter he had no room to concern himself with. He needed to know what was happening *in Pyra*. Only then could they get ahead of Lord Rolan and try to defuse what was quickly turning into an extremely dangerous situation.

The problem was, Sev didn't know how to get the commander the information he sought. Sev and Kade had been sneaking onto the roof night after night, but Rolan had no new visitors and mostly dined alone, in silence—which made what they were doing all the more precarious. Every whisper of fabric or scrape of foot against tile was something Rolan might hear, and then Sev and Kade would be goners.

The realization of what Sev had to do slowly solidified itself in his mind as the days wore on. There was only one way he could truly know where Lord Rolan's soldiers were going . . . and that was to go with them.

He knew that it wouldn't be like last time—he wouldn't be ignorant of what was happening or be saved from battle by Trix and Kade. If Sev were sent back into Pyra, he would be risking his life and facing the very real possibility that he might wind up in a battle *against* Phoenix Riders. Or, quite possibly *worse* . . . a battle against innocent Pyraean villagers.

But what other choice did he have? The commander needed information, and if Sev did his job right, the Riders would know where the attack was headed before it got there. They'd be able to prepare proper defenses or ambush the soldiers before they reached their target. It still might mean Sev's life, but it also meant he'd be preventing death and destruction instead of just causing it. This was what he'd signed up for, wasn't it? Trix had said that as a spy, she was ready for her own demise. Sev would have to be too.

When soldiers from all over Ferro started turning up at the estate, called in for reassignment, Sev saw his chance. He didn't know where they were going or what their orders were, but he did know it had something to do with Pyra.

After dinner he made his way to the captains' office, his palms sweaty. Everything rested on his ability to get transferred to one of these new regiments, and after months of playing the fool with all the soldiers he encountered—not to mention his severe shoulder injury—he worried they'd prefer to keep him holed up inside an estate, where he couldn't make trouble or compromise missions. The only reason he was hopeful at all was because he'd caught a glimpse of some of the new arrivals in the training yard that morning. Many were young and inexperienced, shipped in from the remote regions of Ferro where they saw no action save for drunken cookhouse fights, and Sev had survived the last attack in Pyra—survived facing off against Phoenix Riders. At least that was the official story. No matter what these commanding officers might think of him personally, they couldn't deny his apparent combat experience.

Sev knocked on the door. They called him in, and he found half a dozen soldiers surrounding a long table buried in paperwork, the pages spread between plates of half-eaten food and cups of wine. Sev made his request, heart in his throat—and was surprised by the answer.

"A soldier with real battle experience?" asked the youngest of the captains, who looked to be roughly ten years Sev's senior. "I'll gladly take you over these milk-fed, smooth-cheeked adolescents," he said loudly, the words carrying out the door and down the hall of the barracks, where some of the younger recruits were awaiting their postings. The other captains guffawed, while Sev smiled and hoped they didn't look too closely at *his* paperwork. Sev was tall, but he couldn't be much older than the "smooth-cheeked adolescents" to which the man referred, and Sev's patchy stubble wasn't much to brag about either.

Someone cleared their throat from the back of the room, and Sev spotted Officer Yara. She wore a look of displeasure and pressed herself tightly against the wall—her perfect posture on display—though Sev suspected she was leaning back as far as she could from the mess the captains had made rather than attempting to stand on formality. He realized that she was older than all the others in the room and had fought in the Blood War. Surely she was more experienced—and more deserving of promotion to captain—than these others. The oversight likely had more to do with the fact that she was a woman than it did with her qualifications.

"He hasn't been approved for active duty," Yara said, and Sev wilted slightly.

"He looks fine to me," said the young captain, who was obviously eager to have him.

Yara leaned forward and plucked his paperwork from a file on the desk, though Sev had no idea how she'd found it so easily. "According to the healer's most recent report," she began, staring pointedly at Sev's shoulder while she shoved the paperwork into the captain's face, "you can hardly lift a fork, let alone a sword or spear."

"That's—that must be old," Sev said. He reached out and lifted a mug of ale from the desk, offering her a winning smile even as his shoulder twinged with the effort. Yara was not amused—Sev knew she was a stickler for rules—but the others laughed appreciatively.

"He's fine! And I could use someone with experience in Pyra on my crew," the young captain said, waving Yara off. "I want to make it to those riverside settlements in decent time—surely he'll know the best routes."

Riverside settlements? Was that their next target?

"That information is classified," Yara said, eyes flashing. "You can't just shout it out for any old foot soldier to hear."

The captain laughed. "Oh, lighten up! He won't say nothin'," he said with a wink in Sev's direction. "Besides, that's just one stop in a long line of other targets he doesn't know about, all right? Stop clucking at me like a mother hen."

Yara closed her eyes, nostrils flaring, and Sev sensed an argument coming. He was certain the captain wouldn't have called a male soldier hounding him about proper protocol a "mother hen," and he scrambled to get the conversation back to the issue of his paperwork.

"I'll get her to update it," he said quickly, putting the mug down again. Surely Hestia would do that for him? She had shown him plenty of favoritism. What was one more thing?

"Best get it done soon, then," the young captain said with an indifferent shrug. "You'll be a part of my regiment, and we ship out in three days."

Sev sent a letter to the commander as soon as he got back to his rooms, relaying the information the young captain had let slip: that their next target was the fishing communities located next to the River Aurys. They weren't fully fledged villages, which made them easy targets. Sev cringed at the thought.

Kade didn't make it to Sev's rooms that night. Apparently one of Rolan's hounds was sick, and so Kade was unable to make his usual visit. Sev was secretly relieved; he didn't relish the idea of telling Kade about his plans, and wasn't sure if he even had the strength to go through with them in the first place. He'd heard what their next target would be—wasn't that enough?

No, it wasn't. Sev knew it even without the captain's mention of "a long line of other targets" they'd be hitting. The commander needed someone in the thick of things, and while Sev couldn't report every one of Lord Rolan's movements, he could at least ensure that this particular regiment did not succeed. Still, he knew it was a risk—one Kade would likely warn him against. But that didn't mean he shouldn't do it. And so, when Kade had to spend a second night with the sick dogs, Sev once again kept the information of his decision to himself.

Hestia's next treatment for Sev's shoulder was scheduled for the night before they departed, and Sev had deliberately waited until then to address the topic.

He had been good for the past couple of days, skipping his nighttime antics without Kade to join in, and his shoulder should look better than it ever had thus far.

"Evening, Sevro," she said as she entered his rooms, waving her assistant in with the tray. Sev didn't speak until the man departed and he and Hestia were alone.

"Hestia, I—I was hoping I could ask you for a favor."

She'd been unwrapping a bundle of herbs and paused, peering at him curiously. "Go on, then."

"I'd like to be stationed with the newest regiment, set to ship out tomorrow. But the thing is, to do that—"

"You need my approval," she said, frowning and crossing her arms over her chest. Sev wondered if she knew what Rolan was up to . . . if she had any idea he was clamoring for war with Pyra and the lengths he was going to get it. Truth be told, Sev had yet to figure out how Hestia felt toward Rolan at all. She always spoke fondly of Cassian and his family, but she never mentioned Rolan or gave any indication that she liked or disliked her new employer. But surely her Ferronese pride had her wishing for a local in the position of governor, not a Stellan.

She didn't speak again for a long while. Instead she walked over to the window and stared outside at the darkening sky. When she looked back in Sev's direction, the setting sun cast her face in a glow of orange and purple light. "Why are young men so eager for war?"

Sev lowered his head. Of course Hestia was thinking again about her sons, who had no doubt fought willingly and with great pride during the war. It occurred to Sev for the first time to wonder whose side they'd been fighting on. Commander Cassian had been the governor of Ferro during the Blood War and had thrown his own armies behind Avalkyra Ashfire's claim to the throne. Many defected, unwilling to follow him into what became a rebellion against the empire, but many more continued to fight for him until both sisters died and the war was done.

Sev looked up—it seemed she was waiting for an answer. Could he tell her? He didn't want a war—he didn't want to fight at all—but this was the only way he knew how to prevent it. He was a spy, and never before had it struck him so powerfully what that meant. It meant that the people around you—good people—saw and believed the worst in you because you had to play a part. And right now Sev had to be the brash, foolish young man who, after barely surviving his first fight, couldn't wait to take part in his second.

"They say there's trouble along the border," he said, carefully choosing his words. "And I'm no coward."

Hestia returned to the table with her materials and got back to work. She didn't speak the whole time she prepared the poultice, and Sev got some sense that he shouldn't break that silence—that she was doing some serious thinking.

By the time the bandages were in place and secured, she stepped back.

"I won't do it, Sevro," she said, and Sev's stomach plummeted. No, no—he needed to do this. There was no other way. "You're not ready, and you haven't thought this through. You're young, and brash, and—"

"I'm a soldier, Hestia," Sev cut in. "Stop"—he swallowed around the bubble rising in his throat—"stop *coddling* me. I'm not them. I'm not one of your sons."

Sev couldn't look her in the face. As it was, he saw a flash of shock, followed by deepest pain, before he dropped his head. Why had he done that? Surely he could have talked her around, *convinced* her, rather than going for the lowest possible blow?

When he dared to look up again, Hestia's eyes were bright—but her expression was under control again.

"No," she said softly, before turning away, "you're not."

Sev was surprised by the stab of pain that followed those words. But he supposed Hestia's sons never would have spoken to her that way. And when death came for them, they'd probably thought fondly—longingly—of their mother, and known in that moment that she had been right all along. Sev wondered what his own mother might have said, if she'd survived the war, only to have Sev willingly join it.

"I'll sign your form," she said at last, and Sev's heart did a strange lurch. Even as he flushed with success, dread began to expand there at the idea of what he was about to do. "Because if I've learned anything in this life, it's that you can't stop someone from doing something foolish if something foolish is what they want to do." She returned to her tray, carefully packing away her supplies. "Be cautious, won't you?" she asked without looking at him, and Sev was both distressed and comforted by the idea that she grown attached to him. That she *cared*. "Use your head, Sevro—and steer clear of friendly fire."

Sev replayed her words. "Friendly fire?" he repeated faintly, and she peered at him over her spectacles.

"I know the difference between a crossbow bolt wound and an arrow wound—and in all my years I've never heard of a Phoenix Rider wielding a crossbow."

Sev gaped at her. Did she know—had she guessed that he wasn't all that he seemed?

Hestia returned her attention to her work, then hoisted the tray on her way to the door. "I'll see the appropriate paperwork reaches your captain before morning, and I'll also have someone bring up a salve and some ointments so you can continue to treat your wound on the road. An assistant this time," she said reassuringly, and Sev knew that word had reached her of his hasty dismissal of her attractive servants. "When you return," she began, and Sev appreciated the word, even if they both knew it wasn't a guarantee, "I shall be very cross with you if I discover that you haven't been applying them nightly. Trust me—I will know."

Then she was gone.

Before Sev could do more than stare in shock at the closed door, the tapestry in the next room shifted, and Kade appeared.

He looked murderous.

"When were you going to tell me?" he demanded without preamble.

Clearly Kade had managed to get away from the dogs tonight and had overheard Sev's conversation with Hestia.

Sev didn't have an answer. He'd planned to tell Kade he was leaving eventually—once he had it all figured out—but it had been easier not to. Easier to accept what he was doing when he didn't have to see the fear and doubt mirrored on Kade's face. When he left this estate, he would be truly, completely alone—there would be no Trix, no Kade, just Sev among his enemies once more. It was hard to believe how far he had come in such a short space of time . . . how he'd gotten used to the idea of Kade by his side, of having someone who had his back.

In truth, he didn't want to give it up.

"I wasn't sure I'd be able to go . . . ," Sev began carefully. "I needed Hestia to clear me."

"That woman would do anything for you and you know it," he said, and the statement made Sev feel even worse about what he'd just said to her. He wished he could have told her the truth—that he appreciated her concern more than he could say and that he was trying his best to *stop* the fighting, not participate in it. But Sev was a spy, and as he was quickly discovering, that meant lying to people you liked and respected. It even meant sometimes lying to yourself. "Why didn't you talk to me about it first?" Kade pressed. "I thought we were in this together."

Sev had been avoiding Kade's eye, but he looked up now. "I didn't want to think about it."

"To think about raiding villages and kidnapping animages? About helping to start a war? Because you *have* to think about it. You can't—"

"No," Sev cut in with frustration. Of course he didn't want to think about those things, but that wasn't what he'd meant. "I didn't want to think about leaving you."

Silence.

Kade's voice was softer when he said, "But you will."

"I have to," Sev said, sensing that the fight had gone out of Kade. Sev got to his feet to close some of the distance between them—but not all of it. He wasn't near enough to touch, but he could better make out Kade's eyes in the growing darkness of the room. Kade's arms were crossed, but there wasn't just anger in his face—there was fear and hurt and something akin to panic. Sev wanted to lift his hands and smooth the lines of tension away, but he didn't.

"If I don't do this, I won't be able to live with myself. I've been a coward all my life, and heroics—they don't come easily to me. . . ."

"I've seen you do some heroic things," Kade said quietly, and Sev's chest expanded, filling him up with unfamiliar pride.

"I know this is the right thing—I can't waver now. This is what I'm here for. If I do this right, I can *prevent* war. That's worth any price."

"Are you so eager to follow in your parents' footsteps?"

Sev swallowed. Alys and Sevono Lastlight had died together in a joint fire dive that not only ended their lives and the lives of their phoenixes, but took down hundreds of empire soldiers in the process. Soldiers who would have captured—maybe even killed—Sev and Kade had they not made their desperate sacrifice. There were many times in Sev's life when he'd questioned their decision, when he'd raged at them for leaving him all alone, but never had he considered that he might be doing the exact same thing with his decision to reenter the field. That he might be leaving someone behind.

"They did what they had to do. I hope that, if it comes to it, I can face my end with half as much courage."

"And what about the hostage, Riella?" Kade demanded, clearly reaching for some excuse or reason for Sev to stay. "She won't be out there on some battlefield."

As much as Sev hated the idea that Riella would be forgotten, that she was just another poor animage child swallowed by the empire and its politics, she was no longer technically a part of his mission. If he didn't follow his orders, what was the point of being back here at all?

"Maybe you'll find her," Sev said, forcing a smile. "You're good at finding people who are lost."

Kade shook his head and jerked away in frustration. "That was Trix, not me. She was the spider. . . . You and I were both just caught in her web."

"Maybe," Sev said, taking a hesitant step forward. "But I didn't want to be in that web until I saw that you were there with me."

Kade turned—and was startled at Sev's close proximity. "It's too dangerous, Sev."

"I'll be careful," Sev said. "I promise I'll stay out of trouble."

Kade's expression was bleak. "Don't make promises you can't keep."

He turned and left through the hidden passage without another word.

Sev stared after him until the room grew so dark that he was forced to light a lantern. He packed his meager belongings—including the medicine delivered by one of Hestia's assistants and the box of correspondence supplies from under the tile—and lay down in bed, staring at the ceiling. If he knew where Kade slept, he might've gone into the tunnel after him. But what could he say? Sev hated to part ways like this, but he knew he was doing the right thing—the only thing.

Still, sleep was a long time coming.

The morning dawned bright and clear, and the training yard was a racket of voices and shuffling feet and the clank and jangle of armor and weapons. Near the back of the column was a line of horses for their packs and supplies, and the sight reminded Sev of the last time he'd ventured into Pyra. Days and nights spent under the stars, with Kade and Trix for company. They'd not be traveling high enough to warrant llamas, and a part of Sev yearned for their gentle, woolly company.

Then he saw something that made his heart want to burst from his chest. Kade stood among the group of bondservants who were joining them on the journey into Pyra. Somehow, he'd gotten assigned to the same mission as Sev.

Kade would be coming with him.

He gave Sev a small smile, and Sev couldn't help the wide grin that split his face in return or the surprising prickle of moisture at the back of his eyes.

He wasn't alone after all. Kade still had his back.

I might be prepared to fail myself,
but I was not prepared to fail you.

- CHAPTER 26 -
VERONYKA

WHILE FALLON'S LETTER BROUGHT news of an attack along the Iron Road, when Tristan sent in his hastily scribbled report about the Silverwood, the commander's letter—which arrived several days after that—brought word of more attacks to come.

According to Sev, empire soldiers were expected to strike fishing communities along the Aurys, and rather than trying to fend off the upcoming assault along the river, the commander had ordered mass evacuations. Since things were heating up, he'd also decided to send Beryk to take over command of Vayle and assigned Tristan's patrol to escort the soon-to-be-arriving refugees to Rushlea, where temporary housing would be set up. The Silverwood survivors were to relocate there as well. Vayle was now considered too close to danger and not an ideal place for refugees—or, apparently, Tristan's green patrol.

Beryk and the rest of the commander's patrol—minus the commander himself—were due to arrive five days after the Silverwood attack, bringing with them a contingent of stronghold guards as reinforcements.

Veronyka knew Tristan saw it as a demotion, almost as a reprimand or punishment, even though in this instance Veronyka didn't think that was the case. They *were* the least experienced, and if soldiers were going to continue to come from the south, they needed their best warriors to be first to respond.

Once they escorted the displaced villagers to Rushlea, Tristan's patrol would remain there to help build shelters, run the usual patrols, plus watch the road for any more incoming refugees. Some of Beryk's guards would go with them to help. The commander had slowly been building their ranks at the stronghold since the attack at the Eyrie, with the intention of assigning the guards to villages in cases such as this, when the Phoenix Rider forces were stretched thin and they needed to fill the gaps. The guards would soon be in place in Vayle and Rushlea, along with those already stationed in Prosperity, helping the Riders keep watch and maintain their defenses.

Despite all the action and movement happening *within* Pyra, Tristan's patrol seemed more uneasy about the Phoenix Rider sightings than the soldier attacks—which they had long been expecting. While they spent their days flying patrols around Vayle and the Silverwood and preparing for Beryk's arrival, they spent their nights gossiping.

"But—why would Phoenix Riders attack merchants in the first place?" Anders asked the group as they sat around the cookfire one evening. "Especially if they're supposedly allied with the empire?"

"It was a weapons shipment," Latham pointed out. "Maybe they needed to arm themselves, and Ferronese steel is the best there is.

"That's even stranger," Lysandro argued. "As governor, that shipment would belong to him. Why steal it?"

"Unless the theft was just for show?" Anders mused, but Ronyn shook his head.

"I say it's a false rumor like the attack on the Silverwood. There's a reason they started torching the trees—they want to make it *look* like a Phoenix Rider attack. No doubt this merchant caravan was the same."

When they weren't talking about the strange Phoenix Riders in the south, they were talking about the strange Phoenix Rider in their midst. For months they'd been told they were the only Riders left after the war, and in a matter of days they'd received word of Phoenix Rider sightings in Ferro and a Phoenix Rider attack along the Iron Road, and Alexiya, a brand-new ally, had turned up.

Though they were wary of her, Alexiya was an integral part of their operation as they attempted to get things under control in the days after the attack. She took charge of the Silverwood patrols, knowing the area better than any of them, though her searches had turned up empty since her first foray back into the trees.

Tristan had barely finished reading Fallon's letter when Alexiya returned, landing at the far edge of their camp. Veronyka had hurried over at once, Tristan following behind.

"Did you . . . ?" Veronyka had started, but the look on Alexiya's face made Veronyka's heart sink.

"The forest is completely deserted—no sign of soldiers or any survivors. There are some bodies we'll need to deal with," she said in an aside to Tristan, who nodded gravely. "I followed tracks leading south into Arboria and west to the river—they could be in the capital by now."

Veronyka thought often of that boat making its way into Aura Nova, loaded with innocent captives, where black market traders bought and sold dozens of animages every day. She had seen it happen.

Just like her *maiora* had been taken by an angry mob, so too were animage children stolen from their families on the crowded Narrows or Forgotten District streets. One time, a young boy and girl were snatched right in front of Veronyka, mere feet away, outside a stall at the market. She had tried to reach for them—to cry out for help—but Val had yanked her into an alley and pressed a hand over her mouth. Veronyka had looked imploringly at Val and her grandmother, but they only stood by silently, spectators to the horror. Veronyka had still believed, then, that goodness would always prevail.

She was wiser now, but that didn't shake the guilt she'd felt ever since. She had stood and watched while two children screamed and cried and begged for their parents. She might not have been a fighter or a Phoenix Rider then, but surely she could have done something. And what if

Veronyka, Val, *and* Ilithya had tried to help . . . ? Couldn't they have saved them?

Whether or not she'd been powerless to save those children in the Narrows, she wasn't powerless now—and still she'd failed to protect the Silverwood villagers. Impotent anger was like a flame inside her chest, flaring up or flickering low, but never gone entirely.

Though they'd flown patrols together and slept in the same camp, it wasn't until the day Beryk was due to arrive that Veronyka had a moment to speak alone with Alexiya.

Veronyka was eating her lunch, and Alexiya had just returned from another sweep of the Silverwood. The others were either on patrol or in the village, save for Lysandro, who was napping in his tent.

Veronyka and Alexiya walked to the edge of the clearing where they'd made camp and stood among the shade of the trees.

"Thank you," Veronyka said before Alexiya could speak. The woman seemed surprised. "For helping us—in the fight, and with all of this. I know it's been a long time for you."

"Time wasn't the problem," Alexiya said, watching as Ximn joined the other phoenixes, eating and drinking from their shared troughs. "*I* was the problem. I'd forgotten why I wanted to be a Rider in the first place. Why it mattered." She paused, staring up at the afternoon sky, and Veronyka remember what Alexiya had said about her Arborian heritage. *Stargazers, every one.* "It will be good for me—for us," she said, nodding at Ximn. The phoenix had finished eating and was now chasing tufts of dandelion spores blown off their stems by a gentle summer breeze.

"So you intend to stay? For good?"

Alexiya tilted her head thoughtfully. Then she flashed a bright smile. "These men . . . I think they need to be reminded that the Phoenix Riders are an order that *women* built, hm?"

Veronyka smiled too, before her thoughts turned darker. "Do you think there's any truth to this Iron Road attack? Do you think . . . ?"

"That it could be Sidra and Doriyan?" Alexiya guessed. Veronyka nodded. Alexiya had said they were always together, after all, and were known for their dark deeds. "They are capable of it, beyond a doubt. But I can't think why they'd do such a thing nearly seventeen years after the war ended. Why now? To what purpose?"

Veronyka knew a purpose that might motivate these Riders, one that Alexiya would not consider. . . .

Avalkyra Ashfire.

Could Val be behind this? Could she have hatched a phoenix at last? It had been months since she'd stolen the egg from the Eyrie, which was sufficient time for the creature to be large enough to fly. The thought of Val on phoenix-back sent a sudden stab of fear into Veronyka's heart. Distance had been one of the few comforts she'd had in the wake of Val's forceful intrusion on her mind and Tristan's fall from his saddle. Val had asked Veronyka to go to her, but what if she came to Veronyka instead? What if she turned up in Vayle or Rushlea?

We could do it together, you know. . . . We could save lives, save the world. You and I together could change everything. . . .

The sudden urge to reach out to Val and demand the truth was powerful, but Veronyka clamped down on it in frustration. It was too dangerous, but maybe there was another way to learn more about the Iron Road attack. She would be escorting refugees to Rushlea soon—and Rushlea was the last-known location of Doriyan. She could seek him out as she had done Alexiya, and with any luck, she'd learn if he had anything to do with the attack—or if he knew who did. It wasn't much, but it would help narrow down her list of suspects. And maybe she could convince him to join their cause, the same as she had with Alexiya.

Alexiya seemed to be thinking the same thing. "*He* might be in Rushlea, you know. Doriyan. That's where he's from."

Veronyka nodded. "I'll try to find him and learn what I can." She paused. "You could come with us, if you wanted. He might be more willing to speak to you."

"I think you'd find the exact opposite to be true," Alexiya said quietly, and Veronyka frowned.

"Did you know him?" she asked.

"Not exactly, but trust me when I say he would not wish to see me. Or any Riders, for that matter, save for Sidra. As I understand it, he went into hiding after the war . . . and not from the empire. He went into hiding from his own kind as well. Tread carefully, Veronyka, and bring your mate with you."

"My *what?*" Veronyka squeaked, so loudly that the phoenixes stopped what they were doing and swiveled their heads to stare in unison.

Why do you squawk? Xephyra asked, and Veronyka shushed her.

Alexiya chuckled, eyes dancing, and shook her head. "Forget his father's lineage—he is a Flamesong, and they are loyal and true." She stopped laughing, but the smirk lingered. "They are good-looking, as well," she added, eyebrows waggling.

Veronyka glared at her, but found she rather enjoyed this kind of teasing. It was what an older sister's jibes *ought* to feel like . . . pointed but not barbed. Cutting, perhaps, but never eviscerating.

Not like Val, who was as cold as steel and sliced twice as deep.

"No, I will stay in Vayle for now," Alexiya said. "And when your replacements arrive, I will help—if they'll have me."

Veronyka knew they were in no position to say no—even if Alexiya's existence would be a shock to them, they'd be a patrol member short themselves, with the commander still running point from the Eyrie.

"How did you come to know Ilithya?" Alexiya asked.

She hesitated. "I didn't," she lied. She hated to deceive Alexiya, but she also had too much at stake to start delving into Ilithya, Avalkyra, and Veronyka's own Ashfire blood. "But we have a spy in the empire, and he worked with her, for a time. It's through him we've learned some of Lord Rolan's plans."

"Spies," Alexiya said with distaste. "A necessary evil, but an evil all the same."

Tristan returned to camp then, his gaze searching the clearing until he spotted Veronyka and Alexiya in the shadows of the trees. He made directly for them, and Alexiya snorted.

"You two are more obvious than Princess Pearl and her riverboat captain," she said, shaking her head before strolling away. Princess Pearl was the title character of a famous Arborian Comedy of the same name, and the riverboat captain was her love—as well as a prince in disguise. Veronyka smiled uncomfortably at the realization that the comparison was even more apt than Alexiya knew, and that in her life, Veronyka would be the riverboat captain and Tristan the princess.

"Well, they're still upset," Tristan said as soon as he arrived. He'd been spending most of his time in the village since the Silverwood battle, trying to smooth ruffled feathers and reassure everyone that the situation was well in hand. "About the attack, and about the fact that we're being shipped off again. I tried to tell them it's for the best, but . . ." He sighed, scrubbing a hand through his hair. His face was drawn and pale, and he had dark circles under his eyes—evidence of a sleepless night—but the shadows only seemed to make the soft brown color and long lashes pop.

They are good-looking, as well.

Veronyka banished Alexiya's words from her mind and refocused. "Alexiya will be staying," she said, trying to bolster his mood. "Hopefully her presence will help. She knows the Silverwood better than anyone, and it's thanks to her we scared the soldiers off in the first place."

Tristan nodded, but his expression was dark.

"I know this feels like a failure," Veronyka began gently, and Tristan cast a startled look in her direction. Veronyka understood his frustration with being pulled back—they were finally starting to do some good—but she knew the assignment didn't hit her quite as personally as it did him. She saw the commander's order for what it was—a sound military decision.

"Was I that obvious, or are you . . . ?" He pointed to his temple.

Veronyka smirked. "I don't need shadow magic to read you," she said softly, unable to conceal the affection in her voice.

Tristan dropped his chin, a rueful smile on his face. "I guess I have a tendency to wear my heart on my sleeve," he muttered.

"Your heart—and your head," she said with a laugh. Tristan nodded in grim resignation, and Veronyka realized that he saw this as a defect in himself, so she added, "I like it."

"You do?" he asked, tilting his face to peek up at her.

"Very much," she said, voice trembling slightly. "I like that I don't have to second-guess. That there are no games with you . . ."

Tristan lifted his head, a knowing look in his eye. Veronyka was thinking about Val, and Tristan knew it.

"Anyway," she said, not wanting to go there right now. "I know he's your father, but I don't think this is personal. A good commander wouldn't put his greenest fighters on the front lines—he just didn't know how wide that line was, or how much wider it might grow."

"I know you're right, but we'll stay green forever if he doesn't allow us to fully participate in this war."

"No matter what your father does, I don't think there's any way to keep us out of this forever. We've already seen two battles, and there'll be more to come—whether we want it or not."

"I guess I should be grateful that we aren't fighting battles on every front—that there is a safe space, for us and the refugees, even if it's temporary. The thing is . . ." He trailed off, kicking at a stone on the ground. "I can't shake the idea that my father is planning something . . . *doing* something . . . that he's deliberately not telling me."

"Do you think it has to do with the Grand Council?" Veronyka asked, considering Tristan's words. Commander Cassian's behavior seemed much the same to her as it had always been—he was a stoic man, one who didn't share feelings or information beyond what was absolutely necessary. But Tristan knew him best, and Veronyka trusted his judgment.

Mention of the council meeting caused a scowl to cross Tristan's face. "What could he *possibly* say that would win them over? And who's to say they'll even let him speak? He's a war criminal. He's supposed to be in exile. I mean, these are the people who killed my mother."

Veronyka stared at him. Morra had told her about Olanna's death, but she hadn't considered that those same people still sat in positions of power in the empire—that they'd continued on, while Tristan's mother had paid the ultimate price.

Tristan said it offhandedly, but his throat bobbed in a swallow, and he was determinedly avoiding looking in her direction. This wasn't just about the commander and his youngest—and newest—patrol leader. This was a father and his son, and Tristan feared for Cassian's life.

"I'm sorry, Tristan," Veronyka said, and though she knew she shouldn't, she trailed her fingertips down the back of his forearm until she found his hand, then laced her fingers with his.

He didn't look at her, and though it took him a moment to respond, he squeezed tightly.

"It feels like . . ." He paused, clearing his throat. His voice was stronger as he continued. "It's like he's willingly putting himself in danger. He's being reckless, and of all the words I'd use to describe my father, 'reckless' isn't one of them."

"Good point," Veronyka conceded. The commander was cautious almost to a fault. "So then you have your answer," she said, releasing Tristan's hand so that she could stand before him.

Tristan frowned. "I do?"

Veronyka shrugged. "Either he's behaving highly out of character," she said, her tone skeptical, "or there *is* something he's not telling you— something that makes what he's doing logical."

Tristan's brows shot up—he hadn't considered that. "I suppose that's a comfort," he said wryly, but Veronyka could tell her words had eased his worries somewhat. "Now I just need to find a way to get him to tell me. After we fly to Rushlea, he wants a report. I think I'll deliver it in person."

"What happens to me once we get to Rushlea?" she asked. It had been on her mind ever since the commander's letter arrived. The war was indeed heating up, and Veronyka wasn't a green Master Rider—she was a green *apprentice*.

"What do you mean?" Tristan asked, trying to sound politely puzzled, but of course Veronyka could see right through it.

She actually laughed a little. "Remember, heart on your sleeve?" she asked, and he gave her a resigned smile before scrubbing the back of his neck.

"He said you should return to the Eyrie, but I'm working on it."

Veronyka's heart sank—she couldn't be sidelined, not now, not when she was finally making some progress. She'd managed to recruit another Phoenix Rider to their side—a war hero. That had to count for something.

"When I deliver my report, I'll explain that we can't spare you. I'll make him see."

Veronyka didn't know if he could really pull it off—but she knew he'd try.

"I hope so," she said. "We've got some unfinished business to take care of in Rushlea. I assume your father still has no intention of investigating the Phoenix Rider rumors?"

Tristan shook his head. "Not according to his letter. He's sticking to his original position—no time, no resources."

Veronyka nodded. "Then it's up to us. We'll escort the refugees to Rushlea, and while we're there, we'll pay a visit to another Phoenix Rider on Ilithya's list."

Dear Lexi,

I'm sure you've heard about Queen Lania's passing. It has been hard for Pheronia—she had a difficult relationship with her mother too.

There are rumors that Avalkyra herself is to blame for the queen's death. She and Pheronia have hardly spoken in days. I know Pheronia is reluctant to accuse her sister, and some people close to her whisper Avalkyra might be fleeing the capital and taking her Riders with her. If she goes now, it's not as a princess or even a queen . . . but as a fugitive. Councilors and politicians are choosing sides left and right.

Think carefully before you do the same.

Whatever happens, I'm still Pheronia's bodyguard. I swore to protect her with my life, and I won't let harm come to her—from anyone.

-Theryn

*Suddenly I had a reason to
keep fighting. Strength comes from
within. . . . You taught me that.*

- CHAPTER 27 -
AVALKYRA

IT WAS SATISFYING TO hear rumors swirl about the Phoenix Rider attack on a merchant caravan in Ferro—but that wasn't why Avalkyra was here. She and Sidra had stopped in Runnet for news of the *other* Phoenix Riders, not news of themselves, but Avalkyra supposed that to outsiders they were one and the same.

They heard tales that upward of fifty Riders had descended on the Iron Road, leaving no survivors—glazing over the fact that survivors had certainly been the ones to spread the stories in the first place—and burning what they didn't steal to arm themselves for more attacks to come.

The truth was that there were only two of them. They'd spared nearly a dozen survivors and had left the entire shipment behind for Rolan's men to deal with. He was a prudent man, if nothing else, and quite liked the idea of claiming the stolen shipment on his insurance even while the weapons sat safely in his storerooms.

They'd flown over a contingent of Lord Rolan's soldiers on the way here, and they were due to attack along the river any day now. Other groups of soldiers had been sighted as well, moving into position along the roads to harass the locals and make travel and trade more difficult. It was a two-pronged approach, antagonizing both sides of the border. Avalkyra's attacks were meant to strike fear into the empire's border lords and turn Pyra into a hostile territory, while the soldiers' attacks were meant to draw the Phoenix Riders into retaliating. Avalkyra and Sidra alone were not enough of a threat to mobilize the empire's armies, but a full-scale Rider battle—whoever had started it—would be enough to turn these border skirmishes into an all-out war.

Perhaps it would work eventually, but Avalkyra was dubious. Veronyka had known about the soldier presence near the border weeks ago—Avalkyra had sensed it in her mind when they spoke through their bond—which meant the commander knew about them too. When would he send his Riders out? And would he send Veronyka, who was talented, but young and inexperienced?

He could only remain inactive for so long. Even if Commander Cassian understood what Rolan was doing and what leaving their seclusion and engaging with empire soldiers would mean for the greater conflict with the empire, he couldn't in good conscience leave the people of Pyra defenseless. They were in danger because of him and his Riders, and the commander was a shrewd man. Even if guilt or a sense of duty didn't draw him out, politics would. Avalkyra knew he hadn't reestablished the Phoenix Riders out of the goodness of his heart or out of fond nostalgia. He was rebuilding their order so that he could *lead* them, so that he could reclaim wealth or status or position. If not for himself, for his son. His centuries-long claim over Ferro aside, the commander could make a legitimate bid to govern Pyra, if he chose. The last governors of Pyra—the Strongwings—had been wiped out during the Blood War.

If the Riders survived the conflict that was to come—or avoided it entirely, as the commander clearly hoped to do—he would be the obvious choice.

If they survived. And if the people of Pyra would accept him. Therein lay the problem. To avoid war was to avoid conflict while innocent people suffered. . . . If he let it go too long, those same people would revolt against him should he try to seize power.

He had future ambitions to protect, but also a reputation to uphold.

And no doubt, if the people of Pyra were in danger, Veronyka wouldn't let him rest until he acted.

Avalkyra was counting on it.

When they finally got news from the rest of Pyra, it wasn't from an attack on the fishing villages.

As the hours had worn on in the smoky Runnet cookhouse, Sidra found a man carrying word from the east, and with a bit of ale and forceful prompting, he told them there had been a battle south of Vayle, in the Silverwood, and that the fight had been between empire soldiers and Phoenix Riders. Not the whole flock or even a full patrol, but three Riders—two of whom were *female*. As Avalkyra and Sidra had not partaken in this attack, Avalkyra knew one of them must be Veronyka. The other's identity was uncertain, though considering the location, Avalkyra had a good guess. A spasm of hot resentment tightened her stomach, but she pushed it aside. It didn't matter. What *mattered* was that Veronyka had left the Eyrie.

Even as Avalkyra relished the news, she found herself cursing her ill timing. If she'd known about the attack, she could have been nearby, swooping in to help Veronyka and convince her of her good intentions. But, of course, when she'd allied with Lord Rolan, he'd been rightfully wary of her. As far as *he* knew, she was a turncoat Phoenix Rider. A nobody. Her carefully cultivated anonymity had been her armor and her shield, and she wasn't ready to expose herself just yet. Avalkyra had little appetite for the political gaming; it was all a farce, a parody of the war she'd fought with her sister years before. As a result, the man didn't reveal his grand plans or strategy to her.

Regardless, Avalkyra had expected any strikes he made to come from Ferro in the west—but apparently he had allies in Arboria, too. With the river as a barrier, his soldiers couldn't have gotten into the Silverwood without crossing at Runnet or Vayle, and both locations were far too populated to make their attacks secret.

With a shadow magic nudge from Avalkyra, Sidra pressed the man who'd been relaying the information. He was red-faced and well into his cups, making his mind the kind of place Avalkyra would rather not venture into.

"What happened to the Riders?" Sidra asked him, gripping the front of his tunic to pull him closer. Avalkyra admired her bravery—she could smell his breath from across the table. "Did they chase the soldiers back into the empire? Did they return to the Eyrie?"

The man's eyes bugged slightly, and he seemed to be enjoying himself less than he had been a few minutes ago, when two young women so desperately craved his company that they bought him a pitcher of ale and invited him to their dark corner of the cookhouse.

"Oh, well, the commandant—"

"The *commander*," Sidra corrected, but Avalkyra shoved her shoulder and waved him on.

"Yes—him, the—their leader," the man amended, darting a nervous glance down at Sidra's fist, which was still clutching his tunic, before continuing. "He sent in reinforcements. Apparently it was only the youngsters in Vayle—the new Rider recruits—and so they were sent off north with the survivors. Not everyone made it, mind, and people have gone missing—Miseriya keep them," he murmured gravely, before adding, "The old guard swooped in to set up some kind of watch or patrol or what have you."

Avalkyra leapt to her feet, barely hearing his last words. "Come, Sidra," she announced, and Sidra obeyed at once, releasing the man and following Avalkyra out into the twilit streets. Their phoenixes were hidden outside the town limits—something Avalkyra risked only because Sidra's mount was there to keep her own phoenix from fleeing or giving their presence away.

"To Arboria so soon?" Sidra asked as they climbed a sloping hill into a copse of trees.

They were due to attack a country estate in some Arborian backwater, dispersing their assaults to give the impression of larger numbers and a stronger force. It would be as unsatisfying as the Iron Road attack, but Avalkyra had agreed to it. Knowing what she did now about Rolan's apparent allies in Arboria, Avalkyra wondered if they were meant to encourage loyalty from new allies or ensure the loyalty of existing ones—but it didn't matter.

She had no intention of going to Arboria herself.

"Change of plans," Avalkyra said. They'd arrived at the clearing where they'd hidden their phoenixes, and after a soft whistle from Sidra—and a firm jerk on the bind from Avalkyra—both creatures fluttered forward. "Think you can handle that Arborian estate on your own? Surely that will even the odds and make it more of a challenge for you?"

Sidra's lip curled up in the corner. "Yes, my queen," she said with obvious pleasure. "Where will you go?" Sidra asked, checking the saddles on both phoenixes and attaching their newly replenished supplies from Runnet.

"Commander Cassian is having his Riders escort the refugees north," Avalkyra said, beginning to pace. "He'll have to set up some temporary housing far enough from the border to be out of danger. What's the closest, safest place to take them?"

Sidra considered as she tightened a strap. "Montascent is too far and Petratec is too small—they'd have nowhere to put them." Avalkyra nodded. "Rushlea's the only option."

"*Yes*, and Veronyka will be there with them. I'll filter in with the other refugees—more will be heading there every day—and orchestrate a way to get her alone. Then I'll tell her about the captives."

Veronyka would have already heard the rumors by now—even beyond those who went missing from the Silverwood attack. It was the thing she'd suggested to Lord Rolan during their meeting, an idea that had not yet occurred to him.

Animages—particularly children—went missing all the time during raids. Even without direct orders, Rolan's soldiers would have been rounding them up to sell or trade. There was many a corrupt businessman who would gladly purchase an animage servant without proper paperwork or indentures. It would cost him half what it would to go through the proper channels. But Avalkyra had suggested he give the order to march them all to a single location—somewhere near the border, where they could be properly defended by Rolan's troops—and where he could use them to draw the Phoenix Riders out.

"You want to use them as bait," Rolan had said, leaning forward with a glitter of interest in his eye. "You think the Riders will come?"

Avalkyra had nodded, dark triumph unfurling in her stomach. *I know one of them will.*

Commander Cassian would never conduct such a rescue mission, no matter how much he might want to. It was exactly the kind of thing that would tip the currently tenuous situation into an all-out war, for starters, and he might not trust the information in the first place, assuming it was a trick or trap. But Veronyka would risk anything to free innocent animage children. She would do for them what she would not do for herself—she would sacrifice her standing with the Phoenix Riders and leave her post. Commander Cassian might not be able to believe the rumors, but thanks to their bond, Avalkyra would be able to convince Veronyka of the truth. She would be able to feel it.

Now it was just up to Avalkyra to get her there.

"Last I heard, Doriyan was hiding somewhere near Rushlea," Sidra said, her tone flat and determinedly disinterested—but Avalkyra could feel her investment in the subject thanks to the bind. Sidra and Doriyan had been close, like brother and sister, ever since the Stellan Uprising—though they'd come up through Phoenix Rider training together as well. But something had happened to sever their relationship after the end of the Blood War; while Ilithya had claimed that Doriyan lost his nerve, Sidra clearly believed things might go back to the way they'd been.

If he was truly there, Avalkyra would find him—and see if he was still of any use.

"Complete your mission in Arboria, then fly to the western Foothills and wait for me. If all goes as expected, I won't be alone."

"What of Rolan's soldiers? They won't let us just fly into their camp and free their captives. It'll be a fight."

Avalkyra grinned, hope kindling inside her chest. "I'm counting on it."

With my hand pressed to my stomach,
my world exploded with light.
With purpose. With power.

- CHAPTER 28 -
SEV

THE MARCH INTO PYRA held all the familiar trappings of Sev's last journey there—the thud of soldiers' boots and the clink and jangle of armor; the scent of leather and pack animals and the pervading sweat and salt of unwashed skin.

Pyra was as wild and unruly as Sev remembered—at turns rocky and inhospitable, then lush with trees and waist-high grass.

But while the purpose of his first time into the Freelands was to go unnoticed, Sev's new captain, Dillon—or Dill, as he for some reason preferred to be called—spoke loudly and often about where they were going and what they were doing. Even if Sev hadn't gotten the information before they'd left, he could have gotten it a dozen times since then.

And that was why, four days later, when they arrived at the settlements, they were deserted.

The goal was to ransack the makeshift villages as well as damage the fledgling Pyraean economy. The fish trade was a huge part of Pyra's livelihood and its disruption would affect not only the regular citizens but the Riders as well. Salt fish was one of the primary winter staples in the region, and Lord Rolan wanted to draw the Riders out, assuming a shortage of food stores would be worthy of their involvement.

In order to get there, Sev's regiment had had to cut around a portion of the Foothills between Ferro and Pyra to find easy enough ground for both soldiers and horses to cross—a route Sev had wholeheartedly supported when Captain Dill showed it to him—and that path bought the Riders enough time to react to the news of the soldiers' approach.

After Sev had written his hasty warning and sent the pigeon off, he hadn't known what the commander would do with the information. But when they crested the rolling hills and saw that the settlements along the Aurys were dark and quiet, Sev's breathing had come a little easier.

Rather than attacking or ambushing the soldiers—risking exposure and giving Lord Rolan exactly what he wanted: the Phoenix Riders fighting empire soldiers near the border—the commander had evacuated the riverside communities.

Dumbfounded and furious, Dill had ordered the soldiers to loot and pillage, and while Sev pretended to be as enthusiastic about senseless destruction and stealing from poor people as the rest, he wasn't faking the smile of relief on his face.

For the first time since he'd delivered the phoenix eggs to the Eyrie, he felt like he was truly making a difference.

Much to Sev's dislike, Dill ordered them to camp in the ruin of one of the settlements while they planned their next move. Most of the structures— many of them stone huts that had likely stood here for centuries—were still intact, despite Dill's orders to lay waste to the villages, and some of the soldiers took the opportunity to sleep inside.

Sev found a tiny one-room hut near the water, the dwelling so small and unremarkable that no one had bothered with it. All that remained after the evacuation was a cold box—now empty—meant to store perishable foodstuffs and a rickety wooden chair. Sev was looking forward to having a place where he and Kade might talk in private and was just in the middle of unpacking his bedroll when the sound of approaching footsteps reached him.

A soldier stood at the door. "Captain Dill wants to see you," he said, ducking back out of the hut without another word.

Sev's heart kicked inside his chest. Had he somehow discovered Sev was the informant?

Captain Dill's command tent was nothing like Captain Belden's, which had been dressed with fine furniture and tended by a personal servant. Belden had wanted the trappings of a lord commander, but Dill's tent was modest, messy, and filled to the brim with rowdy soldiers surrounding a wide wooden table spread with maps and cups of ale.

"Sevro! Come in, come in," Captain Dill said, waving to Sev from his seat at the head of the table, opposite the tent opening. The atmosphere wasn't one of taut tension, and Sev allowed himself a breath of relief. Whatever this was, his secret was still safe.

"Thank you, Captain," Sev said, sidling in and taking the seat offered to him by a nearby soldier—a barrel.

"Get him a cup!" Dill ordered, and Sev was soon plied with a mug of frothy ale, poured from another barrel in the corner of the tent. It was cheap stuff, but strong, and Sev knew he'd have to be careful if he wanted to keep his wits about him. Still, he didn't want to appear formal or rude, so he drank deeply and lifted the mug in thanks.

Dill raised his cup in response—then drained it—before handing it to one of his soldiers to refill.

"As I said to you before, I wanted you here because you were one of the survivors of Belden's attack," he said, shuffling papers and putting a map of the lower rim on top. "And I assume you're familiar with this hinterland— or at least more familiar than me."

"Yes, I am," Sev said. He did have some knowledge—he'd been born in Pyra, after all, and had traveled all the way to Azurec's Eyrie the last time he'd ventured here—but he would have agreed regardless. He was in the command tent, and he suspected that after the preemptive evacuation of their first targeted settlements, Dill might keep the details of their next attack closer to the vest. He might not suspect an informant yet, but he would if Sev continued to do his job right. So Sev needed to learn what he could while he could, and the best way to do that was to stay inside this tent and to be invited back.

Dill nodded and took his refilled cup. "I suspect our backward route through the Foothills gave these villagers the time needed to evacuate. They must have scouts we don't know about, or who knows, maybe the birds told them."

He waited for laughter, and after a moment it came—loud and raucous. Sev joined in, then lifted his cup to block his expression. Technically, a bird *did* tell them, but the words were obviously meant to be a jab at animages. Seemed to Sev it only proved how useful the magical gift could be.

Gratified, Dill took another long draft and belched. "So, is there a better way to cross the country?" he asked, indicating the map on the table before them.

"Or a way to scare off the birds?" one of the soldiers asked, grinning. More laughter.

Sev wondered how they got anything done with all the jokes and jabs. He waited until the laughing died down, then cleared his throat to regain their attention. "It depends where you're going," he said with a shrug, keeping his tone as light as he could, burying his desperate need for the information deep down.

Dill picked up a wooden object carved in the shape of a foot soldier—a marker—and plunked it down on the map. Sev leaned forward. The marker was south and west of where they were now, near Runnet.

It was a busy trader's town, nestled in close to a bend of the River Aurys and the Pilgrimage Road, but the marker was west of it, in the wide-open plains that stretched all the way to the Foothills and the border of Ferro. It was prime farming land, and the fruits of those fields traveled both north into the rocky, mountainous region of Pyra and south into the empire.

And they were going to burn it to the ground.

There wasn't a town or settlement there, but the farmers and herders who worked those fields and tended those animals lived in scattered houses that dotted the landscape. There were probably hundreds of people working those lands, while the landowners lived comfortably in a big house in Runnet. They would be safe behind the village's stone walls, and the simple folk who worked the land would be slaughtered.

People just like Sev's parents.

"If you take the road or travel too near Runnet, you'll be seen," Sev said, keeping his voice flat and neutral. He lifted his cup again—finding someone had refilled it—and took several long drafts to steady his nerves. The alcohol was starting to get to him now, making the edges of his vision go soft and hazy as candlelight, but his hands were steady as he traced an alternate route across the paper. "But if we go north before we cut back west, then travel through these trees," he said, "we'll come out on their northern side. If they're expecting trouble, they'll expect it from the south."

The route would take them right past the place Sev had come across Veronyka and her phoenix. He only knew it was a path they could take thanks to the short side journey he'd taken with Kade and a dozen other soldiers to purchase pack animals from Belden's llama breeder. But while it would certainly hide their attack, it would also slow them down. Even if Sev sent the pigeon out tonight, the Riders and unsuspecting farmers could use all the extra time he could get them.

Dill stared at the map, then at Sev, then at the map again. He pointed at the trees. "They look too dense for horses."

"They're not," Sev said. "I took that same route with a llama train. They cut across the ground easily enough."

"It will take us longer . . . ," Dill mused, scratching at the scruff on his chin.

"But they won't see us coming," Sev said, hating himself. What if something went wrong and his surprise strategy succeeded in catching the farmers completely unaware? He would have then aided in their slaughter rather than prevented it.

Dill considered his words, then nodded. "Yes, yes—a worthy trade-off. I knew you'd come in handy!" he shouted, and several soldiers next to Sev slapped him on the back and ruffled his hair. "Lee," Dill said, turning to the man who'd filled his cup, "see to the preparations."

Lee nodded, and that was it. More ale was poured, more jokes were made, but Sev was not dismissed.

In fact, they even toasted him once or twice. They also raised their cups to victory and success and whatever else they could think of, leaving Sev no choice but to raise his cup too. He needed to remain inside this tent—now and in the future—so he needed them to like him, to think he was valuable, even as he hated them and everything they were doing.

The tent soon devolved into the atmosphere of a pub or a cookhouse. Some of the soldiers were quite deep into their cups, chins drooping onto chests or voices raised loudly as they debated this fact or that. Every time Sev tried to finish his drink and leave, someone had filled it again, or traded his mug for a new one. Whenever someone looked his way, he forced himself to smile, to be easy and carefree, though he felt anything but.

Finally, when the man next to Sev actually fell asleep with his forehead on the table, he took it as his cue to leave.

Though he'd felt level enough sitting down, once Sev got to his feet, the drink began to catch up to him. He managed to exit the tent without stumbling or veering off course, but the walk back to his temporary lodgings was another story. He forgot where it was at first, walking several steps in the wrong direction before looping back around. He passed other soldiers but didn't stop to talk or make eye contact. All he wanted was to close his eyes and lay flat out on his bedroll.

How had Trix done this for so long? How had she smiled and served and lived among her enemies year after year? Was it her future plans for revenge that kept her afloat? Or had she enjoyed this work—the long, slow con with the potential for a big payoff?

Sev supposed it didn't matter. He'd offered to spy, and so here he was. The people he cared about—Kade and the Phoenix Riders—needed him, and this was all he had to offer.

When he arrived at his hut, Sev leaned against the doorway, regaining his balance. It was dark inside save for a patch of moonlight that spilled in from a small circular window, but as Sev shut the door behind him, a flare of lantern light filled the space, and he stumbled around in alarm.

Kade rose from where he'd been seated on the rickety chair, the wooden frame creaking beneath him.

Sev pressed a hand to his chest, his blood pounding—first in shock, then in relief . . . then in something like anticipation. "You're here," he said, feeling dizzy with surprise or something else.

Kade squinted at him, taking a step closer. Sev did his best not to sway on the spot. Kade sniffed. "You're drunk," he said. His voice wasn't one of judgment or accusation, but something closer to mild shock.

"Dill keeps a fine table," Sev said, lurching toward the abandoned chair on shaky legs.

"Dill?" Kade asked from somewhere behind Sev. There was a sound of metal against metal, then the slosh of water into a cup.

"Captain Dill, our fearless leader."

Kade crouched in front of Sev and handed him the tin cup, which he took, impossibly thirsty all of a sudden. He drained it in one gulp, sloshing a bit on his shirt. He wiped at it with as much subtlety and dignity as he could manage, and the corner of Kade's mouth twitched.

"Why were you drinking with Captain Dillon?" Kade pressed, trying to regain Sev's fractured attention.

"He asked me there," Sev said, gasping slightly. He frowned down at the empty cup, and with an impatient eye roll, Kade snatched it and went to refill it from Sev's supplies.

"And?" Kade prompted, bringing the canteen of water with him and setting it on the ground next to them as he held out the cup.

"And what?" Sev asked, distracted by Kade's hands, which were large and long-fingered. Graceful, he remembered thinking the first time he'd seen them. Everything about Kade was strong and balanced and perfectly proportioned. Everything.

Kade sighed through his nostrils. "What did you and Dill talk about? Were you a part of his council meeting?"

"Yes." Sev raised his eyebrows to help his eyes stay open. "I know the next target! The farms west of Runnet. That's the next target," he repeated unnecessarily.

"Are you sure?" Kade asked a bit dubiously.

"*Yes,*" Sev said forcefully. "I can't . . . Do you think . . . ?" He trailed off, blinking down into his cup. He did't remember when he'd taken it from Kade.

"Do I think what?" Kade asked. His voice had a softness to it that made Sev think Kade was amused—maybe even charmed—by Sev's helpless drunkenness.

"Hm?" Sev asked, pulling himself back into the conversation with difficulty. He kept getting distracted and losing the thread of their conversation. He should not have had so much ale. "Oh. The letter. I . . . I don't think I can manage, just now."

It was lucky Kade had come—and not just because of Sev's incapacitation. The pigeon had returned to them the day before, and Kade was able to keep the bird close by but undetected. As a trained messenger, it had a specially honed ability to find familiar animages, and while this one had been trained to recognize Sev while he was at the Eyrie—not just physically or even mentally, but magically—it was learning to identify Kade, too. Sev had made sure to communicate to the pigeon that they'd be traveling, so the bird could find them even as they walked all over the lower rim of Pyra. Though Kade had never trained messenger pigeons, Trix had taught him a few things, including how to intercept or divert one.

Kade's lips twisted into a smile. "Yes, I can send the letter. Hopefully it's enough time . . ." He frowned in thought, absently tugging the half-filled cup from Sev's hands and taking a drink.

Sev watched him swallow, watched where his warm fingers caused beads of condensation to leave trails down the side of the cup.

"What would I do without you?" Sev asked, partially drunk and entirely sincere.

Kade laughed and looked away, but Sev caught the way his lips fought back the smile, the way his hand swiped at the back of his neck.

"Come on," Kade said, grabbing Sev's arm and hoisting him from the chair. Sev hadn't realized it, but he'd begun to slouch low in his seat. "Let's get you into bed."

Sev's head and heart whirled into overdrive, but it was clear fairly quickly that Kade was treating Sev as he would a child or a sick person, and not a romantic partner. He slipped under Sev's good arm, remembering better than Sev did sometimes not to move or jostle the bad one, and helped him onto his bedroll in the darkness against the far wall.

The room spun slightly, and Sev regretted the ale. He wished he were here with Kade, alone in this quiet hut, completely lucid and aware of every tiny detail.

"Kade?" Sev said, as Kade moved to stand. Sev couldn't see his face, only his blackened silhouette, gilded by the lantern light behind him.

"Yes, Sev?"

Sev liked when Kade said his name. Not "soldier" like he used to, or "Sevro," as the others called him.

A few moments of silence passed, and Kade's body relaxed, as if he'd thought that Sev had fallen asleep. He turned toward the door, and Sev spoke to his back.

"Will you stay?" he asked softly, so softly that Kade could pretend he hadn't heard it if he wanted to. But Sev had seen the way his body stiffened, the way he froze midstep. He *had* heard it, and now it was up to him what he wanted to do about it.

But the ale was like lead in Sev's veins. The last thing he saw was Kade's dark shadow, staring at him, before the weight was too much, pulling Sev under, dragging his body into sleep.

The next morning Sev awoke to an empty hut, his head pounding and his mouth as dry as the Shadow Plains in the Stellan desert. He blinked, replaying the end of the night, his physical discomfort amplifying as he remembered making a fool of himself in front of Kade.

As he remembered asking him to stay.

Acid roiled in Sev's stomach, more from embarrassment than from the drink, until he sat up and spotted a spare blanket laid out on the ground against the opposite wall and one of Sev's shirts rolled up like a pillow.

His chest swelled.

Kade had stayed with him after all.

*You have not made bearing you easy, my daughter, and
I sense the fire in you. Surely only a girl could be such trouble.
That is good, because you will need to be strong for what is to come.*

- CHAPTER 29 -
ELLIOT

DAY BY DAY ELLIOT found life at the Eyrie just a little bit easier.

Though most of the Riders were gone, he didn't feel lonely as he once had. The commander had trusted him to take over much of the steward's duties now that Beryk had been posted to Vayle, and when he walked around the stronghold, people would nod and smile at him again.

It was also growing easier not to dwell on thoughts of his sister.

She was still on his mind every single day—a ceaseless pressure on his heart—but the weight eased a bit knowing that he wasn't letting his fear and dread cut him off from everything and everyone. He wasn't letting himself be defeated. He was being strong, for her as well as for himself, and it comforted him to think that if she could see him now, she might be proud to call him her big brother. Elliot was trying, and he prayed with all his heart that wherever she was, she was trying too. Trying to be happy, trying to keep her spirits up.

Trying to stay alive and not lose hope.

Though Elliot's newfound positivity was a nice change, it wasn't infallible. He thought often about why the commander was keeping things from Tristan, and he wondered what the commander meant when he'd proposed they "eliminate" certain members of the Grand Council.

Elliot wanted to know more, but he had only small fragments of the whole picture.

And that's all you'll ever have, he chastised himself one night as he was watching Jaxon fly and his mind began to wander. *It's none of your business. You're grounded; you're not really a Rider anymore.*

He tried to reason that his intentions were good, that he wanted to figure it out because he wanted to *help*, but he'd had good intentions before, too. He'd been trying to save his sister's life. Trying to keep his family together. Intentions didn't matter when you did the wrong thing.

He glanced across the moonlit field at Sparrow, who was perched on one of the massive boulders that surrounded the grassy plain, gazing up as if she could see the stars.

Sometimes he wished he experienced the world as simply as she did. It wasn't that Sparrow herself was simple, but rather, she lived and spoke and acted in the most uncomplicated of ways. She understood things about anger and grief and forgiveness that Elliot had not—at least, not until she'd helped him see it—but she didn't let the dark complexities of the world overwhelm or shake her convictions.

She moved through her life with surety, and Elliot envied her. He didn't think he'd ever lived like that.

Maybe her past had helped shape her into someone who couldn't afford doubt, while Elliot's past had made him question everything and everyone around him; it had turned his friends into enemies, his enemies into allies, and muddied the one place he should have belonged: among the Riders.

At last Jaxon swooped down to land in front of Elliot, nudging his head against Elliot's chest in a bolster of support: They belonged here. Jax was sure of it, and no matter what, Elliot would always have Jax, which meant he'd always be a Rider.

"Thanks, buddy," Elliot muttered, smoothing his hand over Jax's feathers, hot from excitement and exertion after his flight. Though it wasn't the same as flying with his fellow phoenixes or with Elliot in the saddle, it was clear getting out into the open expanse of the sky was crucial for Jaxon's happiness, and there was always a difference in him once he'd gotten his exercise. "Ready to go back in?"

Jax crooned, and the sound drew Sparrow. "Not tired already?" she asked the phoenix, and to Elliot's surprise, Jax turned his head and butted her in the chest too. A stab of emotion twisted Elliot's stomach at the sight. He thought it was jealousy at first, but that wasn't quite right. It wasn't a bad feeling exactly, but an intense one.

Sparrow laughed in delight, stumbling slightly from Jax's enthusiasm.

"Easy," Elliot chastised, his stomach still tight, though he was laughing. "You'll bowl her over."

Jax released a huff of air, causing Sparrow's hair to fly up in her face, before turning away. He flapped his wings and took to the sky, heading for the Eyrie.

The silence felt slightly awkward in his wake, and Elliot searched for something to say. He turned to make his way back into the village. "Are you returning as well?" he asked, gesturing to the gate, but of course she couldn't see that. "Back inside, I mean."

She pursed her lips, and he remembered what she'd said about not liking it inside. She shrugged. "Walk with you," she said, more statement than question.

It was easier to be moving together than standing still. Elliot dug his hands into his pockets and breathed deep the warm, sweet summer air, while Sparrow twirled her spear in front of them.

They were just rounding a corner in the village when Sparrow's hand shot out and pressed against his chest, barring Elliot's movement. Sparrow cocked her head, listening to something; then her hand clenched, taking up a fistful of Elliot's tunic and pulling. She forcibly dragged him into one of the alleys that wound behind the houses and workshops that faced the street.

"Sparrow, what—" he began, but she only tugged him harder and with surprising strength, down into a squat behind Lars's shop. She pressed a hand to his mouth—or tried to, her palm landing on his nose instead, and he batted it away from his face. The gesture worked, though: Elliot stopped talking and listened.

It was hot back there, the forge still billowing heat despite the late hour, and the scent of metal and stale smoke clung to the air.

Elliot sensed Jaxon in the air over the Eyrie, wondering what was happening, but Elliot told his bondmate to stay put. Everything was fine. He hoped.

Now that they were still, Elliot could hear voices coming from the metalsmith's shop. It was a low rumble, difficult to distinguish.

He glanced at Sparrow, her face intent as she listened. The other animals that had been trailing her had scattered except for a raven that had been riding on her shoulder. It had flown into the air at Sparrow's sudden movements and alighted on a nearby barrel instead.

Did Sparrow think they'd be in trouble walking the village at night? There was no curfew, not for the servants or the Riders—or whatever Elliot was. He was about to open his mouth again when the familiarity of one of the voices made his heart stop.

It was the commander.

Axura above, he was eavesdropping on the commander again.

He gripped Sparrow's arm and leaned in close. "I am *not* doing this again," he whispered, moving to stand. As he rose to his feet, Elliot found a vantage point through a gap in the back wall, and his eyes fell on a group huddled around a worktable in Lars's shop. Not only was the commander there, but also Lars, and surprisingly, Morra and Old Ana.

The sight of Morra sent a chill down Elliot's spine, and he flashed back to hours of interrogation with the woman. She hadn't been cruel or demanding, wringing the truth from him with threats or even torture—but she had seen through him in a way Elliot couldn't reconcile or explain. She knew when he was lying or bending the truth. He'd tried it only once or twice at the beginning, too overcome with fear and dread to spill every last detail, but the look on her face had been enough to make him reconsider. She always knew exactly what to ask and where to prod when he held back. A shudder racked his body, and he forcefully drew his gaze away from her.

On the table between them was a long object that looked like a cane—simple in design, with a glossy, polished wooden shaft and what looked like a phoenix-head topper made of gleaming gold or brass. As Elliot watched, the commander took up the cane and tested out its height and grip.

"It's finished to look like wood, but it's metal," Lars explained, drawing a finger along the apparently faux wood grain. "That keeps the weight up—they'll never guess it's hollow."

Hollow? Even as the thought entered his mind, the commander took hold of the phoenix head and twisted.

It came off easily, revealing what Lars had said—that the inside of the cane was hollow—and the head itself was loaded with small projectiles. Darts. The commander deftly plucked one from inside and placed it into the cane, raised it to his lips, and turned away from the group. He took aim, released a sharp puff of air into the hollow cane, and the dart flew out the end to embed itself in the far wall.

The commander lowered the cane again, looking suitably impressed.

"I suggest you get in as much practice as possible, Commander," Lars said. "It's a difficult weapon; by the time you've loosed the first dart, the others will begin to react and scatter. Your strikes must be quick and, above all else, accurate. Morra, how fast-acting will the poison be?"

"Ana's plants are top quality, and we've plenty of time. I can make it as potent as you need it to be." She lifted something from the table—another dart from a pile Elliot couldn't see—and inspected it. It was a simple design—long and thin, with a pointed tip and a fletched end.

"Instant," the commander said, and Morra nodded.

Elliot's mind was buzzing. Was this to do with the Grand Council? And if it was, did that mean . . . ? Did he intend to . . . ?

While the group inside the shop turned away from the worktable, their discussion difficult to discern with their heads bent over the cane, examining one detail or another, a shadow hopped onto the worktable. A raven.

Elliot glanced at the barrel behind him, but already knew that he'd find the perch abandoned.

The bird hopped across the surface of the table, picked up one of the darts in its beak, and then fluttered back. The theft went unnoticed by the group inside, and the raven now stood before Sparrow, who was petting the bird praisingly and holding out the dart for Elliot in her other hand.

He took it, wordless, and remained still until the sound of the clandestine meeting disbanding brought him back to himself. The lights inside the forge went out, and all was silent.

Elliot wrestled with what to do about yet more information he shouldn't have, and had taken to carrying the dart around in his pocket.

Apparently, the commander had big plans for the Grand Council meeting—plans that included carrying a concealed weapon disguised as a cane, armed with poison darts.

Correction: *potent* poison darts.

Elliot kept hearing the word "eliminate," kept palming the dart in his pocket. Allies, enemies, majority votes.

He thought that the commander's plans would have nagged him less if it weren't for the fact that Tristan was apparently being excluded from them. Not only was Tristan the last Rider on Elliot's list with whom he'd yet to make amends, but he was also the commander's son. The truth was, it reminded him too much of his own circumstances. Elliot had thought he and his father were as close as a father and son could be—until Captain Belden showed up at their front door. He hadn't known his father had been helping smuggle animages into Pyra, and he hadn't known that people were watching them closely—but his father had. He hadn't been surprised to see Belden that day, even if he had been surprised by what the man asked. Worst of all, it wasn't his father who'd paid the price—it was Elliot and Riella. Elliot had to be the spy, the traitor, while Riella was forced into being a hostage. Elliot knew their peril hurt his father, that he loved his children and feared for their lives, but Elliot couldn't help resenting the man for the risks he'd taken without a thought for the consequences.

He had been furious with his father after Belden left, his entire world upended after he'd had his dreams of becoming a Rider so recently fulfilled. One day Beryk was there, offering Elliot all he'd ever wanted, and then the next Belden was there to take it all away again. Elliot had refused to do it, refused to join—but his father told him it wasn't that simple. If Elliot refused to go, then they'd no longer be of use to Belden. And if they were no longer of use . . . they were as good as dead.

Now, seeing the commander treat Tristan the same way—keeping him in the dark while he gambled lives and made plans his son knew nothing about—put a bitter taste in Elliot's mouth. He felt he owed Tristan a chance to stop his father before it was too late, to give him the opportunity to change his fortunes, the chance that Elliot never had.

Still, he wavered, alternating moment to moment on what he thought he should do. Tell Tristan; don't tell Tristan. Throw the dart away. Keep the dart close. Destroy it. Hide it.

Tristan's absence from the Eyrie saved Elliot from actually having to make a decision . . . until the day he returned.

With most of the Riders gone, Elliot had been helping the weapons masters teach the young apprentices in the training yard.

Afterward, he was just rolling a barrel of practice swords into the storage shed when he bumped into Tristan inside. His patrol was currently stationed in Rushlea after a brief time spent in Vayle, and Elliot hadn't expected to see him here.

Tristan must have been intending to restock weapons or ammunition, but when Elliot entered, Tristan was staring so fixedly at the rack of weapons that he didn't notice Elliot until he was a foot away.

"Tristan?" Elliot said.

Tristan turned; he didn't jump or flinch back in surprise, but he was so absorbed in his own thoughts, it seemed he'd forgotten exactly who Elliot was. "Hey, Elliot," he said casually, distractedly. Then his gaze sharpened and he straightened, as if remembering his usual reserve.

But for that one second . . . Elliot swallowed. It was like it used to be, when he was just one of the others. Beryk's understudy, yes. A bit of a kiss-up, definitely—he hadn't known how else to hide what he was doing than to be an entirely different version of himself—but still one of the Riders. Still a part of the whole.

But now? Elliot was, at best, an afterthought—and at worst, a lingering problem nobody knew how to fix.

"Sorry to bother you," he said, his mood turning dark. "I was just . . ." He gestured down at the barrel of weapons.

"No, you're not bothering me . . . ," Tristan said, then sighed.

He continued to stare at the weapons, the silence stretching between them. "Is everything okay?" Elliot pressed, forgetting his own discomfort. He examined Tristan more closely, but he looked as he always did: stiff postured and clean shaven, his face a mask not unlike the one his father often wore, though Elliot knew Tristan had a harder time hiding his emotions than the commander did.

"Not really, Elliot. Not really. I keep trying to get him to talk to me— to *really* talk to me," he said, and though he didn't mention him by name, Elliot knew he was talking about his father. Tristan and Cassian's issues were well known, and Elliot had very recently overheard the commander willfully excluding his son on important Rider business. "I'd thought we were there, that things were different, but now . . . I'm on the outside again."

"I understand, I think."

Tristan shot him a startled look before he lowered his brows and nodded, surveying Elliot closely. "I guess you would."

"But I earned that exclusion," Elliot said. "You have not."

There was no bitterness in his voice, which actually surprised him. Elliot had come a long way from even a few weeks ago, when he felt his anger and frustration and self-pity acutely. But now he was simply stating a fact.

Tristan's face flickered, a flash of emotions ranging from relief to gratitude to something like regret. The lost look in his eyes made Elliot step forward, reaching into his pocket.

"I . . . I found something," he whispered, his heart racing. Was this a mistake? Would Tristan call him out for stealing and spying and lock him away for good this time?

Elliot placed the dart into Tristan's hand. Tristan stared at it, then back up at Elliot's face. "What is this?"

"Ask your father about it. Tell him you found it in Lars's forge."

"I can't—he just kicked me out of his office, and I have to return to Rushlea before dark."

Elliot chewed his lip, then shook his head. "Find the time. Now, later—just ask him. There's something to do with the Grand Council he's not telling you."

You will need to be stronger than me,
stronger than my sister. You are entering a
world at war and must come out swinging.

- CHAPTER 30 -
VERONYKA

THE JOURNEY TO RUSHLEA had been slow. While Tristan's patrol was mounted on their phoenixes, they had to keep pace with the walking refugees, who were a mix of children, elderly, and everyone in between, as well as the guard escort who had come from the Eyrie. They walked in a disorganized train a hundred feet long, and the Riders often had to encourage the stragglers to hurry up or tell the leaders to slow their pace. When they weren't soaring alongside the group, they would scout up ahead or double back to check that they weren't pursued before circling to rejoin the main group. They camped alongside the road at night, and always had multiple Riders on patrol, meaning sleep was sparse.

Veronyka did what she could to comfort those who had lost family. Whenever she felt angry and powerless, she thought about Doriyan. The two subjects were seemingly unrelated, but looking for him gave Veronyka some much-needed focus and direction. He had the potential to be another ally in a war where every Rider counted, or he could be the missing piece in understanding the Phoenix Rider sightings in the south. Veronyka didn't understand how it all fit together, but finding the exiled Rider was her best chance at learning more.

And she had to hurry. There was every chance the commander would order her back to the Eyrie, and then Veronyka would know what true powerlessness felt like.

Whenever she was anxious, she fiddled with the heavy golden ring on her bracelet. Despite her determination to forget Val and get rid of the trinket, everything had changed when Veronyka unlocked that puzzle box. Now she had one foot in the past, one in the present, and though she continued to block their connection as best she could, Veronyka knew that she'd have to face Val again—that she'd have to deal with the truth that she so desperately wanted to forget.

Tristan had left as soon as they were settled, flying out to the Eyrie to report to the commander the day after they arrived. He also had a list of supplies they needed, and some damaged tack that needed to be fixed or replaced.

Veronyka should have gone with him, as per the commander's orders, but Tristan insisted he'd handle it. Veronyka was secretly relieved. They'd been so busy setting up camp and the temporary refugee village, she hadn't had a single moment to consider Doriyan and where to start looking for him. With Tristan gone, she could spend some time rereading Ilithya's list and figuring out where to start her search.

It would also give them a chance to work on blocking their bond. They hadn't had much time to practice with everything that was going on—not that Veronyka noticed much of a difference either way—but maybe time apart was what they needed to bolster her flagging attempts to control her shadow magic and inhibit her and Tristan's bond.

Tristan had left in the morning, but it wasn't until the end of the day, after aiding with construction, dealing with refugees, and flying patrol routes, that she got a chance to take out the lockbox again and review Ilithya's list. Dinner had been hours ago, and their camp was quiet and cloaked in darkness.

While Vayle was a rocky village, stacked and piled and built tightly together, Rushlea was, by comparison, vast. It sprawled across the rolling landscape, with two central squares that held bustling markets, but in the wake of the empire's attack and resultant destruction, the village was as subdued as Vayle had been, with a similar decrease in travelers and trade.

The Rider camp was on the outskirts of the village—near the refugee housing, but still separate—in a clearing surrounded on all sides by soaring cliff faces and massive chunks of stone.

Veronyka unearthed the lockbox from Xephyra's saddlebag and settled into a grassy hollow to read. It had been a while since she'd looked at the list, and as Xephyra drew close, lending her glow, Veronyka's heart sank at how little information there was on the crinkled and well-worn page.

Doriyan had been a part of Avalkyra Ashfire's patrol and had fought with her from the Stellan Uprising all the way until the end of the Blood War. There were some notes about "resistance" that were written in Ilithya's handwriting, and Veronyka wondered again if Val had used shadow magic to command her patrol. If she had, Doriyan and the others might have been less agreeable once she'd died and there was no one to force their hands.

Disappointingly, he'd disappeared after the Last Battle, and there'd been no sign of him since. The only reason they thought he might be in Rushlea was because he was born here. That wasn't much to go on, and given what Alexiya had said about him being in hiding from other Phoenix Riders as well as the empire, Veronyka's hope of finding him plummeted. She'd have to keep an eye out during her next patrol and maybe ask around about any surviving war vets.

Leaning back against her bondmate, Veronyka sighed and glanced at the lockbox. Besides the list of Rider exiles, she hadn't looked at the contents since she'd discovered her birth certificate. As she did with shadow magic, blocking the existence of the box's contents from her mind felt like the only way to keep herself together. There was no point in dwelling on things she couldn't change and decisions she didn't know how to make, and so denial had become Veronyka's best friend. And since denying herself meant denying Val, it felt like the right—sometimes the only—thing to do.

But if Val was one of the Phoenix Riders that had been spotted, if she was involved in the attacks anyway . . . maybe there were answers to be found within the lockbox. The exiled Riders list had proved fruitful. Maybe there were things she was overlooking. And with Tristan gone . . . there was no safer time to delve into the box's contents.

With a deep breath, Veronyka stared inside.

It was as confusing to her as it had been the first time she'd opened it—a mishmash of information that her *maiora* had deemed important but that Veronyka had failed to understand the importance of. But now that she knew the truth of who she was, maybe she would find new meaning. Much of what was inside included details about the Ashfire family.

Veronyka's family.

Had Ilithya kept this box for Veronyka's sake? Was it less a spymaster's carefully gleaned intelligence and more a box of random memories and keepsakes trying to preserve the history of the Ashfires, when the empire was trying so desperately to erase it from existence?

Ilithya was in Aura Nova at the end of the war—that was surely how she'd managed to find Veronyka as a baby—but the details of her spy work were a mystery. Veronyka did find an autopsy report with Ilithya's name on it, which meant she must have been working as a healer inside the palace. The Nest was large, though, with dozens of healers in its employ. Had Ilithya had much contact with Pheronia? And how had she managed to find Veronyka? The residents of the Nest must not have known Pheronia was pregnant or they'd have turned the empire inside out searching for her—so where did Pheronia give birth? And who had betrayed Veronyka's identity to Ilithya?

She pushed the thoughts aside. It was still difficult for her to reconcile Ilithya the spy with Ilithya her *maiora*, and Veronyka didn't like to dwell on the idea that she had been just a job to her grandmother. She refused to believe their lives together were entirely a lie.

Reading the papers as Veronyka *Ashfire* was an entirely new experience, and every mention of Pheronia or Avalkyra or other Ashfire queens set a bell reverberating inside her chest. These were her ancestors, her family—her people.

There was a bundle of letters written between Pheronia and Avalkyra during the Blood War, and Veronyka trailed her fingertips over the words written in her mother's hand, imagining she could feel her presence through the faded ink. The letters must have been collected and bound together by Ilithya, though Veronyka wondered at how she'd managed it. The letters from Pheronia must have been found by Ilithya in one of Val's hidden bases, left behind after her death, though Veronyka had to admit she was surprised that Val had bothered to save them in the first place. Veronyka knew Val loved Pheronia, but it still seemed uncharacteristically sentimental. On the other hand, for Ilithya to have gathered the letters from Val *to* Pheronia, she must have taken them from the Nest after Pheronia's death.

The letters painted a fascinating, though not entirely surprising, picture of the sisters' lives. Veronyka read them hungrily as they documented the reason the sisters parted ways—Avalkyra had killed Queen Regent Lania, Pheronia's mother and Avalkyra's chosen suspect in the murder of their father King Aryk—the months when Pheronia's anger prevented her from answering Avalkyra's increasingly dark and demanding letters, and finally, when Pheronia replied to Avalkyra, begging for peace between them, though it was too late. Veronyka couldn't help trying to put the letters in order and fit the shadow magic dreams she'd had from Val into the gaps, filling out the timeline and helping her understand the schism.

She was unnerved by how familiar Avalkyra's words sounded, how she refused to apologize or take any of the blame for what was happening between her and Pheronia, and her constant insistence that they belonged together.

Veronyka put the letters down, her heart pounding against her rib cage. It felt as if Val were with her—as if at any moment she'd speak into Veronyka's mind.

She shook her head—she refused to allow herself to reach for Val like she had the last time she'd opened this box. Part of her reluctance to revisit it for the past weeks was fear that she'd somehow make herself vulnerable again. As if the box itself were some tether binding Veronyka and Val together.

Veronyka was surprised at the surge of guilt that rose inside her. By closing herself off from Val, she'd been closing herself off from her mother, too. It was uncomfortable to realize how much the line blurred between Veronyka and Pheronia, between Val and Avalkyra. Were she and Val doomed to repeat the past? Avalkyra and Pheronia split forever after one violent, remorseless act . . . and now Veronyka and Val were similarly separated after not only the poisoning of Veronyka's bondmate, but Val's attempts to destroy everything and everyone in Veronyka's life.

But while her mother's pregnancy—the thing Veronyka assumed was the reason for Pheronia wanting to reconnect with her estranged sister after months of not speaking—became the catalyst for at least one of the sisters wanting to make amends, Veronyka didn't know what it would take for her and Val to fix what was broken between them. A part of her recoiled at the idea, refusing to absolve someone who wasn't sorry and didn't ask for forgiveness, while the rest of her realized that if she didn't bridge the gap and at least try to bring Val back to her side, there would be no one to rein her in . . . no one to stop the second coming of Avalkyra Ashfire and the destruction of them all.

In truth, Veronyka had never felt so alone. This was her family—here, in this box—but the reality of it outside of the past was harder to understand.

As her hand moved idly over the papers and documents within, her fingertips slid over the wax seal on her birth certificate. Veronyka hesitated but found herself unable to look at it.

Finding out her true identity had given her more questions than answers—particularly the blank line where her father's name should have been. Her mother might be dead beyond a doubt, but her father was unaccounted for. He was as unformed and indistinct in her mind as that empty space on her birth certificate. Maybe he was alive somewhere, mourning Pheronia and wishing things had worked out differently.

Maybe he didn't know he had a daughter at all.

Veronyka would have to face who and what she was eventually, but she wasn't ready yet. She didn't know what she wanted from her future, not when so much in her present was demanding her immediate attention. War was happening, even without the news that an Ashfire heir was hiding in Pyra. If she came forward and revealed her true identity, she'd be putting a target on the Riders' backs, not to mention on everyone else in Pyra.

And what of Val? Did *she* intend to come forward anytime soon? There were technically *two* Ashfire heirs in Pyra, and their identities felt like the tipping point, the thing that would turn everything into chaos.

The information was as dangerous as it was life-changing—a weapon to be wielded—and Veronyka had to be certain she knew what she was doing with it.

Tristan returned the next evening, followed close behind by a wagon filled with supplies.

It felt almost strange to greet him—Tristan and Veronyka had spent so much time together, there was actually a moment of awkwardness when he landed before her and the rest of the Riders just outside the refugee camp, smiling shyly.

He clapped the others on the back and shook their hands, but then he and Veronyka were facing each other, and the greetings and pleasantries died on his lips.

"I—hey," he said, aware of his patrol members around them.

"Hi," Veronyka said brightly—too brightly. She wondered if he felt the pull between them the way she did, as if their time apart had only strengthened her magic's desire to be near him. *Her* desire.

They stared at each other a second longer, then, "How was—" Veronyka began, but then Xephyra had shoved her aside in order to butt her head against Tristan's chest.

He let out a startled "oof" in surprise, then laughed and ruffled the feathers along Xephyra's neck, giving her the casual, affectionate greeting he'd been unable to give Veronyka.

Xephyra moved on to Rex, and Veronyka and Tristan shared another lingering look before they joined the others in unloading the wagon.

With the shadow magic link as strong as ever between them, Veronyka had to wonder if her attempts at blocking their bond were actually making things worse, not better, but she quickly banished the thought and refocused on what was happening around her.

Though he showed a brave, indifferent face, Tristan admitted to Veronyka that he'd tried to speak to the commander again about the Grand Council but had been summarily rebuffed. They were next to the wagon of supplies, Lysandro reading from a list while Latham and Anders stood inside, handing out the items one at a time.

"We barely talked for ten minutes," Tristan said, fighting to keep his anger in check as he stacked several crates on the ground, throwing them down with unnecessary force. "Once he had my report and the supply requests, he tried to send me off again. He was annoyed that I'd told you to stay behind, but he was so swamped with papers . . . I honestly think he might have forgotten about it. When I tried to ask him about the Grand Council again, he told me it was none of my concern."

Veronyka added a crate to the pile and straightened, wishing she knew how to comfort him. But after a lifetime with Val, she understood too well what it was like to be constantly lied to—and had yet to discover a solution to the problem.

"After, though . . . ," Tristan started, then faltered, a hand dropping to press against his pocket. He glanced over his shoulder to make sure they weren't being overheard before jerking his head toward the horses at the front of the wagon where they'd be out of earshot. Veronyka followed. "Elliot found me. He showed me this, and insisted it was my father's." He held out what looked like a poison dart for Veronyka to see before tucking it away again. "I don't know what to make of it—the fact that Elliot is poking around where he probably shouldn't, or the idea that my father might be up to something worse than I'd even considered."

"Did you ask him? Your father?"

"I didn't get a chance."

"Maybe when you give your next report in a couple of weeks?" she offered, unsure what to make of it either. She'd never seen any of the Riders train with darts and couldn't fathom what he had in store for the weapon.

Tristan nodded, but he looked defeated. Veronyka knew he expected his father would just lie to him again, and she privately agreed, though she didn't think it was a good idea to point that out right now.

"Did your father happen to mention anything about the missing people?" Veronyka asked, hoping for good news to change the subject. "From Fallon's patrols?"

In addition to the missing people from the Silverwood attack, the refugees from the fishing settlements and evacuees from various other attacks and raids near the border had also reported people lost and unaccounted for.

And not just random people. Animages.

Veronyka had held out some shred of hope that Fallon's Riders might have seen something or found where the soldiers were taking them, but Tristan's expression told her she was wrong.

"Nothing yet," Tristan said quietly. "Apparently this is pretty standard behavior from empire attacks in Pyra. The commander . . . he doesn't think there's anything we can do."

Veronyka swallowed the feeling of impotent rage that rose up her throat.

They'd had a fresh wave of refugees just that morning, and one woman had lost *two* children. Even as Veronyka knew she was helping here in Rushlea, she couldn't fight the feeling that there was more they could be doing.

As they unloaded the wagons, a group of locals had gathered near the edge of the village, watching the action at the refugee camp with suspicion and thinly veiled hostility.

"Who're they?" Tristan asked, nodding in their direction.

"Farmers," said Ronyn, who had come up alongside them. "Half their crops were burned down during the empire's attack, and the rest when the Phoenix Riders came to their defense."

The farmers stood shoulder to shoulder, their clothes ratty and their hair unkempt. In truth, they looked in worse shape than the refugees.

"They don't want us here—the phoenixes least of all," Veronyka added. While things hadn't escalated beyond dirty looks and muttered threats, it was clear that not all the Rushlean locals welcomed their presence. "So we keep them away from the village."

The necessity of it had angered Veronyka at first. Phoenixes had saved these people and this village, after all, but then she realized they were also part of why the villagers were in danger to begin with. This was Avalkyra Ashfire's legacy; this was years of anger and resentment, not mere months.

"It might be a good idea to talk to them," said Latham, who had joined their group along with Lysandro and Anders. "Smooth things over."

"If they hate phoenixes, there's nothing I can do," Tristan said, turning his back on the farmers.

"I think they want to be reassured," Latham pressed. "You could at least meet with them, listen to their complaints—like you did at Vayle."

"If they want to call a formal meeting, I'll attend it. But I'm not going to give in to an angry mob. It'll only encourage them."

"I think ignoring them is a mistake," Latham argued, his jaw clenched. "They could take it out on the phoenixes."

Ronyn shook his head. "I don't think it matters if Tristan talks to them or not. Even if he smiles and bows and curtsies—they *want* to be angry."

Anders laughed at the image of Tristan curtsying, tugging Latham to the wagon to unload again, Lysandro trailing behind.

"Speaking of phoenixes . . . ," Tristan said, when he and Veronyka were alone again. "The commander did get one more piece of news. There's been another Phoenix Rider attack. In Arboria—at some lord's country estate."

Veronyka thought of Doriyan again. They had to try to find him as soon as possible.

"I hope you caught up on sleep at the Eyrie," Veronyka said.

Tristan frowned. "I suppose. Why?"

"Because we're looking for Doriyan. Tonight."

Here follows the account of Della, retired maidservant to Lania of Stel from 153 AE to 165 AE. Below is a conversation overheard by Della on Day 12, First Moon, 165 AE between Lania, Queen Consort of King Aryk Ashfire, and Councilor Halton of Stel, recounted to Ilithya Shadowheart in 169 AE.

Councilor Halton: Thank you for your time, my queen. According to my research, your family has ties to the governorship of Stel—or at least it used to. Perhaps I can help you reclaim some of that former glory.

Queen Consort Lania: I am a queen, Councilor Halton. I need no help from you.

H: A queen consort. This is the reign of King Aryk Ashfire. Your name will be remembered as it relates to his and as it relates to your royal daughter. They will not sing songs about you, Lania of Stel.

L: And what of the songs about your family, Halton of Stel, descendant of King Rol the Betrayer?

H: A betrayer, allegedly—but still a king. We both come from great lines that have fallen into disrepute, and I think we can help each other. I propose friendship, my queen—and a simple exchange. The wheels are already in motion for a Stellan insurgence, but we need to destabilize the crown. We need someone on the inside. Someone with Stel's interests at heart.

L: I don't see how destabilizing the crown benefits me or my interests, Councilor. As you've graciously pointed out, I am a mere consort queen—but a queen nonetheless. And I have a daughter to think of.

H: If there is no king, you are no longer a mere consort. . . . You are a queen regent. With your daughter underage, you can secure a path for her directly to the throne. And remove any who are in your way.

L: You mean my husband? My stepdaughter? You speak treason, sir.

H: I speak the truth. None are closer to these targets than you are, Lania.

L: And you expect me to wield a dagger in the night?

H: I expect you to tip your hand over a cup. I will get you everything you need. It will be quick and painless—for you, at least.

L: Together we kill a king, and I gain sole rule over an empire. Something worthy of a song, as you put it. What do you gain?

H: Your daughter, Pheronia, will marry my son, Rolan. Both our children will be on the throne after you, and Stel will rule the empire at long last.

Already you kick and punch and fight
in the womb. Your father says you are a warrior
in the making, and he calls you his little fire.

- CHAPTER 31 -
SEV

SEV'S REGIMENT DID AS he'd advised, packing up camp the day after their failed attack on the riverside fishing villages and starting the slow crawl north and then west into the cover of the dense trees. Sev's hangover made the first day hard going, but the warm, sympathetic grins Kade shot him every time their eyes met made the discomfort worth it. Maybe he needed to get drunk and embarrass himself more often.

Sev had been surprised to find that there was nostalgia in the journey for him, retracing the steps he'd taken months ago with Jotham and Ott's splinter unit—none more so than when they'd walked into the small clearing with the now-abandoned hunter's cabin. Captain Dill had sent scouts ahead to check their path, but once they were given the all clear, they'd actually taken a midday rest in the soft grasses of the forest glade.

Sev poked his head inside the cottage as he ate a crust of flatbread and found the house was simple and barren—just as it had been before, except that two girls had lived here then. One with a phoenix, the other with a knife. *His* knife.

Kade came upon him, peering inside too. "I guess she's moved on," he said, and Sev gaped. *Kade didn't know*—hadn't been to the Eyrie to see the girl, Veronyka, among the other Phoenix Riders. And Sev had forgotten to tell him.

"She's with them," he said, smiling at the look of confusion on Kade's face. He lowered his voice. "When I showed up at the Eyrie, she was there—she and her phoenix. They're safe."

A stunned smile split Kade's face, and Sev wanted to fix the look in his memory forever.

But then the expression faltered, and Kade shifted his gaze out the window, to the bustling camp of soldiers. Even if Veronyka had been safe, she wouldn't remain so. She was a Phoenix Rider, a warrior, and the empire wanted a fight.

They moved on after that, their progress through the trees hard but manageable. Kade and the other bondservants had their work cut out for them, trying to get the horses through the dense underbrush, but it wasn't long before they'd reached the heart of the wood and turned south toward the farms of Runnet.

With every step they took, Sev wondered what they'd find when they got there. Kade's letter, written and sent after Sev had passed out from the ale the night at the fishing settlements, had had plenty of time to get to the Eyrie, but messenger pigeons were never foolproof. There was always a chance a bird could get lost or shot down from the sky. There was still a chance that things could go awry.

It was a great relief that Captain Dill seemed to be prioritizing stealth over speed; rather than pushing hard to make it to the farms before night-fall, he'd actually slowed their pace and ordered them to camp early for the night, deep in the trees. Then they'd push hard the next day and hit the farms the following evening.

When some of his soldiers argued, he shut them down with one final bit of information even Sev had lost track of.

"Tomorrow's a festival day," he explained. "They won't be in the fields; they'll be off celebrating the end of the Blood War."

There was some laughter and jeering at that. Given what they were doing—trying to draw the Riders into a battle to start a *second* war—celebrating the end of the first one seemed a bit ironic.

"There'll be drinking," Captain Dill continued, "and food and music. It will be loud and they'll be distracted. They won't see or hear us coming."

Sev's stomach twisted. Those poor people, celebrating the return of their livelihoods, many still recovering from all that they'd lost . . . only to lose it all over again. He prayed to Teyke for luck and to Nors, the fair north wind, for friendly skies; he even prayed to Eo, an obscure goddess favored among traders and messengers, for the safe delivery of the pigeon's warning.

"And what about us?" asked another of the soldiers as the mutters and laughter died down.

Captain Dill smiled. "We'll celebrate tonight. Bring out the ale!"

Whatever further resistance he might have gotten was squashed then and there as barrels of ale were hoisted from the backs of the horses and stacked outside Dill's command tent.

The anniversary of the end of the Blood War was celebrated in the empire with all the usual trappings of a festival: food, drink, and entertainment. As a group of soldiers on the march in enemy territory, there wasn't much room for a true party, but the alcohol flowed as they gathered around the campfires.

Sev thought again about his first time traveling Pyra as a soldier, how Captain Belden had forbidden fires at night because he didn't want them to be spotted by Phoenix Rider patrols in the sky. Now they were trying to lure the Riders out.

Despite what loomed the next day, Sev was almost giddy with relief that he'd managed one more night—to delay their arrival and for the Riders to evacuate the villagers.

Lining up with the others, Sev filled two mugs with ale and went in search of Kade.

The bondservants weren't invited to help themselves from the captain's stores, but they'd likely be having a celebration of their own, apart from the soldiers.

Sev found them at the edge of camp, sitting around a roaring fire. The horses were snoozing in a makeshift paddock nearby, next to the tents that held their burdens for the night. These were sturdy packhorses, gentle and steady of temperament, and their soft sounds of sleep filled Sev's ears and his magic, calming him.

Until he neared the bondservant fire. The people sitting there were clustered in a group—all except for two, sitting off to the side, heads bowed together. It was Kade, and next to him was a pretty animage girl Sev had seen before, with golden hair and a bright, carefree smile. She smiled now, laughing at something Kade had said and leaning in close to whisper some response. They both held cups of their own, which one of the other bond-servants came over to refill for them.

Kade was smiling, and as he leaned back to make room for the man to pour, he spotted Sev.

Sev felt utterly foolish, standing there alone with two cups in hand. He did the only thing he could think of, which was to turn around and walk away, quickly, before anyone else saw him.

Captain Dill wasn't nearly as strict as Belden had been—and far drunker besides—but all the same, it wasn't wise to be seen spending time with the bondservants. It was just too out of character for most of the soldiers and would draw unwanted attention. Sev had risked it only because it was a festival day and everyone was already so deep into their cups they probably wouldn't notice or remember.

The darkness swallowed Sev, providing some measure of relief, but then he slowed, realizing he had nowhere else to go. No friends among the sol-diers and no desire to pretend otherwise.

It was lonely work, being a spy. Sev was lucky to have Kade at all—to have a true friend in all of this—and it struck him in that moment how rare that must be. Sev was, unfortunately, quite used to being alone . . . or at least he had been. All his life with no one to trust, no one to care about— and no one to care about him, either.

That was probably part of what Trix had seen in him, what made her think Sev would be well suited to this kind of work. She'd been right then . . . but was she anymore?

Sev realized that he'd never actually "enjoyed" spying . . . not even the feeling it gave him to know he was helping. The thing that had always made it worth it for him had been having something, some*one* to fight for—Kade, and even Trix. They had given him some sense of purpose—an obligation, a duty. But surely there were other ways to do right in the world than *this*.

He veered back around slightly, finding a quiet place behind the horses' paddock, out of sight of the camp. He needed their simple company right now, and as he settled down on a log, alone in the dark, he decided he also needed to get drunk. Good thing he already had two cups of ale. A head start.

It wasn't long until the crack and snap of footsteps in the undergrowth told Sev he was about to be stumbled upon by some soldier out to empty his bladder.

Sev stilled, hoping he wouldn't be noticed—but it wasn't a soldier who rounded the nearest tree.

It was Kade.

Sev felt even more pathetic than before, sitting by himself on a log with a cup in each hand.

"What are you doing?" Kade asked, his voice puzzled. He picked his way over and stood before Sev. It was easier to see his features now, though the only light came from the moon shining dappled through the trees.

"Oh, just . . . ," Sev began, looking around before finally settling his gaze on his hands. "Having a drink."

"I would've thought you'd had enough the other night," Kade said, amusement in his voice.

Sev didn't reply, and Kade seemed to sense that there was something bothering him.

"Are those both for you?" he asked, nodding down at the cups and breaking the silence that was stretching between them.

"I—no," Sev said with a sigh. He looked up. "But I saw that you already had one. So."

"So . . . ," Kade said, crossing the distance between them to find a seat on the log next to Sev, "you decided to come drink alone instead?"

He pried one of the cups from Sev's grip and lifted it to drink, his eyes on the side of Sev's face.

Sev stared straight ahead. "I . . . didn't want to interrupt," he said. He knew he didn't have any right to jealousy—Kade wasn't *his*. Not like that. They were just friends. But his jealousy extended even beyond the romantic, he realized. Seeing Kade and the other bondservant sitting together like that . . . it had been a strange reminder of his own time with Kade in Pyra: days spent with the animals, nights spent sitting together, talking with Trix.

"Interrupt what?" Kade asked.

"You and that . . . other bondservant." Sev finally swallowed his pride and turned, meeting Kade's gaze.

"Mia?" he asked, and Sev swore he could feel the way Kade tried to keep his voice neutral. "She's the hostler's daughter. We knew each other when I was stationed at Rolan's estate before."

Something unpleasant squirmed in Sev's stomach. What did that mean—*knew* each other?

"How?" Sev blurted, and immediately regretted it.

"Pardon?" Kade asked, brow furrowed.

Sev took a drink from his cup, hating himself but determined to know all the same. "Mia—the hostler's daughter. *How* did you know her?"

Kade's confused expression cleared, frown lines smoothing as comprehension dawned. Sev was beginning to recognize the mask Kade wore when he didn't want to reveal his feelings . . . when he was trying to hide something. He tossed a shoulder carelessly. "From working together."

"Is that it?" Sev pressed.

"What else would there be?" Kade countered, his tone a bit defensive now.

Sev squeezed his eyes shut. Why couldn't he just *say it*? Why couldn't he ask Kade if he'd been with the girl romantically, and if he hadn't, if he'd like to be with Sev romantically instead?

The problem was, Kade meant too much to Sev to risk the rejection. Not only was he the only person in this group of soldiers that Sev could trust, the only person who knew his secret, but he had saved Sev's life in more ways than just the literal sense. He had challenged Sev to do better—to *be* better—and after everything that had happened, Kade was the only thing Sev could count on and cling to. And what if Sev had been misreading everything that had ever transpired between them? What if he confessed his feelings and Kade was horrified? Sev grimaced at the idea of how painfully awkward it would be to meet each night with his unreciprocated feelings for Kade hanging over them like a cloud.

Then again, what if Kade felt the same way? Sev's mind wandered, imagining how their late-night meetings might look then. . . .

Sev opened his eyes. "She's beautiful," he said at last, sighing at his own cowardice.

"You think so?" Kade asked, his sharp tone drawing Sev back to their conversation.

"Yes—I mean, to most people, I would think."

Sev wasn't sure if he was imagining it, but he thought he saw a flicker of a smile cross Kade's lips before he spoke.

"This extra night was lucky," he said, and Sev was so painfully relieved by the change in subject that he actually grinned, though of course the topic wasn't funny.

"Do you think it will be enough time?" Sev asked.

Kade took another drink from his ale. "We'll find out tomorrow."

They had a slow start the next day, the ale having flowed a bit too freely the night before. But at last they broke camp and began their march, exiting the thick tree cover in the early afternoon.

The farmers would still be in their fields if it weren't a festival day, but as the soldiers crossed the sloping farmlands that stretched before them, they found the cluster of houses abandoned too. Not a single person nor animal could be seen, and there was none of the familiar noise Sev associated with farm life—the scrape of tools or the creak of the plow, the shouts of farm-hands or the braying of a hound. There was none of the promised drink and food and music, either. Only the swish of the wind across the deserted landscape.

Sev wanted to weep in relief.

Captain Dill forced his way to the front of the group, a dark expression on his face. He cast his gaze wide; to the east was the distant speck of Runnet, barely visible. To the west were the Foothills and the border with Ferro.

"Torch the fields and the houses," he said. "But be quick about it. We push on before word can reach them. Hillsbridge isn't far from here. We'll make quick work of that run-down place."

Sev's smugness at finding the farmlands evacuated quickly vanished. His breath felt ripped from his lungs, his chest rising and falling rapidly as he tried to draw more air. He *needed* more air.

Hillsbridge was his *home*. Hillsbridge had been a small but prosperous farming community once. But then the empire had come, and Sev's parents had died defending it.

And now he would return, an empire soldier, and tear it all down again.

Panic seared Sev's veins, making it hard to think. He watched, numb, as the soldiers around him took up torches and set to burning.

What was he supposed he do?

There wasn't time to write a letter and contact the Riders; there wasn't time to try to warn Hillsbridge. If Sev arrived at Hillsbridge and didn't participate, Captain Dill would suspect he was the informant.

What was he supposed to do?

The soldiers started marching west—to Sev's home, to his past. To his end?

Through the haze of his thoughts, Sev found Kade. They were *both* from Hillsbridge. Sev's parents had saved Kade's life as well as Sev's own. Sev stared at him, desperate for a solution, for a way out of this.

But Kade only stared back, eyes wide with horror.

Already you draw animals near, and
I know that you belong more firmly in
this ancient family than I ever have.

- CHAPTER 32 -
VERONYKA

VERONYKA AND TRISTAN LOOKED for Doriyan the night of Tristan's return from the Eyrie.

And the one after it.

They tried looking during the day, too, but unlike with Alexiya, they had no information about where Doriyan might be hiding. Rushlea was a large village, plus it was surrounded by rocky bluffs, boulder-strewn fields, and thickets of forest growth. There were virtually thousands of places a person could hide if they didn't want to be found, and with a phoenix, his options were even broader. He wouldn't need to walk into town for supplies, or even live in a place that was technically "habitable." He could be perched on some great slab of stone, like the ancient Pyraean queens of old. He could be anywhere.

Because of Alexiya's warning that Doriyan was hiding from the Riders as much as the empire, Veronyka and Tristan usually searched for him without their phoenixes. That, coupled with the fact that the phoenixes weren't allowed inside Rushlea, meant their bondmates often got left behind at camp whenever Tristan's patrol needed to speak with the townspeople or check in with the refugees. Their temporary town butted up against the southeastern edge of the village proper, so Tristan's patrol avoided bringing their phoenixes there if they could help it.

Xephyra hated being left behind and would often treat Veronyka to an endless stream of mundane information when they were apart, including mental images of pretty flowers or oddly shaped rocks. When she didn't know the word for something, she'd shove the image before Veronyka's eyes so forcefully, it was like a moment of temporary mirroring.

That's poison ivy. Stay away.

That's a wasp's nest. Definitely stay away.

That's my dinner—Xephyra, don't eat that!

They did make one exception to the rule, however, just over a week into their time at Rushlea.

It was the twenty-first day of the ninth moon of the year, which was the anniversary of the end of the Blood War. Typically, all work was put on hold for daylong festivities, but Veronyka hadn't expected anyone to want to celebrate in such dangerous times. However, it seemed the villagers and refugees needed an excuse to blow off some steam now more than ever.

Many of the evacuated children had been begging to see the firebirds again for days, and so Tristan had promised that the phoenixes could go to the refugee camp during the celebrations—but only with their Riders.

While at Vayle Tristan's patrol had slept in tight quarters within the circular ruins of Malka's outpost, here they were more spread out, scattered under jagged overhangs or in soft, grassy hollows. The ground grew rockier to the north of Rushlea, leading into Petratec and Montascent, and quarries and mines dotted the countryside. There were several that were still in use, but they were farther north; those nearby were abandoned. Veronyka felt a strange draw to them, these gaping wounds in the mountain. Like much of Pyra, they were relics of another age, when the province was thriving. Now they were evidence of its deterioration.

It was the morning of the festival, and Veronyka sat at the edge of camp under a gnarled old tree, the sun already hot, beating down in a golden haze of light just outside her shady sanctuary. The Riders were normally up and making their way into the village before dawn, but since it was a holiday, they'd been able to sleep in.

"Hey," Tristan said, striding up the slope toward her and popping the last bites of his breakfast into his mouth. The other Riders were still sleeping or murmuring quietly to one another, enjoying the late start. "Do you know what today is?"

Veronyka was poring over the list of exiled Riders, *again*. She kept rereading the notes, hoping for something new to reveal itself, but there were only so many words on the page, and she had them memorized by now.

After days of searching for Doriyan, she had all but given up hope, and Val was at the forefront of her mind once more. People were missing. People were dying. . . . Wasn't it a worthy risk to reach out to Val and simply ask if she were responsible? Yes, it meant sacrifice for Veronyka and Tristan, but they were both willing to do that, weren't they? And now that they understood the possibilities, wouldn't they be better equipped to ensure that what happened during the relay test didn't happen again?

Pheronia hadn't been able to get through to Avalkyra, and thousands died. But Pheronia didn't have what Veronyka had—she didn't have shadow magic. Was the thing Veronyka had always considered a curse the one thing that could save them all?

Sighing, Veronyka put down the list and gave Tristan her full attention. He stood in front of her, oddly formal, his hands clasped behind his back. She thought back to his question and frowned at him.

"Today is the anniversary of the end of the Blood War . . . ," she said, puzzled by the expression on his face.

"It is, but that's not what I meant." He paused, as if considering his words, before adding, "It's also your birthday."

Veronyka stared down at the puzzle box, still sitting idly in her hands. Her extremities felt suddenly numb and weightless. *My birthday*.

Seventeen years ago, fire and ash had blanketed the empire, and Avalkyra Ashfire, the Feather-Crowned Queen, had died. Pheronia—Veronyka's mother—had died too, but with no magic or bondmate, she remained doomed to that fate, unlike her magical sister.

It was also the day Veronyka was born.

She hadn't thought about that, hadn't yet put it together. It felt incredibly sad that she should celebrate life on the day she'd lost her mother. The day her entire world changed forever. While Avalkyra and Pheronia shared their birthdays—if not both their birth parents—and their death days, Veronyka shared a death day with her mother and a death day *and* birthday with her aunt. Again, the lines between herself and her mother, between Avalkyra and Val, blurred, and Veronyka's breath grew sparse in her chest.

She shoved the box aside and put her head between her knees, forcing air in and out through her lips.

"Veronyka—are you okay?" Tristan asked in alarm, crouching to get a better look at her. He held something in his hand, a package of some sort—she could see it pressed to the earth in his haste to scrabble down next to her. His presence, the feeling of his other hand against her back, drew her away from the shallow darkness and back into the light. "I'm sorry. I shouldn't have—"

"I'm fine," Veronyka said, forcing herself to sit up. *Fine,* she added to Xephyra, who had abandoned her breakfast with Rex to flutter nearer, anxiety thrumming in their bond.

"Are you sure?" Tristan pressed, eyes roving her face.

"Yes," Veronyka insisted. Whether she was fine or not, she willed it to be true. "What I'm *unsure* about," she said, nodding toward Tristan's hand and forcing lightness into her tone, "is what's in that package?"

He stared down at it, then eased himself more comfortably onto the ground next to her. He turned the package over in his hands. "It's a gift. But I'm not sure you're in the mood to celebrate. . . ."

Veronyka wanted to make a joke, but instead she gave him the truth. "I *want* to celebrate. It's just strange. . . . I thought I was born early in the year, in the winter, to Phoenix Rider parents who died in the war. I thought I was nobody."

"You've never been nobody to me."

Fire, golden and warm, spread through her body at his words. When she looked at him, their eyes met, and the surge of feeling she sensed there was staggering.

His expression turned guarded as he watched her reaction, but curiosity colored his voice when he spoke.

"Can you hear it?" he whispered.

"Hear what?" she asked, disoriented.

He glanced away from her, enough to break the strong connection and allow Veronyka to get ahold of her magic again. He shrugged, the movement determinedly nonchalant, and swallowed. "What I was thinking."

Veronyka could tell that he'd opened himself deliberately to her, that he wanted her to know—and yet he knew that it was dangerous and that he probably shouldn't have done it. "Not your thoughts . . . ," she began, trailing off as she tried to remember the sensation. "Your emotions."

"And what were they?" he asked. He wasn't looking at her, still forcing that casualness into his demeanor. As if this were idle chatter and not the invasion of his heart and soul.

"Tristan, we shouldn't—it's not safe."

"You're right," he said hastily. "It's just . . . It's kind of amazing, isn't it? It's like what we have with our bondmates. Seems a shame to block something so . . ." He frowned, looking at Rex and Xephyra in the distance, though she could tell he wasn't really seeing them but was searching for the right words.

"Pure?" Veronyka offered, and immediately regretted giving voice to the idea. But that didn't mean it wasn't true. The fact of the matter was, her bond to Tristan was—and should be—as wondrous and awe-inspiring as her bond to Xephyra. It should be cherished, protected, and honed—not treated with such fear and anguish. It shouldn't be a vulnerability but a *gift*.

The problem wasn't with the bond at all; the problem was with Val. Veronyka was punishing herself and Tristan because of her inability to control her own mind.

Resentment flared up inside.

She shouldn't have to sacrifice Tristan in order to keep Val at bay.

"Yes," Tristan said softly. "So . . . what emotions did you sense?"

Veronyka swallowed, dread and anticipation battling within her. "I . . . It all happened so fast," she whispered. This was wrong. This was dangerous. This was thrilling and desperate and achingly illicit. "It's hard to pull the threads apart—to really know what I'm sensing. But I know your words were genuine."

"What else do you know?"

It was Veronyka's turn to look away now, her throat thick. "I know that you feel the same way about me as I feel about you."

The air stilled between them, the distant sounds of the camp and the forest fading away.

"And what way is that?"

Veronyka couldn't do it—couldn't put words to the thing that was in her heart, the feelings that beat through her with every breath. They were bonded, the two of them, and no matter how hard she fought it, nothing would change that fact. She might as well try to erase her bond with Xephyra or banish the magic that flowed through her veins.

Instead of fumbling her sentiments, Veronyka faced Tristan again. She met his gaze squarely and took his hand in hers too—just to be sure. She knew she was playing with fire, that she was crossing a line she might not be able to come back from, but right now she didn't care. It was only fair to give Tristan a glimpse of her heart, just as he'd given her.

He frowned at her, wary of her breaking the very rules she herself had put in place, before a look of awe and wonder swept his features. His fingers twitched within her grasp, his face alight with understanding. She didn't send a specific message—not like she did with Val—and she couldn't invite him into her mind, either, since he didn't have shadow magic. Instead she sent him her memories of their first meeting, all those hours on the obstacle course, and the awful moment when Val revealed her lies. She shared her every feeling, how they compounded, expanded and grew, how they were a living thing inside her . . . just like her bond to him was.

A thousand expressions flickered across his face—surprise, fondness, shock, and even laughter, one after the other, until he started blinking, his focus wavering, clearly overwhelmed by the onslaught of thoughts and emotions. He squeezed her hand tighter, wanting to communicate, but unable to with her grip on his mind.

Veronyka drew herself back from him, closing her eyes and breaking the connection. With an ache, she strengthened the barriers between them and slammed the door shut.

She opened her eyes to find him staring at her. While the tension had left his face, his eyes were soft and clear and lacking any of the uncertainty that had colored them before.

He lifted her hand, still clutched in his, up to his lips and kissed the inside of her wrist. The touch was shocking in its intimacy, his gaze never leaving her face. Veronyka wanted to melt into him and leave the real world far behind.

The world where she was an apprentice and he her sponsor, where he was the commander's son and a patrol leader . . . and she was a poor mountain girl. At least, according to everyone else. In truth, she was heir to the empire, but Veronyka was beginning to think that was only going to make things worse.

"Here," he said, releasing her hand to pick up the small parcel.

Veronyka unwrapped it. Inside was a smooth, sharp object—an obsidian arrowhead. Or at least, half of one.

"It was my mother's," Tristan said, nodding down at it. "Apparently it was a Flamesong heirloom tracing all the way back to the First Riders, but my father said that's impossible to prove. He thinks it's just nonsense my nursemaid cooked up, which is why he let me take it. It wasn't packed properly," he said, lips pursing, "so it broke on the journey to the Eyrie. But now I think on it, I'm glad it split in two." Reaching into his trouser pocket, Tristan held up the other half, cracked clean down the middle, its point gleaming. "Now we can each have a piece."

Veronyka was dumbfounded. Speechless. Birthday gifts weren't a part of her childhood. They'd never had the gold for extravagances, and though her *maiora* always made sure Veronyka got a sweet cake on the occasion, that tradition had died when Veronyka thought she had.

Of course, now she understood that they weren't celebrating her real birthday at all and that their yearly pilgrimage to the Nest on the Blood War anniversary was their true tradition. There was usually food and music and games in the square, along with quiet vigils for the dead. Val allowed them to participate in neither. Instead she and Veronyka stood outside the castle gates, staring up at its soaring peaks. Though the royal residential wing had been uninhabited since the Blood War, the Nest was still the center of the Golden Empire's government. It was a bustling compound filled with politicians and administrators carrying out their daily business in the same halls that had once held Ashfire kings and queens.

Veronyka had thought they were staring at the site of the Last Battle, remembering their parents and all they had lost. But Val wasn't looking at *just* her past—she was looking into what she believed to be her future, and she'd gazed upon it with hungry, covetous eyes.

"I know it's not good for much," Tristan said, shoving his half out of sight, anxiety creeping back into his voice at Veronyka's extended silence.

"It's perfect," she said, pressing it to her chest. She could already imagine braiding it into her hair.

He smiled—a wide, true smile, dimples emerging and eyes bright.

And then, because it was her birthday and because she wanted to, Veronyka leaned forward and kissed him.

She meant to go for his lips, but lost her courage partway and veered off course, finding his cheek instead. But rather than a light peck, she pressed her lips and lingered, breathing in the scent of his skin, feeling the scratch of stubble along his jaw. He hesitated, his throat bobbing in a swallow, before he slowly turned his face, bringing his lips to meet hers. It was soft at first, chaste and innocent, but then, when she returned it, he met her with enthusiasm, his kiss surer, deeper, his hands lifting to grip her face and tangle in her hair.

It was like a spark on dry tinder, every touch like fire on her skin, catching, crawling, spreading across her body. Tristan kissed her desperately, urgently, pressing her against the trunk of the tree behind her.

Despite their physical closeness, Veronyka was doing everything she could to keep her mind locked tight. It was distracting, causing her to lose focus and break the kiss—only to growl in frustration and lean forward hungrily, snatching his lips with hers again.

She didn't *want* to block him out, to keep the rivers of her magic safe and secure. She wanted to drown in him.

Tristan's door didn't just open—it burst wide, flooding her mind. The channel between them was strong and stable, just as it had been on the battlefield, except this time it wasn't one-way. She let him in, but she reached out, too, as she had moments ago. He went rigid against her, his lips stilling as a shudder ran through him. He pulled back, their eyes locking for an instant, so much love and yearning in his gaze that Veronyka felt flushed and dizzy. Knowing his pleasure as he knew hers, she was intoxicated by the visceral twist of emotion and sensation. It was impossible to fully understand everything that was passing between them, mental and physical, but then he was kissing her again, and Veronyka stopped trying.

When she opened her magic to him, other, distant awarenesses began to creep in. Xephyra and Rex were nearby, along with a smattering of other animals and phoenixes. And the other Riders in Tristan's patrol weren't far off. . . .

The realization startled Veronyka. They had felt so completely alone—protected by the shade of the tree and completely absorbed in one another—but they were not. Her hands clenched hard, not remembering she still held the sharp arrowhead. A jolt of pain shot through her and Tristan, and they broke apart.

Tristan blinked down at her, as if in a daze, before understanding the pain he'd felt hadn't been his own. The connection between them trickled and then stopped, like a dammed river, and clarity settled on his features—along with alarm.

He whipped his head around, squinting down the slope at their camp, but the others were preoccupied getting ready for the village celebrations, unaware of their quiet moment together.

When he looked back around, he gave her an embarrassed smile, rubbing the back of his neck. "I—I lost track of myself for a second there."

Veronyka sat straighter, smoothing her hair as she checked her mental barriers. Had that been a terrible mistake? It didn't feel like one. It felt like the best thing that had ever happened to her. "Me too."

A frown settled on his brow, and he lifted her hand. "It's bleeding," he said, removing the arrowhead and peering into the slice on her palm.

"It's not deep," she said, tugging her hand away. "I forgot I was holding it," she added sheepishly.

"I forgot my own name," Tristan said, his gaze dropping to her lips, and the urge to kiss him again was overwhelming.

"Hey, Tristan!" came Lysandro's voice from across the campsite.

"There it is," Veronyka said dryly, and Tristan smirked. He sighed and got to his feet. He straightened his clothes, paying particularly close attention to his trousers, before picking his way down the slope.

It wasn't long before he returned. The others were heading to the celebrations now, and Tristan had informed them that he and Veronyka would catch up.

"Do you need a bandage for that?" he asked, gesturing to her cut palm. She shook her head—it stung a little bit, but she'd already wiped away the blood and tucked the arrowhead inside the thick strands of her braided bracelet for safekeeping. "Good, come on," he said, grabbing her good hand and helping her to her feet. "Let's go to the village."

Since they wanted to spend time with their phoenixes, most of Tristan's patrol could be found in the refugee camp rather than the main village. The rows of tents and makeshift houses were always bustling with people sharing news or meals over cook fires, and it was a loud, crowded place. Tonight it was particularly rambunctious, with music and dancing and barrels of wine purchased by the commander himself.

Veronyka watched as Anders sang a bawdy Arborian folksong, Lysandro blushing furiously while Latham laughed so hard tears streamed from his eyes. Ronyn was discussing the fall harvest with several of the older refugees, all of them with cups of wine in hand, and Tristan was roped into kicking a ball around with a horde of children who liked to shadow his every step. The ball went soaring past his head—kicked wide by an over-energetic child—and he chased it down, glancing in Veronyka's direction. There was a sparkle of laughter in his eye, and Veronyka's stomach swooped in response, as if that glint was just for her.

Closer at hand, Xephyra, Rex, and some of the other phoenixes were playing with the youngest of the children, who tugged on their tail feathers and threw treats into the air for them to catch. The sight made Veronyka think of the animage captives, of the children who were separated from their family—possibly lost forever. She thought she spotted some of the people who had missing relatives, their faces downcast and their voices subdued.

The celebrations in Rushlea were loud as well, and despite their somewhat cold reception, people streamed to and from the village and the refugee camp, turning the two separate events into one oversize party.

In terms of their duties, the Riders had come to an agreement with their guard counterparts from the Eyrie: The Riders got the day off—until midnight—and the guards got the next day. For anyone planning to drink heavily, having the morning after off might be the better shift, but Veronyka was happy to have the day. Her *birth*day. She ran a finger along her braided bracelet, feeling the shape of the arrowhead through the waxy strands. She smiled.

Veronyka was just making her way over to a table laid out with food when she spotted a man standing alone on the far side of the refugee camp. He didn't look familiar, but they were getting new arrivals almost every day. While the first two big waves of refugees had been evacuated in anticipation of an empire soldier attack, other villages along the route had seen them flee and decided to follow themselves. There were some settlements that *had* been attacked—like the Silverwood—as well as traders and travelers along the road who continued to find trouble farther south and so made their way north to the temporary encampment in Rushlea.

Veronyka was ready to dismiss him as just another refugee when she noticed his boots.

They came to midcalf, were dark and well worn . . . and treated with *pyraflora* resin, the fireproof sap favored by Phoenix Riders. It left a distinctive, waxy sheen that was easy to spot if you knew what to look for.

Veronyka gaped, her heart kicking inside her chest. He could have found the boots, bought or stolen or traded for them. It didn't necessarily mean he *was* a Phoenix Rider.

When Veronyka drew her attention back up to his face, it was to find that he'd been watching her, too.

He turned away at once and strode into the darkness of the distant trees.

"Tristan!" Veronyka called, whirling around to spot him. He wasn't far, and when he heard her call his name, he tossed the ball behind him and jogged over.

"Do you w—" he began, but Veronyka took hold of his arm and jerked him after her.

"I think I found him," she said, keeping her voice low as they ran toward the forest.

"Who?" Tristan asked, bewildered.

"Doriyan."

The sounds of music and laughter faded as they reached the trees, following the man deeper into the wilderness. Veronyka had already ordered Xephyra to stay with the refugees or return to their own camp, and despite complaining of boredom for days, Veronyka got the impression Xephyra was tired of being pinched and prodded and screeched at.

Take Rex with you, Veronyka said, as she sensed Xephyra drifting back to the Rider camp. *Stay out of trouble.*

As they picked their way through the trees, Veronyka explained to Tristan in a low voice how she'd spotted the man's Rider boots, and how he'd fled when he saw her attention.

Before long they found themselves on familiar ground; Veronyka and Tristan had been up and down these paths in search of Doriyan's hideout before.

Large chunks of rock intruded on the path up ahead—which was where they'd turned back last time.

This time, however, they watched from a safe distance as Doriyan scaled one of the massive boulders. Veronyka and Tristan waited until he was over, then rushed forward to copy him, pausing halfway to the top and peering carefully over the other side.

There moon lit a wide clearing dotted by more slabs of stone like the one upon which they were perched, while the far side was enclosed by a sheer, soaring rock face, shimmering with thousands of smooth cuts.

It was a quarry. Or at least it *had* been—it looked decades out of use.

Tristan pointed to a dark hole near the bottom of the rock wall where the man disappeared into the shadows. Not just a quarry, but a mine as well.

They climbed down the other side of the boulder—or rather, Tristan jumped and Veronyka followed, only to stagger upon landing and stumble into him. He caught her, helping her to stand upright, and she couldn't tell if she was more embarrassed about her weak jump or the fact that she enjoyed falling into his arms so much.

The remains of a wooden post-and-lintel doorway marked the entrance, but one side of the crossbeam had collapsed thanks to shifting rocks above, partially blocking the doorway. Tristan climbed across it, squinting into the dark interior.

Surely it was safe if the man had walked straight into it with such obvious ease and familiarity.

Tristan drew back, his expression saying much the same thing. He shrugged. *Do we follow?* he mouthed.

Veronyka considered. Never mind the collapsed entrance—it was dangerous to follow a stranger to an unknown location, especially a pitch-black one. She itched to light a torch, but that would alert him to their arrival. Maybe they should have hailed him while they were still in the open, but Veronyka had expected their final destination to be a home, not a hole in the earth.

Hoping her eyes would adjust, she nodded and led the way inside—hand on the hilt of the dagger in her belt. Tristan copied her.

There were more post-and-lintel arches holding up the rock that loomed overhead and carving a hallway into the mountain. Water dripped, and a dank, musty smell reached her nose. The passage echoed around them, repeating their every step and breath, but the noise soon grew deeper—more vast. Up ahead the corridor split. To the left Veronyka sensed an expanse of open air and suspected that was where the miners dug deep into the rocky ground. To the right there was a doorway that led into a room. Her eyes had adjusted somewhat by now, and she saw it was roughly the size of the dining hall at the Eyrie—and Veronyka suspected it had served a similar function here.

Tristan tugged on her arm and pointed to a set of unlit torches mounted on either side of the door.

Veronyka considered, peering around. Obviously the man didn't live here in this darkness—he must have used this tunnel as a passage, a way to cut through to the other side. There were always multiple entrances in any underground space like this, in case of cave-ins, and they wouldn't have much luck finding them without light.

She nodded and withdrew her striker and flint stone; she lit the first torch and was about to light the second when Tristan waved her off. His hand was steady as he used one torch to light the other, the increasing glow illuminating more of the room around them.

The long tables that had filled the room were pushed together in the center, creating a single, massive surface. Scattered there was an odd mix of objects—cups and cracked pitchers, bits of leather, and nubs of charcoal. An arrow, broken in two, lay near the far side of the table. It reminded Veronyka of the arrowhead Tristan had given her, except this was split in the middle of the shaft, the obsidian point still intact . . . as well as the red-and-purple phoenix-feather fletching. There was a high-backed chair at this end of the table, and something about it felt important to Veronyka, though she couldn't say why.

With a hand that trembled slightly, she ran her palm along the notched and partially splintered wood. It had been beautiful once, the wood sturdy and highly polished.

Then her hand dropped to the arrow on the table. The instant her fingertips touched it, the world shifted, stuttered, and a new scene lay before her, falling over her eyes like a veil.

She was in the very same room, but in a different time—a different body. She sat in the high-backed chair and surveyed the scene before her with regal arrogance.

Val, *Veronyka thought.* No, Avalkyra.

She was in Val's mind again—in her memories.

The tables before her were strewn with maps and papers and cups of wine, the room illuminated with flickering, dancing torchlight. There were people on either side of Val, seated in other chairs, but Val's was taller, grander—a throne. She was obviously holding council or court, but everyone's attention was on the doorway. Anticipation hung in the air.

Four soldiers entered—soldiers that Veronyka suspected did not belong to Val. They wore chain mail and armor in the empire style and were studying the room warily, empty scabbards dangling from their belts. Surrounding them were warriors in the Phoenix Rider tradition—leather armor strapped to their bodies and phoenix feathers in their hair. They pointed spears at the soldiers, who were not alone.

Between them stood a solitary figure, cloaked and hooded. Small hands drew back the fabric, and the breath whooshed from Veronyka's lungs.

Pheronia Ashfire. Princess. Queen.

Mother.

Veronyka struggled to wrap her brain around the idea and apply the term to the woman before her. For she did seem like a woman now, her expression grave and her eyes tired, despite her being not much older than Veronyka was now. She had seen this girl—her mother—grow up in different shadow magic dreams over the years, and yet she'd always viewed the memories from Val's perspective. Even now she could feel's Val's righteous superiority, the disdain with which she viewed her sister . . . and the love was still there, though Val fought hard to bury it.

Veronyka tried to detach herself from Val's feelings, to take in the scene objectively. It seemed that Pheronia had come to visit her sister in the middle of the Blood War, journeying deep into Pyra for the chance to speak to her. She was dressed as a peasant, in simple homespun clothing, except for something that glinted around her throat. A necklace. It was gold, a delicate braided chain that draped across her collarbones and connected in the middle at a pair of spread wings—the Ashfire symbol. Maybe, like Val's signet ring, she'd worn it to prove her identity.

Veronyka looked at her mother with admiration. It took guts to journey here into the heart of her sister's domain. The action spoke not of weakness or frailty, but of bravery.

"Sister," Pheronia said, meeting Val's—and Veronyka's—eyes with a cool, confident stare.

"You shall address me as 'Queen.' Now, tell me, how did you find me?"

"You are not the only one with spies, Avalkyra."

Val's nostrils flared at the casual address. "Queen Avalkyra," she gritted out through clenched teeth.

"Has there been a crowning?" Pheronia asked, taking a step deeper into the room. The soldiers she'd brought with her tightened their stances, while the Riders who stood guard lowered their spears.

Val waved them off impatiently. She leaned forward in her chair, pointing to her head, where Veronyka knew there would be a circlet of phoenix feathers. "Perhaps you haven't heard—I am the Feather-Crowned Queen."

A hint of a smile played on Pheronia's lips, and the sight of it caused hot anger to flare inside Val's stomach, as if the gesture mocked her. "Oh, I've heard, Avalkyra. It looks glorious on you—like a Rider queen of old."

Val settled back in her chair, unsure how to take this apparent compliment—seeking hidden barbs or jabs within the words. Eventually she snorted. "What would you know about Rider queens?"

"I would know everything you ever taught me."

"Why have you come here?" Val snapped. "What's to stop me from slitting your throat where you stand?"

"Nothing," Pheronia said simply, palms wide as if to show her vulnerability—and the fact that she was unarmed. "I am here to talk. I think it's about time, don't you?"

"I tried to talk, xe Onia."

"You mean your letters," Pheronia guessed. "I have since replied."

"Too late," Val snarled, and for the first time Pheronia's face betrayed something like fear, or maybe panic.

"It is not too late. I'm here now. Please, Avalkyra, let us talk in private."

"No," Val said, and Veronyka felt the pleasure she took in denying her sister, even if a part of her wanted to talk too. "You may speak here, in my war room, or not at all. It makes no difference to me."

"I know you want war with me, sister, but I do not want war with you."

The other people in the room shifted, and Veronyka wondered how many of them longed for an end to the conflict, the same as Pheronia, despite their apparent loyalty to Avalkyra.

"I gave you a chance at peace," Val said, plucking an arrow from the mess on the table before her. She looked up at her sister. "You tore the treaty in half." Her words were punctured by a loud snap, the arrow shaft broken cleanly in two.

Veronyka had seen that meeting. Val had shown it to her. She and Pheronia had been in a grand chamber—not some dank, abandoned mine—surrounded by their advisers. Val had slid a heavy document across the table's surface, but Pheronia had not signed it.

Pheronia's rigid demeanor softened, and she clasped her hands together, as if to stop them from shaking or reaching out.

Or resting on her stomach. Veronyka wasn't certain of the exact timeline of these events, but she remembered Pheronia's pallor during their last meeting—the way she'd rested a hand on her abdomen as if nauseated. Veronyka stared at the loose-fitting tunic she wore under her thick cloak. Was Pheronia pregnant in this moment? Was Veronyka already an idea inside her mother's belly?

"That was peace on your terms, Avalkyra."

"Queen Avalkyra," Val said stonily.

"And your terms would see me removed from my position, and all those who aided me—"

"Pulled your strings, more like."

"—would be killed. Wouldn't they, sister?"

"So you fight for a throne you do not want to protect people who care nothing for you? When I have given everything for you? For us?"

"You do not give, Avalkyra Ashfire," Pheronia snapped, losing her temper for the first time. "You take and take until there is nothing left. You have all of fire's hunger and none of its warmth."

Val tilted her head, and Veronyka felt the surge of pleasure that swept Val's body at her sister's words. She took the comparison to fire as a compliment.

"You look ill, sister," Val said suddenly. "I've heard things. Whispers. You skip out on meetings, barely speak to anyone, and are living in near seclusion in Genya's Tower. The stress of the war is clearly taking its toll on your weak constitution. . . ."

Pheronia scowled at that, and some steel returned to her posture.

"You know, some say there was once a third goddess in our skies," Val said, staring up at the darkened roof of their stony chamber. "A third sister."

Pheronia frowned, as if confused by the change in subject. With Val's attention diverted, she cast a wary glance to one of her guards, but he only shrugged.

"Before the sun, before the moon . . . before the world itself. Axura, Nox—and Xenith. All were beings of the sky, great winged creatures of light and life and fire. As you just pointed out, xe Onia . . . fire is hungry. Fire takes, fire devours, and Nox always craved more, her desire to consume insatiable."

Val got to her feet then, strolling a slow circle around the chamber. The guard Pheronia had shared a look with before stepped in front of her protectively, but Val made no move toward her sister. She just continued her story, like a bard before an eager audience.

"To satisfy her sister, Axura gave humankind fire, and in exchange they lit burning tributes before her and her sisters every night. It helped, for a time. But when the primitive humans' weak offerings ceased to satisfy her, Nox looked for something more. Xenith was weakest of the three, and so when Axura's back was turned, Nox devoured her and scattered her remains into the ether. Axura, ever sentimental, looked for Xenith all day, but to no avail. Only when the sisters prepared to sleep for the night did she notice the newly made stars—Xenith's flaming feathers—glowing against the endless black of night. Suspecting what Nox had done, Axura banished her to that cold, empty darkness, where she would be unable to quench her thirst for light and fire. There, she learned to live off shadows instead, turning into a shadow herself. But always, the hunger remained."

Val came to a stop next to her chair, but she did not retake it. She ran a hand along its high back, mimicking what Veronyka had done in the real world mere moments before, and studied Pheronia.

"And who am I in that story?" Pheronia asked. "Xenith, the weakest of the three—the one meant to be devoured?"

Val lifted her shoulders in an idle shrug, a slight smirk on her lips, as if the correlation should be obvious.

"That makes you Nox, then," Pheronia said, shaking her head. The smirk left Val's face. "I would rather be devoured by another than live long enough to devour myself. Be careful, sister. What will you do, where will you turn, when there is nothing left to take?"

Val didn't respond, though it was obvious the words had gotten to her. Veronyka felt the unease and mild confusion in her stomach. Had Val not realized that by casting Pheronia in the role of the devoured, she was in turn casting herself in the role of the devourer? Or had the truth of it not penetrated her mind until now?

"Kyra, please," Pheronia said, using a nickname for Val that Veronyka had never heard before. "We need to talk."

"No."

Pheronia studied her for a long time. "If you do not learn to bend, Avalkyra Ashfire," she said softly, "eventually you'll break."

Then Pheronia turned on her heel and swept from the room. The armed Riders glanced to Val for orders, but to Veronyka's surprise, Val let her sister leave.

"But—my queen," spluttered one of the women seated at Val's table. "Surely we should keep her here as a bargaining chip or a hostage—"

Val retook her seat and picked up the broken arrow. "No. Keeping her will change nothing. This war will continue whether Pheronia wills it or not. She is a figurehead, a puppet for the council's machinations. Nothing more."

But she was more—Val knew it, felt it in her bones—and Veronyka knew it too. Pheronia had more strength than Val would ever openly admit, more *intelligence and compassion and reason. Perhaps they would have ruled well together: Pheronia's cool head and thoughtful nature coupled with Val's strength and passion. Perhaps they could have been more than dead queens at the center of an empire on fire.*

One thing was certain: Val still loved her sister in this moment, and for all her darkness, she could not—would not—deal her a fatal blow. Somehow, even this deep into the war, Val still believed she and Pheronia would come out of it together.

Veronyka wondered if that hopeful part of her died along with her flesh, or if she still longed to make peace with her past.

She wondered if there was a chance at redemption for her.

Veronyka was utterly entranced by the scene, but a tug in her mind was drawing her away, like her head was submerged and someone was pulling it out of water.

She gasped as she came back to herself. She was leaning against the old high-backed chair, a mockery of a throne, and the real world revealed itself slowly, blotchy black dots receding.

This room was darker than the dream room because Tristan had lit only two of the torches—one of which was guttering on the ground next to him. He was on his knees, blinking as if he too were coming back from a daze—and of course he was. They were bonded, and Veronyka had given herself up to the vision willingly, *eagerly*.

But Tristan was not alone.

The man they'd followed here stood over him, gripping the scruff of Tristan's collar and holding a knife to his throat.

And next to him was Val.

*They are day and night and scattered light; sun and moon and
        distant stars.*
*They are life and death and what is left; all and nothing and
        everything in between.*

—"Axura, Nox, and Xenith," a fragment from *Songs of the Sky*, an oral
poem attributed to Roza Heartlight, one of the First Riders and the
inaugural High Priestess of Axura, circa 975 BE

You are a daughter of queens.
But so are we. Where did we go wrong?
Was there ever a chance for us?

- CHAPTER 33 -
SEV

THEY CAME UPON HILLSBRIDGE in the middle of the night.

The dogs were first to raise the alarm. Then there was fire, and smoke, and screams.

The farmers scrambled, terrified, from their beds, taking up whatever weapons they had on hand to defend their families. They burst from their homes wielding shovels and pitchforks, while children and the elderly were corralled out back doors or went running, blind, into the blackness of night.

Sev stumbled through it all, detached from his body. He thought he might have floated away entirely if not for the painful spasms of his heart. Every beat rattled his rib cage and sent shock waves through his blood.

Though the farms, houses, and outbuildings had been rebuilt since the war, Hillsbridge was a fraction of the size it had once been. Even when Sev had lived here it was a modest community, its only claim to fame the bridge that gave safe crossing over a branch of the River Aurys and onto empire lands.

But it was still familiar, still home. Sev kept seeing it as he'd seen it as a child—rolling hills and tall trees—and then, in sudden, jarring contrast, he'd see it the way it was the last time he was here. The last time the empire marched on his home. The scent of smoke, the sound of death. Every clash of weapon, every thump of boot, every voice that cried out—then was abruptly silenced. It all blurred together, and Sev felt like a child again. Lost, lost . . . completely lost.

Shouts drew his attention to the distant bridge, and Sev was brought abruptly back to the moment his parents dove from the sky, careening toward that same bridge and the hundreds of soldiers preparing to cross. He remembered the feel of heat on his skin, knowing that the fire was devouring not just the enemy soldiers, but his mother and father. Scorching the clothes from their backs, the flesh from their bones.

And there was a shed—no, there *had* been a shed, now replaced by a burning wagon.

There was the stonework garden path, scattered with leaves—no, there was now a dirt trail, scattered with bodies.

Captain Dillon had split up their forces, and by Anyanke's cruel fate, Sev was assigned to the advance guard.

His hands trembled so violently he could barely hold his spear, his palms slick with sweat, but still his legs marched him inextricably forward into the cluster of houses atop a gently sloping hill. *His* house—the one he and his parents had lived in—was gone, and that was some small mercy. But the houses that stood here now were not so different.

As soldiers to the left and right of him put torches to every surface, great swaths of fire licking across timber and catching on the dry, sunbaked summer grass, Sev was carried with the rush of bodies making for the doors.

His awareness seemed to blink in and out, his vision turning to black-and-white, shadow and flame. Faces were leached of color, of life, and the darkness moved.

One second he was running toward a house, soldiers breaking through a barricaded door, and the next, Sev was inside, and there were bodies, and screams, and the clang of weapons echoing against the wooden walls.

Sev felt frozen, and yet he *moved*, carried along like a leaf on a river current, the stream crashing through doorways and swirling into eddies, room after room, bringing death and destruction in its wake.

He didn't lift his spear or make any move to attack, and yet there were bodies everywhere, appearing out of the shadows like some gruesome nightmare.

Sev stared uncomprehending at a small body on the floor in a back room. Someone had reduced the door to splinters, and the child—for it was definitely a child—lay near the open window, so close to freedom . . . but not close enough.

Horror glued Sev's feet to the ground, and when a villager climbed back in through that same window, murder in his eyes, Sev waited obediently for it.

It seemed only right.

It seemed only just.

Sev had escaped death more than once, so maybe it was his time.

The man raised a hatchet, the kind used to cut firewood or hew logs, but the strike halted with his arm up over his head. A spear protruded from his chest, coming from the doorway to Sev's left.

The soldier standing there still held the weapon in his hands, but when he wrenched it free, the man crumpled, his body motionless next to the child's.

Sev blinked. He was alive, somehow, and the thought did not comfort him.

The soldier next to him was a grizzled war vet. His face was impassive, unfeeling, and Sev was as haunted by it as he had been by the expression of rage and heartbreak on the man now dead on the ground.

"Wake up, kid," the old soldier said before moving off, his voice echoing in Sev's ears as if he were underwater.

Sev staggered away, out the front door, where everything caught up to him all at once. He fell to his knees in the fruit bushes at the side of the house, the sight and scent reminding him of his father's famous blackberry pie.

He heaved onto the dirt.

Sev didn't know how long he was there before a cool hand pressed against the back of his neck, which was damp with sweat. He looked up, startled, to find Kade's amber eyes staring back at him.

The haze that had surrounded him since this fight began snapped and cleared, bringing the world to screaming life around Sev once more.

"Kade," he said, as the other boy helped Sev to his feet. "What are you doing here?"

Kade didn't look like himself—he was dressed as a soldier, with a padded vest, tunic, and weapons belt. He even had a crossbow strapped across his back and a spear in his hands.

The bondservants were supposed to stay back at their temporary camp, managing the horses while the attendants set up a medical tent and prepared food and drink. Murder was thirsty work, after all.

Kade must have somehow slipped away, stolen a bunch of gear, and followed the soldiers.

He didn't answer Sev's question but gestured behind him. The house was bordered by a thick hedge, and if they climbed through, they'd have some cover from the rest of the battle.

Sev followed, glancing over his shoulder, but it was nighttime and the raging fires cast the landscape in two values: light and dark. Right now, at the side of the house, they were entirely in darkness.

They crouched low, facing each other.

Sev unhooked his waterskin and took a quick draft, spitting into the dirt.

"Are you okay?" Kade asked with concern. "Is it the smoke?"

"What are you doing here?" Sev repeated, ignoring Kade's question— he didn't think he could answer it. Sev *wasn't* okay, but it had nothing to do with the smoke. After everything he had been through, all he had accomplished, he was somehow right back where he'd started—watching the empire wreak bloody havoc on the world to which he belonged. His parents had given their lives to protect this place, to protect Sev, and now it was going up in flames.

Sev might be a spy for the other side, but right now he felt like it didn't matter—that nothing he did could ever make up for this.

And for some reason, Kade was still being kind to him.

Maybe he could see the devastation in Sev's eyes, because Kade gripped his good shoulder to draw his attention.

"We can help them," Kade said, leaning close and speaking in Sev's ear. They weren't going to be overheard, but the distant shouts and screams, plus the crackle of the fires spreading across the crops and wooden houses, created a kind of dull roar that made it hard to hear even at the edges of the fray.

The look Sev gave him was a hopeless one. Kade shook his head as if banishing Sev's thoughts. "*Really*," he said forcefully. "The villagers are running into the trees." He twisted to point at a distant mass of darkness that was blacker than the sky. "I think there might still be a safe house."

Those words shook something loose in Sev's addled brain. The safe house. Even when his parents died and this very same farm burned, hundreds of lives were spared because of the safe house, including Kade's. So what if Sev had gotten lost and wound up a war orphan alone in Aura Nova. Others had made it. *Kade* had made it. Maybe Sev could do the same thing his parents had done, and save others even if he couldn't save himself.

"Tell me," Sev said, and he knew his voice was sharper, clearer, than it had been a moment ago. Kade looked heartened.

"The rear guard has established a wide perimeter," Kade explained, pointing into the distance.

"To stop people from running away," Sev said with disgust, following the line of Kade's finger, though he couldn't see anything in the darkness.

"And to snatch animages."

Sev jerked his head back around. "What?"

Kade fixed him with an unflinching look. "You know that's what happens when the empire strikes Pyra," he said steadily. "It's what they've always done. But this time they were ordered to do it. Apparently Rolan's other regiments have already started marching the captive animages toward Ferro."

"For what? An auction?"

Kade's mouth was a grim line. "For bait."

Then Sev understood. This was still about the Phoenix Riders. Sure, attacking Pyra—the place where the Rider order had begun and the place that sheltered their second coming—made sense, but attacking animages, their own *kind*, struck that much closer to home.

"We have to keep the villagers away from the perimeter. If they stay in the trees, the soldiers won't pursue. It would never occur to them that animages can see as well in the dark as any owl or other nocturnal animal. They'll expect them to run away from the fire and into their arms. We can't let them do that. So we'll—"

Kade stopped abruptly, whirling around as a sound reached them from behind the house.

There were three children there—an older boy holding an infant in one arm and the hand of a smaller girl in the other. His eyes widened when he saw Sev and Kade.

"Into the trees," Kade ordered, hands out to show he was unarmed. He'd left his spear on the ground. "Quickly."

When they didn't move, he lifted his pendant—stamped with the terms of his bondage—from underneath his tunic, to prove he was no soldier. The children still wavered, uncertain, but the sounds from the battle were loud and near, and the trees—while dark and wild and farther up the sloping ground—were a quiet sheltering mass.

They started to move away in slow, uneasy steps backward.

"Come on," Kade said, his voice gentle despite the urgency concealed underneath. "Hurry. There's—"

Kade stopped short as a man rounded the side of the house. He was dressed in a long white nightshirt, its hem ripped and spattered with something dark . . . mud, or was it blood? He was bearded and gray, his hair wild and unkempt, but he was broad-shouldered and steady on his feet.

First he saw the children. *Then* he saw Sev and Kade.

"Get out of here!" he bellowed at the youngsters, his voice loud and sudden, causing the baby to cry. He didn't seem to notice. He shoved the children behind him and raised a spear he must have stolen from one of the soldiers, hefting it, point aimed at Sev and Kade. The tip glinted, reflecting the distant light of the fires.

Kade did what he'd done with the children, holding his hands palm out, showing he was unarmed. Sev remained slightly behind Kade, afraid to make any sudden movements. His own spear was gone—he must have dropped it when he'd retched into the bushes.

Also as he had before, Kade reached toward the neck of his tunic, meaning to unearth his bondservant pendant—but the movement drew his hand dangerously close to the handle of the crossbow still strapped to his back.

The man's eyes alighted on the weapon, and he reacted with a sudden, violent lunge.

Sev watched, frozen with shock, as the tip of the spear plunged into Kade's abdomen . . . and then out the other side.

Kade's arm dropped. Then he fell onto his knees.

It was like before, when the world stuttered and blinked in and out of time: Kade was standing there, alive and well; then he was on his knees, a spear protruding from his midsection. Kade's stolen armor wasn't fitted for him and was too narrow for his wide frame. It left gaps. It left vulnerabilities.

Now it was Sev's turn to react with sudden, desperate violence. He knelt, picked up Kade's abandoned spear, and whipped it around.

The man's weapon was still embedded in Kade, and before he could draw it out, Sev had run him through. He didn't aim left or right to avoid ill-fitting armor—he didn't need to. The man wore none. Sev's shot was straight and true.

Blood bloomed across the white nightshirt, and Sev watched as the light died in the man's eyes. Then he wrenched the spear free. He turned before the man's body hit the ground.

The children had long since fled, but Sev didn't care anymore. He tossed his spear away and turned.

Kade was lying on his face in the dirt. Sev's chest tightened, his insides contracting as if cowering from a blow. From the truth.

The spear had become dislodged—whether by the man's efforts or Kade's fall, Sev didn't know, but when he fell to his knees, he felt hot blood soak into his pants.

So much blood.

I should have told him, Sev thought wildly, though his mind wouldn't let him follow that train of thought to the very end.

Sev tore the crossbow from Kade's back and threw it aside, out of the way, before carefully turning Kade over. He didn't bother trying to stanch the flow of blood or check Kade's pulse. His own hands were shaking, his fingers icy with fear and adrenaline, and he couldn't see for the tears in his eyes.

I should have told him how I feel.

Sev did the only thing he *could* do: He crouched, tugged on Kade's unresponsive arm, and hoisted him bodily over his back. White-hot pain lanced through Sev's shoulder, but that was nothing, *nothing* to the pain inside his heart.

With Kade's weight against his shoulders and Kade's blood dripping down his back, Sev stood on shaky legs and *ran.*

*Were Avalkyra and I always meant
to go down in flames?*

- CHAPTER 34 -
VERONYKA

"VAL—WHEN, HOW—" VERONYKA SAID, mind reeling and heart thumping wildly. Seeing Val here, now, almost the exact same age she was then—in the vision—was causing Veronyka's head to spin. And her mother . . . she had been just feet away—Veronyka could still see her in her mind's eye. She had thought often of her mother in recent weeks, wondering what she might have been like, but nothing had prepared her for the scene she'd just witnessed. Pheronia Ashfire had been strong, and brave, and perhaps most surprising of all . . . she hadn't feared her sister. She hadn't backed down.

Veronyka kept staring at the room before her, as if expecting the past and the present to realign themselves or to blur entirely together. Would she look left and see her mother standing there? Something like hysteria lurched up inside her, and she wrenched her mind to the present.

Her eyes landed on the man who had a knife pressed to Tristan's throat. "What are you doing?" she demanded. "Let go of him!"

The man looked at Val, and after a moment spent surveying Veronyka, she nodded, and Tristan was shoved to his feet. He staggered over to Veronyka's side, obviously a bit disoriented, his brain trying to play catch-up with his body.

Veronyka understood the feeling.

"Val," she said again, this time more slowly, her heartbeat steadying somewhat now that Tristan was no longer in immediate danger. "What are you doing here? *How* did you get here?"

"I flew."

"That . . . that means you've got a phoenix? A bondmate?" Veronyka tried but failed to keep the surprise from her voice. She hadn't thought that Val would ever be able to bond again.

"I certainly didn't sprout wings of my own, if that's what you're asking," Val drawled, smirking slightly. Veronyka couldn't tell if she meant to be teasing or mocking—or if there was any difference, when it came to her.

"So it's been you?" Veronyka murmured. "The Iron Road? The sighting in Ferro?" There had been an attack in Arboria North, too, according to the commander. . . . Could Val have been involved in that as well?

Val lifted her chin. "I've been fighting the empire, like I told you I would—like I thought *you* wanted to do."

Veronyka scowled. "We *are* fighting the empire. Just days ago I—"

"Is this what you call fighting? Hiding away in the north and babysitting refugees?"

"Not all fighting is about fire and blood," Veronyka argued. "We're protectors, Val; we're trying to save people's lives."

"This is work fit for any untrained local who can carry a spear—not Phoenix Riders. I thought you wanted to do something real."

"Like what? Attacking merchant caravans and country houses, making us look like criminals and thieves?"

Val smiled again, then turned her attention to the man. "Leave us, Doriyan, and keep watch at the entrance. Take him with you," she added, nodding to Tristan.

So he *was* Doriyan, as Veronyka had thought. Did that mean Val had allied with Sidra as well? Could *she* have been the one to attack Arboria while Val flew here?

"I'm not going anywhere," Tristan said, yanking his arm from Doriyan's reach.

Val rolled her eyes, then nodded her assent at Doriyan, who stepped back from Tristan and made for the exit alone. He looked once over his shoulder—not at Val or even Veronyka and Tristan, but past them into the darkness near the back of the room. Veronyka followed his gaze, seeing a shadowy archway that must lead into other parts of the mine. Were there others lurking in the darkness, or was he trying to figure out which exit to guard?

"Is he the one you've been flying with?" Veronyka asked when the three of them were alone. "He was part of your patrol once, wasn't he?"

"Very good, Veronyka. You've been reading my documents."

"Ilithya's documents," Veronyka corrected.

Val shrugged again. "My associates, nonetheless."

"Reluctant associates, from what I hear."

Val's nostrils flared. "And where have you heard this, Veronyka? His father, the disgraced ex-governor? Or maybe you've been talking to ghosts? Surely you've noticed that most of the people who defy me wind up dead."

The breath left Veronyka's lungs at what she assumed was a jab at her own mother. "Most," she gritted out, "but not all. I'm still standing here. And not everyone on that list bows to you."

Something in Val's gaze flickered, and Veronyka knew she'd struck a nerve. Was it mention of Veronyka's defiance that had gotten to her, or was Val thinking of Alexiya? Val must have had some reason for having her on a list of allies, even if her status as a loyal Phoenix Rider had changed since the war.

"Why did you bring me here? Why send Doriyan to do your bidding and lure me away from the others?"

"I thought . . . given everything you've discovered . . . that you might want to talk."

"To you?" Veronyka asked flatly, and Val's lip curled.

"Who else?"

"Why the vision, then?" Veronyka asked.

"I wasn't expecting both of you," Val said with an easy shrug. "I needed to make sure it didn't turn into a fight like last time."

At the cabin. "Why did you want the lockbox anyway?"

"I thought if I told you the truth, you'd come find me . . . but I also thought you'd probably need proof."

"A lifetime of lying will make people distrust you."

Val smiled infuriatingly at that. "You're one to talk. How long did you wait to tell this one"—she nodded at Tristan—"about your magic? About me?"

"Longer than I should have," Veronyka said, the old guilt rising inside her. "It won't happen again."

"Careful, Nyka, or your closeness will get you into trouble." She paused, realization dawning. "It's too late, isn't it? It's done. That's why he collapsed."

Val was talking about their bond. Veronyka didn't answer, which seemed to be admission enough. Even now Tristan's unease was like a flickering flame next to her, its heat dancing and crackling against her skin.

"That was foolish—he's too weak to fend it off. He'll be a liability."

Tristan tensed next to Veronyka, but she refused to give the words room to breathe. "No," she said at once, shaking her head. "You're wrong."

"I'm right and you know it—all bonds are a liability."

"As far as I can tell, the only bond I have that weakens me is the one I share with you."

Silence.

"That's where *you're* wrong," Val said softly, and Veronyka was amazed at Val's self-restraint. Usually she would have flown off the handle by now. "We make each other stronger. Together, our power would be infinite."

Veronyka sighed. "I've said it before and I'll say it again: We tried that, Val, and it didn't work. Not for me."

"But things are different now," Val said, taking a step forward. "You are an Ashfire. We both are. We belong together."

"You and my mother were both Ashfires. . . ."

"Yes, and apart, we failed."

"Is that why you showed me that vision?" Veronyka asked, unease fluttering in her chest. Val was self-serving as always, but there was some truth in her words. Veronyka *was* an Ashfire, and it was hard to know what that really meant for her and her future. Val was her family too. Did Veronyka owe it to herself—to her mother and all her ancestors before her—to try to make it work with her? "That was the last time you two spoke, wasn't it? That was the end?"

"I already showed you the *end*," Val said, her voice ragged. Veronyka knew she was talking about the moment when Val discovered that Pheronia was pregnant, just as an arrow claimed Pheronia's life and fire claimed Avalkyra's.

"That's not what I meant . . . ," Veronyka said, thinking back on the scene. Truthfully, they hadn't said much to each other—bandying words, false pleasantries, and empty threats—but the interaction felt important. Veronyka remembered the last thing she'd thought, as the vision dissolved around her: that Val wasn't all bad. That she might yet be redeemed.

There was no way that was Val's intention in showing her that particular interaction. More likely, she wanted to prove to Veronyka that she could have killed her sister but didn't.

To Val it was proof that she had been in power all along. That the war was hers to end.

To Veronyka it was proof that Val could show mercy.

"Okay," Veronyka said, crossing her arms over her chest and giving Val her full attention. "You wanted me here—you used Doriyan and shadow magic and who knows what other tricks—and here I am. We're together. Now what?"

"I have information you want."

"More surprises? More life-changing revelations?"

Val looked almost . . . sorry. Almost. "You should not have had to learn your heritage from a box of papers. But no, not that kind of information."

Veronyka swallowed, trying not to show just how relieved she was. "What, then?"

"The animage captives," Val said. "I know where they are."

"What do you mean?" Veronyka said on a breath. "They must be all over the empire by now."

Val shook her head.

"They're . . . all in one place?" Veronyka asked, chest tight. The animage captives had been haunting her for days, but she'd assumed their disappearances were a symptom of the war and the fighting—not a part of it. If they were all together, that meant they'd been taken not by enterprising soldiers looking to make extra money, but on orders. From their leader. "How do you know that?" They had spies of their own, after all, and had failed to receive this intelligence.

Val shrugged. "I have allies beyond the confines of this mine—and this province."

"Not him," Veronyka said softly. What better ally beyond Pyra than Lord Rolan himself, the person responsible for the kidnappings? Val's black eyes glimmered in the torchlight. "Val—tell me you haven't allied with the man who's trying to kill us all."

"Don't be so dramatic," Val sighed. "And he only *thinks* I'm his ally."

"Wait," Tristan said, speaking at last. "You've allied yourself with *Lord Rolan*? But he's an empire governor—he's the thing you fought against sixteen years ago."

"Seventeen," Val corrected idly. "And they didn't call it the Blood War because it was a fight between politicians. It was a fight between sisters. Between blood."

"What do you mean he only *thinks* you're his ally?" Veronyka pressed.

"Come now, Veronyka. You know better than most that I don't do anything for anyone unless I stand to profit from it. I wanted to learn his plans, and I have. Where he will strike and when," she said with an airy wave of the hand. "And where he keeps his hostages."

"Hostages?" Veronyka asked, confused. Then she realized the full truth. "He's using them to draw us out."

Val nodded gravely. "There are dozens of them. Mostly children. Rolan wants to hurt you, yes, but what he wants more is to lure you into a battle. He wants it to be so spectacular that the empire has no choice but to support him. He will gladly sacrifice a few hundred soldiers for that."

"The commander . . . he'll see through it," Veronyka said, but of course Val knew that already. "He'll see what Rolan's doing. He won't play into his hands."

"What a pity—for the animages anyway. And here I thought you wanted to *save people's lives*. . . ."

"You know where they are?" Veronyka asked, an idea forming in the back of her mind—an idea she knew Val was trying to plant there.

"Yes, why?" Val asked, all polite puzzlement.

You know why, Veronyka found herself saying into their bond, and Val grinned faintly at the small victory. "If I go with you," Veronyka said aloud, "will you help me free them and get them to safety?"

"Veronyka, no," Tristan interjected. He gripped her arm, trying to force her to look at him—but she kept her gaze fixed on Val. There was a triumphant light in Val's eyes that said *this* was exactly what she'd wanted.

"I will," Val said at once.

"And will you agree to stop attacking the empire?"

Val's lips pressed together as she considered her response. "I cannot promise that I won't make moves against the empire—*but,*" she said, cutting Veronyka's objection off, "perhaps I could be persuaded to explore other, less violent options."

Val said the words idly, *thoughtfully,* as if the idea were only just now occurring to her, but Veronyka saw the manipulation for what it was: Val wanted Veronyka to think she had no choice but to stay with Val, that she alone could *persuade* Val to give up her vendetta against the empire.

Was there any truth to it? Val was not someone to be stopped or dissuaded, but Veronyka also knew that Val was being sincere when she said she wanted them to be together. *Why* she wanted this was harder to discern, but Veronyka would be a fool not to recognize that she did have some power or influence over her once-sister, just as Val had power and influence over her. Was it simply the bond at work between them, or was it the bond of family? Of blood? Could Veronyka do what her mother had failed to do and stop Avalkyra Ashfire from tearing the world apart?

"Veronyka," Tristan begged. "You can't do this. My father—"

"She does not answer to him," Val snapped, glaring at Tristan before turning back to Veronyka. Her eyes were dark and glittering when she spoke again. "You are Veronyka Ashfire. You answer to no one."

A chill slipped down Veronyka's back as she considered the truth of Val's words.

If Veronyka wanted, she could come forward—could reveal herself to Commander Cassian and the rest of the Riders. Would he and the others listen to her then? Would the truth allow her to do more, to really make a difference? Was she ultimately being selfish by concealing her identity when she knew she had more to offer than what she was currently? Was she being a coward?

Then again, the revelation of her identity could have the opposite effect. The commander might not see her as a warrior and Phoenix Rider any longer, but as a pawn—a chip or bargaining piece. Would she be locked away and kept safe, deemed too valuable to risk?

But this wasn't the empire—Veronyka had no right to anything here in Pyra. Commander Cassian had rebuilt the Phoenix Riders from the ground up, and ultimately it would be up to him whether he wanted to acknowledge her position from the old world in his new one, or if he would rather treat her the same as he always had: as a young Phoenix Rider apprentice. He'd been a governor once, after all—and his family had been kings long before that. The world had changed, and so too had their positions in it. Was there even room for a queen in the new empire? Was there still value in the Ashfire name?

Veronyka believed that people earned their place—and maybe that was part of why the revelation of her identity had rocked her so severely. All that was different about her was a surname. Did it truly change her, or was she the same person she'd always been?

And if she wanted the Ashfire name to matter, wasn't it up to her to make it so?

"Please, Veronyka," Tristan said, pulling her out of her thoughts. He was standing in front of her now, hands on her shoulders. "She's trying to force you into leaving—into thinking this is the only way."

"I'm not," Val said, walking toward them. Tristan tried to cut her off, but Val spoke over his shoulder to Veronyka directly. "I've learned my lesson; I will not force you. You have until midnight to meet me back here, at the southern entrance to the mine. The decision is yours." She darted a last look at Tristan. "And, Veronyka? Come alone."

Val summoned Doriyan again, and he escorted them down a different passage than they'd entered through, which led to the southern entrance. Val stayed behind in the chamber, watching with a crackling intensity in her eyes as they left.

As soon as they were out of Val's sight, Doriyan's demeanor changed. He hurried his pace, glancing often over his shoulder and muttering to himself. He'd obeyed Val so completely that Veronyka had thought he might be under shadow magic influence, but she realized now that she would have been able to sense it. Doriyan was obeying Val of his own free will, which seemed at odds with what Alexiya had said about him avoiding all Phoenix Riders since the war. . . .

"What are you doing, serving her?" Veronyka demanded, whirling on the spot as they reached the cave mouth. She was frustrated and angry and needed to take it out on someone. "I thought you hated Phoenix Riders. I thought you didn't want to be found."

Doriyan looked taken aback. "I didn't."

Veronyka looked around the cavern walls. "Stupid place to hide, then, when everyone knows you're from Rushlea."

"My father," Doriyan said, looking down. "He's . . . not well. He needed someone to look after him."

His melancholy expression threatened to pierce Veronyka's swelling anger, so she looked away from him. "You should have taken him somewhere safe. You should have left."

Tristan stepped between them. "Just forget it—come on, Veronyka."

"What did you just call her?" Doriyan asked, eyes wide. He shifted his attention over Tristan's shoulder. "What is your name?"

Veronyka hesitated, surprised by his reaction. "Veronyka."

He nodded—kept nodding, as if suddenly everything in the world made sense. "The Pyraean form of the name Pheronia."

"What?" Veronyka and Tristan said together. Veronyka took an unconscious step toward Doriyan.

He shook his head, as if trying to clear it, before fixing her with a long stare. "Axura above," he muttered, scrubbing a hand over his face. *"Yes,"* he said, his voice suddenly hard. "I hate Phoenix Riders. You would too, if you'd done what I've been forced to do. . . ."

"Forced?" Veronyka asked. "As far as I can tell, you were just serving Avalkyra Ashfire willingly."

"As far as you can tell," Doriyan repeated softly. "But I'm not talking about *this*, about *now*. I'm talking about then."

"What happened then?" Veronyka pressed. Alexiya had made it sound like Doriyan and Sidra were devoted servants of their queen, but apparently that wasn't true.

"She would have had me be a dog," Doriyan said, jerking his chin toward the darkness of the mine. Toward Val. "Eating scraps and fetching toys . . . burying bones . . ." He trailed off, shaking his head. "For years I tried to get away, but I never could. So I did it—running messages, creeping around the capital . . . that was one thing. Fighting soldiers—that I could do. But dead bodies and newborn babes? Killing innocent people? I did *not* sign up for that the day I earned my wings. I did not sign up for it."

"What bodies . . . what babies?" Veronyka whispered, dreading the man's answer, though she thought she already knew—instinct or shadow magic, she wasn't sure.

Doriyan seemed alarmed that he'd said so much and cast a terrified look over his shoulder into the mine. Val might have used shadow magic to force Doriyan back then, but she wasn't doing it now—there was no presence of Val in his mind.

Doriyan's face scrunched into a grimace, and he jabbed his thick hands through his wild, unkempt hair. He lurched forward, and Tristan stepped between them again as if to block him, but Doriyan paused just out of reach. "I was there the day you were born," he said, speaking rapidly. "I was there. And that woman wanted me to hide you—me and Sidra."

"You mean Avalkyra?" Veronyka asked. But she'd been dead already, hadn't she?

"No, another one of her '*loyal servants*,'" he said scathingly. "Ilithya Shadowheart. We were supposed to hide you from your father so he never knew of you. But he came. . . . He heard the screams and he came. The look on his face, when Ilithya told him that your mother was gone. . . . We watched from the balcony. But that was not the worst of it. *That woman*," he said again, such vitriol in the words that Veronyka swore she could feel the burn of them, "she told him you were dead too. Showed him a cold, lifeless baby . . . one that Sidra had fetched from the morgue. Never have I seen a man weep as your father did. He wandered out. . . . There was nothing left for him in that room, in that city. Sidra was sent away with the living baby—she'd been holding you out on the balcony, a hand over your mouth, though you did not cry."

She stood, frozen, his words washing over her in wave after icy wave. A part of her was desperate to know more about herself and her family. Her parents. But not *this*.

Veronyka blinked rapidly, trying to dispel the imagery floating in her mind's eye, but all she could see was blood and death.

"The thing is . . . ," Doriyan began, voice quiet again. "I was awake by then. Not before. Before . . . there was a shadow in my mind, a hold that I couldn't shake."

Veronyka wrenched herself back to the present and focused on his words. Surely he was talking about shadow magic?

"It was my own fault. I let it happen. . . . I won't let it happen again. Daxos could see it . . . could sense it."

Daxos, Veronyka remembered suddenly, was the name of Doriyan's phoenix, whom they had yet to see. Next to Veronyka, Tristan perked up, as if he knew what Doriyan was talking about.

"And after she died . . . it was gone. I was awake, and . . ." He looked at Veronyka, eyes wide with remembered horror. "It was a living nightmare. After Sidra left with you, I was sent for your father."

Tristan was next to Veronyka now, his arm around her shoulders, but she was rigid as stone.

"Ilithya told me to kill him," Doriyan said, pain marring his features. "She told me to follow and kill him, just to be sure. . . ." He swallowed. "But I did not."

Veronyka swayed on the spot, the relief gushing through her like a flood, and Tristan clutched her more tightly. She felt woozy, disconnected from her body. She had suspected—maybe even hoped—that her father might still be alive, but it was hard to feel glad in that moment. It was hard to feel anything.

"Daxos and I flew and flew . . . and never looked back. But still, this past haunts me," Doriyan finished, eyes staring hopelessly into the dark.

"But . . . why are you serving her now?" Veronyka asked, her voice barely above a whisper.

"I don't have a choice," he said bleakly. "She's got . . ." He hesitated, and Veronyka thought again of Daxos. Where was Doriyan's bondmate? "It doesn't matter," he finished with a shake of the head. "It's too late for me, but not for you. Run—fly. However you can get away from her, do it. The world barely survived Avalkyra Ashfire's first life. . . . I'm not so sure it will survive her second."

Perhaps I fight a losing battle.
I could lament the hand I've been dealt . . .
or I could choose to change the game.

- CHAPTER 35 -
TRISTAN

VERONYKA WALKED BRISKLY, LEADING the way through the trees and back toward the Rider camp, her arms crossed over her chest. Not for the first time, Tristan wished he had shadow magic so that he could see into her mind and understand her feelings. That he could understand what had just happened.

Tristan had been lighting the torches, then . . . it felt as if he were being wrenched from sleep—and maybe he had been, because he was on the ground, being dragged to his feet by that man, Doriyan. It was the same as the day he'd fallen from his saddle during the relay race.

He glanced uneasily at Veronyka.

When she dropped her hands and they hung fisted at her sides, he made to take hold of the closest.

The instant their skin made contact, Veronyka snatched her hand out of reach. "Don't," she said, voice tight.

"You're not seriously thinking about going with her, are you?" Tristan asked, trying to sound reasonable. "She's lied to you so many times before. She's—"

"I know what she is," Veronyka said shortly. "But that doesn't mean I'm not thinking about it."

ey'd barely arrived on the edge of camp when Rex and Xephyra
down from the trees, overwhelming them with heat and feathers.
Sparks danced in the air, and Tristan's heart—already uncertain and tight
with worry—clenched even more painfully in his chest.

He staggered backward, his fear catching him off guard. It was Veronyka's
efforts, not his, that calmed both phoenixes. The coldness left her face at the
sight of him cowering like a child, and he hated how much he needed her
protection in that moment. How rattled he was and how desperately afraid
her behavior was making him. She was always the open one, kind and calm
and earnest, but right now she seemed angry and volatile, teetering on the
edge of a precipice Tristan didn't fully understand.

"Give us a minute," Veronyka was saying to Xephyra and Rex, likely
speaking out loud for Tristan's benefit. His blood was pounding in his ears,
a tinny, ringing sound as he fought to regain his composure. While Xephyra
complied at once, Rex hesitated, tossing his head like an agitated horse.

Go, Rex, Tristan managed, his chest hitching with stifled breaths. *I'm
fine. Just . . . go.*

When they were alone again, Veronyka continued to walk the last few
paces to camp, but more slowly now, allowing Tristan to catch up.

"Are you okay?" she asked, when he fell into step beside her.

Relief washed over Tristan, despite how much he hated that after everything they'd just heard, *she* had to be the one to check up on *him*. Still, the
warmth in her voice was soothing and familiar after the strange coldness
before.

"I'm fine," he said, reaching out for her again. "What about you? Are—"
Again, as soon as his fingertips grazed her bare arm, she flinched back from
him. "Veronyka, what is it?" he begged, tone strangled.

Something was going on here—more than just the stuff with Val.
Tristan knew Doriyan's words had upset Veronyka too, but usually she
wanted Tristan with her—wanted to talk things through. Something about
her demeanor felt directed at *him*.

"Are you angry with me?" he asked hesitantly. It brought him back to weeks ago at the Eyrie, after he'd hesitated during their sparring match. He'd asked her then if she was mad at him, and while he'd wanted an answer that time, he wasn't so sure he wanted her answer now.

She stopped, eyes squeezed shut. "No. I'm angry with myself."

"Because of earlier, at camp?" Tristan asked, an ache building in his throat. "You regret what happened between us."

"No—yes," she said. When she opened her eyes and saw the hurt expression Tristan knew he was wearing, she sighed and turned away. "I did it again, Tristan. I lost control in the mine, and Val got in—and *again* you paid for it."

"But I'm not hurt," Tristan said, relieved to think that she didn't actually regret kissing him. He tried to smile. "I'm fine, and everything's okay."

"Everything is *not* okay!" Veronyka said, rounding on him. "You regained consciousness with a knife to your throat, Tristan! What if Val had given a different order? What if you were dead while I was years away, a lifetime away, stuck in one of her memories? What if I sacrificed *you* so that I could learn just one more thing about my family?"

Her chest was heaving, tears glittering in her eyes. He wanted to hold her, to cling to her, because it felt like irrevocable damage had been done. That somehow he'd already lost her.

"Look, I get it," he said, voice shaking, "and we'll do better. We'll go back to what we were doing before. I'll learn to guard my mind against her. I'll—"

"It's not her you have to guard against," Veronyka said, expression bleak. "It's me."

He stared at her, at a loss for what to say. "Please," he said, because he didn't have any other words. "We'll find a way." *We have to.*

She smiled, but it was a miserable thing. "Don't you see, Tristan? I'm *letting* this happen—I'm letting you in, and I'm letting Val in too. If I keep dragging you with me, you'll wind up killed."

"You're not *dragging* me anywhere, Veronyka!" Tristan shouted. It was unfair. She was taking all the blame, yes, but all the responsibility, too.

Didn't he get a say in any of it? "Don't act like this is all your fault, like I'm some helpless thrall you're leading around against his will. I know the risks, and I'm *choosing* to go through this with you. Wherever you are is where I want to be."

Her face was like a knife to Tristan's chest. The more he poured himself out to her, the more she grimaced, the more she shook her head.

"Tristan!" came a voice from the other side of their campsite. Tristan and Veronyka stepped apart, though of course they weren't even touching.

Anders ran into view. "You have to come to the refugee camp straightaway."

Tristan shook his head. "Not now, Anders. I—"

"There's trouble with those farmers. The phoenixes were getting too close to the village, and . . ." He raised his hands helplessly.

"And what?" Veronyka asked sharply, her anger obviously still close to the surface.

"The farmers have got them cornered against the back wall of an inn, and they're throwing rotten food at us and the phoenixes. It's taking everything we have to stop them from igniting and making things worse. I only got away because I was inside when it started and snuck out the front."

"Stay here," Tristan said to Rex, who was fluttering anxiously nearby, Xephyra beside him. He added internally, *I'll call if I need you.*

"You too, Xephyra," Veronyka added.

They paused at camp only long enough to arm themselves. Veronyka picked up her bow and quiver and a medic kit while Tristan grabbed a set of practice spears, tossing one to Anders, who was slinging a medic kit over his shoulder. Tristan didn't want to escalate the situation, and the practice spears were just simple wooden staffs—good for clearing a path or blocking a blow, but not for taking lives.

As they walked through the refugee camp, the jovial atmosphere from earlier was gone. Many of the occupants huddled together near their tents, watching the commotion near the village.

Tristan spotted the remaining members of his patrol at once, the Riders and their mounts pressed up against a building at the corner of the thoroughfare that led between the refugee houses and Rushlea.

It was clear they'd been ambushed on their way out of the inn; metal tankards of ale lay forgotten on the cobblestones, their contents spilled over the ground, while the door behind them had been barred from the inside, probably to protect the other patrons from the splattered eggs and rotten vegetables that limned the entryway and covered both Riders and phoenixes.

Ronyn was at the front, and he had suffered the worst personal damage—there was a cut along his cheek, and his chest and arms were covered in filth as he held them wide, trying to protect the other Riders and calm the seething crowd. Lysandro and Latham, meanwhile, were focusing their attention on calming the phoenixes—a battle they were losing. The eaves of the inn were smoking, and pulses of heat and feral shrieks—along with snapping beaks and shifting wings—emanated from the center of the group.

As Tristan drew nearer, he spotted Latham's pale blond head bent over his bondmate, hands covered in blood as he plucked shards of glass from the phoenix's trembling wing.

The sight of it sent a fiery stab of anger through Tristan, and next to him Veronyka let out a growl. In one swift move she lifted her bow, nocked an arrow, and loosed it.

The arrow whistled through the air, embedding itself into the sign above the inn, the loud *thump* causing everyone in the crowd below to freeze. They stared up at the quivering arrow, fletched in bright red and purple feathers, then slowly turned to find the source of the interruption.

"Do we have a problem here?" Tristan said loudly, his voice carrying in the silence. He strode purposefully forward, spinning his staff idly—as if it were a walking stick and he was taking an afternoon stroll—though the crowd backed away from him, clearing enough space for him to cut through to Ronyn and take up a position beside him. Veronyka followed, another arrow nocked and ready, and came to stand on Tristan's other side. Anders hurried after them, pushing through to help Lysandro calm the still smoking and sparking phoenixes.

"We've got a problem, all right," said one of the farmers, a woman standing near the front of group. "We don't want these foul creatures near our village."

"That's right," said the man beside her, spitting onto the ground between them. The gob of saliva landed *very* close to the tip of Tristan's boot, and before Tristan's own temper could rear up, Veronyka had whipped up her bow again and taken a step forward.

"Do that again," she said softly, but the words carried nonetheless. A chill ran down Tristan's spine at the look in her eye. "Do it," she whispered, and he believed that she really wanted him to, that she longed to give in to her fury.

"It's okay," Tristan said hastily, putting a hand on Veronyka's weapon and gently lowering it. He stared at her, waiting until she met his eye, but she wouldn't. A part of him was still back in the clearing, still clinging to the threads of their relationship before he lost her entirely, but he had to focus on the here and now. *We can't let this get out of hand,* he tried to convey to her, wondering if she could hear or understand him or if she was trying *not to* and that was why she wouldn't look at him.

Whatever it was, she grudgingly relaxed her hold on the bow, fixing the farmers with a fierce glare.

"Obviously with the celebrations tonight, things got out of hand," Tristan said reasonably. "However, I'm not sure how you expect us to leave the village when you've trapped us against a building." He made his words as cool and condescending as he could manage, as if they'd been spoken by the commander himself, but there was a sliver of anger there he couldn't quite bury. "If you want us to leave, you have to *get out of the way.*"

The man who'd spat at him earlier took a cocky step forward, emboldened by the lack of an arrowhead pointing at his heart.

"I'm thinkin' I'd like you to *make me,*" he said. Tristan tightened his grip on his staff, while Veronyka shifted next to him, ready to use her bow. He sensed the rising tension of the rest of his patrol behind him, knowing they were preparing for a fight.

"What is the meaning of this?" demanded a voice from the back of the crowd—a *familiar* voice. The words echoed off the nearest buildings and reverberated back with such volume and authority that everyone in the vicinity whipped around in alarm. Those at the farthest edges of the crowd moved hastily out of the way as a man strode toward them, the man Tristan knew he would see as soon as he'd heard that booming voice.

Commander Cassian himself parted the crowd with all the ease of a hot knife in butter, revealing a contingent of stronghold guards behind him, mounted on horseback and with weapons drawn.

Whether it was the commander's natural presence, his position as leader of the Phoenix Riders, or the fact that those mounted reinforcements made the angry group of villagers dangerously outnumbered, the crowd of onlookers hastily ducked and scattered. All that remained were Tristan's filthy, beaten-down patrol and a smattering of riled-up farmers who'd failed to slip off or find a way to hide their handfuls of stale bread and rotten cabbage.

"Just a bit of a disagreement," Tristan said, answering his father, though his eyes remained on the man who'd challenged him. "Isn't that right?" Tristan pressed.

The man scowled mightily. "That's right," he said eventually, as if he'd finished weighing his odds and decided he'd best play along. He shrugged as he hooked his thumbs in his belt, nonchalantly dropping a mushy brown apple into the dirt. "It's all cleared up now," he added, fixing Tristan with a beady-eyed stare before slinking off into the dispersing crowds.

"What are you doing here?" Tristan asked his father once the farmers were out of sight. It was just the Riders in the square now, plus a handful of onlookers from the refugee camp. There was a good deal of noise coming from the other side of town where the celebrations carried on unawares, but the usually packed corner upon which they stood had temporarily been deserted in the face of the almost fight. "Has something happened?"

Tristan's father ignored the question, gesturing to his guards, who rode past the refugee camp in the direction of the perimeter watch. Maybe they were here to relieve the original group or to bolster their numbers.

His first task done, the commander took another step forward, surveying their group closely, picking up on every smear of filth and speck of blood. Tristan remained still, refusing to look cowed. He'd been caught in a bit of an embarrassing situation, but he hadn't done anything *wrong* here—he'd had it under control. Mostly.

"Nothing has happened. I'm here because I was requested," the commander said at last.

Tristan stared. Requested . . . by whom?

"Lysandro, see if they'll give us a private parlor, will you?" the commander said, nodding in the direction of the inn behind them. "Tell them they will be compensated for their generosity—and for the damages," he added, his gaze flicking over the building and landing on Veronyka's arrow embedded in the wood.

Lysandro nodded, ducking his head and avoiding Tristan's gaze as he waved for the proprietor to let him inside.

"The rest of you," the commander continued, and Tristan slowly turned around to face him again, "see to your phoenixes and your wounds. Then get this cleaned up."

While the Riders attempted to wash the filth from their skin and Anders swung the medic kit off his shoulder, Tristan bristled. His father had been here for ten seconds and already he'd taken over command and relegated Tristan to a slack-jawed bystander. "I—we're—" he stammered, but his father had said everything he would have.

Lysandro slipped back outside and nodded to the commander, who strode forward and opened the door. "Tristan?" he said, pausing on the threshold. "You have ten minutes with your patrol. Then I'll see you inside."

Before Tristan could speak a word, the door slammed shut, leaving them all standing in silence.

They avoided looking at one another; Ronyn, Anders, and Lysandro examined their bondmates for wounds and wiped them down as best they could before sending them back to camp. Tristan reached out to Rex, warning him of their approach, and received an earsplitting mental screech in response. Tristan rubbed his temple, promising to come back as soon as he could.

Veronyka had a wad of bandages in hand, unearthed from Anders's medic kit, and after giving several to Ronyn for the cut on his face, she hesitated halfway to Latham. It was clear by her stiff posture and uneasy glance that she either hadn't yet asked Latham if she could help tend Xane, or she was wary to do so. Latham was still hunched over his bondmate's wing, though he no longer dug for bits of glass in his wound. Instead his blood-smeared hands were clenched into fists at his sides.

"Latham," Tristan said, walking toward him and gesturing back at Veronyka. "Veronyka has bandages. Let her—"

"I don't care *what* she has," he said viciously, and Tristan froze midstep. He knew Latham didn't particularly like Veronyka, but his reaction was still surprising. He turned away from Xane at last, and after a hesitant shake of his wings, the phoenix took to the sky, leaving only Riders behind.

Something about his confrontational stance and the way he glared at Veronyka . . . it was all Tristan needed to fly off the handle.

"Is there a problem here, Latham?" Tristan demanded. Latham drew himself up, but before he could reply, Anders cut in.

"Hey, guys," he said, hastily stepping between them. "Come on, we're all a little upset, and the commander—"

"Speaking of the commander," Tristan said, seizing on the subject change. "What is he doing here? Who requested him?" He looked around at the group. When no one answered, his frustration rose. "*Someone* requested him," he bit out, pointing toward the inn, "and I don't think it was the farmers."

"It was me," Latham said flatly. "I wrote to the commander when you didn't take the farmers' threat seriously," he continued, his jaw set. "He said he'd come to smooth things over in a few days, and clearly he got here just in time."

"You should have talked to me," Tristan said. He couldn't help feeling betrayed that one of his own patrol members had gone behind his back. "I would have handled it—I *was* handling it."

"I *can't* talk to you lately," Latham argued. "You don't listen. You're stubborn and reckless. I don't know what's gotten into you—no wait, I do. It's *her*."

Tristan—along with everyone else—swiveled to stare at Veronyka, as if there could be some other "her" in their midst. Veronyka's eyes were dark as they gazed back at Latham.

"*She's* reckless, and she's made you reckless too."

"Latham," Tristan said, trying to keep his voice calm. "Come on. I miscalculated this one time, but Veronyka never—"

"It's not just this! You flew into the Silverwood a Rider short and got caught in an empire attack," Latham spat, pacing now. "You're always running off alone together, and tonight is no exception. You *weren't here*."

The words felt like a physical blow to Tristan . . . because they were true. He and Veronyka did often slip off alone together—whether it was to seek out the exiled Riders or to work on blocking shadow magic—and that meant spending time away from the rest of his patrol. And maybe he had been a bit reckless from time to time, but these were *his* decisions, not Veronyka's.

"You want her to be your second," Latham continued, voice incredulous, "when there are far more experienced Riders already on your patrol. You never ask for our advice or our input—only hers."

The others stared at Tristan, and he wondered idly who had told Latham of his intentions to make Veronyka his second-in-command. Probably Darius, who didn't seem to like Veronyka much either. Tristan didn't look at her, though he thought he could feel her vibrating in anger beside him.

"She's not a Master Rider, but you keep arguing with your father to keep her here. You're trying to get us on the front lines—as if we're not fresh out of training. And, oh yeah, let's not forget the way you risked not just our lives but the phoenixes' lives during the attack on the Eyrie."

Tristan stared. Of all the charges Latham was laying at Tristan's feet, blaming him for the fight at the Eyrie was a low blow.

"Latham," came Ronyn's rumble of a voice, his tone reasonable. "Tristan was under extreme pressure during that battle, and our bondmates deserved to fight for us."

"It's not our bondmates I'm talking about," Latham snapped, rounding on Ronyn.

"Xoe," came Veronyka's soft voice. Tristan was surprised by the tenderness in it, but then he actually listened to the word she said. Xoe . . . short for Xolanthe. She was one of the female phoenixes that had been in the breeding enclosure. The one who'd died.

The one who was Xane's mother.

It all came back to Tristan then, the sight of Xoe falling from the sky, the screeches of anguish from the other phoenixes, but none so potent as Xane's. He'd flown over the place where her body landed for hours, refusing to come down. He'd also set up a vigil next to the funeral pyre where they'd burned their fallen warriors, including Xoe, waiting and waiting for a mother who'd decided not to come back. Not many phoenixes knew their parents, not when eggs could go unhatched for decades—even centuries—but that didn't mean they didn't feel and understand the bonds of family.

And the person who'd convinced Tristan to release the phoenixes—even the females—was Veronyka. She'd saved them all, but in war there were always casualties.

"I'm sorry," Veronyka said to Latham, surprising Tristan. When he glanced in her direction, he saw moisture glistening in her eyes. He knew she'd suffered terrible guilt and regret after the attack, and he hated that Latham had just thrown it all back in her face. "I'm sorry that she died," she continued, before her expression hardened. "But I'm not sorry I released the female phoenixes. *You* were the ones keeping them in a cage, trying to use them for breeding, not me. I set them *free*, as they should have been from the start. And when I opened that cage, they had a choice: fight or flight. Maybe they should have left, but they didn't. Xoe *chose* to fight, just like she *chose* not to come back when we burned her body. And I won't let you or anyone else take her sacrifice away from her."

Latham's pale face flushed with color. He looked furious, but also embarrassed, opening his mouth to reply, but Tristan cut him off. "We can't change the past, Latham, and I understand you're upset with me," he said, deliberately trying to take the focus off Veronyka. Latham was treating her as a scapegoat, as someone to take the blame for Tristan's bad behavior— and he couldn't have that. "But you should have talked to me first. Involving the commander in this . . . I wouldn't be surprised if he decides we're not ready and sends us back to the Eyrie."

"Maybe that's not the worst thing," Latham said.

Tristan's anger surged again. "If that's what you wanted all along, Latham, you could have asked. I would have gladly sent you back to safety behind those walls. But not all of us want to cower and hide."

Latham's reddened cheeks blanched.

"Tristan," said the commander, standing in the open doorway to the inn. "Inside. Now."

Tristan hesitated before following his father, glancing at the others— especially Latham and Veronyka—afraid that the argument wasn't yet over. He tried to wrestle back his feelings of hurt and confusion, pausing as he drew level with Veronyka.

"Wait for me?" he asked hopefully, but her gaze was a lifetime away, and she didn't answer.

Commander Cassian led Tristan into a small parlor, the hearth inside dark and the tables empty. Even the main room had cleared out, the fight scaring away customers and earning Tristan a scowl from the owner as they passed through.

"Take a seat," his father said, closing the door behind him and pointing at a chair.

"I'd rather stand," Tristan said.

The commander sighed heavily, pulling out a chair at the end of the table and sitting. He poured himself a cup from a pitcher on the table but did not drink. Instead he lifted his face and surveyed his son. "I get the impression you're . . . less than overjoyed to see me."

Tristan bowed his head. He was at the end of his rope—he'd been through too much today and didn't have the energy for another fight. "Can we just get this over with?" he asked, fidgeting in the awkward silence. "I know why you're here—I know what this is. You're here to tell me I screwed up, that I'm doing it all wrong, that—"

"*Tristan,*" his father cut in, his expression startled. "I didn't come here to rail at you. I came here expecting to have to use some of my old politician's tricks . . . and maybe teach you some of them too. I came here to *help* you."

Tristan had been contemplating his boots, but he looked up at that. He considered with numb shock that perhaps much of what he'd taken as disappointment and criticism throughout his life had actually been his father trying to teach him things. Tristan just hoped he hadn't missed too many of the lessons with his knee-jerk defensive reactions.

The commander leaned back in his chair, scrubbing a hand across his face. "I thought we'd deal with the disgruntled farmers, shake some hands, and reassure them that everything is under control. Then we'd partake in the festivities." He took a drink from his cup at last. "But," he added, and Tristan had known it was coming, "apparently there are other issues that need to be dealt with. You have to tighten your hold on your patrol, son. I warned you there would be resentment if you pursued a romantic relationship with Veronyka. I warned you not to get distracted from your duties."

His voice was low and steady and surprisingly without reprimand or accusation. Still, Tristan turned away, biting his tongue because his father was *right*, of course. Tristan had lost control of them, but worst of all, he'd lost their respect. And he'd somehow dragged Veronyka into it; she was taking the blame for his mistakes, and that was unacceptable. Suddenly everything he'd asked his father weeks ago came back to him, the importance of waiting, of letting Veronyka prove herself—letting them both earn their reputations *before* they became romantically involved. But Tristan hadn't followed that advice, and now not only was his patrol angry with him, but Veronyka was too. Their closeness was causing trouble on all sides, and

Tristan didn't know how to move on from here. He didn't know how to change the fact that he would always choose her.

"Talk to me," his father said, his tone gentle. All his life Tristan had wanted an invitation like this, but instead he whirled back around.

"Like the way you talk to me?"

"Excuse me?"

"I know there's something you're not telling me," Tristan said, his hand sliding into his pocket.

"This isn't about the Grand Council again, is it?" his father asked, exasperation in his voice.

"What you're doing doesn't make any sense. You're a war criminal—you're in exile—and yet you plan on walking into that room with those people as if you're still one of them. You're not, and I don't believe for a second that you think you are. You know arguing our case against Rolan won't work—he has too many allies on the council, and you too few. What are you really planning?"

Something flickered in his father's expression before he shuttered it away. "Tristan, I—" he began, but Tristan cut him off.

"Stop. Lying. To. Me," he said. He was going for the same low, quiet tones his father often used, but it came out more like a growl.

He drew his hand from his pocket, fingers clutched around the dart Elliot had given him. It had been burning a hole in his pocket for days, this single, tangible piece of proof that the commander was hiding something. Tristan hadn't been able to bring it up with his father before he returned to Rushlea, but now he was determined to get answers.

He slammed it on the table. "If your plans for the Grand Council are as you say, then tell me, where does *this* fit in?"

His father stared down at the dart, his usual composure in place, though his mouth hardened. "Where did you get that?" he asked calmly.

Tristan wanted to shake him. Even now, confronted with the evidence of his lies, he had the ability to look unruffled. It made Tristan want to break something. "That doesn't matter," he said. "But I know it's yours.

Now, is there something else you want to tell me about this council meeting?"

His father didn't speak.

"Let me make something clear," Tristan began coldly. His voice was harsh, but to his surprise, it was no longer emotional. He leaned both hands on the table, looming over his father, who raised his chin so their eyes were on a level. Something in the commander's expression was less impenetrable than before, and it was clear he was surprised by his son's outburst—but Tristan wasn't done yet. "I will not follow you blindly. Tell me the truth. *Assure* me that you are doing the best thing for my fellow Riders and the people of Pyra, or so help me, I will unseat you and take your place in command. I swear it."

Adrenaline coursed through Tristan's body, making it almost impossible to stand still—but he did. He didn't move an inch or lower his gaze, his eyes burning into his father's. There was something happening in this room . . . a standoff years in the making, and Tristan would not, *could not*, back down.

Silent minutes passed before, finally, the commander sighed and lowered his gaze. Tristan leaned back triumphantly as his father's attention shifted to the dart on the table between them; he picked it up, turning it over in his large hands.

"Yes, Tristan. I have been lying to you."

"About the Grand Council meeting?" Tristan pressed.

"About the Grand Council meeting," his father conceded heavily. "And about other things," he added, putting the dart down and leaning back in his chair. This time when he indicated that Tristan should take a seat opposite him, Tristan did. His father poured him a drink, just as he had in the dining hall at the Eyrie weeks ago. He put the cup in front of Tristan and refilled his own.

"Everything I've told you about the Grand Council meeting is technically true—except for my intentions in attending."

Tristan stared at the dart, wondering if Elliot was conducting an investigation of his own—and if Tristan should be worried about that. How else could Elliot have come by the dart and the fact that it was connected to the commander? But Elliot was grounded and had no access to the messenger pigeons. . . . Whatever he was doing, it was staying inside the Eyrie, and Tristan decided he was all right with that—especially since it had helped Tristan discover the truth.

"Though the Grand Council is a large and diverse body of leaders, Rolan has managed to curry favor with many of them. Bribes, threats, and lofty promises . . . even these attacks along the border are one of many ways he is drawing the rest to his side. As it stands, he will get a majority vote for whatever motion he puts forward—most likely, war against us and Pyra. However, there are good, decent members of the council. Members who will vote against Rolan and against war. It's simply a matter of evening the odds."

"Evening the odds . . . ," Tristan repeated. "I don't understand."

His father smiled, a slow, feral thing. "As it happens, Rolan's closest allies and confidants are *also* the very same people who voted to have your mother executed." He paused, lifting the dart from the table again and holding it up between them. "It would give me great pleasure to see them once more and to deliver the killing blow."

"You want to kill them . . . in the middle of the Grand Council chambers?" Tristan asked, barely believing his ears. "Surely there are *smarter* ways to assassinate people? Ideally not in a room filled with witnesses?"

"It would require time we don't have and resources we can't afford to take them out one by one. But, in a single move in a single day, I will not only improve *our* chances and our standing in the empire, but I will remove the entirety of Rolan's cohorts, who have long been thorns in the side of the rest of the council. By removing those members, I will give our friends—not his—a chance at a ruling majority. On the matter of the Grand Council meeting, but *also* on other important decisions. The magetax and the registry. The ban on trade and travel into Pyra. And of course, the legality of the order of the Phoenix Riders."

"You expect them to vote while their fellow council members lie dead on the floor?" Tristan asked, incredulous.

"I *expect* the vote to be delayed. I will be held indefinitely while they vote and vet new members, and meanwhile, our faction will have the majority. Rolan's supporters will have lost sway, power—and their lives. New members might just reconsider voting in his favor . . . especially when there will be no one for them to rally behind."

"So you intend to kill Rolan as well," Tristan said.

"My first dart has Rolan's name on it," the commander said, his lip curled.

Tristan gaped at him. Everything his father did was measured, careful, and deliberate. But this plan . . . it was beyond reckless, the very thing his father often chastised him for. And yet it didn't lack for scope or vision. He wasn't just trying to prevent a war or get revenge for the past. . . . He was trying to build the future. Of course he was still using his "politician's tricks," as he'd called them. Still trying to cut deals and cultivate influence instead of dealing with the problem head-on.

"If I manage this, we'll be a part of the empire once again. Pyra will thrive, and the Phoenix Riders will serve a council that is just and capable."

"You don't think there will be kings and queens again?" Tristan asked, momentarily distracted. How might his father's plans change if he knew he had an Ashfire heir on his side?

"There's a reason the Blood War happened, and it had been brewing long before Avalkyra and Pheronia were even born. It is a dangerous thing to have an elite military force sworn to a bloodline—to a single person—over an ideal. The Phoenix Riders would be better, I think, if their loyalty were to the empire as a whole and not some king or queen, who might use their abilities however they saw fit. Just as the Feather-Crowned Queen did."

Tristan considered those words, his mind reeling. But no matter the future possibilities and strategic benefits, what his father was intending to do . . . this plan was murder. It was bloody vengeance.

"Even if you pull this off . . . you're not walking away afterward. You'll be convicted—you'll be sentenced to death."

His father shook his head. "I've contacted some of my own allies on the council, who will stand to benefit from this plan as much as we will. I'll be imprisoned for my actions, not killed. When the dust settles, I will be able to negotiate the terms of my release."

"There has to be another way," Tristan said faintly, staring hard at his father. "You're putting yourself at the mercy of your enemies. If one single thing goes wrong . . . if they go back on their promises . . ."

"It's worth the risk," the commander said simply.

"Not to me, it isn't," Tristan shot back.

"You don't understand," his father said, his voice oddly gravelly. His hand clenched into a fist around the dart in his palm. "I have to—"

"Have to *what*?" Tristan interrupted, angry again. His father's plans were going to get him killed, and Tristan wasn't going to sit here and pretend it was a totally reasonable idea. First Veronyka and Val, and now this. "Protect our interests? Prove a point? I don't—"

"I have to face them again!" his father roared, slamming his closed fist onto the table. Silence pressed in on them, and Cassian's chest rose and fell rapidly as he collected himself. "I *have* to."

"No, you *don't*," Tristan said desperately, but his father's anger had ebbed away as quickly as it had come, replaced instead with cold fury.

"Yes," he said, his voice soft and deadly and dangerous. "I do. I can still see their faces, Tristan." He closed his eyes, and Tristan railed against the tired look on his familiar features, the way his wrinkles and gray hairs stood out in the harsh light of the nearest lantern, casting his father into stark relief. "I can still see their faces when they condemned her, your *mother*, to death. It was unprecedented. It was personal. And they smiled when they did it. I will smile too."

"Will you smile when you're dead and leave us here without a leader?"

"We'll have a leader," the commander said, opening his eyes. They glittered as they settled on Tristan, a fierce mix of desperation and pride in his expression that Tristan had never seen before. It rooted him to the ground, made his chest heave with something that should have been happiness but wasn't. "That's why you cannot be involved in this, son. Why I've kept you in the dark. They need you—the Riders need you."

"But *I* need *you*," Tristan choked out, staring at the table and avoiding his father's gaze, unable to face the vulnerability there. Didn't his father see that if he failed, those same people who'd taken Tristan's mother from him would have taken his father, too? "You can't go through with it. It's a suicide mission."

"No," the commander said, straightening, his voice steadier than before. Tristan chanced a look at him, and his eyes were dry. "I have every intention of returning. Even so, it is perilous work—and I am the only one who can do it."

"And you expect me to . . . what? Stand aside while you take all the risk?"

"I expect you to be a leader, and sometimes that means playing parts we don't want to play or taking a back seat and letting others do the work. Sometimes it means presenting a unified, confident front—no matter how we might feel on the inside." There was censure in his words, along with something that almost sounded like humor.

"You want me to stop fighting with you," Tristan said, more statement than question.

"That would be nice," his father said dryly, taking a drink from his cup.

Tristan ran a hand through his hair, suddenly exhausted. He didn't know how long they'd been talking, but he knew he had to get back to the others. Val had given Veronyka until midnight, and there was the matter with Latham, too. . . .

Tristan had work to do. He had to be a leader.

"I'd better get back to my patrol."

His father nodded. "I will stay here for the night in case there are any more issues. Then I'll return to the Eyrie in the morning."

"You're letting me stay—letting me keep my command?"

A small smile spread on his father's face. "You're the one who's made a mess of things—it's only fair that you should have to clean it up."

Now I fight not for my life or my world,
but for you and yours.

- CHAPTER 36 -
VERONYKA

THE SILENCE AFTER LATHAM'S accusations and the commander's arrival was decidedly awkward.

Veronyka just put her head down and worked, avoiding the others, though she felt their stares. In some ways it was a relief to finally understand Latham's ill will toward her. . . . But that didn't mean she was happy about it. She'd blamed herself for much of the devastation after the attack on the Eyrie, especially with regard to the animal population. Latham was right— it had been Veronyka's idea to involve first the phoenixes, then every animal at the Eyrie. Some, like Xoe and Sparrow's animal companion, Chirp, had paid the ultimate price—but it was because of their involvement that anyone had survived at all. She'd made peace with that, and the fact that those animals chose their own fate.

Still, it was like picking at an old wound, and Latham's words had managed to cut her open anew.

And Veronyka was sick of it.

She was frustrated with Latham and the ungrateful villagers, with the commander for holding her back and with Val for dragging her forward. But most of all, she was frustrated with herself because she *let* these people get to her.

Always a bleeding heart.

Val had said that to Veronyka several times in her life, and now she understood. Veronyka let every cruel word and dire circumstance cut her, make her bleed . . . *weaken* her. But what was the good in that? The next time Veronyka was sliced open, she'd bleed fire instead.

It was time to do something. To take control. She was tired of feeling helpless while Lord Rolan took what he wanted and innocent people suffered. Veronyka needed to spread her wings and fly. She needed to fight.

To her surprise, some of the Rushlean villagers came to help them clean, insisting that the angry faction of farmers didn't represent the whole village and that they were glad the Riders were there—phoenixes and all. Some refugees joined in as well.

When the work was done, the villagers coaxed the other Riders into staying in town, offering up fresh cups of wine and fried pastries, and so they decided to enjoy what time they had left before they were due to relieve the guard shift and pick up their patrol routes once more.

Veronyka felt Latham's eyes on her as she refused her own drink and made her way back to the campsite alone. Despite how much she'd felt a part of their group in recent weeks, she wasn't actually a member of their patrol. In fact, her presence was unwanted—at least by Latham—and she knew she'd overstayed her welcome. Though many at the Eyrie had been stiff and distant with her after her guise as Nyk had been revealed, she'd thought she'd begun to regain their respect in light of their visits to Vayle and Rushlea. She'd done her best, but maybe some things couldn't be helped.

Xephyra and the rest of the phoenixes flew at her when she arrived, their heat up and their feathers puffed out. Veronyka soothed them as best she could, and wary of Latham's bond with Xane, she edged nearer to him and checked his wound. He was a gentle creature, bordering on timid, and he allowed her ministrations. The cut wasn't deep, but Veronyka didn't like to think about what might have been inside the glass pitcher that hit him, so she cleaned the cuts with water from her flask and secured a length of bandage she'd kept from Anders's kit, just in case.

Xephyra watched her, an impatient presence in the corner of her mind, and the instant Veronyka stepped away from the others, she squawked and dogged Veronyka's steps. She peppered her bondmate with questions, and Veronyka did her best to relay the scenes from outside the inn.

Danger? Xephyra pressed, spreading her wings wide and puffing out her chest. Rex copied her.

The danger is over, Veronyka said, swatting at Xephyra's wings, which blocked her path.

Xephyra didn't reply to that, but instead showed a picture of Val's face. Veronyka sighed. She supposed that as far as Xephyra was concerned, the danger might have only just begun.

And she was right, of course, but Veronyka didn't know how to explain it to Xephyra.

Val *was* dangerous—and that was all the more reason for Veronyka to keep her in her sights. Veronyka didn't fully understand what had happened to sever the ties that bound her mother and her sister, but she did know that the wider the gap had grown between them, the harder it had been to bridge. By the time Veronyka's mother journeyed to the mine to try, it was too late.

Veronyka couldn't let things get that far. Maybe freeing the animage captives would help remind Val of who she was and what she should actually be fighting for. Val kept asking Veronyka to join *her,* but if Val joined Veronyka instead—if she helped the Phoenix Riders defend Pyra against the empire rather than encouraging the strife between them . . . maybe Val could earn the position she so clearly coveted: leader. Champion.

Queen.

There was no ignoring Val, that much was obvious, and no matter Veronyka's complicated feelings toward her once-sister, she couldn't deny that Val made a far more desirable ally than enemy.

If she gave Val a chance to be true to her word, they could do some real good together. They could change the world, as Val had said . . . but change it for the better. Veronyka understood for the first time that she had a responsibility—to herself, to her mother, to Pyra and the empire. She had to try. Even if she failed . . . even if it cost *her* something, in the end, it was better than doing nothing. Better than letting this chance pass her by.

Xephyra continued to stare at Veronyka, her head cocked curiously, while Rex, who stood next to her, started butting Xephyra in the side—much the way a person might nudge a friend when they wanted a question asked on their behalf.

"Tristan's fine, Rex," Veronyka said aloud, stepping around them. "He's with his father."

Rex made a sound very much like a *harrumph* and gazed balefully at her. Veronyka smiled a little; Rex knew as well as her that most of the time Tristan and his father spent together, they were fighting.

Veronyka reached out hesitantly; this bond between her and Tristan wasn't just the two of them, but Rex and Xephyra, too. Would something as simple as comforting Rex strengthen the bond between her and Tristan, when it was already dangerously powerful? It felt like they'd already gone off the deep end, and Veronyka had to do the only thing she could think of to put a halt to their connection.

She had to put distance between them. *Real* distance.

Veronyka would go with Val . . . and Tristan would have to stay behind.

Rex stretched out to her, but at the last moment Veronyka dropped her hand.

To her surprise, it was Xephyra who reacted, a low, crooning sound emanating from her throat. Veronyka turned away. She had to steel herself for what she was about to do.

She replayed Tristan's parting words as she hastily packed her belongings.

Wait for me?

His voice had been tinged with hope. Despite everything she'd said to him earlier, Tristan still held out hope. Once it was Veronyka who'd had to remind *him* to remain positive, to see the bright side of things.

As she gathered her belongings, Veronyka felt the hard shape that was the lockbox, stuffed deep inside her saddlebag. She faltered, thinking of what Doriyan had told her, then slid the box open and pulled out her birth certificate.

When she'd first found it, she'd been fixated on her name—particularly her surname—as well as the name of her mother, listed below. The empty place where a father should have been had remained on her mind as well, the chance at a living, breathing relative too much for her family-starved self to ignore.

But it was the signature at the bottom that drew her eye now, the scrawled penmanship familiar. Despair expanded in Veronyka's stomach as she read the name, settling hard and heavy in her lower abdomen.

Ilithya, Acolyte of Hael.

So it was true. Ilithya, Veronyka's foster grandmother, had been the one to deliver her. She had also, apparently, been the one to lie about Veronyka's very existence, hiding her from her own father—and his identity from the world—before spiriting her away. Veronyka was valuable, after all. Even more so if her queen mother and her aunt were dead.

Words Val had spoken once rose to the surface of Veronyka's mind: *No matter how much she liked to play nursemaid, your* maiora *was a soldier.*

Ilithya had raised Veronyka as a pawn to be used in the future. Like a good soldier would.

She probably kept Veronyka to present her to her queen, and when that queen fell, she scrambled for another plan. Veronyka was an Ashfire heir, and she supposed whoever held her held the potential to reclaim the throne. Plus, she had been an animage. Ilithya could have fashioned her into a Phoenix Rider queen and Avalkyra Ashfire's worthy successor.

But Veronyka *hadn't* been raised to be like Avalkyra, no matter how Val railed at all her supposed weaknesses and deficiencies. Her *maiora* had raised her to be clever and compassionate—not a ruthless ruler. It didn't make any sense. Again, Veronyka struggled to see the woman she had loved as the same person who had done such seemingly cold, calculating things. Why be kind to Veronyka at all? Why sneak words of comfort and wisdom to her when Val's back was turned?

Had Ilithya seen the error in her ways as she grew older? Or had Verony-ka's "education" been abandoned when Avalkyra, the true queen, turned up? Maybe once Val had found them, Veronyka had become an afterthought. Maybe then Ilithya had deemed it safe to love her. Or pretend to.

Veronyka gripped her head and focused. None of that mattered right now. Ilithya Shadowheart was dead, but there were others that Veronyka might save.

With any luck, she and Val would be gone for only a few days. They'd free the animages, then escort them safely to Prosperity, or maybe all the way up to Rushlea. She might face punishment from the commander, but if she returned victorious, how angry could he really be? She and Tristan would be reunited, and they'd figure out their next moves together.

This separation would only be temporary.

But if that was true, why did it feel like she was saying goodbye for-ever?

Veronyka put away the lockbox and saddled Xephyra, who was as apprehensive as Veronyka had ever seen her. She was sidling back and forth from foot to foot, while Rex fluttered anxiously nearby. He watched Ver-onyka's every move, inviting her into his mind, but Veronyka drew herself inward and closed her mental barriers as tightly as she knew how.

So tightly that even Xephyra had trouble getting through, and when Tristan stepped up behind her, she had no sense of his approach.

"What are you doing?" he asked, his voice causing her to whirl around in alarm, her heart thundering. The forest was dark and silent around them, meaning the rest of his patrol must still be in the village; Tristan had come alone.

She looked at him, at the deep ridge of his brow, and returned to her task. "Packing."

"You're going to meet her." It wasn't a question.

Veronyka paused as she fastened a strap. "Look, Tristan," she began, but he was no longer behind her. He was several feet away, gathering his pack and folding his bedroll. "What are you doing?"

"I'm getting ready."

"For what?" Veronyka asked, stepping away from Xephyra to better see him.

He straightened, his satchel over his shoulder and a pile of his posses-sions stuffed under his arm. He fixed her with a steady stare. "I'm coming with you."

Veronyka's chest ached, and she had to look down to collect herself. "Tristan . . ."

He came to a stop next to her, adding his burden to Veronyka's pile of supplies. Rex fluttered over, dropping his head to snuffle at Tristan's chest before nosing around the items scattered over the ground. Tristan watched Rex as he spoke. "I already told you: Wherever you are is where I want to be."

The words made the pain in Veronyka's chest expand, cutting her breath short and pressing against her ribs. She was suffocating from a mix of wild pleasure and aching regret. "This isn't like before, sneaking out at dark or taking a detour on official Rider business. I don't know exactly where we're going, and I don't know when I'm coming back."

"But you *are* coming back?" he asked, seeming to forget the question of whether or not he would join her.

Veronyka turned away, strapping another parcel to Xephyra's saddle. "Yes."

He hesitated, as if biting back words he wanted to say but thought better of. "You can't just go with her . . . especially not alone. You're not her little sister anymore. You're an Ashfire heir," he said, lowering his voice. "What if she betrays you? It wouldn't be the first time."

"How? Nobody *wants* an Ashfire heir—not the people of the empire and not the Phoenix Riders either, if what Ilithya's list says is any indica-tion."

She tried not to sound bitter; there was a part of her that knew she could do good if she claimed her heritage and took her place as a leader. She could be a voice for animages across the empire and in Pyra. But given her bloodline . . . there was a very good chance they wouldn't want her. She'd need more than a name to free the bondservants and make the empire safe for animages again; she'd need supporters and allies. The problem was Val; those who had supported Avalkyra wouldn't support Veronyka—especially once Val came forward—and conversely, those who disliked the Feather-Crowned Queen's legacy would be ready to paint Veronyka with the same brush.

"No, but they might want to kill one," Tristan said bluntly. "Besides, just because they don't want Avalkyra doesn't mean they wouldn't want you."

"It doesn't matter. Val wants me with her for now—that means she won't tell anyone."

"For now," Tristan echoed. "But as soon as you do something she doesn't like, you know she won't hesitate."

"Let me deal with Val, all right? I've been doing it my whole life."

"This is just like the shadow magic—you don't *have* to do this alone. And you don't need her anymore, like you used to. You have a place here, duties, responsibilities. They're going to notice when you don't return. Have you even thought about the repercussions?"

"Have you?" Veronyka snapped. Of course she'd thought about the repercussions, even though she'd tried not to. Would they kick her out for abandoning her post? Or would she wind up grounded like Elliot instead? It was a nauseating thought. "I know my place, Tristan," she continued, her voice cold. "It was made pretty clear to me tonight. And wherever I belong, it's not with your patrol."

Tristan closed his eyes in a grimace. "He—they'll come around. I'll make them. And they don't all think like Latham." He took a halting step forward. "Your place *is* on my patrol. You're my second, whether it's official or not. You are."

Veronyka felt tears gathering behind her eyes and bit the inside of her cheek to steady herself. "You keep saying you want to come with me, Tristan, but you haven't thought it through either." Tristan would lose more than his position of he was kicked out. He'd lose his family and the leadership role he'd fought so hard for. She couldn't let him risk all that just for her. "You're a patrol leader. You're the *commander's son.* You can't just up and leave; people are depending on you."

Veronyka thought she might have finally gotten through to him with that one. His expression was bleak and his gaze distant as he let her words settle over him.

"Just forget you saw me again tonight," she said. "When the others ask, say you don't know where I am."

He laughed harshly, the pain in his eyes like a punch to Veronyka's stomach. The bond between them quivered, shook—begging to be opened, so that she might ease his pain. She clenched her jaw and fought against the urge. "How do you expect me to forget?" His voice was a soft, wretched thing, as if he truly had no idea how to go on.

Veronyka lowered her voice to match his. "Please, Tristan. I need to do this. I need to go with her, and I can't keep putting you in danger. I won't have you risking your position for me."

Tristan's head was in his hands, and his voice was muffled when he spoke. "But she's dangerous, Veronyka." He looked up at her, then higher, into the stars. "How can you possibly trust her?"

"I can't," Veronyka said simply. "But I'm the only one who can do this. All those captives . . . I have to try. I can't ignore it, knowing that I can help. I won't leave them to that fate."

Grim resignation shadowed Tristan's eyes. His head dipped toward his chest.

Veronyka stepped toward him and rested her palms on his cheeks, framing his face. His hands rose at once to cover hers, his face lifting desperately. Though fear made her twitchy, Veronyka didn't draw back from the contact. She stared at him for a long time, willing him to feel her sincerity—her absolute belief that she was doing the right thing.

"Remember when you said you trusted me?" she asked. His gaze faltered, and she knew he was remembering their oaths of fealty—their promises to be loyal to each other. "Trust me now," she continued softly, *and let me go.*

She spoke the last few words through the bond before she released her hold and leapt onto Xephyra's saddle.

Please, he begged, though it was inside her head—the last dregs of their fleeting contact.

"Fly," she whispered to Xephyra, head bent low. With a sweep of her bondmate's wings, they were off into the darkness.

Veronyka closed her eyes as they disappeared into the sky, the wind drying the dampness on her cheeks.

You speak so casually about choice, Theryn, when none of us had any. Avalkyra didn't choose to leave the empire—your precious Pheronia chased her from it.

I didn't choose to have my mother cast me out for my magic. I'm a Phoenix Rider. They are all I have, my only family now that Dad is gone. Where else could I stand if not with them?

I can't stand with you, after all. You chose her, an imposter queen, while her soldiers march into Pyra hunting people like me into oblivion.

My choice was made for me, but yours was not.

Don't write to me again. Don't call me Lexi. Next time we meet, you'll be a soldier fighting for the empire, and I'll be a rebel on the other side.

I fight for the future, but Avalkyra fights
for the moment, for the past—for every slight and
crime against her. Avalkyra fights only for herself.

- CHAPTER 37 -
AVALKYRA

AVALKYRA WAITED IN THE gathering dark, her heart hammering blood and adrenaline through her veins.

Veronyka would come. She had to.

And if she didn't . . .

She *would*.

Everything had led to this point—she could see it now, the way their paths had separated but remained parallel, moving in the same direction so they might cross again.

Rushlea, it seemed, was a fortuitous meeting place. Avalkyra and Pheronia had had a similar encounter in this very spot, but Avalkyra hadn't been prepared then.

This time she'd orchestrated the meeting—had forced Doriyan to draw Veronyka's attention and lead her to the mine—and Avalkyra and Veronyka's relationship was not yet as far gone as Avalkyra and Pheronia's had been. There was still a chance. There was still hope.

Veronyka would be *hers*. Her blood, her redemption.

And this world would be theirs.

The creature beneath her rustled and shifted uneasily, and Avalkyra refocused her attention, tightening the bind. Even when she wasn't riding the phoenix, she had to exert an extraordinary amount of effort to keep the animal under her control. The problem was, the phoenix still had not invited her in. So while there was indeed a bind in place, it was weak in comparison to her bind to Sidra, who welcomed Avalkyra's shadow touch. Avalkyra hadn't even bothered trying shadow magic with Doriyan, especially when it became clear very quickly that he regretted what he'd done in her service all those years ago and had no intention of willingly allowing her into his mind. And so Avalkyra had found other ways to force his obedience.

Even though that decision had conserved her shadow magic, her binds to Sidra and the phoenix were threadbare, fraying ropes in comparison to the steel-chain bond she shared with Veronyka. Maybe someday Avalkyra could explain the power of it, could show Veronyka how to wield instead of fear it. Even within her own mind, Veronyka was afraid, as if Avalkyra's intrusions were something she had to block at all costs, as if Avalkyra didn't fear being there herself far more.

It had nearly robbed Avalkyra of her own consciousness to thrust that shadow magic vision upon Veronyka in the mine. She'd thought it would be a good way to put Veronyka on the defensive—as well as give Avalkyra herself the opportunity to take hold of the situation—but she hadn't expected the memory to be more powerful than Avalkyra's own hold on it.

It had been Veronyka who broke them both out of it. All three of them, actually, because the commander's son had taken up residence inside Veronyka's mind—and heart—as well. It was lucky he did not have shadow magic too, or the web between them would be all the more tangled. As it was, he was a helpless passenger, but Avalkyra would have to deal with him eventually. For now she had to tread very softly, treating Veronyka like a wild horse that might be spooked. But once they started to run together, the wind in their hair and their old lives far behind them, Avalkyra would cut the ties and set them both free.

There was a rustle to her left, and though Avalkyra longed to whip around in her saddle, gaze hungrily roving the trees, she restrained herself.

Instead she closed her eyes and let her magical senses broaden. The phoenix tossed her head, and Avalkyra drew her magic back to herself.

"Hello, *xe* Nyka," she said, still not turning in the saddle.

Despite pulling her magic inward and focusing it on her phoenix, she sensed Veronyka's irritation. It flashed between them before Veronyka got herself under control.

"Let me guess," Veronyka said, her phoenix sidling up next to Avalkyra's and bringing them into her peripheral vision. Avalkyra turned to face her. "You knew I'd come."

Avalkyra smiled. "No, Veronyka. But I'd hoped."

Veronyka snorted. "I thought you said hope was foolish."

Avalkyra had expressed some version of that sentiment many times in both her lives. A helpless fool *hoped* for something outside of her control . . . but a queen made it so.

Even still, Avalkyra had made the moves, willed people and events to force this outcome, but she could not guarantee it. She could not *make* it so. All she could do was stand in the shadows and hope.

"Consider me a fool, then," she said.

Veronyka cast an appraising look at her. Avalkyra didn't much care for the feeling of being assessed and measured, so she urged her mount forward, into the sky.

Veronyka followed. She was a natural flyer, and it was clear her bond to her phoenix was as strong as ever, in spite of—or maybe *because* of—the creature's death and resurrection.

Taking the lead, Avalkyra started to steer them southwest when Veronyka cut her off. She flew in front suddenly, then diverted their flight with a familiar Phoenix Rider hand gesture.

Avalkyra was so surprised that she followed the order without thinking, redirecting her flight south.

Once they had leveled off, Veronyka twisted in the saddle. "There are patrols," she said shortly, the words carrying back to Avalkyra on the wind.

Veronyka slowed her pace, bringing them on a level, but not allowing herself to slip behind. Had she sensed Avalkyra's reaction to her taking the lead and was now attempting to rectify the situation? Avalkyra tried their bond, but Veronyka's mind was guarded. Even without shadow magic, her posture was stiff and her chin held high.

"We'll head west before we reach Vayle," Veronyka continued, still shouting the words for Avalkyra to hear.

Use your mind, Nyka, Avalkyra said. *That is how the best patrols did it.*

Veronyka didn't answer.

They flew all night, the wilds of Pyrmont rolling out before them like some vast Stellan rug. After they passed all the commander's Phoenix Rider patrols, Veronyka subtly slowed her pace, allowing Avalkyra to take the lead since she didn't know their destination. They were on the lower rim now, flying over the Foothills in a steady western path.

Avalkyra was focused on their destination, steering them slightly north of where she expected Rolan's soldiers to be. If Sidra had beaten them back—which she should have—she'd be keeping a lookout and would spot their approach.

"What is that?" came Veronyka's sharp voice. Avalkyra pretended not to hear her, and after several silent wingbeats, Veronyka tried again.

Val, she said, and even in her mind her words sounded strangled. *What is that? What happened?*

Pleased to have won that particular battle of wills, Avalkyra looked down. They were passing the wide grassy plains between Runnet and the Ferronese border, and they were burning. Avalkyra couldn't mirror with her phoenix, but it didn't take superior eyesight to guess. . . . Rolan's soldiers had struck one of the smaller farming communities—Hillsbridge, judging by their current location.

It looked like Veronyka and Val had missed the worst of it; there were mostly soldiers visible now, chasing the last screaming villagers as they tried to flee, or burning and destroying what little remained of the structures.

Bodies littered the ground, and while the soldiers made no move to burn or bury them, some were obviously looting.

I told you, Lord Rolan wants a war. He will have it, whether your precious Riders fight in it or not.

That is not a war, Veronyka said, anger radiating from her and her bondmate in a rush of sparks. *That is a massacre.*

Control yourself, Avalkyra said sharply, though she loved seeing the fire in Veronyka, especially when it wasn't directed at her.

Veronyka's outrage pulsed and glowed, like a coal ready to catch flame. She was closer to diving down and intervening than Avalkyra had first realized. Veronyka was a raging wildfire held too long in check. She needed to be set loose.

No, not a wildfire. An *Ash*fire.

That battle is already lost, Veronyka, she pressed on. *Think of the captives. Think of the battle to come.*

They soon left the carnage and the smell of burning wood and flesh behind, and Veronyka's rigid seat in her saddle relaxed somewhat. When Avalkyra was certain the girl wasn't going to wheel around and dive into the fray, she focused again on the landscape ahead.

They weren't far from the border now; Hillsbridge was the last inhabited village before the ground turned rocky and severe, and the Foothills marked the natural barrier between the province of Ferro and the Freelands of Pyra.

Though it was night, her eyes had long since adjusted, and Avalkyra could make out the distant mass of figures looming in the distance. Moonlight glinted off bits of metal and the smooth surface of canvas tents, and smoldering campfires dotted the ground where hunched bodies sat together or lay flat sleeping.

Veronyka leaned forward—she'd seen it too.

While the soldiers were spread across the ground in swaths of mostly indistinguishable shapes—save for the picketed horses and the tents—there was a clearly demarcated center of the camp where a group of larger tents were clustered together under heavy guard.

The animage captives.

Come, Avalkyra said, turning their flight northward before they were spotted by sentries. They'd not gotten far before she sensed Sidra's presence, and a distant shape rose from the darkness below to soar toward them.

Once she saw it was them, Sidra wheeled back around and led the way to her camp. They'd agreed upon this spot before—there was a series of caves hidden in the craggy landscape that had been popular for smugglers to hide their wares before sneaking them over the border. Some had multiple rooms and levels—even doors and locks—because not all the cargo smuggled over the border could be safely stored in boxes.

As they rounded a high thrust of stone, Sidra's fire became visible, casting dancing black shadows across the small clearing with its stony surroundings.

They landed in the open space, sliding from their mounts. Avalkyra was stiff from hours in the saddle and allowed Sidra to take over care of her phoenix. When Sidra reached for Veronyka's reins, Veronyka shook her head forcefully.

"Leave it, Sidra," Avalkyra said, rolling her shoulders and stretching out the ache in her neck.

Sidra stepped back, leering at Veronyka before tugging the reins and leading Avalkyra's phoenix over to troughs of food and water. Veronyka's mount watched them go, her dark eyes glittering with interest. Veronyka ran her hands over the phoenix's feathers.

"What's her name?" Veronyka asked over the hiss and snap of the campfire and the soft crunching of the other two phoenixes eating.

"Sidra of Stel," Avalkyra said, surprised at the question. Veronyka had Ilithya's list, after all, and Avalkyra had just said her name.

Veronyka stared. "Not *her*," she said distastefully. Avalkyra wondered how much Veronyka knew about Sidra's role in her past, or if her disdain was for Sidra's general résumé. Veronyka jerked her chin toward the troughs. "The phoenix."

Avalkyra noticed that she didn't say *your* phoenix. Could she possibly know that what held her in Avalkyra's service wasn't a bond at all, but sheer, endless will?

Avalkyra shrugged. "Who knows?"

Veronyka frowned. "You didn't name her?"

"No," Avalkyra said, flashing her teeth. "*I* didn't." Surely someone had, once. "If you're so curious, why don't you ask her?" Avalkyra suggested disinterestedly, turning away to remove her cloak and unwind the scarf that bound her hair. It had become habit to cover her head in recent weeks. There were precious few people who might actually recognize her face, but now that she was on a phoenix again, she didn't want to invite comparisons to the Feather-Crowned Queen. Well, not yet, anyway.

"You've let it tangle again," Veronyka said reluctantly, as if upset at herself for noticing—and for caring enough to comment.

Avalkyra ran her hands through the mess. "I've had no one to care for it since you left."

"Is that why you returned to the cabin? For a comb?" Veronyka's voice was dry, but it was clear she was fishing for more information about Avalkyra's visit that day.

Avalkyra smiled. "We both know that even if I'd had a comb, I'd not have used it."

The corner of Veronyka's mouth quirked. She schooled her features back to indifference so quickly that Avalkyra might've thought she'd imagined it.

But she hadn't. She knew it in Veronyka's determined nonchalance. She felt it in the bond.

"So now what?" said Sidra, returning to the light of the fire. "You going to let that creature starve?" she demanded of Veronyka, nodding at her bondmate.

Veronyka stared at Sidra, then darted a glance to Avalkyra. She wasn't asking permission or even inviting Avalkyra's advice. She was measuring the situation, her guard still up, her senses all on high alert.

Avalkyra supposed it made sense. She *had* poisoned the phoenix once.

She strode over to the food trough, and the other phoenixes scattered at her abrupt movement. Digging inside, she drew up a handful of plain oats that had been pilfered from Rolan's horse supplies.

Avalkyra put the dry grain into her mouth, spilling some as she chewed slowly, eyes on Veronyka. Then she cupped her hands and drew cool water from the next trough over. She drank, dribbling liquid down her front.

She wiped her face with the back of her hand, then rejoined them next to the fire.

Veronyka wavered for only a second longer before nodding to her phoenix, who fluttered away to join the others, leaving Veronyka standing alone in the darkness.

Avalkyra sank onto a stone, and Sidra did the same.

Veronyka remained standing, wariness in every inch of her, though she must have been exhausted and in need of sleep. It was late, but dawn would soon be upon them, and they'd flown since midnight.

"There are . . . ," she began, her voice hoarse. "There are so many of them."

Avalkyra knew she meant the soldiers. She tossed Veronyka a waterskin, which she caught but didn't drink from.

Thus far, it seemed that Rolan had been sending his soldiers out in relatively small units so they could move more quickly and be in multiple places at once. Judging from the rumors they'd overheard in Runnet, he was also sending out strike forces to harass travelers along the road, like raiders. He wouldn't risk making himself vulnerable in his efforts to destabilize Pyra, so he'd kept the bulk of his forces close to him in Ferro. And now, with the animage hostages in their midst, they were preparing for a real fight with real warriors, not raiding poor villagers.

"There will be more when the empire marches on Pyra," Avalkyra said.

"If," Veronyka clarified, and Avalkyra couldn't help but smile. Veronyka still thought that war was preventable and not inevitable. Avalkyra would love to blame it on the commander, but she knew this particular brand of foolish hope belonged to Veronyka alone.

"So how do we free them?" Veronyka asked. "You said we'd do that, if I came with you. You said we'd free the animages and get them to safety. Tell me how."

Sidra cast a sidelong look at Avalkyra but said nothing. She'd expected a battle between the Phoenix Riders and Rolan's soldiers, not a rescue mission.

"Those soldiers are due to march in the next day or so," Avalkyra said. It wasn't technically true. Surely some of these soldiers would branch off again, but Rolan fully intended to keep the larger portion of his armies near at hand. "We can wait until they leave a skeleton guard behind, then strike."

"March?" Veronyka asked, eyes wide with alarm. "March *where*?"

She almost made it too easy. Avalkyra kept her face expressionless as she answered. "Where do you think?" She shrugged lightly in the way she knew Veronyka hated. "To some other defenseless village. Or perhaps they will march until they find your weakly held defensive lines and force the fight your commander is too afraid to have."

Veronyka's face twisted with anger as she jerked away, hands flying up into her hair in frustration. "Rolan is attacking *us* and somehow we're to blame? We're the ones at fault? He's turning Phoenix Riders into villains, Val, and you're *helping* him do it."

Avalkyra leaned back, crossing her arms and straightening her legs out before her. "You still don't see it, do you?" she asked, somewhat incredulously. Veronyka fidgeted slightly under her stare, anger giving way to unease. Avalkyra shook her head with something like regret, though the emotion felt ancient, dredged up from some forgotten place inside her. "We are already villains. The empire needs someone to blame, and here we are."

"We're only here because of you."

A flash of rage lanced through Avalkyra's chest, but her voice was steady. "Be careful, Veronyka. There are few in this world who are blameless, and while you pass judgment on me and my past, remember that it is your so-called commander who has secreted you all away and trained you for war. He is the one who has mobilized you in opposition of the empire."

"He's not in opposition of the empire—he's in opposition of war. Of senseless violence."

Avalkyra leapt to her feet. Veronyka's lip was curled, her chest heaving with suppressed emotion. Avalkyra walked around the edge of the fire toward her, and though Veronyka looked uncomfortable at Avalkyra's suddenly close proximity, she was too stubborn to step back or shy away from it.

"*He* is—but not you," Avalkyra said softly. She'd stopped in front of Veronyka with her back to the fire, her figure casting flickering shadows across Veronyka's face.

"What are you talking about?"

"You're angry, Veronyka—and you are not opposed to violence as he is. You see that not all violence is senseless. You *want* a fight. You *want* to make the empire bleed for what they're doing here. You want to make them burn."

Veronyka didn't reply, but instead lifted her chin, leveling her gaze at Avalkyra. She *had* grown, since the last time they'd stood like this. Or maybe it was that her back was straighter, her spine stiffer.

"There is another option," Avalkyra said, her voice quiet now. Veronyka's eyes narrowed; she was listening. "We don't have to wait to fight the skeleton guard. . . . We could attack their full force. Wipe them out. We could hit these soldiers before they even know what's happening. We'll make sure no more harm comes to Pyra by their hands, that no more animages are stolen from their beds and dragged from their mother's arms."

The sky was lightening in the east, causing the darkness that enveloped them to shrink and recede. Veronyka's gaze was searching, boring into Avalkyra's—and Avalkyra let it happen. There was no deception in this offer, no lie in her words. Avalkyra hated the empire and would love nothing more than the chance to tear even a fraction of it apart, her alliance with Rolan be damned.

Still, Veronyka did not speak. Avalkyra sensed Sidra's restless attention— she was always chomping at the bit for a fight—but she let the silence hang as Veronyka considered her words.

"That's exactly what Rolan wants," Veronyka said, shaking her head slightly. "You said so yourself. It's one thing to take out a handful of soldiers. . . . It's something else to engage hundreds in a full-scale battle. I won't help him start his war."

"Look around you, Veronyka—the war is happening. You saw Hillsbridge. You saw the Silverwood. . . . The Phoenix Riders have avoided the worst of the collateral damage by evacuating the border settlements, but that won't work forever. The only difference between attacking them now and attacking them *after* the Grand Council meets is that now, at least, we have a chance to strike a real blow against Rolan's limited numbers. Once the full might of the empire joins him, it won't matter how many soldiers we mow down. . . . There will always be more. We are grossly outnumbered. You could arm every man, woman, and child in Pyra, and still the empire's forces would wipe us out in days—and the only reason we would last even that long is because of the size of Pyra. They outnumber us ten to one, and that's not soldier versus soldier. That's ten armed, trained, career fighters against farmers and herders and fisherfolk. The death toll would be catastrophic. The empire is coming for Pyra, and if they do, the Phoenix Riders will not survive it. We'll be wiped from the face of the earth for good."

Veronyka's face looked pale in the golden light of the fire. After several silent moments, she released a slow, shaky breath. She'd come to some decision, though Avalkyra didn't try to dig for it with shadow magic. She just waited.

"We'll need to rest first," Veronyka said at last, the words slightly grudging—Avalkyra suspected she'd rather fly into battle right this instant, despite her bondmate's tired wings and her own exhaustion.

Regardless, Avalkyra's heart leapt at the acquiescence in her tone. "We'll take the day to prepare, and fly out at sundown," she said.

Distantly, the sounds of the soldiers' camp awakening could be heard, a growing rumble punctuated by loud shouts and the clatter of weapons and horses' hooves.

"We have to protect the animage prisoners," Veronyka said firmly. "Keep the fighting away from them no matter what."

Avalkyra nodded, and when Veronyka's head swiveled to Sidra, demanding a response, she nodded as well. Without another word, Veronyka went to her phoenix and unpacked her bedroll. They ventured into the darkness of the cave together and curled up for sleep.

Avalkyra turned to Sidra. "See how she gives orders without fear or hesitance?" she asked, unable to mask the pride in her voice. She suspected Veronyka could hear her—and wanted her to. "She's a natural leader."

Sidra's expression was considering. "A warrior."

Avalkyra shook her head. "A *queen*."

But I have seen war in a way Avalkyra has not as she soars
high above, fierce and untouchable. On the ground, among
the dying, there is no difference between friend or foe.
We are all flesh and blood and fiercely beating hearts.

- CHAPTER 38 -
SEV

SEV HADN'T MADE IT far before he collided with the perimeter guard. It was lucky Kade was dressed as a soldier; as soon as the guard saw Sev's burden—and the blood—he hastened to help, and between the two of them, they crossed the distance to the medical tent much more quickly.

Once Kade was laid out flat on the ground outside with half a dozen other wounded soldiers waiting to be admitted, the healer's assistant at the mouth of the tent directing traffic, Sev frantically tugged off Kade's ill-fitting armor. He still refused to look too closely at Kade, but he knew that being found in stolen gear would require explanations that Sev couldn't give.

When the man in front of Kade limped into the tent, exposing them to the assistant, her eyes narrowed at the gravely wounded bondservant. She directed her unasked question to Sev.

"Two farmers snuck into camp, sights set on the horses. The bondservant tried to fend them off. . . . I got there in time for the farmers, but too late"—his throat had constricted painfully on the words—"for him."

Not too late. Please, gods . . . it can't be too late.

The assistant nodded and pursed her lips, considering the prone Kade. She knelt and pressed her fingers to his neck, pausing for several seconds, then moved them to his wrist. Sev just stared desperately at her face, seeking answers, but she betrayed nothing.

At last she released Kade's arm and turned to Sev. "Well," she said, standing, "take him in."

"He's alive?" Sev asked. He'd meant to shout it, but the words came out in a ghostly whisper.

The assistant gave him a strange look, no doubt confused about how invested Sev was in the life of a random bondservant he'd stumbled upon by accident. "For now. Take him to the empty cot in the corner."

Sev waited outside the tent after that, pacing, ignoring the other soldiers coming and going. His shoulder was locked up so badly he couldn't move it, so he clutched his arm to his side, trying to soften the pain from every step that shook and jostled the joint. He should stop moving—get a compress—but he couldn't. Wouldn't.

At some point his fellow soldiers announced the end of the battle—as if it had even *been* a battle at all. No, it had been an unprovoked attack on a civilian settlement, and Sev had killed one of them. An old man, whose only crime was living here, in Hillsbridge, and wanting to defend some children.

Every time the tent had flap opened—assistants coming and going from the supply tent or helping limping soldiers in and out—Sev craned his neck, trying to catch a glimpse of Kade, but with no luck. He stood far back enough that the harried healer and her assistants didn't notice him, but eventually his failing patience—and the sight of them in blood-drenched clothes—had him throwing caution to the wind and forcing his way inside.

Despite his worries, Sev's intrusion went unnoticed. There were approximately ten cots total; those nearer the door held soldiers sitting up under their own power, with arms and legs in splints or heavy bandages covering surface wounds, but near the back of the tent were the more seriously wounded.

Sev spotted Kade at once, lying still on the bedding, his shirt cut away and his entire midsection wrapped in thick bandages. The healer had washed and stitched him already, and as Sev edged closer, he bent to smell an empty cup, the residue pungent and reminding him of some of the numbing sedative drinks he'd been fed at the Eyrie.

Seeking a place to sit, Sev peered around anxiously, wondering when someone was going to bark at him for being in the way, but Kade was tucked away next to other sleeping or unconscious wounded, and the healer and her assistants were currently bent over someone in the far corner of the tent under a series of bright lanterns, obviously performing some kind of careful surgery.

Sev dragged over a stool and lowered himself onto it—and hadn't left since.

The healer did eventually notice him, along with the assistant who'd admitted Kade in the first place. They said nothing, but Sev thought there might be something knowing in their eyes. They were brusque but not unkind, and told him that if he was going to stay there through the night, he should find a bedroll and lie out more comfortably on the floor.

Sev just shook his head and remained rooted to his seat, staring at Kade's face. He was forced to move when it was time to check Kade's stitches and rewrap the bandages, but he didn't go far, peering over the healer's shoulder as she exposed the injury. The spear had gone through a gap in the side of Kade's armor, leaving a wound between his hip bone and rib cage.

Though Sev hadn't asked, she explained that the damage was superficial and that despite the blood loss and some minor tearing to the abdominal wall, the spear had mostly cut through skin and fat.

Sev gave her a skeptical look—Kade didn't have stomach fat—but said nothing. He knew she'd told him that to relax his jangled nerves, and though he had a hard time believing Kade had little more than a flesh wound, he was grateful.

He was less grateful when she forcibly removed him from the tent at dawn so he could get food, but Sev knew he'd have to check in with his captain and receive his new orders.

He also took the opportunity to find his pack among the supplies and attend to his own injury—something he hadn't allowed himself to do when he was so anxious about Kade. He smeared some salve on his shoulder, the

medicine numbing and cool and allowing him to rotate the joint a bit—
though movement caused dull pain to spread in a wave across his neck and
back. Hauling Kade hadn't done him any favors, though Sev would do it a
thousand times over.

Luckily, the camp was still in disarray when he arrived at the cook fires,
the smoke from the distant burning village drifting through the silence like
fog. Soldiers were clustered in small groups under the hazy early-morning
sun, eating their breakfasts or speaking in low, quiet voices. Many more
were sleeping, sprawled under the scarce trees or clusters of bushes for shade
from the sun, or, in the case of Captain Dillon, snoring loudly inside his
command tent.

Sev got it from one of the other soldiers that they were staying for the
day so they could recuperate and await any possible retaliation from the
Phoenix Riders, but the atmosphere in the camp was subdued. No one
expected them to come.

Though the idea made his skin crawl, Sev wandered the camp until he
found a well-guarded tent near the supplies that could house only one kind
of occupant: prisoners.

The soldiers guarding the door looked bored and didn't object when
Sev nodded at them before poking his head through the flap. There were
fifteen people, mostly children, and Sev suspected they were animages—or
at least animages according to the soldiers who'd snatched them. The strategy for finding animages was simple: The soldiers usually went for children,
who, in their panic, would accidentally call whatever animals happened to
be nearby. Dogs would howl, horses would kick and buck, and birds would
scatter into the skies in a cacophony of shrieks and wingbeats.

The soldiers made mistakes, occasionally grabbing children without
magic, but it wasn't a concern this time. These animages weren't here to be
sold on the black market—they were here as bait, and whether they were
actual animages or not was irrelevant. All that mattered was that the Phoenix Riders *thought* they were.

Most of the prisoners were sleeping or staring desolately at the walls of the tent, their faces soot-covered and their clothes torn and filthy. Sev thought he spotted the boy with the baby—the one who'd fled with another young girl when Kade was stabbed—but he was so covered in dirt it was hard to tell.

Sev leaned back out of the tent. "Won't they slow us down?" he asked the guards next to the door.

"They're leaving separately. A lucky few of us have the *honor* of marching them straight to the border before sundown," the nearest soldier said bitterly. "As if we weren't up all night as well. Now we get to stay up all day, too."

"Just a few of you?" Sev asked, trying to keep his voice from betraying his interest in the subject.

"Why, you *want* prisoner-escort duty?" he asked skeptically. "You're welcome to my spot."

Sev smiled and shrugged in a noncommittal way. His shoulder throbbed. "I'll think about it."

It was as Kade had said—they were marching the animages to the border of Ferro, where hundreds of other soldiers, and even more animage prisoners, were already stationed, in an attempt to draw the Phoenix Riders into a large-scale battle. More death, more locals caught in the fray. How long could Sev keep this up? How many innocent people had to die—some by his own hand—before he was no longer a good guy pretending to be a bad guy and was just a bad guy period? What did it matter to that dead old man that Sev's intentions were good? And what was Sev learning at this point? Rolan's men would have spread the existence of the animage hostages far and wide. . . . Maybe Sev should leave now, before things got any worse.

When he ducked back inside the medical tent, he froze—Kade was awake, propped up on pillows so he could drink from a steaming mug that one of the assistants was holding up for him.

Sev barged through the narrow space, and the healer and her assistants paid him no mind—he was a familiar sight by now.

"You're up," Sev said, standing at the foot of Kade's cot.

The assistant stood and handed Sev the mug for him to take

over—something they'd done several times over the past twelve hours. Hands were sparse and help was always needed, so they'd made it very clear that if Sev was going to be there anyway, he could hold the tray of tools while they applied fresh bandages or refill the water jug while they cleaned Kade's stitches.

Kade lifted his head drowsily, and though his eyes were sunken and his skin chalky, he smiled, and Sev wanted to weep with relief.

"Barely," Kade croaked, and Sev looked down at the mug in his hands. It smelled like broth, and as he lowered himself onto the stool by the bed, he held it out gingerly.

Kade looked apologetic—maybe even embarrassed—and tried to reach for it himself, but Sev waved him off. "Drink," he ordered, and after another moment's hesitation, Kade obeyed.

They sat like that for a time, Sev holding the mug out for Kade to take careful, measured sips. Sev tried not to stare, but he couldn't help it. Warmth was spreading in his chest as if *he* were the one drinking the soup, making the hopelessness of the past few hours dissipate. Kade was okay, and with the proof of that sitting in bed before him, it was easier for Sev to deal with everything else.

"How did I get here?" Kade asked with a grimace. It was obvious that he was in discomfort, and that even the effort of swallowing soup was draining.

"I carried you," Sev said simply, holding out the mug again. When Kade didn't move to drink, Sev lowered it, meeting Kade's shocked eyes.

"But—your shoulder," he protested.

Sev gave him a steady look. "And?" Kade had no response, so Sev added, "I'd have carried you twice as far, for twice as long, with that crossbow bolt still in my shoulder if I had to."

"Thank you," Kade said after several heartbeats of silence, his eyes bright. Sev was uncomfortable with his gratitude, guilt gnawing on him from the inside as he put the mug onto the side table.

"Don't," Sev said, staring at his hands, which had become fists in his lap. "It was *my* fault. I'm . . ." He swallowed and blinked, his vision blurring as tears sprang to his eyes. "I am *so sorry*," he choked out. He pressed his palms to his eyes. "I volunteered for this . . . this stupid mission," he spat, pitching his voice low, though the rest of the tent was filled with the masking sounds of work and low conversation. "It's because of me you got wounded in the first place."

"It isn't," Kade argued, and Sev lowered his hands.

"It *is*," he said firmly. "You said I shouldn't, and you were right, but I wouldn't listen. And now . . . we just burned our *home* to the ground."

"Sev," Kade said again, more forcefully now. He gripped Sev's arm. "We didn't burn anything down. And what happened here . . ." He paused, staring around the tent. He shook his head. "We saved so many lives by doing this—lives at the fishing villages and the farms of Runnet. I'm sorry that we weren't able to save Hillsbridge, but it was worth the risk."

"Worth your life?" Sev asked, voice agonized.

"Yes," Kade said without hesitation. "This is why we came. Not to avoid the awfulness of what Rolan was doing, but to try to fight against it every step of the way. And we couldn't do that safe inside his estate."

Kade's words calmed Sev, even though he didn't fully agree. To Sev, none of this would have been worth it if he'd lost Kade, but as his mind slowly quieted, he became aware of the fact that his wrist was held loosely in Kade's hand. Sev stared at the place where their skin touched. "It should have been me," he said softly.

Kade shifted, sliding his palm against Sev's. "No," Kade said with a gentle squeeze, raw emotion in his voice. Sev looked up into his face, and Kade forced a smile. "You're too skinny. That spear would have cut you in half."

Sev gave a shaky laugh, wiping at the drying tears on his face with his arm. He squeezed Kade's hand back, then, suddenly embarrassed, tried to draw it away—but Kade held fast.

"Wait—don't let go," he blurted, squeezing Sev's hand, though his grip was weakened by medicine and blood loss.

Unable to speak around the lump in his throat, Sev just nodded and laced his fingers with Kade's. "I won't," he said, thinking for a second about the animage prisoners—and quickly squashing the thought.

Kade eased back against his pillows. "I think I need to sleep," he said drowsily, his eyes beginning to droop.

Sev's chest was warm again, as if a bubble of glittering sunlight had wedged itself underneath his ribs. He wanted to stay in this moment forever, holding Kade's hand while he dozed. In fact, he never wanted to leave Kade's side again.

"I think she liked me . . . ," Kade said suddenly, and the words were so jarring that Sev was certain he was sleep-talking. But then Kade shifted slightly and opened one of his eyes a crack. "Mia. Before. I think she liked me . . . but I never liked her."

"How come?" Sev asked, holding his breath.

Kade closed his eyes again, his lips quirking slightly at the corners. "Not my type."

Sev beamed, but only because Kade wasn't looking. He didn't respond, except to tighten his hold on Kade's hand.

The tent was bright with afternoon sun when Sev jolted awake; he had fallen asleep next to Kade's cot, head drooping onto his chest.

There were voices at the mouth of the tent, where the flap was open, filling the temporary infirmary with a hazy orange glow. Two figures stood silhouetted in the sunlight.

". . . waiting for a few more from an intercepted caravan on its way out of Runnet. According to the scouts, there are some wounded soldiers, but nothing too grave."

"I've got a few empty cots," said a woman's voice—it must be the healer. "Are any of the captives wounded?"

The soldier snorted. "Not enough for you to concern yourself. We need to get them to the border as soon as possible."

"I'd like to see them all the same," the healer said firmly.

"So long as you don't delay us."

The flap swung shut, and the tent was plunged back into darkness.

Sev twisted back around to see that Kade's eyes were open—that he'd been listening as well.

"We're going to the border?" Kade asked, trying to sit up and gasping as his stomach muscles protested.

Sev leaned forward, helping adjust Kade's pillows. "Not yet—just a small escort. They want the animage prisoners to get to the border as quickly as possible, and then the rest of the regiment will follow afterward. I think Captain Dillon was wounded and is being treated by the healer in his personal tent. We won't leave until he's good enough to walk or sit a horse."

"A small escort . . . ," Kade repeated, brow furrowed.

"I . . . I thought about volunteering," Sev said, trying to keep his voice neutral. "But I'm not leaving you. Besides, I . . . I don't think I can do this anymore. . . ." He trailed off, afraid to meet Kade's eye, but when he did, there was an unreadable expression there. "I'm not cut out for—for Trix's line of work," he clarified, and Kade tilted his head, considering.

"I'm not sure I'm cut out to be an indentured servant," Kade said, and Sev's heart dropped into his stomach. Here he'd been feeling sorry for himself and lamenting the situation he'd gotten *himself* into—a free man who'd made his own choices over and over again—when Kade had had his choices taken from him long ago.

Sev dropped his head into his hands. "Kade, I—gods, I'm selfish," he said, the words muffled.

"Sev," Kade said, and when Sev peeked through his fingers, Kade was shaking his head. "No—listen, I'm not trying to tell you you're selfish or make you feel bad," he said gently. "I just meant that sometimes life takes you down a different path than you ever intended. You never thought you'd be a soldier—or a spy," he added in an undertone, "and I never thought I'd wind up in bondage."

Kade paused; Sev got the impression he was steeling himself.

"I was twelve," Kade said, clenching the pendant that hung from his neck and staring straight ahead, at the wall opposite. "I'd spent most of my life moving around, shuffling from place to place. Never alone, though. I had cousins, an uncle—all of us who'd survived the raid on our village when I was barely old enough to walk. I never knew my parents, but I had family at least. The safe house your parents protected was the first home I could actually remember, and I'd been happy there. Lots of other kids to run around with, and animals, too. But eventually we had to relocate. I got separated from most of my family. . . . They had to send us where there was work available or where people were willing to take us in."

Sev had distant family that he'd been parted from too, people he'd have no idea how to find again, their names and faces lost somewhere in the memories of a child.

"One of my cousins and I were both offered work on a barge that ferried animals in and out of Aura Nova," he said. "The man who owned the barge was a registered animage, but not the rest of his help. Most of them had fled the war and didn't have proper documentation to even be in the empire, never mind working as animages in and around the capital city. But business was good, and for him it was worth the risk."

"Did you like it?" Sev asked, having trouble gauging Kade's tone.

"I never made it," Kade said with a sigh. "We were traveling south with some traders, and we were attacked. Raiders." Unease coiled in Sev's stomach, and he thought he knew what came next. "It all happened so fast, and I don't even remember deciding to do it, but the next thing I knew, I was running," Kade said, speaking faster now, as if desperate to get it over with. "My cousin Jalen was older than me, but I was taller and faster. He followed, trying to keep up, but he couldn't." Kade's gaze shifted to Sev, his eyes glittering with remembered pain. "They shouted at us to stop, and when we didn't listen, they started firing. Better we were dead than we bring word of the attack back to the village where we'd been staying. These kinds of raiders preyed on convoys heading *into* the empire, never leaving, so word of their attacks might never get back to Pyra, or not until weeks had passed and they'd managed to take down dozens of other travelers in the meantime. I can still remember the sound of that first arrow striking home. The horrible wet thump and the abrupt way Jalen's breaths cut off. I turned in time to see him hit the ground. I stopped running. They bound and gagged me and took me into the empire. Turned out they weren't raiders at all but soldiers hired to enforce the registry. They knew we were animages—had targeted our convoy specifically. They slapped me with a ten-year sentence. I don't know what they did with Jalen's body."

"I'm sorry, Kade," Sev said, and when Kade didn't reply, he added, "It wasn't your fault."

Kade turned amber eyes on Sev. "I think it was—but I've made peace with that. As much peace as can be had, I suppose. I made a choice I'll regret for the rest of my life . . . but I've tried to do better ever since. It's all any of us can do," he finished on a whisper.

Sev gaped at Kade, who was good and strong and heroic, but who had made grave mistakes in his life—just like Sev. As much as he hated Kade's misery, the story made Sev feel less alone. "Is that why you joined with Trix?" he asked. "To do better?"

Kade scratched at his jaw. "No," he said with a snort. "At first I did it for revenge. I had so much anger inside, and it felt good to do something. But eventually I recognized that it wasn't about revenge or even justice. It was about fate."

"Fate?" Sev asked dubiously. "Like Anyanke's threads?"

"As much as I might regret my past . . . it led me to where I am now. It led me to Ilithya, and now it's led me to you. Maybe . . ." He paused, looking at Sev thoughtfully. "Maybe we were meant to be in this place, now—together. Both of us back where it all started. Except this time we're in a position to do something to help."

Sev bowed his head, trying to regain control over his emotions. His insides were in knots—finally hearing the grim story behind how Kade had become a bondservant, facing the fact of their dark pasts but also the idea of their shared future.

Sev wanted to get to that future, but he realized that he couldn't just shed his position and walk away. He couldn't turn his back on Hillsbridge . . . not again. Never again.

Spying had gotten them into this mess, and it would have to get them out again. Sev would have to be a soldier just a little bit longer.

As Kade had said—they were in a position to do something to help. Sev's participation in the attack on Hillsbridge didn't have to be for nothing. He was alive and he was here, and that would have to be enough.

"I've got an idea," Sev said. "A way to get us and the captives out of here. Are you in?"

Kade smiled. "Always."

Sev slipped out of the healer's tent and went in search of the prisoners. It was easy enough to get himself signed up for escort duty—even if he *was* cutting it a bit close. But getting Kade involved was another matter entirely. Even if he could steal more armor and pass as a soldier, there was the problem of his wound. It might not be life threatening, but even a relatively slow walk alongside a wagon filled with prisoners would be a difficult task for him, especially barely a day after he'd been cut down.

Luckily, the arrival of new prisoners added the perfect amount of chaos into the mix. While their own camp's prisoners were already loaded into a wagon the soldiers had stolen from the farmers, the arriving animage hostages were currently being appraised by the healer. Though the soldiers huffed and complained about the lost time, they were also determined to do nothing to help her, so they sat off together eating and paying the examinations little attention. With bandaged animages mixed in with their own, plus a lack of organization, it was surprisingly easy for Sev to slip Kade out of the healer's tent and into the back of the wagon with the other animages. Sev had laced him into a tunic as loosely as possible and wrapped a bandage around his neck to ensure his bondage pendant wasn't seen. With a last squeeze of Kade's hand, Sev released the flap on the wagon and took up his position with the rest of the reluctant escort.

They were out of camp as the afternoon sun beat down on them, cutting a direct path across the rolling countryside toward the soldiers—and prison camp—on the border of Ferro.

These are the costs of war:
a thousand shattering moments of pain
and loss and a lifetime of regret.

- CHAPTER 39 -
VERONYKA

WHEN A PHOENIX RIDER wanted to approach unseen, she flew under cover of darkness. Quiet as a shadow—soft as starlight.

But when a Phoenix Rider wanted to wage war, she flew under the sun. Brilliant orange rays swept across the landscape below, while above, concealed within that shining golden light, soared three phoenixes on fire.

Their approach was simple. Sidra and Val went in first, Sidra to the north and Val circling around to the south. Once they were in position, Sidra and Val dove. As soon as they reached the perimeter guards' sight lines, shouts went up.

Veronyka watched intently from a safe distance, mirroring with Xephyra so she could see what was happening below. Somewhere a horn sounded; the chase was on.

The soldiers hastily assembled units to pursue—in both directions. The camp was too vast for them to notice their mistake, and besides, they were too eager to catch a lone Phoenix Rider to pause to consider that it might be a diversion.

Though Veronyka monitored Val's and Sidra's maneuvers, her real focus never left the captives. They were shut away inside their tents and surrounded by guards, but with the ranks between Veronyka and her goal steadily thinning out, it was time to make her move.

Veronyka withdrew her bow, nocked an arrow, and dove.

Her breath caught as she plummeted, as if the sudden descent had lodged her heart in her throat. With every pump of Xephyra's wings, the guards in front of the prisoner tents became clearer, their relaxed postures, their calm faces . . . their eyes.

Veronyka's palms grew slick. What was she doing?

The right thing, her mind answered. *The only thing.* Otherwise dozens of innocents would pay. And these soldiers weren't innocent, even if they were unprepared. Even if they were just talking and laughing and eating their dinner.

Veronyka watched them, numb, as one by one they spotted her. The illusion of peace shattered in an instant. They leapt to their feet, scrambling for weapons, stumbling backward . . . but it was too late. She had the drop on them. All she had to do was let go.

Let go.

At the last second Veronyka's hands clenched around her bow, and Xephyra swerved wide.

Shouts went up as they soared back around, Veronyka's brain whirling and tumbling out of control.

She'd hesitated. She'd hesitated and lost the element of surprise. But what else might she have lost if she'd continued?

By the time Veronyka and Xephyra were in range again, the soldiers had raised crossbows and spears, ready for the fight—and Veronyka was secretly glad. This she could handle. This she could justify.

When her gaze landed on a soldier near the mouth of the nearest tent, who held an animage girl on her knees by her hair, a knife to her throat, the gladness turned to ashes in Veronyka's mouth.

She whipped up her bow, planting an arrow between the soldier's eyes before he had a chance to make a demand or call out a threat, and Veronyka realized this was something she could *relish* instead. They dared to use innocent animage children as bait? They dared to lure her here?

She would make sure they regretted it for the rest of their very short lives.

The next three guards dropped before the others even realized the first had fallen. The animage girl cried out and fell to the ground, crawling back inside the tent, but Veronyka kept her attention on the soldiers.

When she had killed to defend and protect her friends, like she had at the Eyrie and even in the Silverwood, fear had driven her. It had made her hands shake and her heart pound like a drum inside her chest.

But fear did not drive her now. . . . It was something else. Something that made her aim true and her pulse steady. Something darker. There was a savage glee in hurting those who had hurt others—who would hurt again and again. These soldiers had burned and pillaged, killed and captured, had ripped families and friends and whole worlds apart. Even now, when justice appeared on phoenix wings, they'd used innocent children as weapons and shields.

What drove Veronyka was anger. It was hot as fire and cold as steel. Veronyka was here, but not. Her body was present, but not her heart.

Her heart was elsewhere, buried deep or forgotten behind, she wasn't sure, but what was left was a chilling detachment.

Whenever emotion tried to surface, Veronyka pushed it down and cleared her thoughts, reordering her mind to focus on the task at hand. She couldn't undo what had already been done, but she could make damn sure it did not happen again.

These soldiers weren't just standing between her and her goal—innocent animages. They were *here*, in Pyra, with the express purpose of destroying everything Veronyka held dear. And unlike the Silverwood soldiers, who had been quick to scatter and retreat, these soldiers were here to fight, to hold their lines and stand their ground. They maintained their positions, drawing together with spears and crossbows raised—no matter how many of them dropped—and Veronyka felt her own survival instincts kick in. She wasn't just preventing harm from coming to herself in this instance—she was protecting all of Pyra.

It was surprisingly easy to think this way. With every arrow loosed, it got easier still, because the soldiers were fighting back, and this was war, just as Val had said.

It was kill or be killed.

Xephyra continued to dive and circle, and with a brief instruction from Veronyka, swooped around wider, bursting into flame and trailing sparks and swaths of fire in her wake, catching on tents and brittle grass and any soldiers too slow to get out of the way.

With a ring of fire as protection, Veronyka decided it was safe to land.

She whipped open the flap of the tent, and the occupants cowered from her, eyes wide and hands raised, as if expecting to have to defend themselves. Outside, Xephyra released an earsplitting shriek, and the animages within understood for the first time that the camp was under attack by Phoenix Riders—that this was a rescue.

"Come," Veronyka said, her chest expanding with the hope on their faces. She located two of the adults in the group, then pointed at the children. "Get them ready to walk. Quickly. We don't have much time."

Back outside, Veronyka loosed a few more arrows, filling the gaps in Xephyra's flame wall. She relished the sight of the rippling heat waves, the scent of ash and singed fabric. It was the smell of phoenix battle, the smell of victory.

When all the animages were outside—nearly fifty—with the oldest carrying the little ones or holding tightly to their hands, Veronyka led them to the back of the tents.

The soldiers' camp butted up against the Foothills, which rose behind in great stony spears and slabs of jagged, soaring rock. The Foothills *could* be traversed on foot, though it was slow going, the narrow paths steep and the ground uneven. There were also sudden holes and gaping caves—some made by nature or the gods, some made by humans past and present.

Veronyka ran until she spotted a juncture between two large stones—a path she had chosen from above—the entrance so narrow that the animages had to squeeze in single file. There was no other way to get through on foot, and Veronyka would soon follow in the air to help lead them deeper into the rocky wilderness. With any luck, she could get them to Prosperity before the soldiers had rallied enough for a proper pursuit. If there were any soldiers left.

Xephyra's wall was growing thinner, and soldiers were starting to break through. Veronyka stopped and waved the animages on, pointing at the narrow opening. Again, she spoke to one of the adults. "Take them through, into the Foothills. Keep moving and don't look back." She crouched down and handed him an abandoned crossbow and quiver. "Just in case."

Even if soldiers started to pursue, they'd have to bottleneck and diminish their speed and effectiveness. The animages needed every advantage possible.

The man nodded and shouted at the others, while Veronyka returned to the fight. Picking up a piece of smoking wood, she tossed it onto the now-empty prison tents, watching the fire catch, then spread, licking across the canvas.

Xephyra, she said, calling her phoenix to her side. Xephyra landed in a shower of sparks, her feathers smoking and rippling with waves of blue-white flame. Veronyka climbed carefully into the saddle, feeling the heat against her skin—but it was a pleasant sort of burn. It made her blood run quicker and her muscles tingle.

Wheeling around, she saw the last animages disappear into the stony crevasse, then took to the sky. In the distance, both Val and Sidra were visible again, raining arrows down and flying in dizzying evasive maneuvers. They had known their diversionary tactics would last only until the soldiers spotted the smoke from Veronyka's efforts, and now that they had, the soldiers turned around and regrouped.

Both Val and Sidra were surrounded, but Val was more outnumbered.

With several pumps of her powerful wings, Xephyra dove toward the fight, shrieking as she shot through the sky like an arrow. Val's phoenix cried out in response, and Val turned in her saddle. She was perched atop a thrust of stone, holding a spear with both hands as she tried to clear away the attackers clustered below. One in particular was trying to climb the bluff. Veronyka couldn't figure out why Val's phoenix didn't just fly away, but then she saw that part of a net had caught on her left wing.

Val locked eyes with Veronyka, their dark depths shimmering with reflected phoenix fire.

Veronyka was still speeding toward her. Eyes on her target, she nocked an arrow and pressed the tip to Xephyra's fiery flank. The steel tip was wrapped with phoenix feathers at the base, which caught fire at once—and continued to burn, no matter the speed of the arrow or the integrity of the wooden shaft. Veronyka let the flaming arrow fly, hitting the soldier clambering up the rocky cliff directly in the chest.

Two more arrows, two more bodies, and Val tossed aside her spear with a smirk and hastened to remove the snagging net. Xephyra looped back around, and by the time she steadied her flight, Val and her phoenix were in the air once more.

"Not tired already, are you?" Val asked, as Veronyka wiped the sweat from her brow.

"I'm not the one who almost got caught," Veronyka called back.

Val grinned, then urged her phoenix back into the fray. Veronyka followed.

Flying with Val was not at all like flying with Tristan.

Tristan was steady, balanced—a practiced flyer.

Val was wilder, looser—more intuitive. It wasn't that she lacked skill; it was that she gave herself over to the flight. Her hair trailed out behind her, red as the dying sun, and her body moved and shifted with the firebird beneath her. Veronyka saw the edges of her clothing catching fire, but Val didn't seem to notice or care. She bellowed orders, shrieked battle cries, and laughed with every narrow escape or dazzling recovery. Val loosed arrows with deadly precision and pulled up abandoned spears from the ground in one breath only to throw them down again in the next.

They wove between one another, flying patterns and set pieces without thought or hesitation.

Is this shadow magic? Veronyka wondered as Val corralled a pair of soldiers for Veronyka to dispatch, and afterward, when Veronyka tossed Val some arrows from her own quiver, seeing Val's was low.

Or is this something else?

Veronyka thought the battle would have been won sooner if she could have dedicated herself solely to the fight. But she was always wary of the escaping animages and the way the soldiers continued to push in that direction. Some had already gotten through—Veronyka had quickly shot them down—and more were following behind.

Val and Sidra were busy with a cluster of soldiers trying to flee to the north when Veronyka spotted another group of soldiers arriving from the east. They were far too small to be reinforcements, but they could be advance scouts.

With a stolen spear in hand, Veronyka urged Xephyra toward them. Her heart was pounding, her blood singing in her veins. If they were scouts, she'd make sure no word reached their main force.

She'd make sure nothing did.

The darkness was growing around them, and Veronyka had to break her mirroring with Xephyra in order to properly aim and use her weapons. Her range with a spear was nothing like her bow, so they had to get close for her to take the shot.

Her arm was cocked back, her teeth gritted, when the figure at the head of the column came into view.

Veronyka's arm locked up.

Xephyra's flames lit his face in shades of orange and gold—and his face was familiar.

Sev?

"Xephyra!" Veronyka cried out, realizing that even without her spear, her phoenix was on a collision course.

Lost in the heat of battle, it took Xephyra a moment to notice Veronyka's recognition and panic. She veered just in time, the group before them ducking and cowering as she whipped past, then threw out her wings and brought them to a sudden, shaky halt.

Veronyka took in the scene before her: There were a handful of soldiers, weapons drawn, and they seemed to be escorting a wagon. Veronyka spotted people inside—additional animage captives?

Sev stared at her, the panic on his face telling her that he was undercover here, and how she behaved would dictate what happened next. But she also didn't know who might be his friends or allies among the other soldiers.

Veronyka considered, then shifted her grip on the spear in her hand and swung it wide, clubbing the nearest soldier upside the head.

Chaos erupted after that—Sev leapt on the soldier next to him, knocking him to the ground, while several of the captives poured out from the back of the wagon, quickly ending the fight. Veronyka dismounted, standing before Sev, another boy who looked familiar—though she couldn't think from where—and a dozen animage captives.

The sight of Sev had snapped Veronyka out of her battle fever. She saw what *he* saw—a field of blood and bodies, people screaming and tents smoking, and in the distance, Phoenix Riders raining fire.

"Let's go," Veronyka said, blinking wildly as she tried to regain her composure. "I already freed the others. I sent them into the Foothills and told them to go northeast. There's an outpost. I'll find you again, but if I don't, stay the course and one of the other Riders will find you."

Sev opened his mouth, but Veronyka didn't give him time to respond. Coldness was spreading through her chest, its icy tendrils making their way through Veronyka's body.

Something was wrong—*this* was wrong. They had done what they'd come to do. They had freed the animages. It was one thing to defend their escape and guard them from pursuit, but what they were doing now . . .

Veronyka mounted up, and as Xephyra took to the sky, she sought out Val. The battle was mostly won by now. Sidra was swooping around the perimeter, rounding up the soldiers who were trying to flee, but Val was on the ground in the middle of a group of them.

Veronyka thought that her phoenix must have been netted again—until she saw that the soldiers were on their knees, weaponless, pleading for their lives.

Pleading for mercy.

Faster, Xephyra, Veronyka thought desperately, but in her heart she knew she was too late.

Avalkyra Ashfire did not show mercy.

Veronyka's stomach clenched painfully—with regret for what she had done and with fear for what she had unleashed.

What will be left, when all this is through?
What will survive of our precious legacy?
Our ancient bloodline?

- CHAPTER 40 -
AVALKYRA

AS SIDRA MIGHT HAVE put it, the soldiers were decent sport.

It was certainly more satisfying than merchant caravans, and there was comfort in striking a blow not just to the empire in general, but to Rolan in particular.

Even with one's allies, it was good to maintain a position of power. To exert control. This attack wasn't just a means to gain Veronyka to her side. . . . It was a show of force.

And what a show it was. Avalkyra had known they would fly well together—had expected it, even imagined it from time to time. But *this*? Veronyka made her Ashfire foremothers proud. Her flying was expert, her control over her phoenix impressive—especially given her softer tendencies toward her bondmate. Her fighting skills lacked true polish, but she was good with a bow—a mounted warrior's greatest weapon.

But Avalkyra was most impressed by Veronyka's battle instincts. Her surprising ruthlessness. When she had a goal in mind, she pursued it with determination and precision.

If only she wanted the empire.

No matter. Avalkyra would bring her around. They were circling the battlefield now, rounding up the last survivors for execution.

Surely Veronyka's heart swelled inside her chest, as Avalkyra's did? Surely she felt this pure, singular joy that came from victory hard won?

But despite all the ways she'd surprised Avalkyra, it was still unsurprising when Veronyka started begging for the soldiers' lives.

Recognizing defeat, they had thrown down their weapons and fallen to their knees. Avalkyra had dismounted to walk among them, taking in the familiar feeling of widespread supplication. The way it made her shoulders draw back and her chin lift toward the sky.

But before she could execute them, Veronyka landed before her. She leapt from the saddle, hair wild and eyes round.

"Val," she said, coming to stand next to her. She gazed around at the soldiers who had surrendered—then wider, to the bodies scattered all over the battlefield. She swallowed, returning her gaze to Avalkyra. "*Please*. Spare their lives. We've already won, and they've surrendered. There doesn't need to be any more bloodshed."

She pleaded so sweetly, so earnestly, that Avalkyra was certain it was for show.

The soldiers on their knees raised their heads, fragile hope in their eyes, and Avalkyra saw the way they looked at Veronyka . . . as if she were Miseriya, goddess of mercy, reborn. A spear of jealousy pierced her chest, sudden and deep. It was easy to see how hope could turn to devotion, and then devotion to love. They would love Veronyka, all of these fools . . . and when they bowed for *her*, they would do so gladly.

No one had ever loved Avalkyra that way . . . and they never would.

Avalkyra didn't want to spoil the newfound camaraderie between her and her niece—the sweetness of their victory—but Veronyka had much to learn about war, and who would teach her if not Avalkyra?

Besides, the best way to end the soldiers' love was to end their lives.

Sidra landed next to them. She dismounted and watched their conversation, a knife twirling in her grasp. She had already learned the lesson that Avalkyra was about to teach.

"Mercy is for orphans and old folks," Avalkyra began, turning her back on the soldiers—after giving Sidra a wordless command through their bind—and walking to Veronyka's side. "Not for invading enemy soldiers, armed and trained to kill."

Veronyka looked up at her, expression pained, before shifting her gaze to stare over Avalkyra's shoulder. There was a scuffling sound, then the slice of a dagger and the thump of a body hitting the earth.

Veronyka didn't flinch. Avalkyra was proud.

"Come," she said, pulling gently on Veronyka's shoulder and leading her back toward her phoenix. Sidra would handle the remaining survivors.

Veronyka allowed herself to be steered, then climbed rigidly into her saddle.

Avalkyra mounted up after her and urged her phoenix into the sky. Though the creature was difficult to control at the best of times, Avalkyra had been surprised to discover that, during battle at least, the phoenix seemed to know what to do without constant shadow magic prodding. Her ancient instincts had taken over, it seemed, and the lack of constant controlling left Avalkyra feeling light and exhilarated. She could sense the phoenix coming back to herself, though, and knew the reprieve was coming to an end.

Veronyka followed her, and soon after came Sidra. She had always been efficient.

Avalkyra led the way back to their camp from the previous night.

"We have to get the animage prisoners to safety," Veronyka argued, but Avalkyra wanted to talk to her first.

"We will," she said, steering her phoenix to land atop the stony cave rather than beside it, and Veronyka did the same. They dismounted, and the phoenixes joined Sidra, who landed below, to drink and eat at their troughs. Veronyka stared in the direction the prisoners were fleeing, as if trying to guard them with her eyes, though they couldn't be seen from this vantage point.

"You did well today, *xe* Nyka," Avalkyra said.

"No, I didn't . . . ," Veronyka said, barely above a whisper. "We got carried away. Those soldiers . . . they aren't evil just because they were ordered here by Rolan. They didn't deserve what we gave them."

"What *I* gave them, you mean," Avalkyra guessed. Veronyka was melancholy, and her dark mood was leaching the joy Avalkyra was feeling from their joined fight today.

"They deserved . . ."

"What, forgiveness?" Avalkyra asked, arms crossed. "Is that where you draw the line, Veronyka? Those who ask for mercy get it? But what about those who never get the chance? What about the people *they* killed—or would have killed? Do those potential victims not deserve the mercy we just gave *them*? Because of us, animage children across Pyra may sleep easier in their beds, knowing they are safe."

"Don't," Veronyka snapped, throat working in a tight swallow. "Don't pretend that's why you did this. Don't pretend you care."

"I am not unfeeling," Avalkyra said on a sigh. "I simply understand better than you the cost of war."

"War took away my mother," Veronyka said.

"War took away my *life*," Avalkyra shot back. "It took away my body, my phoenix, my sister. . . . When I opened my eyes again, the entire world was changed. Do not talk to me of loss."

"Fine," Veronyka said suddenly, and Avalkyra narrowed her eyes, suspicious at once. "I won't talk about the past, but I *will* talk about the future. I want my sister back. I want us together, just as you do, except I want us to do the right thing. We make a powerful team," she said, and Avalkyra had never heard truer words, "but it's *what* we do together that matters. Come with me and join the rest of the Phoenix Riders. We can defend Pyra and put an end to this war, like you said. I want that to be enough for you . . . but I don't think it is. Is it?"

Avalkyra leveled her gaze at Veronyka. It was strange to speak so openly with each other. Avalkyra wasn't used to sharing her thoughts and motivations. Two lives fraught with lies and betrayal had made her keep her own counsel.

When she spoke again, she didn't hold back; she said what she wished she had said in a different time, to a different Ashfire. "It's not," she confirmed, and the light in Veronyka's eyes dimmed somewhat. Avalkyra continued anyway. "You and I are meant to rule together. Join me, sister. The world is ours."

Veronyka frowned. "Why? Why *us*—why together?"

"We have a destiny to fulfill."

"A destiny to what? Undo the past? Remake history?"

"To remake the empire," Avalkyra said fiercely, the words rising up in her like a tide, the want, the need, the desire to make it so practically choking her. She flung a hand out, gesturing toward the capital. "The Golden Empire belongs to us both. For so long I thought it should have been Pheronia and me—that I had missed my chance—but this was my destiny all along. To come back, to rule alongside another Rider queen. Together we would be unstoppable."

Avalkyra saw a flash of something like excitement in Veronyka's eyes, and if she released her hold on her phoenix for just a minute, she felt it too. It trembled between them, but like many things for Veronyka, that thrill was tempered by fear. Fear of Avalkyra and fear of herself.

"You think the council will hand it over to us?" Veronyka asked, nodding to the south, in the direction Avalkyra had just pointed.

Avalkyra snorted. "It is not theirs to give."

"But we'd need support, Val. Armies . . . allies . . ."

Avalkyra felt herself lighting up like a phoenix in full flame. Veronyka could deny it all she wanted, push back her dark urges and warrior instincts, but these questions proved that she'd thought about it—that the empire, their birthright, was on her mind as well. Veronyka was on the threshold of accepting it, and all Avalkyra had to do was help push her over the edge.

Avalkyra lurched forward and gripped Veronyka's shoulders. "We'll get them. And those who don't support us will burn."

Veronyka avoided her eyes, but not before Avalkyra saw the regret there—as if her words had confirmed Veronyka's worst suspicions.

"And how many will die for you to sit on that throne? I know you keep saying 'us,' but there can be only one queen. That's the way it's always been."

"We'll change it," said Avalkyra passionately. And she meant it. Avalkyra would share a throne with no one *but* her. As eldest, she would make the majority of the decisions, of course, and would usher them forward with decades of knowledge and experience under her belt. But Veronyka would always, *always* be by her side.

"Answer my question, Val. How many will die for you to get what you want?"

Veronyka's tone was different now, and Avalkyra straightened, releasing her hold on Veronyka's shoulders. "As many as need to. Any and all who are foolish enough to stand in our way."

"Even if that means Phoenix Riders and animages? Even if that means Pyra?"

Sudden rage reared up inside Avalkyra, and she turned away.

"You must know how some of them see you," Veronyka pressed, while Avalkyra's rage blistered and burned. "The great Avalkyra Ashfire, the Feather-Crowned Queen—but also the person who single-handedly destroyed Pyra and the Phoenix Riders, and left animages all over the empire to be outlawed and placed in bondage."

Avalkyra whirled around. "You would lay all the ills of the world at my feet?"

Veronyka shrugged. "If you want to be queen, that comes with the territory. These are your people."

"I *am* queen."

"Then it's your duty to protect them. All of them—friends and enemies alike."

Avalkyra laughed coldly. "Spoken like the child that you are. Shelter my enemies until they grow powerful enough to overthrow me? You do not feed and care for a snake until it's powerful enough to strangle you. You cut off its head."

"And once all your enemies have been eradicated—animages and Phoenix Riders alike—then what?"

"Then I rule."

"Over what? The ashes of the empire?"

"What do you want from me, Veronyka? Softness? Do you wish me as pliant as sweet summer grass? I'd never have survived if not for my *strength*," Avalkyra spat out, that searing rage clawing its way up her throat.

Veronyka slowly shook her head. "If you don't eventually bend, Val, you'll break."

"*What* did you say?" Avalkyra asked sharply. Those were the words spoken by Pheronia all those years ago inside Avalkyra's underground base near Rushlea. "Are you trying to threaten me?"

Veronyka sighed. "What I'm trying to do is see if there's any hope for us. You say you want to rule together, but if you refuse to change, to compromise or sacrifice—"

Avalkyra boiled over. "You want to talk about sacrifice?" she shrieked. "I gave up everything for her! I could have won that war a thousand times, but a thousand times I pulled back. I hesitated. I gave her a chance to see reason—I gave her the mercy you beg for. I gave her my life and I gave her my death, too, and still it was not enough."

Avalkyra's breath thundered in her chest, her ribs rising and falling like the beat of a war drum.

"I am not her," Veronyka said quietly. "I am not the sister you tried to save."

Avalkyra felt a spasm cross her face, no matter how hard she fought against the surge of emotion.

She was angry. She was outraged. Veronyka was a sentimental fool.

And she was right.

Avalkyra kept trying to align her past with her present, kept casting Veronyka into the role played by her other sister. Her first sister. Her true sister.

Her Shadow Twin.

But Veronyka was the real shadow—the echo of the past. She was . . . what exactly? A second chance? A shot at redemption?

Veronyka was an Ashfire, but she was no ally.

She was a rival for the throne, the same as her mother had been, but things were different this time. *Avalkyra* was different.

She schooled her features into blankness and fixed her gaze on Veronyka.

"And I am not the same person who went into those flames. Cross me, Veronyka, and I will not hesitate. Not this time."

"So that's it, then?" Veronyka asked bleakly, disappointment etched in well-worn cuts across her features. She looked like her mother.

No.

She looked like an enemy.

"Get in line behind you or get out of the way?" Veronyka finished sadly.

Avalkyra drew herself up, pleased that Veronyka finally understood. "Exactly."

They stood like that, face-to-face, Ashfire to Ashfire, for several long minutes.

Unease crept in; Veronyka sounded defeated, but she didn't look it. Instead, her eyes were alight and her expression had shifted to one of grim resolve.

Suddenly Avalkyra longed for the days when Veronyka was young and innocent, when she was trusting and vulnerable and unwilling to fight back.

But as she looked at Veronyka now, Avalkyra saw not the child she had been, nor her mother, Pheronia—she saw a new threat. Someone intelligent and powerful and without her mother's shortcomings or her aunt's dark past.

A strange, unfamiliar fear gripped Avalkyra's heart as she realized that if the Phoenix Riders—and the empire—wanted an Ashfire to rally around, it would not be her.

It would be Veronyka.

Bitterness twisted her from the inside out. Avalkyra couldn't let that happen, couldn't let Veronyka grow in strength and support. She had to nip her glorious ascension in the bud.

Avalkyra reached with a tendril of shadow magic—but not to Veronyka.

There were other ways to make use of her Ashfire blood, after all . . . other ways to bind Veronyka to her mission and to bind her other, more willing allies to her purpose.

Val would have to go through with her alliance with Lord Rolan. All the way through.

Perhaps she had learned something from the last war after all.

"So, *xe* Nyka?" Avalkyra asked, and her voice shook ever so slightly. "What will it be?"

"It's like you said to me in the Eyrie," Veronyka replied, her voice steady. "I've chosen my side, and it's not yours. I want to save the world, and you want to destroy it. You don't want to stop the war—you want to win it. And I can't let you. If you won't bend, Avalkyra Ashfire, then neither will I."

Right on cue, Sidra made her move. While Avalkyra and Veronyka spoke atop the cave, Sidra had lured Xephyra inside it, just as Avalkyra had commanded her to through the bind. With the flick of a lever, thick metal bars came crashing down over the entrance, trapping Xephyra inside. The noise pierced the night, sudden and close, and Veronyka's eyes flew wide. She lunged, meaning to jump down toward Sidra, but Avalkyra grabbed her arm.

There was a moment of struggle as Avalkyra reached for the short dagger in her belt.

It was thin and sharp—and tipped in poison. A slash of skin, a sharp inhalation of breath, and then Veronyka Ashfire went limp in her arms.

What will be left for you,
my daughter, at the end of this?

- CHAPTER 41 -
SEV

AS THE FIGHTING DIED around them, Sev and Kade did as Veronyka had told them and ushered the freed animages into the rocky Foothills until they met up with the rest of the fleeing prisoners.

Sev kept seeing Veronyka's fiery descent, kept feeling the heat of the flames and that strange, numb realization that she was about to attack him. He shook his head. She'd recognized him just in time, and then, when she'd seen what he and Kade were trying to do, she'd helped.

Now she was gone—Sev tried to spot her, but there was smoke and fire everywhere, and he had to focus on the task at hand. He clutched a short sword in his sweaty grip, and Kade, along with some of the older animages, held weapons of their own, whatever they could find abandoned on the ground. Kade hadn't been fighting because of his wound, but he held a spear and was using it more as a walking stick than a weapon.

When it was clear they weren't being followed, they stopped their frantic pace and paused in a darkened hollow to catch their breath and distribute some of the provisions they had taken from the prisoners' wagon.

Kade sidled up to Sev, slightly away from the others. "What about us?" he asked, handing Sev a waterskin.

Sev took a long drink, thinking. The rest would make their way to

Prosperity outpost before being reunited with their friends and families, but what about him and Kade? Sev didn't think he was cut out for the spying game, no matter what Trix had thought—or hoped—and Kade couldn't return now that he'd abandoned his position as a bondservant. But if they didn't continue on in the empire, what would they do? Sev thought about the phoenix egg he'd left at the Eyrie. . . . He could claim it and become a Rider or sell it on the black market, as he'd told Commander Cassian. With that much gold, Sev and Kade could live comfortably in hiding—so long as the impending war didn't get in the way.

But Kade would never go for that, and it was a bit of a shock to realize that Sev couldn't do that either. He couldn't just run and ignore what was happening around him—not anymore. It was surprisingly good to know.

Maybe it was like Kade had said: Fate had brought them here, and the path before them offered Sev a way out of the spying game, which he desperately wanted to take. But even if he quit being a spy, he and Kade could find other ways to fight.

Still, Kade needed to recover first. It only made sense to head north to Prosperity with the others, and then go from there. See what other paths presented themselves.

Before he could tell Kade his thoughts, a distant chorus of shrieks drew Sev's attention. Above, Veronyka soared by with the two other Phoenix Riders Sev had seen raining down fire and arrows during the battle.

He was still confused about what was going on—had the commander sent Veronyka and these two others to destroy Rolan's soldiers and free the animages? If he had, why was Veronyka not helping to escort them to safety? And wasn't the point of Sev's spy work to *avoid* a fiery bloodbath like the one he'd just witnessed? Had there been a change in plans?

As he watched, Veronyka dismounted to face one of the other Riders, perched atop a rocky bluff near the edge of the Foothills. Their phoenixes fluttered down among the rocks below with the third Rider, leaving the pair of them alone.

"It's a bit odd, isn't it?" said Kade, coming to stand next to Sev and following his line of sight. "Didn't you say she was the only female Rider at the Eyrie?"

"I thought she was . . . ," Sev said, thinking back to his time there. He hadn't stayed long, but he'd seen the Riders go out on patrol or return from flying practice, walking the stronghold or practicing in the training yard; Veronyka was the only girl he recalled. He knew they planned to recruit with the eggs he'd brought them, but it would be too soon for any of them to be flying and fighting.

"Do you think—" Kade began suddenly, then stopped. There was a loud, echoing *clang*, like a metal door being slammed shut. Then something that looked like a scuffle broke out between the two Riders. Veronyka abruptly staggered back, as if from a blow, before she crumpled into the other Rider's arms.

Sev took an involuntary step forward, but the Riders were hundreds of yards away, visible at all only because of the fires that burned all around, illuminating their surroundings, and the setting sun glowing behind them.

The Phoenix Rider Veronyka had been talking to hoisted Veronyka, unconscious, onto one of the phoenixes and flew away, followed behind by the other Rider. Veronyka's phoenix was nowhere to be found.

The sight of two phoenixes disappearing into the evening sky gave Sev a sudden, powerful wave of familiarity. He turned to Kade.

"The Phoenix Riders who met with Rolan," he said, and Kade was nodding, as if he'd already gotten there.

They watched the Riders fly away, but as it turned out, they didn't go far. With their phoenixes still hot from the battle, they glowed, and it was easy enough to see them alight atop a stone tower to the south, likely at the very outskirts of Ferro.

"The prison tower," said someone behind Sev, and he turned to find the eldest of the animage prisoners standing behind him.

"Prison tower?" Sev repeated, darting a curious look at Kade.

"Well, it started out as an outpost or some such," the man said, scratching his stubbled jaw. "But the governor likes to use it for high-priority prisoners, when last I heard."

The man shrugged and returned to the others, and Sev turned a regretful look on Kade. "I think she's in trouble. Veronyka. We need to help her."

Sev knew that as they were—two exhausted animages with varying degrees of battle wounds—they wouldn't be much help at all, but they could at least scope things out. Then they could try to send a letter to the commander and tell him what had happened in case he wasn't aware of her being here. Their pigeon had yet to return since its last trip, but Sev would worry about that problem later.

Kade, slouched and dirty and stiff with heavy bandaging, looked at Sev for a long while. Then he smiled.

"What?" Sev asked dubiously. He'd expected any number of reactions from Kade—arguments against such a dangerous plan or wiser, more intelligent suggestions—but not humor.

"It's just . . . you've changed," Kade said, unmistakable fondness in his voice. "The last time she was in trouble, when Jotham and Ott ransacked her home, you wanted to look the other way. Now it's *you* who's suggesting we risk everything to help her."

Sev felt his cheeks heat. Was this praise or admonishment? "She saved my life," he said with a half shrug.

Kade shook his head, still grinning. "But that was after you'd saved hers—you're already square."

Sev snorted. "So, what, are you regretting your influence on me?"

"This isn't me," Kade said, expression thoughtful. "I think this was you all along."

Sev was taken aback by that. He remembered himself as a child, rushing into danger without a second's hesitation, wanting to save the farm and his parents with no consideration for himself. Then he thought of his years on the street since, how he'd learned to be ruthless and selfish and cunning. Which was the true Sev? His childhood instincts or his learned behaviors?

"Maybe you're right," Kade continued as they separated from the animage prisoners and picked their way toward the outpost tower. "You were never meant to be a spy. You were meant to be a hero instead."

If I am to become naught but ruin,
may it be so that you can build anew
upon the ashes.

CHAPTER 42

VERONYKA

VERONYKA DRAGGED HERSELF INTO wakefulness, her body heavy and her mind sluggish.

Images from the battle flashed before her eyes—blood, smoke, ashen faces, and bodies pierced with phoenix-feather-fletched arrows. Val with a knife.

Veronyka lurched up, blinking away the last dregs of sleep and staring around, her heart racing.

She was in a wide, round room, its walls made of stone, while several windows—and a walkout to a balcony—offered patches of darkened sky, sliced through with wrought-iron grates in swirling feather motifs. Veronyka had the sense she was high up . . . no trees or other buildings interrupted the view.

She was on a pallet on the ground but had no memory of coming here. She thought back and recalled the stinging sensation of her skin being pierced. She looked down to see a rough bandage tied over her forearm.

Val had cut her.

No, Val had *drugged* her. Veronyka had blacked out soon after that, and now she was here.

When she looked up again, Val was standing in the open doorway that led to a shadowy landing. Veronyka must be in a tower room, probably part of an old outpost. Circular buildings weren't typical in most valley architecture, and stone towers—especially ones embellished with phoenix-related designs—were a Rider convention.

"Look who's finally awake," Val said, and Veronyka stumbled to her feet. Her head spun, and she wondered with blind terror how long she'd been unconscious.

"Xephyra," she croaked. The last thing she remembered was the clang of heavy metal and the feeling of being trapped.

"Relax, she is safe. As are you. It's only been a couple of hours."

"Where am I?"

Val didn't answer that question. She simply strode into the room and paused next to the balcony, gazing through the metal grate with her arms crossed over her chest.

Veronyka clung to the wall next to her pallet, feeling like she should probably lie down again but unwilling to do so in Val's presence.

"You *kidnapped* me," she said. Her mouth was dry, and the words felt like they stuck to her tongue.

Val glanced over her shoulder; then, with a roll of her eyes, she strode to a table underneath the nearest window and poured a cup of water from a pitcher. She handed it to Veronyka, who stared at it warily—Val had just drugged her, after all.

Another eye roll, and Val took a drink before holding it out to Veronyka once more. She longed to refuse it but reminded herself that if she was going to get out of this, she needed her strength back.

She gulped greedily, and Val watched her with mild distaste.

Gasping, Veronyka lowered the cup. "Tell me where I am and what I'm doing here," she said, her voice stronger this time.

"You're in Ferro. And you're here because you refused my offer to work *together*. And so I'll treat you as I've always treated you—like a child who should know better but doesn't."

Veronyka's chest began to heave with her suppressed anger, the sudden burst of emotion making her light-headed again.

"You're here because it is *my will* that you should be, and a queen gets what she wants."

"Not from me," Veronyka said, jaw set.

Val laughed. "Oh, *xe* Nyka, from you most of all. I willed you to come with me—and you left everyone and everything you love behind. I willed you to help me destroy my enemies—and you slaughtered dozens of soldiers in cold blood. I willed you here, into a cage—and both you and your phoenix were only too happy to accommodate me and too stupid to see the trap until it was too late."

Veronyka's hands clenched into fists, heat rising in her face, but Val didn't stop there.

"You believed that I wanted you next to me, like your poor dead mother, when in fact, all I've ever wanted was to have you beneath me, where you belong."

Veronyka lunged at her. She forgot her weakened body and groggy mind—she forgot everything but Val's smug face and the lies spewing from her mouth.

Val was too shocked to react as Veronyka collided with her. Forgetting all her training, Veronyka was fighting on emotion and base instinct alone. She rammed her shoulder directly into Val's stomach, knocking the wind from her as they both went careening onto the stone floor. Veronyka heard Val's head strike the ground with a thud, dazing her, while Veronyka struggled to disentangle herself and get to her feet. Her own head was throbbing in pain from the abrupt movement, but she ignored it.

Veronyka made it onto her knees before Val recovered, her hands scraping and sinking into flesh until finding a grip in Veronyka's hair and dragging her backward with a hard yank. Veronyka yelped and swung out viciously, landing an elbow to Val's jaw that forced her to cry out and release her grip.

Veronyka tried to get up again, but Val took hold of her ankle, causing her to stumble. With a growl of frustration, Veronyka used the leg to pin Val down, straddling her, and cocked back her arm for a savage blow.

Only, the hit landed on *her* face, not Val's. Out of nowhere, Sidra had joined the fray. She must have come in through the open doorway, and without so much as a word or a warning, she cracked Veronyka across the cheek with the back of her hand.

Veronyka hadn't seen it coming, and the impact sent her flying to the side. Hot pain spread along her face and neck at the sudden blow, and she slammed into the ground, seeing stars. She blinked and scrambled away from Sidra, who stalked toward her.

"Not her face!" Val shouted from her place on the ground, and the words seemed odd to Veronyka.

Sidra froze midstride, giving Veronyka a chance to scuttle away. One hit had been enough for Veronyka's eyes to slide out of focus, and she spat blood onto the floor between them.

Val cursed, getting to her feet. "Keep it below the neck, Sidra. He won't want her if she looks like some back-alley brawler."

"Who won't want me?" Veronyka asked sharply, looking between them.

Val smiled, walking over to Veronyka and crouching down so her face was inches away, *daring* Veronyka to strike again.

"Your new husband," Val said, smiling even more widely as a flicker of fear crossed Veronyka's upturned face. "Didn't I tell you, Veronyka? You're going to be married."

"What? Why?"

"Haven't you listened to what I've been telling you? I need to get my empire back, and you're going to help me. What governor *wouldn't* leap at the chance to marry an Ashfire and put themselves on the throne?"

"Lord Rolan," Veronyka said faintly. "Was *this* the basis for your supposedly false alliance? His armies for a queen? Or was this something you thought up to punish me for not joining you?"

Val stood upright again, looming over her. "I promised what I needed to promise. I did what needed to be done. If you were standing beside me, not *opposite me*, you'd have some say in the matter. As it is, you will do what I tell you to do, and while he preens and prances around, betrothed to a princess and preparing for his coronation, I will use his soldiers and his deep pockets to take what is mine."

"You're an Ashfire," Veronyka pointed out. "Why don't *you* marry him?"

Val shrugged dismissively. "They're all far too cowardly to ally with someone like me. As you said yourself, I have a reputation for bloodshed. I doubt any of them would have the stomach to share my crown, let alone my bed. But the daughter of the weak, impressionable Pheronia Ashfire? That is far more appealing."

"No," Veronyka said, standing shakily. She dragged the back of her hand across her lip, wiping away a smear of blood as she worked through all Val had said.

Veronyka was accustomed to being a part of Val's schemes, but when they were young, she'd believed the lie that Val was looking out for her— that her plans were for the best. The night she'd poisoned Veronyka's bond-mate had shattered that illusion, and Veronyka had learned that Val would do anything to achieve her ambitions. To Val, Veronyka was only a means to an end, a tool to be used.

This betrothal should be further proof of that, and yet . . .

"That's not it," Veronyka said, surprised at the revelation. Val gave her a curious look, but Veronyka's attention was turned inward. "You don't need me for this—why go through the trouble? Why chase me across the province when you've had what you needed all along? You're an Ashfire. If you really wanted the throne more than anything, you'd have come straight to Rolan weeks ago and struck up this deal yourself. Don't *pretend* you think these empire lords would be too afraid to do it—we both know an ambitious man would marry you in a heartbeat. Why come for me instead?"

Val seemed taken aback at the question. "What do you—I *told* you. Together, we could—"

"Yes, yes, I know," Veronyka said, waving away Val's words. "We could be powerful. We could remake the past and rewrite your legacy." Val's mouth was open in outrage. She clearly did not appreciate Veronyka's mocking interruption, but Veronyka ignored her. "You became so fixated on that, you put *me* above the empire you so desperately covet. You don't *need* me by your side to achieve your ambitions," Veronyka said, smiling as she shook her head. "No, but you *want* me there. You want it more than anything. . . . You want it more than the throne. You're weaker and more cowardly than the rest of us put together, because all these years later—a lifetime later—and you still haven't learned to stand on your own. You were too afraid to rule alone when my mother was alive, and you're too afraid to rule alone now."

Val slapped Veronyka across the face.

She looked utterly shocked when she did it, as if she were the one who'd been struck, and had apparently forgotten the warning she'd just given Sidra.

Veronyka's head snapped back again, but Val had hit her opposite cheek, causing new pain to flare up and her brain to rattle around her skull. She stumbled backward into the wall and leaned there, gathering her breath.

It had been worth it, though. She'd never seen Val look so shaken.

Panting, Val slowly gathered herself, smoothing her hands over her tunic and pushing her tangled hair out of her face. Piece by piece she put herself back together, her steady, unfeeling mask in place.

"You're wrong. I have always been separate from you and your mother. I have always stood alone. I have suffered much in my lives, but why would I suffer the indignity of a marriage to a valley governor when I could pass that off to you instead?"

The words were sensible, her logic sound . . . but Veronyka *knew* Val and could tell she was lying even without shadow magic.

"It doesn't matter if it's you or me," Veronyka said, still propped against the cold stone to keep herself upright. "The council will never allow it. Besides, one governor can't overtake the empire—if they could, they'd have done it by now."

"You're forgetting the Grand Council meeting," Val said, tone back to her usual brusqueness. "Once Rolan convinces them that the Phoenix Riders are a threat, the empire will send its armies into Pyra. They will send thousands, ensuring they finish what they failed to do seventeen years ago.

And while they are gone and the capital is vulnerable, we will send our allied forces into Aura Nova and take the Nest."

It could work, Veronyka realized with numb horror. The empire was so preoccupied with Phoenix Riders and Pyra, it wasn't prepared for an attack from within. If a single governor focused his attention on Aura Nova, he could easily retake the Nest, the literal and political center of the empire. Holding it would be another matter. . . . But if a rightful heir were crowned, the council would have a hard time undoing it. It wouldn't be *illegal* as much as against their own personal interests.

Lord Rolan would become king—or so he believed—although neither he nor Veronyka would ever actually rule. As soon as they had the Nest, Val would crown herself. Surely Lord Rolan knew that? And would the governor's forces stay loyal to Val once their acting general had been betrayed? It was the empire's gold, not the governor's, that paid their salaries after all. They'd be foolish to desert or attempt to remain loyal to their spurned governor—in fact, Veronyka was quite certain Val would kill the man and install someone of her own choosing in the position. Perhaps Sidra. Would Rolan's soldiers remain faithful to the empire itself, whoever was in charge of it?

"Yes," Val said, obviously delighted with herself and her deceptions. "You will wed Lord Rolan of Stel, governor of Ferro and descendant of King Rol the Betrayer himself, and I will take back what is mine. I'll enjoy sticking a knife into the back of a born backstabber."

"Why are you telling me this?" Veronyka asked. Val never revealed her grand plans to Veronyka. . . . Growing up, she rarely revealed her plans for lunch, never mind the scheme that would put her on the throne. "What's to stop me from telling all of this to my betrothed?"

"It's simple. You tell him, and I'll slit your bondmate's throat."

Simple.

Veronyka supposed it was. This person before her . . . she was not Veronyka's sister, not her friend or her family, whatever blood—and magic—might bind them together. She was Veronyka's enemy, and that knowledge did simplify things.

Veronyka hadn't come forward with her identity or willfully set herself against Val. She hadn't tried to gather allies or make a claim on the throne. And still Val had put them in opposition to each other. Veronyka would be drawn into Val's machinations whether she willed it or not.

Val would never let her walk away.

And so Veronyka wouldn't. She would embrace her true identity and the power—and responsibility—that came with it.

Val intended to rule the empire, cutting a fiery, bloody path to the throne. She'd sacrifice the small amount of peace they'd managed in the wake of her first bid for the crown. And that was only her rise to power. What would happen if Val could command armies and write laws? It was a prospect too terrifying to consider.

For once Veronyka thought she understood the commander's insistence that peace was worth whatever price.

But she would not give Avalkyra Ashfire peace.

Veronyka would fight her every day, in every way she knew how.

"Do we understand each other?" Val asked.

"Perfectly," Veronyka bit out, her teeth clenched.

"That is good, *xe* Nyka," Val said, her face suddenly soft. "I am tired of arguing with girls who look and sound like you."

"You mean my mother," Veronyka said, more statement than question.

"I do," she said, and left the room. Sidra followed, slamming the door behind her and sliding the bolt into place.

Veronyka hurried to the door anyway, peering out the window, but all she could see was the empty hallway. Sidra had even taken the wall sconce with her—not trusting Veronyka with an open flame.

The room was dark and still, yet the walls seemed to pulse, closing in on her a little bit more with each rapid, suffocating breath.

How could Veronyka have let this happen?

Xephyra? she choked through the bond, needing to get out of this confinement—but of course, Xephyra was confined too. Again.

Veronyka couldn't believe she'd been so foolish, selfish—*reckless*, just as

Latham had said—and now here she was, once again a victim of Val, a help-less, powerless prisoner. And for what? Yes, she'd freed the animage hostages, but now she'd taken their place, and she was no closer to stopping this war.

In fact, by allowing herself to be caught, she might very well have sealed Val's victory.

Here, Xephyra said at once, and it was the reassurance Veronyka desper-ately needed and didn't deserve.

I'm so sorry, Veronyka said, but she had difficulty finding words after that. She had forsaken Xephyra by coming here, and Tristan, too. She'd sacrificed her true family for the hope of some shining, intangible thing tied to blood, when all Val had ever done was use their blood—and Veronyka's love for Val—against her.

Family was more than blood; family was the people you chose. And Veronyka had let fear and uncertainty make her lose sight of things she already knew. Just like her fear of her true identity made her lose sight of the fact that she already knew who she was, and no birth certificate could change that.

Without the sconce her room was draped in shadows. The moon's poor, watery illumination striped through the window and balcony bars, remind-ing Veronyka exactly where she was. A cell.

She could sense Xephyra in the distance, just out of reach, but couldn't actually see her. She cast her senses wider, seeking any animal that might be able to help her, but the rocky, arid landscape was virtually devoid of wildlife.

Veronyka slumped down against the wall, her legs still unsteady after the poisoning.

It will be okay, she said to her bondmate, hoping the words would over-ride the anxious terror bubbling just below the surface of her mind. *I will free you if it's the last thing I ever do.*

Images of Rex and Tristan flashed between them, and the sight caused a prickle of tears to sting Veronyka's eyes.

"Yes," she whispered. *I miss them too.*

Then she sat bolt upright, realization shooting through her—Xephyra wasn't just missing them. She was showing Veronyka the way to gain their freedom. She had a bond with Tristan, did she not? Of course, Veronyka had been doing everything she could to stifle that link, but she'd failed at it, just as thoroughly as she'd failed at keeping Val out.

They were miles apart. . . . Even if Veronyka hadn't tried to block their connection, linking with him over such a vast distance would be extremely challenging.

But Val had done it. No matter where she was, she was able to get inside Veronyka's head. Val was an accomplished shadowmage, though—she'd had two lifetimes to master it—and Veronyka was not.

Closing her eyes, Veronyka pictured the rivers, seeing the way Tristan's door shook and rattled on its hinges, begging to be opened. She hesitated, then flung the door wide.

There was a dull rush—the sleepy murmurs and hushed thoughts of people nearby, unsuspecting minds in the city—but Veronyka's heart sank when she felt no sign of Tristan. There was a chance he was sleeping at this late hour, dreaming comfortably . . . not thinking about her at all.

Veronyka shook the emotional thought and refocused. Tristan didn't have shadow magic; his mind didn't know how to sense her the way Val's did. No, this time Veronyka would have to be the one to do the reaching. So she did, following the tendril of their connection, the passage that bound them as thin and tenuous as a cobweb—but just as strong, too. She knew they were still connected and even felt him there, a Tristan-shaped blur in the distance of her thoughts, but she could not get through. There was a fog between them, translucent yet solid, like a milky pane of glass.

A well of despair surged within her. Veronyka understood now why her bond with Tristan was always so difficult to manage; it was new, and she'd never given it a chance to properly form or solidify. From the instant she'd been aware of it, she had fought against it. Thanks to Val's influence, Veronyka had assumed that a shadow magic bond was a vulnerability, but she should have known that Val's way of doing things was the wrong way.

Still, there had been moments—like the battle at the Eyrie and even their kiss just a few short days ago—when Veronyka caught a glimpse of the power of the bond, and it had scared and thrilled her in equal measure. But she'd let fear win out instead of remembering that even her bond with Xephyra had begun as a confusing, overwhelming thing she wasn't entirely in control of. She thought of all the times Xephyra had ignored her wishes, remembered every intrusion or loss of focus. No matter the difficulties, Veronyka had always been open and trusting, and so their bond strengthened and stabilized.

She had never given her bond with Tristan that same chance. Every time they grew closer, every time their bond tried to better connect them and fortify the link, Veronyka had shut it down and blocked it out.

Now, when she needed Tristan the most, she couldn't reach him.

Veronyka's throat tightened, but then Xephyra swept into her mind, her presence as calm and comforting as being wrapped in warm wings.

It will be okay, she said, mimicking Veronyka's words, but Veronyka took heart from them nonetheless.

It will be okay.

Your father wants us to go into hiding—
to leave all of it behind. He does not understand.
You cannot flee from something that is
a part of you.

- CHAPTER 43 -
TRISTAN

TRISTAN LURCHED OUT OF his bedroll.

He stared around the darkness, frantic, confused, as sleep slowly ebbed away.

He'd been dreaming of Veronyka, he thought. It had been an oddly disorienting dream, as if he'd been speaking to Veronyka *through* Rex . . . or had it been Rex talking to Xephyra?

He rolled over and found Rex's giant head mere inches from his face. Tristan yelped, and Rex leapt into the air, squawking and sending up a cloud of sparks. The tiny flecks of fire danced and shimmered into the air before settling on Tristan's bedroll.

He scrambled backward, flinging the blanket aside, but too late—the places where the sparks landed smoked and burned.

Fire! Tristan's mind screamed, the scent pricking at his nostrils and causing a wave of cold sweat to break out over his neck. His heart galloped in his chest even as, one by one, the smoldering dots flickered and winked out.

He forced himself to breathe slowly and find his mental safe house. It was there and it was strong; he only needed to remind himself of that.

Rex, he pleaded through their bond, when the phoenix's emotions continued to intrude upon his thoughts. *Calm yourself.*

Rex fluttered several feet back, tossing his head, and the faint glow from underneath his feathers receded.

All was darkness, and Tristan took a moment to close his eyes and steady his ratcheting heartbeat.

When he opened his eyes, Rex had edged closer again. He was pushing insistently on their bond, nudging Tristan's mind, but Rex's panic made his attempts at communication muddled and unclear.

"Rex," Tristan said desperately, clutching at his head. "Rex, please, I can't—"

But then it came to him in a crystallized image: Xephyra, a darkened cave—and bars. A stab of icy fear pierced Tristan's stomach.

He leapt to his feet and went in search of his father.

Despite intending to leave the morning after the Blood War anniversary, the commander had remained in the village an extra night—this time at Tristan's request—to help with some of the supply replenishment and logistics for the refugees. It felt like a huge step in their relationship that Tristan was able to ask for help without fearing judgment or reproach, and likewise, his father had agreed to remain with humility and good grace.

Maybe they were both maturing.

The commander had taken a room at the inn that had served as the backdrop for the confrontation with the Rushlean farmers, and Tristan wasn't sure if his father had chosen it for simplicity's sake or if he'd wanted to give the owner his custom after a problem with his Riders had chased away their business.

As Tristan wandered into the darkened village, light spilled from the ground-level parlor he and his father had spoken in the night before.

The commander was awake and working, even at this late hour.

Tristan couldn't remember a time when his father was asleep before him—or after him, in the morning—and he honestly couldn't even picture it. Just thinking of Cassian in a nightshirt, tucked under plush blankets atop a heap of pillows, was laughable, as if the commander weren't a real human at all but some unchanging entity in a fixed state.

No, that wasn't true. Tristan's pristine image of his father had been altered since their conversation the previous night, the cracks finally showing in his cool, constantly-in-control facade. Though he disagreed with what he knew of his father's plan—he was forbidden to ask more or talk about it—he couldn't help but have grudging respect for what his father was doing. All this time, Tristan had struggled with the idea that his father was being too safe, too reserved—bordering on cowardice as he insisted over and over again that they couldn't engage the empire, couldn't risk themselves and their position. But what his father was *actually* doing . . . it was anything but cowardly. And though he was obviously personally motivated, he'd thought long and hard about what he was doing, setting up the pieces so that it wasn't just he and the Riders who benefited from his actions, but the entire empire.

Tristan had to admit he was impressed.

It still grated that he wasn't allowed to be involved, but it was nice to know that for once he wasn't being excluded because his father thought him irresponsible or incapable. . . . He was being excluded because his father had faith in him to lead if all else failed. Tristan tried to be deserving of that trust, especially after he'd made such a mess of things with his patrol.

Despite his anger at Latham's claims and accusations, Tristan knew that he *had* lost sight of some of his responsibilities of late—particularly to the other Riders. He'd been so consumed with proving himself a strong and capable leader that he'd become selfish again—just as he'd been before Veronyka arrived at the Eyrie. Tristan had been behaving recklessly, rushing into fights and dispelling with the usual protocols, thinking that he risked only himself.

He'd been wrong about that, and now his patrol was in shambles. Latham hated him, and Veronyka had flown off with her malevolent sister. The others hadn't taken her disappearance well, nor had his father.

Thoughts of Veronyka brought him back to the dream that had awoken him.

Tristan hurried down the dark hallway of the inn, following the light that leaked around the parlor door.

While Rex had calmed down a bit once Tristan woke up, his thoughts were still agitated and insistent, showing repeated flashes of Xephyra, of some dark, enclosed space, and that feeling of being trapped.

Worst of all was the lack of Veronyka. Were she and Xephyra separated, or was Veronyka captured too? Had she managed to escape? Even if she had, there was no way she'd leave her bondmate behind. Wherever Xephyra was, Veronyka wouldn't be far, and if Xephyra was in a cage—that meant Veronyka was unable to get her out. That meant Veronyka needed help.

"Father," Tristan said, knocking gently on the parlor door. Cassian was working his way through a pile of papers and looked up in surprise to find his son standing there.

"Tristan," he said, putting down the document he'd been reading. His face was drawn, his eyes bleary, and Tristan suspected he had no idea just how late it was. He craned his neck to peer out the window at the dark silence of the village beyond. "What are you doing here?"

"Veronyka's in trouble," Tristan said without preamble, his voice tight. He swallowed, trying to keep his and Rex's panic down.

Though there was a new level of peace between Tristan and his father, Veronyka was still a touchy subject. Tristan had refused to give any details about where she'd gone or why, following her advice after all and insisting that when he'd returned to camp, she was already gone.

He kept going over the night's events in his head, second-guessing his choice to let her go and wondering if he should have followed her. There was this tight, tense feeling in his chest all the time now. He'd first noticed it the night she'd told him about her shadow magic—and about who she truly was. For a long time he'd thought it was the idea of her inside his mind that made him feel this constant, pressing sense of panic. But after she'd left, he'd come to realize that it had nothing to do with her magic and everything to do with who she was. He couldn't help but feel like their lives were diverging and would continue to do so, taking them on separate trajectories. He hated to think that their time together was limited, a brief crossing of paths—but what else could it be? She was

Veronyka Ashfire. She was destined for greatness, while Tristan was the son of an exiled governor.

"What kind of trouble?" the commander asked.

"I don't know," Tristan admitted reluctantly.

"And how do you know she's in trouble?" his father asked, casting his tired eyes down at Tristan's hands as if expecting to see a letter or a report there.

Tristan's empty hands curled into fists. "Rex . . . he sensed it somehow. He and Xephyra . . ." He trailed off, afraid to reveal too much, to give his father a sense of just how close he and Veronyka—and by association, their phoenixes—had become.

As close as you can be with someone, Tristan thought, his limbs tingling at the thought. *Bonded.*

The commander sighed, sitting up straighter in his chair. "If you don't know what kind of trouble she's in—or *where* she is, for that matter," he added with a glare, and Tristan avoided his gaze, "then I don't know how you expect me to help you. I couldn't let you go flying after her anyway. You're a patrol leader now. Your Riders need you, this village needs you, and I need you. This is what responsibility feels like. Your underwing *abandoned* her post; by rights, she should be stripped of her apprentice status and expelled from the flock permanently. The Phoenix Riders do not take kindly to deserters."

"She's not a deserter! She's . . ."

Tristan trailed off. A sudden image flared before his eyes, and everything else fell away: Xephyra, the bars . . . and then Val standing on the other side.

He staggered, coming back to himself in a rush. He reached for the nearest object he could find—the back of a chair—blinking until his vision cleared.

Xephyra was imprisoned, but Val was not. That meant Val had turned against Veronyka. And if she had to hold Veronyka's bondmate by force . . .

"Tristan, are you all right?" his father asked, rising from his seat.

"Yes—no," Tristan said. Sweat coated his skin, and he gripped the chair so hard his fingers ached. "We have to help her—she's in grave danger. We all are. We have to go to her."

The commander retook his seat. "*We?* You want me to send our depleted forces away from civilians to find some wayward apprentice?"

"She's not just some wayward apprentice!" Tristan shouted, losing control of his temper. They didn't have time to debate this.

"I know she means more to you, but—"

"Not just me—all of us!" Tristan said, chest heaving. He knew what he had to do, the thing he'd promised not to do . . . but the only thing that could help her. "She's Pheronia Ashfire's daughter."

His father gaped at him. "She's *what?*" he said, voice cracking like a whip.

"She's . . ." Tristan stared at his father, then turned his attention to the table instead. "She's Pheronia Ashfire's daughter. She was born the night the war ended, and Ilithya Shadowheart stole her away."

Tristan darted a glance up at his father. He leaned back in his chair, his eyes sliding out of focus, trying to determine if what Tristan had just said was even possible.

"And there's more," Tristan added. His father's gaze snapped onto him once again. "Avalkyra Ashfire is alive. I've *seen* her, with Veronyka. They flew off together, intending to free the animages that the soldiers have taken captive, but Avalkyra has some alliance with Lord Rolan. I think she turned on Veronyka. Avalkyra resurrected after the Last Battle, and Ilithya raised her and Veronyka together as sisters—but Veronyka never knew her own identity or who her sister was. Avalkyra went by Val. . . ."

"Tristan . . . ," his father said eventually, doubt etched on every line of his face. "You're not making any sense."

"You've never heard of human resurrection?"

His father frowned. "Resurrection? I—"

"Have you or haven't you?"

The commander sighed, scrubbing his face. "Some of the poems in

The Pyraean Epics . . ." He paused, shaking his head. "There are legends of ancient heroes living for centuries, and some of the older timelines of the queendom list Queen Nefyra as ruling for two hundred years. It's most likely a mistake in dating. . . ."

"Or *resurrection*," Tristan argued, though his father still looked unconvinced. Tristan thought of the lockbox strapped to Xephyra's saddlebags, of Veronyka's birth certificate and all the other documents inside—of any way he could prove this to his father.

Then a light went off inside his mind. The exiled Riders.

"Have you heard of a Rider named Doriyan?" Tristan asked in a rush. "He was a part of Avalkyra Ashfire's patrol, and he was from Rushlea."

The commander seemed taken aback at the change in subject and the urgency in Tristan's tone. "Yes, I knew him. We flew together once or twice. I tried to find him after the war, but . . ."

"He's here," Tristan said eagerly. "He's been hiding in Rushlea. I know where. He knows who Veronyka is, who Val—Avalkyra is. He's seen her, spoken to her. If anyone recognizes the reborn Ashfire queen, it would be him, right? And he might know where Val has taken her."

"Tristan—"

"Please," Tristan interrupted. "Trust me."

His father agreed.

They took their phoenixes to the mine, and when they arrived, the place was quiet and dark. A sliver of anxiety wedged itself into Tristan's chest as he realized that just because Doriyan had been here didn't mean he *lived* here. With Avalkyra gone, had Doriyan left as well?

With a glance back at his father, Tristan drew his bow and nocked an arrow, while his father slid a short sword from the scabbard on his hip. Their footsteps echoed as they made their way deeper into the cavern—but Tristan soon noticed a faint glow up ahead. It was coming from the chamber he and Veronyka had had their confrontation with Val, so Tristan slowed his steps, listening hard. He couldn't hear voices or conversation, but as they approached the entrance, Tristan noticed something about the quality of the light. It didn't flicker and dance, like the fire from a sconce or lantern would. It was steady and soft. . . . Like a phoenix not yet in full flame.

With a last look at one another, Tristan and his father stepped through the doorway.

Doriyan was seated on the floor of the cavern, chains binding him to a metal loop embedded into the far wall. Shackled next to him was his phoenix, a thick metal cuff clinking on his leg. He glowed gently, and it was clear by the scent of smoke and the sight of scorch marks along the stone that the phoenix had tried to ignite once or twice to melt his chains, but they were treated with fireproof sap.

"Doriyan?" Tristan said blankly. This . . . Val must have done this to him. Had she captured and chained his phoenix before? Was this why Doriyan had said he had no choice but to serve her?

Doriyan startled at the sudden presence of two people standing before him, and the phoenix squawked and flapped his wings. Doriyan scrabbled backward, as if expecting attack, and his eyes blinked rapidly as they came to rest on Tristan's father. He frowned.

"Lord Cassian?" he said incredulously, his gaze darting to Tristan next.

"It's Commander Cassian now, Doriyan," his father said as he and Tristan approached. It took some time—and a heavy rock—but they eventually managed to break a loop on the chains that held Doriyan, and together all three of them broke the ankle cuff on his phoenix.

They left the dank chamber at once, and Tristan dug through Rex's saddlebags for what provisions he had on hand. As Doriyan drank from a flask and his phoenix ate from a small sack of grain, the three of them took a seat on a cluster of boulders.

Doriyan confirmed Tristan's story, as well as Tristan's assumptions about why Doriyan was serving Val in the first place. Val had chained his phoenix and threatened his life in order to force him to lure Veronyka to the mine, and when she left, she'd chained Doriyan as well.

"I doubt she'd've been back anytime soon," Doriyan said bluntly, and

Tristan was shocked at how he could speak so matter-of-factly about his once-queen condemning him so carelessly to death.

"Do you know what her plans were?" Tristan pressed. "What she wanted with Veronyka?"

Doriyan shook his head. "All I know is that she had some semblance of an alliance with your replacement, the new governor."

"Lord Rolan," the commander said with resignation, glancing at Tristan. Tristan felt a surge of triumph at having his words confirmed, but they still didn't know where to look for her.

"Any idea where they went?" he asked.

"Odds are, they're in Ferro," Doriyan said. "That's where the bulk of his army is, and a man like Rolan . . . I don't think he'd journey far without their protection."

The commander stood and thanked Doriyan for his information. "There is a place for you in my flock, if you want it," he offered.

Tristan was surprised at the offer—despite Doriyan's regrets, he had done awful things in his lifetime, by his own admission.

Doriyan looked surprised too. "I . . . I'll think about it, Commander," he said gruffly.

Cassian nodded, once, before striding back toward Maximian. Tristan hastened to follow.

"I don't get it," Tristan said as they climbed onto their saddles.

"Don't get what?"

"Why she came to him and not to you," Tristan said, voicing the thing that had been bothering him for a while now. "You and Avalkyra . . . you were allies, weren't you, during the war? Why hasn't she contacted you? Why would she seek out Rolan instead of a Phoenix Rider?"

His father toyed absently with a strap on his saddle. "Avalkyra and I did not always see eye to eye," he said carefully. "And, well . . . after her *supposed* death, when I turned myself in to the council and tried to make a deal . . ." He shook his head. "A person like her would never forgive such a thing. She also had great respect for your mother. . . . I wouldn't be surprised if she blamed me for that as well. At least there, I can agree."

"Well, I don't," Tristan said firmly, realizing it for the first time. He knew what people said, and he himself had been angry with his father for a long time for his willingness to work with their enemies. And maybe he found it easy to see his mother's death as a result of his father's actions. To blame him. But doing that turned Olanna into a victim, and that wasn't right. She'd fought until the very end, knowingly taking risks but deeming them worth it anyway.

And his father had continued to fight too, in his own way. His plans for the Grand Council proved that.

Neither way was right or wrong; neither way had been perfect. But they'd both fought, and that was what mattered to Tristan.

Cassian's eyes flickered in the moonlight. "I'm glad to hear that, son."

Tristan cleared his throat, looking away. "You should know . . . ," he began. "Veronyka went willingly with Avalkyra, but whatever peace was between them . . . I think it's over. Avalkyra promised Veronyka she'd help free the animages that Lord Rolan captured, but if that's done . . ."

His father tilted his head, considering. "If Rolan is allying himself with an Ashfire, I think he's making a move on the throne. Which means this war he's orchestrating might just be the beginning of what he has in store." He turned in his saddle. "Come, Tristan. It's time for the Phoenix Riders to fly to Ferro."

Here follows a fragment of an ancient myth, transcribed in the Second Era from an oral account originating from the First Era of the Reign of Queens.

When Nefyra's lifelong love, Callysta, died from an arrow wound, Nefyra despaired.

She put Callysta's body into the Everlasting Flame with her bare hands, heedless of the fire that crawled across her own skin. Cirix, Callysta's bondmate, went into the flames with her and came out a new hatchling. He bonded to Callysta's daughter Calliope, who was the youngest of her children.

Though life went on for the queendom, it did not go on for Nefyra. She stood before the Everlasting Flame day after day, night after night, longing for Callysta. She did not eat. She did not sleep. On the morning of the third day—she was gone. So too was her bondmate, Ignix.

The story ends there, with no further accounts on record. This myth contradicts the widely accepted historical timeline positing that Queen Nefyra ruled for nearly two hundred years *after* Callysta's death.

Many scholars believe this myth is meant to indicate Nefyra's transition into a recluse, who ruled in isolation from within her palace. Others suggest this myth simply truncates the timeline, illustrating Nefyra's death in conjunction with her lover's for dramatic effect, proving that Nefyra succumbed to her broken heart and threw herself into the fire. Others argue she would have walked in calmly, purposefully, knowing that a reunion with Callysta waited for her on the other side, among the stars. There are even those who believe she leapt onto her phoenix's back and flew away, unable to live there among her people any longer.

Like many secrets of the ancient Pyraean queens, the truth is likely lost to us forever.

—"Queen Nefyra's Divinely Long Reign," from *The Lost History of the Ashfire Queens*, by Enzo, High Priest of Mori, 123 AE

The Ashfire legacy comes with us, always.
Everywhere. There is no hiding from it.
No escaping it. It is in our blood.

- CHAPTER 44 -
SEV

BY THE TIME THEY reached the tower on foot, night had descended. It had been hard going, but the most direct route was through the rocky Foothills, and Sev didn't want to risk circling around and running into any soldiers.

As it was, the outskirts of Ferro were surprisingly quiet, with no hint of the battle that had taken place barely a mile away. Or maybe that *was* the hint—anyone with sense had likely fled the area or locked themselves up somewhere safe. They were technically just inside the border, in an area called Copper Hill. The majority of mining activity in Ferro had moved farther west in the highlands or south in the Spine when bronze weapons gave way to steel. Copper Hill was now something of a ghost town, featuring warehouses and processing facilities but little by way of houses or markets.

Still, the nearer Sev and Kade drew to the prison tower—their pace slow and careful as Kade clutched at his side—the more Sev was convinced that something else was going on. Though he could see light flickering from the highest tower room, spilling out from the balcony and several windows, the rest of the building was dark.

Dark and apparently empty. Near a dozen barred windows lined the ground floor, all black and unlit, and the double doors that faced east were shut but unmanned. What kind of prison tower didn't have guards? Even if there were no prisoners, it seemed strange that Lord Rolan would leave the structure wholly abandoned. How easy for squatters to take up residence or for thieves to strip the building and leave it broken and unusable.

Despite the deserted look of the tower, Sev was wary of getting closer. The light atop the tower meant that *someone* was here, even if it was just Veronyka alone and held against her will. But what about those other Riders? What about their phoenixes?

Kade nudged Sev as the light in the topmost room went out, and a minute later, two people exited the building on the ground level. They conversed in low voices as their phoenixes emerged from the top of the tower, where roosts were built into the architecture, and landed in the courtyard before their Riders. The one who'd kidnapped Veronyka leapt into her saddle and flew south, while the other climbed onto her phoenix and circled around the building, coming to land on the tower's highest peak. There she perched, facing north.

Sev glanced to Kade—this was their chance. The front door to the building faced the east; if they skirted around the side of the building and stuck to the shadows, she'd never see them.

With a finger to his lips, Sev stood from where they'd been squatting behind the remnants of some old stone wall that had once enclosed the area. Kade followed, grimacing all the way.

They hurried across the open space between their hiding place and the prisoner tower, then stuck close to the wall as they edged toward the doors. It was so dark that they could hardly see, but Sev still paused against the wall of the building, waiting to see if the Rider perched atop the tower—or anyone else they might have overlooked—had spotted them, but no alarm was raised.

Pausing to catch his breath, he tugged at Kade's tunic, seeing a darkened patch of blood seeping through the bandages on both his front and back. Kade brushed him off.

"I popped a stitch in the fight."

"Just one?" Sev pressed, reaching for Kade's tunic again.

"We don't have time for this," Kade said with some exasperation. Sev could tell he was in pain, but Kade was right—Sev would check on the wound later. For now they needed to see if they could get inside the building, if there was any way to free Veronyka while one of the Riders was gone.

The doors were wood banded in steel, with barred windows cut in each. Sev gently touched the handle, and was unsurprised to find it locked, but when he got on tiptoes and peered through one of the windows, his heart leapt when he saw that it was a simple latch mechanism.

Sev considered their possessions, and his eyes landed on Kade's belt. He reached for it.

"Can I help you?" Kade asked, trying to whisper, though his voice was several octaves higher than usual.

Sev couldn't help but smile at that; he stopped tugging but didn't remove his hands. They stood very close together. "I need your belt," he said quietly.

"What about yours?" Kade pointed out, but he spotted the issue at once. Sev's belt held weapons, while Kade's was a regular bondservant-issue belt and did not. "Fine," he said, though he batted Sev's hands away to remove it himself.

Sev continued to smile until Kade handed it over. The belt had a simple metal buckle, and with a quick snap, Sev removed the prong that bisected the frame, leaving a metal square. He got onto his toes again, then carefully fed the belt through the opening between the bars of the window.

He lowered it until the buckle dangled at the right height, knocking gently against the lock. It took several attempts: once, twice—Teyke help him—*three* times until finally Sev got it into position, sliding the loop of the buckle onto the latch of the door. He carefully adjusted his grip and paused, steadying his breath. This was the moment of most danger, when they would discover exactly how well cared for the lock was, whether it would open silently on well-greased hinges or with a resounding shriek on tarnished, rusted joints. He pulled.

The lock released with a soft click, and Kade quickly took hold of the handle to stop it from rattling any further.

Sev sighed in relief and drew the belt back up, trying not to look too pleased with himself. Kade was watching him, though, so he said, "You learn a thing or two, living on the streets."

Kade raised his brows. "Like how to get a man to part with his belt?" he asked, paused in the doorway.

Sev stepped after him, stopping so that they were chest to chest inside the frame. "No. That's the first time I've managed that," he said softly, and Kade's eyes dropped, an embarrassed smile tugging at his lips.

Inside was as empty as Sev had expected; there was a hallway leading off to the left and a door that led up to the tower on the right. He examined the handle to the tower door, but unlike the exterior door, this lock would have to be picked. Sev could do that, too, if only he had his tools.

Turning, he found Kade examining a table surrounded by chairs and scattered with half-empty cups and a pair of dice. "Looks like they left in a hurry," he said, indicating the disarray. Not only had they left alcohol and a game of dice behind, but one of the chairs was knocked over, and several copper coins glimmered from where they'd fallen onto the floor.

"Look at this," Sev said, spotting a piece of paper clipped to a board that had fallen onto the ground under the table. He pocketed the coppers, too—old habits died hard.

Kade smirked but didn't say anything.

"Prisoner listing . . . ," Sev said, running his finger down a column of names with cell numbers beside them, but all had been "released" and dated except one at the very bottom. "It's her," he said blankly.

"Who?" Kade asked, taking the list from Sev. His eyes bugged. "*Riella?*"

They both turned in unison to stare down the cellblock. "Come on," Sev said, checking the number and hastening down the hall.

"I don't see any keys," Kade murmured, hands flying over every surface as he searched for hooks or drawers along the wall and table.

"I don't need keys," Sev said, jogging back to grab his arm and tug Kade along.

"Criminal," Kade muttered under his breath, and Sev chuckled. Kade had a gift for delicate work and would make an excellent lockpick if he cared to learn, though Sev suspected he wouldn't want to. In his heart, Kade wasn't much for sneaking and stealing. He was an honorable man, and in another life he'd probably have made a dutiful soldier and an impressive Phoenix Rider.

Maybe he still could.

Riella's cell was supposedly at the end of the hall, but again the lack of guards or light made Sev uneasy. It seemed like the soldiers had left without preparations or notice, which made him think that the Phoenix Riders had banished them—more proof that they were allies of Rolan and had authority over empire soldiers. Otherwise there would've been evidence of a fight.

The hallway was dotted with doors, and each had a small window cut out of the wood, allowing them to peer inside as they went. Though Sev knew she was meant to be housed at the end, he made sure to check all the rooms as they passed.

The first few were dark and quiet, nothing visible in the minimal light, but Sev began to sense something as he neared the end of the hall, even before Kade gripped his arm.

"Animals," Kade whispered, a frown creasing his brow. "A lot of them."

They stopped in front of the last door. Sev peeked into the square window, squinting into the darkness. There was definitely something alive in the room, a sniffling, shuffling energy that made Sev's skin prickle. But the longer he stared into the darkness, the more confused he became. There was a dark shape slowly distinguishing itself from the blackness of the room, still as a heap of clothing—and yet not. There was something crawling, writhing overtop of it, and then a pair of eyes blinked back at him.

There was a person sitting on the floor in the corner of the room, covered head to toe in dozens of rats, their furry, inky bodies shifting and scrabbling over one another.

The prisoner got to her feet—Sev could see it was a young girl—but didn't come any closer. The rats dispersed when she stood, though they remained nearby.

"Riella?" Sev asked incredulously.

"Who are you?" she asked warily, her voice soft and young sounding. It reverberated in the empty space, making Sev's heart thud in fear that they would be overheard.

"We're here to rescue you," Kade answered, keeping his voice low. "I'm Kade—this is Sev. We're here on behalf of the Phoenix Riders. We're—"

But the girl recoiled at that, pressing herself against the wall. The rats drew nearer once again, scurrying in a heap over her feet and legs.

"What is it?" Sev asked, and she pressed her lips together, though he could see her chin trembling.

"They said . . ." She cleared her throat, as if it was dry, and Sev wondered how long it had been since she'd been given water. "I saw the phoenixes through the window, and I thought . . ." Her eyes were wide and the bottom lids sparkled with tears. She shook her head and blinked away the moisture. "There were two of them, and they ordered the soldiers to leave. When I heard them, I thought that maybe they were here to rescue me. But then the soldiers left and they walked down the hall, toward my cell. . . ." Her voice quivered slightly. "They asked who I was, and I told them. They were Phoenix Riders! Why wouldn't I?" she asked, almost pleadingly. "They said I might prove useful, but if I made any trouble—if I made a sound— they'd kill me."

Sev remembered that Riella's father worked for the Office for Border Control. It was surely why Rolan had kept her, even when her brother stopped spying for him. Her father would ensure that Rolan's soldiers could come and go as they pleased while the border officials looked the other way.

"We're not like them," Sev said at once. "They're not the same Phoenix Riders we serve—not the same as your brother."

"My brother?" she asked, delicate hope clinging to her words. "Is he here?"

"No," Sev said apologetically. "But we're going to take you to him. Let me . . ." He trailed off, stepping back to squat down and squint at the lock.

It was the same as the door to the tower stairs: a classic tumbler, easy enough to pick—*if* he had the right tools.

"We'll be back," Sev promised, and Kade followed him down the hallway.

"I thought you said you didn't need a key," Kade said accusingly as Sev copied what he'd done earlier, hands skimming over every surface of the table and walls.

"I don't—but I do need lockpicks. Thin strips of metal. Small tongs or pliers, a hairpin . . ."

"Do you think you're likely to find a hairpin inside a prison tower?" Kade asked dryly.

Sev sighed and straightened, stopping his search. "Point taken. Maybe . . . ," he began, scanning the room, until a glimmer of light caught his attention near the front door. He leapt forward, crouching down to lift the piece of metal he'd broken off Kade's belt buckle. It was almost exactly what he needed—*almost*. It was easy to tell at a glance that while it was the right shape and thinness . . .

"Too short," Sev said with a curse, trying it on the lock to the tower stairs just to be sure—but his suspicions were confirmed. He held it up to his own belt, but he knew the dimensions would be roughly the same. If only they could get their hands on a larger buckle. . . .

"A horse's saddle," Kade said abruptly.

Sev's head snapped up. "Yes," he said, nodding. "They must have stables somewhere nearby. . . ."

He strode for the door, but Kade gripped his arm. "What if she hears?" He jerked his chin upward, indicating the Rider keeping a lookout atop the tower above them.

While they could probably pick Riella's lock without the Rider hearing—the tower was easily five stories high—Sev knew that picking the lock on the bottom of the stairs would be far more dangerous. The tower would act like a funnel, amplifying sound, the echoes reverberating all the way to the top. But how could Sev unlock Riella's cell and walk right past the door leading to Veronyka's? Should he do neither, and get a letter to the commander instead? But while Veronyka was obviously being held for some purpose, Riella was a complication, a liability . . . and more likely to wind up dead.

Sev glanced back down the hallway before answering in a low voice. "Now's our best chance to get Riella out of here, while that Rider's focused outside the building. As for Veronyka . . . I won't unlock the tower door unless the Rider leaves. Sending a letter to the commander might be our best option." Kade's expression was pained, but he nodded. "Come on," Sev said, leading the way back outside. "Let's go."

As they suspected, there *were* stables nearby—barely a hundred feet away across the grassy courtyard closed in by the tower and the wings of the ground-level prison.

Sev hurried toward the building, while Kade struggled to keep up. He was fading fast—Sev could see it in the slump of his shoulders and the heaviness of his eyes. His face was looking sallow and drawn too, and Sev hoped it was just exhaustion and not more blood loss. He thought of the popped stitch and tried not to panic, especially when Kade stumbled over a stone in the darkness and clutched at his stomach.

As Kade staggered, Sev slipped deftly underneath his arm, helping to support him.

"I'm fine," Kade insisted, but he leaned heavily on Sev. "Just tired is all . . ." His words slurred slightly, causing more alarm to shoot through Sev's veins.

Maybe, if Sev could convince Kade to leave with Riella, he could attempt to save Veronyka, too, and pretend to be a tower guard if the Rider found him. He still might wind up dead, but if Kade and Riella were safe . . .

Sev couldn't tell if it was his spy's instincts telling him to resume his role as a soldier, or his sudden urge to be a hero telling him to be reckless. A spy was supposed to gather information, stick to the shadows, and let others call the shots. But what if Sev could use his role *as* a spy to be a hero?

Maybe the two weren't mutually exclusive. He wanted to act, to make his own choices—to follow the path that was before him. And maybe that path was leading him back to being a spy.

When they reached the stables, Sev poked his head inside, relieved to see that there were no horses or stable hands. Whatever guards had been inside the tower had probably taken the animals when they were forced to flee, and he assumed they managed their own horses since there were so few of them.

It was dark and cool, and Sev helped ease Kade down onto a barrel before looking around. His eyes lit on an extra saddle on a rack, and he hastened toward it, fingers trembling slightly as he fidgeted with the fat, gleaming buckle on the flank cinch.

The metal was stronger than the prong on Kade's belt, though, and Sev had to break the entire buckle by wedging the handle of a shovel inside and twisting. It worked in the end, but he was sweaty and panting by the time he managed it. Plus, he needed two—and so went to work on the next buckle.

When he finally whirled around, triumphant, it was to find Kade leaning back against the wall of the stables, arms pressed against his stomach.

Any good feeling Sev had at his victory evaporated.

"Kade," Sev said in distress, tucking the strips of metal into his pocket and leaning forward. He put both hands on Kade's shoulders.

"I'm fine," Kade said again, though his eyes remained closed.

Sev's heart clenched painfully. "Just rest a minute. I'll . . ." He stopped. He heard something—distant voices. He darted across the stables to the window.

It was dark, but he could still make out the tower—where *two* Riders now perched. The second Rider had apparently returned from her nighttime errand.

And below, the courtyard was filling with people.

Sev's stomach dropped.

He counted a dozen soldiers on horseback, but they didn't approach the stables or dismount. Instead they'd taken up a sentry position around the prison building, facing south.

They must be an advance guard, and they were waiting for something. Or someone.

Glancing down at himself, Sev began to peel off some of his supplies and extra baggage.

"What is it?" Kade asked, getting gingerly to his feet. "What's happening?"

Sev continued to unload their supplies as Kade peered out the window. His expression was bleak. "How will we get out of here? Riella . . ."

"*You'll* leave through the back door," Sev said, nodding his chin toward the rear of the stables. "And I'll figure out what's going on."

"Sev . . . ," Kade began, his expression tight. But what could he say? Sev was the soldier—and for now he was still a spy. That was the whole point of keeping his cover intact in the first place. For moments like this. He considered the idea that his role as a spy could be donned at will—not an identity, but a single aspect of his character. Something he chose to perform, not something that defined him.

Kade was a runaway bondservant, plus he was too injured to be of much use. If Sev didn't ask these soldiers what was happening, right now, they might miss their chance to help Riella and Veronyka. He had to try.

"Wait until I draw their attention, then slip out the back. I'll meet you behind that broken wall—same place we watched the tower from before."

As Sev moved to leave, Kade gripped his arm. His eyes were wide and fearful. "Just—be careful."

Sev nodded, laying his hand over Kade's for a moment before gently dislodging it. Their gazes locked, and Sev had that familiar twinge that he got whenever they parted—the shadow of the time on the mountain, when Kade had disappeared into the trees and Sev didn't know if he'd ever see him again.

"Stay hidden," Sev added softly. "Please."

Kade took up what he could carry of Sev's abandoned supplies and nodded, moving to the back of the stables as Sev strode out the front. One of the soldiers hailed Sev as soon as he stepped out of the shadows.

Sev gave him a version of the truth—he'd been on prisoner-escort duty until their convoy had been attacked by Phoenix Riders and the prisoners freed. His story veered into fiction then as he explained that he'd been chased back into Ferro, but when he'd arrived here, hoping for safety, he'd found the place deserted and Phoenix Riders in residence. He'd just been looking for a horse when the others arrived.

Word had already reached Rolan—and therefore, these soldiers—about the attack and the Phoenix Riders occupying the tower, and so the man nodded gravely but without surprise.

"The situation is under control. The governor's on his way with reinforcements."

"Lord Rolan?" Sev pressed, wanting to be sure. He swallowed, wondering how on earth they were going to free Riella now—and how they could possibly help Veronyka.

The soldier nodded. "He'll be here before midday."

Such is your inheritance, my daughter.
A name. A legacy. An empire in ruin.

- CHAPTER 45 -

VERONYKA

VERONYKA HARDLY SLEPT.

Sidra was perched outside her room atop the tower all night, keeping a lookout, her proximity like a shadow—because it wasn't just Sidra there, but Val, too. Not her body, but her mind. Val herself had been gone, but even when her physical presence receded, her magical presence remained. Sidra had the touch of Val's shadow magic on her, permanently—Veronyka had been aware of it since their first meeting in the Foothills next to the soldiers' camp.

It was something Veronyka had seen all her life.

Some people—like Tristan—were prime targets for a shadowmage. He was fast and loose with his emotions, quick to anger and frustration, and though Veronyka knew he tried to emulate his father's stoic nature, he rarely succeeded in that regard. One of the first things she'd noticed about him when they'd met was the way he projected. She didn't have to go searching in his mind for his feelings; they were so powerful and insistent that they bumped against Veronyka's mental walls even when she tried to block him out.

It was no wonder their bond had formed so quickly.

Veronyka had asked Val once why she didn't try to control everyone who'd ever crossed their path or stood in their way: the border guards who barred their passage, the landlords who ruthlessly raised rents, or the thieves and cutthroats who stalked the Narrows streets.

"Why not control every animal in the world and have a magically bound menagerie?" Before Veronyka had been able to answer, Val had continued. "It's draining. Connecting with a mind is one thing, but holding it? Influencing it? And for every additional mind you penetrate, your potency weakens. It's like trying to control a herd of sheep versus just a single lamb."

Val had taken them out to the pastures to prove her point, demanding that Veronyka try to take hold of an entire herd of sheep. She had failed, of course.

"You think that is hard, try it sometime with people," Val had said with superiority as they made their way back home. "Human minds are more complex and difficult to get a grip on. Even those as wide open as yours are hard to hold for long, and when you release them, their disorientation is counterproductive. It's a waste of time and energy, and with mixed results. Sometimes it's better to just pay a bribe or draw a knife."

What Sidra had in her mind was more than the usual touch she'd seen before in people Val had manipulated with shadow magic. It was something deeper.

Morra seemed to believe that Avalkyra had used shadow magic on her entire patrol, causing them to fly with expert precision . . . and to obey her with unusual zeal. Doriyan had said as much inside the mine, even if he had no touch of shadow magic on him now. But Val always claimed that using shadow magic on groups was ineffectual. Had she learned a way to negate the usual difficulties of using shadow magic on multiple people at once? Had she found a way to form a long-term connection that *wasn't* a bond?

After all, Sidra had been a part of Avalkyra Ashfire's patrol too, and here she was years later, doing Val's bidding without question, drenched in her magic. Veronyka had to find out more.

When Sidra finally left her perch and came back inside, it was early morning, pale golden sunlight visible through the window and balcony grates, though the tower room remained shadowy and cool. Indistinct voices and the clatter of horses' hooves floated up from the ground below, but they were distant sounds, and Veronyka couldn't tell if they were coming from nearby or just the normal noises of a city waking up all around them. There was certainly no urgency in Sidra's demeanor as she put a lantern onto the table, then crouched to place a bowl of mushy, unsweetened oats on the ground next to Veronyka. Her hand rested on the knife in her belt, but her expression was bored. The dagger was an idle threat—Val would kill Sidra if she did anything to damage her prize.

Still, Veronyka made no move to attack or escape. She'd thought of nothing else for the first few hours of her confinement, but now a calmness had settled over her. There *would* be an opportunity to get out of this. She just had to remain sharp and wait for it.

Or create it on her own.

As Sidra prepared to step away, Veronyka slowly dipped her hand behind her back—there was nothing there, but the movement drew Sidra's attention. The woman lifted her head, scrutinizing Veronyka, seeking her intent and measuring her level of threat. When Sidra's gaze latched onto Veronyka's face, Veronyka seized the opportunity and locked eyes with her.

The channel between them opened immediately—albeit a bit clumsily; Veronyka's attempts at shadow magic were as unskilled as they had ever been. But she was determined, and she held her breath as she slid into Sidra's mind.

She wasn't digging for information or trying to take control; no, she was seeking Val.

It didn't take long. Val's magic was there—Veronyka could taste the iron tang of it and smell the smoky residue like the dying remnants of a banked fire—but Val herself wasn't present. She wasn't actively in Sidra's mind. . . . Rather, she'd left an imprint of herself, a marker . . . an access point . . .

A door.

Veronyka studied it, tried to follow the line of magic where it led like a thread to Val's own mind, but it was clear that while it looked like a bond, this connection was something flimsier. Something temporary and one-sided. Even though Veronyka's bond with Tristan was something he wasn't initially aware of, it ran both ways, and there was a piece of him in her mind the same way there was a piece of her in his.

Was there more than one kind of bond? Val might have put a part of herself in Sidra's mind, but Veronyka doubted very much that there was a part of Sidra inside Val. Besides, bonds were based in love and trust and mutual affection. . . . Whatever this was, it wasn't that.

It was shocking to realize that despite everything, what Veronyka and Val had was indeed a bond. That those elements existed between them.

Or at least they *had*.

Before Veronyka could dwell on that, she sensed Val's presence . . . not in her own mind, but in Sidra's. Veronyka drew back as much as she could but didn't let go of her connection entirely. A second later she understood that Val was summoning Sidra. Without a clue what she was doing, Veronyka took that temporary door in Sidra's mind—wide open and waiting—and slammed it shut.

Sidra wavered, blinking as the command in her mind was abruptly cut off. Yes, Veronyka had closed the door—but Val would just open it again. The question was: Could Veronyka destroy the door entirely?

The sound of agitated footsteps echoed up from the stairwell; Val was coming. Veronyka released her hold on Sidra, who lurched into a standing position, staggering slightly.

Val marched into the room. "Sidra?" she barked, and the woman stood to attention.

It was a testament to Val's arrogance that she didn't even consider that Veronyka might have something to do with Sidra's sudden resistance. She simply scowled at the woman, then jerked her chin toward the stairwell behind her. Sidra obeyed at once.

Veronyka picked up her bowl and started shoveling the cold oats into her mouth without tasting them.

"Are you bonded to her, then?" she asked. She didn't have time to figure this out, and she thought the suddenness of the question might catch Val off guard and trick her into talking.

"Bonded?" Val asked with a derisive snort. "With Sidra of the Stellan Plains? Don't be absurd."

Veronyka nodded at the door, where Sidra had disappeared. "Then how—"

"Ah, *xe* Nyka—you've never understood the complexities of shadow magic. The potential. A bond is an exchange born of equals and cannot exist where there is not trust and respect." She paused, and her expression closed somewhat as she realized she'd admitted to having such a relationship with Veronyka. "A *bind*, though . . . that is a much more useful thing."

"What's a bind?" Veronyka asked innocently, playing to Val's arrogance and belief in her superiority. Apparently the thing she'd just discovered in Sidra's mind had a name. A thought occurred to Veronyka; if Val had been using *binds* on her patrol during the war, that would explain why both Sidra and Doriyan had done whatever she asked without question. Dying likely broke Val's hold on Doriyan, and he didn't like what he'd woken up to. Sidra had maintained her loyalty, and no doubt Val had reinserted her bind on the woman without much difficulty. Doriyan, however, might have fought against it.

"Something you'd never have the guts to implement," Val answered. "A bind is control and influence. It makes true allies of those who would merely be your followers."

"But doesn't that make you vulnerable? Having bonds with so many—"

"It's a *bind*, not a bond, and you don't just put them into *anyone*. It takes time, effort, and familiarity, and too many binds means spreading yourself—and your magic—thin."

"But couldn't another shadowmage use one of those binds to sneak into *your* mind?"

Val's lips twisted into a smug, self-assured smile, as if she suspected Veronyka wanted to do just that. "It's *my* mind—it's where I'm most powerful. *They* would be foolish to try."

Rather than scare Veronyka off, the words resonated down to her very core.

If asked before today, she'd have said one of her greatest fears was having

Val inside her mind. The unwanted invasion and vulnerability of it haunted her every step, but Val's words just now had irrevocably altered Veronyka's understanding of shadow magic. All this time, Veronyka had been focusing her energy on the wrong thing: keeping Val out, so afraid of having her sister in her mind that she'd missed the fact that it was *her* mind, and there, she ruled.

There, she was most powerful.

Val misinterpreted her stunned look. "Forget it," she said. "It's a power you'd never understand."

"It sounds like a one-way bond. It sounds like you *force* people to be loyal to you rather than inspiring it on your own."

"Inspiring loyalty . . . ," Val murmured, shaking her head. "You talk like your mother."

Veronyka had heard Val pass harsh judgment on everything and everyone, but after what Veronyka had seen in that abandoned mine, she knew that while what Pheronia had done was risky—and surely there were other such instances when she tried, perhaps in foolish hope, to reason with her sister—she was not stupid. For Veronyka's entire life, Val had belittled Pheronia and praised Avalkyra. How hollow those words were now that she knew the truth.

"Thank you," Veronyka said, and Val scowled.

Before she could retort, Sidra returned heaving a bucket of water, contents sloshing over the side.

Val turned on her heel and left, returning a short while later holding a long swath of sheer green fabric stitched with gold thread.

"What's this?" Veronyka asked automatically, though she already knew. They were getting her cleaned and dressed to meet her fiancé.

Ignoring her question, Val hung the garment on the back of the door, revealing a dress with of "split skirts," which was a common style among Stellan women. The design allowed the wearer to ride easily—important for a culture so entrenched in horses—while still maintaining a soft, elegant look. Skirts were utterly nonexistent in Pyraean and Phoenix Rider history, impractical for the working classes and downright dangerous for people who rode flaming firebirds. As such, they'd never been favored in the Golden Empire's fashions, though they had been fairly popular in the lesser kingdoms of the south. The weather was often scorching in the Stellan Plains, so flowing, loose-fitting materials were worn by both men and women of that region.

Split skirts became the norm, and clearly, Val wanted to endear Veronyka to her Stellan husband.

Veronyka wanted to remind Val that no matter who her betrothed was, *she* wasn't Stellan—but the words died on her tongue. Pheronia Ashfire had been Stellan on her mother's side, and as for Veronyka's father? She knew it didn't matter, not truly, but something about not knowing her cultural history, her origins, made her feel like a plant torn up by the roots.

As Val tried to straighten the sheer layers, part of the embroidery caught on one of her braids and she cursed.

"Ridiculous," she muttered, and Veronyka was strangely comforted by it. The dress was beautiful, but it wasn't *her*, it wasn't Veronyka. The outfit felt like a costume, like the heavy face paint a player wore on Mummer's Lane.

Worse, it was something a Rider would never—*could* never—safely wear, and Veronyka hated the idea of putting it on, of erasing that part of herself. Deep in her mind, Xephyra crooned.

Sidra returned with another bucket of water and an armful of other supplies, which she handed to Val. Val put the bottommost bundle onto the window ledge, then offered a thin cotton towel and a hunk of olive soap to Veronyka.

Veronyka's hair and skin were sticky with sweat thanks to the late-summer heat and the filth of the battle the previous day. She desperately needed to bathe, relished the idea of feeling clean again—but the thought of what came *after* made her take several staggering steps backward. Panic was clawing at her, a rising tide in her throat.

"No," she said, shaking her head. "I won't do it. I won't dress up like a doll for you. For *him*."

Val glanced over her shoulder. In response to Val's wordless command, Sidra reached into the hallway and took up her bow and arrow, pointing the steel head directly at Veronyka.

"How about now?" Val asked, looking at Veronyka once more.

Veronyka clenched her fists and took a step forward—but not toward the soap and water. Toward Sidra.

Five more steps and Sidra's arrow was pointed directly between Veronyka's eyes. Her heart beat wildly in her chest, but she refused to let the fear take hold.

Instead Veronyka stared at the woman, daring her to do what Veronyka knew she could not. Sidra had hardly reacted to Veronyka's approach, except to tighten her grip on the bow, but now she angled her head to Val, a question in her eyes.

Val hesitated, and Veronyka spoke into the silence.

"You need me," she said evenly. "An arrow through the head—or the arm or the leg, for that matter—would make me a bit unappealing for my betrothed, don't you think? Wouldn't want to look like a 'back-alley brawler,' would I?"

Val's nostrils flared, and she closed the distance between them. She was inches from Veronyka's face, her next words whispering across Veronyka's cheek and stirring her hair.

"Stand down, Sidra," Val said, though she continued to stare at Veronyka.

Veronyka remained perfectly still. The words were what she'd wanted, but something in Val's cool, unruffled demeanor told Veronyka that she hadn't won this battle.

"And take your bow to the phoenix's cell instead."

All the breath disappeared from Veronyka's lungs. How could she have forgotten? She was not here alone.

Xephyra—behave, Veronyka said desperately through the bond, flashing a mental image of what was to come. Xephyra bristled but edged backward, into the depths of the cave.

Veronyka should have known this would happen, that Val would resort to the same tactics over and over to get what she wanted. Veronyka considered trying to shake Val's hold on Sidra again, but shadow magic or not, Sidra would obey.

Sidra disappeared down the stairs, and Veronyka stared after her, muscles tensed as if she meant to follow, but she knew she could not.

Val stepped even closer, the fabric of her tunic brushing against Veronyka's arm.

"One false move—one toe out of line, and I'll have an arrow through your bondmate's heart," Val said, voice soft. "It would give me *pleasure*, and there would be no coming back from it. No bones, no pyre. Do we understand each other?"

Veronyka swallowed thickly, still staring into the empty doorway, though her eyes were unseeing. She was with Xephyra now, ears ringing as she saw Sidra approach the phoenix's cage through their bond. Xephyra ruffled her feathers and cowered back even more, but there was nowhere to hide, and Sidra's arrow was nocked and ready.

"Yes," Veronyka choked out.

"Good," Val said, and Veronyka could *hear* the smile in her voice.

Refusing to look at it, she snatched the cloth and soap from Val's hand and crouched over the nearest bucket.

Movements jerky with impotent rage, Veronyka began scrubbing at her skin and hair.

Val strolled over to the wall, leaning against it and watching with lazy, hooded eyes. "I told you before, loving them is weakness."

Veronyka paused. Distilled in those four words was everything that was wrong with Val.

In *this* life, anyway. Veronyka knew from experience—from the time she'd spent in Val's memories—that her beliefs hadn't always been this way.

"You loved *her*," Veronyka said quietly.

"What?" Val said, straightening from her repose.

"You loved your sister, Pheronia. You loved my mother."

Veronyka had been lathering the soap in her hands. When she looked up, Val stalked toward her so quickly that Veronyka barely had time to flinch before Val slapped the bar of soap from her grip; it dropped into the nearest water bucket with a soft *plunk*.

"Yes, Veronyka," she snarled. "I loved her, and look what happened."

"She's not the reason you died," Veronyka said reasonably, wary of Val's angry face leaning over hers. "Loving Pheronia didn't make you lose the war."

"Are you naive, or just stupid?" Val snapped, turning away in disgust. She began to pace. "If I didn't love her, I'd have done away with her, just like I did her foul, scheming mother. Instead I let her live, and everything I'd worked for my entire life went to pieces. Love is the force that halts a blade and conflicts a heart. Love is the veil that obscures the truth, that turns all the world to darkness until it's too late to see the light. Until you watch your sister die from your own arrow and the anguish of it consumes you."

A heavy silence followed Val's words. They had been strong, terrible words, but none so much as the last few.

Veronyka fought to keep her voice steady. "*Your* arrow?" she whispered.

Val rounded on her. "Yes, Veronyka! My godsforsaken arrow!" she screamed, so loudly that Veronyka flinched. "Does that really surprise you? Does that shatter your illusions of me, your sweet, caring aunt?"

Veronyka supposed it didn't. When she thought back to the vision of her mother's death, she'd felt Val's desperate sorrow—the confusion, the regret. She hadn't *meant* to shoot Pheronia. She hadn't done it on purpose.

And there had been something else there, when her hand had pressed against Pheronia's pregnant belly. . . .

"You didn't learn anything," Veronyka said, her voice trembling slightly.

"Excuse me?" Val barked. She was ready for a fight, whether Veronyka gave it to her or not.

"You loved me, Val," Veronyka said, her words stronger now. "We have a bond, remember? You loved your sister's daughter because you still love *her*, even though she's gone. You loved me the moment you knew I existed. I *felt* it." Veronyka knew Val understood her meaning—she'd felt it with shadow magic. "And even now, in this new life . . . you found me. You fed me, protected me, and kept me alive."

Confusion flickered across Val's features, before her expression hardened once more. "So I could use you now! All I ever loved about you was your Ashfire blood."

The words landed like a blow—just as Val had meant them to—and Veronyka turned away. It didn't matter that Val was lying to herself as well as to Veronyka, that she'd said the words with the sole purpose of inflicting pain. Frustrated tears stung Veronyka's eyes, and she didn't know if she was angrier with Val or herself. What did it matter if somewhere, deep down, Val loved her? Veronyka didn't even know if *she* still loved Val. How many times could a person hurt you and your love for them endure?

Then again, surely only love could make words like hers cut so deeply? Love didn't stop people from hurting each other—love made it easier. Avalkyra had loved Pheronia even as she'd killed her. And Pheronia had loved Avalkyra, even when she walked out of that mine, turning her back on Avalkyra forever.

Even as she lay dying, Avalkyra's arrow embedded in her chest, Pheronia had loved her sister.

If Avalkyra Ashfire was capable of killing the person she loved most, what did that say about her now, a lifetime later? The person Veronyka saw her in shadow magic dreams was not the same person standing before her. They might look the same, talk and act the same, but Val had been through so much since then. There was poison in her heart, a darkness so thick and consuming that no amount of fire could burn it away.

The fact of the matter was, it made no difference whether they loved each other or not. Veronyka had vowed to stand between Val and the throne she so desperately coveted. Love would not protect either of them.

"What about your bondmate?" she asked, still turned away from Val. "The phoenix you rode here? There is no bond without love."

Unless . . . could a bind work on a phoenix, too? Had Val found a solitary firebird and used a bind to make her subservient?

Val snorted at the question. "Conflating love with the bond is the same as saying that iron loves the heat and the hammer that turns it into steel. Without those things, it is lesser, but it does not love them."

No wonder Xephyra chose me over you, Veronyka thought, but didn't say aloud. She was tired of having this same fight over and over again. Instead she applied herself to washing, scrubbing at her skin with savage jerks and dumping half the rinse bucket over her head.

When at last she stood naked and scrubbed raw, Val toweled her off roughly and helped her dress, her touch stiff and impatient. She sighed at the way Veronyka's chest failed to fill out the low-cut design and at the dripping spikes of her cropped hair, falling just past her chin. Val tugged and clawed at the strands, and it took everything in Veronyka to stand there and suffer her ministrations. She just closed her eyes and mirrored with Xephyra, the sight of that nocked arrow a reminder of what was truly at stake.

Finally Val managed to twist a few braids just behind her left ear, leaving the rest of her hair to hang loosely behind. It was by no means elegant, but Veronyka didn't hate it. At least she wore braids and not a veil or a head scarf. It appeared that while Val wanted Veronyka to be appealing to her Stellan fiancé, she also wanted to remind him of who she was—an Ashfire.

Apparently, this concept didn't extend to the braided bracelet Veronyka wore on her wrist. Val lifted Veronyka's arm to stare down at it with a mix of something like pride and disgust on her face. "It's hideous—remove it."

"No," Veronyka said, snatching her hand back. "It's . . . sentimental. Please."

Val rolled her eyes—but she let Veronyka keep it—before making her way over to the window ledge. A square of fabric remained there, and as Veronyka watched, Val unwrapped it like a present, revealing a smooth lacquered box within.

The Pyraean puzzle box.

Veronyka's lips parted. "How did you . . . ?" Then she remembered that Val had drugged her, and she'd been unconscious for several hours. Clearly Val had searched Xephyra's saddlebags.

Val ignored her, opening the box with quick efficiency—no doubt she'd done it dozens of times in her life. She shuffled the documents inside until she found that dreaded piece of paper with the heavy wax seal. She smiled in satisfaction, putting it on the table next to her—but she wasn't done.

Shifting the box slightly and pushing the contents aside, Val slid her hand along the bottom—and a second, hidden compartment sprang open. Veronyka's jaw dropped as Val opened the wooden panel; there, nestled in a worn silk cloth, was a golden necklace.

Veronyka's heart stuttered to a stop. That necklace . . . she'd seen it recently, glimmering in the torchlit cave as it hung around her mother's neck.

"I lost everything else," Val murmured, her voice low, soft, and *almost* tender. "But not this. Ilithya took it before she left the Nest."

Veronyka watched, strangely numb, as Val lifted it from the compartment and put the box back onto the ledge. Veronyka tried to imagine a similar scenario, except in her mind it was her mother offering the jewelry instead. The image wouldn't take, though, and instead she saw herself and Val, but in another life, when they were still sisters—and they still loved each other.

"It's an Ashfire heirloom," Val continued, her tone brisk now as she carried it over to Veronyka. "It originally belonged to one of the Five Brides—Princess Darya—and was a betrothal gift from her Stellan husband. It actually spent most of its life in Stel, passed down to Darya's niece when she failed to have any children of her own." She paused, fastening it around Veronyka's neck before dropping her hands from the clasp and stepping back to consider how it looked. "Pheronia's mother got her hands on it eventually. It's actually of Ferronese make, but famous in Stel for being worn by so many governors' wives. I'm certain he'll recognize it and know at least some of its history."

"You need it to prove who I am," Veronyka said, realizing for the first time what Val might have *actually* been after when she went seeking the lockbox. Not the list of exiled Riders, but the evidence of Veronyka's identity. She'd claimed she'd wanted the box to prove to Veronyka her own heritage, but perhaps she'd had this deal in mind even then.

"Papers lack romance," Val said matter-of-factly, "but this necklace has a storied past, and it says without words that you are connected all the way back to the dawn of the empire. It also shows you are both Pyraean *and* Stellan—even if only a quarter."

"A quarter?" Veronyka repeated, mind suddenly racing. Pheronia was half Stellan, half Pyraean, which meant . . . "My father. He was Pyraean too?"

Val scowled. "How many times do I have to tell you? You are an Ashfire. . . . Nothing else matters. All the rest of this"—she lifted the wooden box, its contents shifting and sliding around—"is worthless."

And then, to prove her point, Val lifted the lantern from the table. Before Veronyka realized what was happening, Val lowered the open flame over the box.

Veronyka cried out in horror, but the contents—old pieces of dusty, dried-out paper—caught fire at once. She had taken a step forward, reaching as if she could stop Val, but there'd been no chance. Instead she froze, watching everything she had from her family disappear before her very eyes. It wasn't as painful as watching Xephyra's lifeless body go up in flames . . . but it was close.

Val hadn't flinched or tried to step back from Veronyka's approach; she just watched the years of Ilithya's work and decades of personal and cultural history burn up, the flames dancing bright and golden over her expressionless face.

When the contents were blackened and smoking, Val lowered the lantern back onto the table and unceremoniously tossed the box into one of the buckets of cold bathwater. It landed with a splash and a gurgle, the water sloshing over the edge. The scent of burned paper and scorched lacquer filled the room.

Veronyka stared at Val. It seemed even the past was not exempt from her callous nature and stone-cold heart.

Before she could say anything, a rumble of horses' hooves echoed up to them. Val stepped toward the balcony, peering down below.

"He's here," she muttered, rushing back inside. She shoved aside the water buckets and kicked Veronyka's clothes to the opposite side of the room. Then, to Veronyka's surprise, Val drew up her hood.

A spark of realization burst to life inside Veronyka's mind.

Rolan didn't know who Val was. He didn't realize that he'd cut a deal with the true heir to the throne and was being offered a weak prize with the spare. Once Val had what she wanted, she'd betray him. Who did he think Val was, then? Some matchmaker? A distant relative, maybe?

Veronyka was struck by the fact that Val rarely did things for no reason. . . . Even burning the contents of that puzzle box had been a form of self-preservation. The items within were too damning, too obviously connected to Avalkyra to be allowed to remain when her identity was still a closely guarded secret. The fact that it wounded Veronyka and taught her a lesson about clinging to the past was just an added bonus.

But Val hadn't burned everything.

Veronyka toyed idly with her bracelet, her hands behind her back. All she had to do to stop this was to reveal Val's true identity.

But with Sidra's bow trained on Xephyra, Veronyka couldn't risk it.

Not yet, anyway.

Veronyka dropped her hands to her sides as Val approached; with a final tug on Veronyka's dress, she swept from the room.

Voices echoed up the stairwell, followed by the clunk of heavy footsteps and the clink and jangle of metal weapons. Veronyka's breaths were shallow, her palms sweaty as she waited.

At last a man stepped into the room. He was tall, almost handsome, with broad shoulders and a surprisingly kind face.

But his eyes . . . There was coldness in them. Calculation. He might have been smiling, his lips turned up at the corners, but Veronyka sensed the cunning in his gaze. Carefully hidden, but still there.

Val was like stinging nettle or thorny rosebush, her sharp edges visible, her threat apparent as soon as you laid eyes on her. But this man . . . he was like winding wisteria or creeping ivy, pleasing to look at but deadly over time, slowly choking the life from everything around them.

"Veronyka Ashfire," Val said, coming to stand next to the man. Veronyka had never heard her full name like that, and those two words were enough to make her already shallow breath even shorter, her head buzzing and faint. "May I introduce Rolan of Stel, governor of Ferro and your newly betrothed."

"Princess," Rolan said, bowing deeply.

Veronyka glanced at Val. She had no idea of the proper etiquette—should she nod, or bow, or curtsy? But Val only lifted her chin and shook her head slightly. Veronyka was an Ashfire; everyone in the world was beneath her. She did nothing but stare.

On each side of the doorway stood two of Rolan's personal guards, while several others could be seen milling around out on the landing.

And one of them was familiar—she'd been face-to-face with him the night before. The moment their eyes met, Veronyka's heavy heart leapt.

Sev.

It was the thing she'd been waiting for, her shining golden chance. Finally she had a plan.

Princess Darya's marriage—the last of the Five Brides—sealed a very precarious union between what was then known as the Commonwealth of Stel and Queen Elysia's Golden Empire. Princess Darya first gained notoriety in Stel by killing Rol, a Stellan king, and so when she became the wife of the newly minted Governor Verlan, many in the province looked upon the match with scorn. Wanting to prove his loyalty to the empire and ingratiate himself with his new king and queen, Governor Verlan commissioned a necklace to present to Darya on their wedding day. He had the necklace made in Ferro, but it was based on a Pyraean design, featuring a variation on the spread-winged sigil of the Ashfire line.

Though by all accounts a decent man, Governor Verlan was ten years Darya's senior, a widower, and had three children from his previous marriage. Theirs was not a love match, and Darya bore no children. Upon her death she gave the famed jewelry to her niece.

From there, the necklace made its rounds in Stel over the years, and eventually back into the direct line of governors. Governor Diana wore the necklace to a meeting of dissident Stellan lords and ladies who wanted the province to separate in the early reign of Queen Malka, in order to subtly remind them of the peace treaty symbolized by the marriage between Verlan and Darya, as well as show where her interests lay—in remaining a part of the empire. She quelled the movement to separate before it began.

Interestingly, the necklace's absence was as significant as its presence. When Governor Ellian's wife did not approve of her son's choice of bride, she refused to gift the necklace to her to wear on her wedding day—as was the custom at the time. She also refused to pass it down to any of her son's children, and it remained locked away until her death. The necklace had now become a symbol of approval and legitimacy within the Stellan ruling line.

By the time Lania of Stel—a beautiful daughter of a once-grand Stellan family that had fallen into poverty and disrepute—got her hands on it, it represented the power of Stel and its importance in the history of the empire. As such, it was an ideal symbol for her daughter, Pheronia, to prove her position and standing not just through her father, but through her Stellan mother as well.

—"Symbols of Power," from *Jewels of the Golden Empire* by Ginevra, High Priestess of Mori, published 172 AE

It is a terrible burden you'll have to carry,
but one I must pass on to you regardless.

- CHAPTER 46 -
SEV

WHEN SEV HAD SNUCK into the tower the previous night, he'd been hoping for a chance to free Riella, and if he was lucky, to either free Veronyka too or to gather enough information for Commander Cassian to help her instead.

What he *hadn't* expected was to find out that Lord Rolan was on his way, poised to marry Veronyka—who was actually Veronyka *Ashfire*, heir to the throne—or to learn that the Phoenix Rider who had imprisoned and handed her over was her sister, Val, the girl who'd threatened to cut Sev's throat months previously. Was Val an Ashfire too, or was the sister thing a lie?

Sev stared, his brain whirling and spinning and tumbling out of control. He realized distantly that he should have put some of this together already—Veronyka had, after all, been raised by Ilithya, Avalkyra Ashfire's spymaster. Was it so far a stretch to believe that Veronyka was an Ashfire kept safe by Ilithya for all those years?

When Lord Rolan first arrived, Sev had shrunk back, not wanting the man to notice his face—though the governor clearly had more important things on his mind. Then he'd simply followed the man up the stairs, pretending he was meant to be there like all the others. With Kade safely away from the tower, Sev could afford to be a bit more reckless.

When he reached the top, he peeked around the wall, heart hammering as he drank in the details. Veronyka stood there, looking stiff in her formal wear and completely different from the last time he'd seen her, mounted on her phoenix and hungry for blood. Her hands were clenched into fists as she faced Lord Rolan, and it couldn't be clearer that she did not want to be here. Sev *knew* that, but it was one thing to know it and another to *see* it.

He had to help her. But how?

The problem was, Sev had to avoid being noticed by Lord Rolan *and* by Val, so he remained lurking in the hallway outside, poking his head in once or twice, but unsure how to proceed.

Just when he decided the best thing he could do was get out of there and get a letter to the commander, he peered through the open doorway one last time. . . .

And locked eyes with Veronyka.

It was a strange thing, but he felt as though her gaze had taken him hostage—as if he were unable to look away, his eyes pulled to hers and held fast like a magnetic current.

Her expression was urgent, almost pleading, and a barrage of confusing sensations and images flickered across his waking vision. He staggered slightly, gripping the wall for support, when at last two clear words distinguished themselves from the deluge, whispered into his mind.

Help me.

Sev didn't understand it, couldn't begin to fathom the how or the why of it, but he knew those words came from Veronyka. Was this some Ashfire trick? It didn't matter.

He nodded. Yes, he would help her. That was why he was here.

Tell me how, he begged inside his mind, but there was no answer.

Something thunked loudly on the rickety table within the room, causing Veronyka's gaze to wrench away with a start. The lawmaker Lord Rolan brought with him had finally entered, dropping his bag onto the wooden surface and unearthing a stack of papers.

Veronyka cast one last frantic look in Sev's direction, and another image surfaced in his mind, clearer than the rush he'd seen before. A dark hole—a cave. And within . . . smoking, burning feathers. A phoenix.

No, *Veronyka's* phoenix.

Sev had forgotten about her. When Veronyka had been taken away, her phoenix had been nowhere in sight.

Now Sev knew what had become of her. She was trapped in a cave with metal bars. There was something else, too, some other instruction or warning, but he was unable to grasp it.

Before he could formulate a question in his mind or figure out what to do next, the image vanished, and Veronyka's attention returned with a snap to Lord Rolan and her sister. Sev watched her swallow, pulse jumping in her throat, while Val said her name impatiently—as if this weren't the first time she'd tried.

A warning bell sounded in his mind a second before Val's cloaked head began to turn. Sev darted back from the doorway and disappeared down the stairs, past the other soldiers.

He slowed his steps and schooled his features into an expression of boredom. When one of the soldiers looked his way, as if expecting news or orders, Sev shrugged and mimed a talking mouth with his hand, rolling his eyes.

The soldier snorted.

Sev wandered to the edge of their perimeter, but as a soldier himself, no one paid him any mind. Then, when the nearest guards bent their heads together in discussion, he ducked behind a corner of the crumbling wall and slipped away.

He came up on Kade from behind, finding him crouched in the same place they'd both been hiding the previous night.

Kade whipped around, the tense look on his features relaxing at once. "Sev. What's happening? What—"

"Come on," Sev said, nodding his head away from the tower. "We've got a phoenix to free."

Sev caught Kade up on all he'd seen and heard as they picked their way over the rocky ground.

He tried to keep the vision Veronyka had shown him—and how, exactly, had she done that?—in his mind, but the details were hazy. One thing was for certain: her phoenix had been locked up somewhere near the place Veronyka had been captured, at the edge of the battleground. Sev wasn't eager to go back, but if they hurried, they could make it there in under an hour.

At least he understood now why she wasn't fighting her imprisonment, despite her obvious desire to. They had her bondmate.

When Sev saw how stiffly Kade was moving, he tried half-heartedly to convince Kade to remain behind—but he wouldn't hear of it, especially when Sev relayed the fact of Veronyka's identity. They were in the middle of something big here, and Kade insisted Sev needed someone to watch his back. Sev couldn't deny that he was probably right. He was out of his element again, not quite a spy and not quite a hero, either. He felt a stab of guilt for not rescuing Riella but tried to focus on the task ahead. Freeing Veronyka's phoenix was the first step—he'd worry about everything else afterward.

It wasn't long before the rough earth beneath their feet gave way to slabs of stone and steep inclines, requiring more climbing than walking. Kade labored, sweat pouring down his face, while Sev kept his eyes cast wide, trying to find the easiest paths, as well as seeking shadowy entryways or clefts in stone. They were probably in Pyra now, the actual borderline happening somewhere within the rising, undulating Foothills that stretched for miles north, south, and west.

As Sev climbed, he tried to recall the last thing Veronyka had been trying to say to him. It had been some kind of warning that had been interrupted by her sister.

Sev soon got his answer.

They crested a rise and spotted a dark hole in the side of a series of low, rocky hills. A cave, striped with bars that gleamed golden in the early afternoon sun. Something was inside, something that tickled the edges of Sev's animal magic and caused Kade to halt and tilt his head. Then there was a flash of brilliant red, caught in a beam of rich, orange sunlight.

A phoenix.

Before Sev could take another step, an archer came into view, standing atop the cave mouth.

There was a swift draw, a shuddering twang, and an arrow flew straight for them.

Will the greatness of our ancient ancestors
cast a shadow upon you, as it does Avalkyra?
Or will the past teach you, ground you,
and light the way forward?

- CHAPTER 47 -
VERONYKA

IT HAD BEEN RISKY reaching out to Sev with shadow magic *right* in front of Val, but Veronyka had been desperate. Things were escalating alarmingly fast, and Veronyka needed to act before it was too late. If she could only get Xephyra out of that cursed cell and away from Sidra, she could focus on herself and her own predicament.

Luckily, as Veronyka's eyes had locked with Sev's—recognition and relief lighting a fire in her chest—Lord Rolan had been prattling on about binding contracts and legal signatures and Val had been distracted by her obvious anger and annoyance.

Veronyka had done the best she could, showing Sev Xephyra's cell and pleading for his help. It was unsettling to realize that her weeks of effort to block and disable her shadow magic in order to keep herself and Tristan safe might be her very undoing. While she'd seen flashes of the magic's possibilities before, she hadn't considered it on a wider scale: long-distance communication and relaying messages or asking for help without ever having to say a word. The truth was, Veronyka had barely skimmed the surface of shadow magic's potential, and she was beginning to realize that she had been desperately wrong to attempt to block it out, just as Morra had told her. Veronyka knew now that it hadn't been as much about her identity and her magic as it had been about fear—fear of her own power. First as a shadowmage, but in more recent weeks, as an Ashfire as well.

Veronyka could afford fear no longer.

She hoped that it wasn't too late and that her mistakes wouldn't mean the undoing of them all.

Though her communication skills were clumsy, Sev had seemed to understand well enough, his mind ready and willing—if a bit unsettled by the sudden intrusion. He had hurried away as quickly as Veronyka could dare hope, and though she'd tried to warn him about Sidra, their connection had been cut short when she realized Val was speaking to her. Sev had made his escape just in time, and now all Veronyka could do was monitor her bond with Xephyra and wait.

So far she'd been able to glean very little—only that Sidra had abandoned her position in front of the cell bars, but that could mean anything. A break to relieve herself, a sweep of the area, or a comfortable seat.

Veronyka didn't allow herself to be hopeful, or to assume. She needed to know beyond a doubt that Xephyra was safe before she risked anything.

It was impossible not to be anxious and jittery, her stomach in knots and her fingers shaking. Focusing on her bondmate was hard enough, but in some ways it was better than dealing with what was happening directly in front of her.

First Val had shown Rolan the birth certificate—a condition of their contract—which was authenticated by a man who had accompanied him. A lawmaker and notary. Apparently, marriage to Veronyka had been a part of their alliance from the get-go, though she wondered what would have happened if she'd agreed to stay by Val's side and willingly fight with her. It was clear either way that Val had no intention of truly honoring their contract, though how far she expected Veronyka to go was another matter entirely.

Once Veronyka's identity had been confirmed, a written contract had been produced. Pages of ink-darkened paper were sprawled across the table's surface, spelling out every dark detail of Val and Rolan's alliance, including

Veronyka's role as the prize to be won, the ticket to Rolan's elevation to kinghood.

There were a few mildly entertaining moments when Rolan confronted Val about the attack on his own men. "Bloody massacre" were his exact words, though it was chilling to see the way he reacted—as a commander, angry to have lost hundreds of valuable troops, and not a human being who'd lost hundreds of people.

Val had let his heated words wash over her, unmoved, before replying simply, "You told me to do whatever it took to get her here—that was what it took."

Veronyka doubted Rolan would keep his position or his head when all this was through. A part of her was glad for Val's callousness, but at the same time, Veronyka knew she'd suffer for it too. If Rolan proved difficult to quell or more intelligent than Val assumed, she might very well hand Veronyka over and force her to wed and bed the man to achieve her goals, even if she never allowed them to be crowned. Veronyka was technically underage and too young to marry, but when an entire empire was at stake, rules could be broken and laws rewritten. There might even be a clause about it in the stacks of papers the two bickered and bargained over.

The notary did scratch some portions out, amending statements or adding new ones.

They ignored Veronyka completely, as if she weren't even there or was unable to understand the proceedings. It never occurred to them that she might want to weigh in on her own future; instead they treated her like a prized horse brought to market.

Still, she did her best to get in the way, leaning over Val's back to read and interjecting with inane questions—anything to buy Sev more time.

"What's a betrothal agreement?" she asked, catching one of the headings. Or, more harrowingly, "What's a consummation clause?"

When that failed, she started pointing out things she knew would irritate Val. Veronyka's title wasn't technically accurate on the documents—they'd called her "princess," not the *crown* princess—which was sure to annoy Val, who was an elitist and a stickler for proper royal naming conventions. Veronyka also noted that Val was listed in the contract as Veronyka's "foster sister"—which wasn't entirely off base—as well as her guardian. Apparently that was all it took to give her complete authority over Veronyka's future.

When looking at the contract started to make Veronyka's stomach roil, she sought other ways to kill time. She asked to use the chamber pot, which was both crass and difficult in her outfit—Val flatly refused—and when Veronyka was finally handed a quill and told where to sign, in a fit of desperation she "accidentally" upended the ink pot all over the pages.

Veronyka thought Val might slap her again. She expected Val would have, whether it compromised her false identity or not, if the notary hadn't promptly produced a second copy.

He was just adding the previous amendments when Veronyka blurted, "Why do we even need this?" All three turned to stare at her, and so she added, "I'm already here, aren't I?"

While Val stared daggers at her, Rolan straightened, a considering look on his face. He had the air of someone who was self-assured, confident—*arrogant*—and did not like to be questioned in any way.

And there was something in his eyes that unsettled her. Veronyka realized then that it wasn't the *look* of them—they were ordinary enough, dark green and wrinkled slightly at the corners—but rather, the state of mind she sensed when she looked *into* them. It wasn't shadow magic, she didn't think, but just natural human instinct. As soon as their eyes met, she sensed the resentment there, the deep-rooted anger.

He *hated* her. It was so clear now, as evident to Veronyka as if he'd shouted the words at her.

A chill ran down her spine.

"Why do we need a legally binding document spelling out our betrothal agreement and the resulting political alliances inherent therein?" Rolan's voice was calm, steady, but tension had begun to gather in the line of his shoulders and the firm set of his mouth. "We need it because of your mother, that's why."

Veronyka frowned at that. What did her mother have to do with it?

"I see no one's told you," he said, casting a look over his shoulder at Val, whose arms were crossed, her face unapologetic. When Rolan turned to Veronyka again, there was no warmth left in him, the cold hatred in his eyes expanding, encompassing his entire being. "Pheronia Ashfire was supposed to be my wife."

Silence followed his proclamation. Veronyka was stunned; she couldn't believe she'd never heard Val or her *maiora* mention the fact that Pheronia had been betrothed. Meanwhile, she'd gotten pregnant with Veronyka by someone else.

Rolan seemed pleased by her apparent surprise. He nodded and began a slow circuit of the room. When he turned away from her, the corners of Veronyka's mouth quirked. Val gave her a severe look, but Veronyka couldn't help it. Everyone had called her mother the Council's Queen, the voiceless, powerless pawn of her advisers . . . and yet Alexiya had said she had a streak of defiance in her and did what she wanted. She'd traveled into the wilds of Pyra with a handful of guards to confront her dangerous, volatile sister, all while pregnant, making a life for herself with the man she chose—not the man she'd been told to marry.

Pheronia Ashfire was no one's puppet.

She'd refused to marry this man, and so would Veronyka.

"It's poetic, isn't it?" Rolan said, pausing to peer out the far window. "You even look like her." He tossed an appraising look in her direction before returning his attention to the window. "And judging by the marks on your face and hands, you are equally stubborn and disobedient. Do not make the same mistakes as your mother did, Veronyka. Trust in your betters to make the right decision."

"If she didn't make those 'mistakes,' as you call them," Veronyka said, lifting her chin, "I wouldn't be here."

"None of us would be!" he spat, the first ripple in his composure. "I'd be on a *throne*, not meeting in some disgusting hovel trying to secure the empire and my future, neither of which would *be* in peril if it were not for your spoiled, selfish mother. For too long my family has suffered insult and disrespect. We were kings once, just the same as that pathetic excuse for a governor, Cassian. And still he spurned my sister—a match above and beyond what he deserved—to run off with some half-wild beast-talker. Then this godsforsaken war took our father from us, so it was up to me to set things right. The weak, bumbling council gave me his position in Ferro, trying to appease me after I lost my chance at Pheronia, but it was not enough. The descendants of King Rol will be kings again, starting with me."

He pointed a finger at himself, chest heaving while Veronyka marveled at the decades of brewing resentment. *This* was why he hated her. She represented the betrayal perpetrated by her mother, which was apparently one in a long series of perceived slights against not only himself, but his sister and his entire family for their lack of title and position since King Rol's death.

"They were clever to hide you," Rolan said, his features schooled into calm imperiousness again. "A helpless babe with a bloodline such as yours? I could've claimed you as my own, called you *my* daughter and ruled in your stead." He adjusted his tunic. "Or perhaps I would have married you just the same. Better a true king than a king-father."

Veronyka realized with mild shock that his words were true. That no matter how much she resented Ilithya for stealing her from her own father, for hiding her away and keeping her safe only to use her as a tool in a decades-old war, Veronyka had been safer with Ilithya and Val than she would have been with someone like Rolan. Ilithya's motives might have been flawed, but she'd told Veronyka to call her *maiora*, had taught her and cared for her, even loved her—Veronyka was certain of it. By keeping her in the dark about her identity, Ilithya—and even Val—had allowed her some semblance of a normal childhood. From what Rolan had just said, that was more than she ever would have gotten from him.

"King Consort," Veronyka said tightly. "Whether you marry me or not, you will never be a true king."

He took a step closer to her, their face bare inches apart. He was taller than her, but she refused to tilt her head up to look at him. "We'll see about that," he whispered.

Veronyka sensed Val out of the corner of her eye and could've sworn she saw something like furious pride in her features. Whatever her feelings toward Veronyka at the moment, there was nothing she loved so much as seeing upstart valley kings put in their place.

"My lord," came a voice from the doorway, and Rolan turned. "Riders have been spotted due north."

"What *kind* of riders?" Rolan asked, stepping away from Veronyka. "Horse riders?"

The terrified look in the man's eyes said it all. "Phoenix Riders."

But being an Ashfire . . . being a queen . . .
is about more than what flows in your veins.
It's about what beats in your heart.

- CHAPTER 48 -
SEV

THE ARROW HURTLED STRAIGHT for them.

Sev already had his hand on Kade's arm, and with the half second he had to react, he pushed, the momentum forcing them both in opposite directions.

Sev stumbled backward and fell, hitting the ground hard and jostling his shoulder in a painful reminder of his last encounter with an arrow.

Despite the pain, he had thoughts only for Kade, and as he looked wildly around, the loud ricochet of the arrowhead on stone sent a wave of relief reverberating through him. The shot had landed somewhere in the distance; meanwhile, Kade must have taken shelter behind one of the spiky bushes or rocky outcrops that surrounded the area. He was safely out of sight.

Assured that Kade hadn't been hit, Sev scrambled to find cover, realizing that he was the only visible target now.

Another arrow zipped through the air, slicing past a cluster of shrubbery to Sev's left and sending him flat to the ground. He gasped, sucking in gulps of dusty air, trying to think. This, surely, was the other thing Veronyka had been warning him about. The phoenix was being guarded—probably by the other Rider that had been with Val.

Sev shifted closer to the cover of the dense foliage, then remained perfectly still, thoughts racing. Even if he'd known there was a guard, he didn't have a shield to protect himself or a bow of his own to make a counterattack. Sneaking up on the Rider would have been his best option, considering his rather limited skill set, but he hadn't known exactly where the cave was. How can you sneak up on something or someone you don't know where to find? If he and Kade had spotted the Phoenix Rider first, they could have better planned their attack. Now Kade was nowhere to be seen and Sev was ducking for dear life. How exactly was he supposed to free Veronyka's phoenix?

Lifting his head to peer through the leafy branches, Sev watched as the woman leapt from the top of the cave, her boots crunching on the rocky slope. Behind her, another phoenix—her bondmate, no doubt—took up her Rider's abandoned post defending the front of the cell. Now even if Sev did manage to draw the Rider off, Veronyka's phoenix would still be guarded.

The Rider's gaze scanned the area, and Sev suspected his stillness made her believe one of her arrows had struck home. As a Phoenix Rider she would be sharp-eyed and accurate—an ideal combination in an archer and an *un*ideal combination in a person trying to kill him.

Sev was tempted to run, but he knew that no matter how fast he went or how much he zigzagged, she'd be able to shoot him down with her long-range weapon with ease. That thought made him pause. How best to disable a long-range shooter? Get close range.

He considered. Even with her phoenix behind her, he doubted she'd venture far from the cave mouth or allow herself to be lured away. She only strayed a bit now because she wanted to find his body, to confirm her kill.

As silently as he could, Sev shifted to put his palms and toes against the ground, while remaining flat on his stomach. Slowly, he tightened his muscles, ready to spring. His shoulder protested in taking his weight, but he pushed the pain aside. As she drew nearer, the scrape of her boots muffling his movements, Sev slid one of his feet up and underneath his body.

She drew level with him, her gaze in the opposite direction. As soon as she turned his way, she'd see him. It was now or never.

Sev coiled all his strength and leapt. She heard him spring up, whipping her bow around, but he was already within the span of her arms. Her eyes bugged out just before Sev's body collided with hers, taking them both off their feet and down hard into the dust. Sev's shoulder screamed at the impact, and the breath whooshed from her lungs in a grunt. Somewhere behind them the phoenix squawked but didn't leave her post.

Keeping her pinned, Sev pushed himself to his knees, wrenching the bow—which would work just as well as a club or garrote wire—from her grip and tossing it aside. She shifted beneath him, hands scrambling next for the fallen arrow and its sharpened tip, but Sev snatched her wrist, halting her reach.

Her other hand clenched into a fist and collided with Sev's temple, the pain sharp and lancing through his skull. Stars burst in front of his eyes, and he swayed, loosening his hold. She took advantage of his unsteadiness, bucking underneath him and rolling to the side.

She reached into her belt, withdrawing a dagger, and Sev lurched away from her sudden, vicious swipe. As he scrambled backward, his hand landed on her abandoned bow. He swung it around as hard as he could, knocking the knife from her grasp.

Sev's head was still fuzzy from the punch, but he tried to clear his thoughts, to *think*. There was no way he could defeat a skilled warrior nearly twice his age. He had to find a way to trick her, to trap or confuse her. There had to be something. . . .

Behind them, Veronyka's phoenix let out a fierce screech, claws scraping and beak snapping at the bars. The other phoenix released a shriek in response, and her Rider stared, a frown on her face, before her head lifted toward the sky.

Sev followed her gaze, his heart jumping wildly.

Five phoenixes were streaking through the sky, their fiery feathers catching the last summer sunlight, glinting orange and gold with flashes of vivid purple. They flew high above Sev's small scuffle and toward the tower looming to the south, partially obscured by trees.

Sev wasn't sure, but he thought he caught Commander Cassian's austere profile among them. Relief flooded his body—he was not alone.

Speaking of not alone, the Phoenix Rider who stood before him recovered from the distraction sooner than Sev. When he lowered his gaze from the sky, it was to find that she had retrieved her knife, and currently had it pointed at Sev's throat.

He raised his hands, realizing belatedly that he must have dropped her bow . . . and it had been picked up by Kade. Out of nowhere he appeared, looming behind her. Before she could react, he lowered the bow over her throat, pulling tight and causing the taut string to press against her windpipe.

"Drop it," Kade ordered. Her face was growing red, her veins bulging as she struggled, and with a last, murderous look, she threw the blade into the dirt.

Kade lifted the bow and shoved her forward. Sev didn't know why Kade had relinquished his hold, but it didn't matter.

She gasped and staggered away, only to put two fingers into her mouth and whistle.

Her phoenix leapt forward at once, finally abandoning her position in front of the cave that held Veronyka's bondmate.

The phoenix darted toward them, and before Sev could do more than gape, the Rider had timed a perfect leap onto her back. Together they soared up into the sky and made straight for the tower.

"Let's go," Kade said, tugging Sev's arm and making for the barred cave. Sev shook the last dregs of dizziness from his head and followed.

He was anxious at being so close to a phoenix—particularly an angry, caged one—and was glad to have Kade's animage abilities close at hand.

Inside, sparks and fire danced. The bars were actually warm to the touch, and Sev cowered from the angry firebird. Kade tried to withstand the heat, but he too was backing away before long.

"Please," Sev called out, after reaching for the bars again, only to have a burst of heat and flame force him to stagger back. "I'm a friend. We're here to free you." The phoenix stopped flapping her wings and tilted her head. Sev took this as a good sign and hastened to continue. "We met before," he added, wondering if there was any chance the phoenix would remember. "Outside your cabin, on Pyrmont. Soldiers were there, and we helped you and Veronyka hide in the bushes."

After a half-hearted head toss—more out of confusion than anger, Sev guessed—the phoenix backed into the dark corner of the cave, leaving them in peace.

Sev released a breath, his fear and residual adrenaline from the fight ebbing away.

The lock was large and heavy but featured a simple mechanism that he'd be able to pick. He dug into his pocket for the buckle prongs and got to work.

Time ticked by agonizingly slowly, and though it felt like hours, it was minutes later when the lock clicked and Sev unhooked it from the latch. The bars were heavy, and Kade helped to lift them, despite how Sev protested. They had barely gone up halfway when the phoenix burst forward from the cave's dark depths, soaring into the sky and following the path the other Riders had taken toward the tower.

Sev tossed aside the lock and pocketed his makeshift picks. After he and Kade shared a tired look, they followed.

Hold fast to your heart, my daughter.
Blood can lead you astray, but your
heart will always beat true.

- CHAPTER 49 -
VERONYKA

PHOENIX RIDERS.

Veronyka's heart sparked at the words, her entire body catching fire, excitement searing in her veins. They were *here*. Somehow, someway, they had come.

Val darted a furious glare in Veronyka's direction, fingers of shadow magic prying at her mind, questing for understanding. But Veronyka hadn't done this.

Her rage shifting into confusion, Val turned away, taking her magic with her.

Veronyka prepared to check in with her bondmate to see if she'd been freed when realization hit. *Xephyra*. If Veronyka and Tristan were bonded, then surely Xephyra and Rex were as well. Had her *bondmate* managed to call for help when Veronyka could not?

More urgently now, Veronyka connected with Xephyra—and a thrill shot through her.

Sev. She could see him outside Xephyra's cage. Where was Sidra? It didn't matter. She must have left, or Sev must have taken care of her.

Limbs tingling, Veronyka watched through Xephyra's eyes as Sev rattled the lock and peered in through the keyhole. That other animage was with him, a bondservant, and again Veronyka was struck by a familiarity she couldn't place.

Sev's expression was determined as he produced several long, thin pieces of metal from his pocket. Lockpicks.

". . . Five by our count, but there could be more coming," one of Rolan's soldiers was saying, drawing Veronyka back to her surroundings. They had thrown open the balcony doors, and several soldiers were standing outside, pointing to the north.

Rolan's expression was thoughtful. He turned to Val and Veronyka. "Luck, it seems, is on our side."

"Luck?" Val repeated incredulously. "They know we're here, and you've got barely thirty soldiers to protect us. These are *Phoenix Riders*. We must leave at once."

"Why on earth would we leave," Rolan began with an arrogant drawl, "when they are about to assure our victory?"

"I thought you assured our victory when you called for the Grand Council meeting. What has all this pointless fighting been for if not to guarantee their votes in our favor?"

"As you might imagine, allies who've been threatened, bribed, and otherwise purchased do not always make the most loyal friends. There's no telling who might offer a higher price or a more dire threat. I'd rather not take any chances. If we engage them, if an entire flock is seen *here*, on empire soil, battling and burning . . . There will be dozens of witnesses. I will no longer need to waste time, soldiers, or gold to ensure we get the desired verdict. They will prove themselves guilty."

"Why do you think they're here in the first place? To do *you* a favor? This is no accident or coincidence. They've come for her," Val said, pointing a finger at Veronyka. "They know who she is, and they know we have her. They could tell the council and ruin everything."

"If they know we have her, it's more important than ever to discredit them. The council will be forced to act. The Phoenix Riders won't have time to make claims or argue their case—war will be upon them."

"I'm telling you, they won't leave here without her. They'll capture us all. They'll—"

Potent relief exploded in Veronyka's chest, and she knew that Xephyra was free, that she was coming for Veronyka.

"She's not worried about me or your stupid plan," Veronyka interrupted, determination flaring to life within her. "She's worried about herself."

Both Rolan and Val stared at her, as if just realizing she was a human person capable of speech and not an inanimate object to be argued over and bartered for.

While Rolan's features were scrunched in confusion, Val's face had gone stiff with shock and rage. There was a flicker in her eyes, and Veronyka knew she'd realized what Veronyka herself just had—Sidra was gone, which meant Xephyra was safe and Veronyka was free. Did Rolan know Veronyka had a phoenix? He was about to find out.

That's right, Val, Veronyka thought through their bond. Val's mind was closed to her, as usual, but Veronyka forced her words through the barrier, finding newly made cracks of self-doubt. *I'm coming for you.*

"What do you mean?" Rolan pressed, glancing between them. "Explain yourselves."

"Don't listen to her—she's deceptive, like her mother," Val said hastily.

Veronyka smiled, ignoring her. "You should make a habit of knowing who you're in business with, Rolan. This isn't just my foster sister. This is Avalkyra Ashfire, the Feather-Crowned Queen. Or at least, she used to be."

Rolan gaped, as if he sincerely couldn't believe his ears. "Preposterous," he said, waving away her words. "Avalkyra Ashfire died during the Last Battle, along with your mother. And even if she didn't . . . this girl can't be older than twenty, and Avalkyra would be in her thirties by now."

"Thirty-five, to be exact," Veronyka said.

"The Riders are coming. We don't have time for this," Val burst in angrily, but Rolan was still staring at Veronyka. Whether he believed her or not, she had his attention, and that was all she needed.

"I never said Avalkyra Ashfire didn't die. She did—spectacularly,"

Veronyka added, and Val's nostrils flared, her lips pulling back from her teeth in a silent snarl. "But she came back. Resurrection. Surely you've heard the stories, phoenixes going down in flame only to rise again, more powerful and terrible than before. Well, animages are just as magical as phoenixes. Think about it. . . . Why would she go through all this trouble to give *you* a throne and an empire?"

Rolan looked at Val, a heavy frown lowering his brow. "She's been promised wealth and position. That's plenty for a nameless Pyraean girl."

"Oh, but she's not nameless. Val. A*val*kyra. You never met her, did you? You met Pheronia, of course, but you never met her Phoenix Rider sister. But do you know who has?" Veronyka asked, taking a slow step toward him. She was speaking calmly, cajolingly, allowing Rolan's mind to catch up with her words. "Commander Cassian, who's on his way right this second. He can confirm her true identity, and so obviously she wants us to flee."

Rolan swallowed thickly, eyes wide and blinking. With a quick gesture, he waved several guards in from the landing. Two flanked Val, while the others remained on either side of the door, blocking any chance of escape. They didn't touch her, but their presence was threatening enough.

"This belongs to her as well," Veronyka said, and before Val could say anything, Veronyka held out her wrist, twisting the golden band of the signet ring until Avalkyra Ashfire's seal with its spread wings was clearly visible.

Rolan snatched Veronyka's wrist, staring down at it, before roughly releasing her.

"I must admit she has the Ashfire look . . . ," Rolan muttered, his voice low and slightly feverish. "But why *hide* it when—" He froze, looking up at Val. "You want to crown yourself. You want to use *my* army and *my* resources, and then, rather than put your niece on the throne, you would put yourself. Why bring her into this at all when you and I could forge a more powerful alliance?"

Rolan's words mirrored exactly what Veronyka had asked Val the night before. Val's eyes sparked dangerously, but she was quick to mask the reaction.

"As if Avalkyra Ashfire would ever stoop so low," she scoffed, still not admitting her true identity, though those words seemed confirmation enough to Veronyka.

"My lord, they're here," another soldier announced. He'd been perched on the balcony keeping a lookout and now rushed in through the door, moving to stand between Rolan and the open air.

A great sweeping wing became visible, followed by a gust of warm wind. Then two massive clawed feet gripped the banister and a leather-clad Rider slipped from the great bird's back.

Commander Cassian, just as Veronyka had hoped.

There was another gust of wind as Maximian took flight, and then several more phoenixes made their perch and unloaded their burdens, the view of blue sky obscured by red feathers. Nearer at hand, Veronyka could hear the creak of crossbow strings and the metallic scrape of steel withdrawn from scabbard, but Rolan held up a hand, telling his soldiers not to attack.

The commander was now joined by Beryk, Fallon—*Alexiya*—and Tristan, whose gaze was restless, searching . . .

Looking for her.

Veronyka took an unconscious step forward, but Rolan's soldiers were in a tight ring around them now, blocking Veronyka, Val, and the governor himself from sight of the balcony. Rolan cast a considering look at both of them before nodding.

"We'll discover the truth now, once and for all." He nodded at his guards, and they led the way outside.

"You're going to walk out there with this paltry escort?" Val demanded, her voice slightly shrill. Veronyka could sense the panic in her, the way her mind—and her eyes—darted around, seeking a way out of this mess.

"No, *we* are going to walk out there," Rolan corrected. "You will come with me onto the balcony, or the deal is off."

In the wake of the Last Battle and the end of the Blood War, the Council of Governors scrambled to get the empire back under control.

But while many of the land's leaders and politicians worked hard to bring order and prosperity back to their people, many others sought opportunity for personal gain. Without a queen on the throne, motions had to be passed by a vote—but any orders or decrees issued *before* the war were given higher priority. If they came stamped with the seal of one of the Ashfire queens, even more so. It was too soon to tell if the royal line was truly broken or if any of the distant Ashfire cousins—real or imagined—wanted to make a claim to the throne. Tales of long-lost Ashfires and secret weddings abounded, and no object proved more valuable—or more difficult to find—than an Ashfire signet ring.

Even edicts stamped by Avalkyra—the rebellious traitor queen—held weight according to the lawmakers and notaries who still held their positions on the council.

While a ring with the spread-winged symbol of Avalkyra Ashfire did appear in the aftermath, only to be quickly debunked as a fake, the seal of Pheronia Ashfire was never seen again.

—"The Lost Ashfire Rings," from *Jewels of the Golden Empire* by Ginevra, High Priestess of Mori, published 172 AE

My heart tells me that where I am weak,
you will be strong. Where I have failed,
you will succeed.

- CHAPTER 50 -

AVALKYRA

THE THREE OF THEM stepped out onto the balcony; Rolan's guards surrounded them on all sides, while Veronyka, their prize, was sandwiched between them.

Before them stood Commander Cassian, leader of Pyra's ragtag Phoenix Rider forces.

Avalkyra steadied her breathing.

It had been harder than she'd expected to walk into the Eyrie all those weeks ago. The place reminded her of her own time in Phoenix Rider training, and it had been strange to see Cassian grown old, wearing the mantle of commander, when Avalkyra had known him back when his father was governor. He had been several years her senior, and she'd watched him train as a Rider, take his position in Ferro, and court her childhood friend, Olanna Flamesong. His cautious politician's nature tempered Olanna's natural fire, softening it—softening *her*—and Avalkyra had hated to see them together.

But all three of their lives had long been intertwined, and both Olanna and Cassian had been on her Rider Council. In her memories, he was still as young as her. He was . . . well, he looked like his son did now. It was what Avalkyra had thought when she'd first seen that brown-haired, brown-eyed boy. Even the touch of Olanna's blood couldn't change all the ways he favored his father.

And his son was with him now. He'd do anything for Veronyka, which Avalkyra supposed was an admirable asset. There were two other male Riders, unfamiliar to her, and then a woman. She was tall, her black hair long and braided.

Alexiya, Rider of Ximn.

In truth, Avalkyra barely knew the girl and hadn't seen her since the war. Of course she was no *girl* now, but a woman grown, and older than Avalkyra by seventeen years.

But *then*, she'd been young and brazen, and she'd looked just like *him*.

If Commander Cassian was guilty of stealing Olanna away, what Alexiya's family had done to Avalkyra's was much worse.

Avalkyra swallowed; she remained cloaked and hooded, her entire body still—but her mind raced. She could avoid these reunions no longer.

She hadn't been able to face Cassian when she'd been at the Eyrie, alone and friendless among Riders with whom she did not, *could* not, belong. Alexiya, on the other hand, was a reminder of the past that Avalkyra would rather forget.

But it seemed that her grace period—her years of hiding in the shadows—was over at long last.

Avalkyra straightened her spine.

The time for bargains and treaties was gone.

Now it was time for steel.

"To what do I owe this most unexpected pleasure?" Rolan asked the Phoenix Riders, smiling jovially, arms spread wide as though in welcome.

The commander took him in with narrowed eyes. "I didn't think you'd be so . . . pleased to see me," he said, his tone equally light, though lacking in the upbeat, almost friendly attitude of Rolan.

"Why shouldn't I be?" Rolan asked, his mouth still quirked up at the corners, as if they were sharing the same joke. He leaned in conspiratorially. "I've been trying to draw you out for weeks now, Cassian. It's a good thing you've finally come—there are almost no Pyraean settlements left."

Veronyka stiffened, and Avalkyra sent an elbow into her side. The girl had to stop exposing every thought and feeling for the world to see. Without their bond, without shadow magic—even without *eyes*, Avalkyra was certain she would have known Veronyka's impotent anger in that moment.

Cassian, for all his faults, was a master of his expression and demeanor. Avalkyra had tried to use shadow magic against him in her youth, but he wasn't worth the effort. Secretive and strong-minded by nature, he was the exact opposite of his son, who was an open book. The only sign Cassian was angry at all was a slight tightening around the corners of his eyes, highlighting the crow's-feet that marked all the years that now separated Avalkyra from her past, from her once-contemporaries.

"Congratulations. You have drawn us out—though I would check that triumphant tone, Rolan. I flew over quite an impressive battlefield on my way here . . . and with no Pyraean settlements in sight."

Rolan's smile evaporated. Cassian was referring to the short work Avalkyra and Veronyka had made of his soldiers. Despite Avalkyra's pride in the destruction they'd wrought, it was hard not to be regretful. Would she and Veronyka never fly together again?

"Rest easy. We are not here for a fight."

"Oh no?" Rolan asked, eyeing the weapons strapped across the arms and chests of Cassian's Riders.

"No. We are here for the girl. There has been no bloodshed here yet, and there need not be."

"Surely you've figured out by now that bloodshed is precisely what I want: Phoenix Riders with blood on their hands—empire blood."

"Be careful what you wish for—it might be your blood that is spilled today. You will have a difficult time pleading your case to the council if you don't make it out of this encounter alive."

Avalkyra tilted her head at Cassian, studying him. Perhaps the years apart had hardened the man, made him capable of more strength than she'd have thought.

Rolan's face was a thundercloud. "You dare to threaten me, *here*, after you've trespassed on Ferronese land? You are a foreign army, and my soldiers stand here in defense of the empire. This is my province now, and while your position was small recompense for what you did to my family, your life would be a more worthy payment."

Tristan's head jerked around to look at his father in surprise, and Avalkyra couldn't help the smirk that crossed her lips. How little these younglings knew about the past and the world their parents had built—the lies and betrayals that served as its foundation.

"As I recall," Cassian began, "your sister never complained. She and I were not a good match."

"My sister is a fool and a simpleton," Rolan said with disdain. "I don't care if she prefers not to wed, living in seclusion away from the court and the nobility—it was not for her to decide. Our elders make decisions, form alliances . . . and it is up to the next generation to see those commitments through. Why, the empire wouldn't be here at all if it weren't for the Five Brides. If everyone flouted their duties and shirked their responsibilities as you did, society itself would crumble."

Though he didn't respond, Cassian wore a look of chagrin. Avalkyra wondered if it was for show, meant to placate Rolan and his tirade.

"But the universe has a way of rectifying such slights," Rolan said, straightening and casting a possessive look at Veronyka. "Anyanke's hand, as they say."

Cassian snorted. "I don't know about Anyanke's hand, Rolan, but you've just shown yours. You covet the throne."

"The throne is mine by rights. The girl is simply fulfilling her mother's broken promise and giving me my long-overdue Ashfire bride."

Tristan's eyes practically bugged out from his head. The fool hadn't yet figured it out, but from the look on his father's face, it was clear that the commander had.

"When the council hears about this, they will come for you," Cassian said with obvious distaste, "and believe me when I say, they do not punish treason lightly."

"You would know all about that, wouldn't you? Don't fret—I'll protect *my* wife, unlike you. And the council won't hear about this because you're the one who won't be leaving here alive."

Cassian took a step forward. He was taller than Rolan and broader of shoulder. The move was one of intimidation, and it worked. "Yes I will. Without my Riders, you have no villains to pit the empire against, no opposition for this war you so brazenly push for. You *need* us."

Avalkyra stared hard at Rolan—he hadn't foreseen this. He'd welcomed the idea of a fight with the Riders, not realizing that it was a fight he couldn't win. He did need them, if his plans to take the capital were to come to fruition. He had to get the Riders out of here while keeping Veronyka, but Avalkyra wasn't sure he could pull it off.

Whatever happened, she could not let Veronyka slip through her fingers again. Avalkyra stretched her awareness wide, seeking the binds she had in place, the only allies she could trust.

"Now," Cassian continued, "if you release her, I may forget what I know about your designs on the throne, and we can let the Grand Council decide how to proceed."

"You are outnumbered here, Cassian. I will dictate the terms," Rolan spat.

Avalkyra had had enough. "She is not yours to barter with," she cut in, looking between both Rolan and Cassian.

A stillness descended on the balcony, and Rolan stared at her with dark intensity, waiting to see if her identity was about to be proven.

Avalkyra had been standing next to Veronyka, partially concealed behind the surrounding soldiers, but now she stepped forward, jerking her arm out of a nearby soldier's reach.

She felt Veronyka's eyes on her—surprised, maybe, that Avalkyra would willingly show herself when the foolish men were doing such a good job of ignoring her presence.

But Avalkyra was done standing by, silent, as Cassian stole Veronyka's loyalty and Rolan ruined Avalkyra's carefully articulated plans.

She paused, bracing herself, then slowly lowered her hood.

Her mess of deep-red hair slid forward, practically glowing in the afternoon sun, while her braids glinted and sparked like a phoenix aflame.

"So it's true," Cassian said, his voice low. "Avalkyra Ashfire. It has been a long time."

There was a ripple of reaction at his words, like a stone dropped into water. The soldiers on the balcony stiffened and stared, while whispers and mutters reverberated outward from there. Alexiya's dark eyes bored into Avalkyra, expression unreadable, while Rolan, on the other hand, looked annoyed.

Avalkyra bristled at the informality in Cassian's words. She lifted her chin. "When last we spoke, you called me queen."

Cassian inclined his head—in recognition of her words, but not in a bow. "A lot has changed since then."

Avalkyra studied him for several weighted heartbeats, then finally looked away. "I was sorry for your wife. Olanna was the last Flamesong—the end of a cherished dynasty."

"Not the last," Cassian corrected, gesturing to Tristan.

Avalkyra didn't follow the movement or look Tristan's way.

"I must admit," Cassian continued, "I'm surprised to see you allying with a Stellan governor—and against your own kind. If I remember correctly, you would rather burn alive than make deals with empire politicians."

Avalkyra's nostrils flared, and she clenched her jaw. "As you said—a lot has changed. When I was a Phoenix Rider, we never backed down from a fight. We did not cower and hide."

"I seem to recall several concealed underground hideaways . . . ," Cassian said.

Avalkyra scowled. "Those were *bases*, not hideaways—and unless you've forgotten, there were many, many fights. . . ."

"I've had enough of this," Rolan snapped, taking an aggressive step forward. Both groups—the soldiers surrounding Rolan and the Riders who surrounded Cassian—reacted to the movement, tension coiling muscles and hands dropping to weapons, but Rolan made no move to actually attack. "There is no walking away from this, Cassian. You are here, on empire soil, when your very existence is illegal—and an abomination."

"I may be *an* enemy of the empire, but Avalkyra Ashfire is *the* enemy. And even if you get your war and your bride, the council won't recognize the marriage or Veronyka's position as heir. No one will accept you as their king. They'll rally together and come for you, and the empire will crumble from within."

"They'll do whatever I tell them to do. Once the empire's armies march into Pyra and I seize the Nest—and its coffers—*I'll* be the one paying their soldiers and passing their laws. They'll have no choice but to support me or be obliterated."

"There will be no king of the Golden Empire unless my terms are met," Avalkyra said sharply. She had been shuffled backward again by the soldiers, but she made sure to keep Veronyka next to her as she spoke. "Sign those papers and our deal stands."

She said the words with conviction, but she knew the situation had already spiraled beyond that point. While she spoke to Rolan, her attention was divided, her shadow magic rushing out of her in a wave. Next to her, Veronyka squirmed, as if she sensed the powerful pulse of magic.

Rolan snorted. "Our *deal*?" he scoffed, fixing Avalkyra with a disdainful sneer. "I intended to march on the Nest long before you turned up—with or without a legitimate claim. Now that *she's* here"—he jerked his chin at Veronyka—"I should kill you where you stand, you dark-magic witch. You wreaked havoc upon the empire for half my life, and now you expect to use *my soldiers* to help you secure the throne for yourself? I have what I need—an Ashfire. I certainly don't need two."

With a signal, one of the soldiers behind Avalkyra gripped her shoulders, while the soldier opposite stalked toward her, a short sword in hand.

Another soldier tugged Veronyka out of the way—or tried to, but Avalkyra held fast to her other arm.

There was a struggle, and Avalkyra used it to her advantage. She lunged, slipping a dagger from the sheath on her wrist and sinking it into the neck of the soldier holding Veronyka, drawing the blade back again before the others on the balcony even realized what was happening.

There was a spurt of blood, splashing onto Veronyka, who stared in shock. Avalkyra, with her hand still gripping Veronyka's arm, flung her around and used her as a shield, blocking the thrust from the soldier with the short sword. He hesitated, unwilling to harm Veronyka, and that bought Avalkyra another spare moment. She spun the knife in her hand and stabbed backward, gutting the soldier who was trying to regain his grip on her from behind. The man keeled over, releasing his hold, and Avalkyra shoved Veronyka aside as she kicked out, knocking the short sword from the other soldier's hand. He stumbled backward, and Avalkyra twirled the dagger in her hand once more before flinging it hard. It spun end over end until it embedded itself in the man's chest.

As soon as Avalkyra made her move, chaos erupted around them. Tristan leapt forward, reaching for Veronyka, but Avalkyra shifted her blood-slicked grip and took up a fistful of fabric, dragging her away by the back of her dress.

There was a steady, rhythmic drumming in Avalkyra's ears—her pulse, mixed with the steady pump of wingbeats.

Below, more soldiers cried out in alarm, having spotted Avalkyra's escape vehicle. Like all outposts, this structure had roosts built into the topmost level of the tower. Avalkyra's phoenix had been perched there all along, concealed within the pillars of the stone architecture, and upon Avalkyra's command had slipped out of the shadows and dove among them.

Avalkyra knew the soldiers would not fire without a direct order, and Rolan was too busy shouting at the soldiers on the balcony and wading through the melee to get to Veronyka. Veronyka fought as well, trying to get away from both sides as they struggled for dominance, still reaching for Tristan's hand.

Without a second's thought or hesitation, Avalkyra pulled Veronyka up onto the railing of the balcony with her. There was a gust of wind, a flash of scarlet feathers—and together they tumbled over the edge.

Day 2, Fourth Moon, 170 AE

I'll call you what you wish, Alexiya, Rider of Ximn—
but you're wrong. I never had a choice at all.
Someday you'll understand.
Your brother, Theryn

My heart tells me you will
rise up and become the best of us.
Last and greatest in an ancient line.

- CHAPTER 51 -
VERONYKA

VERONYKA SAW GROUND, THEN sky, then ground again.

They had been standing on the balcony—both sides arguing and getting nowhere—and then Val had snapped and retaken control. There was blood, and shouts, and the next thing Veronyka knew, she was tumbling backward into the open air.

She landed hard on what turned out to be a saddle, and Val landed on top of her. Before Veronyka could catch her breath they were soaring up again, astride Val's powerful phoenix.

Veronyka was free, but she knew she was not safe—she'd simply left one captor for another.

Val's grip was bruising in its force, pinning Veronyka to the saddle as she struggled to sit upright. The wind was whistling in Veronyka's ears, and the world rushed by at a dizzying speed as she twisted around, trying to see the scene on the balcony they'd left behind. She didn't want to be swept off somewhere by Val, not while Tristan and the rest of the Riders were still in danger. Because of her.

They were flying north, but veering slightly west, probably trying to avoid being spotted by people in the city—or shot down by Rolan's soldiers.

Were there more Riders, too, waiting somewhere nearby? Or had the others remained at their posts in Pyra? Even if there were reinforcements, if they saw her atop this phoenix, would they try to bring them down? Or would they watch them leave, unsure if Veronyka was in the middle of being saved or being captured?

And where was Xephyra?

The phoenix underneath her continued to pump her vast wings, while Val scrambled into a better position, gripping tight to the reins.

Now that she was on the animal, Veronyka realized how truly enormous the phoenix was. There was no way Val had hatched this creature within the past few weeks—or months, for that matter. This phoenix was much older than that.

Was this Nyx, Val's bondmate from before the war? Had she survived after all? But if it was, their bond would have survived too, and Val could have tracked her down wherever she'd wound up. Veronyka couldn't believe Val would have remained phoenix-less for sixteen years if she'd had a bondmate somewhere in the world.

But what about a *bind*mate? Veronyka had already considered the idea when she'd asked Val about her phoenix in the tower. After all her disparaging claims about love and weakness, Veronyka had begun to wonder if there wasn't another way to take hold of a phoenix and bend it to your will. She'd long suspected Val didn't have the ability to bond again, but a bind, on the other hand . . .

A bond was forever—sometimes even after death, like with Veronyka and Xephyra—but a bind was one-sided and didn't require love or affection or loyalty. Judging by how easily Veronyka had tampered with Sidra's mind that morning, binds were impermanent and unstable, and could therefore be blocked and weakened.

Maybe even broken.

Val's magic continued to emanate from her in steady, powerful waves. She was exerting an inordinate amount of magical pressure to keep the phoenix under control, but a sudden jostle dislodged Val's tight hold on Veronyka's arm, and Val was forced to divert her attention to keep both of them in the saddle.

Veronyka took the opportunity to turn her focus to the phoenix.

The poor creature's magical barriers were not entirely sound; generally, phoenix minds were strongly defended and impossible to intrude upon without invitation.

This phoenix was *trying* to reclaim its mental fortitude, but gaps and glimpses kept appearing before Veronyka's magical eyes. Rather than force her way into one of those cracks, Veronyka seized upon a flickering opening and reached out to the phoenix instead.

I think I can help you, if you'll let me. I think I can get her out.

Veronyka glanced down at the ground below, the trees and buildings rapidly fading into a shockingly distant blur. If she *did* break Val's hold, what would happen to them?

The phoenix screeched, banking hard and causing Val to curse and struggle to regain her hold.

Out, the phoenix echoed, her voice booming in Veronyka's mind. She thought Val heard it too, because she shot a look back at Veronyka. *Out, out, out.*

Can you land? Veronyka asked desperately, though the small opening in the phoenix's mental walls was already shifting and disappearing.

Val pushed harder, her magic flowing outward, but after Veronyka's intrusion, the phoenix had started resisting.

The phoenix shook herself suddenly, then twisted in the air and spun, as if she were trying to buck them from her back.

Val pressed herself flush to the saddle—determined to ride whether this firebird wanted it or not—but Veronyka was slipping. She was practically upside down now, dangling helplessly and sliding farther with every burst of wind and jostle of the phoenix's wings.

After a particularly violent gust, Veronyka's leg came loose. She tried desperately to bend forward, to grab hold of something, but the force of the slipstream was too much.

Val cursed, releasing her own hold and reaching back for Veronyka. She grasped the flimsy Stellan dress, tearing it as she pulled. She reached again, this time grabbing a fistful of the fabric—along with the chain of Pheronia's necklace.

"No!" Veronyka cried, but too late—the delicate golden links snapped as the phoenix bucked again, but the momentum actually worked in Veronyka's favor, causing a break in the winds that allowed her body to fold forward. She pressed a hand to her chest, clutching the broken necklace against her skin. It slipped down, between her fingers, and became snagged within the layers of sheer fabric. It would have to do for now.

Val pulled Veronyka's body upright, and Veronyka gripped Val's arm in return, relief sweeping through her.

But that shred of safety was short-lived.

Just as she began to climb up the phoenix's body, clinging to Val's hand while her other sought a piece of the saddle, Val's eyes went wide. She slipped too, her leg—which had been twisted around a strap—dislodged as Veronyka's extra weight pulled at her.

The phoenix spun again, slamming them both hard against the saddle, temporarily breaking Val's hold on Veronyka. Again Val reached, determinedly, doggedly, and regained her grip. Veronyka couldn't help but appreciate her survival instinct.

Val was a fighter, a warrior . . . and unyielding in her will to survive.

Whatever the cost.

When Veronyka's arm began to slide through her fingers again, she met Veronyka's eyes, and Veronyka didn't know if it was shadow magic or the look on Val's face, but she knew what her aunt intended to do.

You wouldn't, Veronyka thought, believing the words even as their tone was more question than statement. Val had raised her, had fed and clothed and cared for her—in her own way. They might not be actual sisters, but they were in all the ways that counted. Val hadn't *deliberately* killed Pheronia, and she wouldn't deliberately kill Veronyka either.

Then Veronyka remembered Val's words from earlier: *All I ever loved about you was your Ashfire blood.*

It wasn't true—Val had been lying. She was an excellent, accomplished liar. Veronyka had a window into her mind; surely she knew the truth?

You wouldn't, she said again.

I would, Val said, the words like chips of ice in Veronyka's heart.

Maybe letting go was the only way. Their love was toxic, after all. Dangerous . . . Maybe Veronyka had to let her go too.

Val's fingers trembled—half a heartbeat of hesitation—and then she released her hold on Veronyka's wrist, letting Veronyka fall into the open, empty air.

Veronyka saw ground, then sky.

Then ground again.

But remember, child: greatness comes in many forms.
Elysia was great. Avalkyra is great. And you too will
be great. It is up to you to choose how.

- CHAPTER 52 -
AVALKYRA

THIS WAS THE TRICK, the thing the stories never told you. In order to survive, you had to be willing to let go.

Sometimes it was easy, the hand cold and limp and slick with blood.

Sometimes it was harder, the hand strong and fierce and clinging to life.

It seemed Avalkyra knew only two ways to live: gripping so hard she strangled or letting everything and everyone go.

Could she start over yet again? Could she come back from this?

Maybe she was already beyond that point. Maybe she was completely and truly lost.

Survive, her heart said.

But Avalkyra's heart had beat so long, there was no fire left. It was a smoking, smoldering ruin.

Not like *her*. Not like Veronyka and her incandescent heart of flames.

Survive, her heart said again. *When there is no light left, live off the shadows instead.*

So Avalkyra chose darkness instead of light.

Was it cowardice that made her close her eyes, or self-preservation?

Whatever it was, she closed them, and she let go.

When Nox decided to expand her dominion beyond night and into the day, she flew down to Pyrmont and found nothing but stones. She offered the stones all she had to give: shadows, darkness, and endless cold. The stones cracked and shuddered, and out came black-winged birds—strixes.

When the days grew shorter and the night closed in, Axura was forced to make a stand. She flew down to Pyrmont and offered the stones all *she* had to give: fire, light, and enduring warmth. Out came red-winged birds—phoenixes.

And so the goddesses reaped what they sowed, each getting back exactly what they gave.

—*Myths and Legends of the Golden Empire and Beyond,* a compilation of stories and accounts, the Morian Archives, 101 AE

It will not come easy.
Nothing worthy ever does.
Like Nefyra before you,
your life will be a trial by fire.

- CHAPTER 53 -
VERONYKA

VERONYKA FELT WEIGHTLESS, FLOATING in a sky of orange and amber, her body gilded by an apricot sun.

Her mind was clear—empty, almost. There was nothing but that sense of being untethered, of existing in an endless, lifeless void. Completely alone.

But then there was a screech. A desperate, angry cry, and Veronyka woke up.

She wasn't alone—she was *never* alone.

She had Xephyra.

Large claws wrapped around her spinning, twirling body moments before Veronyka hit the earth.

With another shriek of fury, Xephyra tucked her feet up against her chest, curling into a ball to protect Veronyka before she crashed hard on her back, sending rocks and bits of debris flying as they bounced and tumbled across the ground.

The impact rattled Veronyka's bones, but she was focused entirely on Xephyra, reaching desperately for their bond. They came to a complete stop, and the stillness of the world, of their minds, made panic surge up Veronyka's throat.

Xephyra! she yelled into their connection.

Not so loud, Xephyra said, and Veronyka almost laughed in relief. She rested her head against her bondmate's chest, reveling in the sound of her heart, the steady rise and fall of her chest, and the warmth of her soft feathers.

Thank you, Veronyka said. Xephyra already knew it—didn't need it—but Veronyka wanted to say the words anyway. She pressed a hand to the front of her dress, finding the broken necklace and tugging it out. She clutched it in her hand.

Are you hurt? Veronyka asked, disentangling herself from Xephyra's claws and sliding down to her feet. She stuffed the necklace into her pocket, then ran her hands over her bondmate's feathers, surveying the damage.

Xephyra didn't reply but suffered Veronyka's ministrations before stiffening in alarm and getting awkwardly to her feet, casting Veronyka off her. Her attention was focused somewhere behind Veronyka, who turned just in time to see Val and her phoenix careening toward the ground.

While Xephyra had taken the brunt of the fall to protect Veronyka, Val's phoenix was clearly intending to do no such thing. She shook her head and flapped her wings in erratic bursts, while Val clung desperately to the saddle until the final moment of impact.

Veronyka staggered back, the force of the landing reverberating through the ground beneath her feet. Her shadow magic leapt forth, reaching of its own accord, seeking Val amid the wreckage barely twenty feet away.

Veronyka's breath was caught in her throat until a surge of terrible anger and annoyance burst through their bond. Val was okay. Reluctant relief flooded Veronyka's chest; she was glad that Val hadn't fallen to her death—and simultaneously angry with herself for caring at all when *clearly* Val did not, having dropped Veronyka from the sky seconds before.

While Xephyra had saved Veronyka's life, Val had managed to remain astride her phoenix long enough to avoid falling from a deadly height or being crushed underneath the massive creature. Still, as Val stumbled from the saddle, blood oozed from a large cut near her hairline, and her body was streaked with scratches and dirt.

The four of them had left the tower at the edge of the city behind, and now found themselves on a gently sloping hillside, crisscrossed with stonework paths—some of which had been torn up with their violent landings. The grassy lawns were surrounded by carefully shaped shrubbery and brightly colored flowers; several fountains splashed and gurgled, while gleaming marble statues sat at regular intervals. A garden. They must have landed in the wealthy sector of Ferro, on the outskirts of Orro, where the rich built country villas atop the hills that overlooked the province.

The lush landscape was utterly incongruous with the sight of Val covered in blood and her massive, angry phoenix rising up behind her, tossing her head and scraping her foot-long talons into the dirt.

There was a marble pavilion raised atop a set of wide steps nearby, with swaths of fabric blowing gently in the breeze, and beyond it, the tower they'd left behind was visible on the horizon to the southeast.

But it wasn't just the tower Veronyka saw.

A cloud of dust was rising from that direction, and shapes soon distinguished themselves from the distant blur.

Horse-mounted soldiers. Dozens of them, riding hard, and coming straight for them.

*I pray you are able to pass
through the flames.*

- CHAPTER 54 -

TRISTAN

STANDING ON THE BALCONY and not talking—not shoving Rolan and his soldiers aside until he had Veronyka safe in his arms—was one of the hardest things Tristan had ever done.

But before they'd left Rushlea, his father had given him stern instructions.

"I know you are emotionally invested in this," he began, and nothing he had ever said had been a greater understatement, "but you must keep silent and let me do the talking. You have to trust me. Understood? Rolan is an egomaniac and as manipulative as they come, and if what you say about Avalkyra Ashfire is true . . . well, whatever Rolan is, Avalkyra is worse."

Tristan had agreed, knowing that the wrong answer might have seen him left behind. But it had been difficult. His feelings were out of control, and he'd had trouble paying attention as his father and Rolan traded words and threats and insinuations.

She'd been *right there*, but she might as well have been miles away.

The intense relief he'd felt when he'd first laid eyes on Veronyka faded with every second that passed, replaced with a tight, suffocating pressure on his chest. She didn't look right, dressed as a Stellan noblewoman with her shoulders rigid and her spine straight, and then Rolan had said the words "Ashfire bride," and Tristan had finally understood.

If it had been hard to stand mere feet away from her and do nothing, it had been harder still to watch her fall over the edge of the railing in Val's iron grasp. To watch her soar into the air on the back of a strange phoenix . . . only to plummet through the sky soon after.

Tristan thought his heart might have actually stopped, his very blood arrested in that one, single, terrified moment. Was that how he had looked, falling limply—and utterly helplessly—from Rex's saddle? Was that how it felt to watch someone you loved die and be completely and utterly unable to help?

But then Xephyra was there—no longer locked up after all—shooting toward Veronyka like an arrow. They met in midair, Xephyra snatching Veronyka in her claws before curling around her bondmate and hitting the ground hard.

Everyone on the balcony stared, thunderstruck.

Had . . . had they survived it?

Tristan's stomach clenched so tightly, he thought he might be sick, but then Val and her phoenix were plummeting after them, twisting and fighting to remain aloft as if buffeted by high winds or dragged down by invisible nets.

Their strange struggle continued until they too came careening downward and crashed somewhere near Veronyka and Xephyra.

There was a breathless, frozen instant on the tower balcony—then everyone moved all at once. Rolan barked orders, and the soldiers turned their backs on the Phoenix Riders and barreled down the stairs. Below, Tristan could hear more shouts and the sounds of horses being mounted up and ridden away, obviously in pursuit.

"Bondmates, now," the commander bellowed. Tristan had already called Rex, summoning him back from the outskirts of Ferro where he and the other phoenixes were clustered together, out of harm's way but not so far as to be unreachable.

They'd flown here as fast as they could, traveling all night and stopping only once, at Prosperity, to tell Fallon what was happening so he could relay it to the others. But by a twist of fate, Beryk was there with Alexiya, reporting on the recent happenings in the east, and they'd all insisted on coming. Darius had remained behind to man the front lines and keep a hold on Prosperity and Vayle, while the rest of Tristan's patrol—who had to finish up their last-minute duties and assign their patrol shifts to the guards—were expected to arrive at any minute. Tristan's Riders might be green and inexperienced, but it was better to withdraw Riders from Rushlea—which was safer than the other locations—than to remove anyone else from Prosperity or Vayle.

Though it seemed like a lifetime, the phoenixes arrived before the horse-mounted soldiers got even halfway to Veronyka and Val. Tristan leapt into the saddle and hastened to mirror, using Rex's superior eyesight to get a better look at what was happening. Both phoenixes were back on their feet, and—Tristan released a shaky breath—so were Veronyka and Val.

Now they just had to beat Rolan's soldiers.

Faster, Tristan said to Rex, who let out a resounding cry and a shower of sparks. One, two, three pumps of his wings and they overtook the commander, who had been in the lead, riding hard on Maximian.

His father didn't object or fight for position, but slid back, filling the spot that Rex had vacated. With five of them, they flew in an expanded arrowhead pattern—Tristan now in the lead, with his father and Beryk to the right and Fallon and Alexiya to the left.

Tristan turned in his saddle and told the others to arrange themselves in a protective circle around Veronyka and Val. It seemed natural to issue orders at this point, and no one questioned it as they arrived at their destination and spread out to take up their positions.

Veronyka and Val had luckily avoided landing in any populous areas— or colliding with buildings—and the Riders found themselves making a stand inside a well-kept private garden.

Or at least, it *had* been well kept. Great clumps of earth were torn up, the stones from pathways scattered across the lawns, and Val's phoenix, who was still behaving erratically and clawing at the ground, was smoking, causing the nearby plant life to catch fire.

Veronyka was on her feet, Xephyra by her side, facing down Val. They seemed utterly unaware of their surroundings, absorbed in some private battle, and Tristan had to trust that they would be okay. Veronyka could handle her sister; the rest of them would handle the soldiers.

But as Tristan and Rex banked and circled around to face the coming cavalry, Tristan knew they had their work cut out for them.

The soldiers separated and approached in three groups, two circling around to try to find weak spots to break through the Phoenix Rider perimeter, while the third halted their progress to form lines. Tristan was facing that faction, aware of the horses that galloped behind him but trusting the other Riders to handle it. Trailing the horse-mounted soldiers were reinforcements on foot, marching alongside covered wagons.

Tristan frowned. Wagons meant specialized weapons and war machines. Catapults, slingshots . . . and nets.

The mounted soldiers didn't wait for them. Instead they unfastened the shields from their saddles and raised them up over their heads. Tristan recalled vividly the stories his father had told about this particular empire tactic.

The soldiers strapped the specially designed shields across their backs, protecting themselves from fire and arrows from above as they rode forward.

The only way to take them down was to fly so low that you were in range of their weapons, or shoot from above and aim at the horses, not the riders. The empire counted on the Phoenix Riders having a soft spot for animals and being unwilling—or at least hesitating—to deliver fatal blows.

But Tristan thought there might be another way. The ground between the line they held in the sky and the ranks of soldiers preparing to ride was grassy and dotted with flowers and shrubs. And despite careful attention, the plants were hot and dry this time of year—and perfect kindling.

Another way to slow a horse's attack was to spook it, and like most normal living things, horses did not like fire.

Come on, Rex, Tristan said, urging him to ignite as the soldiers began their charge. For once in his life, he was not afraid of the burst of heat and crackle of flame licking up his bondmate's sides. He was so preoccupied with the problem at hand, so focused on protecting Veronyka, that there was no room in his mind for fear or hesitation.

Tristan lit his first arrow and aimed it at the stampeding horses—then pointed it slightly lower, at a cluster of bushes closer at hand. The arrow hit, the fire caught, and he repeated the process.

Though he didn't create the perfect line of flames he'd been hoping for, when Rex pumped his wings and pulled them up out of range, he'd managed to create a legitimate obstacle. Many of the horses kicked and reared, staggering into the others, and only a third of the soldiers were able to pass through gaps or push their skittering mounts to leap over the blaze.

But then Cassian was there, swooping down so low and so suddenly that the riders pulled back or dodged to the side, giving him the perfect angle to strike. He took out two soldiers with his bow by the time Tristan joined him, taking out two more.

When they circled back around, the soldiers had regrouped and were preparing for another charge. Tristan and his father shot arrows to keep the fiery barrier burning, while behind them, Fallon, Beryk, and Alexiya executed maneuvers of their own.

Tristan kept a constant eye on the distant foot soldiers and the wagons they brought with them, sensing that what advantage they had now would eventually shift in the empire's favor. He darted looks over his shoulder at Veronyka and Val, too, but they were still facing off with each other. Time slowed during a fight as his mind analyzed every movement and detail, but he suspected that only minutes had passed since they'd taken their stand.

They continued to hold their positions until Tristan noticed Fallon getting into trouble on his right, near the pavilion. It looked like the soldiers were trying to push him back, using the colonnaded, open-air structure as a base to attack from. The roof protected them from Fallon's offensives while their archers were able to squat behind the columns to loose arrows before ducking out of range again.

And worse, Tristan saw that one of the wagons had already arrived, and the soldiers appeared to be unloading its wares inside the protection of the gleaming marble building. He spotted enough equipment to know that a catapult was coming.

Leaving his father to handle the next charge, Tristan nudged Rex toward Fallon and the pavilion.

They swooped in low, causing the soldiers who'd been unloading the wagon to duck and scatter. Fallon used the distraction to fire off a round of arrows before soaring back out of range.

As Rex swooped around, Tristan considered the wagon. If they could set it on fire, they might destroy what was left of the catapult—and whatever other weaponry was inside too.

He craned his neck, trying to see Veronyka, but Xephyra blocked her from view.

It was now or never.

Tristan nocked an arrow as they dove back down. Just as he was about to release, a tidal wave of sound and heat rippled through the air, knocking them off course. Tristan whipped around; Val's phoenix had burst into flames so suddenly and powerfully that scorch marks scraped across the earth in every direction. The air was thick with smoke and sparks and hazy with heat. Tristan couldn't see Veronyka *or* Xephyra.

Panic lodged itself in his throat, when Rex tugged urgently at his mind. Before Tristan could respond or realize what was happening, his world jerked hard to the side, and he almost lost his seat.

Rex's wing—it was caught, snagged by a net.

He pumped frantically, twisting around and brandishing claws and beak, but then a second net flew through the air, catching Tristan this time as well as Rex, and with a final, furious shriek from Rex, they were dragged down to the ground.

This is the cycle, the circle
of life for Ashfire queens, just as it
is for our fire-blooded phoenixes.

- CHAPTER 55 -

VERONYKA

THE STAMPEDING HOOVES ECHOED all around them, a steady rumble like thunder. Both Veronyka and Val turned to look, but then shapes began to distinguish themselves in the sky above.

Phoenix Riders.

They cut the soldiers off and set themselves up in a protective wall, which bought Veronyka and Val a bit of time.

Veronyka's attention shifted back to Val and the angry phoenix next to her. She was struck with a strange familiarity, but before she could get a clear look, the phoenix got to her feet, tossing her head and shaking out her wings.

Then she turned on Val.

The air around the phoenix rippled and blurred, while sparks danced from underneath her feathers.

She was about to ignite.

"Val!" Veronyka shouted, but Val remained rooted to the spot.

The phoenix heard her cry and swiveled her head in Veronyka's direction instead.

Out! the phoenix shouted into Veronyka's mind, repeating her request from earlier.

Xephyra bristled at the larger phoenix's aggressive tone, moving to step in front of Veronyka in a protective stance.

"Xephyra, no!" Veronyka said desperately, brushing aside her bond-mate's wing and coming up alongside her again. The phoenix opposite was ancient and angry, and Veronyka couldn't let this turn into a showdown. "It's okay," she murmured, putting her hand on her phoenix's neck—the feathers rippling with heat as Xephyra's hackles rose. "I want to help her."

Veronyka edged around her bondmate and reached tentatively toward the phoenix, who was shuffling nearer, though her movements were hesitant and twitchy.

Veronyka took her chance.

The phoenix's mind . . . it wasn't open exactly, but Veronyka thought the creature was trying to let her in. Fear made her pull back, again and again—not surprising, given what Val had done to her.

Veronyka didn't make any sudden movements—physical or magical—sensing the firebird's panic. The phoenix was still hot, heat waves and bursts of sparks pulsing from her body, but she hadn't fully ignited. Yet. There was something terrible and broken in those eyes as Veronyka met the phoenix's cold stare, the fire within so blazingly hot that it felt icy as it brushed against Veronyka's senses. Her heat was so near to the surface that the phoenix was constantly fighting it back. One false move and she'd go supernova.

Before Veronyka could do more than a cursory examination, seeking the opening that belonged to Val's bind, Val herself lurched forward.

She looked wild and desperate, blood soaking into her temple and dirt smeared across her skin. Her eyes were bulging and slightly manic, making her terrifying in a way Veronyka had never seen before.

"What do you think you're doing, *xe* Nyka?" she demanded. "That animal belongs to me."

Then she turned to the phoenix and a surge of magic pulsed from her. Veronyka felt it through her bond to Val and through the fleeting connection she maintained with the phoenix beside her. The power of it made Veronyka's knees buckle, waves of it crashing over her and swirling in her mind.

The phoenix screeched and shook her head again, great taloned feet scratching at the ground as she fought off the magical control.

"Val, *enough!*" Veronyka shouted. The phoenix was growing even hotter, and Val's demands were only making things worse.

"Be quiet!"

"You have to stop this."

"Why don't you make me?" Val asked, whirling on Veronyka now, forgetting the phoenix biting and snapping mere feet away from them. She stalked toward Veronyka, her magic pouring into Veronyka's mind, barreling down on her—not like a wave that rose and fell and eventually broke. Like a waterfall, the force of it rushing and relentless.

And despite all instincts to the contrary, Veronyka let it.

She thought of Val's words and realized that if she didn't stand her ground now, she'd be running from Val forever. So rather than blocking or cowering away, Veronyka swung the door to their bond wide and let Val in. She flooded Veronyka's mind, Val's magic like dark, inky swirls amid the pure waters of Veronyka's own magic. It was awful, opening herself to someone she knew meant her ill. Veronyka felt terror and desperate vulnerability, but she quickly stifled those thoughts.

This was *her* mind. Her stony tower. Her domain.

Veronyka drew herself up and focused not on the stones or the doors or other barriers she'd constructed; instead, she focused on her magic. It filled her mind, expanding and surging up from some well deep inside her. Rather than shrinking back as she might have once done, hiding within the barriers of her own mind, protecting her thoughts and feelings, Veronyka reveled in them. She embraced the power and the fear, the beliefs and the memories and the experiences that made her who she was.

She was Veronyka Ashfire. She was an animage and a shadowmage. She was a Phoenix Rider, a warrior—a light in the darkness.

Val was everywhere, her magic potent and malevolent, but as Veronyka expanded, it was Val who was forced to shrink back, to try to gain purchase in shallow recesses and forgotten corners.

What—what are you doing? Val demanded, and Veronyka sensed true fear in her.

Like you said, this is my mind, Val. It's where I am most powerful, and you are not welcome.

This time, when Veronyka's magic swelled, Val tried to stand her ground, to weather the storm, but it was clear the sensation was uncomfortable. She stood before Veronyka, gasping, blinking, as if her mind were being buffeted from within.

Leave, Veronyka said, and it wasn't just a word—it had power. She'd always hated the idea of shadow magic, but that was because she hadn't understood it. What she knew of shadow magic came from Val, who had twisted and distorted its use, turning it into a weapon to be wielded instead of a bridge to connect and a fortress to defend.

Leave, Avalkyra Ashfire. I will not tell you again. And in a burst of rage and iron smoke, Val was expelled from her mind, pulled through their bond as if she were being sucked down a drain.

Veronyka watched her go, felt her mind clear of that dark presence. Then she left the door open, knowing Val wouldn't dare return anytime soon and also knowing that if she did, Veronyka would be ready. Without the effort it took to keep her bond to Val locked and barred, Veronyka felt energized. All this time she'd been hindering herself; now she'd never felt more alive.

Val, however, did not take kindly to Veronyka's newfound strength. She staggered back after she'd been ejected from Veronyka's mind, as if she'd received a physical blow.

The look she shot Veronyka was fierce as phoenix fire, but there was a flicker in the back of her eyes that told Veronyka she was unnerved, too.

Choosing to fight a different battle, she turned away from Veronyka, focusing her attention back on the phoenix.

Their bind was still in place and was probably keeping the phoenix nearby, though the creature continued to shake her wings and expel great puffs of hot air.

The heat was enough to make Veronyka's eyes water, and while her own resistance to fire was strong thanks to her bondmate, Val's would be nonexistent. But no matter Veronyka's magical defenses, they were meant to protect her from *Xephyra's* fire, not all fire. If this phoenix ignited before her, both Veronyka and Val would be scorched.

"Val, leave her," Veronyka pleaded, but if Val was ever going to start listening to Veronyka, it would not be now, after she'd suffered a shadow magic defeat.

"You! Phoenix!" Val shouted, choosing to speak out loud—probably to save her depleted energy. "I order you to calm yourself at once. You *will* obey me or you will suffer my wrath."

The phoenix turned on her, and Veronyka grudgingly admired the way Val stood her ground, despite the sweltering waves of heat that made her hair blow back from her face and her cloak and tunic smoke.

Val did something, some kind of magical push or pressure that Veronyka could feel, and the phoenix twitched and trembled in response, a ripple going through her body from beak to tail.

When the tremors subsided, the phoenix did not back down or cower. She drew herself up to her full, impressive height, towering over Val. This was more than anger—more than rage. This was retribution.

The phoenix filled her chest with breath and screeched so loudly and viciously that flames erupted from her beak, like the mythological firedrakes from ancient folklore. Veronyka had never seen such a sight, never felt such dangerous, dazzling heat. The hair on her arms burned, the fabric across her flesh singed, and she wanted to cry out in horror, but her throat was too dry to speak.

But then Xephyra was there, shielding Veronyka, taking the brunt of the other phoenix's blazing inferno. She spread her wings wide, enveloping Veronyka in a blissful reprieve, though the smell of burning hair and fabric was still thick in her nostrils.

When the flames died down, Veronyka looked over Xephyra's wing to see Val crouched on the ground. She'd managed to throw herself behind a dense scrub bush that was now nothing more than a blackened stump of smoking cinders. Rather than recognizing defeat, Val leapt to her feet and strode purposefully toward the phoenix again.

Veronyka realized then that what she was seeing wasn't fearlessness or bravery—attributes she'd often admired in Val when they were younger. It wasn't even the stubborn willfulness Veronyka had come up against over and over throughout their lives.

This was a child having a tantrum, an emotionally stunted human being who was so used to getting what she wanted, she didn't see that not everyone and everything in the world was for her to command.

Val, don't, Veronyka begged, but again she was ignored.

"I'm not finished with you!" Val screamed, small and spiteful as she marched toward the giant firebird, heedless of the sparks and crackles of fire that coiled beneath the phoenix's feathers. "You are *mine*. Do you hear me? You are—"

A sudden, vicious surge of fire *exploded* from the phoenix, as potent and powerful as a volcano, and it sent Veronyka, Xephyra, and Val flying backward. The air was knocked from Veronyka's lungs, and Xephyra crooned softly, having taken the worst of it across her back.

But Val had no such protections. The phoenix's fire had been directed at her, and she had been walking right toward it.

Veronyka gasped, sitting up, brushing hands across her scorched skin— but it wasn't scorched. Her mind raced, confused—she could feel the flesh melting across the side of her face. But then she realized it wasn't her face at all but Val's, the skin curling away from blackened muscle and bone. The fabric of her clothes melted along with the skin, *into* her flesh; her hair burned away, the beads and charms turning to ash in the wake of that fiery combustion.

Veronyka sobbed, her mind pulling back, retreating from the agonizing pain even while she tried desperately to extend her magic, to remain in contact with Val, afraid every aching second would be the last second, the last moment of Val's life. No matter what Val had done to her, no matter how corrupted she'd become, there was a part of Veronyka that would always love her sister. It was the part of her that was her mother's child, the part of her that had *felt* Val's love for her even as Val denied it. Perhaps she wished she could truly let go of Val, but just as her mother before her, Veronyka would love Val—even as she hated her—until her dying breath.

Tears streamed from her eyes, the heat powerful enough to crush her, some oppressive, invisible force. When at last Veronyka could stand, she searched desperately for Val, clinging to the wisps of their mental bond, the connection eerily silent.

Val was a heap at the edge of a starburst of scorched earth. The phoenix was already gone, soaring away into the darkening sky, while Val lay motionless, her body broken . . . but her mind was not.

There was a flicker . . . a stirring. Val was still here. Still alive.

Painful relief swept Veronyka's body, followed quickly by something closer to dread.

Not even phoenix fire could break the Feather-Crowned Queen, and that meant that something else would have to.

That *she* would have to.

Their bond was as strong as ever, even if opening herself to it meant Veronyka lived in a world of agony. Val herself *was* agony—all other thoughts and feelings and ambitions burned away.

Veronyka moved to walk toward her when Xephyra let out a warning croak. Veronyka looked into the sky, seeing another shape looming, growing larger with every weighted wingbeat. She recognized Sidra in the saddle, riding purposefully toward them.

Barely slowing her approach, Sidra leapt from her phoenix's back, scooped a limp Val onto her saddle, and flew away, the pain and the horror in Veronyka's mind going with her.

Not the memory of it, though. Her stomach churned at the phantom sensation of raw skin and scorched nerves, at the suffocating scent of melting flesh and burning hair.

Veronyka shuddered, gritting her teeth.

Rage filled her, and she turned her attention to the world beyond the blackened grass at her feet.

The Riders were successfully holding back Rolan's forces, but even as she took in the burning battlefield, she sensed everyone's attention shifting away from her and the explosion that had just rocked the landscape and toward the gleaming white pavilion.

She spotted Tristan at once and watched, hot anger turning to icy dread as gleaming metal nets dragged him and Rex down to the ground, where he disappeared in a crowd of soldiers.

Above, the commander had already altered his flight, hurtling headlong toward his son, but Veronyka was determined to get there first.

She leapt onto Xephyra's back, and though much of the saddle had been melted thanks to the other phoenix's blistering fire, it was still functional. Xephyra's feathers looked dull and wilted, and Veronyka's hands shook with aftershocks and rising adrenaline. But when they took to the air, they flew as fast as they ever had.

Rising warmth pressed against the bottom of Veronyka's saddle and the insides of her legs. Xephyra's feathers glowed, then caught, ripples of blue-white flames cascading over their shimmering, iridescent surface and catching on the edges of Veronyka's Stellan clothing. Heat waves bent the air around them, and they left a trail of sparks in their wake.

Behind her, Commander Cassian and the other Riders fell in line, but Veronyka did not slow her pace or alter her trajectory.

The soldiers had seen her approach and were lining up to face her, archers at the rear with spearmen and foot soldiers armed with nets at the fore.

Xephyra saw the glint of that hated metal net and shrieked her fury.

Veronyka couldn't see what was happening inside the pavilion, but the number of soldiers that defended it told her that their master, Lord Rolan, was inside.

And so was Tristan.

*In fact, the ancient Pyraeans called
the birthing bed the "pyre," for from the fire
and pain of that place comes new life.*

- CHAPTER 56 -
TRISTAN

IT HAD ALL HAPPENED so fast.

They'd been fighting—they'd been winning—and then the next thing he knew, that burst of heat and flame had sent him off course. That metal net had snagged them both and ripped them from the sky.

Veronyka. Was she okay? What *happened*?

Before Tristan could do more than try to scramble upright, rough hands pulled at him, tearing him away from Rex. He kicked and fought, managing to loosen one arm's grip before two more soldiers leapt back onto him, dragging him deeper and deeper into the crush of their bodies.

Rex remained behind, trapped inside the net that was being pinned to the ground with foot-long stakes. Rex tried to stand, straining against the metal, but the pegs held fast. He shrieked his frustration, fire and sparks rippling across his feathers as he prepared for a different kind of resistance. Together they fought, refusing to give up. They had to get out of here; Tristan had to get to Veronyka.

But then a hand gripped Tristan's hair and yanked his head back, exposing his neck, where he felt cold steel against his throat. Another soldier with a crossbow took up a stance directly in front of Rex, heedless of the pulsing heat, and took aim.

They stopped fighting.

How had this happened? Tristan had come here to save Veronyka, and now *Tristan* was Rolan's prisoner instead.

Tristan was *Rolan's prisoner.*

That couldn't be right—this couldn't be happening. But even as he thought it, Tristan was dragged by several soldiers inside the marble pavilion where Rolan stood, smiling indulgently, like he'd already won. It would be so easy for him to kill Tristan now, to get whatever justice Rolan felt he was owed, but Tristan knew the man was shrewd. If he did that, chaos would be unleashed, and Rolan would be unlikely to make it out of here alive.

Still, Tristan was glad it was him with the dagger to his throat and not Veronyks. However important he was to his father, he was far less valuable in general, which meant Rolan had lost something in this exchange.

He'd lost his Ashfire.

Before Rolan could speak, a shout went up, and the steady pump of wingbeats filled the air. In the distance, a Phoenix Rider approached.

Veronyka.

Tristan's knees buckled in relief to see her emerge from that explosion unharmed, mounted and riding Xephyra. He could face whatever was coming now that he knew she was okay.

Val and her phoenix, on the other hand, were nowhere to be seen. A million questions flitted through Tristan's mind, but he allowed himself to enjoy the sight of Veronyka flying toward him before Rolan's archers raised their bows and aimed them at her.

"No!" Tristan cried out, but Rolan had already called them off.

His expression was hungry. Veronyka was what Rolan truly wanted, and Tristan was just a means to an end, a way to return things to the way they were before this battle had broken out. Rolan stepped nearer to Tristan, ready to use him as a shield, ensuring that Veronyka didn't try to attack. She was followed closely behind by the rest of the Riders, including Tristan's father, all of whom had abandoned the fight in the face of this new development.

They flew hard in Tristan's direction, but Veronyka led the charge.

She looked murderous. Tristan had never seen her look so fierce, so dangerous.

She was beautiful.

He could see the Ashfire in her as she soared through the air, the legacy of queens going back centuries. The bravery of Nefyra. The strength of Lyra. The leadership of Elysia.

And if history had taught him anything, you did not cross an Ashfire queen.

As Xephyra drew near, she slowed her pace, but only just. Veronyka stood in the saddle, leaping from her back onto the steps of the pavilion without missing a beat. She looked worse for wear: Her clothes were torn and burned in several places, and the scent of smoke and ash clung to her skin, which was covered in bloody cuts and smears of dirt. But she'd gotten away from Val, and she strode forward with unerring confidence, ignoring the soldiers standing on either side, clearing a path, her eyes fixed on Rolan.

A flicker of emotion crossed her face when she spotted Tristan in his clutches, but she didn't waver.

"Ah, my betrothed," Rolan said as she stepped into the middle of the pavilion, forcing lightness into his voice. Seeing that Veronyka was unarmed, he stepped around Tristan, though he made no order to have the knife pressing against Tristan's throat removed. If anything, the soldiers that held Tristan's arms tightened their grip. "I see you're one of them," Rolan added with mild disappointment, indicating the Riders that were flying toward them. "Another detail your *sister* failed to mention."

Veronyka ignored him. "Release Tristan at once," she snarled, "and I'll come quietly."

"A fair trade," Rolan said, tugging on Tristan as Veronyka made to stride forward. Tristan refused to budge. There was nothing fair about that trade, and even if there were, he refused to make it.

"Wait," came a voice from behind Veronyka. Commander Cassian strode up the steps, while Beryk, Fallon, and Alexiya landed behind him.

They, however, remained in their saddles—an intimidating presence for the gathering soldiers, who still outnumbered their own. But these were Phoenix Riders, and if Tristan's patrol arrived soon, they'd be better matched.

His father strode up the steps and put a hand on Veronyka's shoulder, stopping her in her tracks.

His face was pained, and Tristan didn't think it had anything to do with the small wounds he could see on his father's face and arms. Tristan swallowed thickly, blinking away the tears that pricked behind his eyes as he met Veronyka's anguished gaze. He shook his head gently, wary of the knife, and her jaw clenched.

Things were not going to be as simple as that. "I am not a fool, Rolan," Cassian said, his voice steady. "If we make that exchange, you will kill us where we stand. If that fails, you'll condemn us to the Grand Council instead and have our people destroyed by the empire. You have to give us more than that."

Tristan narrowed his eyes at his father. Was he giving up his chance to get revenge at the meeting in order to broker a deal with Rolan now? Tristan knew it was the right thing to do—the only thing, in fact, given their current precarious circumstances—but he also knew what it would cost his father to throw away so many weeks of careful planning. To throw away his chance to face Olanna's murderers.

"More than your lives in this very moment? That's more than you deserve!" Rolan spat, his irritation close to the surface. "I have you grossly outnumbered, Commander. All I need do is say the word, and you'll all be dead."

"Along with your ambitions," the commander said, all the more calmly in the face of Rolan's fury. It reminded Tristan uncomfortably of the way *they* interacted at times—Tristan all temper and bluster, and his father, ever stoic and patient. "We will not accept that trade. Now, offer something else instead."

"You dare to push me while my man has a knife to your son's throat?"

"I'm not pushing you, Rolan; I'm negotiating. You may need to reconsider your odds when my reinforcements arrive, and what a victory now will do to your odds of a victory later."

These words seemed to permeate Rolan's bad temper. He glanced at Tristan, and his fervent, kinetic energy was replaced with wary consideration.

"And, Rolan," Cassian added, his voice somehow both whisper soft and dagger sharp, "if you kill my son, you will *not* leave this pavilion alive."

His eyes bored into Rolan, who was first to lower his gaze. Rolan glanced around, as if sensing that the power had shifted between them, and he scrabbled to reclaim it. He sniffed and tossed his shoulders in a determinedly careless gesture. "You know what I want, Cassian. And since you will not deign to give it to me, I fear we are at an impasse."

Tristan's pulse leapt in his throat, as if in anticipation of the blade. Unless he intended to hand Tristan over for nothing, a stalemate was a very bad thing. If they didn't come to terms now, Tristan would be hauled away who knew where for who knew how long. Or things would devolve into another fight, and not everyone standing in this pavilion would survive it.

"I never said I did not intend to give it to you," the commander said, and all the warm feelings Tristan had been feeling for his father turned to ice in his chest. "You would make a smart match for an heiress," he continued reasonably, but the words were like poison, snaking through Tristan's body, filling him with dark despair.

"No!" he burst out, unable to rein in his anger. "No, Father. That isn't for you to decide! You can't do this. You can't—"

"Quiet, boy," Rolan hissed in his ear, nodding at his soldier, who raised the knife and tightened his grip.

The tears that had stung the back of Tristan's eyes swam before his vision now as he looked from his father's cold, calculating face to Veronyka's expression of shocked horror, which surely mirrored his own. Both their lives were on the line, and they were powerless to stop it.

"What did I ask you before we came here?" his father said quietly.

Tristan wavered. His father had asked Tristan to let *him* do the talking. He'd asked Tristan to trust him.

Tristan took a deep breath and nodded.

The commander turned to Rolan once again. "An arrangement could be made, if the right terms were proposed. You can't expect me to trade a princess for an exiled governor's son, even if he's my own. You'll have to sweeten the deal considerably."

Rolan considered Cassian's words. He licked his lips. "The Grand Council will go as planned," he began, "and you will *not* attend. Your people will be deemed dangerous and a threat to the empire. The armies will march into Pyra to find you . . . and if, in that chaos, you help to put myself and the Ashfire girl on the throne, I will grant the Phoenix Riders full immunity in my new regime. You will be my royal guard and given positions of wealth and status."

"While the rest of Pyra burns and animages across the empire continue to suffer? Not good enough, Rolan."

"*And,*" Rolan added, speaking faster now, "in exchange for your loyal service, I will lift the magetax and free every bondservant currently under term for magic use."

The commander's brows rose, and looks of surprise colored the features of the soldiers who surrounded them. But Tristan was skeptical. They would have to fulfill their side of the bargain first. What would stop Rolan from betraying them once he had his throne and his bride?

"I will see you and your Riders after the Grand Council meeting, *after* the empire marches into Pyra. We'll make the exchange once the Nest has been taken."

The commander lifted his chin. "Agreed."

Tristan's heart plummeted, and Veronyka's head snapped around. She looked stunned, angry—*mutinous*—but then the commander bent his head and whispered into her ear. Bracing words of comfort? Harsh warnings or pragmatic assurances? Whatever they were, Veronyka's vengeful expression faltered, and her eyes latched onto Tristan's.

There was apology in them, and desperate, aching regret. Was she saying goodbye to him now? Tristan couldn't bear it.

I love you, he thought, begging her to hear him, inviting her into his mind and his heart.

And then she was there.

I love you too, she whispered into his mind, his heart, and then there was sunshine on his face and wind in his hair; there was warmth and laughter and everything he felt for her, and her for him. The sensations wrapped him up like a caress, swirled around his body and clung to his skin. *I'm with you,* she seemed to be saying—Tristan had trouble understanding the words as he tried to soak up every last drop of her. *I'm always with you.*

She withdrew from Tristan's mind, and a single tear slid a clean track down her dirty face. Whatever sadness she felt seemed to slip away with it. There was fire in her expression now, her jaw clenched and her eyes burning holes in the back of Rolan's head as he turned, gestured to his soldiers, and they moved to leave the pavilion.

"The phoenix," Veronyka said—her voice cold and clear and ringing.

"Excuse me?" Rolan said, frowning at her. She nodded toward the soldiers near the back of the pavilion, who currently held Rex under guard. Tristan ached at the sight of his fiercely proud bondmate brought low, with metal cutting into his flesh.

"You will release him into our custody," she continued.

Rolan snorted. "So he can burn us all to cinders? I've seen how your pets behave when their master is under duress."

"You will release him, Rolan, or I promise you will regret it." Veronyka sounded like Val as she spoke the threat, and a chill slipped down Tristan's spine.

He thought Rolan felt it too, or sensed something of the danger contained in this one girl. He forced out a laugh, though his mirth didn't reach his eyes. "Consider it an engagement present," he said, nodding to his men.

Veronyka's posture softened somewhat, and Tristan's own tension seemed to melt away. She'd thought of Rex, even in the face of everything, and she'd saved him. Outside the pavilion, stakes were removed and the metallic rattle of nets slinked across the ground. Rex tossed his head and screeched, ready to explode into action, but then Xephyra was there, nipping and clawing and corralling him away from the soldiers and the temptation to tear them all to pieces.

Rolan watched it happen, an unreadable look on his face. As soon as Rex was released, the commander and Veronyka started walking backward, down the steps. Soldiers still flanked them on either side, but they were silent spectators more than threats.

Rolan moved to leave as well, before halting abruptly. "Oh, and, Cassian?" he called over his shoulder. Both the commander and Veronyka paused. "If you cross me, I will ensure the armies of the Golden Empire burn the entirety of Pyra to the ground. You will remember the register and the magetax with misty nostalgia thanks to the bloody vengeance I will bring down upon your kind."

Then Tristan was swallowed into the crowd of Rolan's soldiers, the knife at his throat gone but replaced with twice as many hands, shoving him between his shoulder blades and dragging him along. His arms were jerked forward and tied together, and then suddenly he was hoisted up onto a horse. Footsteps echoed all around him, and voices called out orders. He was in a daze, craning his neck, trying to see, but the Riders were already distant specks in the sky.

Rex reached out to him, hurt and confused as he was ushered along by Veronyka and Xephyra.

It will be okay, Rex, Tristan said, though his words sounded faint even to his own ears, the distance growing between them with every pump of his bondmate's wings and every step of the horse trotting beneath him.

I'll see you again soon, he promised, but there was no response.

From the sacrifice of the mother comes the daughter.
A price paid in blood. Life cannot come from nothing.
Life needs life. Avalkyra taught me that lesson as well.

CHAPTER 57

SEV

SEV AND KADE HAD been watching the tower as they approached with fear and anticipation in equal measure. It was a thrill to see the Phoenix Riders come to claim Veronyka and make a stand against the empire, but as they approached, a fight seemed inevitable, and Riella was still inside the ground-level prison cells.

Sev could sense that his place in this conflict was changing . . . that the conflict itself was changing. The small battles and subterfuges were now turning into all-out war. He didn't know where he fit in that new landscape—but he did know that watching and waiting wasn't it. He had to decide to involve himself once more, or to leave a situation that was out of his depth and get him and Kade to safety. Sev might be able to retain his position as a soldier for the time being, but Kade was a bondservant on the run. His time as a spy in the empire was over.

Before Sev could decide what to do, the tension in the tower exploded. The Phoenix Riders had been facing off against Rolan *without* their phoenixes, no doubt in an attempt to defuse the situation. But then out of nowhere Val's phoenix—Sev recognized it because of the long, dark tail feathers—appeared from the top of the tower, where it had clearly been perched out of sight, waiting to be summoned.

Sev watched, mouth open, as Val *and* Veronyka fell over the edge of the railing, only to land on the phoenix's back and soar away. Then, like a kicked anthill, the soldiers inside the tower poured back outside, running to horses and following Val and Veronyka in hot pursuit. Normally such a venture would be pointless—a full-grown phoenix could outstrip a horse any day—but the sisters had crashed not far from the prison tower, landing in a cloud of dust and sparks a few miles outside Copper Hill. The Phoenix Riders had summoned their mounts too, and now both sides converged on the place where the sisters had fallen, leaving the tower suddenly, conveniently, empty.

"Now," said Kade, his voice flat with shock.

"Now," Sev said in agreement.

They ran the rest of the distance to the tower, the double doors wide open. When they approached Riella's cell, they slowed their pace.

"Riella," Sev called as they made their approach. "It's us. It's Sev and Kade."

While Sev squatted to pick the lock, Kade peered in through the window again. He murmured apologies for taking longer than expected and explained that they had to hurry—the tower was empty, but they didn't know for how long.

When the lock sprang open with a loud clang, Sev stood, and together he and Kade swung the heavy door wide.

Riella's cell was easier to see now in the daylight than it had been in the dead of night; there was a cot, a table, and some other assorted items. She hadn't been shut away in a dank underground hole, but it was still no place for an innocent young girl. Some of the rats were still there, crawling over her ankles, clearly there as a comfort to her.

She'd slung what looked like a threadbare blanket across her shoulder, with assorted items bundled inside like a satchel. She seemed uneasy at the open door and looked warily at the pair of them standing there. Sev knew that he looked too much like the soldiers who had imprisoned her, too much like the men who had dragged her from her home and kept her from her family.

Kade recognized this too and stepped forward. Like Sev had seen him do multiple times before, he withdrew his animage pendant. "I know what it is to be mistreated by the empire. That's not who we are or why we're here. We're both animages," he said, gesturing to Sev, "and we're going to take you to your brother."

Riella stood as tall as her short frame would allow, her fists clenched on her blanket-sack, her chin held high. Her lip trembled slightly, but then she nodded and crossed the threshold of the cell.

Sev led the way, leaving Kade to walk alongside Riella. He poked his head outside the doors and raised a hand for the two of them to remain inside until he'd had a quick look around the perimeter. There were no soldiers, so Sev waved them out.

Riella seemed a bit wobbly on her legs—and Sev wondered if she'd been given any exercise or time outside her cell over however many months she'd been here—so Kade was holding her hand as they crossed the open space toward the old stone wall. The problem was, Kade wasn't much better off than she was, his face tensed in a grimace and his brow dotted with sweat.

Sev paused halfway toward rejoining them, then hastily diverted his steps. "I'll be right back," he called, not waiting for an answer. The court-yard on the other side of the building in front of the stables was empty—of people, anyway—and when Sev rounded the tower, his eyes landed on his target: horses, tethered alongside the wagon that Lord Rolan had arrived in.

He slowed his pace, but there was nobody there, save for three extra horses, not including the pair hitched to the wagon. He was surprised they'd been left unattended, but then again, it had been chaos as they'd spilled out of the tower and chased down Veronyka and her sister.

There was certainly a lot of noise coming from beyond Copper Hill, shouts and clanging weapons accompanied by bursts of roaring flame and violent shrieks. Sev hoped the sounds of phoenixes meant that Veronyka was okay—that Commander Cassian and the others were helping her.

Waves of heat were rippling across the landscape, turning whatever was happening there into an indistinct haze. One burst of heat was so strong it hit Sev like a gust of wind and set the horses to tossing their heads and whinnying in dismay. He turned in time to see one of the phoenixes soar away into the sky, while another—this one carrying a Rider—swooped in to take its place. What was happening?

Sev shook his head and focused on the horses. Kade and Riella were waiting for him.

The horses were tied to a fence post, but Sev poked his head into the wagon first, seeing little by way of supplies, though there was a fine bowl packed with fresh fruit and a ceramic flagon of wine. Sev emptied the fruit into a saddlebag before tossing the bowl back, then stuffed the wine inside as well. It might help Kade deal with the pain, at any rate. It might help Sev, too—his shoulder throbbed with every step he took, and he had to pack the supplies essentially one-handed, his left arm unable to reach or hold much weight.

Luckily, they already had some provisions from when they'd first set out for the prison tower, and Prosperity outpost wasn't too far.

That done, Sev untied one of the horses, gentling him as best he could with his clumsy animal magic. He was just preparing to untie another when a distant thundering rumble, growing louder, drew his attention.

Rolan's forces were returning.

Sev staggered back, forgetting the second horse, and gripped the already freed horse's reins, hastily pulling him around the corner of the building and out of sight. One horse would have to be enough—they'd take turns, or Sev could walk the whole way if he had to.

Sev was glancing back over his shoulder to make sure he hadn't been seen when he spotted Rolan himself at the head of the throng, riding hard with a body thrown over the back of his saddle.

No—not a body. A person. A prisoner or hostage, their hands bound together. Sev ducked low, squinting until he caught a glimpse of the person's face.

He'd half expected it to be Veronyka, though such treatment would be shocking—but not entirely surprising—for Rolan's bride-to-be.

But instead he saw Tristan, the commander's own son, the person who had interrogated Sev upon his arrival at the Eyrie.

The person who had thanked him, sheltered him, and ensured his wounds were treated, even while he and the other Phoenix Riders fought for their lives.

Rolan slowed his horse just beyond the far edge of the courtyard before leaping off and barking orders. Tristan was dragged down from the horse and then left there, lying in the dirt.

The soldiers milled around, checking wounds and saddles and drinking water. They changed out the wagon horses—and Sev was relieved he'd only managed to take one, which had thus far gone unnoticed—while more soldiers continued to ride toward them.

In the distance, he spotted the Phoenix Riders rising up into the sky in two rough V formations. They were flying north, away from the battlefield, but one of them trailed behind the others. They veered wide, closer to the tower, as if trying to catch a last glimpse of Tristan before they left him behind.

Sev thought again about fate, about paths chosen and destinies unfulfilled. Mistakes in both his and Kade's lives had brought them together—brought them to this point. They'd done what they could, made hard choices, always trying to stay together. But there was a new path before Sev, one that Kade could not follow.

Just as when they were children, their lives were diverging again.

The road before Sev wasn't the one he'd have chosen or even wanted to follow, but all he could do was make the best choice in the moment.

Heroes did what needed to be done. Surely Sev's parents hadn't *wanted* to die that day, to leave their son behind. But circumstances had brought them to that point, and they'd chosen to do the right thing—the only thing. Sev didn't *want* to be a spy, but here he was, and here Tristan was too.

Sev couldn't just walk away, and for the first time in his life . . . he didn't want to.

A spy wasn't what he wanted to be, but a spy was what he needed to be.

This time it wasn't about obligations or debts. It wasn't about his parents, either.

It was about choice. It was about doing the right thing. Being a spy had often felt like the wrong thing, but this time Sev had two paths before him—one easy, one hard—and he was choosing the harder path.

And it felt good, even if it would come at a cost.

He turned away from the soldiers, tugging the horse into a trot as he made for the crumbling wall and Kade, who was looking around in wide-eyed panic.

"Sev!" he hissed, his expression a mix of annoyance and relief. "How could you just disappear like that—and the soldiers . . . I heard the hoofbeats. Are they back?"

"Not all of them," Sev said, which wasn't technically a lie. "Besides, we needed the horse." He led the animal over the gap in the wall and toward Riella, who stood with her arms hugging her chest. Her tension eased somewhat at the sight of the horse, though. "Look at you," Sev said pointedly, gesturing to Kade's sweat-soaked tunic and his wound, which had at some point begun to bleed again, a dark stain spreading through not just the bandages but the cloth of his shirt as well. "And she's no better," he added in an undertone, as Riella patted the horse's long, spotted nose.

"Fine," Kade said grudgingly. "Let's get out of here before the rest of them arrive." He took hold of the horse's reins and started to walk, Riella alongside him—until he noticed that Sev hadn't moved.

He frowned and retraced his steps.

"Listen," Sev began, and Kade clearly sensed something in his tone and expression. Could he see the decision that Sev had already made?

"Sev, what're you—"

"Keep walking north," Sev continued, fighting to keep his voice even. He knew the signs of a lie and made sure to keep his gaze steady and his posture relaxed. "Get a head start. I'm going to go back for a second horse."

"*What?*" Kade demanded, outraged. "Absolutely not. It's too dangerous—one horse is plenty. We'll take it in turns. We'll—"

"I'm a soldier, remember? No one will question me. We need another horse. If we take turns, we'll be too slow. You need medical attention, and Riella won't last long on foot," he said softly, though the girl was standing out of earshot. "With just one more horse, we'll be able to get away from here and to safety in half the time."

Kade was shaking his head, gaze frantic. "Sev, it's not—"

"We don't have time for this," Sev said. "Get out of here, and I'll catch up. Don't slow your pace for me. Promise?"

Kade's brow had gone so low, it reminded Sev of when they'd first met, except despite his scowl, his eyes glittered with a mixture of emotions Sev couldn't quite place.

"Do *you* promise?" Kade countered, and Sev knew he was referring to his assurance that he would catch up.

The words were heavy; Kade had told Sev before not to make promises he couldn't keep, and Sev felt the weight on his tongue as he spoke.

"Yes," he said. "I promise that when all this is over, you and I will be standing together on the other side of it." He paused, staring at Kade, unable to look away from his face. "Look, I—"

Then he gripped Kade's tunic and tugged.

Kade seemed startled at first, his body rigid, until the last instant before Sev's lips met his. Sev paused, waiting for Kade to respond, and then a soft, relieved smile lit Kade's features. *Finally*, it seemed to say, just as Kade's arms rose to meet him, pressing hard into Sev's lower back, pulling them together.

Sev couldn't help the rumble that rose inside his chest in response, as low and languid as a purr. He knew he was revealing too much with this gesture—not the fact that the kiss confirmed what had long been brewing between them, but the timing of it. The way it felt like goodbye.

Sev pushed the thoughts aside and felt Kade's mouth shift beneath his, the smile gone as heat built between them, intense and crackling. Sev floated in a haze of bliss, his only vague, distant thought mild regret that they hadn't done this sooner, that they could have been doing this—and other things—every night for weeks.

But how could Sev regret anything when he was here, now, and Kade was his?

At last Kade pulled away. His eyes shimmered in the golden afternoon light, their color soft and liquid and more amber than ever before. "Don't take too long," he said tenderly. He lingered for half a heartbeat, hands heavy on Sev's sides, then slowly backed away.

Behind him Riella watched, eyes wide, but said nothing.

Sev nodded, fixing every detail of Kade into his mind, then turned on his heel and ran back toward the courtyard.

More soldiers had arrived, and it seemed they were preparing to leave—Sev had returned just in time.

Tristan was being hauled off the ground and thrown around like a sack. He was dirty and slightly disheveled—probably as much from the fight before his capture as from his struggle after—and his eyes . . . they were wild, desperate, and haunted. He looked defeated. He looked lost. He looked utterly alone.

Sev unhitched himself from the wall; three quick steps, two deep breaths, and he was among them. Soldiers bumped and jostled, but Sev pushed through them, like a riverboat fighting against the current.

Except Sev was one of them, a boat among other boats, then, and they did not know that while they rushed downriver, Sev sliced up.

He came face-to-face with Tristan as he was being forced into the covered wagon. It took Tristan a few seconds to see Sev—to really *see* him—and then something in his tight expression eased.

Sev gripped his arm as if to help force him inside, but he held Tristan's stare. He wished, suddenly, for Veronyka's ability to communicate without words—but he tried all the same.

We're in this together. You are not alone.

This time Sev wouldn't be a spy because he thought he had to be. He would be a spy because he chose to be.

And as Rolan mounted up and prepared to lead the convoy, Sev knew, suddenly, what he had to do.

Protect Tristan. Make sure they both got out of this alive.

And make sure that Lord Rolan didn't.

Rolan was the cause of all this. Sev could try to learn his movements, to anticipate his strikes and block his attacks, but if he wanted to stop the war altogether, he had to cut it off at its source.

Tristan reached for Sev—or tried—but his hands were bound, and a sharp shove between the shoulder blades had him falling into the darkness of the wagon. Two soldiers went in with him, but Sev remained outside, standing on the side step as the wagon lurched forward.

There were several others riding along as Sev was, heads craned to the sky in case of pursuit. Sev lifted his head too, but he didn't look up—he looked north. To the path he had not taken.

His heart broke a little as he thought of Kade, waiting for him in the wilderness. But they would be okay. Kade knew the countryside and could find the outpost on his own. They had a horse and provisions. Kade deserved a chance to heal—he deserved his freedom.

Despair and desperate loneliness welled up within Sev, and so he closed his eyes and thought of the words he'd spoken to Kade before they parted. *When all this is over, you and I will be standing together on the other side of it.*

The promise held true; Sev and Kade *would* be together at the end this war—but it wasn't over yet.

Day 13, Tenth Moon, 170 AE

She's gone, Lexi. They're both gone.
I don't know what to do.
They're gone, and I'm still here . . . . and I don't
know what to do.

And so I will give you all that I have to give.
Blood, and life, and love most of all.

- CHAPTER 58 -

VERONYKA

LIVE TODAY TO FIGHT tomorrow.

The commander's words—whispered in Veronyka's ear—echoed in her mind. Their meaning was plain and their logic sound, but they were at odds with her heart. This was all her fault. She'd lured Tristan here, and now he was paying the price, taking *her* place among their enemies. And he wasn't as valuable as her. What if Rolan changed his mind? What if he decided he'd rather hurt Commander Cassian through Tristan than uphold his end of the bargain?

Fury simmered within her, impotent and with nowhere to go, like a lidded pot trying to boil over. There was no relief for her, no calming this storm.

Before Veronyka mounted Xephyra, she turned to face the commander. She wanted to scream at him, tear him down for gambling his son's life and negotiating her future.

But then she looked at him, *truly* looked at him, and the words died on her tongue. He appeared utterly defeated, his shoulders slumped, his face gaunt and colorless. And his eyes . . . they glittered with unshed tears.

Veronyka realized that she couldn't be the indignant child any longer—the apprentice or new recruit who raged at the injustices of the world and blamed the commander for her poor circumstances.

She had to show strength. She had to help carry this burden.

She had to lead.

They took to the sky, Xephyra flying close to Rex, snapping at his heels and ensuring he didn't turn back around. Veronyka rode rigid in the saddle, gripping her reins relentlessly tight.

When she was certain Rex was under control, Veronyka nudged Xephyra to slow her pace and veer past the tower—just long enough to see Tristan thrown into a wagon. Just long enough to see that, to Veronyka's surprise and immense relief, he wasn't as alone as she'd thought.

Fallon had flown ahead as the negotiations inside the pavilion came to a close, hoping to intercept the coming reinforcements—Tristan's patrol. He'd found them just outside the city limits and flagged Veronyka, Cassian, Beryk, and Alexiya to land. They stopped to rest for a while and regroup, then planned to fly directly to the Eyrie to figure out their next moves.

The phoenixes needed a break even more than the humans; they'd flown overnight into a surprise battle and now had to undertake another long journey back home again.

Rex, however, was riled up again and refused to settle. Tristan's patrol and their mounts crowded around, trying to calm him, but it was no good. He leapt and screeched at any phoenix or human who got too close, sending clouds of sparks puffing into the air.

Veronyka had been drinking water, trying to put herself together again, but she dropped her flask and pushed forward.

Xephyra beat her to it, taking up a defensive stance in front of Rex and forcing the other phoenixes to clear off. Tristan's patrol backed away too, turning to find Veronyka in their midst. They wore frowns and worried expressions, and Veronyka wondered what—if anything—Fallon had told them.

They craned their necks to look past her, where Cassian was conversing in low tones with Beryk, Fallon, and Alexiya. Veronyka realized they were looking for Tristan, waiting for an explanation, and her gut clenched at the prospect of telling them the truth.

They rounded on her. "Where is he?" Lysandro asked. "Where is Tristan?"

Veronyka shook her head. "He . . . Rolan has him."

Anders and Ronyn wore matching looks of shock, but it was Latham who spoke.

"Are you kidding me?" he demanded, his face livid. "We fly all the way to Ferro for *you*, a turncoat apprentice, and now *Tristan's* the one in danger? We shouldn't have come here," he said scathingly, moving to turn away.

Veronyka's hand shot out and gripped him by the front of his tunic, yanking him back in front of her and pulling his face down to her level.

He looked shocked at first, even offended, until his eyes met hers and he sensed something dark in her, something terrible. His face paled, and he stopped struggling against her hold. Anders, Ronyn, and Lysandro gaped at them, but made no move to intervene.

"Do you think there's even the *slightest chance* that you're more heartbroken than me?" she asked, her voice quivering with rage. "Do you think I wouldn't take his place *in an instant* if I had a choice?"

Veronyka released him with a shove, then realized that the commander's group had joined theirs and that everyone was staring at her.

"But Commander," said Latham shakily, glancing her way before turning his attention back to Cassian. "What happened?"

The commander looked around, and every face stared back, awaiting his answer. "There was an . . . exchange."

"We exchanged *Tristan* for *her*?" Latham asked in outrage. "Why?"

The commander's eyes flicked in her direction, and Veronyka answered for him. "Because I am Veronyka Ashfire, heir to the Golden Empire's throne, and I'm a far more valuable bargaining piece."

She couldn't help the bitterness in her words, but they were true all the same. She met their shocked reactions with cool detachment, looking each of them in the face. Alexiya, however, didn't look disbelieving or even surprised. Her gaze was narrow-eyed and measuring. She'd likely already gathered this information from the conversation with Rolan on the tower—if the commander hadn't told her before they arrived—and she stared at Veronyka like she was trying to see something that wasn't there before . . . as if she was trying to see the Ashfire blood pulsing under her skin. "But make no mistake," Veronyka added, "I will do *everything* in my power to get him back. I swear it." When it was clear no one else intended to speak, she turned to the commander. "Can I have a word with you?"

She walked a few feet away from the rest of the group, out of earshot. After several stunned looks at one another, the others dispersed.

"I'm sorry I didn't tell you," Veronyka said to the commander, without preamble. "I didn't learn the truth until a few weeks ago, and . . . I didn't know how to deal with it, or what I wanted to do. I knew it would change things, and I wasn't ready for that."

He didn't say anything. He looked haunted, as if he'd aged ten years, and she thought his silence wasn't about keeping his usual calm demeanor in place or about intimidating her. She thought that he genuinely didn't have a response.

"I understand," he said at last. "I'm glad that you felt comfortable sharing with Tristan, at any rate. He only told me when he knew you were in danger. Otherwise he never would have betrayed your confidences."

Veronyka nodded, fighting down a bubble in her throat. Talking about Tristan was painful, and she needed to get these next words out. "I want you to know . . . ," she began, searching for the words. "You're the commander here. I'm just—I want to get Tristan back. That's all I care about. For now I'm just another Phoenix Rider in your flock. I'll do whatever you need me to do."

"I welcome your allegiance," he said softly, and the words were oddly formal. Veronyka wondered if he thought she'd challenge him or oppose his leadership, but they both loved Tristan and wanted to avoid a war with the empire—and that meant they were on the same side. "Though you won't be just *any* Rider in my flock." Veronyka frowned at him, uncertain. "I think, given the display I saw today . . . it's time you were elevated to Master Rider. And since you were Tristan's second, and he's not here . . ." He swallowed. "You'll lead his patrol in his stead."

Veronyka stared down at her feet, a riot of emotions swirling inside her chest. Leading a patrol was something she'd long dreamed of, but doing so because Tristan was being held hostage was like a heavy weight dragging down the burgeoning hope trying to rise within her. Would they even want her, after everything that had happened? Veronyka supposed it didn't matter. They were united in their goal of rescuing Tristan, and once they did, he could resume leadership. Once they did, everything would be okay again.

"Thank you, Commander," she managed, her throat tight. "I'd be honored."

As the commander set up rear and forward scouts, Veronyka moved to the edge of the clearing, where Xephyra was still battling with Rex.

Rex was repeatedly trying to take flight, while Xephyra was repeatedly knocking him from the sky—using beak and talons to push him off course or drag him back down.

The waves of heat made Veronyka think of Val's scorched flesh. Her stomach heaved at the memory, but she did not slow her pace.

"Rex!" she shouted, coming to stand between them despite Xephyra's attempts to butt her aside with her head.

Rex screeched, flapping his wings and turning away, but Veronyka pursued him, Xephyra just behind her.

When she finally stood in front of him, they locked eyes, and he showed her his violent anguish, his tumultuous confusion and fear. Tristan had forced him to leave, forced him away even when Tristan was in danger and Rex could help.

Xephyra was trying to comfort and reassure him, but he didn't want to be consoled. Veronyka understood that perfectly.

So instead she made him a promise.

I'll get him back, she said into his mind, making the same promise she had to the others, but putting all her conviction behind the words. *If it's the last thing I do, Rex. You, me, and Xephyra, together. We will get him back.*

She didn't try to soothe him or quell his anger. She asked him to bank it, to keep it hot and smoldering, but not to waste it here, now, against friends. She asked him to save it for when they freed Tristan. Because they *would* free Tristan. Veronyka wouldn't cut deals or negotiate. She would take him back with all the blood and magic and fire in her possession.

Save it for vengeance, Veronyka urged Rex. *Save it for war.*

Know that, my daughter.
Whatever happens . . . you are loved.

- CHAPTER 59 -
KADE

THOUGH THE HORSE MADE travel faster and less exhausting, every bump and jostle as they crossed the rough terrain was like a knife to Kade's stomach. Riding two in the saddle didn't help either.

They'd stopped for water and a few moments' rest just past the smoldering battlefield where Sev and Kade had helped free the captive animages, and when Riella saw the spreading stain on Kade's side, she'd insisted on letting him ride alone for a while. It was sweet, and Kade wanted to refuse—but he couldn't. The truth was, no matter how much riding the horse caused him pain, he could hardly stand, the ground bucking and swaying beneath his feet and his head spinning. The water helped, but Kade knew he needed medical attention. He'd definitely popped another stitch or two, and the blood loss was such that he thought he could feel it dripping down his back and stomach and into the waistband of his pants.

The *beltless* waistband.

Kade craned his neck, looking behind them for the tenth time. Sev should have caught up to them by now. Even if he hadn't managed to get the second horse, he was still the strongest of the three of them on foot.

Unease grew like a weed inside his chest, digging roots deep into his stomach while vines clawed up his throat. What if one of the soldiers had caught Sev stealing? What if the Phoenix Rider fight spread and Sev had gotten caught in the crossfire? Kade looked over his shoulder again and again, but there was no sign of Sev or soldiers.

Evening fell around them, darkening the shadows and making their path treacherous, slowing their pace. Riella climbed back into the saddle, and Kade realized he'd been drooping slightly and she was worried he might fall. While Kade's energy dwindled, even on horseback, Riella seemed to grow stronger. She was awake and alert, eyes fixed on the road ahead of them even while she murmured soothing words under her breath—for the horse or Kade's benefit, he didn't know.

When a haze of light illuminated the path before him, Kade thought he was finally losing his grip on consciousness—but no, the sun hadn't crashed down from the heavens. Phoenixes were descending out of the sky all around them, one after the other, like fallen stars.

Kade was wary until he recognized Veronyka among them and realized these were the Riders that he was meant to deliver Riella to—they were the destination, the end of the journey. Even though his heart lightened at the idea that they were saved, Kade couldn't help the way his head turned away from them, neck craning and eyes searching.

Despite her growing calm and strength, Riella recoiled slightly at the sudden appearance of these Phoenix Riders—no doubt reminded of the ones who'd overtaken the tower. She'd had her arms wrapped gingerly around Kade's middle, but they clenched tightly now out of fear, causing Kade to release a gasp of pain. He pried her hands off his stomach and held them instead, catching his breath as a man called Beryk, the commander's second, came forward.

Riella knew him—she stiffened at first, but then she nodded at his words of concern and encouragement, explaining they were heading back to Pyrmont and how their rear scout had spotted the two of them. Apparently Beryk had been the one to recruit her brother and get them all into this mess, but his face was kind and his eyes shone with both happiness at seeing her and regret at what she'd had to endure.

He was quick to shout orders to the others, who helped Kade and Riella from the saddle and plied them with water and food, while Beryk himself eyed Kade's stomach. Another shout and some spare bandages were bound tightly around his midsection for the journey back to the Eyrie.

"Back to the Eyrie," Kade repeated, as Beryk and his helper—a smiling fellow with big ears—stepped back.

"That's right. It's a long journey, but if we fly all night, we should—"

"Take Riella with you," Kade said, "but I have to stay here."

"Stay here . . . ," Beryk repeated, looking around. They were, quite literally, in the middle of nowhere, in the uninhabitable hinterland of the Foothills.

"Someone has to stay," Kade explained, knowing that he wasn't entirely making sense but determined to get the words out, "in case he comes. He's coming—he said he would."

Beryk glanced at Riella, who was staring at Kade with concern while the other Rider muttered something about "fever" and "blood loss."

"We can't stay here. There are still soldiers spread along the border and Foothills, not to mention any Lord Rolan might send in pursuit. We—"

"But that's why I have to stay," Kade insisted. "I can't leave him here alone."

"Who—" Beryk began, but it was Riella who answered.

"There was a soldier who was helping us. He picked the lock to my cell."

"He isn't a soldier," Kade said sharply. "Not really."

As the others continued to frown and murmur in anxious voices, drawing a small crowd, someone pushed their way to the front of the group.

It was Veronyka.

She whispered something to Beryk, and he and the rest dispersed. Riella didn't move.

"I'm Veronyka," she said.

"I know," Kade answered.

"Sev isn't coming," she said. "He—I saw him, as we were leaving. I flew close to the tower, and I saw him."

Kade's breath stalled in his chest.

"He's fine," Veronyka said hurriedly, and the tension in Kade unraveled like a snapped rope. "He's unharmed. The thing is . . . one of ours was taken. Tristan." Her voice quivered, and Kade realized that he wasn't the only person who'd left someone behind. "Sev was *with* him. And I think he chose to stay. I think he saw that Tristan was in trouble and wanted to help."

Kade blew out a shaky breath. "How do you know?" he whispered.

Veronyka hesitated. "I don't," she admitted. "It's more a . . . feeling."

Kade dropped his head into his hands. He was free—a thing he'd wanted since he was twelve—and yet it tasted bitter on his tongue. He and Sev were supposed to be together at the finish line, and they weren't, which could mean only one thing: The game was not done.

"Will you come with us?" Veronyka asked tentatively.

Kade let his hands fall from his face. Where else could he go? And if what Veronyka said was true and Sev was with the commander's son, then being with the Riders was the best place for him. If anyone was going to fight for Tristan's—and by association, Sev's—release, it would be them.

Riella had remained nearby throughout this conversation, and she was staring anxiously at Kade now, as if his decision mattered greatly to her. He realized that she'd had a traumatic couple of days—well, couple of months, actually—and that any familiar faces were probably a welcome sight to her.

He smiled at her—though it was tired and heavy in the corners—and nodded. Riella seemed to relax somewhat, and Veronyka nodded in return.

"We're going to separate you for the flight, if that's okay?"

Flight, Kade thought, dazed. They were going to *fly* to the Eyrie.

Riella didn't wait for Kade's response. "His stomach is badly wounded," she warned, "so he'll need to be safely secured in the saddle. And you'll need to be careful with him."

Veronyka darted a glance at Kade, lips quirking at the young girl's protective tone.

Kade shrugged, and Veronyka's expression turned thoughtful. "Maybe you can ride together after all. Riella will be light, which will balance your extra weight. And this way she can keep an eye on you."

Kade raised his brows but made no reply, and Riella beamed at the idea that she'd be trusted to care for him.

Veronyka led the way over to the phoenixes, who were clustered together. She stepped aside and swept an arm to indicate her phoenix, who was sidling up to them slowly. "This is Xephyra."

Riella stared wide-eyed at the beautiful creature, and Kade did the same. It was hard not to be both awed and a little bit scared, but after a short hesitation, Riella was the first to make a move, reaching tentatively for the phoenix's head, which was lowered toward her. She stroked the phoenix's feathers, and when the bird's large, scarlet head nudged her gently, she released a bubble of delighted laughter.

Kade smiled, and Veronyka did the same, expression colored with pride and affection for her bondmate.

"Then it's settled," she said. "Xephyra can carry you and Kade, and I can ride my friend Rex."

It took a bit of time for them to pack their supplies and mount up again. Kade was exhausted, but his anxiety at riding for the first time kept him awake and antsy until Veronyka reassured him in a low undertone, "You'll both be strapped in, and I'll be flying right next to you. Xephyra is young, but she's strong, and she knows you're not trained Riders. She'll fly slow and steady."

Kade was tied in first; then Riella was helped up behind him. She pointed out when a strap put pressure on his stomach and asked him if he was all right once they were settled in. Kade didn't know exactly when she'd become the mother hen in their relationship, but he was glad to provide her with something to focus her attention on. She was coming more and more alive with every moment, and he was grateful for that, too.

Veronyka climbed onto the back of a phoenix that had arrived without a Rider—Rex, she'd called him—and that Kade assumed belonged to

Tristan. The phoenix seemed subdued, emanating a dark, brooding temperament, but when Veronyka bent low and whispered something to him, he straightened his neck and stood taller.

Next thing Kade knew, they were off. He didn't need to steer or pay attention to where they were going—Xephyra simply followed the others, which flew in V-shaped patterns. Veronyka was right next to them, as she'd promised, and Kade's entire body felt alive with the thrill of it, the wind whipping against his skin and the rhythmic, soothing pump of the phoenix's wings. He looked back at Riella once or twice, her face filled with awe, and she spent most of the journey with her head swiveling this way and that, taking in the rolling landscapes and the vast, starry sky.

When at last they reached their destination, the sun was rising, gilding the mountain peaks and dancing off a golden phoenix sculpture that rose from behind a stone wall. Inside the fortifications was a series of buildings, and outside, a quaint village. All of it was tucked between spears of the mountain and quite invisible until they'd swept wide and entered from the east.

The phoenixes flew past the stronghold toward a massive structure shaped like an amphitheater, carved from the stone of the mountain and reaching deep into the ground. They landed at the very top, where a small crowd of people had gathered, helping unload the Riders who landed first.

Xephyra took them down slowly, landing on a long plinth and remaining still until Veronyka landed beside them and helped to unbuckle Kade and Riella.

Kade slid down shakily to his feet, the hours of sitting making his muscles tense and sore. His stomach was a constant, nagging pain, and he felt light-headed again as he was forced to stand. He'd only just stepped aside for Riella to climb down when a strangled cry rang out from across the stone walkway.

A young man stood there, eyes wide and body frozen in a half step, as if he meant to run at them.

No, not *them*—Riella.

She looked in the direction of the sound. "Elliot," she whispered. This must be her brother, the one who had betrayed the Riders in an attempt to save her.

Riella stumbled forward, her own legs wobbly after the time in the saddle, but it didn't matter. Elliot ran, shoving people aside, and was there before her knees could hit the ground. He scooped her up, clutching her to him, his face crumpled as tears ran down his cheeks.

While he cried, Riella clutched him tightly, face buried in his shirt. When he drew back to look at her, she smiled, and that only made Elliot cry harder, so she kissed his cheek.

Everyone stood there, watching them; an older Pyraean man wiped away his own tears, a hand on the shoulder of a girl around Riella's own age, whose attention followed their movements, though her eyes were unfocused and distant.

Then Riella disentangled herself and took Elliot's hand, leading him over to Kade. She whispered to Elliot as they approached, and before Kade could extend a hand or nod a hello, Elliot pulled him forward into a bone-crunching hug.

Kade gasped in pain, uncomfortable with Elliot's overwhelming gratitude and his tight grip.

"Elly, be careful—he's hurt," Riella chastised, tugging his arm.

Elliot stepped back at once, face apologetic, but Kade waved him off with a forced smile that was more of a grimace. Elliot led the way down the platform, and Riella took his hand—and Kade's, too. Kade was surprised—and a bit amused—and hoped that Elliot didn't get the wrong idea, but he seemed so utterly relieved to have his sister back that he just stared at her, oblivious to everyone and everything else.

As they made their way into the stronghold to be tended by the healer, rooms and food and baths being prepared, a sense of intense, aching relief washed over Kade. But it was short-lived.

This feeling of accomplishment—of *peace*—was incomplete, because Sev wasn't here with him.

ဆ ဆ ဆ

The next day Commander Cassian visited Kade in the room he'd been assigned inside the stronghold. The healer had patched him up, restitching his wound and rewrapping the bandages. She'd also left a cup of something warm and medicinal smelling, but he hadn't touched it yet—which he was glad of, when the leader of the Phoenix Riders strolled through his door.

Kade tried to sit up, but the commander waved him off. He held a piece of paper in his hands.

"I received a letter from Sev," he said without preamble.

Kade's stomach clenched—igniting a fire along his stitches—as he waited to hear what kind of letter it was. Surely if Sev was in a position to send a message at all, he must be safe and unharmed—but he needed to hear the commander say the words.

"His cover remains intact, and he is with my son."

Son. Kade hadn't realized Tristan was the commander's own child.

"He will continue to report regularly and keep us informed of his actions. He also sent this," the commander said, holding out the paper. "It's addressed to you."

"Oh," Kade said, his mouth dry. He took the letter with trembling fingers. "Th-thank you, sir."

The commander nodded but didn't leave. "Sev made a request, as well," he said, and Kade frowned. "There is a phoenix egg at the Eyrie that belongs to him. He has asked that it be given to you, so that, if you wish, you can train to become a Phoenix Rider."

Kade's fist clenched involuntarily, the letter crinkling in his hand. He was at a loss for words, his mind buzzing and blank. A Phoenix Rider—*him?*

"It is ready for you, whenever you decide how you would like to proceed." The commander cleared his throat and offered a small smile. "We would be glad to have you."

With another nod, he left the room.

Kade's ears were ringing. Barely two days ago he'd almost lost his life serving as a bondservant on the wrong side of a war. Now here he was, back in Pyra where he belonged, with people who would raise him up and give him a place, a purpose, a home. He wanted it, yearned for it so desperately he thought he might choke, but it still felt all wrong. And yet . . . what better way to help Sev than to become one of the phoenix-mounted warriors they'd fought so hard to protect?

Fingers clumsy and vision swimming, Kade unfolded the paper. It wasn't some long, passionate love letter. It wasn't even an explanation—not really. It wasn't written in code, either, but scribbled plainly in Sev's own hand. Two words.

I promise.

Kade took a deep, steadying breath and pressed the words against his chest.

They *would* be together again. Sev, a soldier, a spy—a hero down to his bones. And Kade, an animage, a once-bondservant—and a Phoenix Rider.

The past fades and the future beckons.
Stay strong. Burn bright.

- CHAPTER 60 -

VERONYKA

WHEN THEY FINALLY RETURNED to Azurec's Eyrie, Veronyka was exhausted, bone-weary in a way that made her eyes itch and her muscles ache—but she couldn't sleep. Couldn't rest. Every day Tristan was locked away instead of her was a day she would be working to free him.

She spent the night on the ledge outside Tristan's empty room, sandwiched between Xephyra and Rex. As they sat in silence, Veronyka tugged out the rough, uneven braids Val had given her. She'd already asked Morra for the tools she'd need, and the woman had worn a look of pride as she handed over comb and wax and string. For her first braid, Veronyka attached the arrowhead from Tristan, then, for her second, the pendant from Pheronia's broken necklace.

Veronyka noticed for the first time that there was a heart at its center, stamped into the gold and wreathed in flames. She compared it to Val's ring, and while the spread-wing emblem was the same, Val's was stamped with two *A*s in the center. Each sister had taken the Ashfire sigil and made it her own.

After several moments' consideration, Veronyka pulled out a knife and sliced her braided bracelet from her wrist. She withdrew Val's signet ring and lock of red hair from among the beads and trinkets and added them to a third and final braid. It was heavy, and the weight felt like an important reminder. She swept aside the rest of the hair, along with the other adornments. It was time to let go of the past and look to the future. To the real fight that was still to come.

Veronyka's magic was less hampered now that she'd stopped wasting energy on blocking her bonds and shrinking away from her abilities, but as she reached for Tristan across the vast distance that separated them, their connection was fragile and uncertain. Like when she and Xephyra had been parted for an extended period after her phoenix had resurrected, Veronyka and Tristan would have to rebuild their bond once they were together again. And they *would* be together again.

For now, she could tell he was alive, and that would have to be enough.

Veronyka called a meeting the day after their return. She knew it was presumptuous and that the commander had likely intended to do the same, but she couldn't bear to waste another second. The old her would be hanging her head as she awaited Commander Cassian's punishment after abandoning her responsibilities and running off with Val. But the new her? The one who had put Tristan's life in danger? The one whose own life hung in the balance, her past weighing her down while her future was, if possible, even more bleak? That Veronyka didn't have the energy to focus on things that no longer mattered. Lord Rolan and the empire were coming for them; Val was out there somewhere too. And like a wounded animal, she'd be all the more dangerous in the wake of her defeat. Val's mind had been silent as a crypt on the other side of their bond, and Veronyka might have thought her dead except for the scent of smoke that occasionally filled her nostrils, and the taste of metal that sometimes coated her tongue.

Veronyka found herself wishing that Val had a true bondmate, one that could have protected her from such a savage attack, as Xephyra had done for Veronyka. But after all she'd been through, Val still didn't understand the power of love. It was love that had saved Veronyka—and it was love that motivated her now. Love made Veronyka powerful, not weak. Val could probably live a thousand lives and never truly understand that.

When Veronyka arrived at the meeting chamber, the commander gestured for her to sit next to him, where his other patrol leaders sat. Veronyka didn't know if he'd already told them of her promotion or if they simply accepted the change after everything that had happened over the previous day, but no one reacted as she took her seat and the meeting began.

She'd summoned every single Phoenix Rider at the Eyrie—except for the young apprentices with new hatchlings—along with Morra and Ersken. She'd invited Elliot and Riella—though Riella had been too exhausted to come and Elliot hadn't left her side since her return—and of course, Kade. He would have crucial information about Rolan's estate, the people in the governor's employ, and Sev, their spy in the field. Kade had needed to be helped into his chair, his stomach thickly bandaged, but he'd come all the same.

It had taken some time, but she'd finally connected Kade's face with the memory of him outside her cabin from months previous. He'd been the bondservant traveling with Sev and the rest of the soldiers. It was because of him that she'd trusted Sev in the first place, and hidden from the other soldiers just in time. Seeing him here was like being reunited with some long-lost friend, and she was glad of it. She was also glad that Sev was with Tristan, that neither of them were truly alone.

The talking went late.

They discussed Rolan's terms, the upcoming Grand Council meeting, and preparations that had to be made. There would be many more meetings to come, but knowing that they were actively doing something, not sitting and waiting, caused an immense weight to lift from Veronyka's shoulders.

As she walked out into the courtyard, Alexiya joined her. "May I have a word?" she asked, and Veronyka slowed her pace. They stood next to the empty training area, the courtyard silent and silver in the moonlight.

"You were surprised," Veronyka guessed. "When you found out who I am. I saw you staring at me, looking for her. . . ."

Alexiya shook her head. "No. I was looking for *him.*"

"Him?" Veronyka asked with a frown.

"My brother."

Veronyka's legs went wobbly beneath her, and Alexiya guided her over to a barrel. She plunked on top of it, staring up at Alexiya, who smiled a bit sadly.

"I haven't spoken to my brother in over seventeen years. Not since he started an affair with a princess and chose the wrong side." She shook her head. "He was a fighter too—but a soldier. He was not an animage. In truth, we had been separated long before then, since my father and I left Arboria so I could train to be a Phoenix Rider and Theryn stayed behind with our mother."

Veronyka recalled Alexiya mentioning the fact that she'd left her mother *and* her brother behind.

"Theryn?" she repeated breathlessly, savoring the word. "Is that . . . ?"

"Yes, your father's name is Theryn. I don't know where he is, Veronyka, but I plan to find him. He deserves to know about you—he deserves to know his daughter is alive."

Alexiya's gaze was cast southward, and Veronyka's thumping heart sputtered with sudden anxiety.

"Are you . . . ? Do you have to go now?" she asked. There were a million questions she wanted to ask, and she'd need days and weeks to process the answers.

Alexiya looked pained. "The sooner the better, I think, with war on the horizon."

Veronyka bobbed her head but kept her face downcast, not wanting Alexiya to see the stinging tears that had sprung up in her eyes.

She gathered herself and got to her feet. Alexiya wore a knowing look, and her own eyes were a bit glassy and bright.

Alexiya cleared her throat. "I wouldn't be surprised if Avalkyra's put you off the whole idea," she said, going for lightness, "but I'd very much like to be your aunt, if you'll have me."

Veronyka stared up at the woman, at a loss for what to say. Alexiya was a gift, a piece of her family she hadn't expected to find or dreamed of having. Overwhelmed, all she could do was step forward and hug her.

Alexiya obviously wasn't the overly affectionate type, and she seemed startled at first, patting Veronyka awkwardly on the head before she laughed and gave Veronyka's body a tight squeeze.

"You know, the Pyraean word for aunt is *tiya*," Alexiya said, drawing back.

"*Tiya* Alexiya?" Veronyka said, beaming. "I like it."

Despite Veronyka's exhaustion, sleep eluded her. It was well past midnight when she left Rex and Xephyra together in the Eyrie and wandered the darkened stronghold. Her feet carried her out the gate, through the village, and into the open field where she and Tristan had spent so many nights training.

To her surprise, she wasn't out there alone.

Sparrow was perched atop a cluster of rocks near the edge of the field. Ever since the girl had lost Chirp, Veronyka had failed to see her without at least a few animal companions perched on her shoulders or winding between her ankles.

But tonight she was entirely alone.

"Sparrow?" Veronyka asked, afraid to startle her as she approached. Sparrow whipped around, and Veronyka could've sworn she'd looked hopeful for a moment until Veronyka spoke again. "It's me. Veronyka."

Sparrow deflated. Had she been waiting for someone else?

Before Veronyka could ask, a gust of wind rippled the grass around them—the only warning as a phoenix descended soundlessly from the sky above, obliterating the stars and soaring low on silent wings.

Veronyka's breath caught in her throat, and she stumbled back, alarm coursing through her veins. The phoenix didn't belong to any of the Riders at the Eyrie, which meant it was probably wild.

Wild and dangerous.

As the phoenix landed on the ground before them, something in Veronyka's heart clenched, some unknown dread—then it hit her. This was
Val's phoenix. Well, not *actually* Val's, but the phoenix Val had tried to
control. Veronyka sensed it with her animal magic, felt the familiar coldness
swirling within. Her shadow magic tingled as well, recognizing the bind Val
had placed within.

Though she bore no Rider, Veronyka had the horrible idea that Val had
sent her here.

That she'd come for revenge.

"Sparrow!" Veronyka cried out, reaching for the girl, refusing to take
her eyes from the perceived threat.

The phoenix before them jerked upright and lifted her head, and then
suddenly Xephyra was there, leaping forward with a screech and several
powerful pumps of her wings. Had Veronyka called her? She couldn't be
certain, but the other phoenix flew back several feet in response to Xephyra's
challenge.

"No, wait!" Sparrow said, her brow furrowed in confusion as she tried
to understand what was happening around them. "Don't fight, please."

Her voice held a touch of anguish that reminded Veronyka that she'd
lost the closest thing she'd had to a bondmate during the attack on the
Eyrie. During a fight.

But Veronyka wasn't ready to tell Xephyra to stand down. The other
phoenix's size dwarfed Veronyka's brave bondmate—and yet she didn't
attack or counter Xephyra's challenge. The phoenix was doing the same
thing she'd done in Ferro—tossing her head and moving with erratic
twitches of her vast wings.

She looked confused, like she was trying to shake something loose from
her head.

Something, or some*one*?

Val had interrupted her before, and though Veronyka had glimpsed it,
she'd never gotten a chance to try to remove the shadow magic bind.

"I think . . . I think it's okay," Veronyka said hesitantly. She was holding Sparrow's arm, and she released her grip. She looked toward the village and the stronghold walls and waved off the pair of guards that were pointing in their direction, ready to raise the alarm. A patrol would be due to circle around soon as well, but she thought they had a few minutes. She turned her attention back to the phoenix. "I think she's just scared."

Xephyra snapped her beak and expelled a rush of heat in reply—she wasn't yet convinced the phoenix that had almost burned Veronyka to a crisp could be trusted.

Veronyka closed her eyes and sought their bond, showing Xephyra the memories she had of Xephyra's own explosive arrival at the Eyrie. She'd been confused too, and scared, and had lashed out with flame and fury. Veronyka didn't hold back, letting Xephyra see and feel the fear she herself had felt in that moment. Veronyka tried to explain that Val had done to this phoenix what she had done to Xephyra, using shadow magic to confuse, except this phoenix didn't have a bondmate to help her.

Compassion, Veronyka thought determinedly.

Xephyra huffed, shaking out her wings and casting an appraising look at the other phoenix. The firebird seemed cowed and subdued, emitting low croons deep in her throat.

Finally Xephyra extinguished her own simmering heat and settled back on her heels, her wings pressed to her sides. She looked like a parody of good behavior, but Veronyka appreciated it nonetheless.

With a tentative step forward, she edged nearer the other phoenix. She reached out with her magic and was instantly, powerfully rebuffed.

She caught a clear view of the phoenix's face, though, and suddenly Veronyka knew why she had seemed familiar before. She also understood why the firebird might have chosen to return here, with or without Val's influence.

"Xatara?" Veronyka whispered, and the phoenix's head jerked in her direction. Her feathers puffed up, and a soft croak issued from her beak.

Sparrow straightened. "Xatara?" she repeated, sounding puzzled.

"She was here before the soldiers came to the Eyrie. In the breeding enclosure. She flew away the night of the empire's attack."

Xatara tossed her head, agitated again, and Veronyka took a step back, drawing Sparrow with her.

When Xatara settled, Veronyka tried to reach out again—to tell the phoenix she meant no harm, that she wanted to help—but she was blocked once more.

"She doesn't like you," Sparrow said matter-of-factly.

"Pardon me?" Veronyka demanded, looking down at Sparrow.

She shrugged. "I asked her, and she said she doesn't like you. Called you . . . Blood of the First. Like it was a title."

Veronyka gaped. "Blood of the . . . ," she repeated, stunned, but Sparrow tilted her head at the phoenix, then clarified.

"Ashfire. She called you an Ashfire."

Sparrow didn't seem to understand the significance of that—or didn't care—but Veronyka did.

"She won't hurt us," Sparrow said, misunderstanding Veronyka's silence. "She's just . . . lost." Sparrow took a step forward, drawing closer to the giant phoenix, and Veronyka let her. The phoenix inched forward too, lowering her head and peering curiously at Sparrow.

"Yes," Veronyka admitted, speaking to Xatara. "I am an Ashfire, but I am not like her." She put a picture of Val in her mind and tried to communicate it, though she didn't think she got through. "Your bind—her hold on you—I think I can remove it."

Xatara made no reply, though her dark gaze fixed on Veronyka.

"She will help you," Sparrow said, and Veronyka realized the words were for Xatara, not her. "If she can."

Veronyka marveled at the way Sparrow got through when she could not.

Without warning Xatara stepped directly in front of Veronyka—but while the movement startled her, it was not threatening. The phoenix seemed calmer now and had obviously chosen Sparrow as her ally in this encounter.

Xatara blinked at Veronyka, and sensing a shift between them, Veronyka reached again for her mind.

Thank you, she said, when the barriers were lowered and Veronyka was granted access. She didn't waste time, though she marveled at the phoenix's endless memory and dark, shadowy depths. Instead she did what she'd said she would do and sought out Val's bind.

It was easy to locate now that Veronyka knew the feel of them. And while she'd only temporarily blocked Val's bind when she'd tampered with Sidra's mind in the tower, this time she intended to obliterate it.

The bind was a flimsy thing compared to a bond, and Veronyka suspected it would disappear entirely over time, but she didn't want to risk it. Its presence obviously caused the phoenix distress, and there was no telling when Val might turn up and try to bend the poor animal to her will once more.

Veronyka poked and prodded, trying to visualize the link the way she did in her own mind: as a doorway in a stone wall. Then she yanked off the door and ripped down the frame. There was an imaginary deluge of rock—Xatara's mental defenses shifting and redistributing and settling back into place—and then there was nothing. An impassable wall. A barrier fully mended.

Xatara lifted her head and crowed, a fierce, triumphant sound that echoed across the landscape.

She shook her head and ruffled her wings again, but it seemed more out of relief than confusion. Despite the broken bind and the time she'd spent as a prisoner here, she seemed content to stay.

Veronyka didn't know what to do next, but Sparrow did. She extended her hand, reaching across the gap between them—crossing the physical barrier between them and this phoenix that had yet to be breached.

Veronyka stiffened but didn't move to stop her.

After Xatara stared at the hand for several silent seconds, her gaze darted to Sparrow's face before settling again on the girl's outstretched hand.

She was behaving rather uncertainly—nothing like the raging inferno that had scorched Val, or Veronyka's memory of Xatara's dark countenance—and edged carefully nearer. When Xatara drew almost near enough to nudge Sparrow's fingertips, she hesitated, and though Veronyka didn't pry, she sensed the phoenix's confusion through the lingering remnants of their connection.

Xatara wanted the contact, needed it—and yet she feared it. Looking at Sparrow, Xatara saw something small and precious. Something to protect. But Xatara needed protecting too.

The great phoenix bowed her hand, pushing it into Sparrow's hand, and the girl's face lit with aching, desperate pleasure.

She gasped softly, stroking the phoenix's gleaming beak with a trembling hand. Then she froze, turning to Veronyka. Her smile was brighter than the sun. "Her name's not Xatara," she said, tilting her head as if listening or trying to understand. "Her name is Ignix," she said.

"Her name is—what?" Veronyka said, completely taken aback. "How could you possibly know that?"

"Just told me," Sparrow said, as though it were obvious. Veronyka watched, dumbstruck, as the phoenix nuzzled Sparrow's palm. "She's hurting. She's been hurting a long time."

Veronyka gaped. But . . . this *was* Xatara; Veronyka recognized her face and the feeling she emanated—endless, ancient cold.

Xatara was Ignix.

It was just like Val had said—that it was wrong to cage a phoenix because there was no telling who the ancient creature might be. Had Val not known who Ignix was when she violated the phoenix's mind, or had she been so desperate she simply no longer cared?

Before Veronyka could react, the phoenix—Ignix—raised her head and fixed Veronyka with that fathoms-deep stare. She opened her mind to Veronyka again, and in that instant Veronyka *knew*.

This was indeed Xatara, the same phoenix trapped and caged by Commander Cassian.

This was also the phoenix that had thrown Veronyka from her back and burned Val's face. The phoenix that Val had compelled against her will.

A thousand memories flitted through Ignix's ancient mind, a thousand pains and hurts and devastations. Ignix had flown to every mountain peak and river valley; she had lived with men and women and her fellow phoenixes. She had raised the young in the Aura Nova compound and had watched them die at the hands of the empire. Suddenly Veronyka realized that Ignix hated Val for more than just her bind; Val had been the ruin of the phoenixes and the reason the young hatchlings had been slaughtered.

Ignix had lived through it all, had seen everything, and yet she was afraid.

Daughter of Ashfires, she said into Veronyka's mind, the words so loud and clear her ears rang. *Prepare yourself. Forget your human foes. The true battle will be fought not on the earth, but in the sky.*

What do you mean? Veronyka asked, her shins throbbing with pain as they dug into the ground, though she couldn't recall dropping to her knees.

Avalkyra lives, and she is hungry. Like the devourer before her, she can do naught but consume. The light will not have her, so she will turn to the darkness instead.

You alone can stand
against her.

- EPILOGUE -
AVALKYRA

SIDRA FLEW THEM ALL the way to the ruins of Aura. Avalkyra couldn't recall giving the order; all she could remember was pain.

But she did not cower from it. She relished it, let it feed her, like fuel to the fire.

Fire.

How it had burned, so white-hot that Avalkyra thought she might go mad with the agony of it. Her left eye was swollen shut, and her lashes and most of her eyebrow melted away into the flesh of her ruined face. But what had beauty ever done for her? And if her eye never opened again, what need had she of both when she was a shadowmage and could borrow the eyes of any person she saw fit? Avalkyra could see everywhere and everything.

So why had she not seen this? How had she not known that this would happen?

As soon as they arrived in that familiar, empty city, Avalkyra fell from the cursed phoenix saddle. It was nighttime, the world dark and cool everywhere except for her face, which burned constantly, a reminder of what she no longer was . . . what she would never be again.

"Leave me!" she screeched at Sidra, though using her mouth had been a mistake. Fresh, hot pain lanced through her jaw and the flesh of her face, blood pooling in her mouth.

"The wounds," Sidra protested, even though her bind was still intact. Avalkyra thought of the way the phoenix had acted, the way Veronyka had tampered with their link. . . . This was Veronyka's fault.

All her fault.

Leave me! Avalkyra shouted again, into Sidra's mind. This time the woman did not argue.

Sidra left Avalkyra alone in the place her foremothers had built, the haunting, echoing reminder of all their triumphs and all their failures.

Just as Avalkyra's body was nothing more than a vessel, so too were these ruins. They were the physical remains, the earthbound relics of former greatness, now dimmed and diminished.

The pain throbbed again, and stumbling around in half blindness, Avalkyra kicked and spat and scraped her fingernails across every visible surface. She hated them all. She hated everything.

Before her was the smoking chasm of the Everlasting Flame, though perhaps it should have been called the Temporary Flame, or better yet, the Forsaken Flame. Axura had gifted them with magic and fire only to take it all away again, leaving her people with no choice but to travel down the mountain, seeking their fortunes and getting tangled with those lesser men in their lesser kingdoms.

They never should have left.

Avalkyra never should have come back.

Why should she serve a goddess who did not serve her? Axura had abandoned them all.

Axura had abandoned *her*.

Stumbling forward, Avalkyra tripped, falling down the worn-out steps that led to the edge of the empty pit. The impact robbed her temporarily of consciousness, but when she came to, she found herself on the ground, staring into a dark fissure. It ran straight up and down, twice as tall as she was, but concealed in a niche behind some dusty old statue.

Avalkyra squinted, unsure if her mind was playing tricks on her.

Deep within were a series of smooth stones, packed tightly and stacked ten, fifteen deep.

Phoenix eggs.

Avalkyra laughed. How could she not? She had spent this entire second life seeking a phoenix, trying to make herself whole again. But the world of fire and light had rejected her, and now, in her lowest moment, she'd found a cache of phoenix eggs, enough to create an army that would rival Lyra the Defender's Red Horde.

And Avalkyra could not hatch them.

She laughed again, her barely scabbed-over flesh tearing, blood spilling down her throat, choking her. She crawled forward, prying them out, the raw skin of her hands and arms protesting with every movement.

Still she pulled and scraped, leaving bloody smears across their dull gray surfaces, until they loosened, cascading down from their hiding place. Lurching upright, coated with dirt and dust, Avalkyra hurled an egg against the statue—some warrior queen long gone—smiling savagely as the egg cracked against the golden figure. It might look like solid rock, inside and out, but it was not. It was an egg, and eggs—however durable—would eventually shatter.

She picked up another egg, throwing it against the ground and kicking aside the pieces. She destroyed one, two, three of them, phoenix after phoenix she could never have—so no one would. But there were hundreds of eggs, and Avalkyra had only two hands.

Then she turned, seeing the distant, smoking desolation of the Everlasting Flame. She threw an egg as far as she could, but it shattered on the ground well before it reached its target. With dogged determination, Avalkyra picked up another egg and hitched it under her arm. Then she walked, dragging her feet, her body protesting with every painful step until she stood before that yawning void of nothingness.

With the last wisp of her strength, she flung the egg inside, then collapsed to the ground, chest heaving and head spinning.

Avalkyra's good eye drooped.

She didn't know how long she sat there, if she'd fallen asleep or simply lost consciousness, but she was brought back to reality by a tendril of awareness that whispered across her skin. It prickled at the back of her mind, but it was a strange, unfamiliar sensation.

Avalkyra turned toward the feeling, staring into the inky abyss of the smoking pit.

The abyss looked back at her.

Rising slowly out of the darkness was a feathered creature—a bird—its plumage so black it seemed to absorb what little light surrounded it. The feathers were iridescent, fading to the color of ash and smoke at the tips, and shadows clung to its wings the way fire sometimes clung to phoenix feathers.

But this was no phoenix. This was no creature of the living world.

This was a strix.

Its eyes—deep, dark holes in its face—latched onto Avalkyra's.

And they didn't let go. They *chose* her.

Avalkyra had found her bondmate at last. She had found her reckoning, her ruin.

No. Not just her ruin, but the ruin of all.

She smiled.

TIME LINE

NOTABLE RULERS FROM THE REIGN OF QUEENS (BEFORE THE EMPIRE, BE)

First Era, before dates and events were meticulously recorded (c. 1000–701 BE)

1000 BE – 800 BE	Queen Nefyra[1], the First Rider Queen: Chosen by Axura to be the first animage and the First Rider Queen. Ignix, the first phoenix, was her bondmate.
775 BE – 725 BE	Queen Otiya, the Queen of Bones: Defeated a rival Rider family that tried to usurp the throne.

Second Era, the height of Pyraean culture (701–279 BE)

701 BE – 645 BE	Queen Aurelya, the Golden Queen: Began construction on the Golden City of Aura, from which she derives her name.

---

1 *Despite having died soon after her love Callysta, Nefyra is the only queen mentioned in any stories, legends, or histories from Pyra during this period. Because these accounts were verbal, it is likely there were errors in dating, or perhaps Nefyra's heirs were named for their mother and grandmother, suggesting that Nefyra II, Nefyra III, and even Nefyra IV were the likely queens mentioned in these accounts. There is also the possibility that the line between myth and history has been blurred here, and the songs and myths were intended to depict the First Rider Queen as having a divinely long reign.*

412 BE – 335 BE	Queen Liyana, the Enduring Queen.
335 BE – 317 BE	Queen Lyra the Defender: Mustered the Red Horde, the first-ever gathering of the entirety of Pyra's Phoenix Riders. Successfully defended Pyra from the Lowland Invasion.

Third Era, the decline of the queendom (279–1 BE)

9 BE – 37 AE	Queen Elysia the Peacemaker: Her reign in the queendom was most notable for the loss of the Everlasting Flame and the mass evacuation of Aura. After leaving Aura, Elysia founded the empire and married the Ferronese King Damian.

AFTER THE EMPIRE (AE)

37 AE – 45 AE	Queen Ellody the Prosperous: Reign of Prosperity.
45 AE – 56 AE	King Justyn the Pious: Reign of Piety. Transformed Azurec's Eyrie from a training facility into a pilgrimage site. Built the Pilgrimage Road.
56 AE – 95 AE	Queen Malka the Wise: Reign of Wisdom.

95 AE – 121 AE	King Worrid the Learned: Reign of Learning. Born deaf, he designed a specialty saddle to accommodate his condition. Set up the Morian Archives, making sure the empire's histories were recorded by the priests and acolytes of the god Mori.
121 AE – 135 AE	King Hellund[2] the Just: Reign of Justice.
135 AE – 147 AE	Queen Bellonya the Brave: Reign of Bravery. Lost her arm as a child, became the fiercest spear thrower in the empire's history.
147 AE – 165 AE	King Aryk the Unlikely[3]: The Unlikely Reign.
165 AE – 169 AE	Queen Regent Lania of Stel: Reign of the Regent.
169 AE – 170 AE	Avalkyra[4], the Feather-Crowned Queen. Pheronia[4], the Council's Queen.
169 AE – Present	Reign of the Council.

---

2 *After he married his bold Queen Genya the General in 125 AE, many began to refer to this period as the Reign of the General.*

3 *So called because Aryk was Bellonya's youngest brother, fourth in line for the throne, and only ascended because his older brother and both her daughters predeceased her.*

4 *Neither princess was officially crowned, but both were referred to as queens before their deaths in the Blood War.*

GLOSSARY

GODS

Axura[5]: Goddess of the sun and daylight, as well as life, symbolized by the phoenix

Nox[6]: Goddess of the moon and darkness, as well as death, symbolized by the strix

deathmaidens: Servants of Nox, who lure lost souls into the dark realms

Miseriya: Goddess of the poor and hopeless

Hael: God of health and healing

Teyke: God of luck, a trickster, symbolized by the cat

Mori: God of knowledge and memory, symbolized by the owl

Anyanke: Goddess of fate, symbolized by the spider

Soth: The wicked south wind, likely originating from the now-extinct Lowland civilization

Nors: The fair north wind, of similar origin to Soth, and still prayed to by the people of Arboria North

Eo: An obscure goddess of unknown origin favored among traders and messengers

Xenith: An alleged third sister of the ancient Pyraean pantheon of Axura and Nox

---

5 *"Azurec" in the Trader's Tongue*

6 *"Noct" in the Trader's Tongue*

GLOSSARY

NOTABLE PEOPLE

Callysta: Lover and second-in-command of Queen Nefyra. Callysta's and Queen Nefyra's phoenixes were also mates: Cirix, the first male phoenix, and Ignix, the first female phoenix.

Queen Genya the General: Married to King Hellund the Just. Exiline was her phoenix. Successfully defeated the brigands that terrorized her husband's reign.

The Five Brides: Queen Elysia and her four royal sisters (Anya, Rylia, Cara, Darya). They helped secure peace treaties during the founding of the empire through marriage alliances.

The First Riders: Fourteen female warriors chosen by Axura to fight against Nox's darkness.

King Rol of Rolland: Ancestor to Rolan of Stel and originally called Rol the Unruly, he earned fame—and the nickname Rol the Betrayer—for his famed assassination attempt against Ferronese King Damian.

Rolan of Stel: Governor of Ferro, responsible for the attack on Azurec's Eyrie

Councilor Halton of Stel: Rolan's father

Lania of Stel: Wife of King Aryk Ashfire, mother of Pheronia Ashfire, Queen Regent of the Golden Empire

FAMOUS BATTLES

Dark Days: The dawn of time, when Axura's phoenixes battled Nox's strixes, saving the world from endless night

Lowland Invasion: Attempted invasion of Pyrmont (then the entirety of the Pyraean Queendom) by an unnamed civilization living in modern Pyra's Foothills

Stellan Uprising: A series of lords who banded together in Stel, attempting to wrest several major cities from empire control, eventually defeated by Avalkyra Ashfire

Blood War: The conflict between opposing heirs and sisters Avalkyra and Pheronia Ashfire

Last Battle: Fought in Aura Nova, final conflict of the Blood War

COMMON TERMS

animage: A person who has animal magic

shadowmage: A person who has shadow magic

Red Horde: The first-ever gathering of the entirety of Pyra's Phoenix Riders, under Queen Lyra's reign

False Sisters/Shadow Twins: Siblings born mere moments apart by the same father and two different mothers

Mercies: Phoenix Riders that checked battlefields for survivors and resurrections

Shadowheart: Spymaster, position in ancient Pyra in service to the queen

magetax: Tax charged to animages for the use of their magic

magical registry: Record of known animages in the Golden Empire

bondservant: An animage working off a criminal debt to the empire

mageslave: A derogatory term for a bondservant

dark realms: The endless black abyss where lost souls wander for eternity

Soth's Fury: A series of caves near Azurec's Eyrie, named after the south wind and currently in use as a Phoenix Rider training course

Silverwood: A stretch of forest near the eastern Pyraean Foothills featuring taller, straighter trees likely brought to the region by settlers from Arboria North

Prosperity outpost: Originally built by Queen Lyra the Defender during the Lowland Invasion and updated and heavily expanded by Ellody during her Reign of Prosperity

Copper Hill: A once-thinking mining community on the outskirts of Ferro, now home to warehouses, processing facilities, and an abandoned outpost-turned-prison

GLOSSARY

Shadow Blooms: A spiky black flower that grows only on the upper reaches of Pyrmont, also commonly called "Deathmaidens" after the servants of Nox

PYRAEAN TERMS

aeti: Yes, affirmative

Aura: City/place of gold, and the ancient capital of Pyra

Aurys: River of gold, which flows from Pyrmont's highest peaks down into the valley of the Golden Empire

diyu ma: "Long time," an expression or greeting

impyr: Term of endearment translating to "little fire," originating in a Pyraean song

maiora: Grandmother

pyr: Fire or flame

Pyra: City/place of fire; also known as the Freelands, an emancipated province of the Golden Empire

pyraflora: Fire Blossom, a tree with red flowers symbolic of Pyra. Petals can be made into poison, and sap is used for fireproofing.

phoenixaeris **(s)**; *phoenixaeres* **(pl)**: Phoenix Rider or Phoenix Master

phoenixami: "Phoenix friend," usually meant to indicate apprentices or young, untested Riders, and carried with it the hint of derision or condescension

phoenovo: Phoenix egg

petravin: Rockwine, a distilled Pyraean liquor aged with a blend of local herbs and flowers, made only in the small village of Petratec

sapona: Soaptree, plant used to bathe with

Sekveia: The Second Road, an ancient route through the wilds of Pyrmont that supposedly leads to lost treasure

stellaflora: Pale white Star Flowers used to commemorate the dead

trivol: A three-Rider arrowhead flight pattern **xe:** Prefix meaning "sweet" or "dear"; can also mean "brother" or "sister," based on the gender of the name it's paired with.

xe xie: Generic term of endearment translating to "sweet" or "dear" (xe) "one" (xie)

FOREIGN LANGUAGE TERMS

sia: Yes, affirmative in dialect of Arboria North

verro: Yes, affirmative in Ferronese

ACKNOWLEDGMENTS

I want to thank the usual suspects: my family, my friends—all the people in my life who have accepted that I will fall off the edge of the earth for days (weeks . . . *months*) at a time, will miss birthday parties and holidays and fun nights out, but love me anyway and support me on this path I've chosen with enthusiasm and open hearts.

Thank you to Sarah McCabe, my editor, who helped me wrangle this gigantic book into submission. You have been an invaluable guide throughout this entire, terrifying process, and I'm thrilled we get to do another book together to finish out this series.

Thank you to Penny Moore, my agent and ally, who fights constantly for her clients and has made this dream of mine a reality.

Shout-out to the whole team at Aevitas Creative Management, and thank you to Sandy Hodgman, who has helped *Crown of Feathers* find readers all over the globe.

Thank you to everyone at Simon & Schuster US and Canada, who have done so much for me and my books. Your support has made many of my authorly dreams come true, and I've only just begun.

And finally: Thank you to the readers, bloggers, bookstagrammers, reviewers, librarians, booksellers . . . everyone who has taken the time to gush and shout and recommend *Crown of Feathers*—I can't thank you enough for your support and the endlessly incredible feeling that there are people out there who *get it* . . . who get me and this book and this story I've tried to tell. I love you all.

ABOUT THE AUTHOR

NICKI PAU PRETO is a young adult fantasy author living just outside Toronto, Canada. After getting a degree in visual arts, a master's in art history, and a diploma in graphic design, Nicki discovered two things: She loved to escape the real world, and she wasn't interested in a regular nine-to-five life. Luckily, her chosen career covers both.